# Arkalen

To our parents and to our families, to those who have come before and whose memory we strive to honor.

In particular to my father David Lowell. What would you think of what's become if you could have seen it?

~Andrew Bunny

To my grandfather, Jack Frost, who passed the same week I was writing the final pages of Kargaroth, finishing the first draft of a book that had been in work for nearly a decade of my life.

That week will always be associated with the mixed emotions of great accomplishment and great loss, in a combination that to this day I'm not sure I can adequately describe.

And to my father Jack W. Frost, who was able to read the full Daemon's Song trilogy before his untimely passing, and loved and supported these books in a way that only a father can.

~Mark B. Frost

A Tale of the Great Onion Knighthood

Author / Written by
**Mark B. Frost**

Author / World Builder
**Andrew Bunny**

Icerabbit Publishing

Published by **Icerabbit Publishing 2021**
**Nashville, TN, United States**



Art by **Liza Nazarova**
**https://elizabethn.space**

Maps by **Cornelia Yoder**
**http://www.corneliayoder.com**

Book Design by **Mark B. Frost**

**Library of Congress Control Number: 2020907744**
**ISBN 978-1-7328252-2-2**

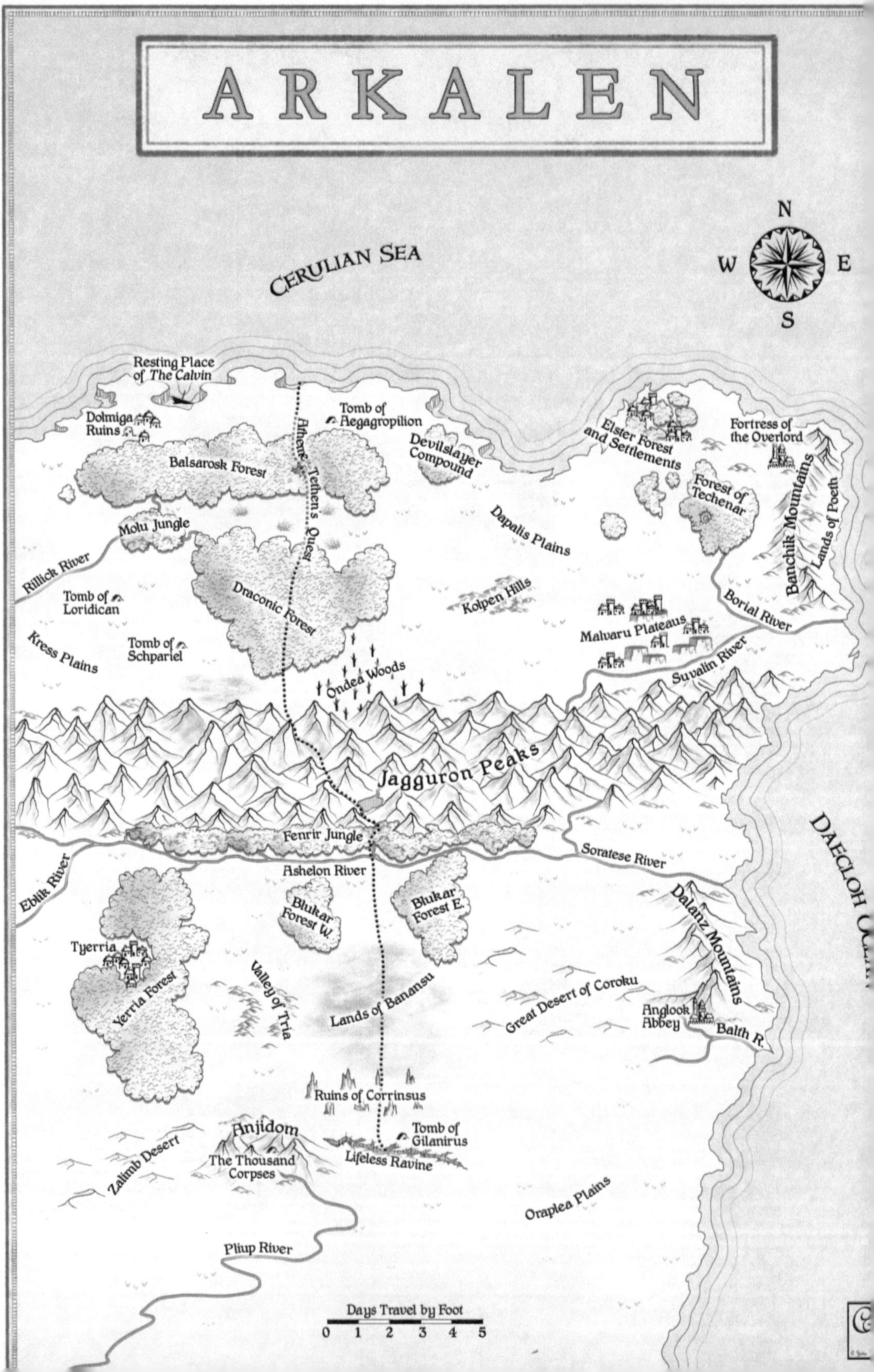

# ARKALEN

CERULIAN SEA
Resting Place of *The Calvin*
Dolmiga Ruins
Tomb of Aegagropilion
Devilslayer Compound
Elster Forest and Settlements
Fortress of the Overlord
Balsarosk Forest
Athene Tethen's Quest
Forest of Techenar
Banchik Mountains
Lands of Poeth
Molu Jungle
Dapalis Plains
Rillick River
Tomb of Loridican
Draconic Forest
Kolpen Hills
Borial River
Malvaru Plateaus
Kress Plains
Tomb of Schpariel
Ondea Woods
Suvalin River
Jagguron Peaks
Fenrir Jungle
Soratese River
DAECLOH O
Eblik River
Ashelon River
Blukar Forest W.
Blukar Forest E.
Dalanz Mountains
Tyerria
Yerria Forest
Valley of Tria
Lands of Banansu
Great Desert of Coroku
Anglook Abbey
Balth R.
Ruins of Corrinsus
Anjidom
Tomb of Gilanirus
Zalimb Desert
The Thousand Corpses
Lifeless Ravine
Oraplea Plains
Pliup River

Days Travel by Foot
0 1 2 3 4 5

# ARKALEN I

## Of Wisdom and Beasts

Chapter 1.

# The Mighty Cerulian

Flagship of the northern empire of Felthespar, the *Calvin* bucked limply against the antagonistic waves of the southern seas. Her journey had been a long one, and damage to the sails and rudder threatened her ability to press onward. The early months had been sailed across smooth waters, a seafarer's dream. Then she had entered the horizon of a southern storm. Mild at first, captain and crew had laughed it off, confident there would be brighter days ahead. Instead the storm had persisted for nearly three months, and its intensity had only swelled. There were occasional lulls sufficient for repairs and rest, but never more than a few days. Nearly a quarter of the crew's full compliment had been lost, tossed from the deck by relentless waves or struck by the unforgiving boom. Both ship and crew alike were now worn and weary from the berating weather.

Captain Yoshim, as exhausted as the rest of his crew, stood at the helm mourning their position. When the storm first began he had been confident they could muscle their way through. After all, they were already near their destination, nine months through a journey that had only taken ten last he had sailed it. Yet three more months had passed and land had not been sighted—not that any of the crew could see more than ten yards in any direction. Yoshim himself was so storm-battered he was no longer even certain if they were on course. He had thought a few times of turning about and attempting to return home, but that would sentence the crew to at least nine more months of sailing. Besides, without their current bearing it would be even more difficult to make the return trip.

He knew their situation, and the outlook was not good. Even if the storm ended soon they could be lost at sea indefinitely, unable to find land before they exhausted the food stores. Staying on their current course and trusting to a combination of his crew's skill and luck gave them their only slim chance for survival.

His first mate—the third appointee this month—approached the helm groggily as the ship rocked under the ocean's throes. Yoshim tried forcibly to muster some shred of optimism, but given the current intensity of the swells he doubted the man brought good news.

"Captain, we've lost the Crow's Nest," the mate shouted over the winds whipping past their ears.

"What?" Yoshim shouted back halfheartedly.

"A fierce gale took it. We've lost the entire topgallant from the mainmast."

"Is the mainsail intact?"

"Aye, we have her still. But the rigging's too badly damaged for us to make use of her. It's safe to say the ship's crippled."

Yoshim sighed slowly. "It was only a matter of time before we suffered a serious blow. Our luck held longer than I thought possible. Was anyone in the Nest when it was lost?"

"We think Hannigan, sir. But given the storm, it's hard to take decent roll."

Yoshim said nothing in return. Hannigan had been a good man—and a brave sailor, evidenced by the fact that he had been willing to take to the Nest at a time like this—but there was no time for grief or regrets now. All of the lost members of the crew would receive a joint funeral once they reached land, if there was anyone left to honor them.

From the fore of the ship came a muffled shout. All Yoshim was able to make out was, "Ree head!"

He turned to the mate, "What was that?"

"One of the lookouts up on the bow. I think he said 'tree ahead'."

The captain felt his heart skip a beat. "Tree? We've spotted land?" More muffled shouts came from the lookouts but Yoshim could not make them out. "Get up there, get the report, figure out what's going on and bring it back to me. It's going to be nigh impossible to make anchor like this."

The mate headed cautiously on his way to the fore. Yoshim endeavored to hold the ship firmly on course, while simultaneously trying to resist holding his breath. He did not know how close to land they might be, nor how many knots the ship was traveling. There was a real risk they might run aground. Only a moment later he saw the first mate running back, screaming at the top of his voice. The winds had picked up and Yoshim was unable to make out a single word. He focused his attentions, trying to catch whatever sound he could. Then the winds reversed for a moment and he heard it.

"Tree in the water! There's an uprooted tree floating off the port bow! We're about to plow right over it!"

Yoshim reacted quickly as he could, swinging the helm hard to starboard, but it was too late. He had barely turned the wheel ten degrees when the ship lurched horribly. The captain lunged forward and wrapped himself firmly about the helm, clinging for his life. A dozen or so crewmen were thrown overboard—including the current first mate—and a dozen more were knocked high enough into the air that they lost consciousness upon crashing back to the ship's deck. The jar from the impact only lasted three seconds, but to Yoshim it felt like an hour. His heart was pounding, his head was pounding, his arms were scraped by the wood of the helm. After things settled his thoughts moved slowly. All he knew for certain was that those who were not already dead would be so shortly.

He pointed to the nearest crewman and shouted, "You there! Get below decks, find the three lords. If they're still alive, put them on the lifeboats. If there was a tree floating out there, then surely land's nearby. Pecoros willing, we may be close enough that they can find a beach."

"Sir, they won't stand a chance on the lifeboats amid these swells!" the man retorted.

"And they'll stand a better chance on a sinking ship? Follow your orders!"

As the man headed to the deck ladder, one of the surviving scouts from the fore reached Yoshim to give him the report. "Captain, we struck the tree by its trunk. There were some roots left and it's torn a large hole in the hull. The tree's lodged there right now and seems to be slowing the ship's descent, but one way or another we're going down."

He nodded soberly. "I had already presumed the worst. Spread the word, tell the men they can try to make a swim for it if they want to brave the waves, or they can stay and go down with her. To each his own."

The man gave a nod, then ran across the deck translating his captain's final edict into a curt, "All hands, abandon ship!"

Elbed Yoshim, captain to the end, stayed with his ship until she sank deep enough that a powerful wave washed over her, wiping aside debris and crew alike. Thus ended the second voyage of Felthespar's mighty ship, and the life of her first captain.

* * * * *

Abaddon Daemon, Lord Templar, Knight of the Sun, and former Champion of Felthespar awoke on the shores of Arkalen to a haze of pains. His eyes stung, his skin crawled, his bones ached, his stomach lurched. He tried to open his mouth, but it was dried by saltwater and clotted with sand. He tried to discover his surroundings, but he could not force his eyes open long enough to see. He brushed his hands against the ground in front of him. Shortly after confirming that he was indeed lying in sand, he felt a terrible stinging, as if he had just poured a considerable amount of salt into open wounds. He fought through the pain and lifted himself onto his hands and knees. He tried once to stand, but was quickly brought back down by overwhelming nausea as he began vomiting a mix of sand and seawater.

After a minute of this, he struggled to keep himself from falling face-first into his own vomit. Instead he rose once more to his feet, this time barely finding legs to stand on. He walked toward land, away from the sounds of the sea. He desired to dive into the ocean and let it wash him clean, but he knew this was not freshwater, and the saltwater would do him more harm than good.

He tried to shed a few tears to cleanse his eyes, but his body was dehydrated and had nothing to give. After a few minutes of forced blinking, he reached the point where he could squint enough to make out vague shapes. He looked around and saw what might be people, merely a few yards in front of him.

"Water, please," he scratched out with a hoarse voice.

One of the shapes came forward and extended a hand. It was too late by the time Abaddon realized that it was not to help him, but to strike him on the forehead with a large club. He fell to his knees, fighting to fend off his assailants for only a matter of seconds, then once again drifted into unconsciousness.

* * * * *

When Abaddon next awoke his pain had dulled. His head ached and his eyes were still sore, but overall his body's healing processes seemed to have made some headway. He was no longer nauseous, but instead extremely hungry, plus the thirstiest he had ever been in his life. He gingerly edged himself into a sitting position on the bed he was in—little more than a sheet tossed over a rock slab—and looked around the room. Across from him sat half a loaf of bread and a bucket of water on a small stone table.

He fell to his knees and moved to the bucket, gathering a small amount of water in the palm of his left hand. First he tasted it. Definitely freshwater, no traces of salt other than the small amount it had soaked up from his skin. He lifted the bucket and carefully poured a small stream over each hand. He washed them as clean as he could without wasting much of the precious liquid, not knowing whether there would be refills coming. Once he was satisfied, he sat the bucket down, gathered another small amount into his palms, and used it to flush his eyes out. It took about five handfuls for each eye before he felt like they were in healthy condition. After this the bucket was half emptied. With no further delay he uplifted it and drank it down to the last drop, careful to pour slowly enough that he did not spill any over the sides.

His ordeal with the water over, he snatched up the bread and returned to his bed to sit, eat, and think. It took him a while to press past basic survival instincts and remember the *Calvin*, Yoshim, and his other companions from the vessel. He had no idea if any of them had survived, but it would be his first priority to find out. After a few further moments of thinking, his hand shot up over his right shoulder. His weapon was missing. His thoughts raced, attempting to recall if he had possessed it when he had awoken on the beach, but the memory would not come. He was briefly upset, then eventually forced himself to chalk it up to lucky circumstance. “Had the sword not come loose, it probably would have dragged me to the bottom of the sea,” he said to himself, trying to find his voice. “I might not have washed ashore.”

He dismissed the matter for the time being, having little else in the way of options. He took the last bite of his bread—already thirsting for another bucket of water—and walked over to the barred window of his stone-walled room.

He was surprised by what he saw beyond the confines of his cell. A series of shabby huts sat around a barren village, serving more as decoration than shelter. Wood and thatch affairs sat sadly as fierce winds whipped through, threatening to pick them up and carry them off. There were a few other buildings akin to the one in which he was imprisoned, though most were run down and looked to be artifacts from a previous settlement.

He surmised that whoever had captured him was likely a group of nomads that had stumbled across an old abandoned city, supplementing it with a few makeshift huts of their own. If these huts were as young as they appeared, then the villagers had actually settled here amid the intense weather that was still raging. Though he tried, Abaddon could not think of a good reason for this. It likely meant the settlers had chosen between a very few, poor alternatives.

A man suddenly stepped in front of the cell's window, blocking his view. It was the sentry assigned to watch over him, finally taking notice that his prisoner was awake.

"So, outlander, you're alive after all," the guard did not try to disguise the contempt in his voice. "I was rather hoping you wouldn't awaken this time. Our chief says we have no reason to kill you. I contend that we have no reason to leave you alive."

Abaddon did not make eye contact, but rather stared upward, trying to gauge the time by the sky. He estimated it was early afternoon, maybe midday. "Could I get some more water?" was the only response he offered.

His jailer huffed, then spat. "You'll take the rations given to you and count yourself lucky for those."

The guard turned from the window, resuming his normal post. Abaddon returned to his bed and had a seat, not wishing to waste energy until he had more time to recover.

He leaned his chin against his fist and speculated, "It's going to be one of those trips."

## Chapter 2.

# Devilslayers of Arkalen

Long before the arrival of visitors from the land to the north, a group of people on the southern continent had banded together to declare war against their own oppressive terrain. They proclaimed themselves the Devilslayers of Arkalen, believing it was in the demise of demonspawn where they would purchase freedom. Their founder was a man named Orikon, a visionary who sought a better world and promised security would one day belong to humans. They had long been a weak force struggling to do good against overwhelming odds, their numbers rarely climbing above a few hundred war-worn soldiers.

Then the first visit of Abaddon Daemon had brought about the destruction of the Lifeless Vortex. This monstrous maelstrom of magical energies had once fed the chaos of Arkalenian demonspawn, making it all but impossible for human settlements to thrive in the inner regions of the continent. After the Vortex's collapse, the Devilslayers' victories began to surge at an encouraging rate, and their ranks expanded. Soon human settlements began to take root and in some cases flourish, confident the Devilslayers would champion their rights. A scant few years had passed, and the once-small band had become the most prominent army on Arkalen.

Two years before the shipwreck which would herald Abaddon's second visit, High Chieftain Orikon led a contingent of his followers to investigate a fresh assault against humankind. Most of the slayers following him were veterans, men and women who had been fighting demonspawn for as long as they could remember, since even before they had joined his ranks. It was the chieftain's preferred recruitment strategy to find warriors already defending their settlements and enlist them into the Devilslayer's ranks, in exchange for official protections extended over their homelands.

According to reports, the attack they were to investigate had been swift and was already ended. All that remained for the Devilslayers was clean-up and medical care for survivors. Orikon did not normally see to recovery operations such as this, but he was the nearest chief and happened to be in high spirits, so he had taken the mission under his own wing and would carry it out with utmost vigor. Half of his troops would see to the damages, while the other half would determine the identity or breed of the attacker. Once they knew what type of demon had done this, they would make an evening of hunting it down and bringing it to justice.

Orikon smiled to himself as he relished the thought. As the ferocity of the Devilslayers grew, demon attacks continued to diminish in frequency and intensity. He felt confident this new attack had ended so swiftly thanks to the creature's fear of retribution. Even so, the High Chieftain would find the assailant and retribution would be had. His warriors would never rest until no demonspawn was bold enough to risk incurring their wrath.

The village they approached sat nestled atop a giant plateau with a gentle slope, one of the many young cities of the Malvaru Plateaus. Orikon's company reached the base of the hill and headed up stoically with a steady pace. When he reached the top of the rise and saw the village laid out before them, he came to a jerking halt.

Running from the right side of his view to his left, the entire plateau had been split down the middle. A gaping ravine was torn through the village, and the ground around it remained scorched. The chieftain quickly dispatched units to help the survivors and bring back a report, then headed himself to examine the rift.

After an hour he had been unable to determine what manner of attack could have caused damage of this nature. One of his best slayers, a man in his late twenties by the name of Kelve Orista, soon approached him with a report.

"Most of the survivors on the outskirts of the crater were unharmed. There were a few burn victims, and a couple of families injured under the collapse of their houses, but for the most part this giant scar in the earth seems to be the full scale of the attack."

Orikon scratched the back of his grayed head. "And the people? Did they see anything out of the ordinary? Surely there was some greater dragon or the like that did this, correct?"

Kelve shook his head. "There doesn't seem to have been. A few reported witnessing a strange man in odd attire, colorful and elegant robes. They said he looked like he might have been foreign clergy. No survivors seem to have spoken with him and after the attack he was nowhere to be seen. May have been in the middle of whatever blast caused this. His presence is suspicious enough that I doubt it's coincidence, but it's impossible to say whether he was source or target."

"Any footprints coming or going?"

"Aye, lots. After the attack, the families with no casualties retreated in every direction. It's hard to read much more than that on the ground. All of the markings seem to have been made by humans, nothing of extraordinary size that we could find."

The High Chieftain detected movement on the opposite edge of the ravine. A man of average height and heavy armor—black leather and plate mail—crouched and gathered up some of the burnt earth, then raised it to his face to gather the scent. Orikon watched him intently for a moment, until the man turned and began to walk away rapidly.

Kelve soon noticed the stranger as well and moved to give orders to nearby sentries. Orikon detected this and swiftly stopped him. "No, Kelve. Leave him be. He's not related to this. Just another investigator, like us."

"Perhaps he knows something we don't. We should question him."

The chieftain thought this over for a moment, then shook his head. "Leave him be. That is an order."

Kelve gave a nod, and after another word from his chief

returned to help the wounded. Orikon called a nearby slayer, one of his fastest runners, and sent him to fetch extra manpower. This entire settlement was going to have to be relocated. It would require weeks of labor. He was slightly annoyed by his inability to pursue whatever creature might have caused this, but this demonstration of power also instilled enough fear to make him think otherwise. He prayed this would prove to be a one-time incident, and not a permanent new threat to humankind.

* * * * *

From atop a lonely hill, Deun Coloran looked down upon another burning human settlement. It was the fourth lead he had looked into this week, and his fourth dead end. The first had been the human settlement in the Malvaru Plateaus, with the gaping rift torn through for no apparent reason. There had been three more attacks since, linked by no discernible motivation or consistent collateral damage. This town was much the same—another random demon attack, more humans slaughtered, but once again the village did not match the pattern of havoc Deun was seeking. He hunted a singular evil with a specific calling card, and these unrelated attacks were merely distractions.

Still he stared down upon the damaged town for a short time, his mind processing the signs of carnage. He had been trained to obsessively catalog details, and it was hard to deny the urges of that training. Besides, he had nowhere else to go now. It had been nearly a month since there had been a sign of activity from his prey, and by now he had no way of knowing to which area of the continent it might have spread.

By the time he was satisfied with his analysis of the former valley settlement, he sensed a figure approaching from behind. His right hand slowly fell from where it had been scratching his chin, resting lightly on the handle of a dagger hidden under the neckline of his breastplate. His left hand he placed on the ground, carefully monitoring vibrations from the steps of the man behind him.

"You're treading on dangerous grounds, old man. I'd think you'd know better than to sneak up on me."

"Hello, Deun. I see you're as quick as usual. Somehow you always beat us to the scene."

The elder visitor wore peculiar makeshift armors decorated with animal hides and pelts. Only those familiar with the Devilslayers would have recognized the ensemble. A thick steel chain served as a belt, and various weaponry pieces hung from it menacingly, most of which were carefully concealed by dangling furs. The placement of the armor was intentional, covering most of the human vital areas but little more. It allowed protection without encumbrance, but served to give the slayer a tilted and unbalanced look. Deun, in contrast, was armored to the core. Every inch of his body from the neck down was shielded either by massive black plates or thick layers of tightly-wrapped leather.

He stood to his feet and drew a cigarette and a match from the base of his glove. He made no effort to disguise the contempt in his voice. "Your men are either lazy or incompetent, Orikon. I don't have your complicated information networks, yet still it seems I'm always a step ahead of you. It's shameful." He struck the match against the back of his glove and lit his cigarette.

The High Chieftain, oldest of Devilslayers at the impressive age of sixty, shuffled his feet humbly. "I do not claim that my men match your merit, young wolf. Nor do any among them claim such honor for themselves. Perhaps if you were to return to us and repay your training, teaching our kind the way they once taught you. We could benefit greatly from your superior skills."

Deun took a long slow drag from his cigarette before answering, "Go to hell. I am no wolf of yours."

In the still-burning village below, activity began to increase as dozens of slayers flooded the area, pulling people from collapsing buildings, evacuating the survivors to safe places and providing medical assistance.

Orikon shook his head as he noted how few had survived. "If you do not help us, why do you not at least help them? You have been here longer than us, no doubt, and in the time you have stood here bemoaning your fate you could have rescued women and children. Lives were lost because of your selfishness."

As the younger man turned to leave he crushed his half-smoked cigarette with a gloved fist and dropped it at Orikon's feet. "I'm no one's hero. My purpose is to end lives, I have no stock in saving them. Good morrow, venerable one."

The elder watched as his ungrateful student turned his back on him once again. A slim girl dressed in the same Devilslayer vestments approached from the town and quickly made her way up the hill. She reached the top just in time to see Deun disappearing into the distance, and her chief watching after the man with a sad grimace on his face.

"Chief Orikon? Are you alright sir?"

"Aye, Detria. I am fine."

"Who was that dark stranger?"

He shook his head slowly. "You may not remember, but he was one of us when you were still very young. He was the strongest of us all, the strongest that has ever been. Until he lost his mind. Nearly a full dozen Silver Pride gave their lives trying to bring him down the day he left in a fearsome rage. Since then he has been little more than a mindless barbarian, wandering the continent aimlessly in search of something that exists only in his mind."

"What drove him to such a rage?"

Ignoring her question, he turned his attention back to the village. "What is the condition below?"

"We're not sure what hit. Something powerful, clearly seeking something. The attack was surprisingly methodical and thorough given the suddenness, as if it were a deliberate search. While well over a hundred people were killed, some quite brutally, none were eaten or had their spirit drained. No jewels or gold or any sort of trade goods seem to be missing, and there's nothing else here that would interest any known forms of demon. In short..."

Orikon interrupted her conclusion. "We don't know what it was. Same as the last three attacks."

"Correct, sir."

There was a short silence. Detria wondered what was going through her chief's mind, but she did not interrupt his thoughts. She glanced back in the direction where the stranger had disappeared and let her thoughts settle upon him for a moment. Soon Orikon spoke again.

"I suppose there is nothing more to be done. Save those we can, salvage what can be, and tell our tacticians to see if they can find out any pattern to the locales of these attacks."

"Sir, if I may?"

He raised an eyebrow in surprise and a slight smile spread over his face. Detria was a respectful and doting follower of the old chief, and it was rare that she spoke her own mind. "Yes, my dear?"

"That stranger, the one who you said was so strong—is he a threat? A danger to the slayers? Or possibly even to others?"

His smile faded as he turned and stared blankly at the horizon. "Go, help the villagers."

She bowed and took her leave. Orikon took a slow breath and clasped his hands before himself in prayer. After several motionless moments he dropped his hands and wiped away a tear.

"I hope you have not finally crossed that line, Deun. For your sake, for all our sake, I hope you have not become the monster you need so desperately to believe is real."

* * * * *

Even as Orikon and his Devilslayers were cleaning up the aftermath of the fourth attack, a fifth had already taken place. The assailant was becoming more efficient, navigating from human city to city in less time. As he walked down the main road of the leveled settlement, he kicked at the nearest straggling body. His mood grew darker with each failed search, and the destruction he left in his wake more vicious. This city had been nearly double the size of the last, yet this time not a single survivor would be found.

It was easy to tell by looking at him that he was not quite

human, yet calling him a demon would have been inappropriate as well. His face was a human's, but perfectly chiseled as if it been etched in glass. He had no expression, no wrinkles; his eyes never blinked. The only part of his face that moved was a small mouth when he spoke. His skin had no color of its own, but rather seemed to reflect color from behind his face, a muddied red tone. His hair, which more closely resembled an odd helmet, was two peculiar plates of rough metal or stone which covered each half of his head, exiting from his forehead and ending in two pinpoints at the base of his neck. His hands bore a similar appearance, muddy-red palms with stone-like fingers protruding forth. He wore layers of thick robes of an unknown cloth—almost like rubber in its consistency, sturdy yet easy-flowing as he moved—with an assortment of red, black, and gold decorations adorning it.

He looked up and watched the columns of smoke rising into the air. The demons of the continent, untamed fools that they were, were already aware of his foreboding presence and hastily retreated from the area. He smiled for a moment at the fear he instilled in them. Then his expression returned to one of rage. He spun about and flung his arm in the direction of the nearest house, and the building exploded into a pillar of flames and rubble.

"My, my," came a soft hiss from the shadows behind him, "that seemed a bit of an overreaction."

He did not turn, but responded coldly, "Is that so? It seems to me impossible that you should know that to which I am reacting. Ergo, there are no grounds upon which you can judge the congruity of said reaction."

"Such nice words, with such an elegant demeanor. You would fool me into believing you were a human of high breeding, had I not already observed that you behave no better than a cur."

The assailant's temper slipped another notch. "Who and what are you?"

The creature stepped out of the shadows and into the open street. "I am demon; Zekraul. Return the courtesy, if you please."

The tall stranger turned and gazed upon his opponent. It was a dark, wiry creature, with little solid form to speak of, and no face visible on his black head save for two indentations which might serve as eyes. His slim body comprised a black crystalline structure, which seemed to shift continuously as if rebuilding itself whenever he moved. "Where I come from long ago, they called me Schpariel," he answered. "I am the First Anointed Godbeast of Gehenna. I am herald of the end of this world, and Elysium beyond it."

His newly revealed opponent gave a sharp hiss and took a step back. "You lie."

"Believe what you will. Whether it is the end of this Morolian plane or not, it won't matter to you. You have the honor of dying here, to quench my wrath." Quickly he reached forward his left hand and gave a snap. A spark shot forth from between his fingertips, and rapidly expanded into a sweeping cone of fire that raced at his foe.

The one introduced as Zekraul leaped forward and plunged his right hand into the flames that threatened to engulf him. His black body shifted to match the red and orange of the fire, and he surfed unsinged along the wave. As he reached the source of the attack, he transformed his left hand into a massive hammer and aimed to smash his opponent. The supposed Godbeast responded by flying suddenly into the air at imperceptible speed. Zekraul was not caught off guard, and swiftly kicked himself into the sky in pursuit.

Stony fingers spread forward and an electric barrier surrounded Schpariel. Upon reaching it, Zekraul placed his right hand onto this barrier and his skin turned to yellow. He latched a firm foothold on the field of energy and struck forward with his left hand. The Godbeast fell to the ground fast, smashing through a small hut. Zekraul shot himself forward off of the energy barrier just before it dissipated, landing next to his fallen foe. To his slight dismay he found that his foe was not fallen, but rather standing unharmed on the far side of the hut.

"I see that you have the power to merge your body with fields of energy," the emissary of Gehenna observed. "That's very handy indeed. You are the first creature of this plane to strike me since my awakening. But as I am busy, I have no taste left for this fight."

"I simply came to introduce myself. This is my continent. I have made my home here for some time, and do not appreciate your unscheduled carnage among my humans. We could perhaps come to some sort of agreement. How about I allow you to stay, if you swear fealty to me and offer me use of your substantial power?"

Schpariel briefly fumed in annoyance, then tapped a foot three times and gave another snap. A long black scepter adorned with a bright sapphire appeared in his hand, which he pointed at Zekraul. Instantly two giant rock slabs shot out of the ground, one on either side of the demon, then smashed together around him. "You merge with energy," the Godbeast taunted, "but it seems you don't merge with rock." He pointed the scepter at the hut through which he had been hurled and it lifted into the sky. Then with a flick of his wrist, he sent the uprooted building smashing into the spot where his foe stood pinned between the two boulders.

Content with his victory, Schpariel turned and disappeared into the depths of a village. As he faded out of earshot, an ebony black hand slowly rose from the debris of the hut. The fingers extended and sharpened, growing into five massive six-foot blades. They swiftly whipped around and shredded the hut and the two boulders that had trapped Zekraul, turning them to shrapnel. Beaten and bent, the resilient demon shuffled into the clear and slowly straightened his shattered spine back into place.

A long, slow hiss emanated from his throat, as if his voice was warming itself up. "Ssss. If that is truly a Godbeast of Gehenna, things are going to get complicated. Perhaps I should consider an extended leave of absence." He looked down at his hand, and with effort transformed it from his usual black into an intense shade of yellow, crackling with electricity. "Still, this power I borrowed may come in handy," he said with a chuckle. Then, like his opponent, he turned from the battlefield and headed along on his way.

## Chapter 3.

# The Crawling of the Winds

As fierce gales whipped across the plains, grass-covered hilltops danced and flowers struggled to resist being torn apart. The weather patterns on Arkalen were becoming more intense, slowly crawling across the continent like some intangible beast. The disturbance seemed headed for the ocean, and was not far from that goal. Now it passed over the easternmost tip of the continent, robbed partly of its viciousness by the tame landscape.

Atop one of these berated hills sat nine men. Their appearance seemed tranquil enough. Dusty grey robes rested loosely over dark tunics and breeches, rippling lightly on the breeze. They were adorned with no other accessories, not even footwear, but a decoration of complex tattoos traced across their skin in its entirety. Their simple attire belied the storm they represented. These were men of war, here to carry their war to a new battlefield.

For seven months they had sought a hidden fortress, and at last it lay spread out before them—nestled in a deep valley, surrounded by hills on the west and towering mountains backed by ocean on the east. High stone walls surrounded several small castle-like buildings, with three huge iron gates providing access. Humans and demons united by some dark pact came and went freely, running questionable errands and labors. It was a base that did not exist, the base of a warlord who did not exist. Finding it had been like hunting a shadow at night, but these warriors of discipline had never lost heart. Now that quest was over, and the next ready to begin.

They had sat motionless for many hours, since long before the sun had first crossed the eastern horizon. As the evening dwindled toward twilight, their tenth finally returned from the city. They sensed rather than saw his approach, as he was masked in a thick layer of mystical invisibility. As he reached them and dropped this cloak, they rose to their feet to hear his report.

Their leader, Tenkahn the Aged, brushed back his grey hood and scratched his head. His formerly light brown hair was fading, slowly turning its way to white. His brethren knew he had demanded too much from his divine blessings in the past few years. They did not know how much longer he, nor any of them, could continue at their current fervor.

"The Overlord is not here," he reported to them. "From what I was able to gather today, he left his second-in-command in charge. All I could catch was a name: Shote."

One of the men stepped forward. "Second-in-command? We have heard nothing of a second-in-command."

Tenkahn nodded. "Only of small surprise. We have heard little even of the Overlord himself. True to form, I gathered only scraps about his second, but it seems clear that he is, in fact, enough of a lesser to the Overlord that even he fears him. For us, this means that if we are to defeat the Overlord—which I believe we must—then we must first be able to defeat his second."

"Then we are to move in now?" another of the monks chimed in. "Even though our target is not within grasp?"

"We will take the Overlord's keep. There are several hundred soldiers and demons here that serve under his command. If the Overlord himself is as dangerous as we have previously estimated, it may prove difficult for us to overcome both him and his armies. As things are, we can wipe out his forces, kill his second, secure his fortress for ourselves, then lay a trap and await his return." The men nodded, and no further concerns were voiced. "Very well. Let us go now. The second is resting, and it should be a while before he responds to our assault."

The ten men gathered in a close circle, and after a few seconds all vanished under a fresh cloak of invisibility. Harsh winds whipped once more across empty hilltops before fading. The storm was moving.

* * * * *

Detria Alsen sat next to a lonely campfire, prodding dying embers with an old sword. Wicked winds were tearing through the forest canopy under which she hid, and she knew it would do little good to try and rekindle the blaze. Even if she did get a fire started in this weather, it would take only one strong burst of breeze slipping through the trees to extinguish it or, worse, spread it.

She had isolated herself from the rest of the Devilslayers. Orikon, the former High Chieftain, had recently passed away. Detria had regarded Orikon as a father, or perhaps the closest thing she had ever known to a father, at least. She knew she had likely not been closer to the man than any of his other apprentices, but she had placed a deep significance on their bond, probably moreso than he had ever placed himself.

Still, it was not his death that had upset her so, nor even the burden that he had likely never cared for her more than his other young wolves. What had outraged her and driven her from the compound was the new chieftain's treatment of the loss. Yasiff and Orikon had long been at odds, with Yasiff accusing the old man of losing his touch with reality and seeing ghosts that were not there. Detria had never understood the context to these arguments. No one, not even Orikon himself, had ever explained his side in a public forum. Yet she placed unshakable faith in her group's founder, and deemed Yasiff out of line for questioning his elder and better. Once Orikon passed, Yasiff had rushed the funeral, offered no words of respect, and had even dared to proclaim aloud, "It was the natural time for him to go. Any later might have been too late."

Detria, always the highest ranking among her pack, a Silver Pride Wolf and slayer with an absolutely untarnished reputation, was now under unofficial chastisement and court-marshal for assaulting the reigning High Chieftain. Once found guilty—which she would inevitably be given her refusal to defend herself—the most lenient punishment she could face was a complete blacklisting and banishment from all Devilslayer clans. The far more likely punishment was execution.

Part of her wondered if she had thrown her life away for nothing. Maybe Orikon really had become unbalanced, as Yasiff claimed. Maybe the old man had begun to lose clarity in his final years. She forcibly brushed the thought aside, knowing she could not give Yasiff the benefit of the doubt now. She had already pushed too far, risked too much. The only path that made sense was to stand firm upon her own integrity, and have faith that she had done the right thing by standing up for one who could not stand up for himself. After all, that was the very idea upon which the Devilslayers had been founded.

A visitor suddenly stepped into the clearing and plopped down next to her. He had not been particularly stealthy, Detria had simply been too caught up in her own concerns to notice his approach. It was Kelve, one of the wolves in her pack. He had long held an open crush on her, so it was of little surprise he would be willing to risk his reputation by fraternizing with a reprobate.

"Hey doll, what are you doing way out here alone?" Kelve had never shown Detria the respect she deserved, but in the past few years she had grown to accept his loose and informal style.

"Kelve, you idiot. I'm about to be executed and that's what you come out here to say to me?"

"Relax, Deets. My old man used to be on the presiding council for serious infractions of slayer law, before he passed. They listen to me, under the assumption that I'm going to take dad's spot soon. In a case like this, you win major sympathy points for defending the honor of a fallen High Chieftain. They've already openly rebuked Yasiff for what he said, chastising him that this whole situation was his fault, and that as High Chieftain he's expected to uphold a higher standard. He's definitely not happy, but he's been put in his place for the moment."

She turned away from him and looked into the embers that had once been her fire. "So what are you saying? This is over already?"

Kelve had been sitting back, leaning on both of his wrists, his legs extended forward and crossed at the ankle. When Detria asked this, he slowly straightened himself into a seated position, legs crossed in front of him and hands together. "I can probably make it go away, if you want. It won't take much for me to push the matter. Question is, do you want that?"

She turned back and met his gaze. She had never seen Kelve look so serious. For the first time, she found herself thinking about how much older he was. Nearly ten years her senior, he had served in the Devilslayers every day of his adult life. Kelve had always come off as comical and lean-spirited, but now Detria wondered if perhaps there were hidden depths to him.

"Why wouldn't I want that? I mean, this is our home, right? It's all we've got."

He glanced to the ground at his side, and for a moment his jovial nonchalance returned. "Ah, sure. Devilslayers are we, yo ho. Fight to save the day, fight to save the world, and so forth." He paused, then slowly shook his head. "But it's not enough anymore. Not for Yasiff. He's stopped believing the world can be saved."

He shuffled forward, bringing his face only a few feet short of Detria's, and now she was certain that his eyes were burning with the intensity of deeper beliefs. "Yasiff doesn't want to save people," he continued. "He wants to rule them. Oh, sure, it's all under the pretense of 'protecting' them. He says the world cannot be saved because people are disjointed, they are chaotic, there is anarchy. He believes if we bring the continent under a single order and control the lives of the people, then we can make their pain go away."

Detria internally admitted that she could understand this ideology. She had seen many brutalities in her time as a slayer, just as many of them the result of human violence as of demon attacks. Still, she could see that Kelve took this seriously, more seriously than he had perhaps ever taken anything, so she decided not to play devil's advocate against him. Instead she offered the nudge he needed to continue his speech. "And you don't agree."

"Yasiff has been seizing power from Orikon for a long time now. Do you know why? Because Orikon had finally started to believe in the Overlord. The old man had spent more than a decade fighting against that myth, then finally in his last days he started to believe it was true. Why the sudden transformation? More importantly, why was Yasiff so vehemently against his transformation? Maybe he had something Yasiff was afraid of. Maybe he had proof."

"The Overlord? Kelve, what are you talking about?"

He gave a slow sigh and scratched the back of his head. "I guess you've never heard the tales. There are stories among the men, stories told over campfires. Stories of a dread Overlord, a single demon entity that is coordinating all of the efforts across Arkalen."

She slunk back with a smug grin. She had known her friend a long time and seen him often taken to flights of fancy, but she could not believe this even out of him. "Doesn't that seem a tad outlandish to you? I mean, they're demons. Why do they need a leader to do the things they do? And what about the humans we see warring among themselves?"

Kelve nodded, his face remaining somber. "I know, I know. I used to think the same things. But now, I don't know. Orikon was one of the smartest fellows I've ever known. I always listened up when he talked. So when he said to me and a few of the other veterans that he was beginning to believe the stories, I took it to heart. Sure, maybe the Overlord isn't behind all of the evil in this world. But just because there's not a single great conspiracy doesn't mean there couldn't be an evil presence at work somewhere, in some of the things that happen."

His eyes narrowed and he leaned in even closer. "But here's what really gets me. Now Yasiff has taken the reins and declared loudly that there isn't an Overlord. He's decided we're not fighting some devil, we're fighting nature itself, human and demon alike. So the only solution is to conquer nature, rule over it. What if that's all this is really about? What if Yasiff doesn't want us to believe in the Overlord, because he *needs* us to think there's no other way to save our world? What if he doesn't care about the truth, because what he really cares about is his own plans to rule us all? Tell me which you would choose—if our options are to either waste time fighting a war against an enemy who doesn't exist, or take away the freedoms of everyone in the world, which is the better path? Which is the path that your conscience can better live with?"

She shuffled back to distance herself from Kelve and thought over his words. "I-I'm not sure."

"Yeah. Same thing I said when Orikon asked me. But now it's different. The slayers were founded on a principle, you know? 'Help those who cannot help themselves.' Be the strong, to protect the weak."

"What are you driving at?"

"I don't know. Maybe you can tell me." He abruptly rose to his feet and brushed himself off, then turned and began to walk away. After a few steps he stopped and, without looking back at her, spoke just loudly enough to be heard over the uplifted winds. "I'm not a leader, Detria. I don't have the backbone like my dad did, like Orikon did. People can't lean on me, because I'll let them down. When things get rough, I'll cut and run." He then turned and looked to her, and the smile she knew so well returned to his face. "But I make a fine follower. I can promise that."

With that, he left. She sat alone, mulling over his words, trying to find the hidden messages in what he had told her. It did not take her long to decipher what the man was asking of her, but it took her the rest of the night to determine how she felt on the matter. As she sat alone in the dark, the storm rolled on, gathering power rapidly as its northern border finally dipped into the ocean.

* * * * *

Atop a single peak separated from its brethren mountains to the south, a serene figure stared outward across the continent. Over hills, forest, and plains alike his gaze penetrated, striking out deep into the far ocean where a fierce tempest now raged. The storm had hit the sea and was rapidly gathering momentum and power, turning into a juggernaut dancing over the waters and ravaging the Arkalenian shores.

The observer's attire was simple. He wore only a long white robe, with sleeves covering his hands and a loose hood draping his visage. Slim rays of sunlight struck beneath the hood's concealing line, highlighting a pale jawline with skin so white it seemed unnatural. He watched the storm for a long time, not really observing anything in particular. Here he stood for a little over three hours.

As the sun began to touch the western horizon, his head jerked back and his body gave a slight shudder. Black clouds began to close in around him, clouds that only his mind could perceive. After a few seconds they gripped him tightly and he was sealed within his own private abyss. The peak of the mountain stood empty in his absence.

His solitude did not last long. Soon an indeterminable voice began to speak. It was heard by neither his ears nor his mind, but somehow filled both at the same time.

*I have waited many years. Tell me your progress. Tell me it is time.*

"All preparations are laid. The necessary relics are gathered, and the first of the Godbeasts roams freely. Now the last components are approaching. The three warriors from Felthespar float aboard their ship, carrying with them the shell of the gods. They're maybe a month's voyage away. That is, if they can survive the storm."

*They must not perish. You must make certain they do not.*

"This storm is not my doing, nor does it bow to my will. If they die, then perhaps it will mean that Nature itself has deemed our plans to failure."

*Nature? Nature is an excuse humans use for their folly. My plans will not fail. I have waited for too long.*

"Very well then. You protect them. There are other events which I must set into motion."

*You would do well to show me proper respect. It would facilitate your future.*

"So you say. However, I am no god. I cannot do that which I cannot." There was a brief silence following this claim.

*See to your errands.*

The abyss gradually lightened, thinning into dust clouds and then fading away to reveal a world soaked in sunset lights. The pale traveler turned and drifted down from the mountaintop. "If this plot is to be my life's culmination, then I will play it out as *I* see fit," he whispered quietly to himself as he went.

## Chapter 4.

# A Grand Escape Plan

A few miles of southward trek from the northern shore of Arkalen, the Balsarosk Forest began. It extended over a decent stretch of the continent, running especially far to the west. This forest had once been made into a fiercely gnarled affair, twisted and corrupted by the currents, a prime residence for demonspawn. But the once-rich Asterian currents did not flow here anymore, so most of the demons had fled, surrendering this region of the continent over to human rule.

In the clear heat of midday, a man walked alone through Balsarosk. He was not one of the continent's natives, and was unaware what he might expect to encounter. He was tall, easily four inches over six feet, with his powerful build accentuated by glistening white plate mail. A sheathed sword rested comfortably on his left hip, and a large and intricate spear was strapped firmly across his back. His face was disguised by a white helmet and light blue face mask, which was matched by several other strips of blue clothing throughout his uniform.

He walked boldly down the widest paths he could find. He did not seem to be taking any particular care with his directions, but his comfortable stride reflected undaunted confidence. It would have been difficult for an onlooker to recognize that he was hopelessly lost.

This man was Cildar Emle, Holy Paladin of Felthespar, Knight of the Sun, and former Lord of the Phoenix. He was far from the familiarity of his homeland, now traveling across a continent upon which he had never before set foot. As he marched, he occasionally allowed his gaze drift to his left side. Every so often he could detect slight movements, or a brief glimpse of a shadow. There was nothing more to indicate that he did not travel alone. He considered his position for a moment, then decided to speak out.

"Hey, Myris." The shadow in the trees froze, disappearing entirely once stationary. When the response came, it echoed across the trail and seemed to come from all directions. This too was part of the shroud of stealth that hid Myris Phare, Knight of the Moon, Lord of the Children of Cain, away from the world.

The hidden figure knew the question on his friend's mind and answered intuitively. "I have detected nothing nearby. There is clear evidence that creatures have traversed these woods, but nothing recent."

"Maybe you should come on out of hiding then."

"Thank you, but I am quite comfortable here."

Cildar nodded. It was characteristic of the Cain to be overly cautious, so he chose not to pursue the topic. They had been following a trail of footprints for a matter of hours. Initially they had hoped these were the tracks of their commanding officer, Abaddon Daemon. There had since been sufficient evidence for them to dismiss that theory. Whomever they were following, the patterns did not match Abaddon's gait. Cildar considered abandoning this trail and returning to the beach to search further, but their previous efforts had been fruitless. It seemed unlikely they would have better success now. Furthermore, though he would not admit it aloud, he was caught up in his own curiosity over their current quarry.

As he was thinking, he found himself stepping out of the forest into a large glade. In front of him stood two robed figures conversing, and far beyond them—an hour's worth of travel by foot—another forest loomed. One of the pair was adorned in solid white with a large hood, and appeared to be a priest. The other was covered in a black, gold, and red affair, and what Cildar imagined to be some sort of strange headdress.

He subtly checked over his shoulder and noted that Myris had not yet exited the safety of the trees. *Good*, he thought to himself, *we still have an element of surprise on our side.* As he was doing this the priest took notice, then turned to his peculiar ally and waved a hand, dismissing him. The pale stranger began to approach Cildar, as the other turned and headed in the direction of the distant forest.

The paladin debated whether he should make an attempt to halt the fugitive, but cautioned himself that he did not yet know enough about these men to make such a rash move. They might pose no threat to him or anyone else, and it would be hasty to begin treating them as enemies.

Still, something about this encounter immediately did not sit right with him, and he decided to be curt rather than courteous. "Who are you?" he demanded of the approaching man.

"How irritating," came the immaterial response. "It seems I cast my net and caught the wrong fish."

Cildar's eyes narrowed and his left hand moved to rest on the hilt of his sword. He was uncertain what to make of the priest's words, but was now confident that he and Myris had wandered into some sort of trap. "I ask again, who are you?"

The man ceased his approach just ten feet shy of the paladin. He leaned his head back slowly, freeing the upper part of his face from the shadows. Cildar was not comforted by what he saw there. Clear white eyes with silver irises stared out from a solid white face. Something about this visage was markedly unnatural, and Cildar felt certain this was no human. "Your friend may as well take his leave from the shadows. His petty tricks do not deceive my eyes."

Without a word, Myris obliged. He leaped from the forest and dropped his stealth guards, landing silently at his compatriot's side. He was a stark contrast to the white knight in appearance. Nowhere near his friend's stature, he stood a mere five foot, nine inches, and was of slim build. He wore a tight tunic and breeches, both dark grey in color, and a long and tattered black cape drifted closely at his back, matching black gloves, boots, and belt. Myris' face was not disguised, and a thick shock of reddish-brown hair sat over piercing brown eyes and a humorless face.

"If you expect me to be impressed, I am not," he announced disinterestedly. "The advantage of sight you possess is not something with which I am unfamiliar."

The man continued to disregard the words of the foreign travelers. "Neither of you seem to have the sword. Does that mean your leader is yet alive? Does he possess it still?"

The knights exchanged glances. Cildar was rapidly tiring of the stranger's refusal to respond to them directly, and decided to treat him in kind. He drew forth his Trine Lance and infused it with a small surge of spiritual energy, causing the crystalline head to flare out as a shimmering white lantern. He leveled the triple-pronged spearhead out and pointed it at his opponent. Following his lead, Myris reached to his back and pulled forth a curved blade about three feet in length, with a handle folded along the inside of it. At the flick of his wrist the pole doubled in length and the blade twisted up, transforming the weapon into a large scythe. The Cain dropped into a low crouch as Cildar widened his own stance, planting his feet firmly.

"I'll ask but one last time," the tall man answered in a low, dangerous tone. "Who are you?"

The pale priest lowered his hood once more, and a smile adorned his cold features. He held forth his left hand and a light breeze began to blow through the area, pooling into his palm. "The Rook and the Bishop would do battle with the Queen?" he muttered halt to himself, then raised his voice to his adversaries. "Though I am the more powerful piece, it would be foolish of me to risk my well-being by facing the two of you without allies. It seems an exit is in order. Give my regards to your lord. I will be coming to see him."

Cildar began to object, but in that instant the stranger turned his hand and slammed his palm to the ground. The ball of wind he had pooled there instantly turned into a tempest, ripping apart the ground and sending a wave of screeching air carrying earthen shrapnel washing over the two lords. Myris endeavored to move in for the kill by using his renowned speed to overcome the attack, but instead he was overcome himself and sent flying back into the forest. Cildar managed to stand his ground, but was forced to raise an arm to protect his face. When the attack subsided and he lowered his arm, the mysterious stranger was nowhere to be seen.

Myris extricated himself from shattered branches and walked over to his ally, brushing himself off. “Annoying,” he commented.

The paladin moved to where the man had been standing and scanned the area hastily, trying to determine which direction the fugitive had taken his exit. His efforts were in vain, so he turned back to his companion. “What of that attack? Anything you’re familiar with?”

“A compact burst of wind like that with no physical rune structure? It is beyond either Cainite or Felthespari sorcery. It seems the type of technique only an adept mystic would be capable of performing at such whim.”

Cildar nodded his agreement. “Though I’m skeptical he’s anything as simple as a mystic. I’d say we’ve wandered into something here.”

Myris closed his Soul Scythe and returned it to his back, hidden beneath his cape. “For better or worse, that was our intent. So then, what is next?”

“He’s looking for Lord Abaddon. Fortunately we don’t know where he is. I’d say we keep trying to find him ourselves, but we’d run the risk of leading this guy right to him.”

“You are assuming he either can or is even interested in pursuing us. And that he poses a significant threat. Just because he seeks the Destroyer does not mean he is prepared for what such a confrontation would entail.”

“Even if that’s not the case, we still don’t know how to find Lord Abaddon.”

“Then we should seek allies elsewhere?”

“My thoughts exactly. Surely there’s someone nearby who knows more about the region than us, and can fill us in on what exactly we should expect from our foes here.”

"Alright. So the next step?"

Cildar placed the Trine Lance on his back and pointed out into the distant south. "We head to the next forest."

* * * * *

Abaddon sat in his tiny cell as the sun rose on the fifth day. Using a tailoring kit provided to him by one of the guards, he had finished touching up his old uniform. It was a simple ensemble, but he was comfortable in it. A tight black silk shirt covered his torso, cut off at the neck and shoulders by sewn-in elastic bands. A pair of loose-fitting black breeches covered his lower body, adorned with a purple belt and sash running along the left leg. Finally, thick white leather gloves and boots—which had lost their clean polish—guarded his hands and feet.

He looked out the window and took note of color of the sky. It was a few hours past dawn, nearing time for the guards to exchange shifts. He was not eagerly anticipating this, and gave a sigh as he rose to his feet.

He moved over to the window and slid his head between the bars. "Old man, wake up," he shouted.

The sentry on duty gave a snort and shot rapidly to his feet, presenting a salute. "Sir! I am alert and awake!"

"Relax," Abaddon answered calmly, "it's just me."

"Heh?" the kindly elder looked back at his prisoner with a bleary smile. "Oh, I see now," he said slowly. "Guess I nodded off again, eh?"

Abaddon gave a nod. "You didn't miss anything."

The man stretched and offered thanks as the prisoner returned to his stony bed. The previous day the elder had been caught asleep by the morning-shift guard and had been chastised sternly, warned that if it happened again he would lose his job. Abaddon had elected to help the weary gentleman avoid further trouble.

Since his imprisonment he had been guarded in shifts. Each sentry took eight hours and did little more than stand outside of his cell window, occasionally passing him some meager rations. His cell was a curious design, in that it had no door. Instead, he had discovered the window itself could detach, providing a narrow access path. Since the floor of the cell was a couple of feet lower than ground level, it created a feeling of being trapped in a small cave.

The first guard shift began at midnight and was covered by the old man. Abaddon had found the elder handy, in that he was an easy source of information. When he was awake he liked to go on long rants, discussing far and wide the events surrounding the village. From these rants Abaddon had learned the settlers here were refugees from some sort of overlord, hoping to escape his wrath by hiding within the shelter of the storms where no sane person would dare to wander.

"So we settled into the Dolmiga Ruins, intending to build a new life here," the old man had explained. "Until you arrived, that is. Something about that big sword they found on your body inspired the young soldiers, made them think they had some sort of fighting chance." Abaddon's interest had piqued at the mention of his sword's survival, but he said nothing. "So it was given to the strongest lad in the village, and he's been training with it ever since. They say they're gonna ride forth and overcome the Overlord himself, tear his whole kingdom down. I don't know about it. Seems to me that we've escaped and we should stay here. But maybe I'm just slowing down. A couple of decades ago I probably wouldn't have hesitated."

The second guard began his shift in the morning. He was a man named Tesserick, and Abaddon had developed a distaste for him. Tesserick made it a point to torment and harass his prisoner rather than simply ignoring him. He had several times now spat into Abaddon's water rations, or thrown his bread into a fire. He constantly taunted the big man, trying to get a rise. Abaddon had, as of yet, said nothing in return.

The third and final guard began his shift in the early evening. A young teenager, clearly equipped for actual battle neither physically nor emotionally. Abaddon had developed a camaraderie with the boy. In exchange for war stories, the young man had made a habit of fetching him extra rations and supplies. It was he who had brought Abaddon his tailoring kit.

"I think the women on the far side of the village have something like what you're looking for," the boy had mentioned when the prisoner had expressed a desire to repair his unkempt uniform.

"How far is it?"

"It'd take me about half an hour to go there and back probably. But I need to go now, before they're asleep." It was about two hours before midnight. If they waited any longer, he ran the risk of being absent when shift change came.

The prisoner merely gave a nod. The boy turned and started to leave, then stopped and began pacing back and forth. "Something wrong?" Abaddon queried.

He looked back at the prisoner with a furrowed brow. "You-you're not going to try to run away, when I'm gone? Are you?"

Abaddon's face remained expressionless. "Not on your watch," he promised.

The lad seemed reassured enough by this and headed on his way. Abaddon had used the opening as an opportunity to sneak out of his cell and down to a nearby spring for a quick bathe, but returned before anyone was wiser. He never bothered to mention his brief absence.

Today's scheduled guard shift came, and Abaddon's tormentor wasted no time in launching his aggressions. "Looks like you missed your opportunity to get out of here, huh, wretch? You should've escaped yesterday when the old man fell asleep. Today he was on the ball."

It was not much of a taunt, but the prisoner's icy patience was finally exhausted. "If I wanted escape, I would need no opportunity. If I choose to walk out of this village this very moment, I will do so."

"Big talk from the caged bird."

He rose to his feet and his eyes flashed dangerously. "I am no bird," he growled slowly, his words emphatic and deliberate. "I am the Daemon."

For a moment the bold soldier considered backing down. He resolved that he could not show weakness to his prisoner, however, and resumed. "Sit down and silence yourself. In a couple of days our tribe will be vacating this town, and you'll be left here to rot."

Abaddon took a moment to reflect on this, then answered, "I have decided to offer you a deal. It's against my personal nature, but I was trained to be merciful to weaker enemies. If you release me from this cell and lead me to whomever has my sword, you'll be alive when the sun rises tomorrow."

Tesserick's voice rose to an outraged high pitch. "You dare give me ultimatums? Who do you think you are?!"

"One chance," he answered coldly. "Cooperate with me."

"You can go to hell!"

He gave a somber nod, satisfied with his own charitable offering. "I expected no more from you."

He thrust his arms out and unleashed a commanding war cry. Tesserick leaped back startled, but began to laugh when nothing happened after several seconds. Then the wind began to pick up, as the earth developed a slight tremor. The jailer's laugh came to a choking halt, and he looked with terror into the cell.

Abaddon did not move, but continued to let his summoned disturbance flow. He had not gathered ether to his body since he had landed, and he was sorely due for a recharge. After half a minute he was satisfied, and slammed his fists together in front of his face. A shockwave released from his body shook the bed from walls of his cell and sent splits along the foundation. This attack did only superficial damage, but the Daemon's rage was only yet building.

Focusing his thoughts, he raised his right fist high and then slammed the ground between his feet. Instantly the earth around him erupted, as pillars of rock twenty feet high emerged and decimated his delicate dungeon. Tesserick ran from the tremors to a nearby weapon rack and seized a huge battleaxe. As he turned back to face his foe, he began to quake with fear.

Abaddon walked through the turbulence of upthrust rocks as they continued to collapse around him. Wind whipped fiercely around his body, creating a visible sandstorm fluttering about his form. One slab of granite came close to smashing him beneath it, but a sudden and seemingly light rap from his knuckles sent the offending boulder shattering into a rain of pebbles.

As Tesserick watched this march, his hands trembled uselessly. Abaddon met his gaze. It was only now that the guard realized how intimidating of a figure the prisoner was. Two inches over six feet tall, he was a fortress of muscle carrying broad shoulders and a head backed by long black hair. As he approached with the supernatural winds swirling about him, his mass only seemed to expand, and his arms bulged tighter as his knuckles turned white from clenched fists. Deep blue eyes swirled with intensity and gave off a light of their own, and Tesserick knew suddenly he was facing no normal man.

"Where is my sword?" the monster slowly demanded with a guttural roar.

Casting caution to the wind and giving himself over to adrenaline, Tesserick dashed in with his axe upheld high, sounding the alarm at the top of his lungs.

Abaddon waited until his outmatched foe was only a yard away, and then took a rapid sidestep to his left, upheld his right arm in a straight line, and dashed directly through Tesserick.

The move was impossible to follow, little more than a sudden zigzagged step on Abaddon's behalf. The freshly arriving guards were witness to a terrible sight as Tesserick's entire torso exploded into nothing but blood, and Abaddon stood nearby in a calm stance, his forearm soaked in red death.

The gathering soldiers quickly decided better of assaulting this man, and instead slipped out of the way and made a path for their own champion. A giant man stepped forth, nearly seven feet tall, made of solid muscle except for a large potbelly. In his right hand he held aloft a huge and beautiful greatsword, five feet of blade attached to a one-foot hilt, with a blood groove running three-quarters of the length of the six-inch-wide steel. From the base of the hilt, two steel spikes ran out at forty-five degree angles. The entire hilt and cross-guard, including the spikes, were wrapped tightly in thick white bandages. All that could be seen was a dark ruby pommel-stone protruding from the butt of the hilt.

All but a touch of rage seemed to fade from Abaddon's visage as he at last saw his sword. He announced calmly to his new opponent, "That sword is bound. Those bandages mean Kargaroth will not taste human flesh this day."

The man's brow sank in confusion, but he chose not to exchange words. He instead seized the hilt of his claimed sword firmly with both hands and charged his enemy.

When he was within range he gave a powerful downswing, releasing with his left hand after giving a sharp pull for extra speed. Despite his size he moved with sharp agility, and the attack seemed unavoidable. Abaddon looked serenely into the oncoming blade, and as the edge was only an inch away from his forehead his body slid two feet to the right. Kargaroth's tip buried itself deep into rock, as the Daemon seized the wrist of the hand holding its hilt and gave a sharp twist. His opponent screamed as his entire forearm was mercilessly snapped. The Felthespari warlord quickly followed up with a firm punch to the potbelly. As the bigger man doubled over in front of him, Abaddon grasped Kargaroth's hilt, lifted it high, then brought the ruby pommel down on the back of his foe's head.

The tribe watched in horror as their champion—defeated in less than five seconds—smashed into the ground with unreal force, his head and shoulder driving a full foot into the dirt.

The former Champion of Felthespar used a leather strap at his back to secure Kargaroth in place, and with a soft sigh turned to leave. First he issued a statement to his onlooking captors. "If this was the warrior you expected to defeat your feared Overlord, then the Overlord himself must truly be a weakling. Else, your hubris knows no bounds."

He left without encountering further resistance, proceeding to step swiftly through an attached forest as the sounds of commotion behind him continued to increase. He suspected he would be pursued if there was a strong leader among them, or if he gave them time to get organized. He decided it best to make his way swiftly, lest he was forced to injure more people.

He was then surprised to sense he was already being followed, albeit clumsily. He increased his pace silently, but his pursuer did the same. Eventually, when he was maybe a mile from the village itself, he turned and stood his ground.

"Who dares hunt me? I grow tired of games."

His answer came shortly, as the boy who had guarded him in the evenings suddenly dashed into the narrow clearing. The boy failed to stop, but rather tripped and fell straight into Abaddon's stomach.

Abaddon had lowered his guard instantly when he saw the youthful face, and when the boy crashed into him the breath was knocked from his lungs. He took a couple of steps back and tried to recover his composure, as the boy struggled to his feet muttering apologies. The winded man made a swift slashing gesture with his open hand, and the boy fell silent.

After a few seconds he had steadied himself and managed to speak unabated. "Why are you after me?"

"Sir, please, I want to follow you. I want to be like you."

Abaddon's left eye twitched. "What?"

The boy sat on his knees and looked at the ground in front of him. "Please, hear me out. My whole life I served in the plantations of the Overlord. When the escape came, I happened to be in the quarters the assault was launched from. I had no choice but to escape with them. I stayed in that village, and did as I was told, and... and..." the boy slowed down, taking a few deep breaths and attempting to organize his thoughts. "When I listened to your stories, about the battles you've fought and the adventures you went on, I came to believe that you don't have to be what your surroundings make you. I want to learn to walk on my own two feet. I want to learn to walk a warrior's path, like you. I'm not very strong, and I haven't learned much about combat. But I want to be stronger. I just..." he took a few extra deep breaths, forcing himself to spit out the last sentence of his speech as his eyes brimmed with tears of fervor. "I want to be strong enough to hold up my own shoulders." He raised his face from the ground, and with effort met the tall man's gaze. "I want to be brave enough to look men like you in the eyes."

Abaddon stared back at the boy for nearly half a minute, drinking in this request. He offered his response with a harsh but not cruel whisper. "The path I walk is the path of death. Both mine and my enemies'. If you follow me, you will surely die."

The boy rose to his feet, but he broke off his gaze and looked once again to the ground. "I accept that inevitability of death. I'm not afraid of dying. I'm afraid that I've never even been alive yet."

Abaddon turned and headed into the forest again, setting half the pace he had been moving at previously. "Do not fall behind. I want to put some distance between us and your former home."

The boy smiled and his hands shook with excitement and fear, both from what he had just done, and of what lay ahead. He wiped his eyes and his nose on his sleeve, and then rapidly set himself jogging to keep up with his new master's gait.

## Chapter 5.

# Of Men and Dragons

"You never told me your name."

The boy looked up from the lengthy bug he had been watching crawl across his boot. Abaddon was at a nearby stream washing the blood from his arm and cleansing his boots and gloves. They had been traveling east for two hours, heading toward the center of the continent. The northerner was trying to regain familiar territory, rather than risk wandering aimlessly in hopes of discovering his fresh surroundings. The last time he had been on Arkalen his journey had taken him on a directly southern route, and he was unfamiliar with these western shoreline areas where the tribesmen had brought him.

"Eiden. My name is Eiden Hoek," the boy answered.

"Have you ever heard of a man named Tenkahn, Eiden?"

He thought for a few seconds, then shook his head. "Forgive me, no. Should I have?"

The man finished with the stream and stepped away, pulling his gloves back on. "It would have surprised me. Still, the question merited asking. Come, we don't know how much farther we have to go. I wish to make reasonable progress before evening approaches."

As they walked, Eiden could not stop staring at Abaddon's now-spotless white gloves. Though a mere fifteen minutes ago the right glove had been coated in blackening blood, it was now impossible to tell they had ever been anything less than pristine.

"Master, if I may ask something—"

"Don't call me master. If you must use a term of respect, 'sir' or 'Lord Abaddon' will suffice."

"Forgive me, sir. If I may, how did you get your gloves so white? All you had was water from a stream. Are they some sort of special material? I know you said that your homeland in the north was advanced in many achievements."

He shook his head lightly before responding. "Do you know much of magic, Eiden?"

"Magic? You mean the powers that demons use?"

"That is a part of it, yes. However the power is not limited to demonspawn. Humans are capable of channeling it as well."

The youth's face lit up, "You mean you used magic to clean your gloves?"

Abaddon shrugged subtly. "I would not put it so grandiosely, but in essence. Listen closely, as I'll only attempt to explain this once. Reality is split into two planes. The world that you know, all you have ever seen or witnessed, is the corporeal, which we call Morolia. There is also a second layer to the world around us. You could think of it as a mystical background, for simplicity's sake. This is the ethereal plane of Asteria. Across both planes, mighty streams of ether run. These streams dictate the laws of reality, and when one learns to interact with and control them, they can be used for virtually endless applications, which is summed up by the term 'magic'."

"How do you learn to see them? How do you learn to interact with them?"

"That I cannot teach you," he responded curtly.

"Oh. Is it forbidden to share your knowledge with others?"

"No. I cannot teach you because I do not know. I am, by birthright, what is called a 'mystic'. My ability to interact with the ether streams is natural, an extension of my consciousness. I reach out and tap the currents of reality as naturally as you might extend your hand to pick up an apple. Because of this, I cannot teach it. I do not understand the process necessary for someone who is not a mystic to learn to manipulate magic."

"Oh." Eiden was disappointed, but let the matter drop. A few minutes later his curiosity again got the better of him. "So when you cleaned your gloves, you just wished them to be clean and then they were?"

The Balsarosk Forest around them had begun to grow thick and cumbersome, so Abaddon answered as best he could while forcing overbearing branches out of his way. "It's not that simple. Magic is not as—well, magical, as you might think. It comes down to a few basic tenants. Morolian ether can be used to manipulate natural processes via white magic, Asterian ether can be used for bursts of energy manipulated via black magic. To fix my gloves, I first used an ultra-thin layer of heat to burn away the residues on the surface. Next I used white magic to draw oils from the ground and applied them to the leather. Then I used another white magic trick to make the leather age rapidly and respond quickly to the treatment."

"I think I'm starting to see. You must be incredibly powerful, with all that magic at your disposal."

They finally pushed their way through the roughest parts of the forest and found themselves in a huge clearing. It ran in each direction, east and west, for as far as the eye could see. On the other side, less than five miles away, another forest ran across the southern territories. Abaddon stopped and analyzed his surroundings, but did not break off conversation.

"Not so much as you'd think. I have never put forth the effort necessary to master the sorcerous arts. I use my mysticism to enhance my physical strength and capabilities or to aid my healing processes, but beyond that my power is limited to a few mere tricks. I don't know enough about white magic to heal someone else, and I'm not even skilled enough with black magic to create a simple fireball."

Instead of turning to the other forest he tacked a course east, stepping rapidly. Eiden was forced to break into a small run to keep up. In a few minutes they reached a disturbance, an uprooted section of ground about five yards in diameter.

"Looks like a demon attack of some sort," the boy postulated.

Abaddon kept looking around, sniffing the air and touching the ground with his fingertips. Finally he wandered back to the outskirts of the forest. He pushed a few broken tree branches out of the way and found what he sought. Eiden followed and looked over the man's shoulder. He noticed a patch of what appeared to be blood, mostly dried up. Abaddon removed his left glove and touched his fingertips to it, then gave it a smell.

"Cainite." He brushed his fingertips off on the ground and restored his glove.

"Cainite?" It took the boy a moment to recognize this word. "Didn't you say those were the ancient enemies of your homeland? Have they followed you to Arkalen?"

Abaddon shook his head and continued searching the ground, lightly pushing Eiden out of his way. "Unlikely." He found a spot that intrigued him, just a few feet beyond the edge of the trees, and stared motionlessly for nearly a full minute. Just as the younger man began to grow uncomfortable, his travel companion finally straightened his back. "Unless I am mistaken, Cildar was standing here, and that blood belonged to Myris. I'm uncertain what they were doing. There are signs of a struggle, but it appears to have been of small scale and brief duration."

"Cildar? Myris?"

As Abaddon answered he began walking south once more, heading toward the new forest. "They are allies, fellow passengers aboard the ship which brought me here. Myris is a former Cainite, a defector."

"Defector?"

"A savior or a traitor, depending on your point of view. He forswore the Cainites and joined forces with Felthespar during the War of the Second Arocaen. His allegiance was crucial to Felthespar's victory. He and Cildar are two of the only men with whom I would entrust my life. I'm comforted to see they have survived. However, I'm not comforted to see they are alone. If there were other survivors, Cildar and Myris would certainly be escorting them."

"You said it looked as if they had been in battle. Should we be concerned about that?"

"For the moment, no. We know too little to begin fretting. We should follow their path and be grateful for our blessings. It's serendipitous that we stumbled across their trail in this manner. I hadn't even decided to seek them out, since it seemed unlikely they had survived."

As they resumed their march Eiden fell into a thoughtful silence, unable to match his leader's optimism. Instead he focused on putting one foot in front of the other. He was accustomed to days of travel from his expedited fleeing of the Overlord's lands, fortunately, and did not yet find himself tiring from their journey.

After an hour they reached the edge of the new forest, which Abaddon stepped into without hesitation. Eiden noticed the man's pace seemed to quicken, and he unconsciously did the same. The Lord of Felthespar's pace continued to increase, however, and soon Eiden found himself struggling to keep up.

"Are we in a hurry, sir? Do you think we're about to catch up to them?"

"No," the man answered quizzically, "right now I'm not hasty for the sake of Cildar and Myris, but for ourselves. I know this forest. Last I was here I nearly lost my life. From this point, be swift and silent."

Eiden gave a swallow and his pulse quickened, but he did his best to do as told. It was difficult for him to move at such a high speed—nearly a full run—and keep himself from making many sounds. Occasionally he would step on an old branch or bump into a low bush or plant, but Abaddon never chastised him.

After another hour of marching they were forced to come to a stop. In front of them, three giant entangled trees grew blocking the path forward. Eiden looked around, but could not locate any easy routes to gain passage.

Abaddon tapped his foot with annoyance. "This happened last time, as well. This forest is difficult to navigate efficiently. Whether by nature or design I am uncertain."

Eiden continued looking around, examining the blockade. The mystic did likewise, but soon gave up and turned to head back the direction they had come. He was about to give an order when the boy suddenly exclaimed, "Up there!"

Abaddon looked to where Eiden was pointing and saw an opening in the trees. It was large enough for two or even three men to pass through, but it was easily forty feet from the ground. He scanned the structure of the trees, and could not find more than a few suitable footholds.

"We can't get up there," he concluded. "Atheme could probably make it, but I'm not as agile as him, especially with Kargaroth's weight." He thought for a moment that he could perhaps give Eiden a boost that high, but it seemed too much of a risk for the youth. Abaddon glanced to him for response, but the young man had already pulled a satchel from behind his back and fetched out a strange pair of gloves with hooks attached, as well as a tightly balled spool of rope.

Without further word Eiden leaped to the trunk of one of the trees and began to scale rapidly. He used only his upper body strength to shimmy up the trunk, leaving his legs hanging loosely below him. Every so often he would pass one of the footholds Abaddon had taken note of and, without thinking, he would use his right foot to spring himself up a few extra feet.

In little more than a minute he reached the opening between the trunks and situated himself, tying the rope off on the sturdiest nearby branch and tossing the end down to the man below. "There you go. That should hold your weight."

Abaddon looked at the rope that had been thrown down to him. It was tiny, only an inch in diameter, but made of a strange black, corded material he did not recognize. It was too hard to be leather and too flexible to be steel. He gingerly placed one leg on the tree trunk in front of him and shifted his weight to the rope. To his surprised, it held firm. He climbed up the tree and joined Eiden without incident.

"What is this?" he asked as he reached the natural balcony.

"Troll leather. It's pretty wicked tough stuff. The Overlord recently added a few trolls to his ranks. They make it from the skin of their own fallen. I stole some when we left, it's too handy to not have around, gruesome as it is."

"That was impressive," he added as the boy reeled up the rope.

"I was a carpenter under the Overlord. I had to learn how to get to inaccessible high places and get over my fear of heights. If I hadn't, I'd have been put to death and replaced with someone who would." His tone reflected surprising apathy over his ordeal, and he paid little attention to himself as he talked. "Since I didn't make much of a soldier, he didn't have any other use for me." He finished fetching his rope and then dropped it down the other side. "Okay, ready to go down?"

Abaddon shook his head. "After you. Going down poses no problem for me." Eiden quickly slid down the rope, slowing himself a few feet before hitting the ground and landing gently. The remaining man untied the rope and tossed it down, then he placed his left hand over his right wrist and concentrated on gathering a stream of ether about his fingertips. When his enchantment was complete he hopped from the landing and slammed his right hand into the trunk of the tree. His fingers split the wood and dug deep furrows in the bark as he slowly slid down to ground level.

When he landed he dismissed the spell, and the tips of his gloves leaked a light grey smoke as the effect passed. He motioned forward wordlessly as he stepped past Eiden, and the boy quickly fell into place behind him.

"That was black magic?" he quizzed as they headed into the newly discovered section of the forest. "I'm guessing you gathered small amounts of power, maybe heat, into your fingertips, and then used it to dig into the tree."

This new area of the forest was sparser than the area before, so Abaddon was able to set a brisk pace. "A well reasoned guess, but incorrect. Do you recall the name I mentioned before? Tenkahn?"

"Yes," Eiden responded.

"Last I was on Arkalen I met him and his allies. They are a band of monks similar to myself, in that they are able to channel the currents on a mystical level. They taught me many of their secret techniques. The one I used there is called Shattering Fingertips. It uses a tremendous amount of white ether, compacted into high potency, to shred apart Morolian matter. The technique is an ultimate extension to the Tiger Claw style of martial arts."

Eiden nodded for a few seconds, then posed another question. "Why use white magic instead of black? Didn't you say black was used to gather energy?"

"Black magic is highly volatile. It would be extremely difficult to prevent it from burning something specific without advanced techniques. In this instance, my own gloves or fingertips. White magic is much more suitable for something of that nature. Forget not, this forest may yet be dangerous territory. Be silent."

They marched stolidly onward another two hours. The area of the woods they had entered seemed to be a windfall, proving less convoluted throughout. Abaddon could not help but think that it felt as though they had stepped over one of the walls in a maze.

Eiden concentrated on marching and sang a few traveling tunes in his head. After the first hour he lost track of time and simply followed his companion mindlessly, bobbing his head rhythmically all the while. When Abaddon finally came to an abrupt halt, Eiden only managed to stop half a foot short of bumping into his back.

"Is something wrong?" he asked in a whisper, fearing the answer was yes.

Abaddon shook his head slowly. "We weren't fast enough."

He turned around and looked over Eiden's head, staring back into the treetops. The youth stepped around to the man's side and looked in the same direction. At first, he saw nothing. Then he began to hear strange sounds, and detect shapes moving along the branches with ease. Once they became aware they had been noticed, the shapes moved from hiding into the light, and Eiden was unable to repress a gasp.

They were large lizards, far larger than any he had ever seen. Taller than Abaddon, and at least as well built. Their bodies were decorated with the sharpened bones of their own kind, and their vicious curved talons extended an entire foot from their fingertips.

The boy swallowed and commanded himself not to panic. In the service of the Overlord he had worked alongside many breeds of demonspawn, so he was not completely taken aback. At the same time, he realized this was not the protected domain of the Overlord, and there was no telling what these creatures might do to two human travelers. He wondered how his new lord's power measured up against this many dangerous foes.

"I can't take them all," Abaddon answered with seeming prescience. "They are draconics. Mutated dragonspawn. They would likely number among the strongest demons on the planet. I was stronger last I was here, and had an ally nearly as strong. Maybe two dozen is my limit, depending on how heavily they swarm me. I might go down without killing a single one."

Eiden turned pale and the forest began to spin in his eyes. "So I'm already going to die?" he asked despondently.

"Don't be so sure. They haven't yet attacked. That strikes me as odd. Stay silent a moment." With effort, Abaddon cast a grey magic spell to adjust his hearing, tuning into the voices lilting lightly through the leaves.

"He seems to be the one," a hidden draconic speculated.

Several voices began bouncing back and forth in response, with little organization. "Then we must leave him alone!"

"The rest will come if we bother him. Remember last time?"

"He is food. Good food. We have not had such food in so long."

"Silence, fools!" a commanding rasp suddenly rang out. "I will go. Do not move."

One of the smaller green draconics pounced forward and landed fearlessly in front of the human trespassers, only two yards away. Abaddon waited for the creature to speak first, hoping he might gain information he could work with.

"We know you," was all the beast offered.

Abaddon's mind raced. There was clearly some backstory here, but he had no idea what it might be. He wanted to offer a confident response, without giving himself away. "Perhaps. I have killed your kind in the past."

A series of shrill hisses arose from the forest, but the green creature on the forest floor raised a taloned hand and the trees fell silent once more. "You are the champion of the Devilslayers, yes? We recognize your aura. It's unique in its potency. We could not not know you." After finishing this speech, the creature took another step forward and hissed violently at Abaddon's face.

The man did not flinch at this display. *Interesting*, he thought to himself. *They have mistaken me for someone else. And on a particularly unlikely basis.* Aloud, offered only a simple, "What of it?"

The creature took another half step forward. "Why do you come to our forest? We have done no wrong to incur your wrath. We have not overstepped our bounds. The ones that we have killed came to *us*. You agreed to leave us the forest territory."

Abaddon glanced off to the side, dwelling on the information he had just been presented. If the draconics were as afraid of these 'Devilslayers' as it appeared, things must have changed radically on Arkalen since his last visit. For a moment he considered using his opponent's hesitation as an opening to leave, but then decided he should not waste this opportunity.

"We're looking for two men. A tall man in white and a shorter in black. I demand any knowledge you have of their whereabouts."

At this brazen display, the voices in the trees began to chime in once more.

"Enough! We owe these humans nothing. Let us eat them and be done!"

"If we eat one, the Devilslayers will find out. They will send armies for us. They will burn the very forest to the ground if they must!"

"Then don't let them find out. Eat them, bones and all, drink their blood to the last drop. Leave no evidence!"

"But the Devilslayers surely already know they came here! If they disappear, we will be blamed regardless."

"What if they die elsewhere? Are we to be blamed then, as well?"

Their leader shivered with rage, then turned to the forest. "Shut up! Speak no more or I start taking your heads!" He spun back to Abaddon. "These men you seek, are they your friends or foes?"

"I'm not interested in your inquiries," he responded coolly. "I demanded their whereabouts."

The draconic was losing his temper. He took another step forward, closing the gap between them to less than a yard. "We have no reason to help you! I should kill you where you stand."

Abaddon took a large step himself, putting his nose only inches from the draconic's fangs. Slowly and deliberately he challenged, "Try me."

The creature's eyes went wild and its breathing rose to a frenzied wheeze. Abaddon worried briefly that he might have carried his bluff too far, but knew he could not show doubts now. The draconic crouched lower and placed his hand around a bone scimitar hanging from his belt, the human raised his right hand to the hilt of Kargaroth, and the cold war continued.

Just as it seemed tension had reached the breaking point, one of the draconics from the forest defied the master's order. A female voice rang out, "We cannot win in this! If he's as strong as they say he will kill many of us! Even if he does not, they will come for us as the others have said!"

The draconic commander turned his gaze back over his shoulder. Trying to save face and make it appear that he was not backing down, he stepped around the big man and began to head south.

"We indeed saw the men you seek. We would have killed them, but it seems they had allies. Many troops appeared and rescued them from us. I'll show you where they left our woods. My hopes are that you will find them and you will all kill one another."

Abaddon waited dramatically for about five seconds, then spun about to pursue the draconic. He gave a snap as he passed Eiden, and the boy inhaled sharply and seemed to reanimate, quickly pursuing the two.

## Chapter 6.

# The Soldiers of Detria Alsen

Near a small evening fire, Cildar sat drinking an unfamiliar fruit cocktail from a wooden mug. He sat alone in a smooth hilly area, with several nearby rock formations serving as company. The armor from his upper body had been painstakingly removed and laid in a careful pile to his right. In addition to the armor, over two dozen daggers, shurikens, short swords, small axes, and other hidden weapons lay organized in neat rows. His left shoulder was carefully wrapped with bandages, and his ribs braced with a splint. His helmet and mask had also been discarded, revealing a head of dirty blond hair and sharp green eyes.

He and Myris had been badly injured fighting a battle against the draconics. Cildar was forced to use his Haste technique, an ability which amplified his strength and speed several times over with grey magic, then used white to increase his rejuvenation to supernatural levels. Unfortunately this had only caused the reptilian warriors to set into him with escalated fury and numbers, and in spite of his defenses they had nearly ripped him in half before help arrived.

He still held his misgivings as to the source of this help. They seemed to be a tribe of nomads, makeshift in both their dwellings and their attire. Cildar had fought wars in many countries, so he was accustomed to nonstandardized soldiers. Yet these men and women did not seem to be soldiers at all, but rather an entire mobile village. They lived in tents of various sizes, tents which even now were being knitted by members of certain families. A few among the inhabitants were sparring, but it was of a light, pleasant nature. Clearly no emphasis was being placed on developing technique or pushing limits.

They shared no symbolic equipment or uniform that might distinguish them as anything more than a random collection of individuals. It varied wildly which among the fighters even wore armor at all, and if so, of what shape or size. As Cildar looked at them now, the sight suggested to him they were nothing to marvel at. Yet only a few hours prior he had watched them drive a force of draconics to a bitter stalemate, something which would have posed a challenge even for his own Phoenix Dragoons.

A young woman made her way over to where Cildar sat. Her attire was a cute ensemble, her long light brown hair flowing down over a nearly identically-colored tabard. The tabard was tied off at the waist by a black belt, and hid a slim breastplate. She wore a pair of fading red shorts that ran down slightly past her knees. Below these shorts her legs were covered by dark stockings damaged by her travels, and then a slim pair of simple brown shoes. The only distinctive part of her outfit was a pair of shoulder pads, golden in color and tied together with chains of the same metal that ran under her neck, as well as diagonally across her waist down to the belt.

As she passed by groups of men a few cheery cries went up. She raised a hand and gave a bow, nimbly sidestepping through groups as she lightly skipped down a small incline to arrive where Cildar had comfortably isolated himself.

She slid a box over to his feet and took a seat on a rock next to him. He first suspected she may have come to flirt with him, given her easy nature with the other men, and was trying to think of the most polite way to cut the conversation short. He nearly blurted out a statement announcing that he was married, but she spoke before he found his words.

“I hope you’ve been made comfortable. That box is a first aid kit, the best I could round up. I don’t know if it’s much, as our supplies are a little sparse right now. Hopefully in the next few days we’ll reach a real settlement, and if you’re still with us we’ll try to gather something more suitable.”

Cildar dismissed his previous thought—internally grateful he had not spoken it aloud—and instead offered thanks as he picked the box up and opened it. It was fairly lacking, as the girl had implied, but there were a few useful herbs he recognized, as well as additional rolls of bandages. He was pleased at the sight of these at least, as had already exhausted his own supply.

"Your shoulder is still in very bad shape," the young woman said with a furrowed brow.

He took a look, and his left shoulder had indeed already soaked his fresh bandages a bright red. He gathered white ether into his hand and began rubbing it over the area, attempting to patch his skin back together. "The damage is quite severe, but it's too soon to change this wrap. I need to give the blood time to clot and the skin to heal. The next exchange will be painful, most likely."

"I haven't seen your friend. Is he okay? His wounds were also grievous, as I recall."

"Don't worry over him. He's resilient." Cildar was lying. Myris was wounded at least as badly as himself, if not worse. Unfortunately his Cainite enchantments made him nearly impervious to white magic, and the paladin was incapable of healing his wounds. Too injured for conventional methods of medicine to be sufficient, Myris had instead gone hunting. The most effective way for him to recover injuries so severe was by using his Soul Scythe. The ancestral Cainite relic was capable of sapping the strength from other creatures and using it to heal its wielder in remarkable ways rivaling even Cildar's own healing. Still, in Myris' condition hunting a creature powerful enough to provide sufficient healing energy could easily prove fatal.

Cildar worried over his friend's return, but did not wish for others to share in that fret. Instead he changed the subject. "Pardon me, miss, but I'm afraid I don't know who you are."

She hopped from rock where she had situated herself and gave an apologetic bow. "Forgive me! Wandering the wilderness does so cause one to forget basic etiquette. I'm Detria Alsen. I'm the leader of... well, us." She raised her arms and nodded toward the camp.

He tilted his head in confusion. "You're the leader? When we were rescued in the forest, I thought I remembered there was a man shouting out orders."

She gave a nod. "My deputy commander, Kelve. When we face the more intelligent breeds of demons, Kelve often assumes the guise of authority. Many species consider a female leader to be a sign of weakness. If I had been the one barking out orders instead of a man, the draconics likely would have never backed down and let us escape with our lives."

"Hm, clever. Your warriors are quite impressive in combat."

"Although not nearly as impressive as you and your ally. The two of you alone were successfully holding off two-score draconics." Her eyes went wide as she spoke. "I've never heard of such a thing! Even the fiercest warriors I have ever known would think it impossible to come out of such odds alive." Cildar gave a smile and rubbed his cheek, but said nothing. The woman returned to sitting on her rock and watched him for a moment, then asked, "So there must be some story to you two. I find it hard to believe such warriors simply congealed out there in that forest. You must tell me something of your origin."

"It's not a short nor easy tale to explain who we are. But if you're curious, I will do my best to relay some rendition to you."

She hopped once more off of the rock and down to the ground, crossing her legs and leaning her elbows against her knees. "I absolutely am."

Suddenly there was a shout from the north. Detria shot to her feet and her face became serious. "What now?" she muttered with concern. Cildar noted how easily she shifted from light and jovial into a stern demeanor fit for command. "Kelve!" she demanded firmly of the approaching man. "Is something nearby?"

Three men approached from across the camp. In the darkening evening it was still impossible to make them out. The frontmost waved a hand and shouted back, "No, everything's fine. We have some more guests."

She turned to Cildar. "Friends of yours, perhaps?"

He carefully edged himself forward and rose to his feet, favoring his left side. "I don't know," he stated. "I don't believe I have any friends here."

Soon the figure identified as Kelve came close enough to the fire that the paladin got a good look at him. He was a tall man, slightly shorter than Cildar at six feet. He had deep black hair, cut short, and was one of the most heavily armored men in Detria's camp. He wore an assortment of earthen tones, mostly green, on a mix of plate and scale mails. Along his belt hung at least a score of tubes and vials of unknown nature. On each of his hips rested a thick cutlass, with blades three feet in length adorned by gilded silver hilts and basket-guards. Cildar surmised that the man's commanding appearance was designed to enhance the illusion that he was the encampment's true leader.

Shortly after identifying Kelve, Cildar was also able to make out the two visitors following. The one on the right was a young lad, maybe seventeen years of age, with hair of a color somewhere between red and brown running to his shoulders. His outfit was basic, little more than dirty white tunic and breeches, and some black sandals that seemed to be at the end of their lifespan. There was a strap across the boy's chest and across his waist. The paladin noticed several satchels of various sizes on these straps, presumably for carrying tools of some nature. Then he turned his gaze to the other traveler.

His eyes went wide and he straightened his back. His shoulder protested the sudden movement, but he ignored the sharp agony. "Lord Abaddon!" he exclaimed.

Abaddon Daemon gave a halfhearted nod as he entered the campsite. He reached back and removed the massive Kargaroth, thrusting its tip firmly into the ground so that it stood upright of its own accord. Detria's eyes went wide as she stared at the most tremendous broadsword she had ever seen, and the newcomer ordered, "At ease, Cildar. Debrief."

Cildar relaxed his stance, then quickly began pooling more white magic and working it over his shoulder. "After abandoning the *Calvin*, Myris and I fought hard to keep our lifeboat upright. Amid the swells of that storm we stood little chance, and were barely able to hold it together for an arduous few minutes. Yet remarkably, we were able to reach the continent's northern coast. It would seem that Captain Yoshim gave up on our vessel just barely too soon, unnecessarily dooming himself and the crew. A hard tragedy to accept, to be sure.

"Upon gaining the shore, Myris and I were quickly driven into the forests for cover and forced to wait until the following day when the weather began to calm. Though we tried our best in the weakening torrents, we were unable to locate any other survivors. We searched for several days, and eventually found the wrecked hull of the *Calvin* itself. It had drifted quite far downshore from us, but had washed up conveniently under a large overhanging cliff. We spent another day concealing it, relocating giant vines, mosses, and other plant life over it, as well as using a series of large boulders to lock it into place so the tides will not carry it back out. With enough manpower and a few weeks of work, we believe she can be made seaworthy again."

"I was not so fortunate," Abaddon replied. "Short though the journey may have been, my lifeboat did not make it to land, but rather was crushed by the ocean. I'm forced to assume the young Jegan commander who traveled with me was killed nearly instantly. I myself washed up on a beach somewhere mostly dead." He paused and pointed to his friend's injured shoulder. "Draconics? Or something else you encountered?"

"Draconics, sir."

"And the Cainite? Does he survive?"

The paladin hesitated, not entirely certain of the answer, which then presented itself. Myris stepped out from the shadow of a nearby rock formation and announced, "I am unharmed." Cildar looked his friend over. He indeed seemed to have regained a healthy color in his cheeks, and his movements were crisp. The dark man gave a deep bow to their returned ally. "It is most good to see you, Lord Abaddon."

Detria exchanged glances with Cildar and inserted herself into the conversation. "Excuse me for interrupting your reunion, but I would still somewhat like to know who you all are."

Abaddon stared at her for a second, then stated, "I am Abaddon Daemon."

She raised her eyebrows and then smiled. "Well thanks. I am Detria Alsen."

"Lord Abaddon is our commanding officer," Cildar added. "He was leading the expedition that brought us here. I don't know who the boy is, though." The young man standing nearby gave a slight wave and an awkward smile.

Abaddon looked over to him, but offered no introduction. "You have not told her anything?" he instead asked of Cildar without inflection. Detria did not find herself enjoying her newest guest's presence. He had an overbearing personality, and she suspected he kept Cildar and Myris in line by means of fear. She was skeptical the man could actually be more powerful than the two warriors, but at the same time she kept glancing to his weapon and reconsidering the thought.

"I was just about to get to it when you arrived," the paladin answered. "We haven't been here long."

"Don't let us interrupt you. We'll settle in and rest." He turned to Kelve. "The boy is tired. He could use some food and water." Detria could not tell if this was meant to be taken as an order or a simple statement of fact. In either case, she felt her patience with the large man slip further. She gave Kelve a nod, and he in turn signaled to a distant sentry watching over the commanders. As Abaddon seated himself on a nearby rock, Detria motioned for the clearly uncomfortable youth to have a seat next to her. Myris, for his part, returned to the shadows, never quite within sight.

With Detria and Kelve listening carefully and Eiden snacking on some food provided to him, Cildar did the best he could to explain their previous lives. He told of the northern continent, of the nation of Felthespar, of their enemies the Cainites. He touched upon how Myris had come to be a member of their nation by means of subterfuge, then changed sides when he would have otherwise been sentenced to death. Detria had commented, with apologies to Myris, that it seemed foolish to accept someone so dangerous into your flock during such a time of war. Cildar had been without an answer to this, but insisted it had since proven to be the correct course.

For a while he became sidetracked telling stories of their friend, the Lord Councilor Atheme Tethen. Only during this part of the tale did Abaddon have anything to say, occasionally correcting a detail or inserting a quote from Atheme. Detria could feel their affection for their detached friend, and she smiled to think of a land where people stood so steadfastly together.

Cildar finally worked his way around to explaining the boat, their trip, and how they had become shipwrecked and stranded.

"So I guess that's it," he finished.

Detria shook her head. "I still don't understand. *Why* exactly are you here? Why did you come back to Arkalen?"

Myris answered in his loquacious friend's stead. "To put it simply, we are here for sport."

"Sport?" Kelve asked in bewilderment.

"For the adventure," Cildar added. "We want to test our limits against grave danger. Which so far, Arkalen has not been short on."

Abaddon had sat throughout all of this with his arms crossed, staring at his feet. As he spoke he did not change position, even to look up. "We had with us a full complement of knights. Good soldiers. If they were still with us, we would probably go to war with the draconic forest and wipe them out. They would have made an excellent starting point, at least. But as we are, we're in no condition to wage war on any sizable force."

Detria shook her head. "There's no need to wipe out the draconics. I mean, that forest is their home. Yes it can be somewhat inconvenient to travel around at times, but they are no threat to the humans of the continent. They're held in check by the Devilslayers."

The big man looked up at this, locking eyes with her. Normally

Detria was unafraid of anyone, but she felt an unnatural intimidation at the cold intensity of his dark blue eyes. "That's the second time I have heard that name. Eiden doesn't know of them. He says where he comes from, he has never heard the term. Who are the Devilslayers?"

She swallowed and broke off his gaze, shaking off her anxiety. "The Devilslayers are the most powerful force on Arkalen. It's a band of over four thousand men and women running the entire stretch of the continent, and always growing. They were formed to protect human settlements and freedom, and hunt devils—human or demon—without mercy."

Eiden's face turned somber and he dropped what little remained of his meal. "Devilslayers," he spat. "Where I come from, they are not the most powerful force. Excuse me." He stood and left the fire, moving to another area of the camp. Detria gave a nod to Kelve and he headed off to escort the young man.

She turned to Abaddon. "Just where does he come from?"

"I'm not certain. He has given me very little detail. All I know is that he's had a hard past, and abides it well. I admire that of him."

She nodded. "It's really no surprise that he was abandoned. A couple of years ago, the Devilslayers began to change. Instead of a guardian role, they began to become more governmental. They started placing taxation and laws upon various villages, and if even a single member of the community defied them they would pull their protection entirely. When this started, I had a large falling out with the Devilslayer's High Chieftain. I left, and thanks to Kelve's influence many of the slayers followed me. We've continued to grow somewhat since then, picking up many the Devilslayers wouldn't let in, due to handicaps such as 'family'. You wouldn't tell it to look at us, but we've actually become quite a formidable force."

"I can vouch for that," Cildar chimed.

"We try to do what the Devilslayers don't anymore. We protect those with no protection. But there aren't nearly as many of us, only maybe six hundred warriors. We're quite strong, capable of battling even an elite squad of slayers. Because of that, they've stopped trying to strong-arm us as they did for many months. But we haven't been able to accomplish nearly as much as them, regrettably." She gave a sigh, then rose to her feet. "If you'll excuse me, it's getting late and there are duties I need to see to. Hopefully you'll be staying with us at least until morning, yes?"

"At least," Abaddon answered.

"Good. I'll look for you at first light. Sleep well. You're safe here."

As she left, Myris muttered to his comrades, "All the same, I believe we will keep our own watch."

His allies nodded, then Cildar turned to Abaddon. "What now, milord?"

"We have no force of our own, no information, and no course of action. Chances are we're going to need to forge an alliance with someone, either Detria or the Devilslayers themselves depending on what goals we set. For now, I say we follow her and see where it leads us."

Cildar smiled at this conclusion. "I'm glad to hear. I rather like these people. They seem hearty, and their spirits are strong."

"Besides," Abaddon continued, "there's something I am curious about. The leader of the draconics seemed convinced that I was someone else. He said my aura was unmistakable. If there's really someone among the Devilslayers with an aura so close to mine, I'm curious to meet him."

"You think him a mystic?" Myris asked.

"Maybe. The ether pole that was once here was highly volatile. Such currents would have doubtless caused some mystics to develop, perhaps well beyond the numbers Itrius normally sees. It's possible there are many mystics here. However, it seems more likely to me that it's either Tenkahn or one of his monks. They are few, but they're a powerful force comparable to a small army. If we could find them, they would be the most suited allies we could make." He paused for a moment of contemplation. "There's something else I need to talk to you two about. Something Eiden mentioned to me."

"Eiden? Is that the boy's name?" Cildar queried.

"It seems there's some sort demonic overlord here. I'm unsure of his reach or seriousness, but he at least has a few hundred human slaves. Eiden was one, until a large band of them made their escape. Once we decide what our alliances are, I believe we should make it a priority to go there and liberate whomever we can."

The three continued to converse for nearly an hour, until Eiden returned to their fire. The lad seemed to have made some friends among Detria's camp already, and his spirits were visibly renewed. He and Cildar chatted idly for a while, the paladin rambling freely on about Felthespar, and Itrius in general. This lasted until past midnight, when Eiden finally settled down and fell asleep. As the night grew quiet, the three veteran soldiers settled up their watch shifts.

## Chapter 7.

# What Motivates the Mighty

As the sun approached a midday position, Detria Alsen marched at the head of her forces. Once on the move, her troops were substantially more organized than at camp. They had gathered their gear and spread the load equally across uniform squads, marching in blocks of a hundred apiece. Detria, Kelve, and their new ally Abaddon marched twenty yards ahead of the front lines. Cildar and Eiden had situated themselves somewhere in the middle ranks, where they chatted idly, and Myris had taken to following at the rear.

Detria could not repress a nagging suspicion that the newcomers were trying to establish some sort of authority by way of their positioning. Earlier that morning she had asked Abaddon about his small crew's intentions, and he had declared that the knights would join her ranks, following her for whatever missions she had in store. Knowing their strength she had graciously accepted this offer, but now felt as though she was being subtly undermined. They were but few, but tactically situated throughout her force in a way that implied they found her leadership inadequate. She tried to reassure herself that these were weathered soldiers, paranoid from years of battlefield experience, but she could not keep from taking some small offense.

When Kelve suddenly dropped behind to inspect the ranks and ensure there were no emergencies, she fought past her misgivings and tried to make small talk with the foreign commander. "You carry an interesting sword," she noted pleasantly. "I've never seen its equal. Though it must prove difficult to wield in combat."

He was silent for a moment, his face betraying no reaction. "Its name is Kargaroth, the Unholy Blade. It does not see combat anymore."

"Oh? And why is that?"

"The bandages."

Her face twisted in confusion. She glanced at the hilt of the sword, which was carefully wrapped about in a thick layer of bandages. "The bandages? What are you talking about?" she asked with a chuckle.

Abaddon gave a sigh and looked to the sky, spending a moment considering his next words. "They're symbolic. I swore I would not use Kargaroth to draw blood so long as those bandages remain on the hilt. It sounds strange, I know. There's a lot of history between the sword and I."

"If you've sworn not to use it, why carry it? Wouldn't it be better left to someone who would use it?"

"Kargaroth represents my past. Its weight is the burden of my memories. There are people I owe—I owe them to carry that weight." He seemed about to add something more, then abruptly change subject. "Where are we going? What is our objective? It's been many years since I was required to march blindly to a destination."

Detria courteously accepted his tacit invitation for her probe no further. "There are reports of a demon attack to the south, just outside of the Malvaru Plateaus. One of our scouts tells us that the Devilslayers have declared the area quarantine. There's only one reason they do that, these days."

"And that is?"

She lowered her head and grinned. "I have a confession to make. This actually wasn't our destination until yesterday, after I met your two friends. They have exceptional abilities that we've never seen the likes of in a human."

"You're referring to their ability to use magic."

"Yes. For two years Arkalen has been enduring attacks we had never before seen. Each one is different from the previous in damage and form, but they are linked by one common factor: they are seemingly without cause or objective."

"Is that not to be expected of certain demon attacks? On Itrius, there is a creature called a behemoth. They usually lie dormant, but when active they go on reckless killing sprees that often claim several villages. Their only objective is their need to sate a berserk rage."

"Things are different on Arkalen. Or at least, they have been for some time now. Demons stick to their territories, and if they attack humans it's for either food or riches, depending on the sophistication of the creature. We've not had attacks as unprovoked as these, nothing like the behemoths you mention. I was hoping your friends could use their magic to look over the area, perhaps divine what exactly happened. If it's something new, like this 'behemoth', they could tell us that."

"Magic is not that simple. It does little more than allow us extra tracking capabilities. However, Myris in particular is the best tracker I have ever known. I'm certain he will lend you his talents."

Detria's shoulders drooped in disappointment. Skilled trackers had already tried and failed to determine the origins of this creature, and it seemed unlikely to her that Myris could provide additional insight with mere skill. She had been hoping for some further benefits from his more mysterious powers.

Abaddon took no notice of her dejection, but continued, "Have you considered that this might not actually be the enemy at work? Perhaps the Devilslayers themselves are responsible for staging these scenes, using them to assert a grip of fear over the civilians they protect."

She was taken aback at this suggestion. "I admit I have my issues with the Devilslayers, but I do not think they are capable of anything so foul!"

He shrugged off her reaction. "It's not an atypical bureaucratic policy. From what I've read, Felthespar's not unfamiliar with the tactic, having actually manufactured a few creatures in the past in order to spread fear across other territories. One of our scholars, a man named Kinguin Peet, believes that the behemoth itself might be a Felthespari creation. Though he's been unable to find sufficient evidence to support his claims, so it's suppressed by the Arcanum High Council."

"I'm surprised to hear you speak so harshly of your homeland. From the conversations last night you seemed very fond of it."

"I am indeed fond of Felthespar. However, that does not change the reality of what the city has been or what crimes it has committed in the past. A government is only as virtuous as its leaders. Not all the ministers of Felthespar have been as honorable as Atheme."

"That aside," she countered, "I still don't believe the slayers are behind this. When the attacks first began I was still a slayer myself, and I remember the genuine confusion our Chieftain expressed." Abaddon gave a nod, but no further respond. Detria happily let the subject drop. The more the big man spoke, the more wary of him she became. His personal loyalties and beliefs seemed vaporous, too easily tossed aside in regard for cold analysis.

She decided to change to a lighter note, hoping to draw some sign of humanity out of his stoic demeanor. "Do any of you three have family back home? I mean, to have traveled across an entire ocean seems so extreme. Were none of you tied to anyone you left behind?"

"I'm uncertain about Myris. He's quite private, though he does share more with Cildar than myself. I've never heard either of them mention his parentage, nor siblings. He did have cousins, but from what I understand they were distant, only really connected because of the shared family name. The name of Phare is the highest nobility of Cainite society. The eldest cousin was previously their Lord Commander, until Myris took his life in our Second Arocaen. The youngest, with Myris' blessing, now leads their people as a King in their new nation of Adonnis."

She spent a moment digesting this information. It filled her with dozens more questions, but she did not desire getting hung up on the matter now. She took note to interrogate Cildar later, as she found him a more compelling historian than his commander.

"And the other two of you?" she prodded instead.

"Cildar and I share a great deal there. Both of our mothers died in childbirth. Though in Cildar's case it was upon his younger brother's birth, so he does yet have some memories of his mother. Our fathers, as it happens, died on the same fool's errand—a mission to kill a monster they stood no chance against. My father led the expedition, sending Cildar's and several hundred others to their deaths."

"I'm sorry. That's terrible. But I must confess, it's a story I recognize all too well. Many Arkalenians, both civilians and skilled warriors alike, die facing monsters they cannot overcome. It's the song of our lands."

He shook his head. "It doesn't bother me. I have no real memory of the events, nor of either of my parents. They're nothing more than specters of a former life. I was raised mostly by my uncle. Although," he chuckled here slightly, but Detria could not tell if it was out of joy or resentment, "he was actually no uncle at all. Rather a political calculation, a man appointed to raise me in order to keep my father's reputation shielded from siring a bastard."

"My god. Again, I'm sorry..."

"Again, don't be," he cut her off. "For whatever reason my Uncle Yovess was granted custody, he cared for me as his own. He was the one soft spot in those early years. Without him, I fear I might have no kindness left in me at all."

"Yet I don't recall any stories of your uncle from yesterday. I assume he has passed on?"

"Aye, but not as you probably think. He and I were also present on my father's fateful expedition. After its decisive failure, Yovess tried to lead the two of us home. The lands there were dangerous, and unfit for travelers such as us. He contracted a disease and died long before we reached our homelands."

"So he died," she asked with a squint, "and you were just a boy... but you didn't?"

"The lands were dangerous. As it turned out, I was moreso."

She raised an eyebrow and gave a smirk. "What's that supposed to mean? Were you raised by wolves or something?"

"After a fashion, I suppose. My first slaughter was a pack of hungry wolves, as a young boy. It was a few weeks after Yovess died, and I was struggling to find purpose. I didn't know where I was or where I was going. Then came the wolves. At first, I was resigned to my death. Until they took the first few bites out of me; that was when I changed my mind. I had found a purpose. It was almost an hour later when the final three wolves decided to retreat, but by that time I was in a foul mood. After that, I hunted *them*. You could say it set a tone."

Detria marched for a few silent moments with eyes wide. She debated internally whether the man might be a habitual liar, but his previous tales had rung with such a clear air of truth to them. Abaddon seemed to detect her discomfort, adding, "But everything worked out, in its own way. I did find my way back to Felthespar eventually, though by then I had forgotten it as home. Atheme found me, and as he did for so many souls, he helped me to become a better version of myself. If you ask me what family I left behind, I would tell you only Atheme Tethen. I miss him every day."

"And what about loves?" she asked, eager to accept the cheerier shift in topic the man had offered. "Do none of the three of you have wives, girlfriends?"

"Cildar has a wife. He adores her dearly. He swore to her, swore to all of us, that after this journey he's going to give up war to settle the rest of his days by her side. It's why he came. So that once he returns he may dedicate himself to her without reservation of spirit."

She bit her lower lip and shook her head sadly. "That seems like such a heartbreaking thing. He left the woman he loves to come here and seek terrors? I really don't understand."

"Cildar has two great loves in his life—Jessandra, and the battlefield. He wishes to give up the latter, but feels that unless he has one final thrilling adventure to look back on, he will never be able to stop his heart from wandering. It's difficult for a man to sacrifice one half of himself, no matter how much more value he places upon the other."

"I guess I just don't understand men," she started jokingly, but her tone quickly became a dire one. "I face grave danger every day of my life. All of my people do. We don't draw any pleasure from this 'adventure', as you call it."

"Some are cast involuntarily into the fates others would seek. It's the cruel twist that keeps us each marching for something other than what we have."

She dwelt on this sentiment for a moment, but was unable to settle her feelings on it. Instead she once again redirected the conversation. "So you told me of Cildar's wife. What about you and Myris?"

"Myris has had loves before. Two I know of for certain, and there may have been others. All lost their lives in combat or war. As for myself, I have been with women, but I have never loved."

She admitted inwardly that she was unsurprised by this personal admission. "And why would you say that is?"

"That's quite a deep matter to pry into, don't you think?"

She had not expected an answer, and felt an odd comfort in finding some sense of predictability in the gruff man. "Come on, you seemed so willing to elaborate on Cildar's motivations, but can't answer a simple question about your own?"

Once more there was silence for nearly a minute, so Detria assumed the conversation had ended. As she checked the front ranks of the troops behind her, Abaddon suddenly resumed speaking. "I am consumed by my violence." She jerked her head back and stared at him, but his face and tone were expressionless as ever, his eyes calmly fixed ahead as though he were merely discussing the weather. "My carnal lust was long ago replaced by an unquenchable bloodlust. When I battle an opponent, man or monster, I am filled with some slight satisfaction. Atheme taught me to channel this killing instinct, that my violence need not preclude some sense of morality. I've tried to honor his teachings to the best of my ability. Yet still I seek what I have always sought—a mighty opponent to push me to my absolute limit and then claim my life." He clenched his left hand and his eyes widened as he concluded his thought. "To die in a haze of blood and violence. That is the fate the Destroyer within me seeks."

Detria almost tripped as she stared at him, then forced herself to regain composure. Once she had done so, she offered, "You're a scary man, you know that?"

"Terrifying, some have said," he responded with disinterest.

Kelve returned from the ranks and gave his report on the condition of the troops. Afterward all conversation ended, and Detria was left pondering the mind of her bewildering new companion.

Soon they reached the outskirts of what appeared to have once been a city. Detria and Kelve brought the army to a halt, as Abaddon sounded a shrill whistle. Myris was shortly at his side, followed in a few moments by Cildar and Eiden.

Detria gave a few orders and then moved to the Itriun commander. "The area beyond this point is quarantined. If the Devilslayers notice us, they'll bring whatever response force they deem necessary. It'd be better for a small group to get caught than a large one."

Myris reached behind his back and drew forth his Soul Scythe, looking to the trees in the nearby area with intent. "I could slay their watchmen, if you wish it."

Detria blinked at the man, unsure if he was serious. Abaddon responded in her delay. "The Devilslayers are not our foes, merely a hindrance. They are equivalent to a local police force. We will avoid them when they inconvenience us, but we'll refrain from direct confrontation."

Cildar nodded his agreement. "Aye. Let's only make the enemies that we must, for now."

"Kelve is staying behind?" Abaddon asked of Detria.

She nodded. "He'll see to the troops here. If things become thick, I've got some flares I can use to signal them to move in as backup, or pull back for retreat."

The man turned back to his own meager ranks. “Cildar, you and Eiden will remain behind as well. Myris and I will proceed alone.”

The paladin bowed slightly, but the youth objected, “Sir, I wish to come along!”

Abaddon shook his head sternly, but was not rude in his response. “You and Cildar are not suited for stealth travel. Myris and I can remain invisible if we wish. For now, we shall avoid any incidents we can.”

Eiden lowered his head. “Yes, milord. Forgive my brashness.”

The warlord turned back to Detria. “We’ll move ahead. I cannot presume how taken you are to stealth, but we’ll keep a close eye on you as we move. If you get into trouble, one of us will assist.”

She was about to object to the notion that she would need help, but Abaddon and Myris exchanged a nod and with a sudden leap vanished into the forest. Detria gave a final order to Kelve, then rapidly followed into the trees herself.

She knew the Devilslayers’ practices well enough to deduce where their sentries might be posted, and easily moved through the woods without incident. In only a couple of minutes she emerged on the far side of the thin forest, into a desolate area that had once been the center of a large human settlement.

At first Abaddon and Myris were nowhere to be seen, and she was surprised to find she had beaten them. She only had a few seconds to ponder this thought, however, when she heard them moving behind her.

“This truly is a high level of damage,” Abaddon speculated.

Detria clenched her eyes to shake off both her shock and her irritation. “Yes,” she responded, “sometimes the damage is quite severe. This was one of Malvaru’s larger settlements. It might have someday turned into a major hub for trade.” She paused and gave a small sigh. “That is, if our lands ever grow to see such days.”

The Felthespari commander walked past her and gave a soft snap. Myris hastened forward and the two began scanning the area. At first Detria followed their lead and gathered what information she could, but quickly decided it was a meaningless exercise. She had already inspected so many of these sites, there was nothing new for her to learn here.

For nearly fifteen minutes, no one said a word. The two men moved from area to area, looking over various spots that had once been buildings, or large craters that seemed situated in strange places. Soon each headed over and gathered around Detria, who had seated herself on a pile of collapsed timber.

"Report," the big man demanded of Myris.

"It moves fast. It is not large, but weighs an inordinate amount. If human, it is heavily armored. If demon, it is very densely built, possibly a creature of stone or metal."

He nodded in response. "The speed is unnatural. It's not swift, but rather seems to be lifted from point to point by some external force."

"Possibly similar to my own speed." Myris raised a hand to his face and rubbed his chin pensively. "Or if not arcane in nature, perhaps some crippled form of flight."

"The spells are what bother me most," Abaddon added to the analysis.

"So you noticed as well?"

Detria moved her head forward, attempting to bring herself back into focus. "Noticed what, please?"

"The damage done here was not a single spell," Myris elaborated. "It was a vast series of spells, somewhere between two dozen and twoscore. Upon analyzing the debris, it appears there was no lag between the castings. Certainly no more than a half-second between each strike. Normally this would be a sure sign of a high number of foes, but all other evidence points to a single caster. Such a feat should be nigh impossible."

She creased her brow and shook her head. "Couldn't he have just been a lot better at magic than you? Casting spells at a much higher rate?"

This time Abaddon offered response. "Not at this level. The amount of ether required to execute this many advanced spells would take a long time to gather. At least a few seconds between each spell, even for a proficient mystic. The alternative would be to have them each matrixed to your spirit in advance, were this creature intelligent enough to do so. But the process of tapping a matrix involves speaking a series of code words, which are usually not brief, and even then the matrix takes time to ground."

Detria followed this as best she could, but feared she was out of her depth. "Couldn't he just have 'matrixed' a whole series of spells together, so they all happened at once?"

Abaddon and Myris exchanged a glance. At first Detria worried they were mocking her, but soon realized by their expressions they were actually considering the possibility. "Not unless the creature knows a technique more advanced than ours," Myris finally answered.

"So what does all of this mean?"

"Best guess? We're looking at someone who wields an artifact of divine or nearly-divine stature," Abaddon proposed. "One capable of storing tremendous matrixes of its own, and responding instantly to the subject's will by way of telepathic link. The Arcanum houses such a weapon, but we never suspected it would have an equal here."

"While that is almost certainly a piece of the explanation," Myris countered, "I personally am more disturbed by the currents. They offer no evidence that any spells were ever cast in this area, via artifact or otherwise."

"The currents?" she asked, beginning to feel overwhelmed by her own ignorance on the subject.

Abaddon began casting around, seeming to stare deeply into the air. "All magic is fueled by ether," he offered in explanation, "which runs in its own currents independent of the air itself. They're intangible, but run everywhere. If a spell is cast, even a small one, it leaves an impression on the currents."

"Normally," Myris continued the thought, "the impression is not enough to decipher much about what spell was cast, only the magnitude. For an attack this large, the currents should be wildly disrupted, to the point of nearly falling apart in the local vicinity. Yet these currents show no impression at all. Aside from the few spells I have used to scout since we arrived, they seem completely untapped."

"I had not noticed until Myris pointed it out," Abaddon confessed, "but he's correct. Based on an observation of the currents alone I would swear magic hasn't been used in this area for at least a month."

Detria scratched the back of her head, feeling she was finally beginning to understand. "That does seem strange. Is it possible that this attack wasn't magic?"

Abaddon turned and began walking back toward the town, so Myris answered in his commander's stead. "Remember, the creature is small, at most ten feet in height. I can conceive of nothing at such size capable of inflicting this much damage without magic."

"Myris," the big man shouted from near the center of the town, "come look at this."

The two dashed to where the mystic warlord stood staring at a dark crater. Detria noticed Abaddon's eyes, and was shocked to see they were glowing as if alight from within.

"What kind of magic leaves a red ether trail?" the man asked of his compatriot.

"There is no such thing."

"Work your eyes, observe the currents here where the largest strike took place."

The former Cainite held his left hand over his face, and when he lowered it his eyes were also glowing. He stared for a second and then whispered, "Impossible."

"Not impossible. Just nothing we've seen before."

Again Detria was forced to interject into their musings. "What *are* you babbling about?"

Abaddon looked to his friend and motioned for him to explain. "There are two types of major currents," Myris answered, "white and black. Sometimes grey currents can also be observed, in a few different shades. Regardless, when one uses Ether Vision, the world is seen entirely in greyscale. And yet I can clearly see hues of red here."

"So there's some new kind of magic you've never heard of?" she asked. "Is that such a big deal?"

Abaddon again began walking away as he replied. "This goes beyond that. Black and white ether are the laws upon which reality as we know it is built. Ether itself cannot be altered, it can only be channeled. White cannot be converted to black, black cannot be converted to white, and red simply does not exist." He paused, casting a glance into the trees to the north. "At least not in Morolia," he whispered to himself. Then added aloud, "We should head back. We can explain more to you at camp, and discuss the matter with Cildar."

Detria nodded, still much confused by much of this, and followed the two soldiers into the forest as they disappeared.

## Chapter 8.

## To Take the Next Step

Poised atop a tall and lonely petrified tree on the southern border of his forest, the draconic Farthas sat chewing on the bone of a former ally, bemoaning his own fate. Twice in the past week his clan had been harassed by humans, and twice they had been denied meals due to the influence of the Devilslayers. The draconics presently held a treaty with the slayers that safeguarded their survival, but as the humans of Arkalen spread it seemed increasingly certain there would soon be no place for their kind. Once humanity had the necessary strength and few enough foes, Farthas felt certain they would come to eradicate his people.

One of his lieutenants—and his mate—a female named Meriosthro, had long been lobbying to lead the tribe from the forest and seek a new home beyond human reach. Farthas had resisted this idea. He warned that if they ran now, human reach would only grow. They would have to run again, and again, until eventually there would be nowhere left. Now he considered a change of heart. With human traffic through the area increasing and his forces growing ever hungrier, it was only a matter of time before an incident broke out, followed by rebellion.

His tribe's self-afflicted losses had risen to disconcerting rates, as well. After many centuries, Arkalenian draconics had evolved far from their dragon ancestors, and had developed the ability to reproduce rapidly. In a way, this had been their race's salvation. In times of starvation when spiritual feasts were hard to come by, the stronger draconics feasted on weaker members of later generations, sustaining their own spirits enough to get by.

With this latest enduring famine, their cannibalism had

outpaced their reproduction. Even without human aggressions, their numbers dwindled. As Farthas stared at the bone he was gnawing to sharpen his fangs, he considered the possibility that he had just eaten one of his own offspring. But draconics were not bound by the familial attachments of humans. It mattered not whom he had eaten; only that he was no longer starving.

He sat atop a tall rock surveying the troops around him as they lazed about. Hungry as they all were these days, there was not much activity. It was best to conserve strength and hope to make a meal out of a passing demon. Thanks to the efficiency of the Devilslayers, even that was becoming an increasingly rare event.

Farthas was startled from his reverie when he heard a voice behind him. "It's sad to see such marvelous creatures fallen so far from nobility."

He leaped to his feet and spun about, seizing the bone scimitar at his hip. Somehow, a human had managed to climb the stony peak atop which Farthas had been sitting, and stood no more than a foot away from him.

"Relax," the man demanded slowly. For some reason the draconic could not resist the command, so he released his grip on his sword and slouched slightly. The intruder was slim, wearing loose robes of shimmering white. Through the shadows of the hood Farthas' demonic sight could make out pale skin and silver eyes, as well as liquescent silver hair. He could also sense the spirit beyond the eyes, and immediately recognized that this was no human.

A sharp hiss rang from his throat. "What does your kind want of ours? Have you come to mock our fall?"

The human mouth twisted into a wry smile and the man gave a bow. "Come, my friend, surely you are not so far lost from Asteria that I am a stranger to you. It's not so unnatural that I would wish to offer your people aid."

"What's your name? Your true name, the name of your spirit itself."

The visitor seemed to debate answering, then stepped forward, right on top of Farthas, and whispered something in his ear.

The draconic gave a hissed gasp and was forced to dig his clawed toes deep into the petrified wood to keep from losing his balance. "Impossible. One such as he could not have fallen from grace."

"I am not fallen. I have simply found a new grace to follow. For the moment."

"We have no desire to deal with you, and no interest in your 'new grace', whatever it might be."

"Of all your people, you and your mate are among the very few who evolved from original dragon bodies. I know draconics are barbaric, but dragons are supposed to be more noble, more intelligent. I'm not here to ask you for anything at all, I simply have a suggestion to offer. Could you not at least hear me out?"

The draconic knew the man was manipulating him, using a reminder of his former dragon self to evoke old emotions. He wanted to be enraged, but could not deny that it felt good to remember majesty he had once held, and be paid the respect that it warranted. "Very well. I will hear you out."

"Slightly north of here, and to the far east, there lies a stronghold. Demons of all sizes live there in harmony, as well as a large supply of human slaves. When the humans grow too old to work, they're fed to the demons most in need of sustenance. The Devilslayers do not know of this place, nor even suspect it exists. And if they ever discover it, it will serve them little good. The demons who guard it are too powerful for mere humans to threaten, no matter how practiced in the art of killing." Farthas hissed quietly, but offered no response. The pale stranger reached into his robes, then pulled forth a paper cylinder and handed it over. Farthas took it—almost involuntarily—but still offered no words. "Consider it, for the safety of your people. Who knows, once you are outside of Devilslayer territory, you may even find a few sources of food for the journey. Wouldn't that be nice?"

The next thing Farthas knew, Meriosthro was shaking him to get his attention. He looked around, but could not locate the strange visitor. He noted the sun had changed position by nearly an hour from where he last recalled it. He wondered for a moment if he had dreamed the peculiar incident, until he noticed the slim document still clutched in his right hand. Quickly, ignoring Meriosthro, he dropped to the ground from his pillar and unraveled the paper. She followed him down and looked over his shoulder in curiosity.

He was looking at a small map of the continent, with a large red "X" scrawled in an area far to the east. His mate asked of him, "What is that, Farthas? Where did you find it?"

He rolled it up and placed it under his hide armor, answering, "It seems it's our destiny, Meriosthro. Gather the brood, I have new mandates to give."

* * * * *

The climate of the southern continent proved to be much more temperate than that of Itrius, and this fact was not lost on the Felthespari visitors. In the early winter months when snow would already be blanketing the land around Felthespar, they were faced with little more than a slight morning chill. Once the sun rose to the midday position even that faded, sometimes shifting the afternoons into a warm but still comfortable humidity.

Fighting off these morning chills, Cildar and Myris sat around a campfire lounging in the first rays of sunlight. The former lounged, at least, having removed his armor and helmet and settling back for a hopefully quiet onset to his day. Myris was more like-minded to Abaddon and rarely relaxed, especially in unfamiliar surroundings.

There had been a few arguments on this subject between the two close friends. The paladin had proclaimed, "This is supposed to be a warrior's vacation. We came to fight, but we also came to experience a new land. Once in a while, you've got to lie back and experience it." Myris was not taken in by this argument, and had more than once accused the man of being uncharacteristically indifferent.

Cildar assured himself that the cause for his detached comfort was their newfound allies. They had traveled together for nearly two months, and Detria's people had proven to be a formidable force. They had already encountered and dealt with several potent demon threats without requiring assistance from the Felthespari—an arrangement which, as it happened, was no mere accident.

"Since we march with them," Abaddon had ordered one evening early during their travels, "we will help if called upon. But we're not here to fight their battles. Besides, it would be unwise to reveal our full strength until we know more of Arkalen's conflicts and alliances."

Cildar suspected this decision had been inspired by a brief argument between Detria and Abaddon a few weeks prior, wherein the small girl had practically threatened to attack the man for undermining her authority. The Felthespari warlord had apologized sincerely, never losing his cool—to Cildar's surprise and relief—and since then their group had resigned themselves to a passive role.

Serving as a distraction from this tension, there was the young Eiden Hoek. At Abaddon's bidding, his compatriots had begun to train the lad in the arts of magic. Cildar had been a little put off by this at first, not feeling up to the role of tutor. He had since warmed to the boy, finding him surprisingly sharp and a quick study. Eiden was already beginning to gain a comfortable familiarity with his spiritual energy, having recently summoned his first Aura barrier. In his other studies, Myris had already taught him several basic cantrips. The boy had memorized them all, and was now advancing into the realm of fire magic.

So Cildar reassured himself that he was relaxing because he was comfortable, because he was safe here with these friends. But in the back of his mind he knew he was deceiving himself. His charade of relaxation was a front to keep from dwelling on his own misgivings, misgivings that Myris remained insistent to force upon him.

Even as he now fought to repress his anxieties, the Cain once more began harassing him. "So exactly what are we waiting for?"

Cildar shut his eyes and leaned back against the small mound he was propped against, listening to the sounds of the campfire and basking in a light breeze. Over the course of the last month they had gradually wandered their way south of the Kolpen Hills, escaping the fierce winds of the storm at the oceanic border. It constantly brought the term "deceptively tranquil" to his mind.

"Waiting? Who said we're waiting for anything?"

The dark warrior was beyond aggravated at his friend's state of denial, and tried to force his way past it. "You know exactly what I mean. We travel with an army who fights demons, yet we do not fight. They seek weak people who need help, yet we do not assist them. At first I believed this was reconnaissance, Lord Abaddon's way of acclimating us to the environs. Now we have even begun retracing familiar territory, and unless I am mistaken we are heading back the way we came only a week ago. We have done nothing more than allow ourselves to melt into a pack of sentries, and we are enabling neither their duties nor their mission in any way. You and I waste our days teaching a young boy to use magic, perhaps in the hopes that he will spread it to others, providing them a new weapon. Lord Abaddon, for his part..." Myris stopped himself, not sure how far he wanted to take his next statement. "Did we really travel the ocean for a full year for this?"

Cildar sat up and leaned forward. He thought for a few minutes, going through a gamut of responses. Myris said nothing further, awaiting the conclusion of his friend's internal debate. Finally Cildar shook off his reverie and gave a nod. "You're right. One of us should speak to Lord Abaddon. This can't go on forever." He grabbed his armor and helmet, rising to his feet as he strapped them on. "I'll do it."

Their commander usually situated himself at the edge of the encampments, watching the horizons as if awaiting some sort of sign. Cildar could not guess how many days it had been since the mystic had slept, but suspected it to be an unhealthy number. Felthespar's former Champion was infamous in his defiance of human limitations, and it could be months before either lack of sleep or food began to take their toll on his gifted physiology.

As expected, he found the man standing alone beyond the eastern tents. He approached slowly, gathering his thoughts and words. As a commander himself, he knew how hard it could be to take criticism. He also knew that Abaddon, while normally cool and reserved, had a few switches that were likely to set him off. The upcoming conversation needed to remain civil, so Cildar knew it was important that he express himself prudently.

"Milord, permission to speak," he requested as he approached.

"Always," came the perfunctory response.

"Myris and I have been discussing our situation, and we begin to grow concerned that perhaps we're not doing enough here."

The man nodded, replying, "As of yet, we've encountered no threats that demand our attention. Between the Devilslayers and Detria's people, it seems this continent is more protected than we assumed. Arkalen was already saving itself from the wilds, even without our presence."

"But there are a few threats we could deal with, are there not?"

"That's a difficult determination to make. We've yet to encounter any such creatures firsthand."

"Yet if we don't do something productive—"

Abaddon suddenly spun about and eyed Cildar evenly. The Dragoon briefly feared he had pushed too far, but the man's tone did not rise. "What would you have me do, Emle? Call off the mission? Turn us around and head back to Felthespar? Yes, I'm beginning to have my own doubts about whether we're needed here. I'm beginning to question the difference we can make. But last I checked, we don't have a ship that's seaworthy, nor do we have a crew which can man it." Then with emphasis, he said slowly, "We have nowhere to go."

And there it was, the fact Cildar had fought inwardly to avoid for so long. They were stranded on Arkalen. The *Calvin* was too damaged, and the three of them could neither repair it nor sail it by themselves. It was possible, likely even, that they were to be stuck here for the remainder of their lives. Though some part of him had already known, suddenly being faced with this reality caused his heart to break as he thought of the wife he had left behind. His eyes brimmed with tears as he pictured her waiting for him for two, five, maybe even ten years before finally giving up hope.

Abaddon was not blind to his friend's pain, placing a gentle hand on his shoulder. "If we're going to accomplish anything here, we need allies. Arkalen may have its own Jegan. For now, I fear we have no choice but to idle as we work to forge alliances."

At the mention of its name, Cildar's mind turned to Jegan. The river town on Itrius held most of the continent's shipwrights and sailors. It was from there that the *Calvin* had been built, and first taken sail. Cildar had made many diplomatic visits to Jegan, and his family had many bonds there. Memories of those times lifted his heart. He tightened both his jaw and his resolve. "Of course, milord. It's as you say. Nonetheless, if we're to make allies of Detria's people, perhaps it's time we render them some service."

"I will speak with her and see," he promised. "Though she has previously expressed a desire for us to not meddle. Perhaps she'll have warmed to us somewhat by now." The paladin gave a departing bow, then went to take a walk by himself. Abaddon watched him leave for a moment, then gave a shout to a nearby hill. "Come out, Phare. I know you were listening."

Myris appeared and walked forward, dropping apologetically to one knee when he was within speaking distance. "Forgive me, sir. I meant no offense, just my old Cainite nature acting up."

"If you're going to spy on *me*, then I advise you to get better at it. Meanwhile, make some use of yourself. Find Detria, tell her I'd like a word with her."

Myris gave a smile and rose to his feet. "As you wish."

An hour later, Abaddon and Detria held a meeting within her command tent. She found this impromptu audience an inconvenience, as normally by this time of day her troops were already on the march, and made no attempt to hide her annoyance. "What do you need, Sir Abaddon? I have no wish to waste much more sunlight."

"My knights have expressed discontent. They grow restless from inactivity. We understand that your people have a specific mission, that it's important for you to protect the inhabitants here. I come to ask you if perhaps there's something more we can do. Perhaps there has been some task, some powerful foe, that you previously thought beyond your mettle. I know we are but few, but don't underestimate us. We will make a difference in the tides of battle."

"A powerful foe?" she looked away from him and seemed to get lost in thought. Soon she looked back with a creased brow, then said, "Do not think me crazy."

He tilted his head at this curious transition. "For?"

"For what I'm about to tell you, do not think me crazy." She leaned forward on her elbows against the small makeshift table serving as her desk. "When Kelve and I first split from the Devilslayers, he used his influence to recruit many of the soldiers who now fight with us. But more than that, Kelve used politics. You see, there were two branches of slayers. There were those who believed in this creature, who is called only the Overlord, and those who did not."

Abaddon raised an eyebrow as she mentioned the Overlord. "If I may ask, to which group did you belong?"

"The latter. I didn't believe in him. I was forced to depart the slayers for other reasons. Mostly, I simply didn't agree with the new Chieftain's way of thinking. But many here still believe in the Overlord. They left the Devilslayers because they believe we're seeking him out. Kelve himself still makes it a priority, always searching out new information. I personally try to avoid the issue, focusing on protecting real people rather than chasing fairy tales."

"So what are you asking of me?"

"You and your men are capable of taking care of yourself, and you're resourceful. That much I have learned of you. If you really want a mission, then I'll give you one. Go prove or disprove the existence of the Overlord. Like your men, many among my troops are beginning to grow restless. They've started to question my conviction to find and kill the Overlord—with good reason, of course. If I send you and your men out to find him, alongside a few of my own most zealous troops, it will do much to improve morale." Abaddon watched her without moving, his expression unreadable. She added, "Though it may sound that I'm sending you on a wild goose chase, I don't mean it as offense."

He shook his head slowly. "I wish only that you had brought this to me sooner."

Detria was surprised by this response. She had not expected the Itriun to take so heartily to the ephemeral cause. "Why?" she could not resist asking.

"You know the boy who travels with me?"

"Eiden? Of course. He's become a friend to many of my people."

"The first several days I traveled with Eiden, all he could talk about was this 'Overlord', it seemed. I told you he had endured hardships. That's because Eiden comes from a village of people who escaped the demon's grasp. He himself is a former slave of the Overlord. And further, he knows precisely where the tyrant's fortress sits."

Detria's blood froze and her breath caught. She stared at Abaddon with her mouth agape, processing this information. If what he told her was true, then not only was the Overlord real, but she had been sitting idly on the key to finding him for months now. She gathered her thoughts and dashed to the tent flap, shouting out to the nearest soldier to find Kelve and send him to her immediately.

Abaddon rose to his feet. "I suppose you'll need to speak with Eiden. I will fetch him." She nodded, but could not muster further response. He paid this no mind and took his leave of the tent.

* * * * *

A week later the Lords of Felthespar found themselves marching at the fore of Detria's forces, heading for war. Abaddon's companions were both pleased by this news—Myris for finally having a cause, Cildar for the distraction. They marched in a single front rank with Detria, Kelve, and Eiden, and kept their attention sharp. Cildar and Myris covered the right flank, and Abaddon himself watched the left with Eiden at his side. The boy grew increasingly nervous as they moved further to the east. He did not look fondly forward to his homecoming.

Eiden's information had been invaluable. He knew the location of the Overlord's base, the composition of his forces, rough troop counts from the time of his escape, locations of barracks and living quarters for officers. He could even sketch out the entire fortress from memory with little detail omitted. Detria had offered him an officer position in her small army for this operation, and after a nod from Abaddon he had accepted.

Their mission seemed a simple one. Reach the Overlord's plantation, start a battle, and take it over. Eiden had explained that the Overlord himself was almost never present, only visiting the fortress when he had new recruits to drop off, then leaving again after less than a day of inspections. Many of the human forces were held against their will, their loyalty only maintained by fear of their demonic ministers. Abaddon had suggested they could utilize Myris' stealth to instigate an internal revolt, or at least turn a few defectors. Either would help turn a siege battle rapidly.

With the exception of Eiden, spirits were high. As they were still far from their destination, many among the troops had taken to singing traveling songs. Detria encouraged it, and she and Kelve even joined in and led a few.

Just before midday they reached the edge of a mighty forest. Eiden came to a sudden stop at the sight of it, getting swallowed by the front ranks of marching troops before Kelve noticed and sounded a full halt. Detria began to question the young man, but Abaddon stopped her and suggested the officers hold their discussions away from the ranks. Since the outset of this excursion, Detria had become more open to heeding the foreigner's council, and she nodded in agreement. Kelve instructed the squad to rest up and re-file, separating into rows of no more than three soldiers to allow easier passage through the forest. The six officers moved to the side, beyond earshot of the nearest troops.

"What's wrong, Eiden?" Detria asked. "Is there something about this forest we should know?"

"This is the Forest of Techenar," he answered with an unsteady voice. "About two years ago, some creature appeared in it. I don't know much about it, but it's supposed to be dangerous, and randomly violent. All of the Overlord's forces were fearful of it. I remember one day it was said the Overlord himself appeared at the fortress beaten nearly to death. He'd been returning with five mighty ogres, all new recruits, and the creature had attacked them in the forest. The ogres were all slain, the Overlord forced to retreat. Nothing more was said on the subject, as far as I know, but after a day's rest he left again. This is a bad way to approach. We should head north, nearer the Elster Forest. It's much safer."

Detria scrunched her mouth to the side, unconvinced. "The Elster Forest settlements are practically Devilslayer vassals. They're recruited from too heavily for us to gather any potent allies there, and we could easily run into one or more full slayer packs. I'd really rather avoid that if possible."

She looked to Abaddon for analysis. He offered, "I don't know much about the Overlord's strength, but I have fought Arkalen's ogres. Anything that could kill five of them at once is indeed a dangerous foe. Still, whatever it is, the three of us should be able to contain it if we can isolate it."

"Good," she responded. "We'll set a fast pace and try to move through quickly."

"We'll put ourselves slightly out front," he continued, "maybe fifty or so yards ahead of the army, as a forward scout." He turned to Cildar and Myris. "Tune your senses, use enhancement spells to keep a close eye on the currents. Stay sharp."

The three Felthespari entered the forest. Detria waited for a report from her front ranks, gave the signal to Kelve, then they headed in as well.

After an hour of marching, everything seemed calm. Detria,

Kelve, and Eiden formed the front row of her forces, and every so often they could make out Abaddon or Cildar's shape through the trees ahead. The former Devilslayer commanders kept their wits about them, making certain no one made unnecessary noise or chatted idly as they moved.

At the advanced front, Abaddon instructed Myris to slip into the trees and scout for anything suspicious. Then he conversed with Cildar. "The currents here have definitely been in use."

The paladin gave a nod. "Aye. Both Asterian and Morolian currents have been quite active. I'd guess whatever this creature is, it's not related to the attack Detria showed you a few weeks ago."

"Disappointing. I would have preferred to put that mystery behind us before proceeding with this Overlord ordeal."

Cildar was about to respond, when suddenly Abaddon came to a grinding stop. The paladin matched the halt quickly, checked his commander's gaze, then began scanning to their right to see what had spooked him. Myris soon landed next to them with a tentative, "Milord—"

"We know," Cildar cut him off, trying hard to gather his spells and focus his senses. He was not as adept at scanning the currents as Abaddon or Myris, and was still discerning exactly what had transpired.

A few seconds ago there had been a large shift in ether to their right, as if a massive battery of spells was being gathered together for a huge release. The three warriors focused on the source of the disturbance, both trying to pinpoint its location and anticipate the incoming attack.

Yet no such attack came. The currents soon returned to normal and the area remained peaceful. Cildar read through the currents as they flowed past, but found no indication of any spells having been shaped. Some creature had certainly harvested a large amount of both planes' ether to itself, but did not seem to have a particular purpose for it in mind.

Abaddon voiced what they were all thinking. "It's a mystic. Or at least, something like a mystic. Tremendously potent, possibly even beyond my own level. That current nearly knocked the wind out of me. I haven't felt an ether shift that intense in many years."

"It could be a lich," Cildar suggested, superstitiously raising his hand to the base of his Trine Lance.

"Unlikely," Myris retorted. "Whatever this is, it was also dealing with an incredible amount of white ether. Liches do not tap Morolian power like that, they can only shield themselves against it."

"It's no nightspawn," Abaddon agreed. "It could be a dragon, but I've never heard of one channeling white ether at that level. Most dragons neglect their Morolian selves."

Cildar drew his Lance and tapped the butt to the ground, and the blade came alive with a holy glow. "Enough theorizing, I think it's time we take to pursuit."

Around this time Detria was within sight. Abaddon signaled to her and she ran forward rapidly, leaving Kelve at the head of the troops. "What is it?" she asked once she caught up to the trio.

"We've located the creature. We're moving to intercept. Take the troops on through, don't linger."

She looked over the three of them in concern. "What if you can't take him?"

Cildar and Myris received a nod from Abaddon, then dashed off to the south. "We find it's best not to consider that possibility. We'll rejoin you when we can. If you reach the Overlord's domain, try to give us at least three days to catch up before engaging his forces. If we haven't shown by then, then we probably won't."

With that said, he took off after his fellow knights. Detria stared in the direction they had disappeared until Kelve caught up with her, then she wordlessly resumed command of the troops and continued on their march.

## Chapter 9.

# The Beast of Techenar

The weather in the lands surrounding the Fortress of the Overlord was calm. The storms had passed deep into the ocean, moving on to claim other countries and isles. Arkalen was free of meteorological assault and the countryside was tranquil, no longer reflecting the turmoils that raged among its peoples.

Atop a hill far away, the man in white robes used enhanced vision to observe the events at the entrance to the plantation, where the western iron doors stood firmly shut. Outside of these, a pair of red ogres conversed with and eventually welcomed an army of draconics into their master's embrace. The robed figure watched until he was certain the draconics' new alliance went smoothly. Once satisfied, he turned his gaze back to the west.

Before he could adjust his eyesight to pierce the trees and spy into distant territories, he found he was not alone. Ten feet from him stood a figure garbed in strange, colorful robes. His ally's stony face could not express emotion, but annoyance could be read in his stance.

"Ah, Schpariel, my friend," the pale man said with a deep bow of respect. "Any luck in your search?"

"There is none." The tone of the response was terse, clearly dissatisfied. "You promised you would do your part. Tell me your results."

"You must be patient. It's not an easy task. There are many sources of information upon which I must draw."

"And yet you waste your time exporting dragon waste to a new sanctuary. How does this help in reaching my goal?"

"Please, they are lowly pawns. I have told you, my sources indicate that Aegagropilion is located somewhere in the central stretch of the continent. To aid you, I have moved obstacles, possible opponents, to do battle with one another here in the east. In this way our search can continue unabated."

The domineering creature was not placated by this. "I am Schpariel, the Dark Wisdom. I did not ask for your assistance in clearing away the insects of Morolia. I will kill the ones who step into my path, and I prefer it that way." He extended his right hand, and a slim black scepter with a large sapphire atop it materialized from the air. "You swore to find me information, and I demand it of you now.

The priest spread his arms wide, a humble smile spreading on the visible half of his face. His hands slipped from the sleeves of his robe, and the skin revealed held the same unnatural paleness as his face. "You draw your Moon Rod against me? Would you kill me in order to sate your rage? I'm no match for your power. If you wish to spill my blood, nothing can stop you. But please remember that I am your ally here. I wish only to serve your cause."

Schpariel gritted his knuckles tight against his rod. A cracking sound was heard, then the staff melted into black smoke and drifted away on the breeze. "Your tongue is as silver as your features. Aegagropilion. Where?"

"If I knew, you would know, be certain. I will redouble my efforts. There are loremasters on this continent who may have the necessary information. That is, if you have not already slain them as insects."

Schpariel swiftly reduced the distance between the two, leaving only a few feet. "Do you mock me?"

"Never, almighty Godbeast. But you cannot deny the possibility. Still, I'm confident that if someone who has died knew something, then someone who lives must know it as well."

Schpariel stared for nearly a full minute, his chiseled face expressionless. "I will return to the central continent and continue my hunt. I hope you can find information for me soon. I am many centuries old, but even my patience can only last for so many years of this idle searching."

The pale figure turned his gaze to the southwest, checking the location of the Felthespari. *If Schpariel heads through them,* he thought to himself, *the casualties will be unpredictable. My plans cannot risk such interference at this juncture*. Then he stated dispassionately to his companion, "May I recommend that you head north as you return to the mainland? You've not given that area much attention in your searches, correct?"

At first Schpariel did not move, seeking signs of deception. Finding no useful indicators in the skilled conspirator, he turned and left without another word, heading northwest as suggested.

As the white-cloaked individual also turned to leave, the air around him suddenly turned dark and seized him. A familiar voice spoke from the void.

*You play with fire. Schpariel cannot be controlled forever.*

"It's not yet time. He will simply have to be patient until I'm ready for him. I need the Dark Wisdom's presence to summon the others, but I cannot yet deal with the chaos Aegagropilion would bring."

*And yet I find myself in agreement with the Godbeast. You waste time with trivialities. What concern of ours is the fate of these draconics?*

"The draconic Farthas is of Asterian heritage, possessing the spirit of a true dragon. I may yet have a need for him, and could not have him carelessly slaughtered by the more dangerous pieces crawling the board. With him safely tucked away for the moment, the Knight is now in play. I must be preoccupied with his actions, and Schpariel must yet await my attentions."

*What will you do if he finds Aegagropilion without your assistance?*

"As unfortunate as that would be, I'm not unprepared for the eventuality. If necessary, I will find them further distraction at that time. Aegagropilion is unimportant in the grand scheme, only Gilanirus matters. Now release me. I do not have time for your inquisitions."

The void faded, and once more green hills lay spread out before the priest. He tacked a course for the southwest and quickly headed along his way.

* * * * *

Myris was first to reach the origin point of the disturbance in the currents. He inspected the spot while awaiting the arrival of the others. It was an enclosed opening between the trees, barely enough room for a few scattered boulders and a small spring. It took only seconds of scouting for him to confirm that someone had definitely been here. Whoever it was, they were gone now, on the move before the Felthespari had even begun their pursuit.

He tried to interrogate the currents, but everything read exactly as he would have expected. Black and white currents had flowed into this location from every direction, emptying into some vessel, most likely a living one. There were no distinct ether disturbances leading any particular direction, and nothing on the ground to indicate where the mysterious figure had gone afterward. Myris' two companions soon arrived, landing spryly nearby and quickly taking note of their quarry's absence.

Cildar knelt and inspected the ground. "Someone was sitting here. Legs crossed, small form, medium weight. All indications are definitely human."

Abaddon stepped over for a closer look. "That confirms this isn't related to Detria's mysterious attacks. That creature was inordinately heavy for its stature."

The paladin rose to his feet and brushed his hands off. "Keep in mind, Eiden suggested there was some *creature* that had been haunting this place for a couple of years now. His description didn't seem to imply a human."

"Yes," Abaddon replied. "We must be wary. We could yet be dealing with multiple enemies."

"I guess the point is, we need to make this one talk."

"Agreed. Myris, can you track him?"

The smaller man had not moved since he had landed, taking his time and enhancing his senses with grey magic, scanning the surrounding area vigorously for clues. "Do not take any further steps," he insisted softly. "Neither of you move." He continued his search, looking for a broken twig, a bent leaf, a light footprint. He sniffed the air, trying to find the familiar vapors of sweat or blood. Eventually he noticed something across the clearing—one of the trees on the east side was missing a small section of bark. It was such a small difference that it could have been nothing. A bird or even a squirrel could have caused it.

Nonetheless, Myris prowled nimbly across the clearing and leaped to the branch of a tree neighboring the damaged one. He spotted footprints, and hesitated only a few seconds to determine whether they were the marks of someone entering or leaving the glade.

"Lord Abaddon, he went this way. He moves in nimble leaps between the trees."

"Scatter, quickly. We'll split paths, each coming from a different angle. Whoever reaches him first, stop him and hold out for the others. Go!"

The warriors did as their commander bade, heading in the direction the Cain had indicated. Myris stayed on point, taking the most direct route based on what few tracks he could find. Cildar remained just within shouting distance, taking the left flank and watching the woods for signs their target had adjusted course. Abaddon, in similar fashion, hung to the right.

They had gone over a mile when Myris came within sight of something ahead. It was little more than a grey speck leaping through the canopy. He checked the positions of Cildar and Abaddon behind him. They were closing the gap on their target, but not quickly. It would take another half hour to catch it at this rate.

He decided to proceed as Abaddon had instructed. He summoned his blessings of inhuman speed, zipping through trees he could only barely see in time to avoid. Within two minutes he was practically atop the fleeing figure, and slowed himself as he shouted, "You there, stand down. We only wish a word."

His prey complied, coming to a dead stop directly in his path. Myris brought himself to a halt five yards away—enough room for him to react to a sudden attack, if necessary—and checked their surroundings. They stood in the midst of a tight grouping of trees with little space. It was a dangerous setting for a pitched battle. Inwardly, he hoped it would not come to that.

He examined the stranger who still had not turned to face him. The figure was of average size and stature, draped loosely in unassuming grey robes and cowled hood, with no footwear at all. Myris recalled the man in white robes he and Cildar had encountered before, wondering if there was some relation between these two—perhaps rivaling religions. He debated whether to begin the interrogation himself or await the arrival of his comrades.

His debate was cut short as Abaddon suddenly caught up with him, landing softly to his right in a burst of speed that even caught the Cain off guard. Clearly the man had been traveling more slowly for Cildar's sake. Myris took an intrigued note of this fact, but kept his attention focused on the figure ahead.

"He has offered me no response," he informed the taller knight. "His attire may indicate some manner of priest."

"Monk," Abaddon corrected.

"Ah. Perhaps he is burdened under a vow of silence, then. I take it you know his order from your previous travels?"

Before Abaddon could respond, the ground beneath the stranger's bare feet crumbled into shrapnel. The robed figure had spun about, launching himself with such voracity that the forest floor had been unable to endure the force. A slower warrior would have been caught off guard, but Myris was able to see the attack now coming his way. He reacted almost instantly, rocking back onto his heels while simultaneously dropping his hands down to the sword at his hip.

Frozen in that instant of panicked perception, he realized his life was in real danger. As he tracked the motion of his hand and scaled it against the progress of the monk's body, he knew he would be struck before his sword had fully left its sheath. Myris wore no armor and had not raised any of his personal grey magic, confident that he could rely on his own speed at this range. If the oncoming punch was magically reinforced, he could easily be killed in a single blow.

As Myris contemplated how powerful the oncoming strike was likely to be, the monk opened his fist, extending his fingertips forward evenly. He came at his target's chest with a five-pronged strike, when suddenly a large shadow filled the space between the two. Also recognizing the eminent threat to his friend's life, Abaddon had thrown himself narrowly between ally and assailant, with no time to manage a defense of his own. Myris heard a deafening boom, then felt a tremendous pain grip his left shoulder. He let out a cry of shock, realizing the force from the attack had struck him straight through his commander's own body.

As he continued to rock backward on his heels, a splatter of the big man's blood drenched his chest. Then Abaddon fell a step back into him, clearly shaken by the piercing thrust. Myris reacted swiftly in spite of his own pain, adjusting his footing and reaching both hands out around the man's waist. With a swift whisper he spoke the keyphrase, "Meselinde o-fladchiar," tapping a Flamewave matrix. From his fingertips a crackling explosion slammed into their foe, simultaneously blasting both Felthespari backward. Myris only barely managed to avoid being skewered by the blade of Kargaroth as the two rolled to the ground. At that moment Cildar joined the fray, falling from the canopy above and releasing an Aura Blast directly into the hooded face. The beam of brilliant white light joined the burning explosion to force the monk away, stifling his assault.

Still dizzy himself, Myris tried to help Abaddon to his feet, but quickly realized the man was unable to stand. Instead he lowered him onto the grass, propping his head against a nearby rock. "Milord, are you alright?" he asked in trepidation. Only rarely had he seen Felthespar's Champion unable to gain his own feet. Blood poured over the man's chin and he clutched at his chest with his right hand. His left arm seemed limp, unable to move. It was then Myris realized what had happened: Abaddon had been struck directly through the heart.

"You can't fight him," the warlord struggled to say between coughs and rasping breaths. "Have to make him leave."

"Myris!" Cildar shouted from somewhere behind him. "I need you to buy me a moment!"

"Forgive me, milord. I shall return to your side shortly." He left his wounded commander where he lay and dashed to join Cildar.

Their opponent had not moved since the first attack, standing several yards away with his arms and head dangling limply. Smoke still poured off his entire body, making it impossible to gauge how injured he might have been by their joint magics. He showed no signs of hostility, but the Felthespari knew now he was too dangerous to be taken lightly.

"If he's still on his feet after that," the paladin explained, "I'm going to need to activate Haste. While I'm gathering spells I'll be completely vulnerable, and I don't think I can dodge this guy."

Myris reached behind his back and drew his Soul Scythe, layering on as much of his own grey magic as his aching body could endure. "I shall do what I can. Do not take long. Lord Abaddon may not be rejoining us for this battle."

Cildar was perturbed by this announcement, but could not spend time dwelling on it. Instead he began quickly gathering holy auras and grey barriers as his dark ally charged the monk.

Myris whipped his Soul Scythe in frenzied patterns, dealing combinations that reduced most of his opponents to ribbons of flesh. The monk had immediately begun moving again once the smaller man reached him, stepping back rapidly and easily ducking the Scythe's sweeps, revealing his body to be neither harmed nor slowed from the previous exchange. Myris felt a slight queasiness seize his stomach as he watched his adversary's movements. Only Atheme Tethen, Knight of the Heavens, had ever been able to avoid his scythe with such effortless precision.

Suddenly the monk gave a swift uppercut with his left fist, striking the Soul Scythe at its joint. Myris' right thumb nearly broke at the impact, and he was forced to release his weapon as it went flying fiercely into the air. Wasting not even a second, the monk followed the attack with a downward right jab to his opponent's face.

But the Cain had known what sort of ferocity to expect this time. As soon as he had felt the impact on his scythe, he had tucked himself into a ball and rolled to the side. The steely fist struck only air, but still a small crater appeared where the knight had just been standing.

Myris swiftly reversed his momentum, rolling back into that crater. His hand already rested on the hilt of his katana, and he taunted quickly, "Taste ice!" as his blade left the sheathe. His Draw Strike technique coated his sword in magical ice and slid freely through the air. A crackle was heard as the katana sliced unhindered through the right side of his enemy's ribs, severing the entire shoulder.

The two combatants paused and stared at each other. The right half of the monk's chest was covered in an expanding plate of ice, and Myris was confident he had cut off the man's arm. He lowered himself into a crouch, positioning his katana to guard himself from the monk's left hand. For the first time, he noticed a series of blue lights tracing along his opponent's skin. Suddenly those lights grew brighter, so bright they could be seen through the man's clothes and even the ice on his shoulder. Myris kept an eye on the currents, and finally he detected Cildar's Haste effect lock into place. He was just about to pull back, when the monk struck hard—not with his left fist, but his frozen right.

The ice covering the silent warrior's chest exploded from the impact of his own blow, and a gush of blood showered from his wound. But somehow the arm did not sever, the shoulder did not snap. Myris was fortunate, as the shattering of the ice had created a backlash of agony and stuttered the sudden swing, weakening the impact to his forehead. Still he was knocked ferociously to the ground, carving a rift as he flew backward through earth and rock until he crashed hard against the base of a tree.

Cildar wasted no time to check on his friend, launching forward within his own storm of white light and laying into the monk's injured right shoulder. A right hook, a left jab, a right jab, a powerful two-fisted downward smash, and then a direct left kick, all landing upon the slice carved by Myris. The monk was sent flying back by this final blow, a slight wince on his face for the first time in the battle, but still his body did not break apart.

The glowing Dragoon did not hesitate, did not know how in his frenzy. He rapidly drew the Trine Lance from his back and cleared the distance he had just established between himself and his target. He began tearing into his enemy vigorously, attempting to forcibly tear the rune-covered neck from the adamantine body.

As blood ran over his eyes, Myris watched this fruitless assault. The monk had fallen back into his defensive patterns, nimbly dodging all of the Felthespari's attacks with little noticeable effort. Myris tried to rise to his feet, but the world began spinning and he fell back to the ground. He heard Abaddon whisper hoarsely from somewhere behind him, "Phare, come here," but he did not yet have the strength to obey.

After one particularly fierce lash from the Trine Lance, the monk launched his counter. Cildar believed that in his Hasted state he was prepared for anything; he could not have been more mistaken. The monk slapped the forest floor with an open palm, and a solid stone spike jutted through the grass and tore into the paladin's chest, lifting him bodily into the air. His solid white breastplate held firm and protected his life, but it did not prevent him from being winded by the strike.

The monk leaped forward and gave a swift chop to the base of the stone spike holding his opponent transfixed. The pillar's base exploded and Cildar was sent flying from the tip. In but a second, there was a gap of five feet between the shining paladin and the floating remainder of rock. The monk took a step forward and struck this stone with his left palm, hurtling it instantly into

Cildar's face with such force that it disintegrated on impact. The stricken warrior was sent reeling back, his face turned into a blood-soaked mess, his life saved only by his helmet.

The monk took another short dash—this time bringing himself within range of his falling foe—and gave a powerful downward chop to the plated chest with his right fist. The paladin's body was sent splintering through earth, and did not halt until it was buried four feet deep. There was a flare of white light from the hole as the warrior's Haste collapsed, and then silence.

Again the monk halted his assault, standing idly and staring at nothing. Myris was surprised to find Abaddon now standing at his side, the man's entire torso drenched in blood from his wounded chest.

"Can you cast Flare?" he asked weakly.

The Cain tried to clear his head, but was certain he had a concussion. It took him effort to answer. "I do not know the structure, but I possess a transference scroll given to me by Kinguin."

Abaddon gently lifted a large rock the size of his head. "Put it on this, quickly." Myris drew the scroll from a pouch and wrapped it around the stone. He gathered an ether spark to his fingertip and touched the paper. It quickly burned up, leaving an intricate rune structure decorating the object's surface.

The big man gripped the rock in his left hand and shouted to their opponent, "Tenkahn! You *will* stand down." He then placed his right hand over the stone as well, speaking the simple activation phase for one of the Arcanum's most complex spells: "Flare!" He chucked the rock through the trees, straight at the monk.

The warrior identified as Tenkahn raised his left hand out high, intending to catch and crush this projectile with ease. When it was within a few short feet of his open fingers, the spell placed on the surface caught. Even imbued upon such a small object, the reaction of this legendary spell was overwhelming. The currents for miles around gave a sudden sharp pull, hastening to empty themselves into the stony vessel. Tenkahn himself was disoriented, and fell back a step as if hit by an uppercut. Nearby, Abaddon similarly lost his strength and collapsed. Another second passed and the rock had absorbed all the ether its small frame would allow, and exploded with uncharacteristic force for a bomb of its size.

Myris, Abaddon, and even Cildar were struck by a light rain of sharp shrapnel. Tenkahn himself was blown a full ten yards away, cracking through several rows of thick branches until finally coming to a snapping halt against the base of a distant tree.

The stinging pain of the cuts inflicted on him brought Myris out of his stupor, and he carefully climbed to his feet. He first checked his comrades. Abaddon had lost consciousness, and even more blood had poured from his mouth and chest. Cildar had also been awakened by the shrapnel rain, and climbed gingerly out of his shallow grave.

The Lord of the Cain next checked the state of their opponent, and was dismayed to find the monk had also regained his feet. His left leg and arm seemed shredded beyond conceivable repair, and runes all over his body were revealed and glowing with intensity. As Tenkahn tried to gather fresh currents, Myris realized that this rune structure was keeping the man alive, holding him together. He surmised that the runes were a suit of armor far more powerful than any made of steel. However, with the currents still raging in the chaos from Flare, the monk soon seemed to recognize his runes were no good here. Still exhibiting remarkable alacrity, he leaped into the forest and disappeared from sight.

Cildar had not noticed this event, but walked carefully over to Myris, announcing, "I guess we won."

The shorter man shook his head wearily. "We only drove him away. Somehow I do not believe any significant injury was done."

The Dragoon considered a response to this, then dismissed it. "How's Lord Abaddon?"

"Perhaps that is something you should be telling me."

Cildar knelt to their commander's side and began casting scanning spells. After a few of these his pace began to quicken, and after a few more he seemed near panic. "This is dire. The muscles, arteries, and veins around his heart are all practically destroyed. His condition's worsening, and this is more damage than his natural healing abilities are able to outpace."

"Can you help him? Stabilize him?"

"This sort of internal damage requires serious surgery, and I'm no surgeon. The best I can do is a very poor patch job. But he's already comatose. I don't think there's time." He kept searching, simultaneously working waves of generalized white magic into Abaddon's chest. He reached up at one point and removed his own helmet and face mask, giving himself room to breathe and see more clearly. A few minutes later he also tore off his blue gloves, to allow his spiritual energy to pool directly into his hands and fingertips for more precise manipulation.

More silent minutes of this activity passed. Then Cildar announced, "His heart just stopped." Myris' breath caught in his throat. He knew that Abaddon's injury was his fault, that his life had been bought at the price of his lord's. "I'm going to have to perform a Phoenix Shadow," Cildar proclaimed, interrupting his thoughts.

His despair briefly faded, and he resumed breathing jagged breaths heavy with hope. "Phoenix Shadow? What is that?"

"It's one of very few forbidden white magic techniques," the paladin answered as he made his preparations. "It allows the sacrifice of most of one person's physical and spiritual strength in order to temporarily resuscitate another's. The Church banned its use decades ago, but the Council of Paladins still teaches it. It's especially important among my knights. Risking one's own life to save another is the very foundation of the Phoenix Dragoons. The spell won't actually work any healing. After a few minutes the life that I transfer will be lost entirely, wasted. The only thing this does is buy me time, hopefully granting me enough of a window to heal Abaddon into sufficient shape to survive without it."

"Then use my strength, instead of your own."

"Myris, this technique is not without real risk. There's a chance that in its mere activation you may die."

"Then it is far more reasonable to use it on me rather than yourself. If I die, then you can still heal Lord Abaddon. If you die, then all that remains is myself and two corpses." Cildar hesitated, still not certain he was willing to endanger another of his comrade's lives. Myris insisted, "We really do not have time to debate this, do we?"

The paladin nodded and quickly proceeded. "Give me your arm." Myris complied, and Cildar drew a small knife and a strip of bandage from his belt. With two quick slashes, he made a small incision into one of the wrists of each of his friends, then tied the two together. He motioned for Myris to sit, then placed a hand on both of their stomachs.

He shut his eyes and entered a trance, carefully controlling the white magic needed for this technique. As he did so, he said a traditional prayer to sharpen his mind. "Birthed by ash, die by flame, spirit and body yet remain. Child knows not mother's face, but Phoenix fire is saving grace." He pressed hard into his friends' abdomens, and suddenly a blinding orange light enveloped all three. Even as Cildar pushed, Myris felt a harsh pull rip something from his body. His Cainite spiritual defenses flared instantly, shielding him from giving away too much of his life's energy. He saw the flash of orange, which soon turned into a blinding fire that swallowed his vision. Then he fainted and fell back into the cool embrace of the ground.

Cildar had observed the donation of life that passed from Myris, as well as the resistance the Cainite spirit presented. He was optimistic that his friend was mostly unharmed, despite his collapse. He had no choice but to accept this, for he could not presently offer Myris aid. The transference had worked, and Abaddon's heart beat once more.

The Dragoon dived into his work without hesitation, stopping only long enough to cast an induced coma over his patient to ensure the man did not accidentally awaken. He estimated that he had only ten minutes to complete his work before the Phoenix Shadow would fade and Abaddon would drift once more into the abyss. He bit his lip until it bled, not noticing the pain, and prayed to Pecoros that his skills as a healer were sufficient for the task.

* * * * *

Hours later, Cildar sat around a small makeshift campfire watching over a conscious and recovering Abaddon. Myris had left to retrieve his lost Soul Scythe, and had been gone for quite a while. Cildar suspected his friend was again hunting some large game for strength. The Cain had nearly made a full recovery, having only collapsed from duress after the Phoenix Shadow due to the slight concussion he had received from Tenkahn. Once the paladin had rested from healing Abaddon, he had bandaged Myris up easily enough. Now the wiry hunter needed only for his spiritual strength to recover.

The Phoenix Shadow had saved Abaddon's life by slimmest of margins. During those borrowed ten minutes, Cildar had healed with more combined skill and luck than ever before in his life. Even with that—a performance even a true priest would have admired—the mystic had hovered on the brink of death for nearly an hour after the Shadow had faded. Cildar had stayed at his side, laboring loyally to keep him infused with white magic. Finally the mystic's own formidable natural healing processes had come roaring back, repairing the damage at a faster rate than the paladin could even match.

Now they rested. Cildar estimated it would be a few days before Abaddon was in good enough condition to move again, but he also knew it would be unlikely for the warlord to sit still for that long.

Even though the healer inside of him rallied against him, he could not help but voice his thought. "So what's next?"

Abaddon took a few deep breaths to steady himself. "That was Tenkahn," he answered, "the monk who saved Atheme's life and mine numerous times last we were on Arkalen."

"I'm assuming at the time, he was less apt to the random bouts of berserk violence?"

The man nodded. "Something's wrong with Tenkahn. I didn't get a good look, but it seems that his rune structure has accelerated beyond his control."

Cildar scratched the back of his head. "What exactly is that rune structure, anyway? I've never seen its like."

"It's some sort of human enhancement script, supposedly a gift from their god. It transformed Tenkahn and his monks into mystics of my caliber and enhanced their physical attributes excessively."

"So there are others?"

"Last I knew, there were nine others."

Cildar did not know how close Abaddon had been to the monks, but he decided to ask the uncomfortable question. "Do you think in his mindless state, Tenkahn slaughtered his own allies?"

"It's possible. They never traveled alone before. Tenkahn was always the strongest, but he was never nearly as strong as the thing we fought today. That Tenkahn could have easily wiped out the ten monks I once knew."

Around this time Myris returned from his search, taking a seat on the ground without a word. Cildar offered him a nod, then continued the previous conversation. "I don't think the three of us can beat him."

"You're probably right," Abaddon answered with a sardonic tone. "We've already bought Detria the chance she needs to get through the forest. If we want, we can just move on, reconnect with her forces and forget about this whole mess for now. Who votes that we take that path?"

There was silence for half a minute. Cildar exchanged glances with Myris, then gave a sigh. "We're all idiots."

Myris gave a slight smile. "Which is how we wound up here."

"Glad we're in agreement," Abaddon said stoically. "We can't let him get too far, so we'll move out in an hour."

"Lord Abaddon—" Cildar tried to object.

"I don't want to hear it, Emle. Myris, your blade has tasted

Tenkahn's blood, right? Can you track him?"

Myris drew his katana from its sheathe and worked some complicated Cainite tracking spells on it. It took a few moments of work, but finally he answered, "I have it attuned. So long as he remains within range, I will be able to use the blade to follow him."

Carefully, Abaddon rose to his feet. "Good. Get some rest. I'm going to scout the battle site one last time. As I said, we leave in an hour." He delicately began to walk away, revealing uncharacteristic vulnerability.

Cildar shook his head, overwhelmed by the man's stubbornness. He turned to his remaining ally. "Do you think we have a shot at this?"

"I dare not count Lord Abaddon out in any battle. However, it does seem that we are at a decisive disadvantage. Unless we come up with something ingenious, I do not foresee victory."

The Dragoon opened his right fist and stared at his palm. "You're right. We're going to need something new."

Myris gave his friend a strange look, but did not press further. Soon Abaddon's time limit ran out, and with but a word the three hunters were once more on the move.

## Chapter 10.

# Spellsmith of the Phoenix

The Felthespari lords came to a stop deep within the eastern tract of the Forest of Techenar. According to Myris their quarry had ceased moving, and they would reach him in only fifteen more minutes of travel. Cildar had signaled the stop, and Abaddon pressured the paladin to make it quick, his anticipation for the upcoming battle already palpable.

"What is it?" the warlord demanded. "This is a prime moment to strike, you had better have a good reason for risking it."

The former Champion's eyes were wide, his muscles tense, and the fingers on his right hand twitched in preparation for an attack. Cildar took a breath and steadied himself. He had seen the man like this before other battles. Normally Abaddon was cool-headed to a fault, and his calm and apathetic demeanor had alienated many allies. But there had always been moments when his warlike nature consumed him, when he became a force fit only for death. It was these periods of berserk rage that had earned him the name "Destroyer", and a legend that spanned every corner of Itrius.

Cildar could not be certain what had triggered this sudden regression in his commander's demeanor. It might be heightened stress from his current injury, or even a traumatic reaction to his recent near-death experience. Perhaps it was nothing more than the excitement in finally facing a worthy foe on their journey, or perhaps concern for the monk himself, whom Abaddon still considered a friend. Whatever the case, Cildar was concerned that it would now be difficult to press past this rage and force the man to adhere to a sound strategy. The Dragoon knew the words that he chose here would be as critical to their mission's ultimate success as any combat prowess. He trusted to his intuition, deciding to drop formality and address the man as an equal.

"I'm risking it because I need you to stop and think this through. I know you're eager to throw yourself into the fight, but right now we can't afford recklessness. Last we faced him this guy bested us soundly, and you and Myris are still hampered by injuries from that very exchange. Even if the three of us are a match for him on our best day, this isn't that. We need a sound tactic, or we go no further."

Abaddon's shoulders relaxed and his hand stopped twitching. "You doubt our ability to take him?"

"I am not saying that," he answered with a sigh. "Like yourself, I've come to seize victory. Tenkahn's too powerful for us to defeat as he is, but he's also not of his right mind. His advantage is strength, but our advantage is intellect. We still possess the ability to plan and form strategies *before* entering battle. We must use that for all it's worth."

The man stood silently for several long seconds, then gave a slow nod. "You're right," he conceded.

Cildar was put at ease by this reaction. "So where do we start?"

"The first question," Myris began, "is the end result we seek. Do we wish to save him, or slay him?"

"As Cildar says," Abaddon responded, "I don't believe he's of right mind. It seems to me that his rune structure is out of control. If we can restore him to himself, if that's even possible, he would be an ardent ally."

"Which is something we could certainly use," the paladin chimed in. "But how do we stop that rune structure?"

Both men turned to Myris, who raised an eyebrow. "I am no runemaster like Kinguin or Relm. I can but propose theories, and they may be flawed ones."

"You're the only runemaster here," Abaddon replied, "so it's your advice that we'll be following."

The man gave a sigh. "If I had to guess—and it seems that I do—I would say the rune structure covering his body is a linked entity. I noticed that when it flares it does so in unison, as though it were one giant construct. It seems as if the structure itself is only a single rune phrase, completely unbroken by any sort of grammar."

Cildar rubbed his chin in thought. He possessed enough of a theoretical background in advanced heraldry to comprehend this analysis. "That's highly unusual. Especially for a structure spread over such a large surface."

Abaddon exchanged glances with the two of them. "What does this mean for us?"

"As Cildar said," Myris continued, "it is highly unusual for such a large structure to be a single phrase. Usually enhancement scripts are broken into several phrases, so that if one part fails the other parts can continue to function. This is especially important protection on breakable objects, where large chunks could be damaged or outright removed. Tenkahn would seem to lack this sort of failsafe. If we can find a vulnerable point of the rune structure—a place where a single mark is the only link joining the construct as it flows—and we remove it, we will break the structure entirely. If my theory is correct, it will simply shut down and cease to function."

"As far as plans go, it should be a simple one to execute," Abaddon responded.

"Not quite so," Myris rebutted. "The rune structure seems to have been designed with its own weakness in mind. In the last battle I severed the monk's arm at the shoulder, but it did not break off. The structure flared up and bound him together tightly, preserving both its host and itself."

"I remember that," Cildar added. "Even after a flurry of my own attacks, I couldn't seem to fracture the spot Myris had sliced. It was like the cut had never been made."

Abaddon crossed his arms and bowed his head for a moment of thought. "A straight cut must be too thin," he proposed. "The flow of ether that holds the runes together can bridge a slim gap. But you did slice him, which means his body can be pierced in spite of the runes' protection. We need to isolate a larger link and remove it entirely. If necessary, we remove an entire segment of Tenkahn's body. Hopefully not enough to be fatal, but enough to interrupt the power conduit for his rune structure."

"Which sounds quite a bit more difficult," Myris complained.

"My mysticism makes it easy for me to subconsciously study the flow of ether through and around him. Even in the heat of battle, I can find us a suitable target. But Tenkahn is not apt to stand idly by and allow us to perform surgery. Whatever strike we are to make, it must be both precise and sudden."

"I can do it," Cildar interjected. "I have a new technique I've been working on for the past couple of years, I think it'll work. But it takes me a long time to build up, and I won't be able to fight while doing so."

"Phare and I can cover things until you're ready."

"I'll need to know where to strike. My technique meets your needs for precision and speed, but it will not destroy a particularly large area. Four square inches, at best."

Abaddon paused for a moment, then asked, "Do you have a dagger I can borrow?" The Dragoon drew forth and handed over a slim knife, which the big man placed into his belt. "I'll find the spot. When you're ready, I'll mark it with my own blood. Keep your eyes sharp. Everyone set?" They nodded their response. "Then let us waste no more time."

In a matter of minutes they reached Tenkahn, who stood in the middle of another small glade as though awaiting his rematch. Abaddon gave his allies a few hand signals, then faced the monk as Cildar stood a step behind, already channeling white ether. Myris slunk into the trees on the edge of the glade, awaiting opportunity.

Abaddon first tried to establish diplomacy, though he suspected it was a vain effort. "Tenkahn, do you recognize me? I am Abaddon Daemon. We were allies once. Parley with me."

The monk's response was a physical one, quickly sweeping both fists above his head and then pounding the ground before him. From where he watched, Myris noted that the man's movements seemed even faster than before, his pauses shorter.

Abaddon offered a sharp reprisal, dropping to his knees and driving both fists into the dirt similarly. As his strike reverberated, Tenkahn's technique took effect. The ground around the glade shattered and began to uplift, as great pillars of deep earthen rock climbed to the surface to destroy the area. A second later Abaddon's counter triggered, the shockwave from his fists echoed Tenkahn's own, and the massive quake was brought to a halt. The forest floor was left cracked and shattered, areas overturned and exposed, smoke pouring out from the competing pressures of the warriors' abilities. Nearby uprooted trees began to crackle and collapse, and it was many minutes before the glen recovered from the chaos.

Tenkahn did not stutter, giving a short dash forward and lashing out with his left hand. This punch was several yards short, but Abaddon did not have to adjust his eyes to know that a large dose of pressurized wind was coming for him. He checked over his shoulder swiftly, noting Cildar's position. He could not dodge the attack without endangering his friend, so instead he rapidly removed Kargaroth from his back and stabbed it into the ground in front of him.

The invincible blade held firm against the monk's burst of energy, and Abaddon dashed to his right and came in at Tenkahn from an angle, leaving the sword where it stood planted. The monk twisted at the waist and answered this charge with a swift right hook. The Knight of the Sun tucked his legs up and allowed himself to fall forward, feeling the energy from Tenkahn's fist tear into his cheek as he edged past the killing blow. Once clear, he slammed his left foot forward into the ground and, using his left arm as a counterbalance, delivered a powerful uppercut into his foe's rib cage.

Tenkahn's counter had left his right side unguarded, and he was knocked bodily into the air by the Daemon's wicked strength. As the monk attempted to position himself midair, a dark blur appeared in front of him. Myris had found his opening, and executed a rapid Draw Strike of Fire. A swift rake of flame tore into Tenkahn's chest—magically augmented to slice deep through the armored skin—and the man was blasted across the glade.

Abaddon made a motion with his left hand, then he and Myris dashed across the clearing, positioning themselves so that Cildar was no longer in the line of combat. Tenkahn gave a nimble roll as he landed and regained his feet. He stared at his opponents impassively as flames from the Cainite katana slowly burned the tunic from his shoulders and chest. A thin line had been carved across his tattooed chest, but once more the rune structure roared brighter and held his flesh together tightly.

"That is impressive," Myris muttered as their enemy paid no mind to the fires still dancing across his body.

"The rune structure affords him a great deal of immunity," Abaddon added.

Myris returned his sword to its sheath, keeping his hand on the hilt. "I wonder if he fares so well against a blast of li—"

Before he could finish this sentence Myris realized that Tenkahn was on top of him again, lashing out with a sudden punch. He attempted to unsheathe his blade and use his Draw Strike for defense, but he was not fast enough. Just as he was sure that the rune-covered fist was to tear his head from his shoulders, Abaddon's foot struck the monk's wrist with a ferocious high kick. The Daemon then slipped his left arm to the inside of Tenkahn's right, twisting the arm around and locking his fingers tight into the base of the runed neck.

Abaddon attempted to aim for Tenkahn's ribs again, firing a low right hook, but this time was unsuccessful. The monk used his free hand to latch onto the mystic's forearm and clenched like a vice, bringing the blow to a halt a few short inches from his abdomen. The monk lifted his opponent's captured arm, twisting and attempting to snap the bone, as Abaddon's fingers bit deep into his foe's shoulder and fractured his clavicle.

As the two warriors stood inflicting excruciating pains on one another, Myris drew back. He debated whether he should make an attack, but feared for Abaddon's safety with such meager proximity. He did not have to debate long, as the Daemon soon brought the stalemate to an end.

He stepped forward and slammed his right boot down in a crushing blow on his opponent's bare foot. At the same time, he released with his left hand and gave a swift shove to his enemy's shoulder, knocking him off balance. As the monk fell away, Abaddon turned his extended fist over and gave a jagged sweeping blow to the man's chin. Tenkahn lost his grip and fell to the ground a few feet away.

The Daemon gripped his right forearm in pain and breathed heavily, already exhausted from the short exchanges. Tenkahn lay still for only a moment, then slammed the back of his fists into the grass at his sides. Two slabs of earth on each side of Abaddon suddenly uplifted and clapped together, crumbling from the impact with which they slammed into him. He reeled a step back, then placed his right hand on his thigh and stepped down hard with his heel. A narrow stony spike instantly shot from underneath the middle of Tenkahn's back, lifting him by his spine and tossing him into the air. The monk curled into a ball mid-flight, bringing himself into a tight spin until he returned to land, whereupon he thrust his fists into the ground at each of his sides. Two waves of earth circled about and closed on his opponent. Abaddon quickly leaped back, straightened both of his arms, then unleashed a wave of condensed, focused air from each fist.

Most of the monk's attack collapsed, successfully countered by Abaddon's release of kinetic energy. Myris watched this in awe, amazed at the destruction he had witnessed in the past ten seconds. He had long known of the earth- and wind-shifting techniques the Daemon had learned during his previous trip to Arkalen, but never before had he seen their capability when used without reservation. Only now was he beginning to realize how powerful the man's mysticism had allowed him to become. In the wake of two warriors fighting at this level, his own presence seemed a meaningless distraction.

Tenkahn's face remained expressionless, whereas Abaddon was

panting and bleeding from impact wounds across his body. Myris edged toward his friend's side, but was cautious not to get too close. He did not fear for his own life, but was concerned that his involvement now would be more hindrance than help.

"Are you alright?" he asked with apprehension. The big man nodded slowly. "Is it just me, or is he getting faster?"

"And stronger, unless I miss my guess," Abaddon responded. "His runes are definitely in some sort of overload, and it seems to be spiraling to an extreme. He's already reached the upper limits of what I can handle. If his body keeps accelerating, he's going to surpass me."

Myris tilted his head. "Are you saying you will be unable to defeat him?"

Abaddon squinted in irritation. "I'm saying that I can't match Tenkahn on his own terms for much longer. If this continues, I'll be forced to kill him." He turned and looked over his shoulder, shouting, "Cildar! Are you nearly prepared?"

The man in question had not moved from his original spot, and now his right hand was held out in front of him, glowing with a piercing white aura. His left hand clutched his wrist firmly, attempting futilely to steady his shaking arm. "I will be. Just tell me where to strike," he answered with a wavering voice.

As Abaddon had exchanged rounds of blows with Tenkahn, Cildar had been slowly focusing his energy to pool into his cupped hands. He had previously removed his gloves and stashed them away, allowing more unhindered control over the flow of the white ether. He drew in external amounts of ether as he could afford them, pushing the constraints of his spirit to its limits. After what felt like tensing his spiritual muscle until it was ready to rip, he finally succeeded in bringing all of his formidable holy power gathered into his hands alone.

This left him dizzy and exhausted, but he had to immediately dive into the next phase of the technique. He began shifting the weight of the power from his left hand into his right, straining to keep it from running back up his right arm. After finishing this step, he arrived where he stood now—using his left hand to brace his right arm, focused on holding the gathered energy from falling apart and flying in every direction, as his hand glowed with fearsome power.

After the beckon from Abaddon, he began the final step. He created a small web of energy running along his outstretched fingertips, and began leaking his concentrated holy might into this web. The transfer was rapid, and soon a single spark floated lightly above the palm of his hand. It was tiny, no larger than a fly, but its intensity made it impossible to look at directly, and it cast a ring of light around the paladin's entire forearm.

With that, it was complete. The House of Emle's newest ultimate technique, which he had named Shock. He took a few deep breaths to steady himself, still consumed by maintaining the slim shell that held his attack in its compact form. By concentrating all of his spiritual potency to a single point he left himself vulnerable. He no longer had enough reserves remaining to use defensive white magic, nor to heal himself, nor even enough to link to his Trine Lance.

As Cildar put the finishing touches on his move, Abaddon charged forward and rejoined Tenkahn in exchanges of blows. The Daemon managed to hold his own for a while, occasionally drawing back a few feet to dodge a flurry of the monk's waved punches. Abaddon could feel that his previous injury was beginning to wear him down, and he had nearly exhausted himself in trying to mirror his opponent's techniques. The mystical combat abilities were highly demanding, and he could only hope that soon Tenkahn himself might also succumb to exhaustion, given how careless he was being with his own energy.

On the seventh round of these exchanges, the warlord stepped back as the monk launched immediately into one of his kinetic bursts. Abaddon evaded the attack, the same step he had used half a dozen times now. He was about to move back in for a renewed direct assault, when he heard an explosive roar behind him. He turned to look too late, as pillar of rock collapsed down upon him.

He had no time to counter the move, so he crouched and dipped his head, bracing himself poorly for impact. Where he expected pain, he instead heard a second jarring explosion, and looked up to see Myris standing in the shredded remains of stone.

In the lull that followed, the Cain gave a nod. "I saw the pillar forming before you had noticed it," he explained. "I intercepted with an icy Draw Strike."

"He used Pulsing Fist to trigger a Tremoring Fist," Abaddon explained, turning back to keep an eye on his adversary. "I didn't know such a thing was possible. The amount of power and concentration it would take is staggering. I thought I was wearing him down, but I begin to fear that in his current state he has no limits at all."

Even as he spoke, his mystic vision suddenly fixated on something burning bright with ether lines. At the center of Tenkahn's chest, where Myris had burned off the man's tunic, there was a single rune bridging two sides of the structure. Abaddon had once had these runes carved into his own body, but he did not recall such a single thick mark occupying the center of the chest. He adjusted his eyes to filter out the Morolia currents and focused on the Asterian black ether. As he did so, it became clearer that this particular rune blared with vehemence, a dozen times more intense than the lines carved across Tenkahn's body, but it was messier. It drew in black ether at rates unhealthy if not outright poisonous for a Morolian creature, and showed no indicators of stability.

He looked to Cildar, who seemed ready to strike. The target was chosen. It was time to see where Tenkahn's fate would lie.

"Myris, go!" the warlord barked.

The Lord of the Cain did not hesitate, even knowing how imperiled his life was. As the wiry man charged Tenkahn, Abaddon swiftly drew Cildar's knife and slashed the tips of the index and middle fingers on his right hand. Myris was struck only once and sent flying from the monk, who quickly shifted targets and came straight for his more worthy rival's head. The Daemon took this punch bravely, then reached up and placed a thick stroke of fresh blood over the rune he had chosen.

Tenkahn's blow was a particularly vicious one. The impact traveled through Abaddon's body and caused the ground at his feet to erupt into debris. He mustered enough strength to pull off one final technique as he fell, placing his left palm on his tormentor's stomach and then punching the back of his own hand. A cyclone of wind seized the monk and carried him into the air, and as Abaddon hit the ground he shouted out hoarsely through a mouthful of his own blood, "Cildar, finish it!"

Tenkahn landed solidly and inspected the area. His two combatants lay on the ground where he had discarded them, and a third warrior stood across the glade with a strange light floating menacingly in his right hand. Abaddon noticed the monk's eyes lock onto the Dragoon, and muttered a curse under his breath as he struggled to rise.

"Myris, on your feet. We have to hold his attention."

The shadowy warrior obeyed and rose to his feet unsteadily, bracing the side of his face with both hands in abject agony. As Tenkahn turned back to the two dark warriors, unsure which to finish first, Cildar turned his hand and pointed his open palm at the monk.

The sphere of light surrounding his arm grew and flickered with intensity. He focused it forward slightly, and a small point of light appeared on Tenkahn's chest, dead center of the bloody mark Abaddon had made. Beneath his mask, the paladin smiled to himself and began boasting aloud.

"There's no dodging this, monk." The berserk fighter immediately shifted his attention to the speaking opponent. He dropped into a slight crouch, preparing to move. "That won't do you any good," Cildar continued. "By the time you even know that this attack has been released, it will have already pierced you."

Abaddon coughed up another spurt of blood, then demanded, "Release, Emle! If he doesn't kill you, I'm going to!"

The paladin dropped his smirk and brought forth the full brunt of his concentration. Cautiously, tenderly, he slipped his focus to the front of the pinprick of light, tying his mind to the slim shell that held it together. Then, as tightly as he could, he pierced the front of the shell and commanded it to collapse, releasing the light stored within.

No one, not even Cildar, expected what happened next. From the nearly invisible point of light floating by his hand, a hundred bursts of concentrated white magic shot in every direction. The release of the power within could not be focused, could not be restricted to a single direction. In the instant he had attempted to open the shell, the backlash of holy energy had destroyed it. It was as though he had released a hundred Aura Blasts raining down upon himself and his comrades.

Myris' Cainite instincts warned him of the impending danger, and reacting reflexively he drew his katana and, with a flurry of swings, blocked nearly half a dozen beams of magic headed his way. His katana cracked and smoked from the blasts, but did not shatter. Abaddon sidestepped one particularly large concentration of blasts, then crossed his forearms in front of his face and was met by a barrage cutting into his arms and ribs. Cildar himself was knocked back by the force of the release, screaming in agony at the intense white cannon blast that recoiled through his arm.

Chaotic as it was, the attack could not be called a failure. Before the paladin himself had realized what had went wrong, before the Cain's spiritual warding had ticked, before the entire glade had been fully painted by the light of the attack, the core of Shock had already passed through Tenkahn and traveled half a mile. Cildar's boast had not been an idle one—no living entity could have dodged that attack. A small tunnel, no more than two inches in diameter, had been torn through the monk's chest. The rune Abaddon had targeted, as well as the blood that had marked it, were disintegrated and erased from the world.

As the aftershock ended, Myris looked around. A huge pillar of light exploded far beyond the reaches of the forest. It looked to be almost ten miles away, and had to be at least half a mile wide.

Cildar sat up nursing his injured arm. The pillar that shone above the treetops faded, Tenkahn gave a groan and fell onto his back, and Abaddon and Myris turned and glared at their comrade.

"What?" the Dragoon chuckled as he struggled to talk through his own pain. "Too much?"

* * * * *

Farther to the east, Detria Alsen and her forces had arrived within sight of the Overlord's compound. A huge red ogre stood on each side of a massive iron gate, and Detria had carefully positioned the army so that a hill sat between them and the ogres' line of sight. This gave their scouts a perfect vantage point to keep an eye on things, without giving any information to their soon-to-be besieged foe.

They had only just arrived, slightly over a day's worth of traveling since she had parted paths with Abaddon. He had told her to give them three days to catch up, and she had decided that his three day window began now. Though she had clashed with the warriors from Itrius a few times, she now lamented their absence. The Lord of Felthespar had exhibited a clear intuition for how to wage wars and sieges, and Detria could not help but feel unprepared without their counsel in the upcoming excursion.

Kelve went through and chatted with various regiments, boosting morale. This was not really needed. Most of these soldiers had been longing to find the Overlord for years, desperately wishing to believe he was real. Discovering his existence now proved they had not spent the past few years of their life as fools. For some of them, it vindicated their enmity with the Devilslayers. For others, it proved that there was a chance that, maybe someday soon, Arkalen could be saved. The chaos of the continent seemed unmanageable and untamable, but the Overlord himself was something they could fight, something they could kill to make their lands a better place.

Kelve soon returned and joined Detria, slipping her a quick kiss on the forehead and then sitting down across from her with a grin on his face. Normally she would have punched him in the knee for such a cheeky display, but her eyes lingered on the forest in the southwest. Kelve watched her for a few moments, then gave a sigh.

"So which is it, then?"

She turned and furrowed her brow in confusion. "What?"

"It seems to me you've developed a liking for one of our new friends. Is it the noble white knight, the mysterious ninja, or their brooding leader?"

She rolled her eyes. "Shut up, Kelve. I'm just concerned because they're allies."

"Interesting, because in all the time I've known you, you've never shown concern for an ally before. Remember, we were in the Devilslayers together for years. Many of your best friends often went off on dangerous missions, gone for days at a time, and you never batted an eye."

She shook her head in agitation. "Devilslayers are trained for danger. I knew they would probably be fine. And if not, I couldn't worry about every slayer that went off on a mission."

"Don't smokescreen *me*, Detria. Those guys are way out of our league. At least the paladin and the small one. I don't know how their leader fares in combat, but as for the other two," here Kelve slowed his words for peculiar emphasis, "I doubt even Deun Coloran himself could go toe to toe with them and survive the encounter."

Detria turned her full attention to her lieutenant as he mentioned this name. The man's tone was jovial, but his eyes were somber. She stared at him hard for several seconds, then asked, "Then you noticed it too?"

He tilted his head and sucked through his teeth. "It matches the description from Yasiff's warrants."

Deun Coloran, the former Devilslayer High Pack Leader. Yasiff's very first mandate as High Chieftain had been to declare the man as the prime threat to Devilslayer order. All slayers had been placed on maximum alert to watch for him, and told of his strange movement style. Though he was a former slayer, Deun did not wear their light leather and fur outfits, but had converted to a full set of the sturdiest armors. He had a tendency to shift all of his weight onto his right leg, and traveled through most areas in low bounds, only occasionally dropping his left foot for balance. Even for someone decked in plate mail it left a minimal trail, difficult to follow or notice, but once spotted it was impossible to mistake.

Detria had already noted several peculiar tracks in the area matching the Devilslayer reports, but she found it difficult to be confident with as much foot traffic as her small army had already created. If Kelve had noticed as well, it was far less likely that she had made a mistake. His scouting abilities were significantly more advanced than her own.

"The great rebel Deun," she said with fascination in her voice. "What do we do if we see him? Capture him? Kill him?"

Kelve leaned back and crossed his arms. "We probably would if we were Devilslayers. Of course, we're not. Personally, I want to know what all the fuss is about. What makes the guy such a big threat? Or is there something darker afoot, and the Devilslayers are becoming less trustworthy as they become more prominent?"

Before Detria could respond to this, there was a strange phenomenon. In the Banchik Mountains to the east, a slim pillar of light was suddenly visible from a vast distance, stretching from the base of one of the peaks and climbing as far into the sky as the eye could follow. It lingered for only a few seconds, then faded. She exchanged a curious glance with Kelve, who gave a shrug. "I hope that's not the signal of anything dire," she said half to herself. She made a motion to her old friend, and the two of them moved to start disseminating orders of stealth and caution.

## Chapter 11.

## Farthas the Lost

As Abaddon's party spent the better part of a day recovering from battle, a pale shadow observed from the trees with an equal mix of amusement and dissatisfaction. Though the Felthespari were weakened, it seemed yet unwise to engage them in combat. Instead the figure turned his course back east, returning to the Fortress of the Overlord. He had gone scarcely half a mile when a sudden darkness seized upon him, halting his feet where he stood. His eye twitched at this increasingly irritating phenomenon.

"What do you need now?"

*The monk failed. The Daemon was not subdued.*

"I'm aware of that. Nothing within my scheme happens beyond my attentions. It seems I had slightly underestimated the potential of the Rook. I have changed tack to use this to my advantage, and if not for this interruption I would even now be setting new events into motion."

*This is not part of the plan. Daemon was to be separated from the sword. What do you intend to do about that?*

"Something. Eventually. It's a minor setback, nothing for you to concern yourself with, certainly."

*You underestimate the man. He is dangerous, less apt to be controlled than most of the entities with which you are meddling.*

The silver-haired servant gave a deep sigh. "You concern yourself with my ability to manipulate Schpariel, you concern yourself with my ability to manipulate Daemon. Did you or did you not select me for a reason? Do you or do you not have faith in my cunning?" No response sounded in the darkness. "I understand that you place a great deal of value upon the success of this mission.

But you should recognize that I do as well. From now on, unless you have something important to speak of, cease this incessant paranoia. You are behaving like a human," he finished with contempt.

*So be it.*

"Hold. Before you disappear in typical fashion, I do need one thing."

*Speak.*

"I need a Crucible of Anji. An active one."

*The acolytes of the one calling himself 'Overlord' possess one. Like you, they are in the business of collecting ancient artifacts.*

"How convenient. I was heading that direction anyway."

*They will not release it easily.*

"Nonetheless, they will release it. Now please, I must be on my way."

The darkness slipped into serpentine strands and slithered away. Once more the conspirator was on the move.

* * * * *

While his tribe adapted merrily to their new lifestyle inside the Overlord's domain, Farthas was becoming increasingly rankled. The draconics had been given their own series of tenements, in the form of a few small barracks in one of the recently expanded courtyards. A feast of a few live humans, no longer fit for work, had been served to them. The other breeds of demons here welcomed them and treated them with respect, all the while swearing constant fealty to the Overlord's name.

The atmosphere was loose and agreeable, but there was a distinct taste of oppression Farthas could not ignore. The various demonic leaders swore this was the promised land, that all the Overlord asked was the willingness to put one's neck on the line in the fight against humans. This was something most of them had been doing anyway, with less success. Here, they claimed, there was sight of enduing victory over the merciless human cults.

Offsetting these assertions of liberty, there were the Robed Ones. They were small creatures, no larger than most humans, their bodies cloaked wholly in solid black cloth. Whenever one would come close, the resident demons would grow quiet and say nothing. When a Robed One spoke directly to a demonspawn, even the most ferocious would grow docile and acquiescent. Farthas was as of yet unsure what to make of this phenomenon, but it left a hollow feeling in the pit of his stomach.

After a brutal argument with Meriosthro, he had separated himself from his tribe and taken to wandering the citadel that embodied the heart of the fortress. It was truly a magnificent structure, towers and parapets jutting high into the sky. To the demons it was a work of fear and wonderment. To Farthas it was a structure humans would have built, and there was nothing to admire in that.

As he walked through halls decorated with tapestries—more human accouterments—the draconic thought back to the words he had exchanged with Meriosthro. He knew that many of her points were valid, as they always were. The leaders could not show irresolution to their people; draconics were not taken to flights of irrational or unfounded fears. To most of them, this seemed a good place, a place where they had allies and a fine meal. That alone was enough to make them turn a deaf ear to unsubstantiated concerns.

Lost in his thoughts, he turned a corner and stepped into what might have been a large banquet hall. The room stood mostly empty, except for a strange assembly gathered around a large table, too large for some of the attendees. A few ogres—two blue and one red—took up one side of the table. The other side was composed primarily of animal aberrations—pig-men, bear-men, and the like—demon species who did not even merit a formal name. Two members of the congregation Farthas found especially surprising: at one end of the table sat a vampiric, and at the other was a were-creature with a triangular array of eyes, and a pelt of alternating scales and fur.

"A fenrir," Farthas muttered to himself at the sight of the latter.

"I heard they were wiped out by the humans. This one seems to have evolved beyond its beastly form."

One of the ogres gave a hearty laugh at the sight of the draconic and invited him over to join them. Farthas presumed they were eating, but he struggled to imagine what so many dissimilar creatures would share for a feast. He had already gone most of the way across the room when he realized angrily what was happening. They were gathered about the table not for a feast, but rather to play games and gamble, a distinctly human activity. Farthas would have lashed out and created a scene, but the sight of three ogres with their clubs in close proximity kept his temper silent.

The friendly ogre continued to motion for him to join. He had no intention of playing human games, but he had walked too near now to pretend not to notice. Instead he wandered over by the fenrir, politely declining to take a seat or participate in the game. He watched for a few minutes, then tried to begin a quiet conversation with the wolfen creature.

"I'd heard there were many varieties of demon here, but I never expected to see your kind."

The wolf gave a large fanged smile, revealing deep rows of razor-sharp teeth. "I have no kind. I am the last of fenrir. Years ago, just before the demise of the Lifeless Vortex, my people were slaughtered by the interlopers. A few packs scattered packs remained, but not many. When the Devilslayers began to seize power, we were too weak to fight back. We were hunted and wiped out. I alone survived."

"How is that?"

"I possess the exceptional ability to think, and use logic. It's something my brethren lacked. When enemies came to kill us, I had the foresight to run and hide. I've lived many long years in that way. Some here say I'm a coward. I prefer to say I will live forever."

"That's a haughty boast, even to those of us of dragonspawn descent."

The fenrir gave a soft, contented rumble. "I suspect part of my own roots may be draconic in nature. Like your kind, fenrir do not get ill, they do not die of natural causes. As long as I can avoid death using my so-called cowardice, my life will never cease."

Farthas sneered. It was bad enough that these demons acted like humans, but to have also become such unapologetic cowards—it was too much for him. He began to wish he could have a word with this Overlord regarding the makeup of his army. "I thought one of the terms of staying here was to be willing to risk one's life in battle at a moment's notice? Is that not the arrangement?"

The canine head gave a slow nod as he watched a set of six dice hit the table. "And if the Overlord ever tries to cash in on his side of the bargain, he will suddenly find me mysteriously absent. For now, this place is merely a sanctuary for me. What about you, a once noble dragon? Tell me, do you intend to sacrifice your life for the cause of a lord you've never seen, a cause that you've never even heard?"

Farthas gritted his teeth and turned away. Though he hated to admit it, the fenrir had pinned him quite uncomfortably between two options he found equally despicable. His eyes roamed for a minute, then he changed the subject. "What about that one?" he asked, pointing at the dark specter at the other end of the table.

"Ah, the vampiric. The Overlord has even seduced a few servants of the night to aid him. He promises them power, to assist them in evolving to the next level, freeing them of their weaknesses if they serve him well."

"Liches?"

"None so far. Rumors are that the Overlord has tried to make deals with a few and nearly lost his life in the attempts. Whether they are true or not, no one can say. The Overlord is so rarely here it's hard to know which bits and pieces of him are real, and which are the fabrications of the nightmares he has instilled over his subjects."

Farthas was relieved to hear there were no liches in the compound. Draconics and liches shared in the same meals. In the same way that a starving draconic might feast on another for temporary sustenance, a lich would devour an entire nation of draconics just to increase its power by a small fraction.

He had more questions, and found himself growing at ease with the cynical fenrir. "Yes, what's with that? For what reason do these demons exhibit such fear, anyway? Are the Robed Ones so dangerous as to make even an ogre quake?"

The furred beast looked around quietly. Finding no one was watching him closely, he lowered his voice even further and answered, "The Robed Ones are nothing. They are simple acolytes of the Overlord, fragile and weak. One of his few laws, however, is that no demon disrespect said acolytes. A few have, on occasion, and were reported upon the Overlord's next visit. Their cries were heard across the citadel for five days straight before they were finally freed of their torment." He tilted his head and gave Farthas a devilish grin. "Some say if you really wish to learn more about the Overlord, the only way is to kill a Robed One. Then you'll get all of the personal time with him you could want."

Farthas sneered again. With the effort this Overlord placed into maintaining authority by fear, it seemed unlikely that he was actually a warrior of any merit. Farthas thanked the fenrir for the information, gave a civil nod to the rest of the congregation, then turned and left the banquet hall out the nearest exit.

He wandered aimlessly about the citadel's corridors for another couple of hours, still pondering his argument with Meriosthro, still smoldering at the sights of demons commingling like humans. Eventually he cooled enough to determine that the outlook for his potential life here was not so bad, and he only needed time to adjust. He turned around to head out of the castle and back to his barracks, then realized he had no idea where he was.

He stood within catacombs that looked to be archaic, centuries old. He must have been wandering through for at least half of an hour without noticing his surroundings. "Peculiar," he hissed to himself. "I wouldn't have expected this keep to be so ancient."

From where he stood he could see down at least seven passageways, but could not make out what was at the end of any of them. He started to proceed back the direction he had just come from, when suddenly he detected movement. A figure in black robes stepped out of a doorway somewhere and headed swiftly down one of the passages. It was taller and leaner than most Robed Ones, wearing clothes somehow neater in cut and moving with alacrity and decisiveness uncharacteristic of the hunched acolytes.

"You there!" Farthas shouted, hoping he might ask for the quickest way to the keep's exit. The figure did not slow, however, and soon was gone beyond his view. He hastened to follow, simultaneously curious and aggravated by the stranger's rush.

This chase went on for nearly fifteen minutes. Each time Farthas decided it was time to give up and go find his own way, he would catch a sudden glimpse of the robed figure dashing down a stairwell or through a door. He followed until he had climbed down a flight of stairs and stood alone in a large, empty entryway. One solitary wooden door stood before him. There were no markings, nothing to indicate any special significance save its bizarre isolation. Farthas was confident he had seen the suspicious stranger come this way less than five seconds before him, but the door did not look as though it had been opened for some time.

He sniffed around, but caught no scent of life. He scratched at his leathery neck and debated his next course of action. He had no real reason to be here. He could hope to accomplish nothing by opening the foreboding door and entering the chamber beyond. And yet he was more lost than ever, and without assistance might not see the light of day for weeks.

He convinced himself to reach forward and test the door. "I just need some directions," he rationalized to himself. "That's all." The latch was not sealed and ancient wooden structure opened easily, so he stepped into the dimly lit chamber beyond and quietly slid the door shut behind him. His draconic senses had no trouble mapping out the room he had entered. Several Robed Ones dashed about here and there, checking strange machines and pouring potions into tubes. Farthas remained where he had entered and watched, too entranced to speak.

Soon the Robed Ones grew tired of their labors. Half a dozen of them turned and went to the opposite side of the room, then pushed aside a sliding section of wall. It revealed daylight, and they stepped outside and let the wall seal itself behind them. Farthas was pleased to see his way out, but he was also bewildered. He had descended so deep it seemed impossible that he could still be at ground level.

A large table with a dark sheet cast over it served as the focal point in the laboratory. All of the machines seemed wired to this table, all of the tubes eventually carried their respective chemicals to it. Since the Robed Ones seemed to have taken their leave, Farthas slid forward to inspect the predominant fixture.

He walked around it and investigated, but could determine little. He glanced at the devices decorating the room, but they indicated nothing intelligible to him. Finally, letting his curiosity get the better of him, he stepped forward and placed his hand on the cloth covering the table.

At that moment, two Robed Ones walked into the room from a side hallway Farthas had failed to notice. Seeing the position of his hand, they instantly gave a garbled shouting noise and dashed at him. He leaped back from the table and instinct took over, as the closest Robed One stabbed at him with a flimsy surgical knife. The draconic easily sidestepped the blow, dug his claws into the acolyte's neck, and gave a sharp twist. He simultaneously drew the bone scimitar from his side and with a swift lash sent the second cowled head tumbling to the stone floor.

Farthas stood over his vanquished foes. He thought for a moment of the fenrir's warning, but shook it off. No one had witnessed his actions, no one even knew he was here. Even if the Overlord was a creature to be feared—a matter over which he still had his doubts—there was no way the draconic commander could be tied to these deaths.

He moved to take his leave through the sliding wall, when suddenly he caught a glimpse of the severed head lying on the ground. Shocked by what he saw there, he swiftly ripped off one of the acolytes robes. His stomach turned, both out of disgust and of fear for the monster that could have committed such an act.

The Robed Ones' bodies comprised a jumbled mismatch of various human and demon pieces. There was no consistency, no coordination. Head, arms, torso, legs—no part of the body was fashioned of a single unit. Terrible attempts at stitching seemed to barely hold them together, and their faces were twisted in constant expressions of anguish and despair.

"You're wondering what they are, aren't you?" a voice suddenly sounded. This voice was deep and hoarse, echoing from the darkness around the laboratory. Farthas began stepping backward, trying to hide the fear in his own voice.

"Who's there?"

"The golems of the Overlord. You're wondering what they are," the voice repeated slowly. Farthas' eyes detected movement, as the cloth covering the table began to slide onto the floor. Some large demonspawn had been lying on the table and slowly, deliberately, it turned around and placed its feet on the ground.

"They are the prototypes. The experiments. The necessary failures." The demon stood to its full height, a shadow hovering over Farthas. The draconic was a domineering figure himself, nearly seven feet tall, but this beast stood easily at eight, with a build reflecting an even mix of agility and strength, unlike the brutish ogres. "Building them taught the Overlord what attributes come from which creatures, and how best to mix the creatures to maintain and enhance those attributes. Using what he learned in creating them, the Overlord managed to craft perfection. He managed to create *me*."

The beast took two lumbering steps forward, clearing the gap between himself and Farthas effortlessly. As he did so, the dim light from the candles in the room highlighted his features and gave the draconic a better look. It was a minotaur. Farthas doubted his eyes at first, as they were demons of legend, only myths. The horns of a bull decorated the head, set over the intelligent eyes of a human. The skin appeared to be twisted from that of the ogres, blue and sturdy, wrapped tight about a frame of demonic muscles.

The legs and feet were shaped like that of a were-creature, vaguely human, but the demon remained standing only on his toes. The hands were large, muscular like an ogre's, but with nimble and precise fingers more akin to a human's. Despite being laid out on the table as he had been, the minotaur did not seem to be a fresh creation. He was gravely injured from some previous battle, his entire body covered in deep, stitched gashes and bruises. Many of his bones were set with iron bars to hold their shape, and an iron frame was wrapped around the left side of his torso as if holding his rib cage in place.

Farthas was unable to prevent himself from sputtering uselessly, "Wha-what are you?"

The great beast looked down on him and sniffed with its huge snout. "I am Shote," he continued to speak slowly, but the volume of his voice increased to a low bellow. "In the Overlord's absence, I am ruler here. You have violated our laws. You must die."

The draconic gave a leap back and drew his bone scimitar. If he could stay outside of the minotaur's range, he was certain he could deliver enough slices and blows to bring the demon down. Wounded as it was, and unarmed, Farthas had no doubts he would prove himself a match.

Shote eyed the bold lizard for a moment, then took a slow step back himself. Farthas smiled at what he perceived to be hesitation from his foe. Then the minotaur reached off to the side with his tremendous right arm, and from the shadows drew forth a two-handed greataxe, which he wielded comfortably in one hand.

Farthas' smile faded. Against this monstrous axe his scimitar would serve little use. Shote gave a light practice swing with his weapon, then announced, "I do enjoy a good execution."

* * * * *

Within the shadow of the Overlord's lands, Eiden sat alone practicing the techniques taught to him by Cildar and Myris. The veteran warriors had only shown the boy a few minor spells, but he drilled himself at least a dozen times on each one every day, swearing he would prove himself to his tutors next he saw them. He had even begun experimenting with his own alterations and improvisation, hoping to show off something new. He felt it unlikely that he would truly discover anything unknown to the Felthespari with his still-limited experience, but he hoped with the zeal of youth for such a possibility.

He was currently practicing one of the heraldry spells taught to him by Myris. The Cain had called it a Feeler, and told Eiden it was a good skill for a tracker to use when he believed his target was already nearby. The spell would detect if there were living beings within a certain range, using pulsing sensations to report the findings to the caster. Eiden had been attempting to amplify the effect and alter the feedback, creating a spell that would enumerate all of the surrounding lifeforms and give detailed information on their arrangements. He thought it might be useful for generals like Kelve and Detria to keep tracks of troops, if he could ever get it to work right.

At the moment that was seeming progressively less likely. The spell had been working fairly well earlier, but for the last hour or so he had been receiving irregular feedback impulses. His head was beginning to hurt, and he was uncertain how safe it was for him to keep pursuing the matter. He tried one last time, focusing hard on the direction that seemed to be giving him trouble.

The spell was reporting a hundred or so lifeforms standing near a tree a few yards from Eiden, where the hill's slope met the edge of the Techenar Forest. The boy stared at the forest, still confused by his results. He gave a slight sigh, stood up, and walked over to see if he could get a better reading by casting the spell in the problematic spot.

As soon as stepped past the tree, he found himself staring directly at black steel. Eiden was not taken to sudden reactions to unexpected circumstances, a conditioning from his hard life. Instead he calmly looked up at the face of the heavily armored warrior before him and gave a polite nod.

“Oh, so there is someone over here,” he said in a satisfied tone.

The man’s face was grim and his eyes narrowed. His right hand strayed near the hilt of a dagger, but then he seemed to think better of spilling unnecessary blood. “How did you know of my presence?”

Eiden thought for a moment, then responded, “If you don’t understand, it’d probably be hard to explain.”

The stranger took a step back, putting a comfort buffer between the two of them. “It’s insignificant anyway. Why is this army here?”

The youth looked over his shoulder at Detria’s forces. “We’ve come to wage war against the Overlord in his fortress.” He suddenly realized that he had never seen his former slavemaster in person, and the blood drained from his face. He desperately wanted to ask if this stranger was actually the Overlord, but he was terrified to hear the answer.

His worries were soon put at ease by a chuckle from the knight. “What a waste. The Overlord is nowhere near here, boy. He almost never is. I’ve hunted him for years and never caught him at his home.”

“Ah, I see.” Eiden swallowed and forced his voice to remain even. “We know this, actually. I’ve... got quite a history here myself. But we plan to take the fortress anyway, so we can set a trap and await his return. Perhaps you should join us? You seem to have your own agenda against him, unless I’m mistaken. I mean if you’ve truly been hunting for years, seems like maybe it’s time to try something different, right?”

The man stared over Eiden’s head, in the direction of the Overlord’s compound. For a few seconds there was silence, only crickets and the owls of the forest could be heard. Then he responded, “That plan will never work. The Overlord is too crafty to fall for something so simple, once you hold the base you will never see him again.” He turned, bracing his full weight carefully on his right leg, then holding his balance for a moment. “I’ll wish you success, as you may well drive him into the open for me, but

I'm not interested in his agenda or his lands, only the Overlord himself. Watch yourself, boy." With that, he leaped into the forest and disappeared from sight.

Watching him leave, Eiden scratched the back of his head in confusion. "I wonder why he showed up as a hundred men to my Feeler?" He gave a shrug, then returned to his private campfire to continue his studies.

* * * * *

Farthas lay in a slim stream, coughing as a river of his blood intermingled into the soothing waters. The sliding wall within the catacombs had led out from the base of the hill upon which the fortress was built. After a brief exchange of blows the draconic had slipped through the door and, tossing a few Robed Ones from his path, made his escape. The minotaur's previous injuries proved to be more serious than either contestant had thought, forcing him to abandon pursuit with a winded collapse.

But the damage had been done. Only a single blow from the massive greataxe had landed, but the force had nearly torn Farthas apart. His left arm, three ribs, and even his bowels had been left lying in the floor of Shote's chamber. His reptilian skin began to feel cold, and his damaged lungs had ceased their breathing.

Still the resilient draconic was not finished, as his body struggled to drag himself across the stream to the far bank. This was his limit, however, as he collapsed there, unable to move. In the distance he spotted a dark, robed figure approaching him. "Robed Onesss," he hissed quietly. Again he struggled to put his limbs into motion, but to no avail. His final reserves of strength were fast fading.

As the figure approached, the appearance of his robes gradually seemed to shift. By the time he reached Farthas they were a brilliant white, shimmering in the reflected sunset lights.

"It seems that our time apart has not served you well," the pale figure conjectured.

Farthas forced his lungs to start working again in order to speak his piece. “You. This is all your doing.”

“Please, don’t be ridiculous. I suggested for you to come here, not to probe into the Overlord’s secret affairs.” Farthas spat weakly and let his head slip back to the ground. “Your time is short, it seems, so let us not waste it mincing words. I have been given the power to save lives of inhabitants of this plane. All I ask is a price, a favor which you cannot know in advance. Would you like for me to save you?”

“You owe me,” Farthas responded weakly, already feeling the grip of Asteria tugging once more on his spirit as his body shut down. “One way or another, you did this to me and we both know it. You owe me my life back.”

The silvery stranger hesitated for a moment, then responded, “Perhaps you are right. I do owe you. For you, and you alone Farthas, I will spare your life and ask nothing in return.”

He reached into his robes a drew forth a strange artifact. It was a solid grey orb, nearly six inches in diameter, decorated by a gilded demon with its arms and legs wrapped tightly about the sphere. After receiving a tap from one of the pale fingers, the metallic demon opened its mouth and gave a slight hiss. The eyes started to glow with a bright white light, and Farthas could not resist looking up into them. After a further few seconds he gave a fierce scream, the light burst forward and enveloped his body, then all was quiet.

The bleached priest looked down at the now saturated orb, which had changed from grey to a deep black. He returned it silently to his robes with a smile, then stepped over the remains of the draconic’s lifeless body in order to take his leave.

## Chapter 12.

## I am Demon

Myris and Cildar had extricated themselves and rested twenty yards from where Abaddon watched over their unconscious nemesis. The two knights knew if the berserk monk awoke for a renewed battle, they would be of no help in their current condition. Cildar did not even have the spiritual capacity remaining to heal his own wounds. Instead the two lords conversed, ruminating on the results of the recent battles.

"Is your arm going to be alright?" Myris asked.

The backlash from Shock had rendered some unexpected side effects. The Dragoon's arm had been so thoroughly basked in Morolian ether that the metabolism of the limb had super-accelerated. In mere seconds, his fingernails had grown to six inches and the skin had aged five or even ten years, developing a slightly grey tint due to the unnaturalness of the change.

"I'll be fine," Cildar assured as he snipped away the extra-long nails. "Once I have enough strength to work some basic healing, I can reverse most of this. Some of the damage to the skin will probably be permanent, but not much worse than a severe sunburn."

They fell into silence for a moment. The Cain's eyes drifted over to the two mightier warriors. Neither captive nor watchman gave even the slightest hints of movement. Had Myris not already known where they were, he might have been convinced he and Cildar were alone.

"He is going to get back up," he stated in a matter-of-fact tone.

The paladin nodded. "According to what Lord Abaddon says,

most likely. That rune structure is still active. But he also said it doesn't seem to be overloading anymore. Maybe Tenkahn's mind will be restored, and we'll have ourselves a new ally."

"That could merely be a result of him being unconscious. We lack sufficient data to know otherwise. This is not worth the risk. We should kill him while he lies."

"It's unlike you to be so nervous. Take heart, we won. Things are looking up."

Myris' head snapped around to glare at his friend, and he spat angrily, "No, *you* won. Yourself and Lord Abaddon. Do not patronize me. I served no use."

The taller man creased his brow in concern. Myris had always been a tad moody, but Cildar had never seen his spirits this foul. "Come on, now. We all did our parts, the way we always do."

"When it was your task to hold the monk at bay, you were able to stand your ground with your Haste technique. I had neither the strength nor the stamina to hold him off for even a moment. It has become clear to me now. I can no longer fight at a sufficient level to aid you and Abaddon."

"Myris, you know we need your skills. Your natural speed is virtually unmatched, your Draw Strike technique is vicious, and your mastery of heraldry is far beyond ours. Not to mention the versatility of your Cainite magic."

The disheartened man rose to his feet and stared blankly into the forest. "That you are even forced to justify my presence is a sign of how far I have fallen." He turned and left, walking soundlessly into the trees.

Cildar almost shouted after and rose to follow, but could think of nothing further to say. His attempt to raise his friend's spirits had only dashed them further. He scratched his head with his good hand and whispered to himself, "Maybe he'll get over it his own way."

As the paladin was distracted with concern, the aforementioned fallen monk finally opened his eyes and gave a soft sigh. Abaddon did not budge, watching his former ally cautiously. Tenkahn looked around and soon noticed the man sitting nearby. He offered a forlorn smile.

"Master Abaddon? Have I passed on, and you somehow await me at the other side?"

"It's good to hear you speak," the warlord answered in his stolid baritone. "Hopefully it means we won't need to fight again in the near future."

Tenkahn attempted to lift himself up onto his elbows, but Abaddon gently pushed him back down. "I don't recommend that. Even for men of our fortitude, you've suffered a grievous blow. There's a sizable hole in your chest. It'll be at least a few hours before your runes will be able to repair that damage sufficiently."

"I fought you?" he asked in confusion. The mystic nodded his response. "And you won, of course," Tenkahn continued, pausing to chuckle weakly. "Your strength is peerless as ever. As I was, no one should have been able to defeat me."

"I had help. It was Myris' plan, and Cildar's technique that stopped you." He tilted his head and continued slowly, "*I* would have killed you."

"I do not doubt your word. It seems I owe your friends a debt of gratitude."

Abaddon narrowed his eyes and kept his voice serious. "You said 'as you were'. That 'as you were', we should have been unable to defeat you. What did you mean by that?"

The monk leaned his head back, staring into the evening sky and allowing his mind to pour over past events. "My thoughts are yet hazy, but last I recall, my order and I were preparing to wage war against a demon called the Overlord. We had long been seeking his fortress, and had at last located it. I went in as an advanced scout and discovered that the master himself was absent." Abaddon observed intently as Tenkahn's story echoed Detria's own mission, but did not interject. "Expecting an easy victory, we launched our invasion. We were unprepared for what happened.

"We broke our way through wave upon wave of demonic and human troops alike, easily slaughtering familiar foes with our art.

Victory seemed within grasp, but the Overlord had a second-in-command we had not heard of before that day. A mighty beast, a minotaur as in legends calling himself Shote. Upon his appearance the battle waned and the lesser soldiers retreated away. My men and I turned our assault eagerly, foolishly. Shote was more than a match for all of us. He killed the other nine as I watched, unable to stop him. He took our attacks without flinch, breaking the bodies of my men with twin greataxes he wielded with terrifying skill.

"No creature—even a legendary one—can face the full might of the Monks of Tria and come away unscathed. Shote himself was finally brought down, but at a terrible price. I alone survived of my men. When the remaining forces renewed their campaign against me, I did not have the strength to fight on alone and was driven into retreat. My injuries were, of course, too grave, and I collapsed in the hills surrounding the citadel.

"Then a strange event unfolded. A monk not unlike myself, garbed in bright white adornments, appeared and offered me aid. He said, 'I have been given the power to save lives of inhabitants of this plane. All I ask is a price, a favor which you cannot know in advance. Would you like for me to save you?'

"And he did. He saved my life. But the price he asked afterward was too great. He commanded me to activate the final rune of Tria—the rune which is called Merciless, though it is from the God of Mercy herself." As he spoke, he touched the area of his chest that had been wounded by Shock. "Somehow, though I desired to resist his order, I could not. I suppose it was some spell placed upon me as he healed me. Unable to stop myself, I activated the Merciless Rune as beckoned. That is where my memory ends."

Abaddon absorbed this information in silence for a moment. Arkalen was crawling with puzzles, and he did not yet have enough pieces to discern their full nature. "What is this Merciless Rune?" he queried as he continued to ponder.

"As you yourself know, the runes decorating my order's bodies enhance our characteristics. Strength, speed, intellect—all parts of the human form are made more efficient using Asterian alteration.

The Merciless Rune magnifies this effect. It makes the body so efficient that it begins to burn itself up. Muscles are made so strong that even punching deteriorates them slightly. Speed is made so fast that the skin tears itself in order to move. And the mind is made so efficient, so precise, that all logic and reason is eventually lost out to baser instincts.

"A monk using the Merciless Rune's blessings can maintain a set purpose for maybe an hour, but no more. After that, everything is lost to rage and survival. Often we will continue fighting anything we find, as battle is such an ingrained instinct that it remains one of the mind's final anchors. But in more peaceful times, monks under the influence of the rune were said to become cowards, retreating to distant places and hiding until their bodies burned up from Asterian magic."

Abaddon glanced across the glade to where Cildar sat alone. He stood, giving Tenkahn a friendly nod. "Rest now, friend. In the morning, we'll march."

The monk furrowed his brow. "Have you already some plan? Whither are we bound?"

"A squadron of allies awaits near the Fortress of the Overlord. One of the demon's escaped slaves travels with them, and he contains much information on the inner workings of the keep. With our combined strength and knowledge, I doubt it will pose much difficulty to overtake it."

Tenkahn weakly returned a few determined nods, then lay back and closed his eyes. "I owe it to my fallen brethren to try at least once more." He quickly became lost in thought, and soon fell asleep. As Myris returned from his outing and rejoined Cildar, Abaddon approached them to report on the vanquished monk's condition.

* * * * *

In pale moonlight, the demon Zekraul slipped quietly between the trees of the Techenar Forest. He traveled alone, using the darkness to gather his thoughts. Since his confrontation with the creature named Schpariel some two and a half years ago, Zekraul had done much research on the Godbeasts of Gehenna and their relationship to Arkalen. All of his findings had been intriguing, but none particularly helpful.

Centuries prior, the Godbeasts had invaded Morolia with intentions to use it as a stepping stone to their ultimate goal of Elysium—the outer plane on the far side of Asteria. The Muses of Elysium had responded to this threat, summoning forces and sending them to Morolia to ward the Godbeast's path. The Elysian armies slew the Gehennans and imprisoned them forever in the rocks of Morolian soil. The Elysians returned home across the Veil, and the story should have ended there.

Yet Zekraul had seen Schpariel. He had fought this creature—albeit briefly—with appearance and abilities consistent with the Dark Wisdom of lore, though perhaps dulled by ages of imprisonment. So he was left to debate whether this was truly the second coming of one of the supreme Godbeasts, or some dedicated impostor.

It was an important question to answer. Zekraul had spent his entire life being wary, only picking the fights he was certain he could win. The Schpariel he had faced years ago did not seem terribly dangerous, but was certainly an even match for him at the time. If truly the Godbeast, his powers would only have grown. Even worse, it was possible that other Godbeasts might yet be resurrected as well. If there was any chance of that happening, Zekraul had one and only one plan in mind: to get the hell off of Arkalen.

As he moved through the trees, he began to grow discomforted. He focused his senses, trying to determine what subtle change in the atmosphere was bothering him. Not paying full attention to his own steps, he was surprised to hear the sudden snap of a branch at his feet as he entered a small clearing.

There were muffled sounds in response to this snap. Zekraul froze in place and carefully scanned the area. Though it was nearly pitch black with the treetops hiding the crescent moon, his demonic senses were not hindered. He detected indicators of recent battle, and across the clearing lay a human who seemed to be asleep. He took a few steps in the direction of the sleeping form, examining carefully. The man's chest was bandaged, and his attire was the shredded remains of a monastic robe.

"Telaric nosfricte," a quiet voice hissed into the darkness. Zekraul quickly tried to pinpoint its origin, but the sound was magically guarded and seemed to echo throughout the trees around him. Suddenly the area exploded with light, shining down from nearly a dozen large orbs that surrounded the clearing. The demon was not moved by this display and maintained his composure.

"Someone wants to play?" he remarked coldly. "I'm assuming the unconscious one didn't do that. I made the mistake revealing my presence before I knew of yours, but that's okay. Merely adds spice to my fun, really."

His opponent at last appeared, stepping forward between two particularly large trees. It was a tall man, garbed in brightly-colored but dirty armors. A blue face mask matched gloves and boots, and a sturdy three-pronged spear was strapped across his back.

"Another human," Zekraul taunted. "A slight disappointment. Are you anyone of consequence?"

"I'm the one who took *him* out," the man responded, giving a nod in the direction of the unconscious body.

"Is that supposed to impress me? That one human was able to best another?"

He gave a casual shrug in response. "Don't know. Thought it might."

Zekraul gave a strange hissing laugh, amused by his new playmate. "Most nights I'd leave you alone, perhaps try to give you a slight scare and watch you flee. But tonight I am in a poor mood, and skinning a cocky human alive always does wonders for my disposition."

"I never expected anything less." The knight reached his right hand behind his back and drew forth the spear. He gave the shaft a tap against the ground, and the three prongs at the top came alight. He leveled the weapon forward softly at Zekraul. "After all, you are demonspawn, and I am a holy paladin. We are born to dance, aren't we?"

Had he possessed a mouth, Zekraul might have smiled. Instead he stretched his right arm out to his side, level to the ground. Several audible pops and grinding scrapes were heard, as slowly his arm began to thin and his hand lost definition. He raised his left arm as well, creating a straight line between the two, and the noises of activity increased. He gave a cry that was a mix of roaring and hissing, and finally a single large crack was heard. The bar formed by his arms separated from his back, falling to the ground.

He paused briefly for his opponent's reaction, but the man had not budged an inch, staring at the armless torso with patience and determination. The demon released a second hiss, and his chest slowly expanded outward like a balloon. When it was nearly double its original diameter, there was a fresh pop, followed by a grotesque ripping noise. Two new arms burst from his shoulders, dripping with a green substance that might have been blood.

The adaptive creature bent down and picked up his previous arms. When touched by his fresh hand they began to further transform, tightening in and compacting into a twisted black staff. He raised it high and then gave a firm tap to the ground, mimicking the knight's earlier motion. Upon impact, the head of the staff exploded out into three viciously hooked blades, a crude mockery of his opponent's weapon.

He leaned his spear forward to point at his opponent. "Let's see now if your skills justify your ego. But first, names. One must always exchange names. Even the least civilized among us can observe that courtesy, yes?"

"I am Cildar Emle, Lord of the Phoenix."

"I am demon; Zekraul. I have no other names in your tongue. Are we ready now?"

"Come as you will."

Zekraul commanded his legs to twist about slightly, generating springlike tension. As he did so, his opponent made a strange pronouncement.

"Mal-oste haruste."

As part of his unique nature, Zekraul was extremely sensitive to the movements of energy. As the foreign knight uttered this peculiar phrase, he suddenly erupted with a piercing light, completely robbing the demon of his senses. It flowed outward from the man's body in every direction and somehow seemed to even permeate it, as if his corpus itself had somehow been swallowed.

Zekraul was uncertain if this effect was intended to distract him as badly as it did, but he bravely endeavored not to reveal his disorientation. He released the compressive force in his legs and sprang at the location where he was certain his last opponent stood. He performed a fierce upward slash just before closing in, hoping to lock the knight into a defensive position or, even better, throw him off balance. Instead his mock-Lance passed through empty air, causing the demon himself to lose balance. He hissed in frustration, disappointed but not surprised.

He summoned a fresh surge of concentration and tried to calm his senses, which raged even worse now so near to the overflowingly luminous knight. He sensed a flash of movement at his side and, without turning his head, focused in on the man coming at his left flank. The human's spear was leveled out before him, balanced on both hands and glowing with a huge holy aura. Zekraul had relocated his foe, but had no time to react to his seemingly impossible burst of speed. Just before coming into range, the soldier gave a sharp twist of his body and thrust his weapon into the black crystalline shoulder.

The demon was stricken as if by a battering ram, and his body cracked and launched across the glade. He smashed into a tree on the far side with his other shoulder, rendering both of his fresh arms shattered. His assailant stood idly behind with the explosive aura pouring out for a few more seconds, then it suddenly dissipated entirely. Cildar tried to hold his stance resolutely, but was already beginning to breathe heavily.

Zekraul did not fail to notice this. Clearly the knight had hoped to win quickly with an unrestrained assault, but was too weak from previous battle to continue in this manner for long. The demon stepped away from the trunk he had shattered and slowly adjusted his arms into their proper shape, healing the large gap tore into his shoulder with effort.

"You're something else for a human, I'll give you that. I suspect that yesterday, or tomorrow, you would have served me quite a thrashing. But that's not the case tonight, is it? I'm not one of those overzealous fools with some sick need to fight opponents only at their full strength. No, to the contrary, it will only make me enjoy your suffering even more knowing what a rare treat it is."

He dashed forward again, repeating the exact same attack he had opened with. With his enemy's clearly faded reserves, he felt assured he would not see the peculiar radiance that had distracted him before. His gamble proved shrewd, and this time as he performed his uppercut Cildar stood his ground and attempted to block with the Trine Lance. There was a satisfying clang as demonic strength easily overpowered human, launching the hands gripping the Lance up over the man's head and leaving his abdomen exposed. Zekraul did not wait to regain control of his own spear, but instead leaned forward, headbutting the plated chest so hard he snapped his own neck. The paladin's armor was not sufficient to absorb this impact, and he was sent flying back onto his haunches with the breath knocked from his lungs.

After setting his head back into proper alignment, Zekraul moved in for a quick finisher. He wanted to at least incapacitate the speedy human enough that he would not cause further nuisance, and prevent resistance to his torturous intentions. He dashed forward and gave a quick jab with his spear aimed at the man's lower spine, just between the gaps in his armor.

To Zekraul's annoyance, his attack did not connect. A sudden wall of earth arose between him and his target, erupting with such force that it destroyed his spear. The demon leaped back—only narrowly avoiding the thrust himself—and turned to locate its source. The previously unconscious man was on his feet now, and the wall of rock seemed to have originated from his fist planted in the forest floor.

"Might I offer you aid, good sir?" the monk asked in Cildar's direction.

The first soldier stood to his feet and gave a nod. "I'll be honest, Tenkahn, I'm not at the top of my game. I could use a hand."

The interloper's response was quick—almost too quick for Zekraul. The monk dashed through the wall of rocks he had just formed and it collapsed as he passed it over. As soon as he was directly in front of the demon, he gave a spinning roundhouse kick. Zekraul managed to step back in time to duck this, but it was rapidly followed by a powerful series of jabs and hooks. The crystalline creature danced between the fists, sensing the force of these blows as they brushed near his armored flesh. He could tell that a direct hit would be dangerous, even for a creature of his resilience.

Seeing a brief opening in the pugilistic patterns, the demon gave a long jump away and chucked the remains of his spear at the warrior. The back of the monk's right hand deflected the bar by turning it instantly into dust, to Zekraul's concern. The man's face remained deadly serious as he suddenly made a crouching motion, pointing his open palms at the ground in front of him. Zekraul waited anxiously, but there was no reactive effect to this motion. Then the monk dropped to his knees and punched down with both fists. Still, no reaction. Finally, he lifted his fists and punched them together, allowing the right one to slide over the top of the left. Tenkahn, like Cildar before him, was already panting heavily. Their wiry adversary felt a wave a relief in realizing the monk too had oversold his ability.

Then the anticipated attack finally came. Two earthen fists ejected from the ground on each side of Zekraul and slammed together, trapping him into a giant artificial boulder. He was not totally unharmed by this attack, but it was nowhere near enough to wear down his constitution. He exercised his shapeshifting and transformed his entire body into a multi-directional explosion of steely spikes. As the shell around him collapsed, he returned to his natural form. He was surprised to detect he had begun to give off a quiet involuntary hiss. It was a sign that, like his opponents, he was beginning to tire.

As the rocks fell around him and cleared his path, he noticed yet another human now standing before him—a man garbed in dark attire with a shock of hair covering the upper part of his face. He stood before the beleaguered creature calmly, as though there by accident. He did not even look at Zekraul, but rather stared off to the side with disinterest. His left hand rested on the sheath of a small katana at his side, but his right hand hung loose near his right hip. He seemed unprepared for combat.

The demon's patience slipped at these continuing interferences. "What is this?" he hissed. "Another insect crawling out of the woodwork? Who knew, step on one bug and so many come out to defend his honor."

The newcomer's right hand moved. It was a blur and none of Zekraul's enhanced senses could follow the motion. The hilt of the sword was seized tightly and instantly the demon's world turned to fire. Flames filled his empty eye sockets as they engulfed his head, and he stumbled back with a roar of dismay. He tried to shift his armory skin to absorb the heat with his innate abilities, but the flames faded before he had a chance. As his senses returned he ceased his retreat and stared at the trio of humans watching him, rage filling his thoughts.

He began the process of transforming the fingers on each hand into massive blades, preparing to dash forward and shred his opponents. It was then he heard a short tap echo behind him. He patience slipped another notch, and he swiftly spun his head around a full rotation—breaking his own neck once more—and glared at yet another new human standing there. This man was much bigger than the previous, but equally calm and disinterested, with a tremendous broadsword resting across his back.

"What?" Zekraul roared at him, already braced to spin about and turn this new target into ribbons with his clawed nails. In response, the man used his left hand to crack the knuckles on his right. Then in a mere fraction of a second, that right fist was planted firmly into demonic jaw.

Time seemed to stand still for Zekraul at the instant of this impact. The punch itself was not felt, it was more like a gentle push, forcing his head backward. Pain was felt, however. Not only his head, but his entire spine began to twist away from the blow, the casing of his torso snapping and splintering as it rotated. Wave after wave of pressure continued to rip through the rest of his body, exploding every vulnerable point in his gravelly skin and causing his still-transforming hands to completely shatter into thousands of pieces.

The instant ended. The part of the demon's body that remained intact slid across the grass, coming to a gradual halt near the other humans. He lay there motionless for half a minute, hissing loudly in exhaustion. As his opponents began to gather around, he lifted his broken frame and did his best to piece it back together, discarding the fragments that were unusable.

"To have sunk so low that I was beaten by a pack of half-dead humans. This is not a day that Zekraul will soon live down."

With that admission, he twisted his legs once more into powerful springs and launched himself straight into the air. The humans reacted quickly, as the knight with the spear ran forward and shouted at the large man in black, leaping up onto his offered hands and then springing skyward in pursuit.

By this point Zekraul had anticipated such tenacity, and began to channel his secret ability. His skin tone shifted, assuming a yellow pigment across his entire body. This was a charge he had stored for over two years now, reserved only as a desperation move. Right as the knight was in range, already thrusting out with his spear, the demon released his attack.

A large electric barrier perfectly encompassed him, creating an energy bubble where he floated. The Lance was caught in the field, and a tremendous jolt of power stolen from a Godbeast rocketed Cildar straight back to the ground below. Zekraul carefully refocused the energy of the barrier to his fore, then released it in a huge sweep across the battlefield below.

The humans were forced to take cover and protect themselves as best they could. Myris grabbed Cildar and dashed behind the largest tree he could reach, Tenkahn punched the ground with both fists and summoned a cage of boulders over his crouched body, and Abaddon threw his arms high and erected the strongest grey magic barrier he could muster. When the light from the attack faded, the ground around them had been burned up, the trees were crisp or slightly aflame, and the demon Zekraul was nowhere to be seen.

## Chapter 13.

# Wisdoms

In the aftermath of battle, Cildar and Myris stepped forth from between the trees to examine their campsite. The effect of the Cain's Light spell had flickered out and, as he did not have another copy matrixed, he was forced to draw the rune structure in the air. Once his hand stopped moving the area again lit up as if by daylight, clearing out the deep mire of night.

Their companions shortly joined their side. The four exchanged glances and each gave a reassuring nod of his own condition. Myris cast cold spells to extinguish a few flames that threatened to spread into a wildfire, while the paladin healed some minor burns which had resulted from the jolt of the demon's final attack.

Suddenly the tranquil moment was interrupted by a gurgling yell, as Abaddon gripped his chest and fell writhing to the ground. Cildar ceased what he was doing and came quickly to the man's side, scanning for injury. Myris and Tenkahn watched in concern and bewilderment as the paladin worked a minor healing. Soon Abaddon was breathing normally and staring into the night sky, a few beads of sweat on his forehead.

Cildar delivered his prognosis. "The internal wounds you suffered from Tenkahn aren't healing adequately. Because of your mystic fortitude your condition isn't degenerative and you don't seem to be in immediate danger, but without surgery your heart isn't fit for you to exert yourself in battle. If I were a priest, I'd recommend no strenuous activities at least another six months."

Abaddon narrowed his eyes and growled, "Good thing for me you're not a priest, right?"

His physician gave a frustrated sigh, but did not argue further.

Tenkahn interjected, asking, "What wound? What have I wrought?" Cildar shrugged in response, not having witnessed the attack himself.

Abaddon answered for himself. "It was a modified version of the Pulsing Fist. Rather than releasing a sole kinetic wave from your punch, you opened your fingers and created five compact waves, each with force beyond what I've previously seen you summon."

The monk spent a moment in contemplation. "The Merciless Rune's gifts are truly generous. If I tried to execute such a technique as I am now, I would exhaust all my strength in but a single strike."

Cildar ignored their aside and resumed his warning. "With your heart in this condition, you risk going into arrest when you use your full strength. If you *are* going to fight, I'd say you can't go anywhere beyond maybe sixty percent of your abilities. Anything further will cause too much strain."

Abaddon sat up carefully, still gripping his chest. "So half power, then. Fine. For the time being, I'll have to rely on the strength of you and Myris."

"And myself," Tenkahn raised a fist and proclaimed firmly. "My debt to you has increased, Master Abaddon. I shall repay it."

The warlord nodded his gratitude. "For a while, hopefully that will be enough to carry us."

* * * * *

With the threats of Techenar Forest bested, the warriors of Felthespar settled down once more to rest their battered bodies and await the light of a fresh dawn, hoping in their weary condition there might be no further disturbances until they reunited with their allies. Yet even as they wished for a moment of peace, within the confines of that same forest an event was occurring with unfortunate timing. The Veil—the almighty celestial wall that divided the four planes—briefly gave way, opening a portal for travelers from beyond Asteria. They appeared one by one, materializing in a storm of lightning and heat as the power that carried them disintegrated the Morolian plane where it collided.

They were each over seven feet tall, with bodies sharing similar builds. They were twice the size of a typical human, with muscular and imposing frames. Even this domineering stature belied the enormity of their strength. These bodies flowed into iron robes and sashes, which were not actually clothing but rather living exoskeletons. Their composition was somewhere between natural and mechanical, and it echoed in their movements as well as the tone of their voices.

The first of the six began to move, checking his control over his hands and legs. Two black-laced eyes were sunk into a solid white face, with steely red iron spikes serving as a decoration resembling hair. His robed exterior was the most elegant of the six, capped by enormous silver shoulder pads with an iron sash running between them. The robes themselves were a plain white, encrusted with golden trim. As he spoke, his voice was a clear and solid boom. There was no waver, no shifts in cadence as he gave orders with confidence and efficiency. "Speak," he demanded of his five comrades, "in turn. Identify yourself, confirm that you function."

The ally to his right checked the movement of his limbs and then announced, "Kiastos functions."

It continued in this fashion around the rest of the circle, each verifying that their bodies were intact and then announcing their names. After Kiastos there was Valinoru, Keldana, Torlen, Dosiros. Then the first spoke once more.

"Melukah, of the Sun, also functions. Our reincarnation is complete. Let us begin the next circle." He held his right hand forward and a large pool of white energy appeared in their midst. Each member reached out and touched it, channeling a portion of their strength into the sphere. As this light faded, three majestic staffs materialized hovering in the air, solid wooden bars with resplendent ornamental heads. They varied slightly in design, but followed the same basic pattern—a large golden ring, symbolizing the sun, with a latticework of beams tying it together internally or protruding out beyond the circumference.

The staffs spun about within the ritualistic circle for a moment, then stabbed forcibly into the ground. The light fully dissipated and the staffs grew dormant. Melukah spoke once more. "On this plane, three Staffs of Sun is all I can manage. We will move in groups of two, and each will take a staff." Valinoru, Dosiros, and he each dislodged one of the artifacts from the ground. "Fan out, gather information, and track him down as quickly as possible."

Valinoru offered a bow to their leader. "Eternal Melukah, which Godbeast do we pursue?" His voice was cool as a summer's breeze. It could have easily fooled one into believing he held no malice.

"Schpariel, the one who has been called 'the Dark Wisdom'."

"His power is least of the three," Dosiros observed, his voice a crackling but hoarse roar. "If we can kill him before any of the others are resurrected, this should be a swift war. Barely even worthy of the term."

"Waste no more time!" Kiastos boomed out in a deep bass that shook the ground at their feet. "I ache for the hunt." Melukah waved his hand to confirm, and the three pairs parted ways and dashed into the forest around them.

The Divine Wisdoms of Elysium had come to Morolia.

* * * * *

Tenkahn led the way as the small troop cut through the forest, on course at last for the Fortress of the Overlord. Cildar and Myris flanked him just a step behind, while Abaddon lingered at a distance. Everyone was silent, but the Felthespari's spirits were bolstered by their success since parting paths with Detria. They looked forward to reuniting and sharing the good news.

Such was not to be their fate. Less than an hour into the morning they crossed paths with two creatures, strange in appearance. Both were large beasts, powerful bodies constructed of iron. One stood at an imposing eight feet, and the other only a few inches above seven. The larger was adorned in sashes and robes of a reddish tint, the smaller in a twisting patchwork of black and grey. The thing that struck most was their odd mockery of human features. Eyes, nose, and mouth were carved into motionless faces, with prominent inanimate decorations of stone that resembled hair. The larger creature had a large waving swath of red granite, flowing up to the left side, and the smaller had a carefully carved design resembling a straight but long bowl cut. The red-tinted monster held in his left hand a magnificent scepter, glowing gold with a light so bright it was impossible to look directly upon.

The human quartet came to a stop then took a few steps back, not sure what to make of this spectacle. The creatures eyed them evenly for a moment, then the larger spoke. "You humans, you smell of Gehenna. Are you allied with Schpariel?"

At the back of their ranks, Myris and Cildar heard Abaddon whisper to himself, "The red ether."

The Dragoon took mental note of this, but chose to focus on their adversaries before the situation turned. "Who is Schpariel?"

This response did not have the desired effect of opening diplomatic banter. "Blah," the crimson colossus responded. "Useless as ever. I'll cut them out of our way."

Tenkahn raised his fists slightly and the three men collectively took a step forward. Simultaneously, the smaller creature moved around and placed a hand on the larger's chest. He scratched the back of his head with his free hand. "It's really quite a waste, yeah?" His voice was a cadenced hiss with only a backdrop of a tenor hum. "Do we have to? They are just humans."

"I cannot abide the smell of Gehenna. It fills me with the rage of the flames!"

His compatriot sighed and dropped his hand. "Why must I be paired with the most irrational of Wisdoms? Valinoru and I get on so much better."

The other ignored this comment, slamming his right fist into his chest and bellowing aloud to his enemies, "I am Dosiros, of the Flame! Meet me in combat or die without honor, the choice is yours!" Cildar drew his Trine Lance and an enchanted broadsword of the Knighthood—known as a Morabet—as Myris drew and extended his Soul Scythe. The two came another step forward to bring themselves in line with Tenkahn and awaited the assault. "Three against one, eh?" Dosiros commented with a chuckle. "Fair enough by Wisdom standards. See what you think of this!"

He pounded his chest once more, and the upper portion of his body became swathed in dark red flames. He grabbed the flames into the palm of his hand and threw them once to his left side and once to his right. In a few seconds, two fiery copies of his outline stood on each side of him.

With a bloodcurdling roar he charged through the trees, leaving twin trails of fire behind his mimicking doppelgangers. The humans also charged. Once there was about three yards remaining between them and their opponent they leaped into the air, hoping to catch him off guard.

Dosiros was unfortunately not caught off guard, immediately leaping into the air himself and dragging his clones with him. He smashed hard into the Morolians and sent them flying away, straight over the onlooking Daemon. Dosiros then made a strange motion with one arm, and the two fiery copies flowed to his body. There they formed into giant flaming wings, which then carried him after his opponents. Abaddon watched as the Wisdom flew overhead, then calmly turned his attention to the other.

The remaining deity shook his head. "The most irrational of us, but his extreme power cannot be denied." He gave a conservative bow. "I am Torlen, of Sound."

"What do the two of you want? Why are you fighting us?"

"Ah, I don't know. It's not important. *You're* not important. But I should probably follow the Flame's lead and kill you. Otherwise he may become cross with me. I don't have the energy for dealing with that. Easier to kill you than put up with his temperament."

He raised his left hand and it became encircled with solid white rings that pulsed along his forearm. Then he charged at his opponent, coming in at a low dash. Abaddon waited until the Wisdom was within range, then quickly slammed his right fist into the ground. Torlen was caught unprepared by a sudden upheaval of dangerous stone spikes, and only barely managed to launch into the air and soar over his foe. As soon as the Wisdom landed, Abaddon turned and delivered a perfect straight punch to his head. Torlen jumped back directly away from the move, but was stricken with a sudden impact in spite of several feet of empty space between the contestants.

He stumbled from the blow, surprised that he had been punched by the air itself. "The human knows tricks," he announced with a hint of admiration in his tone. "You attack like both Kiastos and Valinoru. Such abilities are beyond the range of typical human achievement. Are you perhaps an Avatar? Still, you are no Wisdom. Your technique should not be compared to theirs." He raised his right hand in front of his chest, palm pointed outward, and spoke, "Silent Fist." His palm began to radiate with a soothing purple glow. He raised his left hand out forward, still encompassed by the white rings, and once again dashed to his foe.

Again Abaddon attempted to shield himself with the Tremoring Fist of the Monks of Tria, but this time to no avail. Keeping his right hand close to his chest, Torlen softly laid his left fist on the closest rock barring his way. Instantly the entire structure was gripped by white rings, then ground into pebbles and dust. He closed on the human and swiftly placed his right palm onto the warrior's chest.

Abaddon was not intimidated by his foe's daunting stature. He grabbed Torlen's outstretched arm by the shoulder and gave a powerful right hook to the face, and then another, and finally a difficult right uppercut.

Torlen gladly took the opportunity to leap away and reestablish some distance from his opponent, staggered by the force of these blows as his body's durable frame began to fracture. Even as he marveled at the impacts he had just experienced, he knew this battle was already over. The assassin's touch had been landed. He continued to hop back until a solid ten yard buffer had been established, then prepared himself for the finale.

He dropped his enchantments and raised his arms in a basic boxing stance. "You are able to strike at a distance," he announced over to the man, "but I imagine that distance is quite limited. You use ether to carry the force of your blows over the air itself, in carefully maintained waves of energy. It must be difficult to coordinate both Asteria and Morolia so effectively. Your species is uniquely gifted to play with the power of two schools of magic at once. By necessity, my own technique is much simpler. I am the Wisdom of Sound, you see. When I touched you a moment ago, I synchronized with the frequency of the imprint left by your existence upon the plane. I may now cause you harm from any distance, by using a concentrated burst of sound. Thusly."

In demonstration, he threw a punch blindly into the air in front of him. Almost instantly a wave of impact exploded from Abaddon's entire back and fell him to his knees. Torlen continued his taunt. "I can strike like this all day. I could even run a mile away and continue to abuse you. From this moment, you will never come within range of attacking me."

Abaddon gripped at his chest as he tried to muster a response. Instead he coughed up a large amount of his own blood and then collapsed face forward onto the ground. The Wisdom of Sound was surprised by this swift victory. He edged forward cautiously, wary of a trap. When he was within reach he gave a light kick to the sheathed broadsword resting on top of the man's back. Receiving nothing in response, he gave a subtle shrug and exited the area.

When he rejoined Dosiros, the bodies of the other human warriors were scattered about the forest floor, also unconscious. Torlen was surprised to see that none had been killed. He pondered the possible reasons for this.

Dosiros quickly gave the answer to this unspoken question. "I hope your opponent was more interesting than mine. The littlest one gave me trouble briefly, but once I caught him he fell with a single blow, same as the other two."

Torlen gave an unconcerned shrug. "Mine seemed as though he would be an interesting opponent, but I think he may have been sick or something. Like yours, he collapsed after only a single hit. Not even a very good one. Just as I was getting ready to start enjoying myself."

"Perhaps all Morolians are so flimsy compared to us."

"Maybe so. And perhaps that will inspire you to not waste any more of our time with them?"

Dosiros' chiseled mouth moved just enough to make a smile. "Very well. From now on, it's all business. Let us find the Godbeast."

* * * * *

Abaddon regained consciousness briefly, staring at a sun sitting at the top of the sky. He was shocked to find it was nearly noon, and attempted to raise himself to a seated position. The pain in his chest quickly drug him back down, and he once again coughed up a fresh splatter of blood as his insides burned.

"It seems the Knight is not doing so well."

For the first time, he noticed a white robed stranger standing a few feet in front of him. He started to try to speak again, when he noticed the object held in the man's left hand, pointed at the sky.

Kargaroth had been removed from the scabbard at his back.

In spite of the pain gripping his chest he forced himself to spring forward and throw a straight punch at the cloaked head. In spite of his physical injuries, pure mystic will made this blow imperceptibly fast. Even so, his opponent managed to duck, quickly turning and dashing several yards away. Abaddon moved to follow, but his fervor had pushed his body more than it could presently manage. He returned to his knees, vomiting blood and fighting for consciousness. The monk's hood had been disintegrated by force released from the failed attack, and his pale face was revealed plainly, framed in silver hair and accented by silver eyes.

He wagged a chastising finger in Abaddon's direction. "Still so dangerous, even when so battered. I was confident an encounter with the Wisdoms would herald your removal from the board, but as always the Knight proves to be the most unpredictable piece."

Through his coughs, Abaddon managed a coarse, "Who?"

"You wish to know who *I* am? That's a difficult query, and I'm not sure how wise it would be to give information to one such as yourself. I wonder, how many secrets of the dark gods are still locked within that mind of yours?" He paused for a moment with a wry smile, but then shook his head.

"How I wish we had an opportunity to truly converse," he continued, "but I am far too busy just now. Nonetheless, I suppose as I take the shell of the gods from you I do owe something in return." He narrowed his eyes and bowed his head slightly, dropping his voice to a near-whisper. "I am Akatriel the Lost." As he finished speaking he leaned his head back and gave a slow sigh. "I do not enjoy uttering that name. Bittersweet, it burns my tongue." He looked once more to Abaddon and shook his shoulders, cleansing the effect. "You and I are not yet done with this game, Knight. For now, please sleep a while longer."

He raised his free hand and gathered a small amount of silver electricity into it. With a flick of his wrist he sent it into the man's chest. Abaddon tried to fight through the paralyzing effect and rise to his feet, but his strength was gone and instead he fell unconscious to the ground once more.

"Now," the remaining figure mused to himself, "I must stash this sword where it will not be an immediate nuisance. With the Wisdoms' arrival events will accelerate quickly. I must find Schpariel and show him to Aegagropilion, or the situation may spiral beyond my control."

He turned from Abaddon's body and began walking away. He paused for a step, waiting for the familiar black cloud to envelop him and reprimand him needlessly. It did not materialize, however, so he wound his way westward with a broad smile across his face.

# Chapter 14.

## Lost Wolf

The morning of the third day since their separation, Detria and Kelve sat by a campfire awaiting the return of the Felthespari. Kelve had not spoken a word all morning, but Detria knew her friend was tired of waiting. There had already been arguments over the timing of the first assault, with the man repeatedly warning that eventually they would be noticed by someone among the Overlord's forces. Detria had taken a firm stance, insisting the sanctity of promises made to allies was more important than any individual battle.

In truth, she was terrified of the undertaking they were about to embark upon. She had never desired to believe in the Overlord, or his army of unified demonspawn. Now that she knew the legend was real, her mind kept rehashing the campfire tales she had heard since her resignation from the Devilslayers. She wanted to assure herself these were exaggerations, that no demon could be so powerful, so malicious; just as she had once assured herself that the creature was not real at all. She had been wrong before. How could she now know what to believe?

She uttered a soft sigh. Knowing she could not freeze out Kelve all day, she decided to open the matter for earnest discussion. She turned to him and opened her mouth, but was immediately cut off by a sentry shouting in their direction.

The approaching man was chasing after a taller soldier wearing black plate mail, wrapped in leather armors at the joints and exposed regions. The dark stranger came to a stop a few yards away from Detria's small campfire. The sentry moved between his commanders the intruder, panting with effort.

"Forgive me, I was unable to stop him."

Kelve rose to his feet. "I imagine you were." He waved his hand, motioning for the sentry to move aside. The man complied, still trying to catch his breath. "Hello, Deun."

The mailed warrior stared at Kelve hard for a moment, searching his memory. "Kelve Orista."

Detria was struck wide-eyed by this exchange. She rose to her feet as well, stepping close to her friend's side where she whispered, "You did not tell me you knew Deun Coloran personally!"

He gave a shrug and voiced his answer aloud. "We're not close, or anything. When we were young we trained within the same pack. Honestly I'm surprised he remembers me. It's been a long time."

"You were a threat," Deun retorted. "I remember threats."

Kelve flashed a winning smile. "High praise."

"If I had known this encampment was aligned with the Devilslayers I would have debated approach more ardently."

"We're *former* Devilslayers," Kelve retorted, "and if there's any dishonor in that, your share is every bit the equal to ours."

Detria's immediate instinct was to chastise her lieutenant for his effrontery. She did not revel the thought of a conflict with Deun, having heard he was a match for any ten prestigious Devilslayers. She repressed this urge and held her tongue, trusting that Kelve's history with the man would work to their advantage.

It seemed that his tact—or lack thereof—had indeed paid off. The armored warrior bowed slightly and answered, "Perhaps then each of us should not hold the other accountable for past mistakes. You recognized the Devilslayers for what they were and took your leave. I respect that. What transgression did Orikon finally commit to force you to see the truth?"

Kelve turned to his commander and offered a hesitant shrug. Detria shook her head back and forth for a pause, considering her answer. If Deun's enmity was primarily with Orikon, a tacit admission of her group's loyalty to the former chief could burn the scant goodwill only just established. On the other hand, while there were many rumors on the talents of the former Devilslayer champion, one of the most persistent was the man's uncanny ability to discern whenever anyone was lying to his face. Concerned over the risks of any answer, she finally confessed, "He died."

Deun froze. Detria watched closely, but the man's face betrayed no response, even his breathing seemed to have halted. His response, when it finally came, was a measured one. "So the founder passes, and the Devilslayers must adapt to their first change of regime. Who stands to fill the hole left by the old man?"

"Yasiff Oturl."

"Yasiff?" he exclaimed loudly, his face finally flushing with emotion. "What fools—" he stopped and took a deep breath, biting back his irritation. "It doesn't matter. It's no longer any concern of mine. If anything I take solace in knowing there's less reason than before to even consider looking back upon that accursed order."

Detria was pleased the man's wrath had not been directed upon her group, but was beginning to grow anxious with the delicate nature of this conversation. She almost demanded of Deun why he was there, then thought better of it. Instead she gave Kelve a slight nudge and a symbolic nod, signaling for him to carry the negotiations in her stead. She took a step back, allowing the illusion that he was in charge. She had long ago learned the most important trait for a leader was recognizing the situations to lend someone else the reins.

As it happened, Kelve proceeded exactly as she would have herself. "Why did you reveal yourself? We were aware of your presence in the area, but never expected a visit."

Deun turned his body slightly away as if preparing to leave. Detria feared that Kelve had made some mistake, but the visitor did not break off conversation. "There are four bodies in the forest. Human. They may be allies of yours. I'm uncertain. Regardless, they've been beaten very badly, and it's important for me to speak with them so I can determine who they fought and, if possible, where he went. I assume there are medics among your camp?"

Kelve glanced back at Detria for this, not sure how she would wish to proceed. She stepped to his side once more, whispering, "*Four* bodies?" His only response was another shrug. She returned her attention to Deun. "Yes, we have medics. Whoever they are, we will do our best to aid them."

The solemn warrior gave a nod. "I'll wait at the edge of the forest. Send at least three strong soldiers to help me carry the bodies. Hopefully between the four of them, at least one survives long enough to talk."

He took his leave without further etiquette. Detria sought Kelve's counsel on the matter for a minute, then signaled for the bystanding sentry to fetch some soldiers.

* * * * *

Caught up in the feverish grip of forced unconsciousness, Cildar Emle dreamed. There was nothing remarkable to this dream, nothing altered or created by the overactive imagination. It consisted solely of images from the fight he had recently endured, memories of the creature that had harmed him—memories of the Wisdom named Dosiros.

Random pieces of the battle flashed through his mind, with no organization or clarity. After knocking Cildar, Myris, and Tenkahn over a small expanse of the forest, Dosiros had followed after them carried by reaching, fiery wings. He landed and taunted them, demanding they entertain him. Tenkahn stepped forth first, attacking with his mystical might. Cildar took the opening as a chance to activate his Haste technique, as Myris began layering his own grey magic together and bracing for his Draw Strikes.

The Wisdom had blocked all of Tenkahn's blows with a single hand, then gathered a ball of light to the head of the staff he wielded. He seized the monk by the neck, then bashed the staff over his head. A huge explosion had followed, after which the durable warrior was left lying in a smoldering crater. At this time the paladin had completed his Haste and charged recklessly into the fray, with Myris dashing at his side to assist.

When they reached their foe Cildar attempted to unleash a flurry of strikes from the Trine Lance, while Myris executed an almost constant string of the Draw Strike of Ice. The Wisdom took all of these attacks handily, then raised the staff over his head. This was the last sight Cildar could remember before being engulfed by pure heat and light.

As this last image began flashing through his head on a continuous loop, he awoke with a yelp. Detria Alsen quickly came to his side, soothing him and easing him back to the ground. She removed a cloth from his forehead and replaced it with a fresh one soaked in cool water, then offered him a strange bitter root he did not recognize to chew on.

"It'll help with the pain," she promised. "You're burned over your entire body. We've done the best we could with the salves we have available, but you're still unstable."

"The others?" He found his voice frail, and his lips and tongue ached as he forced the words out.

"You're the first to regain consciousness. Myris has a severe concussion, and maybe a fractured neck. Abaddon has been hard to diagnose. He seems fine on the outside, but his recovery has been slow. He doesn't seem to match your fortitude."

Cildar raised an eyebrow at this misjudgment, but did not correct her. "What about the fourth?" he groaned.

"He seems alright." She hesitated, her eyes flickering in the direction where Tenkahn's body must have been. "There was an ugly gash across his forehead. It looked like it should have been fatal. He's recovering nearby, with a full contingent of men overlooking him. Just who is he? Do we need to be worried? Is he the one that injured you?"

Cildar shook his head. "He's fine, don't worry. If you had seen what did this to us, you'd know."

"The creature Eiden had talked about? The Beast of Techenar?" she asked in a knowing tone.

He hesitated to give his answer. He had believed Tenkahn to be the creature haunting the forest, but now there seemed to be potential evidence otherwise. He was unsure what to make of that situation, and even moreso of the creatures calling themselves Wisdoms. The only thing he knew for certain was that he did not want Detria knowing about the monk's formerly berserk state, since it would only make it more difficult for her to accept his presence.

Whether it was the truth or not, he knew the answer he had to give. "Yes."

Detria noted his hesitation, but elected not to interrogate him for the moment. "Rest now. There is a man who'd like to speak with you. He's the one who found your bodies and brought you here, so I've agreed to humor his request. He told me to tell him as soon as one of you awoke, but I don't think you're ready yet. I'll detain him a bit longer."

He nodded his agreement. "Whatever he wants, Lord Abaddon may have his own answers to give." The woman left, and he returned to chewing on the root he had been given. Soon the bitter sap began to ease his pain slightly, and was able to drift into a more restful sleep.

* * * * *

Cildar slept most of the day away peacefully. Every few hours he would awake for brief periods and treat his burns, using light healing auras to accelerate his skin's natural recovery processes. As he was sleeping somewhere around midnight, he was awakened by hushed voice. He looked to his right, where he could barely see a man in dark armors crouched on his knees, clearly trying to keep out of sight of the nearby sentries.

"I need to ask you a question," the man spoke. "It is not much, a mere token. The chieftains here are uncomfortable with my presence and are making this more difficult than it needs be. I don't desire to be here any more than they want me."

"I'm not certain I can speak freely," Cildar answered.

"Listen, you are a knight, like myself. We both share the honor of combat. Surely you can see that some things are simple, harmless. All I want to know, all I am asking, is what did this to you? I could tell from the marks of battle it was something of considerable power. Describe the creature or, if you have it, just give me a single name."

"I have a name," he responded. The man's eyes went wide, and he seemed on edge for the information. The paladin took a pause to consider whether or not there could be negative consequences to this. He ultimately decided it was his own free will as to whether he wished to cooperate. "Dosiros, the Wisdom of the Flame."

The man fell back onto his haunches and his shoulders drooped. "Unbelievable," he said half to himself. "Another dead end. I was so certain I had found him this time."

"Who are you looking for, exactly? Maybe I know something."

The visitor's tone changed to one of irritation, and suddenly he sounded only barely willing to tolerate Cildar's presence. "I'm seeking the same as you. The same as everyone on this side of the continent. The head of the Overlord."

The Dragoon gently eased himself up onto his elbows and into a sitting position. "Then you are right, you seek the same as us. Ally with us, join our cause. You look to be a warrior of merit. We can use every sword hand we can get."

The man rose to his feet and said with contempt, "Do not misinterpret our similar intentions. I am no friend of yours."

"As you will," he answered with a gentle nod. "Regardless, thank you for bringing us here. It seems likely we would not have recovered without aid."

The dark knight turned and walked a few steps away, then stopped and said quietly over his shoulder, "Do not confuse that, either. Had I not been certain you had seen the Overlord himself, I would have left you rotting in that forest. I've only wasted time here."

He took his leave, and that was the last Cildar would ever see of Deun Coloran. As the paladin watched the warrior vanish, he heard a voice from the shadows behind him.

"Not a very pleasant fellow. Though I suppose I lack the right to judge."

He turned around to see Myris walking over to him. He smiled warmly at the sight of the shadowy figure. "I'm glad to see you're alright."

The Cain had his head wrapped in a thick layer of bandages, and a roughly crafted collar gripping his neck. He was clearly irritated by the dressing, but seemed disinclined to remove it. "That man, did you notice anything peculiar about him?"

"You mean aside from the obvious personality problems?"

Myris paused for effect before answering. "He was a mystic."

Cildar did a double take, glancing to where the man had disappeared from beyond sight already. "Are you certain?"

"My Cainite enchantments allow me a few luxuries. One is that I can generally judge the potency in the spirits of others. If he's not a mystic, then he's a mage of Kinguin's level. That seems less likely, especially factoring the general lack of practitioners on this continent, and that Lord Abaddon was already keeping an eye out for a stray mystic."

"So he must be the Devilslayer's champion. That would explain the tense relations between him and Detria. Perhaps he used politics to strong-arm his way into the camp." He thought for a moment, then said, "But I thought the Devilslayers didn't believe in the Overlord."

"He seems to be attempting to kill the Overlord all on his own. Notice his refusal to join us. Perhaps he's been sent as an assassin because the Devilslayers don't want others knowing of his existence."

Cildar went to scratch the back of his head. The pain of his blistered skin was far too intense, and he quickly gave up on the gesture. "I don't know, I'm not sure it fits. We're speculating too much here. We should wait for Abaddon to recover."

"That's actually what brings me this direction. His heart is acting up again. I doubt he'll recover without your help."

The paladin sighed softly. He had rested long enough; it was time to get back to work. He gathered an Aura, checking the potency of his spirit. He found his holy energy mostly restored, with full command over his healing abilities.

"Let me patch up my own body enough to dull the pain, then I'll head his way."

Myris gave a deep bow, then left the healer to his work.

* * * * *

The following day passed without incident. The Felthespari continued to rest, weary from their recent struggles and demoralized by defeat. Abaddon did not regain consciousness. Detria updated her troops, announcing that the first attack on the Overlord was further postponed. They handled the news surprisingly well, their patience still healthy. They had waited long to merely find their foe; they were not disturbed by the brief delay before the next step.

Once Tenkahn regained consciousness Detria held several discussions with him, delving deep into his knowledge of the Overlord. Unfortunately he knew nothing more enlightening than what she had already gleaned from Eiden. The boy himself passed most of the day with Myris and Cildar—when the paladin was not busy administering to Abaddon—showcasing the fruits of his studies.

Myris clued his pupil in on the problems he had been having with his modified Feeler, explaining that the spell responded to the imprint left by a human's Asterian presence. Because of this, the more adept with black magic a person was, the more distorted their image. He elaborated that this was why the Feeler had never been developed beyond its basic form. Eiden was disappointed to discover his idea was futile, but the Cain encouraged his creative thinking, assuring him that it was the most necessary quality for one who wished to become a master of the heraldric arts.

Abaddon finally awoke sometime during the following night.

He did not say anything, giving only a reassuring nod to Cildar and motioning for the man to go get himself some sleep. The weary healer took his leave and Abaddon lay there alone until morning, staring at the sky lost in thought.

The next morning a large meeting took place in Detria's makeshift command tent. Kelve, Eiden, Tenkahn, and the three Felthespari were all in attendance. Detria alone was seated in her chair, as the others either sat on the ground or remained standing around the edges of the tent. Kelve joined the ones seated, a gesture to make them feel more comfortable in the cramped tent.

Detria nodded when everyone was settled and began preparations. "I understand that a few of you are still injured, and that may play a factor into the strategy here. We still have the element of surprise. I considered for a while that we might use this to our advantage, but I've decided against it. I think first an initial skirmish is in order. Line our troops up, charge in, see what kind of defenses we encounter. Between myself, Kelve, Cildar and Myris, I'm confident we could keep any dangerous forces at bay long enough to sound the retreat when and if it becomes necessary."

Cildar gave a nod from where he sat. "You can count on us."

She almost gave an optimistic reply, but was cut off by a gruff bark from Abaddon. "No, you can't. We're leaving. Emle, Phare, we're done here."

"What?" Detria exclaimed, baffled by this sudden announcement. "You can't leave! You promised you were going to help us in this invasion."

"I don't recall making any promises to that effect," the big man countered coldly. "I told you we would join you for a time and help as we could. Now things have changed. We can no longer linger here."

Detria stormed to her feet and slammed her hands against her command desk. She was so enraged she was unable to find words to speak. She had postponed her war waiting for Abaddon's return, trusting to the strength of his compatriots. She had awaited even further for his own recovery, out of respect for his authority over the two warriors, and now he was attempting to take them away at the moment she needed them most.

Kelve spoke in her place as she fumed until her face turned red. "Forgive my brashness, sir knight, but why exactly have things changed?"

"The Wisdoms are here," he announced dramatically.

The weight of this pronouncement seemed to be lost on the other occupants of the tent, who exchanged only puzzled glances. Myris, standing in the back corner, was the first to break the awkward pause. "You speak as though you know them, milord."

"Only of the things Relm taught me." He stopped and looked to the others present, crafting his words for his audience. "I know not all of you have studied advanced theories of cosmology. I'll try to keep this simple. Our world as we perceive it comprises two planes which overlap, Morolia and Asteria. There are, however, planes beyond this, with which we cannot interact. One of those 'outer' planes is known as Elysium, ruled by a collective of creatures known as Wisdoms. They are deities on their world—for all intents and purposes, gods."

Detria smiled and raised an eyebrow, her rage suddenly cooled by disbelief. "Really? So you can't help my people in a real war with an enemy sitting right in front of us because we're being invaded by alien gods?"

Tenkahn contributed his own skepticism to this version of events. "Yes, with due respect, my faith lies only within the goddess Tria. I cannot accept this claim of these Wisdoms, whom I have seen in the flesh, truly being gods."

Abaddon sneered in mild irritation. "Make what you will of claims as to their divinity, it has no bearing to the point at hand. These are, at the very least, godlike creatures who have come to Arkalen on some sort of hunt. The destruction which they are capable of cannot be overcalculated."

"A hunt?" Kelve asked with curiosity.

"The Wisdom calling himself Dosiros spoke of Gehenna,"

Abaddon continued, "another of the outer planes which has been involved in an ongoing war with Elysium for literally thousands of years." He looked up to Detria. "I told you before of the curious case of the red ether. I feel confident now to say that it was Gehennite ether, and its source is now the prey of the Wisdoms."

She raised a hand dismissively. "Good. Let them have it, then. We will wage our war here, and these 'Wisdoms', whatever they are, will take care of the other mysterious plague of Arkalen, which the Devilslayers have been unable to solve. So far nothing you've described sounds to me like anything less than a blessing." She smirked once more, adding, "Possibly a divine one."

Abaddon narrowed his eyes and shook his head insistently. "None of you seem to have noticed that my sword is gone." Myris gave no reaction to this, but Cildar was taken aback. Indeed, the paladin had not noticed the absence of Kargaroth. "After my defeat at the hands of the Wisdom Torlen, a stranger in white robes with silver hair and eyes appeared and relieved me of Kargaroth. Due to the extreme width of the blade, the sword weighs an enormous amount. Nearly fifty pounds, far beyond any normal sword. Yet whoever this was, he held it easily in one hand and was still nimble enough to dodge me at my quickest. His appearance was human, but given the other forces at play here I reserve my doubts."

There was quiet digestion of this for a moment, with many in the tent already feeling overwhelmed and inadequate. Tenkahn then stood up and looked to Abaddon. "Silver hair and silver eyes? You describe the same man that spared my life, as I told you before. The man who activated the Merciless Rune."

Cildar glanced at the monk, then exchanged a look with Myris before any further questions could be asked. "We ran into him too, actually. Before we rejoined with you, Lord Abaddon. Before we even encountered the draconics." He thought back to that encounter, his mind racing. "He mentioned you, come to think of it. Even talked about Kargaroth itself."

"There was another with him," Myris reminded.

"Yes." The Dragoon's eyes darted back and forth, doing his best to recall details. "He was strange in appearance. Large build, robes colored in red, black, and gold. I remember his hair had an unnatural quality to it, and his face..." Suddenly he stopped and jerked his head back.

He looked again to Myris, who finished the thought for him. "It was a Wisdom."

Cildar nodded slowly. "We didn't know anything about them at the time, but it was definitely a Wisdom. The same odd makeup as the two we encountered in the forest."

Abaddon stared at the ground, mulling over this new information. "So Akatriel is aligned with the Wisdoms. This worsens matters further."

"Akatriel?" Kelve asked.

The Felthespari warlord nodded. "He told me his name as he took Kargaroth. He said it was the price he offered. Does it mean something to you?"

Kelve thought for a few seconds, then shook his head. Detria chose that moment to refocus the conversation. "You've talked a lot," she said with a chuckle, "and yet still not managed to explain to me why it's so important that you leave now. Are you suggesting this is all somehow dangerous to us? Even more dangerous than the Overlord? We know the threat he poses. What makes you so sure it's worth abandoning him to pursue these other events we know so little about?"

"The Wisdoms are powerful enough to level anything standing in their path, and they have already expressed a contempt for human life. If they're hunting one or more Gehennans of comparable power, the crossfire of such a struggle could consume cities, possibly even continents. That aside," he paused, considering the choice of his next words, "anyone who knows enough about Kargaroth to desire stealing it causes me a grave concern."

"I thought the sword powerless," Cildar queried, also rising to his feet. "Didn't you and Atheme destroy it? Or at least," he paused and debated his words as well, considering the company in the tent, "robbed it of its threat?"

"Kargaroth may no longer hold power of its own," Abaddon responded, "but do not devalue it as a threat. With sufficient cleverness and resources, it could be fed via another source. The blade still holds the memory of what it once was, and the channels necessary to shape its lost techniques. Its true nature could yet be resurrected. Under no circumstances will I allow it to remain in the hands of the Wisdoms."

"What true nature?" Detria asked. "What is Kargaroth, exactly?"

The room was silent for half a minute. With no answer forthcoming, Cildar offered a slight bow to her, as if in apology. Then finally he turned back to Abaddon. "We're with you, milord, as always. Where do we head next?"

"If you intend to battle these Wisdoms," Tenkahn proposed, "you will need a mighty weapon to use against them. My attacks caused Dosiros no harm whatsoever. While I stand firm in my faith, I readily confess that this creature was powerful like nothing I have ever seen."

Abaddon shook his head sadly. "Kargaroth would have been the only weapon, I fear."

"Perhaps that is why it was stolen by their ally," Myris interjected. "To cripple us in our time of need."

Kelve stood to his feet at this point. Eiden clumsily followed his lead, so as to not be the last one sitting. "There may be one other weapon," the former slayer offered.

"Kelve, no," Detria begged, already sensing his intent.

"I'm sorry, hon, but this seems serious enough to merit last resorts."

"Tell me what you know," Abaddon insisted firmly.

He started to answer, but Detria swiftly cut him off. "Fine, fine. If it has to be said, I'll tell it." She gave a sigh and dropped back into her seat. "It's just a stupid legend, one of the many that float around the continent. When I was a Devilslayer, I was designated as one of their loremasters. I was taught a lot of useful things, like the nature and evolution of various demonspawn on the continent. I was also taught many less useful things. Among those was the tale of a sword buried within the central continent, holding the power to 'slice through anything'. It is named Arda. The legend claims it came from another dimension and is imbued with powerful demonic magics."

Myris turned to Abaddon. "From 'another dimension' could imply that the weapon is Asterian, or perhaps even from one of the outer planes. If such is the case, there is a small chance its powers are not exaggerated."

"We have to try something to level the field," the big man answered with a nod. Then he looked back to Detria. "Can you tell us how to find this sword?"

"I think so. It might take me a while to remember, but I can probably draw up a map."

Kelve rejected this idea. "I think you should go with them," he said instead.

She was taken aback. "What are you saying? That we should just cancel this war? What will the troops think of that?"

He paused before responding, "I didn't say I think *we* should go with them." She stared at the man blankly, so he continued. "Look, I can't claim to understand everything that's going on here, but I think it's safe to say that something certainly is. Abaddon's probably onto something when he thinks these Wisdoms, whoever or whatever they are, need to be stopped. It's not worth the risk to give them a vague map and send them on their way. You learned the route by rote, so only by actually traveling it are you likely to remember the necessary details."

"And the assault on the Overlord? Of all people, I thought you were one of the most anxious for this."

"I am. So entrust the war to my command. Just temporarily. I'll lead in your absence and await your return eagerly. No matter how we approach it, this siege is not likely to be quick. I can lead the early stages while you're away."

As there was a long delay before Detria's answer to this, Eiden stepped over and bowed before Abaddon. "Sir, I wish to follow you as well."

"I appreciate your spirit, but do not believe that would be for the best. Don't take offense, but your skills do not benefit us where we're going. Here, for this war, you are invaluable. You must stay where you are needed."

The boy creased his brow. He felt uplifted by the man's words, but was still disheartened to know he would once again be unable to travel with the Felthespari soldiers. Tenkahn sensed his disappointment and gave him a light pat on the back. "You will not be alone, son." He turned to Abaddon with a more serious tone. "I must also remain. As I said before, I owe it to my lost brethren. I must see their final mission completed."

"I never expected anything else from you, Tenkahn," he answered kindly. They shook hands in farewell. "I'm sorry to part paths with you so soon."

Everyone turned to Detria, awaiting her decision on the matter. "I'm gonna need some time to think on this," was all she offered. The group quietly dispersed, with everyone leaving the tent except for her and Kelve. After a few more words of encouragement and reassurance he also made his exit, leaving her alone to her thoughts.

* * * * *

A few hours later Detria sat at the top of the hill, staring down at the Fortress of the Overlord as if it held the answers she sought. To her surprise Abaddon soon joined her, taking a seat at her side.

"You're a contemplative leader," he opened. "I have much respect for that."

She twisted her mouth up in annoyance. "But time is of the essence, right? Something to that effect?"

He diplomatically ignored this barb. "You're worried about leaving your people behind, are you? Perhaps making them feel as though you've abandoned them?"

"How is a leader supposed to walk away in a time of need? I know most of them chose to be here. But still, I led them here. I assembled this group. I've guided their footprints up until this point. To simply walk away now, after bringing them this far—"

"You need only go so far as to show us the sword. Once that's done, we'll make certain you return to your troops for this battle."

"Thank you, but that doesn't change my dilemma, really."

He leaned forward and locked eyes with her, holding her attention firmly. "I know I have put you into a difficult position. For this, I apologize. I can sincerely say I wish it didn't have to be this way, that I didn't need your assistance. However, for a very few of us in this world, we're put into the unique position where we must neglect what we care for most in order to protect it. I'm uncertain what end Akatriel is working toward. However, I am more certain that unless he is stopped, it will end in such a way that will claim the lives of you and your people, if not all of Arkalen. I'm not asking you to abandon their cause, but this has become a war on two fronts. I'm simply asking you to aid our side for the moment, so that we might win both. If I believed your absence here would truly cause your forces to lose their war, I wouldn't ask this of you. But from what I have seen Kelve seems a capable leader, and I know Tenkahn's merits well. They will do fine for the short time I'm asking of you."

She shook her head, her determination wavering in the face of his. "We don't even know if the sword is real."

"If it proves otherwise then I'm the one who will bear the consequences. One way or another, Cildar, Myris, and I are going after Akatriel and the Wisdoms. I am simply trying to increase the odds of our victory."

She gave a slow sigh. She still did not know if she believed in the same reality as the foreign knight, but felt as though she had been swept up in a tide of events she could not struggle against. "Very well. Can you at least give me a day to say goodbye to my troops? We can leave first thing in the morning."

He stood, brushed himself off lightly, and shook his head. "No. We must go. Ready yourself as soon as possible. I would like to leave within fifteen minutes. The sooner we depart, the sooner you return."

# Chapter 15.

## Godbeasts

Schpariel stood upon the deck of a foreign ship. The vessel was hidden at the entrance to a small cove, locked into place by a series of large boulders. The Godbeast could not determine the ship's origin, nor how it had become beached in such a manner. Its presence had served some small convenience, allowing him to pinpoint a series of caverns which ran into the cliffs behind it. He had searched these for days now, but found not a single clue to his objective.

He had since looked over the vessel itself, idly seeking to unravel its mystery. The wood was young, and clearly the ship had not been here long. This further suggested it was unrelated to his search, much like everything else he had found. He stepped to the edge of the hull and glanced down the side, seeing a large script in human language reading "Calvin".

He considered for a moment destroying the ship with a large fireball, or perhaps a summoned meteor. He ultimately decided against this. By giving in to the whims of his temper, he had been burning his magic at an alarming rate since his resurrection by the silvery stranger. The stores of his Moon Rod were beginning to fade, and could not quickly be replenished while on this plane. Unless he began conserving energy he would soon find himself in a vulnerable state, especially as he had thus far been unable to resurrect either of his brethren.

He turned to leave, but was surprised to see the robed figure standing on the ship's deck nearby. He was impressed the pale human had been able to sneak up on him, but his expressionless face did not let it show.

"I have been seeking you for days," his visitor announced with distress in his voice. "Why do you waste time staring at the ocean?"

Schpariel was once again forced to repress his desire to summon a meteor. "Why are you here?" he responded stoically.

"The Wisdoms have arrived. Time is up."

The Godbeast froze in place, weighing the ramifications of this. Of all his order, Schpariel was the one most weakened when separated from Gehenna. For the Wisdoms, he was easy prey. Inwardly, a slight shiver of panic and despair began to seize him. Outwardly, his stony expression remained unreadable. "Have you found them? Either of them?"

"I've been unable to locate Gilanirus or any word of him. I don't know what the Wisdoms did with him after his defeat during the last Divine War. However, I have at last found Aegagropilion."

Schpariel's despair abated at this news. "With Aegagropilion's aid, the Wisdoms' presence could be turned to an advantage. We must go as swiftly as possible."

"He's not far from here. We head eastward. The Wisdoms have appeared deeper inland, so we have some time to work with. Let us not waste it."

Without further word the two leaped from the deck of the wrecked ship and headed east, angling slightly inward on the continent.

* * * * *

Nearly two weeks of travel had nearly put Abaddon and his crew back within sight of the inner continent. They had passed through the emptied Forest of Techenar without incident, and with no sign of the Wisdoms. Now they proceeded at a staunch pace across wind-whipped brushlands. Detria did not admit it aloud, but she was still hazy on where they were going. She led them in what she hoped was an appropriate direction, keeping an eye out for the first landmarks that would put her on the correct trail.

She spent most of the day marching at the fore with Cildar,

chatting amicably. The tall man was always pleasant company, filled with stories and histories on hundreds of topics. Myris occasionally joined the two for conversation, or spent time scouting the area ahead for danger. Abaddon, for his part, lingered back nearly ten yards. Detria was glad the warlord had chosen to isolate himself, as she was certain he would have asked for details on their path.

The day's march passed mostly without incident. At one point Detria led them into a bog and—unwilling to admit she had come this far by accident—commanded them to force their way through. It was an unpleasant experience for everyone, and afterward she felt guilty and useless. She knew that sooner or later she was going to have to admit she was leading them aimlessly.

They settled down for the evening, yet still no one had pressed her for more information on their destination. They stopped on a small patch of rocky ground near the outskirts of a strange jungle. As soon as they made camp, Abaddon disappeared into this jungle without a word. Detria fretted over this, but Cildar and Myris both assured her it was normal behavior from their commander.

As the sun set, they continued chatting under darkened skies. Myris passed around some strange crystallized bread, very sweet in flavor. He explained it was an old Cainite traveling snack. He had prepared a batch during their time with Detria's troops, while he had access to the necessary supplies. During a lull in the conversation, as Detria sat enjoying the treat, she noticed Cildar looking her over with a strange creased brow. She blushed at his inspection and then demanded, "What?" in a stern voice.

His eyes went wide and he gave a small bow. "Forgive me, but I notice you don't seem to carry any sort of weapon on you, unless it's well hidden."

She laughed, pleased that his intentions were so innocent. "It has been pointed out before. The Devilslayers craft masterful weapons, and all are expected to carry at least a dannig. It's a unique customizable weapon, sort of a simple adjustable polearm. But it breaks down into a lot of separate components to carry around, and that's a lot of added weight. I was trained by a more resourceful master, and have never particularly concerned myself with maintaining my own arsenal. In truth, there's no weapon more appropriate to any battle than your opponent's."

Cildar rubbed his chin. "An interesting philosophy. Arguably a near-pacifist one, in that you don't wish to apply any more force than necessary to overcome your enemy."

Myris chimed in, "I can see the wisdom in it. The Devilslayers lack the artificers and enchanters which are so abundant in Felthespar. As they lack any means to mass produce weapons of mystical qualities, it could come up quite often that the best weapons available to them are, in fact, the ones stolen from some of the more advanced demonspawn."

Detria nodded to this. "And it's only a matter of time before the battlefield is littered with the discarded weapons of their dead."

"And yet," the Dragoon argued, "it leaves you dangerously vulnerable for the initial stages of combat, does it not?"

She smirked in response. "You'd be surprised how many opponents hold back when facing an unarmed foe. Some from a misguided sense of nobility, but most simply become overly confident. Which are you, Cildar Emle?" She rose to her feet and motioned him forward, a confident smile on her face.

"Is this a challenge? That would be unwise."

Her smile broadened. "Would it? Do you have a heart cold enough to defeat me so swiftly and soundly? Somehow I'm skeptical, oh noble paladin."

He chuckled quietly in spite of himself. "Alright, alright. Why not?" He reached to his back and removed his Trine Lance slowly, intending to bring it down and point in her direction threateningly.

Before he was anywhere near her, she surged forward, landing several blows into his armored chest. Cildar endured the blows with a look of bemusement, then lashed out with a sudden left hook. Detria answered this with a simultaneous uppercut to his unarmored jaw. Somehow she avoided Cildar's own blow, although he missed how as he staggered backward from her strike. When he looked up, she stood across the clearing with a lovely broadsword leveled forward, pointed menacingly at him.

Recognizing the blade instantly, his hand quickly dropped to the holster on his hip. “My Morabet!” he objected.

His opponent shrugged. “I did warn you not to hold back. Now you’ve lost your window to defeat your weak little unarmed opponent.”

Cildar tilted his head slightly. “Have I?”

He rushed forward and unleashed a series of blows with his spear, staying slightly beyond the range of the pilfered Morabet. Detria evaded his blows carefully, blocking a few with the blade. Cildar quickly realized he held overpowering advantages in both strength and speed, and eased his aggression. Within seconds of him doing so, Detria flung her left hand forward, filling his eyes with sand.

He stumbled a step back, once more feeling his armored body pelted with blows. He dared not strike out with his spear and risk injuring the girl, and instead spent a moment focusing white magic to clear his vision. He then took a large leap away from her, covering several yards. No sooner had he done so than she sent a scattering of small blades spinning in his direction. His sharp reflexes quickly picked out the most dangerous of the projectiles and deflected them with his Lance. As they fell to the ground, only then did he realize they were shurikens from his own arsenal.

His lip quivered in mild annoyance, and he reached for his favorite long dagger to arm his off-hand. Finding the weapon missing, he looked up to witness Detria now armed with it, using it to compliment the stolen Morabet.

“My, my,” she said with a broad smile, “you are a generous armory, aren’t you, Mister Emle? I look forward to finding out what other weapons you have hidden in that unassuming regal attire.”

Cildar stared at the young girl in shock for several seconds. Then, becoming aware of the situation, he leaned his head back and laughed loudly to the sky, entertained. “You are something else. I knew your people were skilled, but I never would have thought one among you could hold serve against a member of Felthespar’s own Phoenix Dragoons.”

She took a cautious bow, still keeping the two stolen weapons pointed at her foe. “It’s the way of the Devilslayers to find victory against superior opponents. It’s the battle to which we are most accustomed.”

“Still,” he retorted, “you must recognize that you’ve only lasted this long because I’m holding back and not using all of my skills and magic against you.”

“But that was the point of this demonstration, wasn’t it? To prove to you that even the mightiest foes make foolish decisions when they feel they have their opponent hopelessly outclassed.”

He returned his Trine Lance to its holster at his back. “Aye. And well demonstrated, it was. I wonder if you would fare so well against another master of the deceptive arts, however.”

The paladin took his seat on a nearby rock, as Myris rose to his feet and stepped forward, drawing the slim katana from his side. Detria smiled and gave another bow, “Lord of the Cain, wasn’t it? Come then. Let’s see if you can steal these blades back for your friend.”

This friendly sparring went on for many hours, even past midnight. Neither Cildar nor Myris were willing to test their true might against Detria, and she used this against them time and again. She drew them into situations where they had no choice but to strike a crippling blow, then turned the tables when they held back at the last second. On a few occasions an argument arose as to whether or not she was defying the spirit of sparring. She insisted that only victory mattered, and using any knowledge of an opponent’s weaknesses against them was fair play. Cildar and Myris found it impossible to win these arguments, and so the games continued.

When they finally settled down to call it a night, Cildar volunteered to take the first round of sentry duty as Myris settled in for a nap. Detria sat alone for a while, staring at the night sky in contentment at her day's performance. She knew the two Knights had never used their magic against her, but she had represented her people as tactical and resourceful. Against these warriors—which were akin to Arkalen's heroes of legend—she felt she could have done them no greater honor.

It was only a matter of time before the scope of their situation once more took precedence in her mind. She began pouring through the information about Arda repeatedly, finding nothing of further value. She sat doing this for nearly an hour, before finally exclaiming, "Dammit!" aloud in frustration.

Instantly Myris hopped out of his sleeping bag and extended his Soul Scythe, asking, "What? Who?"

She blushed bright red and apologized for disturbing his sleep. "I'm sorry, Myris. I was just thinking aloud."

He shook his head and muttered something she did not catch, then spent a few moments wandering around the campsite. Soon he seemed to wake himself up fully, then moved over and had a seat near her.

They sat together in silence for several minutes, Detria growing increasingly uncomfortable as time passed. Finally he began to speak.

"You hide something."

She blushed again immediately, but did not lose her outward composure. "Huh? Why would you brandish such an accusation?"

"As Cildar pointed out before, I am a master of deception. And please, take this as a compliment—but you are not." She swallowed hard, trying to clear a lump in her throat. The dark man continued, "You have been uncomfortable since we split from your unit. In the beginning I chalked this up to a certain level of codependency upon your soldiers. I have since begun to doubt that surmisal. In particular, you have shown a marked discomfort with Lord Abaddon and his reactions to you. You do not seem quite as worried about either Cildar or myself, but Abaddon's very presence plagues you."

Detria turned to him and eased a few inches away. "And just what are you implying?"

He turned to meet her gaze, his brown eyes piercing beneath a shock of dark bangs. "You are a good person, Miss Alsen. Unfortunately, I find good people disappointingly easy to read. Do not become defensive. It will benefit neither of us. As near as I can tell, you have become insistent upon proving yourself a worthy member of our small group. Admirable, without question. But while you have garnered a certain amount of respect from me and Cildar, you remain unclear where Lord Abaddon stands. You fear he will see through you and recognize that you are lost. With respect, you underestimate us all. We have each known you were lost, from the very beginning."

"Excuse me?" she retorted with a sharp tone.

"I did ask that you not become defensive. Listen, no one here will judge or attack you for the situation we are in. It is a desperate situation, of making beyond our control. We all await the same thing—for you to gain your bearings and lead us on the right path." The young girl turned away once more, staring at the night sky. The Cain persisted further. "The three of us, we each have different tactics. Among his more notable positive traits is Lord Abaddon's patience. He will easily remain aloof for weeks, perhaps months, waiting on you without offering criticism or advice. Cildar, for his part, does not wish to upset you or risk harming your confidence. He, likewise, will remain silent on the matter until you find your own way."

"And you?" she asked, unable to prevent a slightly aggressive tone from slipping into her voice.

"I recognize and sympathize with your plight, but also cannot lose sight of our own. Our time here is limited. We are in a reactive state, attempting to keep up with the activities of the Wisdoms. The longer we wait, the more ground we stand to lose. As such, I wish to help you. Understand, this is not to undermine you. I will make no mention of it to the others. I simply need to right our path as swiftly as possible."

After this declaration the two sat in silence for several more minutes. Finally, Detria began to explain. "The legends my people pass down are complicated, often conveyed in obtuse manners. Location, in particular, is rarely immediately decipherable, especially from an arbitrary starting point on the continent."

He nodded. "Understandable. Conveying such information in a consistently reproducible manner is difficult without a map."

"Oh, but there are maps," she corrected. "Devilslayer loremasters are expected to memorize and catalog each one, along with the various poems and songs that represent the paths. Unfortunately the maps are not of the land itself, but of the positions of the stars and constellations at the time the maps were formed. Given that the stars are constantly in motion, this makes the information highly unreliable."

"Fascinating," he responded. "Tell me, are these maps easily taught to another?"

She frowned. "I suppose so. Loremasters learn them, and are also expected to teach them. How does that matter?"

Myris reached his hands forward and muttered a few incantations. Soon a peculiar sphere of light appeared around the two, mimicking the lights of the stars above them. The Cain began making a few motions and the fake stars in the sphere responded, moving about slightly.

"It is important for Cainites to have an advanced understanding of sidereal time in order to hold their bearings. If you can give me an approximate date for when your specific map originated, I can use this simulation to play it back, compare the location of our current stars, and hazard a guess at where we're heading. It will only serve to get us near our destination, but I assume from there your poems can guide us the rest of the way."

Detria stared at the ethereal structure for nearly a full minute, finally shaking herself free of her trance and responding. "If you can get me close, I can get us there. Myris, this is incredible. Your powers are unbelievable."

He gave a modest shrug in response. "Do not give me undo

credit. It is no more complex than the information you have memorized yourself. Given sufficient time to study the heraldric arts you would find this a parlor trick. I will aid you in finding our path, but make no mistake, you are the one who bears the key."

She gave him a soft smile in response. "Thank you. It's good to know I don't need to guide us alone."

"As promised, I will say nothing to Lords Cildar and Abaddon. But I hope someday, you will find the confidence to place your trust in them as well. I understand secrecy better than anyone; do not take that as mere boast or arrogance. But I swear to you, there are none on the celestial sphere more worthy of your trust than these men." He turned his vision from her and looked to the ground, his voice growing quiet. "In truth, they have saved me from my own secrets, in ways I cannot explain."

Detria spent a moment considering a response. Ultimately she decided against it, and instead began reciting information on the location of Arda, guiding Myris to use his heraldric arts to reproduce the information in his illusory sphere. They were at work for nearly an hour, until finally they felt they had divined a reliable direction and distance to travel. It was only shortly after this that Cildar returned from his watch, asking Myris to step in.

As the Cain moved to assume sentry duty, Detria at long last settled in for her own night's sleep. A smile rested comfortably on her face as she replayed her battles with Cildar, and her work with Myris. She did not know when Abaddon would return from his wandering, but felt at last that when he did, she could face him with courage and lead the party once more to their goal.

* * * * *

Far beneath the surface, a magnificent altar of Anji loomed. It stood over twenty feet high, wrapping around the back of an open chamber. Before it stood rows upon rows of bleachers, seating arrangements for the faithful. Beyond it loomed cliffs, leading farther into underground catacombs. The interior of Arkalen was a veritable beehive of these chambers, carved out centuries ago by the continent's preeminent warring factions, the servants of gods long since forgotten.

Schpariel sneered as he stared at the markings on the altar in front of him. He knew the cult of Anji all too well. During their last war, the Wisdoms had allied with creatures of both Morolia and Asteria. Two in particular had given their side the strength necessary to overcome the Godbeasts. One had been a human Saint of Anji, terrible in might. The Saint had stolen an artifact from Schpariel and turned its power against him, in the end bringing about the Dark Wisdom's own demise.

He forced himself to drop thoughts of the past and focus on his present. "Where is Aegagropilion?" he demanded of his shrouded cohort. "I see nothing here."

"He lies beyond the altar, in the canyon below," the robed figure responded. "We must reach the other side."

They walked across the room, stopping directly before the center of the huge wooden structure. Schpariel raised his left hand and gathered power, preparing to summon his Moon Rod and reduce the altar to splinters. Akatriel grabbed at the Godbeast's wrist and shook his head. "That will not be necessary."

The pale priest reached his right hand forward and touched the altar. A small section of the wood turned into a bright blue light, then faded entirely. A path was revealed just barely large enough for the taller creature to pass through. Akatriel proceeded distractedly. Schpariel paused, ever more curious as to his strange ally's origins, then followed.

They walked for nearly a mile before reaching the edge of the vast stone plateau upon which the altar was seated. Schpariel looked eagerly into the darkness below. It was pitch black, and even his Gehennite eyes took a few seconds to adjust well enough to see. Once the image became clear, his enthusiasm faded once more to the old taste of rage. Below him stood an empty pit, filled only with the peak of a single underground mountain.

He reached over and seized Akatriel by the throat, lifting him a foot off the ground. "This is treachery," he roared, losing his poorly held resolve. "Aegagropilion is nowhere to be seen. Why have you led me astray once more?"

Akatriel's hood fell back, and his cold silver features remained calm as ever. "As it turns out, we lacked an important piece of information. After your imprisonment in the last war, Aegagropilion stole the form of a mighty gold dragon. His power increased radically, as did his size. This is why we've been unable to find him. We were seeking a creature in similar stature to yourself, yet when the Wisdom of Stone imprisoned Aegagropilion, it was within this very mountain that he was sealed."

Schpariel dropped the man to the ground. Once more he raised his hand and gave three sharp taps with his foot, followed by a snap. The Moon Rod materialized in his iron grip. "If that is indeed Aegagropilion, then a taste of Gehennite ether will resurrect him to this world!" With that, he heaved the Moon Rod vigorously into the pit below.

The azure crystal decorating the staff crashed through the peak of the mountain and vanished. For about half of a minute, there was no response. Akatriel shuffled forward, staring below for a hint of activity. Then a reaction began. As if warmed by some hidden heat source, the rocks below began to shimmer a bright red and melted into lava. The lava flowed inward, condensing down, wrapping tight around a bright blue, shimmering light that could only barely be seen through the light of the superheated rocks themselves.

When this display ended, the entire mountain was gone and the Moon Rod nowhere to be seen. All that remained was a single lonely figure, no more than five feet tall, standing in a smoking crater at the base of the pit. For a time there was no movement. Then the rocky frame began to twist about, cracking and shedding its outer skin of stone scales. Arms stretched out, sinewy and ill-defined in shape. A head reared forth, shaped like the giant beak of a great owl with tendons of sinewy flesh hanging out from behind. The creature raised its hands in front of its face. Fingers spread forth, turning into iron claws at the tips. He brought them to his face and tore twin holes for eye sockets. After another moment of resting, two tawny eyes materialized there and stared out, splitting the darkness.

"Aegagropilion," Schpariel shouted from above, "come here and join your brother."

The beast gave a fearsome shriek, then made a run for the base of the cliff. Just as he was about to run directly into stone, four pairs of monstrous spider legs exploded from his ribs. The spiny legs tore into the rock wall and scaled it nimbly, making it to the top in well under a minute.

Akatriel retreated away from the edge of the cliff as the small Godbeast blasted over the side. He was a bizarre creature. His entire body other than his head appeared as nothing more than a tightly weaved patchwork of muscle and sinew. His color was a mix of greens and blacks, giving him an almost plantlike appearance, but his structure was clearly mammalian. The eyes, which had become a brighter yellow now, were the familiar slits of a cobra.

Instantly Aegagropilion latched forth at Akatriel with the four spidery legs on his right side. The robed figure reacted quickly, releasing a blinding white light that disintegrated the legs. Just as sudden as the first set, the second wave of legs struck. Akatriel was not able to block this round, and his chest and stomach was pierced through four times.

He coughed up a small dose of his own blood and whispered coarsely, "I suspected this might happen," without emotion.

"What is this?" the resurrected creature demanded of his fellow Godbeast.

"I know not his name. Yet he is, for the moment, our only accomplice. Please do release him. We have yet to reach the juncture where we can afford his death."

"I could devour him." As he talked, Aegagropilion spoke slowly, but deliberately. The lower part of the beak-like head pulsed, as if a mouth beneath it was struggling to escape. His voice held a gravelly quality, and the pitch seemed to shift slowly, but randomly, from high to low.

"I know you hunger when you awaken, but do remember some of your formerly elegant composure," Schpariel chastised.

"A Godbeast without power is of no use. As I am, I'm no more powerful than a meager hellspawn. I must *eat.*" As he spoke, he slowly began drawing Akatriel near.

Schpariel raised a hand and sent a blue fireball into Aegagropilion's face. The creature reeled back, the spidery legs collapsing back into his body as he lost his concentration. "The Wisdoms are here!" the taller Gehennan shouted. "We cannot afford to be reckless."

The strange monster froze, staring at Schpariel pensively. "The Wisdoms? You resurrect me late in the game, brother."

"I have long sought you. It's only due to the Silver One that I find you at all." He made a motion to where the white robed figure had been standing. They both looked, and the priest was nowhere to be seen. He had made his exit swiftly, to avoid further risk of the Godbeast's hunger.

The pair said nothing of the man's disappearance. Instead Aegagropilion asked, "Are the Wisdoms still in league with the human and the dragon?"

The Gehennans turned and began to head back toward the altar as they continued to converse. "They have long since passed. From what our human cohort tells me, many of the gods of Asteria have been killed by their own internal wars. If we can defeat the Wisdoms, we will be unchecked. Though without Gilanirus, I don't know if we can survive."

"I know where our Lord sleeps."

"What?!" Schpariel exclaimed, a rare change in his normally emotionless tone.

"I was the last to fall in our previous war. I witnessed the cursed Kiastos imprison Gilanirus after his defeat. He is far to the south, hidden away in a tremendous ravine. The Wisdoms tore a hole in the Veil near there, creating a giant vortex of ether to shield and hide the area from Morolian creatures. For us, it should pose no nuisance."

"Then let us make our way there, so that we might renew our war in earnest."

"Not yet. The Wisdoms know the location as well as I, and if they are already here they will be watching for us. We're too vulnerable to make it. First, I must find some creature of power. Do you know of any on this continent?"

By now they had reached the back of the altar of Anji. The pathway still stood open, so they passed through unhindered. As they did, the strange wooden structure closed off behind them, sealing the way once more.

Schpariel answered, "I may have encountered a few."

* * * * *

Abaddon and his companions stood at the entrance to the crypt they had uncovered. There could be no doubts it was concealing something of value. A tremendously dense boulder had been placed in their way, and it had taken Myris a barrage of powerful explosive spells to crumble it away. Now they stared into the gaping maw before them, certain that more obstacles awaited.

Myris took a step forward and gave a bow. "Lord Abaddon, if you have no objections I will proceed first. I have the sharpest reflexes and am the most suited to detecting traps, or attempting to dodge them if activated."

"Get on with it," the big man answered callously. "We'll follow."

Detria knew Myris' claim was true, but still she felt her temper slip in reaction to Abaddon's cold words. The Cain had repeatedly proven himself a resourceful and clever man, and she could not tolerate Abaddon's easy dismissal of the asset he commanded. She held her tongue, still not confident in her place within the group's dynamic, but made a mental note of the incident.

They headed down a narrow staircase, single file. Myris walked a full fifteen yards ahead of the others, placing small, lingering spells of light on the triggers for traps he found. Their pace was good and their scout did not miss a single trap. Detria began to believe their descent would be unremarkable, and marveled further at the Cain's prowess.

Then a disaster struck. Despite his best efforts, at last Myris missed a trigger. Fortunately he himself stepped on it, which saved the lives of the rest of the group as they were so far behind. Cildar shouted a panicked, "Myris! To your right!" as the tunnel turned into an array of hundreds of rusted steel nails and pinned the dark man to the far wall. Detria released a shrill scream that echoed throughout the caverns, mixed with the sounds of rusted metal grinding.

His friend's warning had alerted Myris in the precise nick of time. He leaped to his left and seized his katana. He produced his fastest Draw Strike—of Ice—and severed the four spikes headed directly for him. After the four swings he knew his time was up, so he dropped the katana to his feet and wrapped his arms around himself, compacting his size as much as possible.

So there he was, pinned against the left wall, a solid row of needles to his left and right preventing escape. The ones he had destroyed had stopped only a few inches short of him. One pressed into his right thigh, not firmly enough to break the bone, but enough to cause him a sizable amount of pain.

He turned and gave an agitated look to Cildar. "Would asking for a little help be out of order?"

The paladin came forward to the outermost spikes and gave a swing with his Trine Lance. Two fell to the ground at his feet. He counted the number between himself and his imprisoned ally. "This will take all day. Myris, do you know if there's a release?"

"I didn't even see the trigger. Obviously."

Cildar grimaced at his accidental barb. "Fair enough." He turned and looked over his shoulder. "Lord Abaddon?"

The mystic warlord came forward and gave the structure a study. He held a hand up and placed it against the right wall, closing his eyes as if deep in thought. He stood silently in this manner for nearly half a minute before answering.

"Up there," he pointed to where the wall met the ceiling. "Just a few feet from us, there's a large gear that's exhibiting a great amount of tension. I think if we shatter it the spikes will retract to their resting position."

Cildar gave a nod. "On it." He sprang up and began scaling the spikes, leaping nimbly from one to the next. When he was near the ceiling, he drew his Trine Lance again. He gathered a powerful white aura around the tip, then lunged at the spot Abaddon had indicated.

He leaped back to the ground below as the spikes retracted nearly as quickly as they had emerged. Myris fell to his knees nursing his injured thigh, and retrieved the katana he had dropped. Cildar spent a few moments attempting a healing on his friend's leg as Detria praised both of their abilities.

After everything had settled Abaddon moved nearby and looked down at Myris. "I trust your near-death experience has not shaken you too much for you to continue acting as our guide."

The Cain stared back levelly. "Never."

He returned a nod. "Then let us proceed."

Detria bit her lip at the man's continued disrespect toward his comrades, but remained silent as Myris and Cildar did not take up for themselves. They continued their walk, heading down winding spiral staircases with no rails, and across narrow stone bridges above deep catacombs. After the first corridor the traps were few and far between, and Myris was far more attentive to miss none.

In another hour they reached the final chamber. Or rather, what they assumed was the final chamber, as a deep slope of solid ice ran behind it. The chamber was noticeably cooled thanks to the presence of the underground oddity, and Detria caught herself shivering more than once.

Myris stepped forward and examined a large stone box with a table sitting behind it. "There are words, but I cannot read them."

Detria joined him and looked over the text he had referenced.

"This is an old Arkalen language. It's not really used anymore, but I can translate, I think. 'Here lies Loridican, Saint of Anji, slayer of Schpariel. His name is recalled by the wise.' Hmm, kind of a strange message."

"Schpariel," Myris commented. "The Wisdom Dosiros used that name. It seemed to belong to the creature he was hunting. For it to appear here is either too strange a coincidence, or evidence of a truly ancient Gehennan—one not nearly so slain as this tomb would imply. Has the name appeared in any of your legends, Detria?"

She gave a shrug. "I've never heard it. Nor that of Loridican himself."

Abaddon tapped his foot in impatience. "Where is the sword?" he asked with disinterest.

At his commander's beckon, Myris stepped around the coffin and examined the table behind it. He placed his hand on the surface and the table suddenly fell into an underground opening.

They all jumped back, expecting a trap. Myris muttered a curse under his breath, his hand already resting on his katana's hilt. After a few seconds, the table slowly rose from the ground once more, this time with a shimmering white armlet sitting alone on its surface.

Abaddon stepped forward, edging his way past Detria and Myris. He carefully lifted the armlet and inspected it. At his touch, a series of dark lettering scrawled across the metal. He looked back to the rest of the party. "This is certainly not a sword, and doesn't appear to be either human or demonic in origin. There are magical signatures placed upon it. If I'm correct, they read, 'Forged by Barricus to give the Devil's strength, even beyond the Gates of Hellfire'." Myris edged forward, intrigued by this cryptic promise of power. The mystic commander went back to examining it, holding his hand near the surface. A soft glow of red surrounded the armlet. "Gehennite. This Band of Barricus will do us no good." He walked over to the edge of the icy slope and moved to toss the artifact over.

Myris dashed forward with an uncharacteristic shout. "Lord Abaddon, please!" The taller man paused, raising an eyebrow. "I wish to study the relic, if I may. Perhaps Gehennite technology can be turned to our side. It could help us against the Wisdoms, in theory."

"Then it's yours." He tossed the bangle over, then stepped around Myris and addressed Detria. "Are we missing something? Did the legend somehow become confused?"

She thought for a moment. "I remember the legend of a Saint's tomb, and an artifact lying within. I must have confused the directions for the Arda with this place." She gave a bow and spoke more rapidly, fearing a tongue-lashing from the brooding figure. "Forgive me, I am sorry. I believe I remember the other legend now, though, and if you'll bear with me I think I can get us there quickly. It shouldn't be far from here."

Abaddon gave a shrug with one shoulder. "Don't worry about it," his tone was as impassive as ever, and Detria would have mistaken his words for cruelty had they not been so kind. "Little was lost, and something was gained. We have witnessed that there is at least some truth to these old fables, and Arkalen possesses artifacts which are truly extraplanar in origin. Even if we still do not find the sword, we have proven that seeking it was no fool's errand."

He turned and left the chamber, disappearing into the darkness beyond. Myris hid the armlet deep within his cloak, then followed. Detria walked over to Cildar shaking her head.

"You keep some eerie company."

He chuckled and placed a hand on her shoulder. "Don't take them as seriously as they come across. They seem gloomy, but they're not so bad. Trust me, everyone's happy right now. As Lord Abaddon said, in his own way, our hopes are much higher than they were before. So let's go find this Arda and discover what it's really capable of."

She gave him a smile, and they too carefully made their way out of the chamber.

## Chapter 16.

# The Generals of the Overlord

Kelve Orista sat alone, staring down the hill at the ironclad fortress below. He silently bemoaned his misfortune of having to lead Detria's forces into combat. Playing commander as a bluff or during a meeting was one thing, but he had never been comfortable with responsibility of this nature. He kept mentally running through the ranks of his immediate subordinates, wondering if he could pawn the reins off to one of them. Then he alternately debated handing matters over to Tenkahn or even Eiden. After all, he reasoned with himself, they were both more familiar with the Overlord's territory and tactics. They seemed natural choices for leadership.

But he knew this was foolhardy logic at best. Another command switch, especially to an outsider, would be hard on morale. The troops here looked up to Kelve. The same illusion that Detria used to convince enemies that he was an adequate leader had also worked on her own people, and they would follow him as loyally as Detria herself.

His thoughts turned briefly to running away. After all, it was his nature to shirk duties, then apologize with a flashy smile afterward. He could easily abandon this mess and return later, which would greatly simplify his position. No one would expect him to play leader after such a move. It sounded so ideal, and in a way he yearned for it. Only the thought of the disappointment on Detria's face kept him from placing serious merit in the notion. He could not betray his promise to her.

"Why did I tell her she should leave?" he muttered to himself.

In his head, he answered his own question. He did not

personally place any value in Abaddon Daemon's quest, nor the threats presented by whatever unorganized demons the foreigner hunted. Rather, he had felt Detria would be better served by remaining in the company of the Felthespari. He knew how his friend operated. She would have led the initial charge at the fore of her army, throwing her own body into enemy forces as a sacrificial lamb. Though she would never have acknowledged it, her life was too symbolically important to be thrown away so recklessly. Her demise in the early stages of the war would have been a crippling blow for morale. Even if absent, the knowledge that she was out there, the hope that she would soon return, would stoke the flames of their soldiers' passion and keep them fighting at their peak.

Beyond that—though he admitted it to himself far more quietly—she was too precious to Kelve for him to watch her die. If half the stories the Devilslayers told of the Overlord and his armies were true, then Detria's small band of outcasts were hopelessly unprepared for the malevolence they were about to face. There was a real chance they would all die here today, as soon as they raised the Overlord's ire. At least now if the worst were to happen, Kelve could die knowing he had done his part to protect his commander and his love, as he had so sworn.

He sighed and reached into one of the pockets on his uniform. From here he drew forth a cigarette and a match. It had long been forbidden for the Devilslayers to smoke, but the prohibition had made it a certainty. Kelve tried to refrain from the habit, but he could never resist at least one long draw before a battle.

As he sat smoking, relaxing, he felt the presence of someone approaching from behind. Out of habit he nearly panicked and hid his cigarette away, then he suppressed the instinct, irritated at himself. Tenkahn walked up to his side and gave a polite nod, then stared down at the fortress himself.

Kelve rose to his feet and dusted himself off. The command meetings had already been held, the plan of attack already laid out. In one hour, his troops would make their first attempt to get inside of the fortress walls, prepared to beat a hasty retreat if necessary.

Eiden had told of a lever just inside the main door that would cause it to open, which stood unguarded most hours of the day. The red ogres outside the gates served as the only watchmen, and it was their responsibility to summon creatures to open the doors from the inside. If the ogres could be killed before sounding the alarm, there was a chance that someone could slip over the wall, find the lever, and open the entrance without drawing attention.

The former slayer's nerves began to rise as battle approached. He did not fear combat; like all Devilslayers, he had long become desensitized to it. The din and chaos of battle was almost melodic to him, a lullaby that would calm and steady him once the fighting began. It was the weight of command that continued to exacerbate his anxiety.

No matter what storm raged within him, Kelve Orista had never allowed it to leave so much as a ripple on the surface of his outward calm. As always, he put on his best nonchalant smile and addressed Tenkahn in a careless tone. "Ready for the fight?"

Instead of answering the question, the plainly dressed warrior shook his head solemnly. "Two red ogres will inflict substantial casualties upon your forces. You are weak on range, and close quarters combat with them will be deadly. I doubt they will be killed before those on the inside are roused."

Kelve put his hands behind his head and chewed on his lower lip for a moment. "You were thinking, perhaps, of a more intimate approach?"

"If I go alone, the battle will be much quieter. They will also be less likely to suspect a full invasion, and may simply try to kill me rather than alerting the fortress."

As they continued their discussion, Eiden wandered nearby and gave a bow to each of them. Kelve gave the boy a nod as he asked the monk, "Can you take two ogres by yourself?"

"It has been a long time since I was forced to fight without my ally monks, but I believe I am a match for two simple demons."

"Actually," Eiden interjected, "red ogres are cyclopes. They only have a single eye, which is capable of delivering a powerful paralysis spell. When they outnumber you, you can't possibly win."

Tenkahn spent a moment in recollection before responding. "I remember this effect. When I traveled with my brethren, we were not vulnerable to such a strategy. I may have overestimated my ability to stand alone."

Kelve gave a sigh. He had hoped to rely on the monk's strength to easily dispatch the ogres. Since that was no longer an option, he decided it was time to end his internal uncertainty.

"That's fine," he said to Tenkahn and Eiden both, waving his hands in frustration. "Don't worry about it. It'll be easier if I do it."

Tenkahn furrowed his brow. "Forgive me, Master Orista, but I do not see what makes you believe you can succeed where I would fail."

As the monk spoke, Kelve drew a syringe from a steel case on his belt. He removed the protective cover from the needle, then removed two small colorful tubes from the belt as well. Rough sponges blocked the bottom of each tube, and he stabbed the needle into one, filling the syringe. He then inserted it into the base of his bicep and released the liquid into his bloodstream. He repeated the process with the second vial, then returned each of the tools to his belt. His head began to spin for a moment and he nearly fainted. Once he was certain he was steady on his feet again, he gave a nod to Tenkahn.

"The troops should already be prepared for battle. When I have killed the ogres, sound the attack. Bring them down to the fortress walls to await the opening of the gates."

Without a further word he proceeded down the hill, his head pounding from the effects of the drugs he had introduced into his system. In the way Detria was a master of Arkalen lore and history, Kelve was a master of biology, chemistry, physiology, and medicine. He knew all about the paralysis effect of the cycloptic ogres. They used an electrical discharge that entered the body's nervous system through one of the five senses. Blocking one was not enough—as long as you could hear, see, even taste, your system would be put into a brief shock.

So Kelve had vaccinated himself, using two of the dozens of chemicals he kept with him at all times. The first weakened all of his senses, putting him into a mild delirium. His sight and hearing began to go fastest, so he had quickly injected the second drug. This one drove his neural kinetics into a near frenzy, allowing him to fend off the comatose effects of the first injection and make do with the limited senses he had remaining.

In the end, the combined effect of the two injections would make him immune to the crippling effects of the ogres. However, his reflexes were reduced to less than half of their original precision. Since a single mistake was enough to prove fatal when facing off against two ogres, he was treading dangerous ground.

The sentries noticed him when he was a still good distance away, and moved themselves a few yards from the fortress walls. Kelve was pleased to see they did not attempt to alert those on the inside. When he was almost within their striking range, the ogre to his right smashed the ground in front of him with its huge club, bringing his march to a halt.

"Who goes here? This territory is under private rule," the beast bellowed.

Kelve bowed, keeping his eyes on the ogre to his left whose club still rested on his shoulder. This creature seemed more relaxed than his partner, decidedly unconcerned with the human's presence.

He straightened his back and gave his most winning smile. "I'm just a visitor. Please, I come with presents." He slid a hand slowly beneath the green scale plate covering his chest. The cyclops to his right did not seem to trust this move and responded quickly. The creature opened its eye wide and gave a hoarse rasp, bearing down a blast of pressure against the human. Kelve froze in place, allowing a look of panic to seize his features.

The ogre retracted its club and sneered. "We do not deal with uninvited humans. Your kind cannot be trusted."

Kelve's expression faded to one of amusement and he tilted his head to the side. "Sounds like you've got me pegged."

With a quick swipe he removed his hand from within his armor and shot it fiercely in the direction of the belligerent ogre. A tiny knife attached to a leather whipcord shot forward, heading directly at the beast's eye. The ogre quickly raised its club to block the attack, but Kelve was ready for this. He gave a swift yank on his end of the cord, which caused the knife to change course enough to miss the club. He followed with another whipping motion, sending the blade lower.

The tip of the knife hit the ogre's shoulder. No more than three inches long and half an inch thick, the needle-like projectile only barely bit into the leather flesh, embedding itself just enough to break the skin. Still the cyclops roared in outrage, stomping his feet on the ground in temper. His cohort laughed at his misfortune, teasing, "Ha, you let the puny human cut you with his puny knife." Kelve turned his attention to the mocking ogre, drawing one of the twin cutlasses that rested on his hips. The demon watched the man draw his sword, still laughing. "Go ahead, aren't you going to finish him?" he taunted his friend.

The injured creature never offered a response. Instead a gurgling sound escaped from his throat and he fell awkwardly onto his side, never to rise again. The remaining cyclops gaped in shock, then looked back to the human with a look of anger.

"What?" Kelve teased while tossing his cutlass back and forth between each hand. "Haven't you ever heard of a pressure point? If you hit some creatures in the right place, seemingly harmless ones, you can cause some amazing things to happen. Sometimes even instant death. With ogres, there just happens to be a spot on the shoulder." He lifted his cutlass and pointed at the remaining creature's right shoulder. "Yours is next."

The ogre wasted no further time with words, charging forward and swinging his club with both hands. Kelve quickly reached behind his back and freed a small grappling hook, attached to a five-foot length of leather cord. He began running to one side, and once the club was overhead he swung the grapple and latched on to the wood, using the strength of his arms and legs simultaneously to rocket himself off the ground just before impact. The earth crumbled with the might of the ogre's two-handed blow, sending up a shower of dust and debris. Kelve held his breath so as to not choke on this cloud as he dashed up the wooden surface. He delivered a rapid slice at the base of the ogre's right thumb, then retreated away at a full sprint.

Like his fallen comrade, the ogre bellowed in rage at this minor wound. He raised his club high over his head with his right hand, charging forward to swing at the human once more.

He did not make it far. After only proceeding a few steps the club slipped from his grasp and fell to the ground behind him. He stopped his charge and looked around, confused by his sudden clumsiness. He attempted to seize the club and lift it once more, but was dismayed to find that his arm no longer responded.

"Right about now you'll be losing the ability to use your arm," Kelve explained to the bewildered cyclops. "I may have lied when I said I used a pressure point on your friend. Things of that nature are far too unreliable for combat. I prefer the simple nature of a potent poison. Ogres have a redundant circulatory system, which increases the spread of any blood-borne pathogen. A stab to the shoulder kills in about ten seconds. A slice to the thumb, maybe twenty."

The creature turned back to Kelve and reached out with his left hand, but his time was up. His glazed eye shut, and he joined his partner by sinking into death's embrace. Kelve sheathed his cutlass and drew forth another grappling hook, dashing over to the castle's stone walls and scaling them quickly with the twin hooks. In a few moments Tenkahn had led the troops to the front gates, which opened to greet them.

* * * * *

Akatriel stumbled into a cavern and collapsed onto a small wooden table. This was one of many locations across the continent he had chosen as a base. It was nothing more than a small cave, but sealed away from both weather and intruders by powerful magics, and decorated with a few stolen refinements that pleased him. It was here that he came when his power was running low. He was driven here now by Aegagropilion's assault, forced to rest and allow his wounded frame to heal.

He carefully settled himself into a plush chair and began to gather power, patching the holes in his torso with effort. It took him the better part of a day to recover adequately, then he allowed himself to take a rare moment to relax.

As he did so, he took inventory of his plans and tools. The Crucible of Anji was filled with the soul of the draconic, Farthas. The last remaining Ion of Kentral was in his possession. Kargaroth rested behind a wall in the very cave he sat in, shielded away from the grip of its master in order to protect the Wisdoms from his wrath.

Nearly three years ago, he had found the Moon Rod—supposedly lost forever—and used it to resurrect Schpariel, to incite the attention of the Muses. Finally the Wisdoms had arrived and the Godbeasts were on the move. The conspirator was well aware that Aegagropilion knew Gilanirus' true location. The Gehennans would seek out their lord, and once he was resurrected the game would begin in earnest. Once the Spectre of Gehenna was arisen, Akatriel could not afford for anything to go wrong.

All that remained was the question of the less predictable creatures, particularly the humans. Akatriel had once planned to twist Abaddon Daemon for his own devices, leveraging the northerner's incomparable talent for dealing death. He no longer considered that a prudent course. The Felthespari mystic had once been linked to the entire pantheon of dark gods, transforming him into a divine consciousness known only as "Hell". As the pale priest had taunted, he did not know what secrets were yet locked away within the man's mind. It made it impossible to predict what Abaddon might realize, and when.

He had gambled by telling the man his own name, a test to see if there was any glimmer of recognition. There had been none, so for now he did not seem a threat to Akatriel's greater plans, but that could yet change. Instead the conspirator had found a simpler pawn to suit his needs, though more groundwork there would yet need to be laid. With Kargaroth graciously falling into his grasp courtesy of the unintended confrontation with the Wisdoms, the Daemon's further involvement could only prove to be a complication.

Still, Akatriel did not take unnecessary risks. If his new pawn did not prove himself worthy of the task, he might yet have need for his original Knight. So he could not kill Abaddon, but he could not allow the man to interfere freely with his agendas either. "The Rook is the key," he whispered to himself. "He can remove the Knight from play. At least for a time. I must move."

He rose to his feet and checked his health. He was still weakened, but he could not allow it to show. For the manipulator, the illusion of strength was everything. He did his best to shield his body from further bleeding, used a flush of magic to bleach his robes back to their purest whites, and left the cavern.

* * * * *

In a cold room, atop a turret decorating the keep of the Overlord's courtyard, his commanders sat eating their dinners. The Overlord maintained a wide diversity in the species of his officers, in order to give each faction assurances they were well represented. In the end, however, these generals had only minimal authority, as all were the subordinates to the Overlord, Shote, and even the Robed Ones.

A blue ogre, with three prominent eyes decorating his forehead, took up the largest portion of the room. Like most of his species, his chosen weapon was a club, but his was hewn from solid steel rather than wood. It was slimmer than the clubs of most ogres, and the front face was decorated with a series of long iron spikes. He was Kogonbo, General of Ogres, and even though he was among the largest of his kind, he also held a rare intellect. Because of this he preferred to linger back from the front lines, sending his demonic ranks in as a wall of brute force.

In the corner of the room, hiding quietly in the cool shadows, was the General of the Vampirics, a wispy creature named Kaltheria. She was a shadow wight, evolved past the need for a physical body. Her spirit was held on the Morolian plane by magic alone, and her own forceful will. Just a whisper from her voice could cause a man to freeze with fear, and a mere touch would drain his life away.

Fenrir, who had taken the name of his extinct race as his own, was also counted among the commanders. He had been appointed as General of the Were-Creatures. He despised his position, and his underlings, considering himself an evolutionary masterpiece compared to their kind. But he did enjoy the extra laziness and quality meals that came with the officer's rank, so he kept any complaints to himself.

There was also the General of Trolls, Dokitir. The trolls were a race oddly evolved from the ogres, having shrunk in stature to a size not much larger than the average human. Still, their bodies retained many characteristics of their ancestors, and they were notorious on Arkalen for being virtually unkillable. Their skin could deflect a knife, and their bones a sledgehammer. They had lost a majority of their brute strength, yet were still slow in movement and reflexes. To adapt to these limitations, they had turned to a mastery of shadow magic. Dokitir was one of the oldest trolls, and his adept use of shadow magic made him a fearsome adversary, even as he was beginning to lose his once formidable resilience.

Meriosthro had been promoted as the newest commander, General of the Draconic Forces. Though draconics were usually emotionally detached, Meriosthro was having a difficult time adapting to Farthas' disappearance. He had been by her side for several human lifetimes, and she was suspicious that some among the Overlord's creatures were somehow responsible for whatever had happened to her lost mate. In light of Farthas' loss, she had been selected by the Overlord's generals to join their ranks. Her people had initially been outraged by the notion of a female commander, but she had used these objections as an excuse to turn her grief into rage. Blood had been spilled, and since then not a word had been uttered on the subject.

The final commander, First General under Shote himself, was perhaps the most out of place of all the leaders. It was a slim human female, no more than thirty years old. Her name was Tessena, and she had climbed her way to the top the only way that a human could in this demonspawn fortress: by being the most cunning, the most ruthless, the most deadly of all the Overlord's servants. Her blond hair was cropped off short, just above shoulder length. She wore crude leather shoulder pads, which held a black silk cape that flowed down to her lower back. Her armor was composed of the thickest leathers, all dyed black or dark blue, and though her right hand was unadorned, her left hand and forearm was covered by a thick cerulean gauntlet. Across her back was strapped a small, single-headed axe, the only visible weapon she carried.

There was another human in the room, but he was not a commander. He was Tessena's henchman, Gariso. He was a muscular man, but not extremely intimidating. He wore a large black overcoat, and little of his body could be made out. He wore no hood and, like Tessena, wore blond hair down to his shoulders. Gariso's weapon was a peculiar one, little more than a large spar of wood, eight feet long and a full foot in diameter. Two large triangular handles were affixed near one end, the first placed one foot from the sharpened wooden tip, the other three feet down. Gariso's ability to wield the weighty staff came from his most unusual feature—at some time in his past, his arms had been removed and surgically replaced by the arms of a green dragon. No one was sure how these arms functioned, but there were rumors they had been a gift from the Overlord to the human soldier to repay some past favor. His strength was infamous among all of the fortress's denizens. He had once punched an ogre in the stomach for insolence, bringing the creature to its knees in tears.

As the generals sat eating their meals—each of a different nature—they heard a few loud thuds echo outside of the fortress walls.

Dokitir shot to his feet, prepared to sound the alarm. "What was that?"

Kogonbo waved over to him with a smile. "Relax, it's those two cutups, Khidor and Boffos. They're on guard duty today on the west wall. I'm sure they're clowning around."

Everyone settled back to their meals, ignoring further disturbance. They ate in peace until half an hour later when an alarmed cry suddenly drifted up from the outside.

"Invaders! Humans from the outside have invaded the courtyard! Hel—gack!" The cries ended with a sickening gurgle as the man was felled by some assailant.

Tessena dashed to the window and inspected the situation. Her panic quickly settled and she straightened her shoulders. "Well this is a rather pathetic invasion force," she announced to the others. "Only about five hundred humans." She watched events outside for a moment longer. "Our nearest men have engaged them in combat. Though few, it does seem the invaders are well trained."

"How is our defense faring?" Dokitir asked.

"They're carpenters and gardeners, not warriors. So how do you think it's going?" Her voice suddenly turned from sarcastic to booming and authoritative. "Get some soldiers down there and stymie this invasion! Send the newest forces, the draconics and the trolls. Your people have yet to earn your keep here. Now is your chance." Dokitir and Meriosthro left the room, as Tessena mumbled to herself, "Two assaults against us in as many years. I think maybe the protection of the Overlord is growing weaker." As she continued her vigil, she suddenly recognized a face that put a tinge of fear into her heart.

She rapidly signaled for her companion to come to her side. "Gariso," she whispered to him, "one of the monks is here again.

Last time a mere ten of them killed over half of our forces. We still haven't recovered. I only see the one, but he is an imperative threat. Go down there and kill him, if you can." Her lieutenant nodded and left the chambers. "Kaltheria!" she shouted next. The wight sitting in the shadows rose to her spectral feet, her only indication that she was listening. "Go speak with the Robed Ones, find out Lord Shote's condition. Surely they have nearly repaired him to the point that he can join us once more." Kaltheria did not respond, but instead took a step backward and disappeared into the stone walls.

* * * * *

As she dashed from the banquet chamber, Meriosthro found herself dwelling on many of her old arguments with Farthas. *If we retreat now, they will come for us,* he had prophesied. *They will hunt us to the ends of the earth until there's nowhere left to run. We cannot afford to show such cowardice!* She could not help but fear that her lost love had been wiser than she had reckoned, and was dismayed at how soon the humans had followed her kind here.

She parted paths with Dokitir as each of them ran to their respective barracks. Upon arriving Meriosthro drove her tribe into a frenzy, offering promises of fresh meat and spirit, and they dashed to engage in combat.

When they reached the courtyard, the invaders had driven off or killed the Overlord's slim human forces, and were attempting to get organized and choose a potential building to capture.

Meriosthro smiled as she recognized this. "They're looking for a target!" she called to her warriors. "Give them one!"

The draconics dashed forward with bloodcurdling shrieks. The humans were somehow not caught off guard. The front rows fell back a few steps and raised a wall of kite shields in front of them. Meriosthro ordered her soldiers to attack low and go for the legs. One human stepped forward, however; a man in brown robes. The draconics continued their charge, and when they were about ten yards away the man suddenly pounded the ground with both of his fists. A solid sheet of earth tilted up and pointed at the draconics, breaking their charge abruptly and causing many of the front ranks to be crushed and killed.

Meriosthro was not startled by a simple trick, though she was amazed to see such a demonstration of power from a human. She leaped high into the air when she reached the earthen wall in front of her and went straight for the man who had summoned it, fighting to distract him away from her people.

The rest of her forces were slower to adapt, slowly scaling the upset section of earth and coming at the human troops a few at a time. The invaders were easily able to pick them off like this, and though every so often a draconic would kill a human, another simply fell forward from the second row to take his or her place. Meanwhile the draconic forces fell to crippling injuries at a rate of half a dozen a minute.

Meriosthro recognized the fighting style and accuracy of those humans. In her mind, there was no question—this was a force of Devilslayers. They knew the few weaknesses in the draconics' bodies and were exploiting them. She wished to shout fresh orders to her troops, to command them to regroup and simply walk around the obstacle they currently wasted so much effort scrambling over. Unfortunately, the monk she had placed herself into combat with was proving to be too much for her. Her claws did little more than scratch his flesh, and it was everything she could do to avoid his punches. He caught her in the shoulder with a glancing blow, and her entire left arm became paralyzed with pain. She drew a bone scimitar and continued to fight with her right hand, but she knew her time holding this stalemate was numbered in seconds, not minutes.

Then help arrived. A massive figure in a black overcoat came from the back of the courtyard and slammed into Meriosthro's opponent at amazing speed. As the stricken warrior reeled back in surprise, Gariso reached up and snapped two links at his shoulders. His sleeves fell to the ground, freeing his dragonkin arms. He began attacking the monk with a flurry of shattering punches, the huge log that served as his weapon still strapped to his back. Remarkably, the monk was not overwhelmed, and evenly returned Gariso's attacks even as he was forced back from the battle site.

The two pummeled their way across the courtyard, sending out shockwaves of power that left Meriosthro quivering for a moment. She came to herself, resumed command of her eager but shortsighted troops, and redirected them around the earthen slab.

* * * * *

Eiden stayed close to Kelve's side, assisting the capable leader in any way he could. He tried using a few of the spells Cildar and Myris had taught him—a fireball here, an Aura Blast there—but he could not tell if he was making any difference. His attacks seemed to distract the draconic forces, which might have been a good thing, but Kelve Orista himself was so deadly Eiden could not be sure it mattered.

The former Devilslayer wielded one of his cutlasses in his right hand, leaving his left free in case he needed access to his countless potions and powders. Every time a draconic came close to him, he gave a quick slice to their neck or a stab to their stomach and the creature would slink to the ground, gargling a sickening green foam. Every dozen or so kills, Kelve would draw a strange cloth soaked in a dark liquid from one of the tubes on his belt, then renew the coating on his sword.

There were only a few hundred draconic warriors, so the humans held the advantage in numbers. Some among Kelve's forces knew what it took to cripple the thick-skinned draconics, and the rest knew what it took to keep themselves defended or out of range. The tides were turning slowly, but the invading forces were definitely going to come out on top.

Eiden paused for a second and checked the surroundings. "This is too easy," he fretted. "Kelve!"

The captain slew a few nearby draconics, then came close

enough to hear the boy. "What is it?"

"This isn't right at all! When I left there weren't draconics here. These must be new recruits. We haven't even seen any of the Overlord's main army."

Kelve gave a concerned nod. His spirits had been raised by the thought of a quick victory, but there was no doubting Eiden's word on the subject. He began to carve his way through the enemy ranks, trying to gain a vantage point on the outside so he could see where the next wave might come from.

Eiden did not notice this change in tactic and remained where he was, fighting near a small blockade of his allies. It was not long before these fighters had been cut down, and Eiden suddenly realized he stood alone with a wave of draconics coming for him. He cast the last spells he had matrixed and managed to slow their approach. He had dealt no actual harm, however, and one stubborn draconic came on, a bone sickle held in his hand.

The youth gathered the last of his spiritual strength and released an Aura Blast directly in the creature's face. The draconic came to a halt and tried to guard its head. There was a few seconds of silence, then the reptilian soldier opened its eyes to find itself wholly uninjured. Eiden's white magic simply did not have the potency to overcome even a draconic's meager defenses against such a spell.

The beast lifted his sickle over his head, and Eiden braced himself for death. He was surprised to find that he was not afraid, only anxious for it to be over quickly. That was not to be, as Tenkahn rejoined the fray at that exact moment. A swift backhand to the draconic's stomach left it paralyzed in pain, followed by a punch to the throat that sent the creature's severed head flying back into its allies.

Tenkahn gave the boy a polite nod. "You are of not much use in combat, are you, son?"

"Forgive me, no."

"Your knowledge makes you too important for us to lose you so easily. Try to refrain from such close engagements with our foes. Know where your value truly lies, and do not be ashamed of it."

The monk then sensed danger. He grabbed Eiden and leaped into the air as a beam of wood crashed down where they had been standing. The area was filled almost solely with the draconic troops, and several of them were crippled by the blow. Tenkahn landed out of range and dropped Eiden, then turned to face the return of Gariso.

"Monk!" the Overlord's human champion roared. "I will not be so easily beaten!" He was bleeding from gashes and burns all along his chest and face, though his scaled arms were unscathed. Clearly his battle with Tenkahn had been a taxing one. At last he had drawn his weapon, and now used it as a massive bat. The eight-foot shaft contained an inner spar, which came out from its wooden encasing when Gariso turned the two handles in a certain manner. This fifteen foot range, backed by the strength his unnatural arms allowed him to throw into the blows, made Gariso the only human the demonspawn army feared.

Tenkahn moved away from Eiden and closed in on his worthy rival, bringing himself within reach of the spar. Gariso pulled his weapon back and flipped the length over his right shoulder. He held it firmly by both handles, and used the sharpened short end to make rapid stabs at his enemy's head. The monk dodged these blows with little effort, waiting for the inevitable finisher. As anticipated, Gariso took a dash backward, planted his feet firmly, then while holding his back hand firmly in place, pulled down hard with his front to bring the mast into a spin.

A crushing blow headed Tenkahn's way. The monk did not waver in his stance, fully intending to take the hit. He raised his arms above his head and locked them into a tightly coupled cross, closing his eyes and chanting loudly, "Iron Fortitude!" His arms became encased in an extra thick layer of runic power, and he awaited the impact.

The impact that came not small. The strength of a dragon, coupled with the mechanical advantage of the fifteen-foot lever, was enough to cleave a stone wall in twain. Tenkahn's body reverberated from the attack until his protective field shuddered and collapsed, throwing a tangible shockwave into the area around him. Dirt and draconics alike were blown back by gale force winds, as the Monk of Tria sank into the ground beneath him until he was submerged to waist level. Yet when things had settled, the rune-coated arms had not given way. Tenkahn looked up to his foe, neither smiling nor frowning, and rapped his knuckles up against the pole. The wooden structure hummed for a moment, then the monk thrust upward with bodily might.

The entire length of Gariso's sturdy weapon exploded into splinters, cutting into his exposed chest and knocking him back. As he tried to recover from this shock and reestablish control over the situation, Tenkahn had already cleared the distance between them. The monk's fist crashed only once into the warrior's exposed rib cage. After an explosion of blood splattered from the man's back, he fell onto his face and the battle was ended.

Tenkahn gave a bow to his fallen opponent. "Your arms hold unnatural strength, but the rest of your body is not cut to match. As long as you hold such weaknesses, you cannot fight with me."

Just as it seemed all was well, the trolls arrived.

* * * * *

Kelve had moved himself successfully to the outskirts of the battle and continued to lay into the draconic forces from his own vantage point. Using his poisons, he continued to inflict steady casualties almost unchecked, until Meriosthro noticed him. The draconic leader quickly moved through her troops and leaped at him as if from nowhere, catching the human commander off guard and delivering a fierce rake across his face.

He fell to the ground as his vision washed over with blood. He knew he had to react fast, without mistake. He reached to his belt and drew forth one of his chemical powders—praying to every god he could think of that he picked the right one—and splashed it into the cuts on his face. The dust mixed immediately with his blood, forming a temporary clot and filling the wounds. He then did his best to wash his eyes out with his own tears, stumbling to his feet and turning to his ambusher.

Meriosthro preferred to fight weaponless, using the six-inch claws on her left hand instead. But she had seen already that this human posed more of a threat than most, so she drew her bone scimitar and armed her right hand as well. She did not understand how the man had managed to slay so many of her troops, and had no desire to take the time to find out. Her foe wore armors on his chest and stomach, but her draconic claws could slice through those as easily as mere paper. She dashed forward while he was still recovering from her first strike, and attempted to use her clawed hand to disembowel him.

Kelve hopped back from her attack and gave a swift spin with his sword, chopping hard into the back of her hand. Meriosthro's skin was much thicker than most of her kind, and she only endured a minor scratch from the powerful swing. She did not allow herself to slow, lunging forward with her scimitar. She managed to catch the man's leg at the thigh, slicing the muscle, but she had left her head open. Kelve delivered a powerful wallop to the back of her skull with his sword's hilt, and she tumbled onto the ground face-first.

The former slayer continued to back away, putting a wide distance between himself and the draconic lady. She shot instantly back up to her feet, prepared to come at him in rage, when suddenly she noticed something. Her ancient dragon instincts alerted her to a life-threatening danger. From the scratch on the back of her left hand, a heated sensation was beginning to spread. In that instant she knew how Kelve had felled so many of her soldiers; she knew that she was the next to fall.

She hesitated only a few seconds, but there was no debating what she had to do. She took her sword—carved from the bones of her own people—and placed the base of it right up against the inside of her elbow. She took a deep breath to brace herself for the pain, then with a sudden rip she sliced straight through. Her forearm and favorite hand, with the claws she had worked for decades to shape just right, fell to the ground below with a splattering of her lost blood.

Her eyes brimmed with tears as her body rocked with the pain. It took a lot to seriously injure a draconic, but this wound was sufficient. She would not be able to fight against the human commander any further, not if it meant avoiding even a simple scratch from his blade.

Finally Dokitir arrived with his trolls, hitting the invading forces from the opposite side. Meriosthro knew the trolls had a reputation for being slow, but she had never suspected it would take them this long to join the fray. Now that they had arrived, however, it was quite a sight to behold.

Their approach was not slow at all. In fact, it was so sudden that Kelve was unable to alert his soldiers to the new threat. Fifty trolls were mounted on four-legged, short-haired beasts, which moved across the courtyard at a breakneck speed. Each troll held a long spear of black energy in his right hand—a technique of their perfected shadow magic—and a light purple barrier surrounded and protected the fronts and flanks of their mounts. When they reached the human troops they caused a huge amount of chaos, killing the immediate back lines and knocking many of the remaining troops to the ground from the impact. Now the invaders stood trapped in a pincer between troll cavalry and draconic infantry. They still held the advantage in numbers, but after several minutes of fighting not even a single troll was killed or dismounted, as their magic proved too much to overcome.

Kelve decided it was time for the retreat. Meriosthro had relocated herself away from him, pretending pridefully to have forgotten his presence. Since he was beyond the main skirmish, he had time to work. He took a gourd from behind his back and began pouring a large pile of black powder onto the ground. Once this was done, he soaked the powder with a purple liquid from one of his many vials.

This was one of Kelve's personal inventions. He knew only little of magic, and had known even less before encountering the travelers from Felthespar. But he had long understood that demons used the power found in nature, drawn from the very air around them to feed their spells. He had spent most of his younger life trying to find a way to disrupt this effect, and five years ago he had finally perfected it. He was not entirely sure how the chemical reaction he was about to set off worked, but he knew its result.

He backed away from the powder and struck a match, once again uttering a quick prayer. He tossed the match in the direction of the pile and immediately began to move toward the front gate of the fortress, sounding the retreat at the top of his lungs.

As his troops began to shift for the retreat, the trolls moved to cut them off. Then Kelve's powder caught the flame of the match, and there was an explosion of light. A pillar of black fire shot straight into the air, then seemed to explode into every direction, tracing eccentric spiraling patterns throughout the area. When the black fires ran through the human and draconic units it did no damage, they could not even feel the magical flames. But when it struck the trolls the reaction was instant. Their ethereal weapons and barriers collapsed, and many of them fell to the ground clutching at their eyes and ears as if stricken.

This bought the humans the distraction they needed, and after giving one final push to the already disoriented draconics they fell back and passed their leader at a run. Kelve verified Eiden's survival and escape, then stopped Tenkahn as the monk came nearby.

"Can you do something about this door?" he asked.

Tenkahn inspected the structure briefly, then gave a nod. "Go without me. I shall follow."

Kelve gave him an encouraging punch on the arm, then exited out the front gate. After the man was gone, Tenkahn began gathering energy carefully. The ether in the area had been badly disturbed by whatever Kelve had done, so the monk was forced to spend longer than usual preparing his attack, but his runes soon adapted. The draconics and trolls were already heading his way, hoping to cut him down and follow the human forces onto the plains. He completed his preparations, and swung the fiercest punch into the ground he could muster.

The entire face of the fortress' wall became engulfed with reaching stone spikes that emerged from beneath the ground. The gate's control mechanism was torn to shreds, and the iron doors that stood open were easily ripped off the hinges from which they hung. Marveling at this display of power, the Overlord's forces halted their charge, no longer so eager to catch up with the man who had summoned this fearsome spectacle.

Tenkahn hastily made his way through the open door as pieces of the stone wall began to collapse around him. He only narrowly evaded a crushing demise, but in the end he burst forth on the other side, giving a nod and a smile to the afternoon sun as he ran to regroup with Kelve.

## Chapter 17.

# Chamber of Arda

Two evenings following the discovery of the Band of Barricus, the four pilgrims took a brief respite from their travels. Cildar and Myris were putting in an intense training session, as their companions watched from where they sat near a small campfire. There was no conversation for a long time, as Detria was still wrestling with misgivings. Eventually she grew tired of the sounds of sparring and of shockwaves reverberating through the trees, so she attempted to initiate a dialogue.

"You're a commander, right?" she asked suddenly of Abaddon. He did not turn to her, as was typical. She had noticed it was rare that she seemed to gain his full attention. "Have you been so for a long time?"

"When I first arrived in Felthespar I was apprenticed under Atheme Tethen, by his own will. Not long after that, he rose to the rank of Lord Grand Councilor. Though I take no pride in it, Atheme's position of power enhanced my own status to an unfair degree. In spite of my youth and relative inexperience, I have been a Major over a decade now."

She nodded, musing inwardly that this explained the man's poor leadership style. She almost refrained from voicing the thought, but her conceit got the better of her. "So you would admit you're not really fit to lead."

"I might have once admitted such. But that has not been the case for a very long time."

She leaned back on her hands, trying to get more comfortable. "Are you so sure?"

"The quality of a leader is deceptively simple to measure. It's reflected in your followers. One must merely ask of yourself, 'Do my people believe in me?' You may not be aware of this, but technically I do not outrank either Cildar or Myris. We were, each of us, full members of the Grand Council, and Majors in the Military. Yet if I give either of them an order, even if I command them to die for me, they will do so. Do you know why?"

Detria creased her brow, genuinely bewildered by this statement. She had been convinced Abaddon's authority over the other warriors was a result of some political stature, and their sense of propriety. Discovering they were equals in Felthespar's hierarchy only cast more doubts on her understanding of their dynamic. "Because they fear you?" she answered hesitantly.

He shook his head. "Fear rules only to a point. One can find the strength to overcome fear when confronting death; especially men of their character. No, if I ordered them to die, they would obey because they trust me. I have led them many times. I have made the hard decisions a leader must make, and I never waver in my resolve. Cildar and Myris have faith that when I do something, I do so deliberately. Even when they most doubt me, they will still follow. That speaks sufficiently to the quality of my leadership."

She thought over this for a moment, getting lost in the man's words as she so often did. She shook it off, then countered, "Then why do you treat them so cruelly?"

Here Abaddon finally looked at her and raised an eyebrow. "I recall no cruelty."

"When Myris was injured by the trap, you practically insulted him! I felt awful for him."

He turned his head back to the campfire and stared complacently for a moment. "What you perceive as cruelty, others may not. When Myris asked to lead us, I did not concur in order to appease his ego. I did so because he was the best suited to the task. After his injury, that was no less true. We needed him at the lead. Trying to indicate otherwise, to pretend that we could proceed without him on point, to even acknowledge that his wounds might have rendered him somehow replaceable—that would have only diminished his esteem and highlighted his failure. He had to resume course, for all our sake. I treated him as such because he is essential. Every soldier, from the captain to the lowest ranking squire, feeds on the belief that they are valuable, that their presence makes a difference. Few make the difference of Myris Phare."

Again she felt overwhelmed by the certainty in his words and found it difficult to form an argument. She thought for another few seconds before finally reaching one. "Still, you didn't have to use such a stern tone. You could have made certain he was alright, maybe showed a hint of softness."

"You think so?" he responded. He lifted his gaze from the campfire and stared into the sky, clearly thinking over some event from his past. "There are times that a leader can show softness, friendliness. But in the midst of battle or during times of adversity, a leader must be the rock that his soldiers anchor against. My cold treatment of Myris may have angered him, I acknowledge. But that anger made him harder and gave him resolve. Internally, he swore to himself that he would not make another mistake. Because he had the resolve for this, as well as the capacity, he did not."

"So you think maybe this restored some of his confidence?"

He gave a shrug. "I cannot know for certain. With any person, it's merely a best guess for what will give them strength." He stopped there, and for a few moments they both sat in silence. Just when Detria had decided the conversation must actually be over, he spoke up once again. "What of your followers? If their faith in your leadership was truly put to a test, would the ties of loyalty bind them to you?"

She gave a sigh and bit her lower lip. "I don't really know. Maybe you're right. Maybe I accuse you of being a poor leader when I'm the real impostor. Kelve is the one who spurred me on, who handed me the mantle of leadership. I've never been sure I belong there."

"If the teacher does not believe she is a teacher, then how can her students?"

"There's a lot of difference between a teacher and a leader."

Abaddon rose to his feet and dusted himself off, giving her a polite bow. "That depends on what kind of leader you are." This said, he left camp and joined Cildar and Myris in their sparring, taking a few moments to criticize each of their techniques in turn. His tone was harsh and reprimanding, and as Detria listened she felt she should hear the same cruelty she had before, yet somehow that was no longer the case. As she watched him berate Cildar for improper use of his forearm for defense, she felt instead that she could hear a strange sort of love in his gruff voice.

She frowned as she observed, still questioning Abaddon's thoughts on the nature of leadership, as well as her own. She could see now that even if Cildar and Myris were the man's political equals and his combat superiors, they were not quite equals to his will. With his clarity of thought and impassive stubbornness guiding them, there seemed nothing the three knights could not accomplish. It was little wonder they were willing to hunt even creatures they feared may be gods. Though she still did not understand the relationships of the strange trio, she fervently hoped that she might before their time together ended.

* * * * *

Another day of traveling, another series of easily detected traps, and another hour spent weaving through underground catacombs led the group once again to an entombed monument of a bygone era.

Unlike the previous crypt, this was no shrine to a fallen human warrior. The area they had reached was a long, narrow corridor. The back of the chamber was not open here, but instead ended in a rather intimidating series of serrated blades. The blades were closely knit, mounted on steel bars that formed a latticework across the opening. It hinted that passage beyond might be possible, but was certainly not encouraged. The walls on each side were decorated with a series of tapestries, and below each tapestry sat an oddly shaped stone, each a different color and design. At the end of the chamber, below the wall of blades, a circular recess in the stone beckoned.

It did not take the group long to comprehend what the room's designer had intended. "It's a puzzle," Detria voiced the thought they all shared. "The tapestries seem to be some sort of clue."

Abaddon gave a low growl and began moving across to the circular cavity in the floor. The others followed his lead. Detria assumed he wished to look for more hints before beginning to solve the puzzle. Instead, however, he passed by the absent piece of flooring and headed stubbornly for the wall of blades, eyeing it as if it had dealt him some personal wrong.

"I hate puzzles," he announced plainly after a minute of this glaring.

Detria gave a light shrug. "I'm sure it's not that hard to solve. These places haven't been heavily guarded. I can't imagine this obstacle would be much more difficult."

As they spoke, Myris had already begun to inspect the tapestries. "The difficult determination will be what sort of clues these represent. I have seen similar puzzles designed by ancient Cainites. Admittedly we are a deceptive lot, but often it is not what the art represents which is the clue, but that which it hides. There could be subliminal messages in some sort of ancient language or number system. Given our collective unfamiliarity with ancient Arkalen tongues, this could prove to be impossible."

Cildar shook his head in disagreement. "I'm with Detria. I doubt we're dealing with anything so cryptic. It's more likely this is a simple historical puzzle. I say we just need to put the pictures in chronological order, then arrange the gems as such, and we'll figure it out."

"And yet, we are dealing with a culture that has shown a clear penchant for traps. If we solve the puzzle wrong—and in this case, 'wrong' could simply mean the obvious solution—it may very well trigger a trap that might claim our lives, or destroy the sword."

"Maybe," the paladin continued to argue, "but when we reached the final chamber for the Band of Barricus, we didn't have to deal with such a thing. When you triggered the release mechanism on the altar, the armlet was simply revealed to us."

"Even if your logic is sound, this is not yet the final room. That lies beyond the wall of blades. Moreover, it is possible the sword was considered a more valued prize, as its powers are simpler to use and more dangerous. We have come too far to risk playing into the hands of someone else's design without a greater understanding."

"Myris is right," Abaddon interjected loudly. "I am no longer content to play games as my prey continues to escape my reach."

Suddenly a soft breeze began to build in the chamber. Detria glanced around for a source, before realizing the disturbance was moving into Abaddon himself. A slim white aura had appeared around the man's body, and his clothing began to jostle as the intensifying winds seemed to be attacking him directly.

Cildar immediately recognized what was happening and took several steps forward. "Milord, don't forget your heart. I do not believe now is the time to test your full might."

"If I am yet unsuitable for combat, better to learn so here than at the hands of a Wisdom."

The Dragoon rubbed his chin for a moment, then nodded. He took Detria by the arm and gently began to lead her back toward the area with the tapestries, where Myris awaited.

"What's he going to do?" she asked in confusion at this exchange.

"I'm not certain," Cildar answered, "but if history is any indicator, probably something violent."

Abaddon stood in what appeared to be tranquility for nearly a full minute more. Then with a sudden roar he lifted his arms into the air and locked his fists together. He dove straight into the serrated blades with a sweeping blow, carving a huge path in the middle of them. He spun about and backhanded through the wall once with his right arm, then again with his left. Blades shattered at his rage and flew every direction, the shrapnel causing Detria to leap farther back with stunned profanities.

"Yep," the paladin remarked. "That's about right."

The mystic halted his fury long enough to look back and offer a nod. Behind the first wall of knives, another identical one could be made out. Already a deep slice had been carved into his cheek, and blood flowed from it freely. He did not seem to mind, and the fire in his eyes revealed his intentions all too clearly. "You three wait here," he ordered primarily in Cildar's direction. "Watch the girl, stay on your toes. When I have determined the path ahead, I'll come back for you."

He gathered himself and then dove once more into the structure. As he disappeared from sight the continued sounds of pounding and shattering steel could be heard. Soon that too faded to a dull echo in the distance.

Myris gave a slight sigh and returned to inspecting the tapestries while they waited. Detria was surprised by this display of physical might, and voiced it to Cildar.

"Did—did he just punch straight through beams of solid steel? I can't believe he's that strong."

He coughed and then stared at her with wide eyes. "Lord Abaddon? Surely you jest. His strength is legendary."

She shrugged at this reaction. "I've only seen you and Myris in battle. It seems like Abaddon's been injured ever since I've known him, with his heart condition. Which I guess, what, he's just over now?"

"I guess we never really talked about it," Cildar responded uncomfortably, "and I don't really like speaking for Lord Abaddon on the subject. But you should understand, he isn't like us. Technically speaking, I'm not sure we're actually the same race."

"What is that supposed to mean?!" she practically shouted.

"Lord Abaddon is what is known as a mystic—a native magic user. Everything you might think you understand about humans, it only roughly applies to him. You've been judging him to be weak because of the damage he sustained in Techenar, but the fact is, that injury would have killed anyone else instantly. Probably would have left their body in multiple tattered remains. Since then he's still continued to fight, and travel, and hunt, where any normal person would be resigned to years of bed rest for even the slightest hope at recovery. In spite of that, in just a few short weeks he's nearly recovered back to full condition. If I wasn't so numb to it after all these years, I'd be marveling at what a miracle he is."

She spent a moment absorbing this information. "Huh. I see. What a remarkable gift, to be able to heal at such a level." She spent another moment in thought, then added, "And truly I must admit his brute strength is impressive." She nudged the man with her elbow and gave him a wink. "But come on, be honest. If you really cut loose, like against the draconics, you and Myris could beat him in a fight, right?"

The paladin scratched the back of his head, thinking. "The two of us together? I don't think so..."

"No!" she interjected. "Not together. I meant one-on-one. With all of your magic and techniques, either you or Myris are more than a match for him, aren't you?"

He laughed earnestly. "I fear you have some grave misconceptions as to Abaddon Daemon's strength. Across much of the continent of Itrius he is known only as the Destroyer. Entire armies have retreated from his mere presence, and they were right to do so. I've never beaten him, not once in my entire life, even at my fullest power on my best day. In honesty, I don't believe I've ever even come close."

She furrowed her brow in concern and astonishment. "Oh," was her only response. Ever since witnessing Cildar and Myris battle against the draconics in their forest, she had believed the two warriors must have been the strongest alive, modest and noble in the respect they showed for those they recognized as superiors. It was a stretch of her imagination to believe that Abaddon—that anyone—could be so mighty as to defeat these two heroic knights at the same time. She could not even depict in her head how such a battle might look.

Myris soon returned from his investigation, reporting his findings to Cildar. "These tapestries are interesting. They seem to depict legendary battles of a conflict similar to the one in which we have become involved. The Wisdoms are prevalent in many of the events, but only rarely seem to participate in battle themselves. There is a human warrior of some origin, shown wearing the armlet we found in the last chamber. I can only assume he is the one named Loridican. In some paintings he seems to be allied with the Wisdoms, while in others he is prominently shown fighting against and, it seems, slaying one of them. There is also a painting depicting a ferocious battle between two dragons, a silver and a gold, and another painting where all the creatures are depicted in a huge battle royale, save the Wisdom slain by Loridican. He is absent, replaced by a fearsome beast even larger than the dragons, covered in armor and wielding a tremendous katana."

The paladin tried to absorb this barrage of information. "It's difficult to make much from it. The Wisdoms fought a great beast? It almost makes you wonder if we should be on their side. And apparently a human was, once upon a time. But when and why did Loridican switch sides? Is he the reason the Wisdoms showed us such unprovoked malice? And what about the dragons? Who did they seem aligned with?"

"I find it impossible to determine from the limited events depicted here."

Just then a chiming of metallic sounds were heard, as Abaddon emerged from the opening he had forced his way through. He was soaked in both red and black blood, and three large parallel rips had been carved through his uniform and across his chest.

Myris tilted his head at the sight of the returning man. "Were there complications?" he asked, clearly amused.

The warlord returned a nod, almost giving in to a slight smirk. "A blue dragon had taken up camp in the far room and made it his home. I tried to persuade him to leave it to us for a few moments, but he was intractable. After negotiations broke down, I was forced to send him back to Asteria."

"Excuse me, sir," Cildar nodded and pointed at Abaddon's right shoulder. One of the long knives from the wall was stuck in there, running down into his arm.

The man looked at it and responded quietly, "Right." He grabbed the blade and removed it with a sharp yank. A fountain of blood burst forth, and he placed his left hand firmly to cover the wound. "Come on, let's go," he ordered and turned back into the tunnel he had carved.

Cildar twisted his neck to one side, causing it to release a loud popping sound. "Well the good news is, I think his heart's probably okay now."

The path Abaddon had taken was deep and winding, requiring several minutes to walk. Detria took care not to get herself cut on the piles of blades lying at her feet, though the Felthespari seemed to take no notice. When they emerged on the other side, their attention was immediately seized by the room's most prominent decoration.

This new room was a semi-circular chamber with vast balconies of seats rising all along the curved walls. In the back, at the furthest point of the circular perimeter, a giant statue had been erected. It was well over twenty feet tall, and resembled a knight decorated in full plate mail, with a large helmet that resembled the head of a dragon. The armor covered two massive arms, but the statue also had almost a dozen other pairs of arms of varying sizes coming from the torso. Each of these hands held a sword of appropriate size. In addition, over a hundred swords were stabbed through the mighty stone figure. The arms, legs, torso, even the creature's head were all pierced repeatedly by swords, daggers, and sabers of all sizes and designs.

Detria took her eyes from the statue long enough to glance to her left. There, the bruised and ripped body of a large blue dragon sat lifeless. She stared at it open-mouthed, more disturbed by its presence than the statue. Try as she might, she could not draw up the mental image of a mere man entering combat with a dragon of such size and emerging not only victorious, but virtually unharmed. Staring at this evidence, she began to place more stock in Cildar's description of the strength of Itrius' Destroyer.

Abaddon motioned for Myris to take the lead, and the Cain

warrior moved to the fore. They made their way across the room slowly, Myris sniffing for traps. There were none to be found. As in the previous tomb, this final room was clean of deception.

When they reached the statue at the back, Detria stared at it in admiration as Abaddon attempted to make out some text inscribed on a block at its feet. He finally gave up on the endeavor and turned to her.

"Can you read this text, as you did the last?"

She stared at him for several seconds before responding. He seemed so normal, so small. She had seen him bleed. She had seen him bedridden. She knew he was just a man. How could he hold such inhuman power? How could he be a dragon in a man's flesh?

She dropped the thought and gave him a slow nod. "I think so. Let me take a look." She studied the words for only a few moments before she began to translate. "Here fell the Tyrant, he who was called Gilanirus. Slain only by an alliance of the three worlds, the Lord of Gehenna sought to rule all with his might. Seek him not, for he is hidden beyond the reach of the mighty."

Cildar stepped forward and gave the statue a light punch on the knee. It did not budge from the impact, nor did the frame shake. "It's solidly built, at least. Is that all it says? What about the weapon that's supposed to be here? Are we at the wrong place again?"

Abaddon shook his head, answering in Detria's stead. "I don't think so. I sense some object of power nearby. Foreign power." He reached up and placed a hand on the shin of the giant leg, focusing his energy for a few moments. It took a while for his spell to take effect, but when it did the entire statue lit up with a bright red glow, as well as the swords buried in its frame. His face turned into a sour grimace. "Oh, someone just wants to ruin my day," he exclaimed in frustration.

Myris chuckled at the predicament they were in. He summed up the situation with a sardonic smile. "Given a hundred swords frozen in stone, how do you find the one which can cut through anything?"

## Chapter 18.

# Carved into Cold Steel

Tessena was not happy with the results of the first battle. Not only had the invaders managed to escape with negligible casualties, but the front gate had been damaged and now stood wide open, welcoming the next assault. Additionally, Gariso had sustained serious harm, his weapon had been shattered, and the Overlord's newest general had lost her left arm.

The other generals had been assembled into the main courtyard, forced to look upon the site of their humiliation. Tessena herself lingered back, just within the cooled stone hallway of the main keep, staring outside to where the gathering of demons awaited her. Her demons, she told herself. Her subordinates, the emissaries of her will. They feared her. They respected her. They would hear her.

It was a mantra she had to repeat to herself often. The glove resting on her left hand was a legendary artifact, and while it made her dangerous far beyond any normal human, it offered no protection. For most of the demonspawn under her command, she would make an easy kill. She had only survived this long through a combination of skill and luck and, eventually, the Overlord's own grace. She had to maintain her composure, to maintain her arrogance, to maintain her authority. But as she did so against demons as ferocious as the other Generals of the Overlord, she knew she also courted death.

Even in this she found the thrill of adrenaline, then the rush granted in rising above the constant threats upon her life. Tessena had learned to master these feelings, for both the good and the evils they stirred within her. A few more seconds of meditation and her uncertainty was gone, replaced only with bitterness at her army's—*her* army's—defeat. With her jaw now set in iron she headed down the hall, the setting sun reflected within her glinting eyes.

Upon reaching the courtyard she paced for a few moments about the clump of generals standing there awkwardly. They knew a chastising was in order, and they knew they had no choice but to take it. She drank in this heaviness that permeated the air, letting it stoke the fires of her ego. When she felt once more fully the First General to the Overlord, she began.

"From what we've seen," she spat at them in contempt, "we're only fighting five hundred humans. Yet somehow, you mighty demons managed to get yourselves spanked. We all know just how dangerous humanity can be. There are hundreds of thousands of them across Arkalen, and gathered together they are an army we cannot overcome. Some of you are quivering in your boots already, so fearful that our day of reckoning is upon us. But let me be perfectly clear: this is no reckoning. This is a slap in the face, intended to insult, not injure. Five hundred mortal warriors is not the blight that is going to end the rule of the Overlord. Let's go ahead and dismiss that thought from the minds of your underlings, with utmost finality. Now, assuming that's their actual numbers and they're not still hiding reinforcements, then what are ours? Troop counts!"

Kogonbo was the quickest to answer. "At last ranks check, we were running around thirty ogres. Bear in mind, of course, that my two sentries were lost in this previous battle."

"It's not forgotten," she snapped back, then shifted her attention to the next general. "Fenrir?"

"Five hundred and fifty of the lesser demonspawn," the wolfen creature answered disinterestedly while cleaning his teeth. "But considering they're not much more useful than our human carpenters in real combat, you might want to only count half of them."

Tessena ignored the comment about the human forces with

difficulty and gave a nod to Dokitir in turn.

"A hundred trolls. But you know we work best mounted, and our stables are only up to maybe fifty."

"Then fifty of you will have to learn to work with what you have, or serve as meat shields. Meriosthro already reported to me that we have about two hundred and fifty draconics remaining. I checked for myself and there are about fifty chimeras available, if we can get the damned beasts to cooperate. There are also four hundred human troops, most of whom are poorly trained. I'd rather not throw them onto the battlefield unless it becomes an absolute necessity. In fact, I want to reroute resources to protecting them, keeping them away from the battle lines at all times. They're more useful maintaining the keep than they are as a pile of dead, especially considering the structural damage we've already sustained. Kaltheria, what of your kind?"

The shadow wight stepped from the protective shade of the castle walls with an aggravated hiss. She could abide the sun, but that did not mean she enjoyed being out in the daylight. "The Overlord has gathered less than a hundred nightspawn. We are few, but we make a better fighting force than a measly four hundred humans, or five hundred werebeasts."

Tessena gave a nod, conceding the point. "And what of the acolytes?"

"The Robed Ones?" Kaltheria responded. "There are no more than two dozen of them. But they're of no use at all in combat. The Overlord has even forbidden the notion."

Tessena barked angrily at this misunderstanding. "I know the Robed Ones do not fight, moron! I wish to know what they told you when I sent you to them this morning."

Slowly, the wight faded from view. The human general looked around, then heard a cold whisper originate from above her shoulder. "You would do well to hold your temper with me, womanling. You may be feared by others, but that gloved hand of yours cannot kill me when it cannot touch me." Kaltheria then reappeared where she had been previously standing, answering casually, "Lord Shote will not be ready for another month, at best. His recovery must be handled properly."

The First General was unmoved by Kaltheria's threat. The two led with a similar style—a lot of fear and spectacle, but only rarely resorting to actions that might compromise the delicate balance of power. Tessena might even have respected the shadowy commander, had she not found nightspawn so overwhelmingly creepy.

She summed the numbers quickly in her head. "So we stand at a good fifteen hundred troops. We should be able to handle these humans with those numbers. I don't want to take chances to play games, though, especially with our front door standing open. They're surely tired from today's fight. We won't allow them to recover tonight. Kaltheria, prepare fifty of your nightspawn for an attack. I'll gather the chimeras myself. Those of you who fought today, take this time to rest. If we keep our forces in rotation, we should wear these fools down before this has become an earnest war."

Her orders given, she turned and stormed to the chimeras' quarters without awaiting reply. As soon as she reached the front door of the large barracks, it slammed open and a mighty creature stepped into her path. It had the body of a lion, with the head and wings of an eagle. It was a pure griffin, one of the rarest variants of chimera. His name was Ontarshiss, and he served as General of the Chimera Forces.

"What do you come here for, General?" the beast asked rudely. "I don't believe we have business. You know I don't like unannounced visits."

After her clash with Kaltheria, Tessena was not in the mood for further disrespect. She unwrapped a slim ribbon from her left fist and immediately her blue glove lit up with a harsh light. She pointed her open palm forward at Ontarshiss and commanded, "Unless you want to test my rule, show me the proper respect as your superior officer."

The noble beast stared at the glowing hand for a moment, then gave a bow of his feathered head. "What are you orders, mistress?"

"Gather your chimeras. We have a foe to strike. Is Manticore prepared?"

"He will still not speak." The golden bird cocked its head to the side and gave her a funny look. "Perhaps you'd like to meet with him? Show him your hand?"

"Just get the others ready," she spat.

Ontarshiss backed into the building, using his front claws to slam the door shut in Tessena's face. She took a deep breath, satisfied in her day's performance and now prepared for the attack that would come that night.

* * * * *

Abaddon sat back staring coldly at the statue before him, displeased that his efforts to avoid such games had been denied. Cildar and Myris had inspected the monument for over half an hour, exchanging and discarding ideas. Cildar had attempted to remove one of the embedded swords, and it had required all of his strength, with maximum grey magic blessings. Once finally removed, the edge of the blade was jagged and ruined, and he could not insert it back into its groove.

As the two soldiers continued their inspection, Detria moved to Abaddon's side and had a seat on the floor next to him. She could not predict his reaction to any comments she might make, so she went with the innocent, "So what do you think?"

His response was a pensive one. "The entire structure is definitely charged with Gehennite energy. However, I think it's mostly runoff. If this was Asterian magic and I were a more expert mage, or a devilspawn who knew how to work Gehennite ether, then perhaps I could pick out which area is the most saturated. As it is, we have no way of doing so."

"There's always the brute force option. Remove every sword, try to cut something with it, see how it does."

"I also debated having the four of us each draw two swords at a time and attempt to fight with them, seeing which blades cut other blades. However, by my count there are a hundred and thirty nine swords in that statue. As difficult as they are to remove, it could take a long time. Time is not on our side right now. The Wisdoms already have a head start measured in weeks. Every minute left to their own devices, I grow more anxious."

"We could try melting all of the other swords at once and hope the magic one survives. I assume Myris could manage such a spell?"

"Tempting, but we cannot guarantee that just because the sword is enchanted it has sufficiently enhanced durability. It might only be as strong as simple steel, with its blessing concentrated on the nature of the cutting edge. In which case, we could destroy it and never be the wiser. Unfortunately, I believe that very outcome may be the intent behind this design. A security mechanism to prevent the unworthy, those who rely solely on violent force, from gaining the power of the sword."

At this moment, Cildar successfully drew a second weapon from the statue. He stared at it in annoyance, tired from straining his muscles even under enhanced conditions, and gave it a firm swing against the statue's right leg. The blade shattered, snapping off and zipping across the room. Detria was startled by this, but the shrapnel had flown harmlessly off into the distance.

This incident seemed to renew Abaddon's interest. He quickly rose to his feet and moved to the statue, viciously drawing another sword and cracking it against the opposite leg. Again the sword shattered and the length buzzed into the shadows.

"The statue itself is the key," he announced. "It's made of a material too powerful for these swords to cut. Do you realize what that means?"

The paladin dropped into thought, but Myris slid forward and offered the answer. "The swords could not have been inserted into the statue after it was built."

Cildar snapped, catching up to them. "That's why the blades are ruined. The statue was molded around them."

"Except for the Arda!" Detria exclaimed in excitement.

Abaddon gave a nod. "Arda would have been inserted after, to protect the sword from sustaining damage or becoming stuck. The rest of these blades are bonded to the structure soundly, but Arda merely rests in a stone sheath."

Detria's excitement faded and she scratched the back of her head. "That's good and all, but it doesn't give us a clue as to how we determine which one is Arda more quickly."

"To the contrary," the big man responded. He held out his right fist and gripped his wrist firmly with his opposing hand, focusing his power tightly around the fist. After a few seconds of concentration, a visible stream of air could be seen coiling around his arm. Cildar and Myris took several steps away from the statue, easily guessing at what came next. "If Arda was inserted after," Abaddon continued, closing his eyes as he channeled ether, "it means the sword's mystical properties were used to cut through the statue and it will be the easiest to remove. It also means the statue has but a single weak spot in its structural integrity. Myris, adjust your vision, stay sharp."

The Cain raised two fingers in front of his face, uttering a strange language under his breath. "Diannar tolok," he chanted with a rich tone to his voice, and his eyes became lit with a powerful yellow light. Detria furrowed her brow, still perplexed as to their new plan.

"Tremoring Fist," the mystic exclaimed. He leaped ten feet into the air and gave a ferocious punch to the belly of the statue. The entire chamber floor began to shake violently at this impact. A startled Detria seized onto Cildar's shoulder in order to hold her balance. The quake soon settled, and Abaddon returned to the ground with a light thud. He looked to Myris, awaiting his analysis.

"There's a crack," the man soon announced. "Up there, near the right shoulder."

"Then that's our sword." Abaddon gave a nod, and the nimble Cain warrior leaped up the side of the statue, using the protruding hilts for steps.

Myris soon seized the hilt of the sword in question. It was stabbed perpendicular to the line of the floor, running through the statue's chest toward the right leg. He began to pull in an attempt to free it. As Abaddon had predicted, the weapon slid easily, unlike the previous ones. Myris drew until two feet of steel was visible, then began to reach a hand out to grab onto the blade. Just before his fingers closed he hesitated and pulled away. If this sword could truly slice anything, it would surely have no trouble with human flesh.

He paused and considered his options. With his awkward positioning, poised on two protruding hilts, it was impossible for him to draw the blade any further, but it had not yet come loose from the statue. He took note of the fact that the sword was like a katana, with one cutting edge. This edge was facing him, pointed toward the entrance of the chamber. He gave a shrug and seized the hilt with both hands, and then leaped directly back away from the statue.

His idea worked. The sword sliced without resistance through the material encasing it, coming free into his hands. As he worked to reposition it, though, he found himself with a problem. The sword, from hilt to tip, was over nine feet long. He panicked during his fall, and once certain the weapon was free of the statue he gave it a shove and separated himself from it. He used a Cainite warding spell to slow his descent at the last moment, landing lightly enough to not sustain injury, as the giant length of steel crashed onto the ground in front of him.

Abaddon wasted no time, retrieving the weapon and lifting it. The hilt was of average size for a single-edged sword, approximately a foot in length. The Arda was crafted in every way as if it were a standard katana, except for the excessively long blade. He raised it high over his head, the blade parallel to the ground, and inspected it.

"This is ridiculous," he voiced aloud, "and I say that as the man who wielded Kargaroth for nine years."

He turned his new weapon on the statue, delivering a flurry of rapid slashes. Never once did the blade hesitate in its bite, even against the monument that had previously shown itself nigh indestructible. As a pile of metal rubble came crashing to the ground, Abaddon carefully tucked the Arda into a leather chamber on the back his belt. With a sharp tug he twisted it around, adjusting the tube until the tip of the blade pointed at the ceiling, its hilt resting directly behind his left thigh. He held onto it with his left hand so it did not fall, then turned to the rest of the party.

"The blade's bite is as true as in legend, it would seem. No scabbard will bind it, so I'll have to design a clip to hold it in place. For now, let's get out of here and make camp."

* * * * *

The group made camp not far from the cavern's opening and spent the next couple of hours allowing Abaddon to work on a holding mechanism for Arda. He had collected a few parts from Cildar and Myris, including a small broken dagger he used to craft spare metal connectors. He had made good progress and the device was largely working, allowing him to quickly sheathe and unsheathe the sword from his back without much risk. Still he continued to fine-tune his invention, attempting to make the clip rotate freely between specific angles without going further.

The other Felthespari had grown bored and moved to scout the area, looking to renew their supplies of food and water with any resources they might find in the region. Detria had considered joining them, as she knew her own survival skills and familiarity with Arkalen's plant and wildlife would have been an asset. Instead she had elected to remain behind and observe Abaddon's work.

She spent the first hour of his labor in silence, watching his craftsmanship and impressed by his ability to create and work with such small gears with nothing more than the scant supplies in his possession. He gave her a brief explanation of the mechanical prowess of Felthespar, and attempted to explain to her some of the basic principles he utilized, but she only half listened.

The truth was that she had been struck by Cildar's earlier words about this man called 'Destroyer', and his unworldly power. She wished to attribute such an assessment to the paladin's flair for the dramatic, but her vision was haunted by the corpse of a blue dragon, seemingly murdered by this man in a matter of mere minutes. Detria had spent most of her time in Abaddon's presence writing him off as a spoiled noble, incapable of serving adequately over the two remarkable Lords in his company. She realized now that she had held the flimsiest of reasons to do so, and had allowed prejudice against him to flower too easily.

She replayed previous conversations with him, some from their early travels, some more recent. Abaddon was a difficult man to understand, and this made him difficult for her to like. As the events of the day had served to convince her that he was something entirely other than she had believed, everything he said was now painted in a different light. She found herself desiring more conversation with him, so that perhaps she might resolve her conflicting impressions.

"Cildar tells me you're strong," she opened weakly, unsure how to enter the conversation. "Stronger than him and Myris put together."

"Easily," he answered.

She repressed an immediate sigh of disgust. Her attempts to make amends were off to a poor start. She bit her lip and turned away slightly, trying to think of a better way to approach the discussion.

He looked up at her and raised an eyebrow, briefly pausing his work on the device in his hands. "You're annoyed."

"No," she argued. "I mean, you're just agreeing with what Cildar said. Why would I be annoyed over that?"

"Yet you are, nonetheless. Your emotions have left a clear mark on the currents around you."

She blushed and rose to her feet, fiddling her hands nervously. "What are you saying? You can read my thoughts?"

"I'm uncertain if such a thing is possible. If it is, I don't have my skills honed to that level. I can only pick up impulses, occasional flashes of strong emotion. It's not unlike how a wolf might smell your fear, or how an emotionally perceptive person might closely read the movements of your face. You're clearly irritated with me. It must be substantial, if I'm able to detect it."

"Alright, fine! I'm frustrated! I've tried to get along with you. I really have. But you can't just talk like a normal person! It's like you think there's no need to consider your words more carefully. I'm sure where you come from you're an accomplished man who's shown a great deal of respect, but you do absolutely nothing to endear yourself to anyone around you. You are so impossibly conceited and sometimes I hate you for it!" She suddenly heard her own words, and covered her mouth with her hands as tears began to brim in her eyes. Abaddon continued to stare at her evenly, offering no reaction to her outburst. "I'm so sorry," she stammered, "I didn't—"

"Stop," he suddenly silenced her. "I don't wish to hear insincere apologies. I much prefer your honest admonishment." He turned back to the device in his hands, resuming his work. "You're not wrong about me. Do you know what they call me back home?"

She moved to one of the nearby rocks and took a slow seat. "The Destroyer. Cildar told me. That's a pretty dark mantle to wear, even for someone as unsociable as you."

"Death is where I excel in life. There was a time in my youth that I might have become a better man. You might even have liked me, had we met under different circumstances. But that's not the path I took, and I stopped trying to recapture it long ago. Instead I invest myself ever deeper into war and conflict, where the man that I am can thrive."

"Until you're dead," she added. "That's what you said before, right? Until you achieve your 'glorious death'. Isn't living your life already obsessed with your own death an empty endeavor?"

"I don't expect you to understand. I appreciate your assistance on our quest, but our time together has come to an end. I have Wisdoms to hunt, and unfortunately I have neither the time nor the disposition to convince you to like me."

Detria sat in silence for nearly a minute, watching the man's hands at work. "But I want to," she finally replied. His fingers ceased moving once again and he glanced up. "Your men love you. Cildar and Myris. They're amazing. I've met many prestigious warriors from living among the Devilslayers, but never anyone like those two. You're right, in what you said before—they would follow any order you gave them. They would march on the gates of hell at your command, without so much as a doubt." She leaned forward and rested her chin on her hands. "I want to understand this about you. I want to know what strength of character it takes to inspire men like them."

"Only a moment ago you hated me for my conceit."

She blushed. "Maybe I still do. Maybe because I fear it reminds me of my own weakness."

To her shock, he gave a half-smile in response to this. He sat down the device he was working on, continuing to stare at it as he spoke. When his words came, their gentleness shocked her. "I despise weakness, Detria Alsen. I have had my skin consumed by the flames of dragons. I have been betrayed by the frailty of flesh, and had my very freewill robbed from me. I have been broken down by..." he paused, choosing the next word carefully, "monsters. I have suffered violations you cannot imagine." He looked to her, and she almost thought she saw a hint of tenderness in his normally cold eyes. "I cannot let the weakness win. Enduring is all I have left. It's all I have done for so long, and it's the only way I know to teach my knights the path forward."

"Well," she responded quietly, "that is truly a defiant way to live. If nothing else, perhaps I understand you a little better now." She paused, then shook her head slowly. "But I cannot be that cynical of a leader. I respect your approach, but just as you cannot change who you are, neither can I change myself. I still believe in the march toward the light. As Devilslayers, we were trained to build a better world. Though I may no longer follow them, I still follow that creed. You may lead in your way, ever preparing to carry your people through the worst our world has to offer. But I still wish to lead mine toward the best. Simply enduring is not enough."

He stared at her thoughtfully for a moment. "There is more strength within you than you let on. Perhaps you are right about me. Perhaps the path I walk is too dark, too cynical. Perhaps one day, I will follow yours instead." His tone remained calm and serious, and Detria blushed so hard at the sincere compliment that she could not breathe. He offered nothing further, but instead returned to his work. As she sat in stunned silence, Cildar and Myris suddenly returned with the spoils of their search, in good spirits. She soon found herself drawn into conversation with the two men, but her thoughts never fully turned from their brooding leader.

Within another half an hour Abaddon completed his mechanism for Arda. By pointing the massive blade at the sky, he minimized the difficulty the sword posed to carry. When he was finally satisfied with his apparatus, he gave out fresh orders.

"Now we test this thing. We'll find our first Wisdom and kill it as a show of strength. Hopefully this will draw the attention of the others, possibly buying us the ability to negotiate with them and find out what they want." Myris nodded in eager agreement, as Cildar slammed his fists together in anticipation. Abaddon held up a hand, stifling their celebration. "Not so fast. There is the small matter of Detria."

The woman looked back and forth to them, unsure what he meant. "Me?"

"We promised you we would only detain you as far as Arda itself," he explained. "Now one of us must see to it that you are safely returned home."

Hearing this, Myris bowed his head slightly. "Lord Abaddon, I will escort her. Cildar's services would be more suited for a battle with these titans."

The warlord waved this idea off. "Not this time. Cildar, you will guide Detria home. The Cainite comes with me."

"But sir!" the Dragoon began his objection.

"My decision is made. Besides, isn't it part of your paladin's oath to help damsels in distress, or something to that effect?"

He gave a huff and crossed his arms. "I think you're confusing me with a fairy tale. But I'll do as you command." He turned and gave a deep bow to Detria. "Forgive me, madam, it's not your company I regret. It's the enticing scent of upcoming battle that makes me eager."

She gave a smile. "Don't worry about me. I guided us here, I know the way back. You three go on and I'll find my own way. I'm not some weak girl who needs watched after, if you'll remember our last fight."

Cildar hesitated, seeming to consider this offer. His nobility got the better of him, and he answered, "No, Lord Abaddon is right. With creatures like the Wisdoms about, none of us should be traveling alone. It's not a matter of protecting the weak. Two sets of eyes and ears serve as a more complete defense."

After a few more moments of discussion everyone was convinced this was the right course. Just before they left, Detria reached up and gave Abaddon a hug around the neck. "Thank you for your words. Please, don't lose your life on your adventures." She pulled back and gave him a smile. "I'm only just beginning to get used to your gloomy disposition."

He gave her a gentle smile in return. "Then for you, I shall offset my plans to die in a haze of glory for a time. I promise you will see me again."

She and Cildar headed on their way, and the remaining knights watched them leave. When they were finally gone, Abaddon turned to Myris with a nod.

"Shall we hunt Wisdoms, then?"

The Cain echoed the nod, and the two dashed rapidly on their way.

## Chapter 19.

# On Wings of the Night

As the Devilslayer outcasts recovered from battle in the light of the setting sun, their commanders sat around a campfire drinking a bottle of wine. Kelve had declared it a rare occasion for celebration. The first battle had gone well, and he wished to capitalize on the victory to keep morale soaring. While the commanders appeared to be laughing it up and partying alongside everyone else, they were actually engaged in deep discussion on the upcoming battles.

Kelve spoke on behalf of his lieutenants. There were several present, but they remained quiet, placing confidence in him as their representative. "So let's see if I understand this," he was currently saying, "the Overlord had gathered somewhere over two thousand troops. Given the ranks of shadow wights, cyclopes, chimeras and the like, he had a force that could have damaged even the Devilslayers. Then Tenkahn's men attacked. Between the ten of them they killed over half of this army."

"Demonspawn pose little threat to my order when we are at our full strength," the surviving monk added.

Kelve gave a nod. "Then this 'Shote' got involved. The monks were defeated, the Overlord was spared further losses, but Shote himself was killed."

"Maybe," Eiden interjected. "Shote's death was never confirmed to the servants. I don't know if this was just to keep up appearances, or if he actually survives."

"Alright. So Shote may or may not be dead. In either case, the Overlord seems to have added the draconics to his forces. That, in addition to his usual influx of new recruits, has swelled his numbers back up to somewhere near fourteen hundred by our estimations." No one seemed to think of anything further to add, so he proceeded to the next topic. "Eiden, tell me about the trolls, and those beasts they were riding."

"They're called horses. When the Overlord captured the eastern human lands here, we had domesticated some of the wild beasts and trained them to work as mounts. The Overlord seized the most magnificent of the creatures and decided to keep them for his own purposes. Eventually, when the trolls joined, the Overlord gave them reign over the stables in order to offset their lack of mobility. Trolls are very resilient and difficult to kill, and they're effective casters. They work well as either short- or long-range troops."

Kelve leaned back and rubbed his eyes, not willing to delve any further into the topic. "What's our next move? We've got the gate held open, so hopefully we've helped to eliminate the advantage of the walls."

"Somewhat," Tenkahn rebutted, "but they can always stick three or four ogres in the entryway to block our path. That serves as effective a barricade as any."

"I've thought over that," Kelve replied. "I think given the herbs I currently have available, I could whip up enough ogre-slaying poison to coat fifty arrows or so. We only have ten or eleven capable archers, though. There's a good chance that if the trolls notice our archers bringing ogres down, they'll go after them. There's not a lot I can do to protect us against demon magic. That interrupt effect I used today requires a very rare flower's pollen, and after one use my reserves are tapped."

"It is a difficult issue," the monk agreed. "We are outmatched in both range and brute strength. They have but a few trolls, and even fewer ogres. We could defeat those forces if we could give them focused attention, but the Overlord also has ground forces sufficient to hold our warriors in check while his ogres and trolls pick us off. By any analysis, it seems we will need to sit back and hold them at siege."

"That won't be easy," Eiden argued. "In addition to the three visible main gates on each side, there are exits along the mountains behind the keep, underground tunnels that wind their way out. I've never seen one of them myself, since they fell outside of the range of my maintenance zones. But I know that the Overlord's acolytes use them to gather fresh supplies and food stores when needed."

Kelve shook his head at this news. "And we don't have a large enough force to spread around the castle and make certain they don't use these exits. If we had our own mages we could place them there to attack anyone who tried to leave, but as things stand..."

The conversation continued in this manner for a few more hours. When the night sky was beginning to reach its deepest pall, Kelve waved off further debate and everyone began to depart for their tents. Not even a minute after this, a series of startled cries began to arise from within the camp. The first few noises were either muffled or incomprehensible, but then one rang out that Kelve understood all too well.

"Nightspawn!"

He and Tenkahn reacted fast, attempting to charge to the sounds of the disturbance. This soon proved impossible, as cries and the sound of scuffles were already coming from every direction. Kelve quickly surmised what had happened—the creatures had already spread themselves deep throughout the camp and were attacking at random.

"Everyone, break camp, pull back!" he ordered, turning about to shout at various parts of the army. "Pull back! Toward the Overlord's keep!"

His people responded quickly, organizing and backing carefully through the night. Kelve dashed into his tent and drew forth a large sack of chemicals, then returned outside. Once he was certain a majority of his soldiers had gone beyond the commander's campfire, he threw the bag of chemicals onto it.

The reaction was a slow one. The flames gradually rose and began to shift in color, fading until they were a bright yellow.

Once the fire had become a pillar nearly ten feet high, the cries piercing the night began to change into deep banshee wails. The attacking nightspawn lost their stealth cloaks and become visible, their skin blistering from artificial solar energy. Kelve's forces immediately launched their counterattack.

But victory was not to be so easily purchased this night. Kelve froze in place as he began to distinguish a series of cries originating from the skies themselves. He tried to decipher this new disturbance, but it was Eiden who was first to recognize the threat.

"Chimeras!" the boy warned. "They've unleashed the chimeras!"

Dozens of large winged creatures began to drop from the sky. They were bigger than horses, with the bodies of either lions or bears. Most had anywhere from two to five heads, sometimes of a variety of animals. Their wings were also different from one creature to the next, some resembling the feathery wings of an eagle, the leathery arms of a bat, or the clear blades of a dragonfly. One of the first to land charged straight at Kelve, tucking leathery wings around its body as protection. The head of an eagle sat between the heads of a lion and a goat, and the long necks of two giant snakes grew from the chest, writhing and snapping at their prey.

Kelve drew his sabers and dove into the beast, immediately slicing both snake heads off in a single swipe, then dodging around his assailant and stabbing deep into its stomach through the leather shielding. He dislodged his blade and moved a few steps away, only to find the beast charging him eagerly once more. Either his poisons had no effect on this particular monster, or a complex immune system allowed it to resist longer than most.

The chimera rushed him swinging claws and three sets of fangs. He was not perturbed, easily outmaneuvering the onslaught. He used the cutlass to his left to block the claws and sidestepped the nipping maws. Patiently he sought his opening, then with a swift lash severed the goat-like head.

Though it was not the central head, the chimera crashed to its knee and slipped into a brief paralysis. As it tried to regain its stance and recover from decapitation, Kelve wasted no time. Two more quick slashes, and the chimera had gone from five heads to none. The human commander located his lieutenants and bade them to spread word through the troops, alerting all that removing one of the chimeras' heads would stun them momentarily. Those trained as Devilslayers knew to never allow an opening such as this go to waste.

The battle continued in an unstable manner. The lack of arms made it difficult for the chimeras to guard their necks, so the humans were occasionally able to score a decapitation and bring a beast down. Still, each chimera troop proved to be a match for five or even ten soldiers, and the nightspawn continued to wreak havoc in the background while the humans were distracted by the larger creatures.

Once Kelve was confident in his troop's ability to handle themselves, he set himself apart and began to hunt. He knew that organized nightspawn were invariably tied to a single leader, usually a shadow wight or lich with stronger will than the rest. If he could find and kill the leader, its death would resonate throughout the ranks. With luck, they might scatter and abandon their cause. He worked his way cautiously through waves of the chimeras, until finally one fixated on him and would not be dissuaded. This creature was a bit different than its kin, and had two heads of a giant lizard. Kelve did his best to slice through the scaly necks, but he could not pierce the rough hide.

The beast lunged forward and latched onto his left arm and shoulder with one of its mouths. His armor spared his life, but he screamed as fangs tore deep into his flesh and scratched at the bones underneath. The other neck reared back and braced for a strike, aiming to rip his head cleanly off.

The former Devilslayer thought fast, dropping the saber in his free hand and reaching quickly to his belt. He drew a thin vial and tossed it into the lizard's open mouth. The serpentine head instinctively bit down on the vial, shattering the fragile glass. As soon as the chemical there mixed with saliva, it expanded into a thick foam, filling the creature's maw and leaving it disoriented. Kelve drew a dagger from his hip and thrust it into the open eye of the head still latched onto him. The lizard's fangs released and tore away, causing the man to collapse in dizzying pain. He reached to his belt and swiftly gave himself an inoculation, increasing his recovery rate and dulling the pain, but he would not have the strength to fight for another few moments.

Fortunately he was not abandoned. As the one-eyed head sought to bite into him once more, Tenkahn dashed between the two combatants and knocked the searching fangs away. He turned and delivered a powerful blow to the creature's chest, and Kelve watched in awe as the chimera's own skeletal structure compressed and snapped within it. The monk then swung out with his left hand, mercilessly tearing off the two heads and leaving the crippled body lifeless.

As the injured commander recovered and rose to his feet, Tenkahn alerted him to the situation at hand. "We stand to win this, but by the time we do we will have lost half of our forces. We need to go for their commanders and rout them quickly. There's one over there, and the other is there." He pointed in turn to each of the Overlord's generals. One was a slim human female, the other a shimmering nightspawn with only a vague shadow of humanity remaining. "Choose your poison, poison-master."

Kelve took a deep breath and steadied himself. He ran a smooth cream over his chest, patching his wounds for the time being. "I want the nightspawn. I know how to deal with her kind. The human general is all yours, but be wary. I'm certain she wouldn't be out here with this crew unless she was dangerous on her own merit."

They exchanged a nod, then split to deal with their respective foes.

Tenkahn moved to intercept Tessena. She was rallying the chimeras in an attempt to coordinate them to defend one another, but having little success controlling the stubborn beasts. Just before the Monk of Tria reached her location, he bore witness to a terrible sight. Tessena lashed out with her left hand and seized one of Kelve's soldiers by the throat. Her glove lit up, and a shadowy rune structure traced its way across the man's skin. It took only a second, then his entire body exploded into black dust and drifted away on the wind.

For one of the few instances in his vast life, Tenkahn hesitated to proceed. He had seen this power before, and it was a match for his own. There was a real chance that he could die here, and the Monks of Tria would be no more. It was his sworn duty to prevent this eventuality above all other things.

Then he saw Eiden charge forward to attack the woman. He found himself shocked by the boy's lack of self-preservation. Kelve had warned Eiden several times how important his life was, and that he was to avoid the thick of these battles. In spite of himself, Tenkahn hesitated no longer and moved to the fray.

Tessena used her left hand to catch a spear that Eiden attempted to use against her. The weapon exploded almost instantly into dust, then she reached forward to end the insolent boy. Tenkahn intercepted them barely in time, and the gloved hand latched instead onto the monk's forearm. There was a crackle of magics colliding, then a small explosion separated the warriors.

Tessena and Tenkahn swiftly recovered their feet, but the younger man remained on the ground. The monk decided Eiden was probably safer this way, so he did not draw attention to him. Instead he quickly spoke to the Overlord's general in order to hold her interest.

"I know this power. That is a Hand of Ramsa."

She responded with a flirtatious smile. "Yes. An ironic gift from the so-called God of Kindness. The hand kills any foe without causing pain. But I only care about the part where it 'kills any foe'."

"You are certainly no servant of the God of Kindness."

"Well observed. During some of the Overlord's early raids, I killed a village of the god's servants. This was the last of their precious divine artifacts they had to their name, but they were too noble to use it against me. It was this pathetic morality that cost them all their lives."

Tenkahn slowly brought his fists together in front of him and gave a bow. "My power is also of divine origins. We shall see today whose blessing is mightier: Tria, or Ramsa.

The opponents stared each other down for only a second more, then dashed forward wildly. Tenkahn stopped just a few feet short and punched the ground, using his Tremoring Fist to bring an explosion of stone against the girl. Tessena, in response, reached out with her left hand and touched the rock wall threatening her. It disintegrated instantly, and with a nimble dash she closed in on her foe and clutched his bare chest.

In just that quick of a moment, there was nothing further Tenkahn could do. The powers of the glove merged with the energy of his runes, and a battle of divine magics began. At first he believed he could weather the attack, but gradually he felt his strength depleting. Soon he noticed a slim line of black runes beginning to spread from his chest. He knew that once they had encircled his entire body, he would be lost to this world.

Across the battlefield, Kelve's battle with Kaltheria had proved to be an equally brief affair. Exchanging few words with the wisp, he had launched his assault with blades and vigor. The nightspawn had not been fazed by these blows, and unleashed powerful fear spells against him in retaliation. Kelve had already inoculated himself against these effects, so he remained undaunted. He reached behind his back and drew an intricate leather glove, placing it over his right hand. He then renewed his attack with only the sword in his left. When he swung this new glove, it released a concentrated powder from his fingertips. This powder turned into fire each time it came into contact with the nightspawn's skin, and for a moment it seemed as though he had Kaltheria on the run.

Then the wight vanished from view. Kelve did his best to anticipate the next attack, but his efforts were in vain. Kaltheria appeared behind him and placed her spectral hands straight through his back. He screamed as a paralyzing cold filled his entire body, then fell to the ground at her feet in agony.

He stared up with tears in his eyes as she hovered over him. "Your human reliance upon your senses leaves even the most clever of you vulnerable. How do you stop me when you can't see me?"

He coughed and gave a weak smile. "I can see you right now," he responded with a bob of his head.

"It's the last thing you'll ever see."

"I doubt that, really." With a sudden movement from his right arm, he launched the glove off of his hand and at Kaltheria's face. He surged past his pain and shot to his feet, swinging his saber just before the leather gauntlet would have made contact.

As the blade slashed the leather, the powder contained within the glove's secret pouch splashed everywhere, covering the shadow wight's body. Her shimmering black skin exploded into brilliant white fire, and her screams were so intense they nearly drove Kelve mad. The nearest dozen nightspawn were killed by this brilliant burst of energy, and after a few seconds Kaltheria's visage faded from the Morolian plane for the final time.

The wight's death delivered the effect hoped for. The remaining nightspawn troops mourned the loss of their master with a final howl, then faded into the shadows and abandoned the battlefield.

As Kelve was doing his best to fend off the paralysis spell still inflicting his system, Eiden rushed to him and warned that Tenkahn was in serious danger. The injured commander began hobbling in the direction of the monk as best as he could, bracing himself against the youth for support.

When they were within a few dozen yards of the combatants, he saw what the boy meant. Black runes from Tessena's glove had traced themselves half of the way across Tenkahn's body, shutting off the blue light from his own runes. Kelve did not understand exactly what this meant, but it was clear enough that the monk was unable to defend himself.

He gave a sigh, but wasted no time. He separated himself from Eiden in order to put on a show of strength, then reached to his belt and drew forth a large sack filled with a special refined sand.

He next removed one of his many vials and placed it deep inside of the sack. He was using up many of his most valuable resources rapidly, he knew, but he could not afford to hold out now.

He handed the sack to Eiden, as he did not have the strength to throw it. "Toss that at them," he commanded. "Try to hit directly between them, or at least near. Tenkahn's runes will hopefully shield him, if they have anything left."

Eiden did as he was bid, throwing the bag with all of his strength. It fell a bit short, nearly a yard from where Tessena stood, but still achieved the intended result. The vial burst as the sack hit the ground, the liquid mixed with the powder, and an explosion of pure sound sent the two warriors flying away.

Kelve and Eiden moved to the monk's side and helped him to his feet. It was not long before the runes of Tria resumed their normal shine, so the three commanders turned to face Tessena and awaited her next move. As she began to approach, one of the chimeras landed next to her and whispered something in her ear. It was a majestic griffin, more beautiful than most of its brethren. The First General's face contorted to anger at the creature's message. She spat in the direction of Tenkahn, then mounted the griffin's back as it lifted into the air with magnificent wings.

Soon the rest of the chimeras followed the griffin's lead, and the battle was over as suddenly as it had begun.

* * * * *

By the time the small army had recovered and settled in to rest, the eastern skyline was already beginning to brighten. Kelve sat in his tent with Tenkahn and Eiden. He had been forced to remove his armor, and hours had been spent treating his wounds from the vicious chimera bite. Tenkahn was regaining strength slowly, and warned it could be days before he would be at his physical prime again.

Several lieutenants gave their reports to the monk, then left to take turns resting. Only Kelve, Eiden, and Tenkahn remained in the small tent. There were several minutes of silence, then the commander finally forced himself to ask the hard question.

"How many men did we lose?"

"Your troops are reliable, sturdy," Tenkahn answered. "There were only seventy-five lives lost. Other than those, most of the injured will probably be able to make a return to combat within a week. Everything counted, I'd say our long-term losses will be about a hundred fighters."

As Tenkahn suggested, these numbers were impressive given the nature of the ambush they had endured. Kelve's spirits were not lifted, however. "We can't win this war," he replied despondently.

His companions exchanged a look. The monk replied, "Their demons aren't a match for my strength, and you have proven yourself a deadly foe. As well, your soldiers are resilient and handle themselves well, hiding behind their defenses until opportunity presents itself. We are not hopelessly outmatched."

"The battles we fought today and tonight put us somewhere above four hundred warriors still standing. I've used up a vast amount of my combat arsenal, and don't have the time or resources it would take to rebuild. You were placed into check by the woman Eiden calls Tessena, and are now weakened from the experience. We still aren't entirely sure how many reserve forces the Overlord has hiding behind those walls. Not to mention what would happen if either Shote is still alive, or the Overlord himself were to return." He paused for a few seconds, but there were no counters made to his argument. "We have to retreat. It's the only rational thing anyone could do."

Tenkahn encouraged their weary leader to get some rest, then he and Eiden took their leave of the command tent. After walking a few yards together, the monk halted and began addressing the boy.

"What do you think of the words Master Orista speaks?"

Eiden stared for a moment, chewing on his thumbnail as he thought. "He's right, isn't he? Running away is the only rational option."

The elder chose his next words carefully and spoke slowly, "He's not wrong."

The youth gave a sad sigh. "I wish there was something I could do. Something more."

"Do you?"

"Of course! If I hadn't wanted this to succeed, I would never have come back here. I hate this place. I hate even being here. But I want to see good triumph over evil." He blushed, recognizing the naivety that could be read in that statement. "I mean, I don't know if we're good, exactly. But I truly believe in the evil of the Overlord."

"You know you're useless to us, don't you?"

Eiden's eyes went wide with shock. He had been treated with the utmost respect by everyone since he had joined Detria's camp, and had not expected such harsh words. "What? Why do you say that?"

"Your only use is your knowledge, son. If we had that information written in a book, we would scarcely need you. You serve no use in combat. Your arm is weak, your leg is slow, your reflexes are poor."

He hung his head, feeling a weight of shame settle onto his shoulders. "I'm trying to learn magic..."

"We will all be dead long before your magic is any use in this war. That which a mage requires beyond all other things is experience. It is that which you lack the most."

Eiden hung his head deeper and gritted his teeth. He dared not respond, for fear that he might sob. He had tried to do his best. He had come so far. He had been encouraged by men like Abaddon Daemon, and Cildar Emle. He had been told by great warriors that he could make something of himself, and he had started to believe those words. But deep down he knew the monk was right. His limitations were too apparent. He would never be more than what he was. Never of more use than a simple carpenter.

Tenkahn continued, "But you are not without strengths. You are courageous. I have seen you charge opponents you knew you could not stand against, and fear did not fill your eyes. From your studies, I know you have discipline. You have a sharp mind and a quick wit. And you have the zeal of youth. When Master Abaddon entrusted you under my care he said, 'The boy seeks the strength to stand on his own two feet. Help him find it.' I didn't understand what he intended at the time. Now I believe I do. Is this true? Is this strength what you seek above anything else?"

Eiden's eyes were now brimming over with tears, and he could not repress the quake in his voice as he spoke out with conviction. "I want to be like him. I want to be like Lord Abaddon. I want to be like you, and Kelve. I want to be something I can be proud of."

"And would you give your life over to me? Would you give what it takes to get there?"

He looked up at the man with hope in his heart. He did not understand what was being asked of him, but he was prepared to believe. "You can make me stronger? Like Abaddon?"

Tenkahn nodded seriously. "I can remake you into a warrior even the mighty Abaddon Daemon would grant respect."

The boy nodded in acquiescence, clenching his teeth to keep his jawline solid. The monk returned the nod softly, motioning for Eiden to follow him beyond the confines of the camp.

## Chapter 20.

# Valinoru, Who Rides the Wind

In the heart of Arkalen, paths began to converge. As Schpariel and Aegagropilion worked their way south to find Gilanirus, Abaddon Daemon and Myris Phare approached from the west. The three groups of Wisdoms had spread themselves wide across the continent, still seeking Schpariel, still unaware they were too late to stop the resurrection of the Second Anointed Godbeast.

South, beyond the forests of Arkalen, a towering mountain range loomed. This range had long stood as a firm divider of northern and southern regions of the continent, and was known to its inhabitants as the Jagguron Peaks. To the south it was bordered by a large jungle. To its north a dull petrified forest stretched, spanning the distance between the Jagguron and the forest that had once been the home of the draconics.

It was amid these arboreal sediments that a visitor arrived. Kiastos, Wisdom of Stone, landed from a tremendous leap. He crashed hard into the arid soil, throwing up a cloud of dust. His body was decorated with intricate grey ornamentation, a fancy series of spikes and grates that rose from his back and shoulders and framed his skull. Unlike the other Wisdoms, the lower regions of his body were not crafted into a robed design, but rather showcased two distinct legs. The flesh on his arms and legs had a cracked and faceted design, giving him the apparent texture of large, earthy crystals.

His partner soon joined him, although his entrance was much more discrete. A light breeze blew across the field, then a brief whirlwind formed. The wind faded, and Valinoru was left standing in its place. He was built with a large muscular frame, even larger than the intimidating Kiastos. The Wisdom of the Wind stood at nearly eight and a half feet tall. His designed was simple, a perfect template for his brethren deities. No false hair decorated his head, and instead of a mock-up of eyes, a solid black visor covered the upper half of his face. His Staff of the Sun was strapped casually behind his back, dormant without the Wisdom's touch.

"Have you found him, Breezy?" Kiastos queried his wise partner.

Valinoru was ruffled by his nickname, but did not chastise his ally. He knew the brazen brute would have only fed on his displeasure. "For certain, I should say. There are two bodies of significant power to our north."

"It seems we overshot him in our vigor."

"We're the northernmost unit. The others already lie beyond the mountains. If we don't intercept him, they will not."

Kiastos punched the ground, causing a light tremor in the area. "Good. I wouldn't allow them to steal my satisfaction anyway. Just point me the way and I'll end Schpariel's journey."

"As usual, you pay minimal attention to my words, Kiastos. There are *two* bodies of power to our north. I cannot discern which is Schpariel."

"That should be easy enough. Which is more powerful? This is Morolia. The inhabitants here shouldn't measure up to a Godbeast."

Valinoru took a moment to extend his will through the winds. The Wisdom of Stone did his best to hold his patience for the several minutes it took his ally to complete this analysis. Finally, he announced, "The presence to the east is stronger, but he's not alone. There is a single weaker to the west."

"Huh. A difficult decision. More likely Schpariel is the weak force to the west. But this fills me with curiosity. What Morolian force is more powerful than the Godbeast?"

"You can investigate that if you wish. For safety's sake, I'm forced to suggest we split up and each intercept a different group. Either of them could be the Godbeast. It is our sacred mission to make certain he's eliminated with utmost efficiency."

Kiastos gave a slow nod. "Very good. Hopefully that Sun Staff will make you powerful enough to fight at nearly my level. Ha." He leaped into the air with vigorous might, heading north and slightly east.

Valinoru shook his head as his comrade departed without requesting detailed directions. "He will likely be lost for hours before finding his target," he bemoaned. "So imbecilic." He raised his hands and was engulfed by a fierce gale, then faded from visibility once more.

As the two Wisdoms departed the scene, Myris Phare emerged from beneath the shadows of one of the anciently deceased trees. "It seems the game is on," he whispered to himself. "I must report to Lord Abaddon at once."

He masked himself in cloaks of enchanted stealth and sped back to the forests in the north, praying he might reach his commander before the winds themselves.

* * * * *

Abaddon moved through the forest slowly, the Arda tucked away at his back. He had separated from Myris hours ago, and so wandered aimlessly as he awaited the Cain's return. He was unable to sense the presence of either the Gehennans or the Elysians, so he was forced to fall back on more traditional tracking techniques. So far, this approach was granting him no favors.

He hoped Myris was faring better. The man's supernatural speed allowed him to cover ground at a better pace, but the faster he moved the more his Cainite stealth deteriorated. The gravest risk was that he would stumble across the Wisdoms and be noticed before he could safely return.

A light breeze rustled the treetops. Abaddon glanced skyward, trying to catch a glimpse of the sun to gauge the time. Suddenly, he sensed that he was not alone. He froze in place, straining his senses to their apex.

He felt a shadowy presence to his right and his nerves were set at ease. “Myris,” he greeted his friend. “Any luck?”

“They come for you.”

The big man gave a thoughtful pause before answering. “Unfortunate. I was hoping for an element of surprise.”

“They have separated. Apparently there were two bodies of interest for them. I strongly suspect you are one of them.”

“Then this may yet work out for the best. We stand better odds against a sole Wisdom than a duo. Which one comes for us?”

“I cannot say for certain. I do have names. Valinoru, and Kiastos. One of them approaches. Valinoru is capable of masterful levels of stealth, as well as piercing it. I was able to adapt my methods sufficiently to prevent his detection, but only just. Kiastos is far less clever, but gives the impression that his strength would be substantial.”

“Then I suppose we wait and see who comes. You know the part you are to play?”

“Yes, milord.”

“Then go. Make yourself scarce.”

As the mystic warlord situated himself boldly in the widest clearing he could find, Myris took up station within the surrounding trees. The Cain brooded as they awaited the Wisdom’s arrival. During their initial approach, Abaddon had explained why he had chosen the slim man’s presence over that of the Phoenix Dragoon.

“I don’t need the advantages Cildar offers,” he had posited. “Even with his blessings of Haste, he’s too similar a fighter to myself. What I require is not more strength, or endurance. The Wisdoms are going to have us outclassed in those regards, there’s no changing that. Your talents for stealth, tracking, and speed will better serve us here.”

Myris had been uplifted by these words, until learning exactly what Abaddon had planned for the upcoming battle. He had been instructed to hide in the woodland shadows, awaiting an opportunity for a sneak attack. The former Lord of the Cain recognized this supporting role as another indication that he was steadily running out of usefulness to his friends. Though he would serve his assignment to the best of his ability, and without complaint, his heart was breaking as the ascension of the other Lords of Felthespar left him behind.

Shortly, a powerful gale ripped through the area, tearing the leaves from many of the trees. For a few seconds all was quiet, then a cyclone materialized several yards in front of Abaddon, fading slowly to reveal Valinoru. The Wisdom towered over the man, and the match seemed easily set from the start.

"You stand here as if you anticipate me, Morolian," the elegant voice greeted. "Or perhaps you are simply cast with grave misfortune. Tell me, do you await another?"

Abaddon did not budge, staring the intimidating creature down evenly. "Oh no, it's you I've sought. I trust you are Valinoru?"

"*You* have sought *me*? Folly, thy name is—tell me, what is thy name?"

"I am Abaddon Daemon."

The Wisdom cocked his head. "Should I recognize this name? To me, it holds no special significance."

"Not yet. But with this sword, I will carve it into your flesh."

The man reached to his back and drew forth Arda with a twist, then dashed with the sword held straight out to his right. Valinoru had ample time for a response, raising his right hand forward and gathering a sliver of wind there. He slammed his arm forward in the direction of his attacker and an imperceptible blade of writhing air shot forth, perpendicular to the ground.

Abaddon could not see this slim projectile, but he had no doubts something was coming his way. He instantly halted his charge, crossing his arms in front of his face in a hasty attempt at defense. The line of deadly divine wind crashed into him hard, knocking him back a clear twenty feet. It took all his concentration to prevent himself from falling into a roll, knowing he would likely skewer himself with Arda if he lost his footing.

Valinoru observed his opponent, impressed that the human had not been ripped clean in half. Nonetheless, Abaddon's forearms were bleeding from wide gashes, and part of his chest had also been torn open.

The Wisdom speculated, "You must have used a powerful coating of Asterian barriers to guard your flesh. It's rare, though not unheard of, that a human rises to the level that he can survive a strike from a Wisdom. I would ask you, at this point, to make your escape. As a Divine Wisdom, I cannot be seen to retreat from a mortal. But you are unique, with potential perhaps to be even more than you are. I prefer not to destroy specimens worthy of further study."

The mystic took a moment to gather his breath and allow his innate healing to make headway against his injuries. "Your disposition is certainly more agreeable than Dosiros'."

"You have encountered and survived The Flame, as well? What business have you with us Wisdoms?"

Abaddon lowered his weapon and softened his stance. "I wish to negotiate some small treaty between our planes. I know you're hunting something, related in some way to Gehenna. I'd be willing to assist you in this hunt, in exchange only for a recognition and avoidance of human casualties."

Valinoru paused a few seconds before replying. "You greatly intrigue me. As a matter of etiquette, your proposal has been considered and rejected. Any assistance a creature as weak as you might bring to our cause cannot offset the inconvenience of us being distracted by concerns of collateral damage. As you have revealed that your true intentions are to interfere in our most sacred mission, I shall be required to kill you after all."

"I suspected you might feel that way," he answered, once again tightening his battle stance.

"You survived my first attack, but sustained considerable injury in doing so. If this is your limit, you will wear down far before you ever reach me."

The Wisdom raised his hand and gathered another invisible blade. Abaddon's cold mind recognized the truth in the deity's taunt. Valinoru's attack was conceptually simple, but a devastating combination of range, stealth, speed, and power. If he could not quickly devise a way to counter it, he would be crippled or even dead before this fight could begin in earnest.

He stared at the Arda and analyzed his plight. The sword granted him a generous three yards of range, but he was still over fifteen yards away from his target. Given the damage he had already taken in spite of his grey magic, it was unlikely he could stubbornly charge his way through.

The Wisdom unleashed his strike with a subtle flick of the wrist, and another blade of wind closed on the human champion. Abaddon briefly considered a sidestep, but knew an evasive defense against blows he could not see would not last him long. Instead he straightened his back and held Arda high, chanting the sword's mythos. "Slice through anything!" he bade.

He delivered a rapid downslash, unleashing a wave of kinetic force echoing from his weapon. This was his own technique, modified from the teachings of the Monks of Tria, which he only rarely found opportunity to use. The timing of his attack was perfect, as Valinoru's speedy blade had already nearly reached him. He felt a solid thunk of resistance as Arda came into contact with the maliciously crafted gale, then the sword ripped cleanly through, also slicing into the ground before him. Still his counter proved insufficient; a painful grip seized his right shoulder and left thigh, tearing chunks of flesh from the bone.

He fell to his knees in agony. Valinoru chuckled and said something Abaddon did not hear, his mind distracted running calculations. The first attack had been a vertical line, hitting his body directly in the center. The second, however, had seemingly come at a diagonal. Arda had sliced through and destroyed the middle section, leaving the outer edges intact, and apparently no less dangerous.

"So," he muttered to himself, "I'm able to dispel the attacks, I just can't tell how they're coming at me."

A wicked smile spread across his features as he rose once more to his feet. This would have been an impossible battle for any other man. The Wisdom's ability to strike with invisible blades of untold force was too much to counter, too much to survive. But the mystic held one advantage he had not yet played. He had nearly used this to overcome Tenkahn's Merciless Rune, until Cildar had talked him down and convinced him to take a more measured approach. Standing now against an actual deity, it was time for Abaddon Daemon to stop holding back.

He held the Arda in front of him, gripping the hilt with both hands. He shut his eyes and took a deep breath, leveling his nerves and soothing the pains of his body. Valinoru seemed content to watch, entertained by his small opponent's persistence.

Winds began to rise around Abaddon's body, then blew out in all directions. At first they were soft, but soon they swelled in intensity, rattling the trees and blanketing the surrounding areas of the forest.

Valinoru scanned this tempest, but could find nothing of interest hiding within. He was impressed that the man was able to affect the winds, but it seemed nothing more than an arrogant flexing of mystical muscle.

"Would you fight me at my own game?" the Wisdom asked with genuine interest.

"Not exactly," Abaddon answered. The winds suddenly quieted, and he slowly opened his eyes. They were shining with an intense blue light, and similarly his skin had developed an odd coating of white energy rippling across it.

Valinoru braced for an assault, but it did not come. His curiosity was piqued and he was anxious to see what new surprises the interesting human held in store, so he once again gathered one of his deadly blades. It formed quickly, and he sent it speeding toward his foe at tremendous velocity, a dozen times faster than the previous two.

From where he stood, Abaddon was now able to see the path of the blade. It rotated in the air as it approached him, but he easily calculated the angle he needed to parry. When it was within ten feet of his chest he lashed out with Arda. His blow was overwhelming, and the gusty energies collapsed and scattered. A few residual shards crashed against him, but they lacked the strength necessary to tear through his grey magic.

He began walking slowly toward Valinoru. "Would you like to try that again?" he offered ominously.

The Wisdom grunted and raised his left hand as well. He launched a series of the bladed strikes, alternating the use of his hands. He released over a dozen of them, but each time Abaddon delivered a quick sweep of Arda and the attack was destroyed. The whole time he did not change his pace, but continued his gradual march across the glade.

Valinoru ceased his attacks and demanded, "How?"

Abaddon halted his approach once he was within five yards. "It seems each Wisdom has their own specialty. You may be a master of the wind, but you are still on Morolia. This is my plane, and she responds to my will. In order to see your attacks, I released the limiter that keeps my mysticism held in check. I then bound the currents in the area to my will, tying them directly to my mystic vision. Each time you bend the wind, I see it reflected in the Morolian ether. Your trick is too simple."

When he finished his explanation, he charged forward with a two-handed grip on Arda. Valinoru released two final blades, but Abaddon knocked both of them from his path with rapid strikes, then delivered a sweeping slash at his opponent's waist. The Wisdom proved too quick for this, rising into the air at a blinding speed. The mystic did not lose him, however, still following the impulses fed to him by the currents.

As Valinoru released a harsh blast of slicing gales down at his adversary, the man launched into the air himself and went into a tight spin. The length of Arda lashed out and tore apart all of the approaching strikes. Abaddon soon reached the Wisdom at the pinnacle of his jump. He brought himself out of his spin, reversed his momentum, paused for a fraction of a second to adjust his aim, then released a ferocious uppercut with Arda's blade.

Valinoru used heated air currents to pull himself away from the eager edge of the sword. The human's brief pause had given him some clearance, but not enough to escape to a safe ten feet. Arda struck his stomach and tore up through his chest, eating through his left shoulder and destroying the decorative shoulderpad that served as protection.

The combatants crashed to the ground below, and Abaddon immediately regained his fighting stance. Valinoru shuddered silently for a few moments before rising to his feet. He bowed to his adversary. "I find myself in amazement. I didn't anticipate a human of this era would cause me significant damage. When the internal cavities of my body are exposed, I lack the focus necessary to control the winds. I shall be forced to return to Keldana."

Abaddon narrowed his eyes in thought. "You use your own internal system of currents to reflect your control over external ones."

"Gaining comprehension of this is most unfortunate for you. Had you begged me for clemency previously, I might have been inclined to grant it. As things stand now, I must eliminate you in order to preserve my secret."

Valinoru reached his left hand behind his back and seized his Sun Staff. He held the resplendent weapon high, and the golden surface began to brighten with rapidly increasing intensity. Soon it was all Abaddon could do to look through the light and keep his eyes locked on the Wisdom.

"You will find this weapon is far more merciless than I myself," the deity continued. "Defended even as you are, a fully charged blast of its robust energy will devour you from this plane. If you want a chance to survive it, you would do best to strike before I complete its charge."

Abaddon did not attempt to strike, however, instead waiting stoically as the Wisdom readied his attack. It was another twenty seconds before the Staff seemed to finally reach its maximum charge, flashing out once with a pure glint of heat. Valinoru did not extend his opponent a final chance, but instead began to swing the Staff forward and release its blast.

Just before he could trigger said release, some slim metallic object flew from the forest and crashed into the top of his weapon. Whatever it was became lodged there, and a strange crackle emanated as energies began to mix. Valinoru endeavored repeatedly to command the Sun Staff to release its fires, but it would not respond. He turned his gaze to where his opponent had been standing, only to find the human was now gone. He had only another second to ponder the events at hand, as the Sun Staff finally unleashed its attack in an unfocused explosion.

It was nearly an hour later when the flames in that section of the forest finally died down enough for the Felthespari to return to the clearing. The mysterious object that had signaled Valinoru's demise had been Myris' Cainite katana, imbued with the energies of his Draw Strike of Lightning. The Cain had witnessed the power of these Staffs when Dosiros had used it to defeat Cildar. Based on his observations, he had theorized that if struck with sufficient power at the right moment they could be forced into a meltdown. His speculations had proven as shrewd as ever, but even he had not suspected how much destructive might the golden weapons were capable of gathering. The resultant explosion had set not only the surrounding trees and grass aflame, but even the air itself had burned for several minutes.

Abaddon inspected the body of his foe, verifying his victory. His concerns were quickly put to rest. Valinoru's left hand had been wholly cremated, as well as a majority of his torso. What remained of his body was left in two separated pieces. The shoulders, right arm, and head were intact, but separated from the stomach and legs. The black shades that had once covered his face had been burned away as well, revealing a disturbing absence of eyes. The rest of his head appeared to be mostly intact, but was scarred and cracked by heat.

Myris, for his part, examined the remains of the divine staff. The glorious weapon had also incinerated itself, and only a few pieces of broken gold steel could be found. The man soon located his katana. The slim sword had been enchanted and endowed with peerless durability for its previous lord, but the blade's resilience had not served it this day. The only visible remains was a portion of the hilt, and as Myris attempted to pick it up, it too collapsed into fragments in his hands.

Abaddon gave his ally a nod. "Well struck."

"It was at an unfortunate cost. That katana will be impossible for me to replace without access to goods from Adonnis."

"Perhaps, but we've established the strength of our arms. I'm confident the Wisdoms will soon be aware of their brother's demise."

"Where do we go next?"

"I am uncertain. Perhaps our next course should be to rejoin with Cildar. Attempting to face more Wisdoms on our own is too risky. We held out well, but I'd say there was some providence in us facing this Valinoru."

Myris nodded his understanding. "Dosiros seemed more solidly built, and his talent for destruction less limited. We are unlikely to be lucky enough to force another to charge their staff to the point that they kill themselves."

"We'll need every edge we can afford. Come, we move." He walked a few steps, then realized his companion was not following. He turned back to see the man staring at his own feet, clenching his fists. "What now?" the warlord asked impatiently.

"Lord Abaddon, forgive me, but... what was that? That power of yours. I have never seen anything like it, not since the day... since you struck me down with Kargaroth. Cildar and I long have known you were still stronger than us, but this... this was something beyond that."

The big man creased his brow in concern. He had known this conversation would happen eventually, and had long dreaded it. He walked a few steps back to his friend, speaking in his softest tones. "I'm sorry, Myris. I've not wished to deceive the two of you."

The shorter man did not move, insisting again, "What was that?"

"You perhaps remember years ago, when I was young, I created a limiter technique. It was designed to allow me to repress my natural strength just enough to prevent lapsing into berserk rages, as I was wont to do in those days. After the events of the Kargaroth, when my mysticism was weakened nearly to the point of atrophy, I continued to use it, simply out of habit. At this time it began to take on a different nature. Or perhaps I myself did. The more the limiter constricted my mystic abilities, the more rapidly they expanded. Once a year I have to reinvent the technique, doubling its effectiveness to constrain my advantages. Still they continue to grow, whether I train them or not.

"I'm not a modest man, Myris. You know that well. I don't hide my powers away because I'm ashamed of what I am, nor from fear of using them. I simply desired to still have challenges in this life. I had always intended to return to Arkalen without the overwhelming might once afforded to me by Kargaroth. But by the time Leprue passed and I was finally ready to leave the Grand Council, it was too late. I had once again become too strong. So I've kept my limiter tightly in place, never mentioning it, so that I might fight alongside you and Cildar as a peer. I didn't know how to even discuss the matter with you. I never wanted either of you to feel insulted."

"So," the Cain responded slowly, "you never needed us."

After a long pause, he answered with a simple, "No." Myris' breath caught in his throat, stricken by the stinging honesty of the admission in spite of expecting it. "But I wanted you both at my side. I know that cannot easily salve your pride."

Suddenly Myris began to chuckle. He took a step back and raised his hand to his forehead, then threw his head back, laughing loudly to the sky. Even the normally unshakable Abaddon was startled by this response, widening his eyes in concern at his friend's behavior. Finally Myris settled down and began speaking. "All this time," he said, still laughing between his words. "I have been so worried that you and Cildar were leaving me behind, attaining strength I could not hope to match." His laughing finally stopped fully, and he breathed heavily for a moment. "But that happened years ago. You left Cildar and me both far, far behind you." He once more looked to the man, locking eyes. "Does Atheme know?"

"He suspects," he replied, shaking his head lightly. "I ease off my limiter slightly when we spar, just enough for him to feel the change. He can't match me anymore. I didn't want him to know. Not for certain. Some part of Atheme has always feared me, though he's never been willing to talk to me about it. Since Hell, I don't know how he truly feels. It's another conversation I've never known how to enter."

There were a few moments of silence, then Myris began to walk, moving past his friend and whispering, "At least there are others who can share my humiliation. In a way, I feel less alone than before."

Abaddon lingered behind for a couple of minutes, allowing the crestfallen man to place some distance between them to gather his thoughts. Then he exited the clearing as well, and the two warriors made their way back northeast. After they had been gone for the span of ten minutes, a pale, cloaked figure entered the vacated clearing. Flowing white robes posed a stark contrast to the blackened forest surrounding them.

Akatriel approached the dead Wisdom and looked down at his damaged corpse. "What grace is delivered to me this day. Who would have guessed that the Knight and the Bishop would hold the strength to topple a Wisdom? Pawns though they are, I thought their might so fearsome. Being a god isn't what it used to be in this world."

He made a quick chopping motion with his hand, and a blade of silver energy ripped Valinoru's head from the scorched shoulders. "Convenient as this was," the conspirator mused to himself, "it unfortunately proves that I can't leave the Knight roaming unchecked. His movement is too erratic, too difficult for a Queen to counter." He lifted the severed head and stared at it, a smile playing on his colorless features. "I must place you somewhere for safe keeping, then swiftly capture my next piece." He headed on his way, seeking the nearest entrance to one of his underground chambers.

* * * * *

So fell the first Divine Wisdom of Elysium, slain by the hands of two humans. As the story was told in the ages to come, all who heard would doubt its credibility. But none were more left aghast than those who witnessed the battle from far across the Veil, in the ruling halls of Elysium itself. A Council of Muses was called together and warned of the changing tides on the Morolian plane. Since the other Wisdoms could not be stopped and could not be controlled, a new course of action was decided upon.

As the Muses did not have the privilege to travel to Morolia, it was time to bring the humans to Elysium.

## Chapter 21.

## Kiastos, Who Cannot Break

Melukah, Wisdom of the Sun, self-proclaimed ruler of all Elysium, stepped to the edge of a large ravine and stared into the depths below. He felt many things as he stood in this place once again, but pleasure was not among them. As he reflected, a light rain began to fall over the area. He waited in silence for the precipitation to finish its course, at which point the Wisdom of Ocean stood next to him. Keldana's frame was small for her kind, only seven feet tall and slim, wearing robes that were an alternating blend of solemn blues and whites with a green trim. Of all Wisdoms, only Keldana's eyes and hair—which were both bright blue in color—were carved to resemble a human female's.

When she spoke, a soothing voice backed by a wavy static originated from the motionless face. "Dosiros and Torlen are north, in the jungle. Lost, perhaps. They don't seem to be making much headway. Valinoru and Kiastos didn't even cross the mountains. They have instead turned and returned to the north."

Melukah nodded. When last the Wisdoms had visited Morolia, it was in this very ravine where the body of Gilanirus had been hidden away. The six Elysian divinities had then united their powers, tearing a hole in the Veil between Morolia and Asteria in order to create a tremendous Ether Pole, unparalleled in its size and intensity. Somehow the Pole was now gone, and the Veil seemed to be healing. At first Melukah had feared this to be a sign of Gilanirus' revival, but he had since verified the Tyrant's body remained entombed in Kiastos' stone prison.

"Sooner or later, Schpariel will come here," he announced with confidence.

Keldana nodded. “By that time, Aegagropilion may have been revived. Is it not dangerous to allow the Great Beast to feast?”

“We will place our trust in the others for that. Aegagropilion may become strong, it is true. But I fear nothing like I fear Gilanirus. We must see to it that he is not reached. We shall remain here, ever vigilant.”

Keldana’s head suddenly jerked to the north. She stared hard, trying to understand the message she was receiving. “Valinoru is injured. Gravely.”

“Dead?”

“No. His soul remains bound on this plane.”

“Then it was not the Godbeasts he fought. If he is in dire need of repair, he will seek you out. Valinoru moves at the speed of the winds. We need not go to him.”

“Then we are truly to wait here and take no action?”

Melukah nodded and sat to his knees on the ground, crossing his arms. “Unless you begin to feel the situation to the north is becoming beyond our control. Keep your watchful eye over things.”

Keldana gave a bow and raised her arms. Rain began to fall around them, and her summoned clouds floated slowly north.

* * * * *

The demon Zekraul skulked silently through the forest that had once been home to Arkalen’s draconics. The reptilian creatures were nowhere to be seen, and the demon became curious as to what events had led to their absence. He allowed himself to be distracted briefly by the mystery, crawling over the forest looking for clues.

Unfortunately he made for a poor tracker. Instead of eyes, only two empty indentations accented his malleable face. This was a telling sign of his most prominent weakness: Zekraul did not possess the ability of sight. He had learned to cope with his limitation. Indeed, he had adapted to the degree that his enemies could not even tell he was blind. The basis of his powers was his ability to control and manipulate energy, and he had twisted this affinity to detect any slight change in heat sources around him. In addition, he had set the peculiar frame of his body to be sensitive to sound waves carried along the air. Utilizing both his sonar and his thermal senses, in some ways his vision was more finely tuned than that of his enemies' eyes.

Yet even with these advancements, certain things such as searching the grass for signs of past events, or trying to find a tool laying on the ground, still proved extremely challenging for him. Without movement or heat sources to rely upon, his search was little more than an exercise in futility. After two hours of this he gave up with an agitated hiss, standing for a moment scratching at one of his eye sockets with a hooked claw.

As he stood mourning his handicap, he detected vibrations in the air. Two creatures were approaching the section of the forest where he idled. He wasted no time, quickly shimmying up a narrow tree and hiding himself in the branches. It was not long before the creatures made their way into the area. The demon instantly recognized the thermal signature of the creature on the right. It was the entity claiming itself to be Schpariel, First Godbeast of Gehenna. The second, Zekraul was certain he had never encountered.

They continued their walk casually, and the crystalline lurker began to think himself safe from detection. Then for no apparent reason, the pair came to a stop directly beneath him. He forced himself to repress a nervous hiss and waited.

The new creature turned to Schpariel, who had apparently signaled the halt. "What is it?" the lanky monster asked, "Why do we rest?"

"We are not alone, Aegagropilion," the Dark Wisdom answered. "Something is nearby."

In the branches above, Zekraul was seized by a paralyzing fear. Not only was he at risk of detection, but Schpariel had just spoken the name of the second legendary Godbeast of Gehenna. It seemed that he was about to face not only one, but two Godbeasts in battle. It was the first time in the demon's entire life he was overcome with panic. All he could think to do was pray for escape from this situation, but the only gods he recognized stood directly beneath him.

Schpariel's next comment did much to alleviate his terror, slowly replaced by a building curiosity. "One of the Wisdoms is approaching us."

The other Godbeast shuffled forward, staring hard into the forest. Zekraul listened intently to their conversation as his nerves settled.

"How long?"

"He will reach us in only a few minutes. Perhaps three."

"Can we run?"

"I cannot tell which Wisdom is coming. If it's the Wind, Sound, or Ocean, escape is an impossibility."

"We have not the power to confront them!"

Schpariel paused for nearly a minute, thinking the situation over. Then he turned and faced his ally directly. "You must return the Moon Rod to me. I will need its remaining stores for this battle."

Aegagropilion took a slow step away from his comrade. "You know I have not yet feasted, Schpariel. It is the power of the Moon Rod alone that currently supports my strength. Without it I will be useless."

"As will I! But the Rod falls under my dominion. I loaned it to you as a gift, as a blessing, but now I demand it restored."

The two Gehennans stared each other down for another half minute. Zekraul was mesmerized by the scene. He could not imagine what held Godbeasts themselves so terrified. He had never heard of these 'Wisdoms' they seemed to fear. The thought of creatures with such might intrigued him.

Finally the stalemate came to an end. Aegagropilion reached into his chest and drew forth some sort of tool. Zekraul's substitution for vision could not make it out, but he surmised it was the Moon Rod in question. As the device was handed to Schpariel, the second Godbeast advised him on their course. "Very well. But let's do this my way. I will first fight the Wisdom alone. Weak though I am, I may yet find a way to overcome. You remain hidden. If I fall, strike quickly before you are noticed. There's a chance you'll be able to catch him unawares and defeat him. If so, it will fall upon you to resurrect me once more with the Rod."

"This is surely as sound of a tactic as we shall find. Let us go. We should try to initiate the encounter on our terms, rather than wait to be discovered."

The pair dashed rapidly to the south, and Zekraul dropped from the tree. He released a long hiss of relief and sat contemplating for a moment. "Though I could use this moment to escape," he mused, "I would prefer not to lose sight of these Godbeasts so quickly. If they're truly about to enter combat with a creature more dangerous than they, it would serve me well to witness. I may learn that which is necessary to defeat them, or if my cause is without hope."

With his resolve set, he swallowed his fears and moved once more to the treetops, traveling quietly in the direction the two Gehennans had disappeared.

* * * * *

Kiastos moved through the forest at random, wholly uncertain where he was going. He knew he was near the Godbeasts—partly because of Valinoru, and partly because of his own instincts. Each Wisdom was granted power to pinpoint the location of a nearby denizen of Gehenna, but the Wisdom of Stone's third eye held the dimmest sight.

Nearly three hours after he had separated from Valinoru, he came to a stop. The sun had worked its way toward the western horizon and night would soon blanket the area. Kiastos debated if he should double back and regroup with his partner, but his third eye insisted that Godbeasts were near, and drawing closer. He could not bring himself to give up on the hunt.

It seemed that fortune was on his side. As he considered the approaching nightfall and how it might hinder his search, he was attacked from the fringe of his sight. A tremendous scorpion tail tore through the base of several trees and struck with speed beyond what he could follow. His shoulder was pierced by the arachnid stinger, and he was knocked forcibly onto his back and pinned there by a crushing pressure.

Kiastos gave a grunting laugh that sounded of grating rocks. He leveraged his Elysian magic, and the crystalline structure of his hands transformed into immutable stone. He reached up and gripped the segmented appendage, then effortlessly ripped a large section of it to pieces. As he rose to his feet, he observed the shattered remnants of the tail transforming into strange green tendons, as the remainder retreated rapidly back into the darkness of the forest.

"Bless Elysium," Kiastos grumbled into the void, "I am caught by surprise. I came hunting for Schpariel, and it seems I've found the Great Beast Aegagropilion."

The Godbeast in question lumbered forward, his body's form dramatically altered. In addition to the scorpion tail now attached to his lower back, his arms had been transformed into giant sleeves consisting of hundreds of long, hooked blades. His legs had shifted into bizarre mechanical apparatuses, large hinges running from his torso to hook into two huge cylinders that formed the lower legs. Four of the monstrous spider legs had returned as well, exiting from his back and anchoring into the ground behind him to lend speed and flexibility. He had increased his size until he could stare evenly at the Wisdom, and his chest he had changed into a solid block of steel armor.

Kiastos chuckled at his opponent's appearance. "You've fallen far since our last war, Aega. Forced to rely on your own strength these days? It will not suffice here."

The Godbeast flexed his body, and the damaged segments of his tail regrew from a thick tangle of green plant matter. "Kiastos,

Wisdom of Stone. I remember only little of you, but count myself lucky it's you who has found me. You were the slowest of all Wisdoms. My strikes will land easily, as did the first."

Kiastos looked down to the deep gash that had been ripped into his faceted shoulder. He reached up and touched it with his right hand. Immediately his entire shoulder was petrified, encased by a thick layer of grey rock. When he removed his hand the stone shell crumbled away, revealing the area now uninjured. "It will do you little good," he retorted. "Something else you should have remembered—I alone can heal without Keldana's presence."

"Then let's see just how much you *can* heal!" Aegagropilion shouted as he renewed his assault. His spidery limbs lent him speed, propelling him across the battlefield in an instant. As he reached Kiastos' position he gave a sweeping punch with his right arm. The Wisdom countered with his left arm, which was now encased in a thick tomb of stone. The huge fist easily shattered the myriad of blades the Godbeast had summoned, knocking the fractured arm off harmlessly to the side. Aegagropilion swiftly attacked with his other arm, aiming for his opponent's head at close proximity. Kiastos raised his right arm to the side of his face just in time, the armored limb blocking and snapping the eager razors.

The Great Beast was not discouraged by his apparent weakness in the face of Kiastos' defense. He dropped down onto his mechanical legs, latching them to the ground and bending forward so that his knees pointed at his foe's stomach. Instantly the kneecaps erupted, and two iron spikes burst forth and slammed the Wisdom's body. Aegagropilion swung his spider legs forward and speared them into his enemy's side, simultaneously dissolving the hinges that anchored him to his own legs. He lifted himself above the Elysian's head and pointed what remained of his arms forward, exploding the blades into a flurry of shrapnel. At the same time he swung his scorpion tail beneath his hovering body and dug the steely tip deep into his target's throat. Finally the metal plate forming his chest began to ripple as he released a fierce cry, and his torso changed into a single massive spike which struck Kiastos in the center of his forehead.

The Godbeast grunted in satisfaction as the tip of his final blow disappeared into the Wisdom's skull. He knew it was not enough to finish this opponent, but his successful onslaught would certainly give him the upper hand, especially against one already so slow as Kiastos.

"Get off me," the Wisdom muttered as he reached up with his left hand. He gave a calm shove, and his assailant was forcibly detached.

Aegagropilion tried to catch himself with his arachnid legs, but was surprised to find the ends had been shorn off. Instead he collapsed to the ground with an awkward roll. When he came to a stop, he looked up to his adversary with rage filling his amber eyes.

"Fall!" he demanded with a voice that rang across the clearing.

In response, Kiastos reached up and brushed steel dust from his enemy's final spear from his forehead. When he did so, it revealed a large patch of stone. Aegagropilion inspected the rest of the deity's body, and noticed the same traces of stony armor in every other spot he had attempted to strike.

Realization finally dawned on him. Not a single one of his attacks had actually pierced the Wisdom's frame. His tail, his arms, his legs, the spikes he had created—all had been crushed ineffectually against unyielding defense.

He gathered himself slowly. The remaining pieces of his body shapeshifted back to his original sinewy flesh and merged into his abdomen. He formed his normal arms and legs, then rose steadily to a standing position. "I don't understand," he said in a more subdued tone. "You wear a second layer of armor beneath your skin?"

Kiastos smacked his chest with his stone fists. "Wrong. You underestimate me so terribly. It's true that I'm the slowest moving of the Wisdoms. But that weakness was a price paid for another strength. I have the slowest body, but the fastest mind. I can summon my magic in a narrow slice of a second, and harden any part of my body about to endure an attack. You thought your first attack hit me because I'm so slow. It's never wise to reveal your true strength on your opponent's first blow, so I saved it. Unless you can move much, much faster, you can never touch my flesh."

The newly formed Aegagropilion charged once more. He stretched his hands out into large tents, larger than his entire body. He launched himself at the Wisdom of Stone and wrapped these around him. The Great Beast lashed his canvas tighter and tighter about his foe's body, attempting to bind him down. For a moment it seemed his ploy had worked, then Kiastos began to stretch and adjust within his thin cocoon. Scores of stone spikes burst through the encompassing sheets, and the Wisdom slowly shook away the remains.

Kiastos was revealed covered in his stone shell, every inch of his body coated a dull but durable grey. He laughed as his enemy began backing away from him. "You have to make contact with my flesh to taste my soul, correct, Beast? You'll find only cold stone awaiting your touch."

He surged forward and delivered a slow punch. Aegagropilion easily ducked under it and swung out with his right arm, which transformed into the head of a tremendous war hammer. The fake steel crumbled against real stone, and the Godbeast swiftly turned and distanced himself several yards.

He tried to take a moment to rationalize the balance of power. "I see you know my limitations, but I know yours as well. In addition to being the slowest of your kind, you're much slower when encased in your invincible armor. I also know you Wisdoms use these fake bodies to prevent needing to fully cross the Veil. As long as you've not wholly manifested, your physical strength is reduced. I might not can defeat you at my current power, but tell me, Kiastos of Stone, what are you going to do to me?"

The Wisdom raised his arms partially into the air and gave a slight groan. Slowly, the stone skin covering his body slid up until only his fists and forearms were still shielded. When this was finished, he glared at his opponent. "I think I'll try this."

He punched the ground at his feet with his left fist, and immediately began running forward. Aegagropilion started to react, but was caught by surprise when the earth he stood upon suddenly turned inside out and locked in around his feet. As he tried to separate the upper and lower parts of his body, he realized that Kiastos was already atop him. Heavy stone hands crashed forward and locked tightly around the ensnared Godbeast's body. He reacted quickly, sending vines creeping up the Wisdom's arms in an attempt to reach flesh, but Kiastos extended his shielding back too fast for the vines to overtake.

As the Great Beast attempted to bring his powers to bear and conquer his foe's flesh, Kiastos was doing the same. Slowly the green texture of Aegagropilion's body began to harden and shift to dull tones. It was not long before he felt his strength draining, and the vines that had crept all the way to Kiastos' neck suddenly backed away and slid slowly back down the hardened arms.

There was a minor groan, but no other sounds of resistance as Aegagropilion was slowly transformed into a single stone mound. Kiastos stepped back and shook his head, disappointed but not surprised by the ease of his victory.

As he dismissed his stone armors and allowed himself to relax from the stresses of battle, he was granted an unfortunate sight. Directly across the clearing from him stood the Godbeast Schpariel, his fabled Moon Rod already pointed at the Wisdom for some unseen attack.

Kiastos instantly threw his adamant shell back up. In his mind, however, a sliver of panic struck. His shielding became progressively stronger the longer it was active. Against a famished Aegagropilion it had been sufficient even in instant flashes, but if he was struck by one of Schpariel's more potent spells after only freshly raising his defense, he was certain it would not hold.

This panic lasted for a couple of seconds, then faded. Nothing had happened. Schpariel and he stood eyeing one another, but no spell had been cast. Kiastos sat confused, until he heard the Dark Wisdom complaining.

"Curse you, Aegagropilion. You kept the real Moon Rod the whole time. Now I see your mind."

The Wisdom breathed a sigh of relief and again dropped his armors, leaving only his fists encased. Without his magic, Schpariel could not even fight a partially manifested Wisdom. If the Godbeast tried to run, Kiastos would simply imprison his feet the same way he had with the previous. This was surely his lucky day. Two Godbeasts defeated as easily as lowly lemures at his feet. He had completed the entire mission of the Wisdoms on his own. The angelspawn would be singing folktales of this for centuries to come.

Now it was Schpariel who seemed panicked. In his terror of the Wisdom's approach, he threw his Rod with all of his limited might, tossing it at his approaching foe's face as a tiny spear. Kiastos chuckled and held his left fist up, allowing the Rod to stab uselessly onto stone flesh. He lowered his arm back to his side and continued his approach, taunting, "Betrayed by your own brother, Schpariel. These are the reasons that the Godbeasts will never prevail against the Wisdoms. We are united of a similar mind, and a similar cause. We don't share your cowardice and selfishness."

Schpariel's set mouth gradually twisted into a large grin. "No, perhaps your words ring true, Kiastos. Fortunately for myself, you do share the vice of arrogance. It has been my salvation this day."

The Wisdom stopped in his tracks and tried to decipher his antagonist's taunt. Then he glanced to his left arm and his eyes filled with disbelief. Long green vines had grown from the Moon Rod where it was anchored to his stone flesh, and they had made their way to his shoulder. He attempted to solidify his arm and strip the vines, but his magic would not respond. Before he could think of something more to try, the vines rapidly lunged forward and struck into his neck and face.

Schpariel watched as Kiastos roared and thrashed weakly for a moment. Soon this ended. The vines continued to spread, wrapping slowly around the Wisdom's stone mask and shattering it. When the mask was gone, a human face slowly faded into its place. The skin was a dark grey, and though its shape resembled the destroyed mask, it was clearly flesh. The protruding vines sank into the armored frame and faded away.

The grey lids opened, and black eyes slowly shifted to a bright amber color. "Schpariel!" it spoke. The voice was Kiastos', but there was a background cadence that the Dark Wisdom could not mistake.

"Aegagropilion," he answered. "Good to see that you live, brother."

"Not for long. This is too small a portion of my essence to bind this body. I'm struggling to hold him at rest. Bring the statue which contains my flesh. I can use this arm to free his imprisonment, but you must make haste!"

Schpariel did as beckoned, quickly moving to where his cohort's original body had been sealed. The structure was sealed tightly to now-petrified ground, so he was forced to break through the statue at the waist. He brought the upper half back near the paralyzed Wisdom and sat it down.

Kiastos' left arm reached involuntarily forward and touched the boulder. The rock's structure melted away and dust leaked onto the ground below. When the process was complete, a large ball of vines exploded forward and wrapped themselves viciously about the Elysian's legs. Schpariel stepped back and watched the transformation play out. Slowly, the Wisdom of Stone's body was changed. The general shape remained the same, but the outer shell was replaced by sinewy green flesh, and the small amber eyes that decorated the face became huge. The elaborate decorations and elegant details that had once signified a Divine Wisdom were erased, melting into a supple body more suitable for a changeling.

The reborn Aegagropilion stretched his newborn body and gave a roar that shook the surrounding trees. He looked at his hands and gave a slow smile with his fresh face. "Let's try out the strength of this Wisdom." Gradually, with effort, his fists began to transform into solid stone. He walked across to where the lower half of his former body still stood imprisoned, and with a cry slammed both fists into the stone structure. Shrapnel rained down everywhere, and Aegagropilion laughed. “His talents are a bit reluctant to my will yet, but that will come in time.”

Schpariel stepped forward and placed a hand on the broad shoulder of the Godbeast, who now towered over him by more than a foot. “I’m please that your plan worked out, though I am annoyed at your refusal to share it with me beforehand. Now if you are quite finished, I would still like the return of my Moon Rod.”

Aegagropilion tilted his head and squinted one eye, but did not argue. “Having been sufficiently fed at last, I need it no longer. It’s yours again.” He held his right hand forward, and the slender black rod topped with a sapphire rose slowly from his sinewy palm.

Schpariel seized the artifact and gathered a small store of power to it, then attempted to dismiss it into hiding amongst the ether streams. He was pleased to see the staff disintegrate, and knew that this time his brother had kept his word.

“This is a considerable turn of fate,” Aegagropilion announced. “In the last wars I was never able to absorb one of the Wisdoms. With these powers, we should prove a menacing force once more.”

The smaller Godbeast nodded. “Perhaps, but something worries me. We defeated Kiastos because he had the audacity to travel alone. What caused such a change? During our last conflict the Wisdoms never traveled in groups less than two.”

“They didn’t know of my resurrection, I’m sure. Most likely they thought you traveled alone and were not concerned with your soloing abilities. Kiastos did seem surprised to see me when the battle was met.”

“Still, Kiastos always traveled with Dosiros. Where is the Flame gone?”

Aegagropilion paused and thought this through, at last understanding Schpariel’s concerns. “What do you believe is happening?”

“I cannot know. However, it seems that if a Wisdom pair split, it must have been for a reason. If Kiastos came for us, Dosiros must have gone for something else. Perhaps something else that was a threat."

"A threat to them? Or a threat to us?"

"That would be a good piece of information to have, now wouldn't it?"

There was another long pause. Finally the Gehennans exchanged shrugs, then slowly proceeded on their way, cautious of what awaited them in spite of their victory.

Once the site of their battle stood empty save stony debris, Zekraul slid forward from the shadows of an ancient oak and released a long hiss. "Sssss. These Wisdoms have such strength. And Aegagropilion has the ability to merge with other creatures, take their form, steal their magic as his own. How can I, the marvelous Zekraul, use this situation to ensure my future? Perhaps there's a way. I must be careful, stay close to them, be watchful. Godbeasts of Gehenna, I don't fear you anymore. Now that I understand you, it's only a matter of time before your lives serve me."

## Chapter 22.

## Fall From Grace

As the sun dipped below a canopy of skylines obscured by trees, Cildar suggested he and Detria drop camp. She rejected his call for rest, insisting they could travel a few more hours before tiring out. He had learned not to underestimate the young woman's resolve, so he nodded his acquiescence and they continued stolidly along their way.

They had maintained a good pace since parting paths with Abaddon, and were now on the northeastern fringes of the Draconic Forest. Another week of marching would land them near the Forest of Techenar, at which point they had agreed to separate. Cildar felt confident the Wisdoms would have evacuated the eastern regions of the continent by now, so after crossing the Dapalis Plains he would double back and head south, leaving Detria to her journey.

They traveled onward until two hours after the sun had set. It was approaching late winter and sunset still came early, but the evenings were warm and their march was not uncomfortable. They reached the edge of the forested lands and stepped through, happily greeting the short stretch of plains that lay beyond.

But it was not the plains alone that returned their greetings. A white figure, seeming to reflect daylight even on the darkened landscape, offered an elegant bow to the pair of travelers.

"The Rook, and the princess he escorts. It was most gracious of you to come to me."

Detria reached to her breastplate and drew forth two small knives. Cildar was briefly taken aback to discover she had managed to keep weapons hidden from him this entire time, but had no chance now to comment. Instead he reached to his back and unhooked his Trine Lance from its grips, swinging it forward and pointing it at the pale visage before him.

"Akatriel, isn't it?"

Beneath the silky hood, the paladin detected the movement of the colorless face twisting in displeasure. "Oh dear. The Knight is spreading my name amongst the pieces. Troublesome. It goes to show what happens when you try to play too strictly by the rules."

Detria remained in nervous silence as Cildar continued the exchange of words. "What do you want here?"

"Why think you I want anything? Perhaps this encounter is pure mishap."

"Then get on your way, and we'll do likewise."

Akatriel shrugged, the playful humor draining from his voice. "I was merely presenting a possibility. This encounter is not mishap. You stand in the midst of a very important chain of events. I have spent nearly a decade orchestrating it, and now you northerners are becoming quite a hindrance. I confess I'm improvising a bit at this point, but your actions have forced me from my preferred design."

Cildar calmly waited a few seconds, considering his options. At the same time he began layering white and grey magic onto his body. Once he had made his decision, he charged Akatriel and executed a series of sweeping strikes with his Trine Lance, shouting back to Detria, "Run, clear this place!"

"I can help you!" she contended, moving to follow a step behind his charge.

"Just go!" he demanded, not taking his attention from his assault. "Take to your people first!"

She hesitated in her resolve. Cildar had already driven back Akatriel far, and the cloaked figure made no efforts at counterattacking. The Dragoon continued his charge, slowly rotating his adversary until his view to the north was blocked, allowing Detria a clear path to continue her way east. She saw this opening provided for her and finally broke into a run. "Don't you die, Cildar!"

The two white-garbed figures stood staring at one another calmly as Detria made her way. As her footsteps faded from earshot, Cildar swore, "You will not have her, Akatriel."

The priest reached up and slid his hood back, giving a quiet laugh at this statement. "Rook, what in Morolia makes you think I have any interest in her?"

The paladin took a few cautious steps back, no longer certain in his chosen course of action. "I assumed you were here attempting to forestall the defeat of the Overlord."

Akatriel narrowed his eyes, still smiling. "No you didn't. You have no reason to believe that. What you did was, you allowed your misguided sense of chivalry to blind you, then rushed on instinct to 'save the princess'. I have no interest in the self-declared overlord of nothing, or his little castle. I aim to change a world, not a continent. The events I have set into motion will wipe away the Overlord and his games alongside all others."

"So you're planning an apocalypse? Doesn't that seem a tad unoriginal?"

"And boring, I would add. No, what I'm planning is quite different altogether. A return to the classics, if you will. But you concern yourself in matters too far beyond you." He raised his right hand and gave a snap. A series of silver lightning bolts began to strike from an electrical field condensing over Cildar's head, forcing him into an evasive retreat.

When the storm ceased, the Dragoon gathered a stream of holy energy into his left arm and unleashed an Aura Blast. The attack was far more powerful than he had intended. The white beam was over two feet wide and carried a strange red flicker, and was so intense that the ground beneath it singed from its passage. Akatriel smiled and threw his arms wide. When the white bolt struck, only his cloak remained, and the attack passed harmlessly as though an ordinary white sheet blocked its path. After the holy energy dissipated this white cloak regenerated its midsection, expanded, and Akatriel reappeared inside of it.

Cildar was caught off guard by his own spiritual strength he had just exhibited. He stared down at his left hand with a creased brow. "Have I somehow increased in power?" he whispered quietly to himself. "Is this another aftereffect from Shock?"

Meanwhile, Akatriel volunteered the nature of his peculiar evasion. "From what I'm told, you once fought a lich, correct? If that's true, then I'm sure you are familiar with their shadow miraging technique. It's a difficult trick to pick up, but I've become handy enough with it."

The paladin dismissed his quandary and glared at his foe. "You claim to know much of my life for someone who was separated from me by an entire ocean."

"My resources are varied and deep."

"You're right, I did face a lich. Unfortunately for you, I defeated that lich, and already know how to counter this trick."

"Oh? Well that you must certainly demonstrate for me."

Cildar layered additional grey magic blessings onto himself and gathered a burst of white ether. As he threw up his Auras, his body illuminated with a light more intense than even he had anticipated. His magic held its cohesion, though, wrapping about him tightly. Once he was confident his defenses were in place, he spoke the keyword to tap the Phase Shift matrix which would lock together Haste.

"Mal-oste haruste."

The hurricane of power coursing through his body was overwhelming, and the world around him turned shimmery and unstable. With intense concentration he brought his vision into focus and braced himself for a charge. He was surprised to find that instead of launching at his opponent at full speed, he merely stumbled forward a few awkward steps. He tightened his grip on his Trine Lance and tried to think clearly, but felt a distinct sense of panic sinking in. Haste had never before gone wrong for him, but he knew a failed casting could only mean death.

Akatriel did not leave him languishing under this concern for long. "Having a bit of trouble? You've lived up to your selection as the Rook. Powerful, but predictable when isolated. You think yourself so clever with your ability to assume a false mysticism. In order to survive your suicidal technique, you soak in all the surrounding ether you can reach in order to anchor your spirit on the Morolian plane. But it appears you lack the basic sense to check said ether first, to ascertain whether it's safe for your consumption. Were you not so overzealous in your role as a defender, you might have suspected something amiss when you fired your first attack." He paused to reach into his sleeve, pulling forth a smooth red stone. "Since my arrival here, I have been lacing this area with trace amounts of Gehennite ether using this."

Falling to his knees, Cildar struggled to bring his vision into focus once more and examined the ether around him. Indeed, he could detect thin red streams still drizzled throughout the area.

Akatriel continued, "When not metabolized properly, red ether is poisonous to most species. You haven't taken in quite enough to kill you, but you'll remain paralyzed for the next few minutes. Long enough for me to remove your piece from the board."

He returned the stone to his sleeve, and in its stead pulled forth a small black orb. He pointed the orb in the direction of the paladin's kneeling form, then gave it a light tap. The mouth of a golden demon wrapped about the sphere slowly opened, and a black beam of light fired forth into Cildar's chest. He tried to struggle to his feet or shout his defiance, but found both his limbs and voice had become paralyzed.

He began to feel as though his eyes were closing against his will, as the beam of black light continued to pour into him. The waves of holy energy dancing around him were dyed first to a dark grey, and then to a black tint, until his entire form appeared to be drenched in darkness. As the stricken man's body shifted, the orb held in the conspirator's hand lost its own gloom. After a minute of this strange transference the dark stream of light flickered out, and Cildar was left soaked in a black shade.

Akatriel watched in curiosity as the paled orb in his hand slowly crumbled into dust, the gilded demon melting away into a thin liquid. "Only enough strength remaining for one use," he remarked. "Disappointing, but adequate." He wiped his hand clean and then looked to the kneeling Dragoon before him. "You should be better now. Try to stand."

As bid, the man slowly rose to his feet, his breathing heavy. The only speck of white remaining throughout his entire form was the head of the Trine Lance, which still shone with a bright luminescence. Cildar looked first at the Lance in his right hand, then at the black glove covering his left. He began opening and closing his fingers as if mesmerized by the motion.

"Farthas," Akatriel called to him soothingly, "how do you feel?"

He brought his gloved fist to a tight grip in response. "Why do you call me that? My name is Cildar Emle, Lord of the Phoenix." He ended his statement with a nod, as though reaffirming his own conviction on the matter.

The robed figure reached up and scratched his chin. *Peculiar*, he thought to himself. *The Crucible should have given dominance to the spirit with superior pride and clarity, yet it seems the draconic's mind has been swallowed by the Rook's. This could complicate matters for me.* Aloud, he questioned, "Will you continue your assault upon me?"

The man hesitated to respond. Finally he answered uncertainly, "No. Upon reflection, I'm unclear as to why were fighting. You've not yet shown yourself to be my enemy, Akatriel the Lost."

The priest gave a subtle sigh of relief. "This may yet work," he mused quietly to himself. "He has maintained some portion of Farthas' characteristics. Their wills must have been an extremely close match. I'm uncertain if that colors negatively upon poor Farthas, or exalts this Son of Emle." He raised his voice once more so the man could hear. "You are correct, Cildar, I'm no enemy of yours. In fact, I've given you a generous gift. Can you feel it?"

"I feel... something, I admit. I'm struggling to place my finger on it, but something is different. Something feels... lost."

"That's incorrect. I have taken nothing from you, rather I have *added* onto you. I've made you into something more, a perfect merger of the two dominant species of our world. I might even argue that you're an improvement upon Elzaniru's own work. The few measly decades of life you've experienced thus far may seem diminished now, but that's only because you have been granted a greater context through which to view it. Let it happen, let your mind grow, let your perceptions expand."

The man took in a slow breath, allowing himself a moment to relax. "Yes, I feel it now. I have been petty. I've concerned myself with matters inconsequential, lost in the blink of an eye. I was soft, passive, my ideas built upon ludicrous foundations of propriety. I am beyond those trifles. I am enduring, I will live forever. A creature such as myself should have no desire for the accolades of these small and brief mortals."

"Well spoken. I have merged two souls within your powerful body, giving birth to something new. You are equal parts Morolian and Asterian spirits. As a corollary, it's necessary that you forever remain in your mysticized state. If ever the condition you call 'Haste' subsides, you won't have enough strength to hold your Asterian half in place, and you will die. With time your spirit will adapt beyond this; given enough, your form will become permanent. You are the Dark Paladin, my own brainchild, a volatile mix of a human's potential backed by the wisdom of a dragon."

The man continued to stare at his own gloved hands, still familiarizing himself with them. "If I remain in this state for too long, mightn't I become a lich?"

"Possibly. Is there some concern with that?"

"To the contrary, I should have embraced it long ago. I invented Haste to make me into something more. I should have never hidden from its possibilities." He stepped away from Akatriel and turned to face north, toward the sea. "But what am I to do with this new power? I came to Arkalen for idle fun, yet somehow found myself serving Lord Abaddon's agendas, forsaking my own. I am Emle; how did I come to bow so readily before the whims of another man?"

Akatriel could not repress a broad smile. This was the

opportunity he needed, a chance to plant a seed of guidance in his new creation. "A poignant observation, no doubt a result of the fresh clarity I've given you. Return, then, to your own desires, and not another man's. Return to your hunt for fun, Cildar Emle. Free yourself from the tyranny of Abaddon Daemon."

The tall man straightened his back and flexed his shoulders. "Yes," he said, drawing out the syllable. "What better prey could there be? In younger days I chased after Lord Abaddon. I should have never stopped. I will chase him again. I will hunt *him*! My mighty adversary was always right in front of me, and I was too much the fool to turn on him and sate my need for sport. It's so clear now."

"But Abaddon Daemon is a ferocious prey, to be sure. First, I should like to see the full extent of the might I have graced upon you. Attack me, if you might indulge my curiosity. If you cannot best me, then you are not prepared for the Daemon."

Cildar tilted the Trine Lance and crouched to a defensive stance. As he did, the waves of black energy surrounding him flared up and emanated outward. Then with a sudden burst of speed, he charged his target and thrust. Akatriel shifted rapidly to his left side, gathering a charge of lightning to release. The Dark Paladin roared, "Too slow!" and lashed out with a high kick from his left leg. The pale figure was struck hard in the jaw, and sent plummeting across the woodland floor.

Akatriel brought himself to a halt, launching a series of huge arching bolts at his assailant. The black figure charged forward through the attacks fearlessly, allowing them to rip through his body without response. A trail of blood smeared the grass behind him, but he shouted, "No pain!" as he reached his target and attacked once more.

Several rounds of Cildar's rushes—answered by waves of white lightning—followed. The pale priest was agile beyond human limits, but the Dragoon's ferocity left him at a loss, so it was only a matter of time before he was finally struck. Akatriel summoned a flash of blinding light covering the area and attempted to vanish within it, leaping four yards behind his creation's back and gathering more ether.

But Cildar's drenched black eyes were immersed in Asterian currents, and not bothered by the Morolian disturbance. He quickly turned and blasted once more to his opponent, spearing the robed chest with the Trine Lance.

Akatriel managed to slide just enough to avoid a direct blow, but one of the ribs on his left side was completely disintegrated by the might of the thrust. He shrieked, "Enough! I yield!" hoping it would end the exchange, but within his moment of panic, he felt certain he was doomed.

To his surprise, Cildar did stay his assault. He backed away and returned the Trine Lance to his back, then bowed softly. Akatriel placed a powerful barrier over the damaged part of his flesh, halting the ravage of holy poison delivered by the Lance. He rose to his feet and returned the bow.

"I'm no match for you," he spoke without pain or waver in his voice. "A final word of caution: that spear you use has a peculiar trait. It can banish all powers not of the Morolian plane. If you ever attempt to tie your soul to it directly and wield its full potential, you will be destroyed and the former Cildar Emle restored."

The Dark Paladin answered with a nod, "I understand what you mean. I know my Lance well. I won't allow it to destroy me, only my foes."

"Then go. From this moment forth, you're on your own. I will seek you out no more."

The black figure dashed into the forest, eager to begin his hunt, and disappeared quickly into the darkness of the night. Once he was gone safely beyond earshot, Akatriel collapsed to his knees with a gasp.

"Damn my overconfidence! I was in no shape to tangle with him after the wounds I suffered from Aegagropilion." He bit his lower lip as he sought to repair as much of his body as possible, attempting to cleanse himself of the Trine Lance's magic. "Still, I never imagined the Rook was capable of such speed. The humans involved in this game are more formidable than could have been anticipated."

At that moment, a black cloud began to engulf his body. Akatriel hung his head and began to chuckle, unable to repress himself. Once the darkness had completely closed on him, he spoke before being addressed. "It's been a long time since you meddled. Is there some sort of problem, or are you just a fool?" he spat. "You're not catching me at a good time. I've set the Rook against the Knight and Bishop, and now there are others I must gather. My time is so very crucial right now, I pray you waste it with reason."

*Aegagropilion has absorbed the Wisdom Kiastos.*

"Yes, a strange stroke of luck thanks to the interference of the unpredictable Knight. In addition to my having already foreseen this event, it is good news rather than bad. The Godbeasts have yet to fulfill their role, so it's important that they are not slain. Better to lose a single Wisdom than all the Godbeasts. This doesn't explain your need to bother me."

*One Wisdom is gone. Once consumed by Aegagropilion, their souls serve no use. We will need four for the endgame.*

"I think I understand now. Let me think a moment." He grew quiet, lowering his head further. He sat breathing heavily for a few seconds, trying to catch his breath against his weakness. "Ah! It has occurred to me that six minus one is only five! Which, as it happens, is still greater than four." His temper finally snapped and his voice rose to a shout. "Why do you plague me? Do you think I've come this far to fail on such a simple detail? Be gone!"

*When this finishes, you will pay me back for your insolence with years of servitude.*

"I am older than you, and I will outlive you," he spat through gritting teeth. "My ears are not brought to fear by your threats. If you want this done, you'll leave me alone for my work."

The cloud dissipated, leaving Akatriel sitting alone once more in the forest. It took another ten minutes of intense healing before he felt at last in the condition to move again, then he slowly stumbled out of the area on route to his next task.

* * * * *

Keldana opened her eyes and turned to her lord. "Kiastos has fallen."

Melukah had remained motionless in his seated position for nearly an hour, resting his body now that the sun had gone down. "The same as Valinoru?" he asked aloud. Inwardly, he wondered what creatures were out there capable of injuring his Wisdoms.

"The inverse. His body yet functions, but his soul has been dispelled. He's lost until he can be reincarnated in Elysium."

Melukah did not move, pausing for effect. "Aegagropilion has joined us, then."

"And he must have Kiastos' power now. Perhaps we shall move?"

"No. I still wish to watch over Gilanirus. Dosiros is more than a match for Kiastos. He can handle this situation by himself. Even if he could not, Torlen is by his side. There is no danger there."

Keldana nodded and returned to her duty as watcher.

* * * * *

Dosiros and Torlen had taken a similar stance to Melukah and Keldana, settling down in the once-threatening Fenrir Jungle. Dosiros, like Melukah, was certain the Godbeasts would eventually come this way, and preferred to wait them out rather than continue scouring the continent and risk passing them by somehow.

Torlen was not a fan of this plan, as he preferred to remain in motion. He stood a few hundred yards separated from Dosiros, just within range that the two could sense each other's presence. The Wisdom of Sound was still rankled by his reassignment. Kiastos and Dosiros had proven to be a troublesome duo, so the Wisdom ranks had been reorganized in an attempt to keep at least one level head in each pairing. Torlen had always appreciated Valinoru's company, as well as his travel and combat styles. He was not warming to his fiery new associate.

As he stood musing over previous wars, he detected a strange signal on the airwaves. At first he thought it was nothing, merely a magnetic anomaly in the area. Then it began to repeat and become more insistent. He focused his attention to it and began to notice a pattern. Slowly he recognized it for a message, then began decoding it.

*Torlen. Valinoru has fallen to the hands of humans. We beseech your favor. Find the humans and mark them so that we may bring them to Elysium and judge them for this crime.*

He listened to the message a few more times, but no further information was contained. He reached up and scratched the back of his head. "A human defeated Val? That seems impossible." He hummed to himself for a moment while thinking. "I see. The Muses contacted me because they knew I couldn't resist my curiosity on the matter. They aren't wrong. I suppose I'll head north and investigate."

He moved to Dosiros and reported that he would be briefly absent. The Wisdom of the Flame did not seem to care one way or another, so Torlen channeled ether into his legs and, using a burst of sonic waves to carry him, launched into the sky and flew toward the Jagguron Peaks.

## Chapter 23.

# Lord of the Wolves

Deun Coloran stood at the base of the most prominent peak of Jagguron. Since departing the small camp of Kelve Orista, he had sought out the Overlord with renewed vigor. His quarry was difficult to track, especially when suspicious someone was seeking him. But it had been more than two years since Deun had been close, and it seemed the Overlord had finally dropped his guard. The former Devilslayer had found a clear trail in the Draconic Forest leading south. His spirits had soared from this fortune, and he had rapidly followed the tracks.

His boon was a temporary one, however. The trail was visible for less than a mile, then disappeared. Deun had continued traveling along the course the tracks had indicated, marching through a brief stretch of plains that stood between the forest and the mountainous Jagguron Peaks.

Since then nothing had revealed itself. There was a small petrified forest to Deun's east—possibly the former southern tip of the Draconic Forest—known as the Ondea Woods. He had explored a short expanse of the area. There were signs of activity and large creatures coming and going, but nothing seemed to denote the presence of the Overlord. Dejected, he had traveled farther south and arrived at the Peaks.

His instincts beckoned him to cross the mountains and head into the southern part of the continent. It would make sense that the Overlord might have taken to those regions. It could explain why Deun had been unable to locate him for these past long months. But the southern reaches of Arkalen still belonged to the wilderness, and made for a hard journey. Even with the collapse of the Lifeless Vortex, there were few human settlements south of the divider of Jagguron.

He was not unfamiliar with this southern stretch. He had been in command of the contingent of Devilslayers responsible for wiping out the fenrirs, and various other powerful breeds of southern demons. Afterwards, the Devilslayers had given up on occupation of the southern lands. Without close human settlements, Deun would be committing himself to a long period of isolation and risk. It was a foolhardy gamble to take, with no hard evidence that his prey had truly migrated south. It was rare for him to resist his instincts, but the stakes seemed stacked against him.

His blood froze as some peculiar intuition alerted him that he was not alone. Deun had never understood his intuition, but it had never misled him where danger was concerned. There was something nearby, and it was powerful—powerful enough to pose a real threat to him. He reached to the hilt of the longsword on his back and tightened his stance.

"That won't be necessary," a soothing voice assured. "I'm not your enemy."

He nimbly spun about. There was no one there. A stretch of empty plains ran between him and the draconics' former homeland. Then a shadowy figure appeared, distorting his view of the distant forest. The image shimmered and soon transformed into a man in solid white robes, his hood tossed back to reveal a pale face with a warm smile.

"Who are you?" Deun demanded without releasing his hilt.

"Merely an adviser. I don't know if you're aware, but there are many events crawling their way across Arkalen's surface. You are one of the important players in these events. You've yet to play your part."

"You accuse me of having some sort of fate, priest? I don't place stock in nonsense of that nature."

"You say, yet I cannot believe that. Certainly not with your gifts."

"Now you claim to know something about me?"

The visitor raised his hands before him and crossed his fingers together lightly. "Let us see. You were born in a small village near the eastern edge of the continent. Your brother was ten years your senior, and quite ambitious. He joined the Devilslayers at a young age, and you idolized him as a child. But your brother refused to stay under the control of the Devilslayers. He desired to come home and use his skills to protect your village, so he did. When you were eleven years old, a new demon referring to himself as the Overlord and his small army of acolytes—at the time little more than a wandering band of nomadic were-creatures—attacked your home. Your brother fought the Overlord face-to-face and gave his life, your parents were kidnapped into the Overlord's servitude, yet you miraculously escaped while the rest of your village perished.

"You were found and taken in by the Devilslayers. Your brother's transgression against them was forgiven and you were given the chance to set things aright. When the Lifeless Vortex collapsed, it was you and High Chieftain Orikon who led the push for humans to take the continent back. It was Orikon's sharp wit and your strong arm that made it possible. It wasn't until you had been a slayer for thirteen years when you came across some information about your past.

"It turns out the Devilslayers had been tracking this group of demons and had even anticipated the raid on your village. They sent a young pack leader named Yasiff Oturl to lend aid. But because of your brother's desertion, Yasiff abandoned your people in their time of need. He felt it important to send a message, to highlight the repercussions of shunning Devilslayer order. In the chaos of the attack, the pack leader and his unit waited nearby, stumbling across you. Realizing your identity, they hoped you could prove to be as talented a killer as your elder sibling, so they saved you from your family's fate. This of course paid off, and you became a warrior to match your brother's caliber, rapidly becoming the champion of the clan.

"Until the day Yasiff was foolish enough to admit this to you, in a poorly advised attempt to inspire some measure of gratitude. In a rage, you attacked and killed the Devilslayers who had been involved in your raising. All except Yasiff himself, whom you only managed to injure. Then Orikon stepped in with his full ranks of Silver Pride bodyguards. You were unable to reach either the High Chieftain or Yasiff, though you killed many as they barred your path. Since then, you've sworn to kill any Devilslayers who stand in your way, and you spend your days and nights hunting the accursed Overlord who took your brother's life, so that you may avenge his spilled blood.

"So now, would you say I know you?"

Deun squinted and clenched his jaw. He had shown no emotion or reaction to hearing his own history so callously detailed. He dropped his hand from his sword's hilt and drew a cigarette from the base of his glove, lighting it slowly. After taking a long drag, he responded, "I would say you know a lot about business that's none of yours."

"Then you'll humor me for a moment longer?" As there was no response to this, the pale stranger continued his tale with a smile. "There's yet more to this story, which even you are not aware. Why is it, you think, that you're such an elite killer? Why is it that, even though you were trained as a Devilslayer, you're more than a match for a dozen of them?"

"It's in my blood. My brother was also a fierce warrior."

"Yet your father was a peasant. A farmer. And your mother's heritage similarly dull."

"What would you imply, priest?"

"Your power, Deun Coloran. The Devilslayers thought that because your brother was strong, you would be as well. They thought this because they understand so very little. Your power is a fluke. It's coincidence. It's only by the slimmest margins of fate that you happened to turn out as you are. Bloodlines, heritage, the endurance of the human spirit—these things have nothing to do with it."

"Yet my brother's strength, from what I am told, was a match for my own. How can such a thing just be coincidence?"

"You're correct, your brother was like you. You were both exceptions. You're evolved humans. Your brother had a rare gift—the sight of a seer. He never did learn to properly channel this gift, or he could have ordained many things, possibly even preventing his own demise. Even without developing it, his magical sight allowed him to perceive a few seconds into the future, making him a warrior of incalculable merit. When your brother left the Devilslayers, they thought they would take you and anoint a new champion. At virtually any other moment in history, this notion would have been a foolish one, and you would have been doomed to be a disappointment.

"The potential to be a seer exists in many bloodlines, but it's only one in every thousand for whom the sight is unlocked. Since your brother's had been unlocked, it was a near certainty that yours would not. But in this one case, something else happened. You, Deun, were born as a mystic, a gift surpassing even that of seerism. Your mysticism, in addition to giving you peerless strength, also forced open your seer's eye. Perhaps it was the spot where the two of you were born, or the strange mix of your mother and father's genes. In any event, like your brother, you were given the potential to break the mold that limits human achievement."

Deun finished his cigarette and snuffed it out on the ground. "Thank you for your theories, but I'm truly disinterested. I must be getting back to my hunt."

"Come, listen but a moment longer. I can be a potent ally if you but humor me." Deun again did not respond, nor did he move to leave. "You are an exceptional mystic. In addition to your normal gifts of inhuman strength, speed, regeneration, you also have the gift of the seers. You can see between the narrow cracks in reality, to foresee glimpses of future events. You've always ignored your exalted sight, but it has saved you nonetheless. Have you ever been cut by enemy blade? Has even a demon, no matter how fast or strong, laid a single scratch across your flesh?"

The armored man hung his head in thought. The stranger's words were true, but he confessed to nothing. He had no desire to believe he was something special. He was a warrior because he had always been. He was strong because his brother had been strong, because it was in his blood to be a great warrior. He had always believed these things were as simple as they seemed. He was unwilling to let go of that so easily.

The stranger continued, "I wish to help you, Deun Coloran. I wish to aid you in your hunt. When the time comes, your powers could be a valuable asset for me."

"I neither need nor want an ally." Now knowing his visitor's intent, he turned away and began to move off to the east, uncertain of his destination, but certain that he was done with this conversation.

The shrouded stranger suddenly slid across the clearing faster than Deun could follow, appearing directly in his path with an upheld hand. The warrior jumped back and again his hand flew to his hilt. He had never before been taken by surprise at an opponent's speed.

"I know you don't seek a partner. I'm not offering anything of the sort. More of a mutual arrangement. An exchange of simple favors. If I can deliver the Overlord into your hands, can you offer me a favor in return?"

The dour man slowly drew his sword, a slim but powerful black blade, only two inches wide with an engraved silver handle. "I offer you this: bar my path no longer, or perish by my blade."

"You wish to go through me? You're heading east?"

"What if I am?"

"Surely that's not what your vision tells you. You must learn to obey your seer's sight. You will find the Overlord in the southern lands. If you want to finish your quest, you must cross the mountain range here. It's there that all of the events of Arkalen will collide. It's there that your fate will conclude."

Deun paused for a second, his face set in emotionless iron. "Leave me."

The stranger gave a deep bow, gently favoring his left side. Deun picked out the subtle motion, suspecting the man had sustained a recent injury. “Very well,” the stranger acceded. “I do hope our paths will cross again.”

Without walking, the pale figure faded slowly from sight. The mystic seer remained exactly where he was for nearly ten minutes, waiting until he felt he was truly alone. Once his instincts assured him his visitor was gone, he returned his sword to its sheath and turned to the south. Deun Coloran would cross the Jagguron Peaks.

* * * * *

Detria had not gone far since her departure from Cildar. After running less than half a mile she began to tire and slowed to catch her breath, her body still weary from the day’s march. She knew she was not far from the fight, so she was surprised by the absence of the sounds of battle drifting across the plains. She began to think the situation might have been less serious than they had assumed, and wondered if it was safe for her to go back.

Then she had received unwelcome company. An entire pack of Devilslayers, twenty soldiers strong, rose from hiding within the brush around her with weapons drawn. Detria cursed under her breath. She could not believe she had let herself grow lax enough to not check for sentries. She calmed herself and tried to play the matter off casually. If they thought she was a civilian, they would have no reason to bother her.

“Hello,” she greeted with the most cheerful tone she could muster. “You’re Devilslayers, right? I’ve heard about you. I’m trying to get home to the lands in the west, and there was a monster of some sort back there. You can offer protection from such things, right?”

“Knock it off, Alsen. It’s not going to be that easy for you.”

She glanced over to the man who had spoken. Again she cursed under her breath. “Mek Tellish. It figures I’d run into one of my pupils. How fares the clan since Yasiff took over?"

Mek gave her a bold smile. "Better than yourself I'd say, teach. Since you left, Yasiff thought up this little list, see: high priority but high risk targets. To be dealt with only if a convenient situation arises. I'd say that with us having you outnumbered twenty to one, this is about as convenient as it gets. Seize her!"

Four men came forward and grabbed at her. She thought for a moment to defend herself, but she knew Mek was right. If she struggled, she only increased her chance of taking on injury or even death. This would have to be a political battle.

"Mek, please don't do this," she begged as hands latched onto her arms. "You don't understand everything that's going on. There are events outside of the Devilslayer's hands right now, and I can't be detained! Kelve and I have found the Overlord's fortress. He's waging a war right now and I have to go to him. I have to help them!"

"Sorry lady," the smile had faded from Mek's face, as he was handing out orders to a few of the other Devilslayers. "You've got your agendas, and I've got mine. Even if what you say is true, if there are events going on that the Devilslayers don't know about, then that's just one more reason I should take you to Yasiff for interrogation."

She hung her head and bit her lower lip. When a prisoner was taken directly to the Devilslayer's High Chieftain, it always meant the same thing. There would be a week of intense questioning, followed by at least a month of gruesome torture, possibly more depending on how badly the prisoner was judged in need of "cleansing". As a Devilslayer, Detria had never been able to stomach even watching the torture from afar. Now she would be living through it.

Mek seemed to notice her despair. As she was carried away by the slayers who held her, he leaned in close and whispered quietly, "I'm sorry it has to be this way. If I were to let you go, my men would report me and it'd be me serving in Hell's Cell instead of you."

Her only response was a weak-willed spit in his direction, then she was drug toward the north.

* * * * *

Yasiff Oturl, High Chieftain of the Devilslayers, sat in a large wooden chair decorated with various animal and demon pelts. The High Chieftain had never been such a ceremonious figurehead in the past, but Yasiff had expressed the need to exalt the position, in order to reflect a stronger sense of organization among the tribe. Today there was a broad smile on his face, as the deserter Detria Alsen was brought to her knees before him.

"It has been a long time, Wolf," he greeted her.

Once the guards moved aside, she stubbornly forced her way back onto her feet and glared at the chieftain. "My name is Detria. Use it. I'm not under your hand any longer. You're imprisoning a civilian. Have the Devilslayers become so dishonorable?"

"We adapted to meet the times, as we always have. If we're to save Arkalen from the evils consuming it, we must be willing to seek those evils out diligently. We can't hand out immunity from our rule. If we did, those who were immune would be the very ones who would oppose us. Only by bringing everyone into line equally, and fairly, can we remove injustice."

"As ever, *you* do not seek to remove injustice. You seek to become injustice! You would rule humanity just the same as the demons you swear to kill."

Yasiff rose from his throne and roared, "We *are* justice! If not us, then who? Who will protect the people? Who will preserve the order that is so delicately slipping away?"

Detria ground her teeth in frustration. Yasiff was a madman. It was clear that power had only intoxicated him, forcing him deeper into his insane ideology. "Why did you bring me here? I have my own life now. I have no business with any of you."

"It's been reported to me that you have engaged in war against the Overlord. Is there any truth to this? Or is it only the latest rumors surrounding a creature which does not exist?"

"I haven't seen the Overlord himself, but I have seen his home. A large fortress filled with armies of demons. Kelve Orista and my troops wage war with him even now, and I was trying to return to them when your zealots apprehended me without reason."

"Their reasons were simple. They have orders to apprehend all treacherous deserters. In the past, Devilslayers deserting the clan has led to many bad situations. I've passed a new law stating that those who leave the clan must be cleansed. You left before this law was passed. You have not been cleansed."

"This is insane! The Devilslayers were founded to protect the people of Arkalen. By your own code and bylaws, you should help me now. Gather your men and come with me, help us take down the Overlord's armies! If you do so, then I'll suffer whatever consequences you feel are necessary. But surely saving Arkalen must come first, even to you, Yasiff."

The Chieftain sat down and rubbed his chin. "The Overlord, if he truly exists, is indeed a threat. If there's a demonic fortress, as you claim, then the Devilslayers should know about it. We should take it. But now is not the time. Such things must not be done hastily. There's time for the council to debate this situation. Until they come to a decision, you'll remain here. Take her!" As the guards seized Detria, she dug her fingernails into her palms with such intensity that her hands bled. Yasiff announced loudly, "Detria Alsen, I sentence you to three months of correction. When you emerge, your spirit will be cleansed of the crimes of your past."

As she was led away, she quietly answered, "For your crimes, you'll never find forgiveness. I swear to it." He chuckled at her insolence, then called for the council to assemble to him, in order to debate these new claims of the Overlord's presence on Arkalen.

Detria Alsen would endure Hell's Cell.

## Chapter 24.

## Manticore, King of Chimeras

Tessena sat in her private quarters perusing paperwork. Since their arrival she had overseen several skirmishes against the force besieging the Overlord's land, and had debriefed every surviving troop herself, carefully documenting their comments and discoveries. By now she had built an overwhelming dossier of information, some reliable, some useless. Sorting it out was proving to be quite a task.

These struggles aside, she was convinced she had learned enough to begin the next phase of the war. The invaders were united under a man named Kelve. This Kelve, as well as most of his troops, seemed to be well trained and resourceful. In spite of their small numbers, they had an excellent working knowledge of how to exploit any weaknesses in the demonic ranks. Only the trolls seemed to be an exception to this. Even the diverse chimeras had been dissected and analyzed for all possible weaknesses by now and, willful creatures that they were, they refused to return to combat under Tessena's lead.

Truthfully, the Overlord's army was not in good standing. The death of Kaltheria had triggered the desertion of the majority of the nightspawn. Tessena had done her best to convince the remaining to stay, but after scarcely a week they had followed their absent comrades. In the skirmishes since, ten of the ogres had been either slain or critically wounded by some still unidentified poison. This left the remaining ogre troops hesitant to march out and make easy targets of themselves.

With the ogres and chimeras striking out of cowardice, only the expendable were-creatures, the meager trolls, and the inexperienced draconics remained at Tessena's disposal. She had assigned Gariso to train up a regiment of competent human forces. This endeavor was not going well. The people serving under the Overlord up until now had been used as a menial labor force, and they lacked the edge or instincts required to make good soldiers. Tessena was frustrated by witnessing the shortcomings of her race, but she did not blame them. It was their mistreatment, and their captors, who were responsible. The invaders outside her walls were clear evidence of just how capable humans could truly be.

So she was left with roughly eight hundred dependable troops. Her demons should be more than a match for half as many humans, she was certain of that. But there was likewise no question that her generals were not a match for the enemy's champions. Kelve had a talent for finding a way to kill any foe he faced, and Tessena had seen for herself the strength of the Monk of Tria, if left unchecked.

A knock sounded upon her door, pulling her from her thoughts. She shouted for the sentry to enter. After doing so he gave a quick bow, then announced, "Lord Ontarshiss is here to see you, milady."

"Good," she answered. "Send him in."

The sentry carefully made his way out, and the majestic head of the griffin edged slowly into the room. He tucked his wings in tight about his body, carefully entering until the door could close behind him. Once it was shut, he stubbornly threw his wings wide. All the papers on Tessena's desk went scattering across the room.

She bit her lip and leaned her head on her fists. "Seriously?"

"You are the one who had the gall to summon me into your chamber," Ontarshiss retorted.

"Fine. I'll deal with this later. Listen, it's time for Manticore to take the battlefield. The Overlord calls for his strength."

Ontarshiss chuckled lightly. "Really? Last I checked, my scouts assured me the Overlord is not in the area. I doubt he could have slipped in under my aerial gaze."

"As General to the Overlord himself, I carry his word."

"I am also a General. And since I also carry his word, I say the Overlord says Manticore is not yet ready. It seems the Overlord is of a split mind."

"You mock these matters too lightly, bird."

The griffin surged forward, bringing his razor-tipped beak only inches from her face. "You take my race too lightly, monkey."

Tessena slowly raised her gloved left hand and stroked the side of Ontarshiss' neck, locking one of her fingers underneath the ribbon that kept the glove's powers dormant. "So will we kill each other here and now?" she said in a silky voice. "Is that how this meeting will end?"

Ontarshiss hesitated for a moment. "I could rip your neck open before your magic could seize my body."

"Then do it," she whispered.

They eyed each other steadily for a moment, then the chimera sniffed and backed a safe distance across the room. "Say what you will, threaten me if you like, it doesn't change the fact that Manticore will not enter battle. I was chosen to serve as our people's ambassador to the Overlord, but Manticore is still our king. I do not command him."

"If he doesn't enter battle today, then I'll bring this matter before Lord Shote."

Ontarshiss' breath froze. "You bluff. The minotaur fell in the same battle that Manticore was wounded. Shote lives no more."

"Like Manticore, Lord Shote has spent much time recovering. He's not expected to rise again for a few more weeks. I would hate to see his disposition if I have to awaken him early over a matter of insubordination."

"I do not lie when I say I cannot control Manticore," Ontarshiss answered, his tone now acquiescent. "What would you have me do? My wings are tied."

"Tell Manticore that we need him only for a small thing. Only a single human must be slain at his claws. Once that's done, he may sleep once more. Surely he can accept those terms."

Again Ontarshiss paused in thought. "We shall see," he said

without confidence. He bade the sentry outside to open the door and gingerly took his leave.

The General smiled in the wake of her political victory, then sent a summons for Gariso. Her companion arrived a short time later and the two discussed tactics for a while, after which she grew quiet. Tessena's rule was predicated on a certain amount of manic energy, constantly battling against egos and tempers wildly unchecked. Only occasionally—and only around Gariso—did she take a moment to slow down. When she did, the stress and despair of her situation overtook her like a wave.

Her human champion had seen this behavior many times before, and did not fail to address it swiftly. "Relax, Tess," he chided. "I'm sure you're saying the same thing to yourself already, but sometimes it's easier to hear from someone else's mouth—you're going to do fine. You're the First General for good reason. You're the only one who can lead them to victory here. They know that."

"This is the worst we've faced, Garr. Not since we've been here has the Overlord's defenses been this weak, this beaten down. I'm expected to shoulder that. Any failures will be on me. When Shote awakens, when the Overlord returns; either way, they'll make me pay for all that's gone wrong. Even if they couldn't have done any better themselves. Sometimes I think this is why they promoted me. So that some day they'd have a lowly human to blame, to sacrifice to preserve the Overlord's own reputation. I hoped that day would never come."

"I think you're right. But I also think it doesn't matter. No one ever thought a human could become one of the Overlord's champions. No one ever thought a woman could become one of his favorites. No one ever thought you'd become the highest ranking soldier in an army of demonspawn. They've always expected your failure. And you never live up to that expectation."

She smiled, her spirits renewed. Gariso always had a way of making her feel like she belonged. Perhaps it was the way in which he symbolically bridged the divide between human and demon, or perhaps it was merely in knowing she had another of her own kind standing beside her. Either way, she knew she could never have come this far without him. "I want to win this, Garr. I want to capture these invaders. A large number of them, maybe a couple of hundred. I want to add them to our ranks, so the Overlord sees for himself that human lives can have value even to him. I think in a way, this is the opportunity we've been waiting for. It's time to remind all these demons here why they fear humanity, that we're not just a bunch of carpenters and masons. This is an opportunity to make our people real equals. We don't have to just be slaves."

"So that the Overlord might prevail? So that he might conquer the continent? And inflict his cruelty on more humans? I'm not saying I disagree with you, Tess, but I need to know, is that the outcome we truly desire?"

She bit her lip in determination. "I can't think that far ahead right now. I have to help the people here, in front of me. Our people. Our families. I have to stop the abuses they endure every day, by whatever means."

He nodded. "I'm with you. As I've always been."

She stood to her feet and slammed her fists into the desk in front of her. "Then for now, let's strike a blow in the Overlord's honor."

* * * * *

Kelve made rounds about his small camp, trying to hide his concern. Since the last major battle with the Overlord's army, there had been an almost unending onslaught of smaller assaults from the fortress. Nothing had been sent that his people were unable to handle. Usually only a hundred troops of some particular mix, a select two or three of the Overlord's races. The battles were short ones. Kelve kept his most weathered former slayers to the front lines and casualties were kept at a minimum, but the enemy forces also fought conservatively, retreating after losing only small numbers.

This had been going on for eight days now. Only the previous evening had Kelve finally figured out what was happening. After the battle where the nightspawn commander had been slain, the enemy was taking the small human force seriously. Now they were judging his capabilities. The forces being sent out were tests, rulers by which to measure his ability to handle various combinations.

So now, in addition to being outmatched in terms of number and variety, his forces were outmatched on information as well. The enemies held a better analysis of his army's limitations and ranks, erasing the advantage Eiden's knowledge had previously granted. Kelve had already burned most of his own trump cards, but had no idea what horrible secrets still awaited him behind the stone walls of the fortress.

As though these concerns were not enough, Eiden himself had been missing since the nightspawn attack, along with Tenkahn. Neither Kelve nor any of his lieutenants held any clue what had happened to the two. At first he had hoped they were merely out scouting the area, with the monk having borrowed the youth as a guide. After eight days of such absence, he instead began to fear that somehow the enemy had captured his two most valuable assets.

Things being what they were, Kelve had reached an inevitable conclusion. It was time to retreat from this place. He had held out in hopes of Detria's return, but he had no idea how far she had wandered or when she might arrive. He had to ensure that whenever it was, she still had an army to come back.

One of his lieutenants approached and stood at his side, saying nothing. Kelve used the man as a mirror against his own doubts.

"Colbiss, is this battle hopeless?"

"We were taught things are never hopeless for a slayer, sir. Slayers no more we may be, but I believe our strength of heart remains undiminished."

"There is a loser to every battle," the commander responded. "That means that for everyone who has ever participated in a war, half of them should have surrendered before they did and spared themselves further casualties. If we're going to be the losers in this battle, then our options are to flee now while we have enough soldiers to deter a force from following us out, or to continue fighting until we're all dead."

"But only in the latter course is there even the possibility of victory. If we retreat, we guarantee loss."

Kelve shook his head slowly, surprised at the resistance he was facing. "Would the men all stand as firmly as you, Colbiss? Do they not fear annihilation?"

"The troops believe that we have held out well against a superior force, and that our quality will outmatch their quantity. You have led us brilliantly, and we still have allies left to join. Lady Detria and the knights from the northern continent may yet return. We have proof of the Overlord's presence. Maybe word will spread, and allies from the west will come. Maybe the Devilslayers themselves will send aid. If we stand here, others will be encouraged to stand with us. We will prevail, even if it is perhaps posthumously."

Kelve twisted his lips in thought, but did not argue further. Word could not spread across the continent. Other than Detria, they were completely isolated here. No one else, not even the smallest human settlement, even knew of their struggle. Even if Detria did return, she would not be bringing Abaddon and his friends. Help was not coming.

Instead of voicing these concerns, he gave Colbiss a smile and an order, sending him off on a small errand. Kelve knew the smart thing to do. The smart thing was to retreat. Head inland, gather fresh forces, spread the word of their enemy. The smart thing was to manufacture the scenario that Colbiss and his people already believed in.

Yet he could not. He could not order the soldiers to give up their hope, when it had been bought at such a high price. He resolved himself to be the leader they wanted, the leader who stood on faith rather than reason. He was certain he was committing to a path that would consume his life, but Kelve had always been the man to choose inaction when it was an option. In this scenario, it seemed that the course of inaction was to stay and fight it out.

He looked to the fortress. As Tenkahn had predicted, four giant ogres had been put on guard to replace the destroyed front gates. Kelve knew this did not matter, since he had no intention of launching a frontal assault. As he watched, two of these ogres stepped aside and allowed a small entourage to leave. It was only two figures. Kelve wanted to believe this was a positive sign, perhaps a diplomatic meeting. With the advantages all in the hands of the Overlord, however, such a thing seemed unlikely.

He signaled for his lieutenants to gear up and be prepared, but headed alone down the hill to meet the approaching foes. Before he had even gone halfway, he could make them out. One was Gariso, the bestially-enhanced human warrior. The other was a chimera, but certainly no ordinary one. This creature was far larger than the usual breed, nearly half as large as an ogre. It had only one head, the twisted, disfigured face of a demonic lion, with teeth that stretched out over half of the head's height and gave the creature a terrifying permanent grin. The body was leathery, like that of a dragon, but a dull grey color. It looked as though some strange, twisted stone had been wrapped about it and called flesh. The only other features decorating the beast were the huge wings of a vampire bat, and a scorpion's tail. Kelve could tell this chimera was one to be feared.

He met the two only a few yards out from the base of the hill, checking surreptitiously over his shoulder to see his soldiers lining the hilltop. He started to open negotiations, but Gariso beat him to the matter.

"There is no battle for today, human leader. We offer your forces a chance for rest. If you can buy it."

Kelve squinted. "Buy it? At what price?"

A malicious smile spread across Gariso's cold features. "Our terms are simple, and undeniable. If your champion can defeat our champion—the Manticore—in combat, then we will not attack you again for three days. If, however, your champion falls, then

Manticore and I will run free throughout your forces, slaying as many of your men as we feel suited."

"And if I were to choose to bring my forces down here to stop you now?"

Gariso laughed heartily. "Try it if you want. That only hastens us to our victory condition. Manticore and I wish to kill your men. Isn't that right?"

The chimera's eyes flashed darkly. He had not moved since they had stopped their approach. When he spoke, it was a screeching, deeply toned voice, so gravelly as to be nearly incomprehensible. "I have been awakened early, and I will taste flesh before I sleep again."

Gariso nodded, assuming this response was close enough to agreement. "So what will it be? Send your monk out, or we will set amongst your troops."

Kelve ran a dozen plans through his head, nearly panicking at this sudden development. With Tenkahn absent, he had no way of meeting the situation. "Wait," he suddenly countered, "you said champion combat."

"I did. What of it?"

"Then let me stand in as champion."

Gariso scowled. He had been given very specific orders, and this development did not sit well with him. "Why would you stand in? You're no equal to the Monk of Tria."

"I'm the captain here. I won't ask one of my men to risk his life in this manner alone." He could not confess Tenkahn's absence to the enemy, but did not know how long he could avoid the truth on the matter.

"Then when you die," Gariso answered, "Manticore and I will devour your men freely."

Kelve knew this statement was likely, but he was out of options. He had to hope that somehow he could find a way to defeat the chimera by himself. That was the only chance he had of keeping the situation under control. He gave a stubborn nod and dropped his hands to the hilts of his cutlasses.

Gariso shrugged. "Have things your way. Manticore, finish him!"

The chimera looked to Kelve and gave a sniff, then emitted a strange garbled cough. He turned his back to Gariso and walked a few feet away, then sat down, curled up, and seemed to go to sleep.

The Overlord's human champion sneered. Manticore had agreed to come onto the battlefield on the promise that he would be given a worthy adversary to play with. Clearly, Kelve was not satisfactory. Gariso reached up and released the snaps that held his overcoat in place, raising his scaly arms forward and pointing them at Kelve. "I don't need the help of this beast to handle you. You will die here, one way or another!"

Kelve gave a sigh of relief. While he knew this would only stall the upcoming fight, it was a reprieve for which he was nonetheless grateful. He charged the half-man, half-dragon warrior brandishing his sabers. He swung in furious arcs, appearing to make a wild charge. It was, in fact, a carefully calculated move, designed to test the warrior's ability to defend against a flurry.

Gariso had no trouble with the barrage. The thick scales on his arms deflected the blades without even taking a scratch, and he was easily able to find some position to ensure Kelve's swords never touched flesh on any other part of his body. The former Devilslayer finished his rush ineffectively, then Gariso came at him with an equally fierce counter.

Kelve had seen the man in combat before, and had a pretty good idea of how he worked. His punches were fast and strong, but they were always straight. He never threw hooks or uppercuts, only jabs and crosses. Even with the fierce speed of these blows, Kelve was able to predict their trajectory before they were thrown. The battle was at a stalemate.

Fortunately for Kelve, he thrived well under stalemates. He crossed his swords at his waist and delivered two symmetrical uppercuts with the blades. The sudden fierceness of the strike forced his adversary to back a step away. The human commander did not waste this opening, stabbing one sword into the ground at his side, then seizing a vial from his belt and throwing it hard at his opponent.

Gariso blocked the vial with his fist and it shattered at the impact. A cloud of noxious blue liquid spilled everywhere, covering a majority of the man's face and upper body. A burst of red smoke poured from the liquid upon contact with flesh, and he gave a fierce scream as his body was attacked by the most powerful acid of the Devilslayers. The red smoke that poured from the acid was a poisonous gas in and of itself, capable of killing any creature for a ten yard radius. Kelve quickly took a needle to his leg and inoculated himself from the effect, then watched to see if there was enough of his foe left to continue the fight.

When the smoke cleared, Gariso stood unharmed, repressing a grin. Kelve quickly retrieved his abandoned sword and felt his pulse increase. Had that batch of acid been bad? Had he made a mistake in the mix? It had been so long since he had made a faulty potion, he could scarcely imagine how it had happened.

"If that's how you thought to win this," Gariso announced, "you're in for a disappointment. Acid? Pah. The blood of a green dragon is made from acid. Their breath is poisonous fumes." He lifted his arms high above his head, flexing the hands open and closed. "These arms changed the chemistry of my body. In order to even survive them, to be able to live with them, I had to become immune to poisons, to venom, to acid, to gases. None of your debilitating tricks will work on me."

Kelve took a deep breath and blew it out loudly. "I do hate to hear that."

Gariso charged again, and the impotent exchange of blows resumed. As neither contestant made headway, it was an alternating dance of attack and defend. Both warriors knew the eventual turnout of this. Kelve was pressing his entire body in order to keep up. Gariso, however, was relying only on the strength of his unnatural arms. Kelve's muscles would exhaust long before the sinews of that scaled flesh. Another five minutes, maybe ten, and he would slow down too much. He would not be able to avoid a punch somewhere. Once struck just a single time, the battle would be all but over.

He weighed his options carefully. Manticore still had not moved, apparently bored by this demonstration. If Kelve could find a way to defeat his current foe, there was a possibility the situation would go away for now. Gariso's weaknesses were many, and easily within reach. If the chemical master could find a way to get his swords past the defense of the arms, he could drive his opponent to collapse. He had always avoided using his drugs for self-enhancement—as the side effects were often too devastating to make the temporary edge worth it—but it seemed now he had no choice. If he was going to overcome this enemy, he needed a window of opportunity before his strength depleted.

He created distance between himself and his assailant with a quick flurry of strikes, then prepared his injection. Then suddenly, another idea crossed his mind. He returned the needle to his belt and grabbed his two swords, then charged again.

The bestial solder waited patiently to see if his opponent had some new strategy to offer. He was not left waiting long. When Kelve was only a yard away, he flung the sword in his right hand at the man's scaly shoulder. Gariso used his left arm to block the attack, its green hide still easily deflecting the edge of the cutlass. As Kelve approached, aiming a sweeping blow from his remaining sword at his foe's waist, he whipped his right hand back to his belt. The Overlord's champion used his free arm to block the cutlass, then gave a grunt as Kelve's elbow crashed into his chest.

Gariso released a guttural bark of annoyance. He seized the top of his foe's head with his left hand and sent the man flying away from him. Looking down at his own torso, he saw an emptied syringe protruding from his stomach. He removed it and crushed it effortlessly in his hand, then tossed the device to the ground.

"I already told you, your poisons and chemicals won't affect me."

Kelve rose unsteadily to his feet. A few gashes had been cut into his head by the clawed fingertips, and blood drizzled over his eyes.

"I think this one will," he offered as a retort.

Gariso spat, walking over to the man's discarded cutlass. He picked the blade up and snapped it easily with his hands, then tossed the pieces aside. "Now you only have one sword to defend yourself. You can't hold me off like this. Your gamble has failed you."

The defiant warrior shook his head, taunting, "You're not seeing the big picture yet."

The irritated champion charged to resume the fray, throwing another set of his overpowered punches. Kelve focused on trying to dodge one hand, while using his blade to keep the left dragonkin arm in a state of defense. It was a more awkward exchange for each contestant, Kelve constantly on the defensive, Gariso having to carefully alternate between defense and offense.

Then something changed. Gariso's movement began to accelerate. He lost focus for a moment, and Kelve's cutlass found an opening to bite into his chest. The Overlord's champion did not feel the pain and surged forward recklessly. His fury only increased, and it was not long before he sent the remaining sword flying away.

Kelve backed away as fast as he could, but his opponent leaped at him with a roar. The former Devilslayer dropped to the ground and rolled underneath the man, causing Gariso to trip and fall forward onto his face. He quickly shot back up and charged in his rival's direction, slamming down at the ground with both fists. Again the smaller man narrowly evaded, scurrying like a frightened animal to get away from the attacks.

Gariso laughed and foamed at the mouth, certain that he was the victor and all that remained was to finish the matter off. His enemy was finished; he had lost his weapons, reached his point of exhaustion, and had nothing left to give. As the altered human charged one last time, he knew there would be no dodging this next surge of blows.

But Kelve would not give up so easily. As the first three punches came from Gariso, he used every instinct he had to find an evasive pattern. It seemed for a moment that his feeble attempt to duck and weave would hold. Then Gariso snarled and gave an unexpected strike. He opened his left hand wide and gave a sweeping uppercut to Kelve's midsection. The commander's reflexes failed him at last, and the dragon's claws scraped greedily along his rib cage and over his chest, sending a huge chunk of his flesh and blood—as well as chips of bone—flying into the sky over his right shoulder.

Kelve gurgled and threw himself flat onto his back, his last pathetic defense. As Gariso backed a few steps away and readied himself for the next charge, a strange dizziness gripped his head. He tried to shake it off, but it would not fade. His legs soon lost their strength, and he fell onto his knees. As he tried to overcome this as well, a strong bout of nausea gripped his abdomen and he began vomiting furiously.

When he recovered enough for this to stop, he sat shaking uncontrollably. "What did you do?" he demanded.

Kelve gasped a few strenuous breaths, doing his best to answer as he used a medical clay to prevent fatal amounts of blood loss. "You're immune to debilitative effects, so I tried a different route. I gave you an accelerator that caused your body to go into an adrenaline overdrive. In spite of your alterations, you're still vulnerable to your own biology. Adrenaline overdose can be a very crippling condition."

As the wounded man climbed slowly to his feet and retrieved his sword, Gariso attempted to make a brash insult. Instead he began to vomit again, and with a final overwhelming rush of dizziness, lost consciousness.

Finally seeming to take notice of the battle, Manticore rose to his feet and gave a drowsy shake. "Enough of this," he bellowed out with his rattling voice. He twisted his body slightly in Kelve's direction, and the giant scorpion's tail smashed into the ground.

The human commander was thrown from his feet as the earth around him upheaved from the swift strike. Manticore gave an agile hop and landed a few feet from where the man lay, the permanent grin offset by cruel eyes.

"If you are to survive this, human, you're going to need more champions."

Kelve struggled to redouble his efforts and make a move, but he was well past his limit. With his wound from Gariso, even maintaining consciousness would soon be too much for him.

He shortly realized that would not be a problem. Manticore raised one front leg and opened a series of long serrated claws. He lifted his fanged paw high over the human's helpless form, and sounded the roar that was to be Kelve's death-knell.

As the crushing blow came down upon him, Kelve held his breath and waited for a new, albeit brief pain to seize him. Less than a foot from impact, Manticore's arm suddenly veered from its natural course, missing his target's body by mere inches. The chimera reacted swiftly to this involuntary change, using a fierce thrust of his wings to send himself a full ten yards away.

Kelve sat up, trying to discern what was happening. A voice sounded from the air around him, though he could not place its source, answering Manticore's previous taunt.

"Then he shall have them."

Manticore's eyes shifted to an unnatural green luminescence. "Show yourself, coward, if you should face me."

A grey robed figure materialized two yards in front of Kelve. His vision was blurry, and he stammered weakly, "Tenkahn?"

A hand landed on his shoulder from behind. "I am here, Master Orista."

He looked behind him to see that, indeed, Tenkahn was at his side. "Then who..."

The stranger in front of him answered for himself. "I am Gaius, second servant to Tria. Rest easy, Master Orista. Your courage will not go unrewarded this day." The man turned, offering Kelve a nod and a bold smile.

The commander gasped in shock at the site of the man's face, familiar yet now unfamiliar, covered in glowing blue runes.

"Eiden?!"

## Chapter 25.

# Awaken, Dark Paladin

Myris and Abaddon moved through an unnamed forest sat on the Depalis Plains, meandering at a slow pace. They were unconcerned over making time, as their mission was one founded on inefficiency. They were heading northeast to rendezvous with Cildar, who would be returning southwest if he had already parted with Detria. Once the three Felthespari linked up, they would turn about and head south. Whether they reunited sooner or later, it was an equal waste of time.

Abaddon did not allow himself to dwell on the matter. He needed time to carefully deliberate his next move against the Wisdoms. Part of him regretted each wasted second, but he had already once been bested by the deities. His death as a result of his own impatience could serve no end. Even in the aftermath of recent victory, he was not convinced that either Arda or the release of his limiter was enough to level the playing field. He hoped the death of Valinoru would be enough to strike similar uncertainty into the other Wisdoms. His best option was to give his enemies time to grow anxious.

Myris was even more distraught than his commander. He was loathe to face the matter, but without the Draw Strike technique taken from his deceased Cainite cousin, he was even more of a handicap to his friends than before. His Soul Scythe had the ability to drain energy from the enemies it struck—particularly those of powerful magic—but it served little use against creatures as overbearing as the Wisdoms, entities so powerful he could not lay a scratch on them. He could not even be sure the relic worked at all against extraplanar life.

Until now he had been forced to bolster his strength by hunting animals and weak demonspawn as he could find them, but these proved an inadequate source for the Scythe. Its ability to heal his wounds was exhausting itself, and he feared he might soon suffer a blow from which he would be unable to recover.

Myris believed he had devised a resolution for his personal crisis, but he was wary of committing to it. During occasional reprieves from his traveling companions' company, he had been studying the Band of Barricus. The foreign accessory promised to grant the wielder "the Devil's strength", but Abaddon had attested that as a Gehennite artifact, it would not serve them.

In spite of this, the Cain believed he had found a way to harness the armlet's promised blessings. The risk of the procedure was high, and he could not help but recall Abaddon's own experiences with the dark gods of Kargaroth. Myris' own soul had been altered to be resilient against such corrupting sources of magic, as he had been conditioned from a young age to wield Kargaroth himself. He had no way of knowing if those enchantments would hold against Gehennite influences, or if the armlet was even capable of such influence. For now he had postponed the issue, awaiting such a time that it became a necessity. With the revelation of Abaddon's limiter still hanging over him, he felt his decision might be forced in a matter of days, if not hours.

The two stoic men marched onward, each lost in their own thoughts and plans for the future. They were nearing the western border of the small forest, when both men came to an unexplained stop. Myris looked to Abaddon for an order, but was only given a headshake.

The unseen disturbance revealed itself, as a tall man in black armors dropped from the canopy. He stood slowly from his crouched landing. This unexpected guest looked much like Cildar, yet not. He was covered in a Hasted aura, but it had shifted to a deep black, and his clothes had changed to match. He stood staring at the two warriors awaiting their reaction, which never came.

"I should have known," he murmured in disappointment.

"Nothing ever takes you two by surprise. I had hoped for something more entertaining."

They ignored this comment, as Myris addressed his commander. "What do you make of him?"

"He's not Cildar," Abaddon answered. "His spirit's incorrect. Stay alert. I have no doubts this will come to blows."

The visitor raised a hand and pointed firmly at Abaddon. "I understand why you might think that, Lord Abaddon, but you're mistaken. I am Cildar, but released of the restraints which have bound my will in the past. Free of the conditioning of my father, of my training, of the Military, of the Paladins. For the first time in my life, my fate is mine alone. I'm no longer bound to your mission. Instead, I've found a new one. I've come here to prove the Scion of Emle is truly your worthy rival, surpassed by no warrior of Felthespar."

Abaddon narrowed his eyes. "Something has happened to you. Did you speak with someone?"

"Speak? I suppose you could say that. Clarity was granted to me by the one named Akatriel. For this, I'm grateful to him, and spared his life."

"Akatriel," the big man hissed between gritted teeth.

Myris drew his Soul Scythe and took a tentative step forward. "Lord Abaddon, perhaps I would serve as a better test of his claims."

As his commander briefly thought this proposal over, Myris opened the blade of his Scythe and extended the handle, presuming his request would be granted. Cildar, for his part, began fingering the hilt of the Morabet on his belt.

Just before the clash, Abaddon gave his response. "No. This is my duty."

"Duty? But sir—"

"Stand down, Phare."

The Cain collapsed his scythe and reluctantly backed away. Cildar responded with a light chuckle. "Excellent," he announced eagerly. "No reason to hold back against you, big guy." He gathered fresh ether and launched himself high into the air, clearing over twenty feet, then dropped down at his opponent with a powerful hammer-kick from his right heel. Abaddon made no move until just before the point of impact, then he rapidly reached up and seized his assailant's calf in two spots. He delivered a vicious twist and sent the man spinning hard into the ground.

The Dragoon recovered as soon as his back hit the earth, altering the momentum of his spin and sweeping back up into the air. He awkwardly launched another kick at his opponent's face, which was narrowly evaded. With effort, he swiftly righted himself in midair, then delivered a fierce punch. Abaddon used a forearm to block this blow, as was anticipated. Cildar used the impact to knock himself back from the man, caught his feet, then surged forward with a series of jabs.

Abaddon continued to dodge these blows for a moment, then made a downward swipe at his foe's head. Cildar crossed his arms and caught the blow in the nook, twisting rapidly to shuck the punch off to his side. He then responded with a backhanded swipe at his adversary's face, which the man evaded with a quick jerk of his neck. In that instant, the Dragoon used his left hand to draw his Morabet and sliced at his target's unarmored chest.

Again Abaddon stepped back, but this time was not quick enough. The blade bit into his mystically shielded flesh, leaving only a scratch, but one deep enough to draw blood. Cildar gathered a stock of energy into his right hand and pointed it forward, unleashing a darkly tinted Aura Blast.

The Daemon took the blow boldly, but he was pushed back several feet and winded. "You're channeling your training well, I see," he remarked between strained breaths.

"I won't play the student in order to appease your ego anymore. With Akatriel's gifts, my body and mind are linked as never before. I'm faster, sharper, capable of utilizing every technique and trick that I've ever been exposed to in my entire career as soldier, paladin, Dragoon. You won't find the weaknesses to which you are so accustomed, Lord Abaddon."

Felthespar's Champion took a step forward and glared for a moment. Slowly, his eyes began to glow with an unnatural light. Soon a strange steam began to rise from his skin, and the air throughout the area felt began to feel stifling.

As the man's hair began to lift of its own accord, carried by a breeze which could not be felt, he responded slowly with an ominous tone, "Weaknesses? Who needs them."

With that, he vanished. Only through sheer instinct was Cildar able to guess the incoming strike. He launched himself into the air, as the ground around him exploded into debris. Chunks of dirt and rock flew a dozen feet upward as his feet hovered only inches above the point of impact, still rising from his jump. By the time his mind was able to process the sight of Abaddon's fist connecting with the ground, the airborne soldier could already feel shrapnel rolling along his face and arms. He adjusted himself and attempted to swing the Morabet before his momentum carried him out of range.

The mystic warlord did not glance up from where he crouched, but delivered a swift sweep with his left hand in mere fractions of a second. The enchanted blade snapped under the force of that impossibly fast blow, and Cildar was caught in a gust of wind and tossed across the battlefield. When he landed, he instantly reached to his back and drew the Trine Lance, leveling it forward and preparing for the next lull in the battle.

There was no lull. Seeing the Lance, Abaddon immediately reached back and drew the Arda. As his domineering opponent disappeared from his sight once more, Cildar muttered a quiet curse. He gave a panicked roll to his right, hoping the oncoming man would open with a downward thrust. This guess again saved his life, as the ground where he had been standing instantly split into a wide crater. He regained his feet and dashed, only barely escaping range as his foe lifted Arda and gave a swift cut at his back.

The Dragoon tightened his grip on the Trine Lance and redoubled his blessings, attempting to succumb even deeper to his

Hasted condition in hope of gaining the necessary speed to match his rival. Abaddon casually raised Arda, angling the length of the blade away from himself, and began slowly walking in his foe's direction. As he did, the steam rising from him freshly erupted and turned into a thick, visible grey ether. His eyes became brighter, and his hair and clothes moved about as if being attacked by a gale.

The Dark Paladin backed away as the overcharging mystic approached. His deepest instincts warned him that something was wrong. He had always known Abaddon was a warrior to be feared, and had never doubted that defeat was a real possibility. But it should not have been like this. Not with his dragonkin-enhanced Haste granting him skill and speed far beyond his previous heights. He should not have been so hopelessly outmatched that he could not even see his opponent's moves, that even a single blow from the gloved fists seemed ready to shatter his bones. Something about the man had changed. This was not the fight Cildar had come to pick. "You won't kill me!" he shouted defiantly, doubting the words even as they left his lips.

"Cildar Emle was my student, my ally, and my friend. Whatever has happened to him, I owe it to him to preserve his memory. Whoever you are, you claim to be Cildar. Whatever acts you would commit would sully his reputation and impugn his honor. If Cildar could ask it of me, I believe he would beg me, plead me, to prevent that from happening. I will kill you to protect the name of Emle. I will murder you as a final favor to Cildar. I will *destroy* you," he slowly tilted his head to one side and clenched his jaw tight, "because it's what I do."

Upon hearing this proclamation, Myris took an anxious step forward. Much like Abaddon, he was unclear on what had happened their old friend, but he was not nearly so set in his resolve. He was not prepared to give up on Cildar's life, when they had not yet even sought another solution. He thought to move to stop the Daemon, but with Arda in the man's possession it was more likely the Cain would only join their dark visitor's demise.

The new Cildar, for his part, roared and thrust with his Trine

Lance. Abaddon watched calmly as the tri-pronged crystalline spearhead approached his face, beginning a gentle sweep of the Arda across his path. The Dark Paladin recognized that Arda would take his head before the Lance would reach his opponent's, and was forced to leap into the air. The mystic knight turned and followed his path, making a few slow swings with his katana. He was mocking his prey, reminding him that death was near at hand.

Upon landing Cildar again attempted to come at his foe with the Trine Lance, this time angling the blow in low. Because he had turned to follow the leaping Dragoon's path over his head, Abaddon attempted to counter with another downward swing of Arda. Cildar had gambled for this very response. He forced himself to sidestep to his right as he held his spear steady.

His optimism got the better of him. Abaddon was only wielding Arda with his right hand, and the left remained free. Before the tip of the Lance would have come into contact with his ribs, he reached out and gave a firm tap to the shaft of the spear, just below the blades. With his limiter unleashed the mystic's strength dwarfed Cildar's even with such a conserved motion, and the Lance shot off course. The charging man could not stop his momentum, and soon was within range of that same left hand. Abaddon closed his fist and planted a firm blow into the plated chest.

Cildar went flying away, his sturdy breastplate dented and cracking against his sternum. He landed hard with his back against a tree and fell to the ground coughing blood. It took all his focus to remain conscious and ensure he did not lose Haste. For a moment he began to feel the enchantments slipping in spite of his efforts. He realized that, one way or another, he was about to die. If Haste fell apart the Dark Paladin would be no more, far too soon.

His panic gave him resolve, and shortly he had pieced himself together enough to look up. Abaddon was again walking toward him, the Arda angled out to his side once more as he allowed the tip of the blade to pass casually through the trunks of a few bordering trees. Cildar stared at the towering figure approaching, looking deep into dark blue eyes that glowed steadily. *I cannot beat this man*, he thought in a haze of terror. *He's too strong, he's too fast. There is no fear in his eyes!*

He rose to his feet and placed the Trine Lance in its grips on his back, then began removing hidden knives and throwing stars, flinging a full barrage in his domineering adversary's direction. These weapons were not enchanted, however, and crashed ineffectually against thick grey magic barriers.

Then the warlord charged forward and swept out with Arda once more. Cildar leaped into the air, seized a branch in a nearby tree, flipped up onto it, and launched himself again. Abaddon stopped and braced his legs, whispering quietly, "Now you die."

As he dug his feet in and was about to leap with a final killing slash, Myris suddenly appeared before him and grabbed his arms. Even Abaddon was thrown aback by the suddenness the Cain had used to intercept him, nearly striking out.

"Please, Lord Abaddon! Do not do this!"

"Why do you interrupt me?" he bellowed.

"I understand your need to protect Cildar's honor, and share it. But I cannot commit to his death under these conditions. He might yet be saved from what has happened to him. We do not know!"

Abaddon raised his eyebrow, but nonetheless returned Arda to its clip at his back. His eyes lost their glow and the visible surges of ethereal power faded from his skin. "Nor do we have time to learn, lest you forget."

"I beg of you, allow me to follow him. I will fight him on my own. I shall find out what was done to him, I will find a way to undo it. Cildar has a wife who awaits him, he has a home to return to. I cannot allow him to end in this way. Not slain by the hands of allies."

"We don't have time for games, Phare. We're in the middle of a critical mission, and Cildar is now a handicap to that mission. As your field commander, I can't allow you to abandon me for your personal crusades." The smaller man hung his head and gave a heavy sigh. After a few seconds of silence, Abaddon raised his right thumb to his mouth and bit carefully, drawing blood from the tip. He reached forward and traced a deep red line across Myris' forehead. The Lord of the Cain looked up with wide, shocked eyes. It was an old Onion Knight ritual, one not been used in centuries. "With this mark of shame," Abaddon declared, "I cast you out as a Knight of Felthespar. Until your honor is restored, you serve Pecoros no longer."

Myris took a step back, weighing the ramifications of this action. Then he gave a solemn bow. "Thank you, milord," he whispered.

"I'm no longer any lord of yours, Myris. Serve yourself well."

Wasting no further time, the outcast man turned and dashed in the direction Cildar had disappeared. Abaddon shook his head slowly. "One of my Majors is a traitor, and the other banished." He walked a few steps away and then stopped, whispering to himself, "But perhaps I will yet again see my friends." He headed back to the south, resolved to face the threat of the Wisdoms alone.

Across the forest, Myris also stopped for a moment in contemplation. He reached into a satchel at his side and drew forth a dark piece of cloth, staring at it for several seconds.

"If Myris Phare is Onion Knight no longer," he finally said to himself, "then Myris Phare the Cainite will make his return." He opened the cloth and wrapped it around his head. It was a dark cowl, composed of interlaced folds of black and purple silk. With the hood on, only his eyes remained visible. He touched his forefinger from each hand to his eyelids, and gave a soft sweep. Two bright flames appeared hovering over his face, hiding the last visible traces of his humanity. He gave a soft laugh and faded slowly from view.

The Cainite would hunt the Dragoon.

* * * * *

"Gaius, finish this opponent quickly," Tenkahn ordered of his student.

While the young monk obediently charged the Manticore, the elder carefully helped Kelve to his feet. The former slayer was still reeling and tried his best to make sense of things. “Tenkahn, what has happened? Who is this Gaius? What did you do to Eiden? Is he dead?”

“Nothing so ominous has occurred, my friend. The boy has merely sworn oaths to Tria now, and so I have given him her blessings and inducted him into our order. He took this path upon himself of his own free will. Though he may not look it, that is still the Eiden you knew.”

Kelve watched for a moment as Gaius and the mighty Manticore exchanged blows. The young man was extremely quick, effortlessly avoiding the sweeping claws and barbed tail. His blows were also quick, and his form good, but these impacts did not seem to cause much harm to the chimera’s leathery hide.

“Is he as strong as you?” Kelve queried.

“In ways, he is stronger. Eiden had a limited practice with magic, as you know. The rune structure I gave him unlocks the full potential of one’s spirit as it stands at that moment. Since Eiden had already expanded his spirit, albeit only slightly, the rune structure has increased his power many times over that of a human who had no practice with magic.”

“So he *is* stronger than you. What fortune this is! With two monks of Tria on our side, we might have a real advantage here.”

“You misunderstand somewhat, Master Orista. Gaius has more potential than I, it’s true. But as things are, he knows only a scant few of Tria’s techniques. Even those he can only use at their most novice level. Worse, my own power is currently sapped from the stress placed by the bestowing of the runes upon another.”

Kelve hung his head and let himself slip a bit further into unconsciousness. “So we’re still in trouble.”

The monk was about to answer, but three lieutenants arrived to carry their commander away for medical treatment. Tenkahn relinquished the man over to their care and turned to observe the battle at hand.

Gaius' speed served him well, and the Manticore's roars of outrage increased as its attacks continued to miss. During one such outburst, the beast reared back and struck with its tail's full strength. The young monk dodged, but the earth about him began to shudder and quake. Tenkahn began to move in to assist, but the youth quickly slammed his palms to the ground at his feet. There was a secondary tremor, and the quakes ceased.

"Impressive," Tenkahn remarked to himself. "He used a Tremoring Cancel in the midst of combat. The boy truly does show marked potential."

Unfortunately, Gaius' quick reaction threw off his focus. Manticore lashed out with his front claws, ripping deep into the monk's arm. Tenkahn had previously warned his apprentice, "These runes will protect you from most impacts, but they will not stop the slice of a blade."

The stricken monk leaped away from the creature and nursed his wounded arm. His bicep had been cut nearly clean through. It was all he could manage to channel energy, increasing his healing to the area. On the Manticore came, swinging claws and snapping out with fangs. The novice's shift to healing had slowed his step, and now several times his dodges fell short, leaving him with fresh gashes on various parts of his body.

Tenkahn shook his head. The boy showed potential, indeed, but was nowhere near ready for combat against this mighty a foe. The more he healed, the more damage he sustained, creating a vicious cycle that could only lead to loss. Fortunately the Monks of Tria had a further trick to play. With the presence of at least two blessed warriors, they could pool their spirits and activate the penultimate technique of their runes.

"Gaius," Tenkahn called out, "to me! We will finish this united."

The student did as commanded, leaping high into the air and gliding backward to land in front of Tenkahn. Manticore attempted to charge the pair, using its huge wings for extra bursts of speed. The elder monk gave a hand sign, and the runes on each flashed once in unison. Then he slammed the ground at his feet with a fist.

Both monks vanished, and in their place a wall of earthen spikes was sent racing at the charging Manticore.

The ferocious chimera turned about and used its tail to smash the attack coming its way, but could not discern what had happened to its opponents. The blessings of Tria once more masked her disciples in a cloak of impenetrable invisibility. It would not last long fueled by the spirits of two monks rather than ten, but for a single foe they did not require much time.

Within seconds, the Manticore's wings and tail suddenly exploded from his back, ripped away by a gust of unseen force. The beast spun about and attempted to latch onto something, anything, with its claws. He succeeded, in some sense. His own tail was shoved forward and forced onto each of his hands, binding and tripping him. He fell forward onto his face, screaming in rage. A series of painful blows crawled across his torso and he screamed again, this time coughing up gallons of blood. Finally a decisive colossal blow—the simultaneous impact of four fists—struck the creature's back. His spine shattered, he gave a final sputter, and never again did his dark eyes set sight upon a Monk of Tria.

Gariso had recovered enough to witness this killing blow, invisible though it was, and beat a quick retreat back toward the fortress. The monks' cloak dissipated and Gaius turned to pursue the retreating general. Tenkahn forbade him, insisting it would do more good to let the Overlord's morale suffer at the tale.

An hour later they sat in discussions with Kelve in his tent. The man's recovery from the wound Gariso had given him was not going well, and he had developed a fever. He had dispatched scouts for some herbs, but it was becoming increasingly difficult for him to think. Soon he would be in insufficient condition to whip up the potions necessary to fend off his malady.

Tenkahn exchanged a few words with the attendants overseeing the captain's recovery, ultimately declaring he must confer with the fading man before he might lose consciousness. After dismissing the orderlies from the tent, he spoke softly to an audience of Kelve and his lieutenants. "Master Orista, I fear I have a confession.

Normally the rune activation ritual does not take quite so long as our absence. That is not all Gaius and I have been about for the past few days."

Kelve breathed heavily and tried to adjust his back. He was sitting in the floor of the tent, wrapped carefully in several blankets. "More bad news?"

"Not this time, I don't believe. We felt a force approaching from the west. Rather, Gaius felt the force. We went to see if it was some manner of reinforcement for the Overlord, hoping to waylay them before they could become a more serious threat. To the contrary, it was a rather large group of humans. They say they are former slaves of the Overlord who left some time ago. They have been hiding in fear since, until they decided they could no longer live in such a cowardly way. Though there is but a thousand of them, they have bravely returned, determined to take back their former homelands here in the east."

Kelve coughed lightly. "A thousand? What are you saying to me? Are you telling me we have a thousand reinforcements coming?"

"So I am. They are no comparison for your current soldiers, nor will they likely ever be. But with a careful training regimen, I believe we could slowly begin integrating them into our ranks."

Kelve nodded and waved at a couple of his most trusted lieutenants. "Look into it." He glanced to Tenkahn and the new Gaius, then smiled through his pain. "We will do the best we can. I must rest, it's all I can do right now. If I pass, you and Colbiss are in charge here, Tenkahn." He let his head slip back, then slept. The two monks stepped outside and made a small campfire nearby. They spent the remainder of the night watching closely over their injured friend.

* * * * *

Within the Overlord's fortress, there was much bickering over the news brought back by Gariso. Blame was being passed around in raised voices, and Tessena was hard-pressed to maintain control over the situation. Even the normally pensive Kogonbo was in an uncharacteristic huff.

As foul words were being shouted over other, fouler words, a sudden boom sounded at the back of the room where the generals were gathered. They turned to look at the entrance to the hall, and each of them felt their blood grow cold.

The entryway had been slammed shut as Shote had entered the chamber.

Marks of his injuries still showed on his body, where stitching was carefully holding his blue skin together. His movement was careful, limited, and he was not wearing armors as he once did. In addition, only one of his two greataxes was strapped to his back, as he was not yet ready to bear the weight of both. He wasted no time with formalities, walking slowly across the room to his generals as he spoke.

"Why do you fail to crush those who defy your Overlord? These failures, these shortcomings, make the Overlord look to be some joke, one who can be trifled with. Anyone who opposes his will should be taken care of swiftly, instantly. Your inability to do so is pathetic, and in his absence I stand enraged in the Overlord's place." He moved straight to Tessena, bringing his large nostrils close to her face and breathing hard, letting her feel the heat of his breath against her forehead. "As First General, it's you that carries the failure of your underlings. What excuses will you feed me?"

Gariso stepped forward and placed a hand on Shote's arm. "Tessena, all of us, have done the best we can. You judge us too harshly!"

Shote did not look at the interfering human, but his eyes flashed. "Best?" He then moved suddenly, faster than any of the generals in the room could follow. His hand flew to his back and freed his axe, and within an instant it was planted in the ground at Gariso's feet.

But Shote was not a creature taken to taunts. His axe had landed at Gariso's feet by taking the most direct route—straight through

Gariso himself. There was silence for a moment following the ringing sound of the axe striking marble, then slowly the man's body fell into two halves, as his blood and organs splattered across the floor. Tessena backed away in a mix of loss, disgust, and fear. Shote's mood was rarely sated by a single kill.

In spite of this show of strength, the dreaded beast had strained himself. Several of his wounds had reopened at his sudden movement, and he breathed heavily as he holstered his axe. "All of you will do well to remember this: while the Overlord is not here, I *am* the Overlord. Rid this place of the filth that infests our walls."

He took his leave to the sound of silence. Once he was gone the generals dispersed and each went to their own devices, seeking a distraction to recover from the experience. Tessena alone stayed in the room, her face pale, tears streaming down her cheeks. She was certain that if she did not get rid of the invaders before Shote's next awakening, her life would be the next claimed by his axe. Some part of her mourned Gariso's death; but moreover, she mourned her own.

## Chapter 26.

# Release the Might of Barricus

To the west of what was once the forested land of the draconics, the desolate stretch of the Kress Plains began. Beyond these was a small desert, and beyond that lay the rich oasis of a land filled with life. These western areas of Arkalen were an image of the past, a painting of how the continent had been before the destruction of the Lifeless Vortex, free of the influences of either the Overlord or Devilslayers. Here, Arkalen was an island from the larger world, absent the superpowers of foreign nations and planes vying for supremacy.

This was not to suggest that the land was a paradise. Humans and demonspawn alike shared this realm and, as is their way, warred constantly amongst themselves and against each other. There were sprawling cities and rural protectorates that formed human capitals, but mirroring stretches of chaotic valleys and barren hillsides served as demonic domain. In a way they had reached an odd sort of symbiosis, insomuch as predators and prey ever can.

The stable and pristine nature of this region blossomed from the insecurities of the Devilslayers. Their reach was not quite long enough to extend across the desolate plains and desert, and their grip not yet tight enough to lay claim over the fortified human territories. It was rumored the Overlord did much of his recruiting from the rich demonspawn habitations in this area, but he similarly could not assert power here with his citadel situated so far in the east.

At the eastern edge of the plains leading to this land, a dark figure stepped forth from a fold in the air. He tapped a few scanning matrixes and scoured the ground for its recent history, then frowned in displeasure. Myris Phare had chased Cildar for weeks now, cutting rapidly through plains and forests alike until he had arrived here. Even with the Cainite's unnatural speed on foot, his old friend's newfound ability to maintain a constant state of Haste had made pursuit difficult. Myris found himself reminded of Atheme's stories of pursuing the Hell Knight into Revian. He wondered if Cildar also recalled those tales, and if perhaps this was the reason he headed west.

He edged his way back into the forest behind him, contemplating carefully. He had been charting the rate of his gain against his quarry, and was certain that from where he stood now he could overtake the Dragoon before the week's end. There were two flaws to this plan. The first, a minor one, was that he would lose the element of surprise. It would require a substantial amount of Cainite magic to remain shrouded in invisibility on sunlit plains or desert. In order to preserve his stealth he would need to move at a slower, steady pace as he crossed the open regions. If he wished to catch Cildar as swiftly as possible, he would be forced to approach undisguised.

Little could be done about this, it was a simple matter of making a choice. The second problem was far more urgent: once he caught up, Myris had no clue how he might attempt to save Cildar, or reverse whatever had been done to him. He could not even be sure such a thing was possible. He had to accept the possibility that Abaddon's original course would ultimately prove to be his only choice. Whatever was going on with Cildar, Myris refused to accept that this was truly the man he had grown to admire. Any actions, any atrocities committed by him, would stain the name of Emle. In the end, if he was forced to kill this creature in order to protect that legacy, he would reluctantly do so.

Or at least, he would commit to the attempt. But Myris could not best his old friend in combat so long as Haste was active, and this he knew beyond doubt. If he still held possession of the Scroll of Flare given to him by Kinguin, he could have arranged an interrupt, incapacitating the man long enough for easy victory. Without it, he was required to rely on his own combat skills. Those were insufficient for this task. Cildar had surpassed him long ago upon the invention of Haste, and in spite of years of effort he had never again been able to bridge the gap between their respective strengths. If anything, it had only grown wider as the Lord of the Phoenix had refined and perfected his Hasted blessings.

Myris sat on the ground and crossed his legs, shutting his eyes and uttering a brief prayer to Vaelius. He reached into one of the many secret pouches shadowed by his outfit and drew forth the Band of Barricus, then attached the steel halo over his forearm. The armlet was large, only barely fitting between his wrist and elbow. It was also too thick to fit properly, but he ignored the discomfort.

His eyes still closed, he brought his fingers together gently in front of his face and focused his consciousness deep within himself. Years ago, Myris had been struck by the awakened Kargaroth. The bite of the Unholy Blade had destroyed his spirit, the interface to both Morolia and Asteria. Without it, he could draw neither life nor power from the mirrored planes. The most gifted priest of Felthespar, Cardinal Aveni Landes, had crafted the wounded man a new spirit based upon Aveni's own. Over the years Myris had grown accustomed to this prosthetic spirit, and by now was quite comfortable using it as though it were a natural extension of himself.

But it was not. It was an implant, a foreign body within himself, and as such he could easily feel it out. He could see the energies, the infinitesimal lines of power the Cardinal had carved within his body, in stark contrast against the Cainite spiritual enchantments of his birth. Several lines of energy flowed into the matrix of his spirit. Some were fed by Morolian ether, which was channeled into his chamber and from here used to support the functions of his body. Others were flows of Asterian power drawn across the Veil, feeding the umbra where a mage's matrixes were stored.

Myris had a theory. Since his spirit was no longer a part of his being, and therefore not solidly anchored as those found in nature, he believed he could use Cainite magic meant for self-alteration to twist the ephemeral lattice. If done with sufficient precision, he could perhaps alter the interface enough to establish a connection through the Veil in a different direction—to Gehenna.

The consequences of failure for this experiment were both obvious and stark. Without a functional spirit in place, he would lose his ability to channel ether. Once that was lost, he would be unable to reverse the effect, and in time would die from spiritual starvation. There was no one here to aid him, no one to save him if he made a critical mistake.

Even as he reminded himself of the consequences, he was already resolved to taking the risk. He could not allow Cildar to gain more distance on him while he idled in indecision. Cautiously, he examined every aspect of the bright facsimile, memorizing the flow of the lines. He had studied spiritual theory when he was a young Cainite warrior, and understood the principles of the procedure he was about to attempt.

A human's spirit had two types of interfaces. Draws gathered in specific types of ether, and channels shaped the ether in a manner similar to rune structures. Myris' own spirit had three Morolian draws, two Asterian draws, and a single channel which allowed him to use Cainite and grey magic. For his procedure to work, he had to realign the flow lines of his spirit so that, in exchange for other draws and channels, he gained two draws in Gehenna. He knew he could survive with only one Morolian draw remaining, and he needed to leave an Asterian draw so he could still have access to his matrixes. That left him a slim margin of error to work within.

He began by studying his body's natural intake of white ether. He carefully noted where each ether flow attempted to link to his chamber, and which links were successful. Then he gathered a small amount of black ether, again taking note of the dozens of points where the ether attempted to enter his umbra. Finally he attempted to reach out with his thoughts and link to the Band of Barricus. It required several attempts, but finally the artifact offered a weak response. In his mind he saw the slight flicker of red energy lines attempting to pour into his soul. No connections were established, but he knew now what he had to achieve.

In spite of his resolve to make haste, he spent nearly an hour studying the flow lines of the ether. He would have only one attempt to make this realignment. As an additional complication, he had to craft two different untested matrixes before he proceeded. One would shift his spirit toward Gehenna, and the other would reverse the effect afterward. If either was anything less than perfect, he would seal his own doom. Once he was certain he had found an alignment that would open the necessary lines, he formed his matrixes and braced himself. He took a deep breath, then with a rush of panic-induced adrenaline said the release words chosen to tap the first matrix.

"Mutance crimsonus."

In an instant he lost his grip on reality. He was stricken blind, deaf, and all of his external senses and feelers to the world around him—including his vision into his own mind's eye—shut off with a clenching pain. He was lost for only a matter of seconds before his body adapted to the shock, but when he came to himself he felt like he had been in agony for hours.

Slowly he rose to his feet and looked around. He felt no different. He attempted to gather ether for a spell, but found that he could not. Clearly he had lost his Cainite magics, if nothing else. He looked to his arm. To his surprise, the armlet had changed. It had constricted and reshaped itself, and now fit over his forearm perfectly. The steely band had even thinned, becoming far less intrusive. This seemed a good sign, but still he could detect nothing more.

Then he noticed something peculiar. An unnatural haze surrounded his body. Gradually he brought it into focus, though it was a difficult chore. A slim aura of red ether covered his entire frame. He stretched his right hand out, and watched as the ether around it shaped into claws. He made a fist, and the ether reshaped into a block not unlike the head of a sledgehammer.

He looked to the sky, still trying to determine what he had

done to himself. There he saw birds flying overheard. Seven birds, but they all hung as if suspended in air. He could make out the movement of their wings and was convinced they were moving, yet it seemed so very slow. He looked over the ground and located a small rock, then attempted to pick it up. As soon as his fingers closed about it, the stone crumbled into pebbles. He was surprised, and very gently picked up the next one. He gave it a light flick into the sky, and rapidly the stone left his hand and tore through one of the birds, killing it instantly.

As he was growing to understand what had happened to him, he turned to a nearby tree and lashed out with his hand. The wood crumbled like weak glass at his touch, and he turned to another tree, then another, laying into them with ferocious blows that shattered and leveled their trunks.

*Is this what it is like for Lord Abaddon?* he thought to himself as he marveled at his own strength. *Living in a world of tissue and glass?* As the ancient forest behemoths collapsed around him, he easily walked from their paths, entertained at the futility of their attempts to crush him.

Content for now with his analysis of the powers granted by the armlet, he tried the all-important final step of his experiment. He needed to be certain he could reverse this effect. He again attempted to make contact with his umbra and access his matrixes. It was more difficult than he remembered it ever being, a dozen times harder than the first matrix he had ever used as a trainee. Finally he managed to peer weakly into his stores. Once he felt the connection was solid, he spoke his second keyphrase.

"Mutance azurey." Again he was struck with a brief paralysis. This one was less jarring than before, and soon the red aura faded from him and his body was left feeling oddly diminished.

As his aura faded, a horrible numbing pain sank into his arms. He looked down to notice, in surprise, that his hands were shredded and bleeding, and his forearms had large wooden splinters lodged in them that he had not felt before.

"Hm," he muttered to himself, "it seems the armlet affords me a great deal of power. It increases my speed to its heightened potential and allows me to maintain it, to even think at that level. Given the generous blessings of speed I hold, that is a significant edge. My strength is also increased by magnitudes, but my endurance is not cut to match. Using the gifts of the Band, I could tear myself to pieces before even realizing I was injured." He looked around the small area of the forest, smiling broadly at the damage he had done. "I must make certain that my enemies fall apart before I do."

He drew forth his Soul Scythe and siphoned a small amount of power from the weapon to heal his wounds as he removed the wooden fragments. The Scythe had not absorbed substantial magics in some time, and its reserves were finally depleted. He hoped that soon he would have an opportunity to kill again. For now, he headed from the forest into the plains, and dashed at his highest speeds to intercept the Scion of Emle.

* * * * *

The two Godbeasts of Gehenna arrived at the northern border of the Jagguron Peaks, prepared to head to the southern regions of the continent. They had tacked their course off slightly to the west, avoiding the petrified forest from which the Wisdoms had approached. On their current path, the Draconic Forest headed right up to the mountains themselves, separated only by a small expanse of plains. Lord Grand Councilor Atheme Tethen had once run for his life carrying the injured Saint Sinjuin Serene across these very plains, leaving Abaddon Daemon behind facing the forest's ravenous denizens alone. Such adventures were long since past, and these plains had stood empty for many moons.

Today, however, their loneliness was given reprieve. A figure stood awaiting the Godbeast's arrival, brightly decorating the normal emptiness of the grasslands. The Gehennans were briefly startled at the sight of unexpected company, but shortly recognized the presence of their elusive ally.

Aegagropilion spoke first. The Godbeast's appearance had changed slightly since he had absorbed Kiastos, gradually becoming once more thinner, sleeker, and more flexible. Though he still wielded the formidable might of the devoured Wisdom, his body was slowly reverting to its natural state.

"Ah, the Silver One," he hissed. "Schpariel told me you aid us, yet I have not seen you since my awakening. I would rate your service most poor."

In response to this jab there was an agitated movement beneath the hood masking Akatriel's features. "I trust that since you have eaten you are in more sociable spirits, Great Beast."

The Godbeast gave a chuckle at the sound of his informal title. "You put up with a vast amount of insolence from your underlings," he commented to Schpariel.

The Dark Wisdom waved his comrade to be silent and took a step forward. "Why are you here, now? Dare you stand to betray us? Our powers have only increased since last you toyed with me."

"Such a needless accusation! I have no intentions on betraying you, almighty lords of Gehenna. I'm only here to ask where you're going."

Schpariel puffed loudly in irritation. He began to suspect the pale priest had served out his usefulness now that Aegagropilion was restored. "We are on our way to resurrect Gilanirus, thanks to no help from you."

The small figure raised his head and looked over his shoulder. "And you intend to head over these mountains?"

Schpariel tapped his foot twice and gave a quiet snap, summoning the Moon Rod into the open hand behind his back. "So we do. If we have to knock you from our path, then so much the better."

The conspirator shook his head slowly. "I'm not your obstacle. I only wish for you to witness something."

He pointed to the sky without raising his eyes, and the two Godbeasts followed with their gaze. For a moment there was nothing, as Schpariel prepared a spell to disintegrate his annoyance once and for all. Then a sudden burst of light and sound lit up the entire sky, blotting out the sun with a black haze and sending the trees in the forest behind them thrashing, trunks and limbs snapping under the pressure of the air itself.

Schpariel dropped his spell and stood silent. Both Godbeasts knew what they had witnessed, but only Aegagropilion retained enough composure to speak it.

"Torlen, Wisdom of Sound, moves."

"But where is his partner?" asked Schpariel once he regained himself. "Where's the Wisdom of the Wind? Why does the Sound move alone?"

Aegagropilion nodded, but did not answer. This was twice now they had observed this peculiar phenomenon. It was becoming evident that the Wisdoms were preoccupied by more than just their hunt for the Godbeasts. If the Elysians were working a larger game on Morolia, it seemed a certainty it could only end in disaster for their ancient rivals.

Their visitor offered an explanation, exploiting their misgivings expertly as ever. "Valinoru, like the other Wisdoms, awaits you beyond these mountains. Torlen moves for his own reasons, carefully controlling the playing field and setting it against you. He will not be absent long before he returns to the south. You see, the Wisdoms also know where Gilanirus rests, as they're the ones who placed him there. They know your mind. They need not seek you out, as you will come to them. If you cross the Jagguron, you'll be set upon and torn apart by an ambush you cannot face."

"It's different now," Aegagropilion argued. "I have absorbed the power of a Wisdom myself. I am prepared to face them."

Akatriel slowly shook his head. "You think you've grown, yet it's only in arrogance. There's a difference in the Wisdom you have defeated, and those who await you beyond. Something you seem to have forgotten." He raised his head until his silver eyes showed, staring at the Moon Rod Schpariel had idly allowed to drift to his side. "Perhaps you can guess, Dark Wisdom?"

Schpariel fell a step back. He had his own memories of battling with the Wisdom of Sound, and they were not welcome ones. His confidence in he and his brother's combined strength faded rapidly. "The Staff of the Sun."

Akatriel nodded, allowing the shadows of his hood to hide his face once more. "Perhaps you don't remember the bite of the Sun, Aegagropilion. In the last war you took the form of a gold dragon and used its shimmering scales to reflect the beams of divine light. But you will not find a gold dragon in the mountains beyond me. When you reach the southern lands you'll face enemies who, in one hand, hold the power to wipe you from this plane. With all of your might, what will you do in the face of that death?"

The Godbeasts offered no response. They had not encountered a Wisdom who possessed a Sun Staff since their resurrections, but they knew well the nature of the weapons. The divine powers of Melukah were astonishing, and while the heat of his Staffs was injurious to all creatures, they were particularly attuned to slay the denizens of Gehenna. When their light combined with traces of red ether, it formed a radiant poison that destroyed spiritual and planar bindings. Even a Godbeast could not long survive an assault of that nature.

"You are hasty for Gilanirus' awakening, I know," Akatriel continued, "but this is not the time to lose patience. You know where the Final Godbeast sleeps, he will go nowhere." He turned his attention specifically to Schpariel. "I have a proposal you might consider. To the northwest there is a land less desolate than the remainder of Arkalen. There a plethora of demonspawn species thrive. Take the Great Beast there and let him feed for a few months. Find the nests of the demons of greatest power and make them your own. Once you feel you have achieved might similar to that you held in the last war, you may return to face the challenges that await you here."

Schpariel gave a nod and turned north. Aegagropilion became enraged at the prospect of turning around, but he followed his brother and voiced his complaints as they moved, rather than dealing further with Akatriel.

Once he stood fully alone, the pale figure collapsed to his knees. His life still leaked from his wounds, and he could not seem to staunch their flow. All the threads moved according to his plan, tied carefully in place. It was serendipitous that his master had forewarned him of the approach of Torlen, else he was not certain how he might have delayed the Godbeasts and their crossing of the Jagguron.

He stumbled to his feet and headed to the peaks himself, scaling toward one of the many hidden caverns that served him.

* * * * *

Myris caught up with Cildar just before the final stretch of the narrow desert. To their west, a substantial human city was within sight. The Dragoon had halted his march when his pursuer had come within range of his senses, waiting patiently for the man's arrival. Now they stood facing each other in silence, each with his own certainties about the battle that was about to take place.

Cildar was the first to break the silence. "I suppose you're the forerunner. Does the Daemon follow your path?"

Myris gave a slow shake of his cowled head. "Lord Abaddon has his own path to follow. I have been cast out as an Onion Knight for my refusal to walk at his side. I alone hunt you."

"Then we are the same now, and there remains no reason for us to fight. Join me, Myris, and we'll do what we came to Arkalen to do. We'll have our sport."

The Cainite tapped his foot in thought for several seconds, considering this quite seriously. "No, my friend. As enticing as your offer is—especially when weighed against my own fear of our upcoming confrontation—there is something wrong with you. If I were to turn a blind eye to that, I would be no true friend at all."

"That fear of yours is well justified. I've long held the advantage over you. I may have been sorely humiliated by Lord Abaddon—clearly he was hiding some deeper strength I never dared imagine. But with due respect, don't let that lead you to draw false confidence as to your own chances against me."

Myris began to slowly circle his opponent. "It is true that Cildar always held an advantage over me, but he was never able to kill me."

"I never *chose* to kill you. That was practice. In all the time we've known each other, we've never had a real fight. If you attempt to waylay me now, I can make no guarantees that you'll come out alive. The Lord of the Phoenix standing before you is far mightier than the one you knew. No longer a simple paladin of Felthespar, I am the Dark Paladin. I stand alone, a council of one."

"Dark Paladin?" Myris stopped his strafe and began to laugh quietly. "I would dare say you begin to muster in on my territory, Cildar. A bit melodramatic, perhaps?"

The tall man gave a slight shrug in response, smirking beneath his mask. "I didn't come up with it, but it's starting to grow on me."

"Akatriel, yes?" Cildar offered only a nod, so Myris continued, "What did he do to you? Why do you so eagerly turn your back on everything you hold dear?"

"I could ask of you the same question."

"But you would not waste the breath. You know my answer."

"Because you were never truly loyal to Felthespar," he replied with a sneer in his voice.

"No. Never, truly, to Felthespar. Only to you."

Cildar paused and the two stood in silence for several long seconds. "Must we really do this?" he asked softly.

"Tell me what happened to you, and we shall see."

He sighed in response. "Akatriel expanded my mind. He enhanced my spirit with the properties of an ancient dragon. You question why I've abandoned my loyalties, Felthespar, our quest... as I am now, those things all seem so trivial. Within my mind I see the vast expanse of centuries without end. Long after Felthespar has crumbled to dust, long after the memory of Vesovius Emle is lost to the waters of time, I will endure on."

"Even if what he told you is true and not merely some

sophisticated brainwashing, you are still a man, not a dragon. Your body will still die."

"Not so. Haste is far more than it has ever been credited. It can be a pathway to immortality. Immersed in Asterian currents as I am, I'll transform myself into a lich. Before, such a process would have had its risks. But with the spirit of a dragon grafted onto my own, I'm not only guaranteed to survive the transformation, but to grow even mightier as I endure it. I confess there's a dark irony in a former paladin becoming a lich. Which is why I have forsaken that title, and taken so readily to my new one."

Myris nodded somberly. "Well then, you have given me unfortunate clarity as to what I must first do. If I am to save my friend, to find a path back to the real Cildar Emle, I must first preserve his humanity. Since you clearly will not drop Haste eagerly, I shall be forced to beat you out of it."

"Try your damndest, Myris."

Without further precursor, Cildar sprinted forward and launched into a flurry of punches. The Cainite relied on his footspeed for evasion, making straight dashes of three feet in seemingly random directions in order to avoid each strike. It was a difficult maneuver to maintain. Though Myris' blessings granted him bursts of speed even beyond his normal impressive levels, when moving at his apex his vision was unable to keep up. When he used the full capacity of his blessing of speed, he was fighting blind.

These bouts of blindness made it difficult to predict the next incoming attack. He successfully managed to avoid the first dozen blows, then his opponent backed off. Cildar already knew of the weakness of his ally's legendary speed. He shook his head sadly at the Cainite's pitiable attempt to present himself as a capable opponent.

"What now, Phare? We keep this up until you mistime my attack? You've yet to make even an attempt to strike me. You won't be beating me out of anything, like this."

Myris stood catching his breath. Even the few seconds of

sprinting he had done had strained his body. It would not be much longer until he began to lose alacrity. As he had always suspected, he had no chance at weathering the wrath of the Hasted warrior.

"I see no need to delay this further," he announced aloud. He raised his left arm and slid back the black sleeve. The Band of Barricus was revealed, with slim lines of red runes tracing down its shell. Cildar recognized the artifact, but had no idea what to expect from it. "Mutance crimsonus," Myris stated calmly. The white metal of the armlet turned into a dull pink, then harsh and scratchy red. Soon that color surrounded the Cainite's entire body, filling him with Gehennite fury.

Myris himself was not aware of the physical transformation enacted by the Band's powers, but Cildar now witnessed it firsthand. Myris' body expanded in muscle mass, swelling to the point that it forced his loose outfit taut. Through a few slices in the dark cloth, patches of his skin could be seen. This skin was no longer flesh-toned, but rather a peculiar pale red with dark veins crawling across it like webs. The illusory flames that once hid his eyes faded as well, revealing that his eyelids—much like his clothing—were stretched tightly open. The center of the eyes were a solid black, but the whites had been completely overrun by jagged red lines that appeared to be steaming blood.

No more words were exchanged, as Myris could not resist his adrenaline long enough to speak. Instead he rapidly cleared the distance between the warriors and planted his fist firmly into his foe's dark jawline. Cildar was wholly unprepared for the ferocity of this move. As his body was sent flying back, he felt his opponent's crimson aura continue to assault him, slicing and stabbing into his neck and chest with blasts of heat.

He landed on his feet and attempted to prepare a counter, but was not fast enough. Myris was instantly on top of him, a knee already buried into his plated stomach. The frenzied Cainite bounced back onto his hands, then fiercely lashed out with his legs, striking the taller man's chin with both heels simultaneously. As Cildar's feet left the ground the smaller man also threw himself into the air, somersaulting and catching up at only a three-foot height. The manic warrior lashed out with his right hand and slashed at the Dragoon's masked face, sending him spinning back into the ground below.

Cildar tore his shredded mask from his helmet and drew the Trine Lance into his right hand. It was clear there would be no breaks in this battle. Myris' raw strength was not at his level, but the Cainite's speed was more dizzying than any he had ever before witnessed from the man. As he tried to gain a bearing on his opponent, he was struck hard from his left. A series of four punches and then a high kick connected to the exact same point in his armor, the dent previously placed there by Abaddon. These punches shattered the plate, and the final kick struck deep into the man's abdomen. Myris' foot became lodged in the opening torn into the mail, and he used it as an opportunity to boost himself up over his adversary, then come down with a two-fisted slash across the Dragoon's throat. The two were ripped free by the impact of that blow, leaving Cildar stumbling away and attempting to quickly mend his collapsed windpipe with white magic.

Even in the intensity of this fray, and despite his injuries, the Dark Paladin found his opportunity to strike. As Myris attempted to regain his stance after having his foot dislodge from the mail, Cildar spun about and gave a booming swing with his Lance. The Cainite's razor-sharp reflexes allowed him to lean out beyond the range of the blow and it did not touch his flesh. However, as white wind released from the Lance's tip intermingled with the Gehennite energy surrounding him, the two powers dissipated.

Myris fell to the ground as violently as if he had been struck physically. Cildar did not waste time, but charged forward once again, this time swinging his Lance down at the fallen man's head. The Cainite used his left arm to dig into the ground and throw himself fiercely to the side. As the Lance passed by his right side, barely missing, once again his aura of fury fluctuated and weakened. He landed gently and attempted to charge before his enemy could recover from that swing, but already his speed was not what it had been a moment ago. Cildar gave a nimble leap back and another swing, this time at the man's neck. Again Myris only barely managed to dodge, but again the energies of the Lance assaulted the vapors of Gehenna and evaporated them.

As his Gehennite powers were weakened, Myris' body became increasingly gripped by exhaustion and pain. As this final stroke of wind passed over his face, he felt the breath taken from his body and could not find the strength to recover. His mind flashed in panic, and he fell back on one of his oldest combat instincts—he reached to his back and drew his Soul Scythe, making a sudden swing at Cildar's chest.

The Dragoon had no trouble dodging the desperate attack, as the Soul Scythe had never been an effective weapon against him. However, this time the result was different. Similar to the Trine Lance attacking Myris' aura, the Soul Scythe seemed to latch onto the black streams surrounding Cildar's body. It sucked these energies away and drank them into its dark blade, feeding them to its master.

The Dark Paladin's might diminished slightly, and Myris conversely was given the strength he needed to rebound. He took a deep breath, redoubled his speed, and charged at his opponent with a flurry of blows from the scythe. Cildar stayed on his toes, carefully blocking each attack with a mirrored blow from his spear. As they continued to exchanged strikes, each warrior began to lose vigor. Their attacks became slower, and the reverberations from their blows less intense. After a few more weak swings they backed away from each other panting heavily.

It was only seconds before their respective blessings restored themselves. Cildar's black aura darkened once more to hide his white clothing, and Myris' red aura became hungering flames dancing across his shoulders. They straightened their backs and stared at each other evenly. The Cainite first voiced what each was thinking.

"I hold the edge. Your Trine Lance dismisses my powers, but my Soul Scythe feeds on yours. As this battle continues, my strength will increase as yours fades. In time, I will become too fast for you to keep up. Once my blade bites into your flesh, it will be finished."

"Yes, it appears my ascent to lichdom has had an unexpected consequence. Now that my body is drenched in equal doses of Morolian and Asterian ether, your Scythe is able to feast upon me. What strange fate. Though you would never have stood against the Lord of the Phoenix, you pose a vile threat to me as the Dark Paladin."

"I will restore you to your former mind, or I will kill you. You cannot run from me. You lack the speed. One way or another, this is already over."

The man shook his head slowly and looked to the village to his right. "Looks like a happy settlement down there, doesn't it?"

Myris narrowed his bloodshot eyes. His thirst for battle was beginning to overtake his senses once more. "Who cares?" he growled.

"Certainly not I. Human lives are so brief, already practically extinguished in the long view of history. But I suspect you do. After all, you were taught by the nobles of Felthespar, myself included. Taught to protect the lives of the weak. Can you ignore that instinct?"

"I am a Cainite warrior. The weak mean nothing to me."

The new Cildar gave a wicked smile across his bleeding face. "This will be a good test of that, I'd say."

He returned the Trine Lance to his back and raised his right hand toward the village. Quickly he began to release a volley of blackened Aura Blasts, ripping through houses and trees in the village, striking a few stragglers he could see in the streets. He fired nearly thirty shots as Myris watched horrified—unable to believe any version of Cildar capable of such an act—then turned and began to run away.

The frenzied warrior started to give chase, then heard the sounds of screaming children as their house started to collapse around them. He also heard his former friend shout back as he was still retreating, "Choose your path wisely, Myris. Are you Cainite or Onion Knight?"

Myris' rage clouded his vision and he could not bring himself to move. He screamed and clawed at his own temples, then took a deep breath to settle as best he could. He groaned quietly, "Mutance azurey," to himself, and the gifts of Gehenna slowly faded from him.

Once he felt his blood pressure drop to a normal level, he carefully thought over the decision he faced. It only took him a few seconds, then he was on the move.

An hour later he had saved most of the villagers Cildar had placed in peril. A few of those struck directly had died from their injuries, but Myris had been able to get the rest into stable condition using the medicinal herbs he had held onto for himself. After receiving a few cautious words of thanks, he headed back to the border and stared for a long time in the direction his opponent had disappeared.

For the first time, he began to believe the man he knew as Cildar Emle, Lord of the Phoenix, Holy Paladin of Felthespar, would not make a return to this world after all.

* * * * *

Akatriel collapsed in his small cave with a deep sigh. He concentrated his efforts on calling out over the Veil, summoning his master. It took a long time, but finally a deep black cloud encircled him and he went blind.

*You summon me? An unexpected change in our etiquette. Does cowardice dull your insolence?*

"I need strength. I have wounds I cannot outpace. I can't die now! There's too much to be done still!"

*You know I cannot give what you ask. That body has its limits, and you have taxed them needlessly. You have no choice now but to let it sleep.*

"You don't take this seriously enough! I cannot sleep now! The pieces can't be left to fend for themselves, the Queen must remain in play. Without my authority the board will descend into chaos!"

*I take this very seriously. But you have ignored my warnings. You paid no heed to my words. Even now you do not listen. I do not have the power to grant what you wish. You have no choice but sleep. I am displeased with this, but the failure is your own. If our plans fall apart because of this unfortunate turn, I will make certain that you pay the price.*

The voice and the darkness faded, and Akatriel was left sitting alone with his rage. He shouted at the walls of the cave, demanding that they listen to him, to grant him his request. But none heard his words, no one felt his wrath. Soon his strength gave out from his tantrum and he collapsed to the ground. He gurgled weakly for several minutes, until finally his body shut off and he slipped into a deep coma.

And the Silver One slept.

## Chapter 27.

# Torlen, Whose Touch Kills

The Wisdom of Sound dropped from the sky and landed with a thud in the midst of Morolian hills. He looked about in disdain at the disorganized manner in which the land bent and rolled. In Elysium, everything fit within a strict order, an ideal society built upon structure and discipline. It was a world as Melukah saw fit.

Torlen respected this vision of a pristine world. It fell into line with his own beliefs in synchronicity. He had stood loyally alongside the Supreme Wisdom centuries prior, when Dosiros and Kiastos had attempted to overthrow the Sun's rule. Dosiros had advocated order through violence and oppression, having grown bored of Melukah's quiet regime. The insurgents had been unable to seduce a third Wisdom to their cause, and their uprising had eventually been quelled.

Fortunately, the Wisdom of the Flame no longer possessed the audacity to challenge the Sun. When a Wisdom was slain in both body and spirit, they did not reincarnate in such fashion as the Godbeasts of Gehenna. Instead they had to be revived through a ritual of the Muses, and once reborn they lost the memories of their previous cycle. Dosiros, as a result of his recklessness, was currently the youngest among the Wisdoms. Melukah alone had never died.

The Sound shook thoughts of home from his head and turned his focus to his present situation. He had located the sparse remains of Valinoru's body a few hours prior, in a large forest to the west. His inspections had told him two humans had been involved, then had left the scene heading northeast. Valinoru's head was missing, with his divine spirit still likely bound to it. A Wisdom whose body had been damaged to this extreme was unable to recover, even just to detach from their shell and return to Elysium.

It seemed unlikely the humans fully understood what they had done. It was more probable they had taken the head as a crude trophy, as was their manner. This explained, at least, why the Muses had made this such a priority. Without intervention, Valinoru's spirit could be trapped on Morolia for centuries. With a better understanding of his mission in hand, Torlen had then resumed pursuit to the northeast. There he discovered in annoyance that the humans had separated, with one doubling back and the other traveling into the west.

After debate, he chose to follow the prey moving southward, since that was the direction of the other Wisdoms. It was a gamble, but if he chose wrong Torlen would simply kill this human and move on to find the other. Nothing was lost except for time, and he moved fast enough to make up any lost time.

Then he had sensed something oddly familial. He was unable to immediately identify it, but he knew there was something nearby that was akin to him. So he had dropped into the Kolpen Hills, waiting patiently in an attempt to determine if the source was moving. He judged now that it was not, though he could feel it was nearly right atop of him, no more than a few yards away. This left him with the conclusion that his quarry was watching him, as well.

"Come out," he bluffed to the air. "I hear you. You cannot hide from the Wisdom of Sound."

Behind him there was movement. A creature stepped out from behind a series of boulders at his left flank. He turned confidently to face it. It was a human—most likely the one that had defeated Valinoru—but it was a different thought altogether that went through his mind as he recognized the sight standing before him.

"You're the human I killed before," he remarked.

It was indeed the same man he had fought shortly after his arrival in Morolia. There was little change to his appearance, except that he had changed weapons. Instead of the silver greatsword, he was now wielding an extremely long katana. The weapon was strapped to his back, the vast length of blade pointed toward the sky behind his left shoulder. It was a sword whose origins Torlen knew all too well. The sight of this blade caused him far more unease than the man carrying it.

"My kind do not come back from the dead," the human replied. "You failed to kill me."

"And you killed one of my kind in response, with *that* sword, no doubt. A show of power, perhaps?" The man met his gaze levelly. Clearly he did not fear the Wisdom, in spite of their previous encounter. Torlen found himself almost amused.

"I needed to make certain you understood that I merited your attention."

"And you did so by killing one of my brethren with no cause?"

"Last we met, you Wisdoms tried to kill me and my friends on sight without provocation. You would dare accuse me of having no cause?" Torlen stood silent for a moment, basking now in full amusement. The man continued, "You and I need not fight again. I defeated Valinoru to establish grounds for equal communication. In our previous conversing you seemed more reasonable than your cohort. Perhaps we can establish diplomacy between our peoples."

The Wisdom tilted his head slightly. "While I'll readily admit to being 'more reasonable' than Dosiros, that doesn't mean I'm willing to forgive you for assaulting one of my own."

"You started this aggression," the man growled. "My actions were a reasonable defense."

Torlen took a step forward, crossing his arms behind his back. "Let's assume, for a moment, that I'm willing to entertain this idea of yours. What is it you desire from us, Morolian? Some kind of lowly mortal wish?"

"You're foreigners to this land, and have shown no respect for it. I simply wish to understand your goals. I might even assist you, in order to expedite your departure. But no matter what, I must ensure that you don't cause unnecessary harm to innocent life."

There was another pause as the two warriors stared each down.

Then Torlen continued, "Let me level with you, mortal. I might personally be willing to come to some kind of peaceful arrangement with you, but Dosiros will now want you dead even more than before. And ultimately any pact you might make with our kind must pass through the Sun. Even if you killed Valinoru, Melukah will still see you as a lowly Class Eight. He will not open dialogue with your kind."

"At least tell me of Akatriel. Are you allied with him? Do you know why he has taken my sword?"

"Akatriel is on Morolia as well?" the Wisdom pondered, placing a finger upon his chin. "Interesting. What is he about, I wonder?"

"So you don't serve the same agenda after all."

"To be honest, I couldn't say. Akatriel is a bit of an enigma, which I'm sure you can attest to, if you're aware of him at all. In either case, I'm afraid there's nothing further for us to discuss. I've been sent to punish you for your crimes against Valinoru, and there's really no sense in stalling the matter further."

"So in spite of my efforts, it is to be war between us, then."

Torlen gave an echoing laugh. "You stand alone, Morolian! How would you start a war against the Wisdoms of Elysium? Perhaps you don't understand what you propose. You would aspire to conquer gods!"

The human reached his right hand behind his lower back and seized the hilt of his sword. He gave it a twist and removed it from its restraints, bringing it forward and holding it angled upward at his side. "I have conquered them before."

This claim was made with a dry, serious expression, and Torlen was uncertain how to interpret it. Clearly both opponents were now determined to enter combat. The Wisdom raised his left hand and his forearm became encased in white sonic rings. This technique was his first stage, a primarily defensive ability that allowed him to crush objects with dense lashes of sound.

As he began a series of internal processes to synchronize himself with the surrounding area, he made one final query. "What have you done with Valinoru's head?"

The man gave what appeared to Torlen as a genuinely confused squint. "His head?"

"I inspected his remains, and it's missing. There were two of you, yes? One of you must have taken it. Some cruel ritual of your kind, perhaps?"

He shook his head. "When my ally and I left Valinoru, his head remained behind. We do not dishonor the corpses of the fallen."

Torlen sensed no treachery in these words. This left him at a bit of a loss as to his ultimate purpose here. Nevertheless, the Muses had entreated him to send a human to Elysium. No doubt they wished to conduct their own interrogation on the matter. He would do as they had asked this one time, then turn his attention back to the Godbeasts. If for no other reason, his assassin's pride demanded he defeat this opponent with more finality than their previous meeting.

"You killed Valinoru," he announced, "so I will not take this battle lightly in spite of our first. If you're unable to live up to my expectations of you, death will be swift."

His target offered no response other than bowing his head slightly. Soon a rustling breeze seemed to hit the man, and his body began to emanate a peculiar grey light. There was the sound of a peculiar release of pressure, then vaporous ether trails covered his shoulders. When he looked up, his eyes had become shimmering blue pockets of energy. Like the Wisdom, he would not be taking this battle lightly.

The human rushed forward with a speed uncharacteristic for his species. He brought his left hand across and seized his sword's hilt with a two-handed grip, beginning a swing that would connect with the Wisdom's chest. Torlen was not one to be bested at speed, however. He raised his right hand and released a wide net of sonic waves, casting it over his assailant. The human's sharp velocity was dulled by the thick net, and the Sound easily stepped from the path of the slowed strike.

The incredible length of the blade had forced the deity too far out of range to land a punch. He did not mind this, and again pointed his right hand forward. The human's chest and torso were seized by a blast of sound, blowing him several yards back and driving him to his knees.

During their first altercation, Torlen had planted a Seed of Synchronization into the man's spirit. This touch was the assassin's second stage. Only one with exceptional insight into the ways of Elysium could locate and remove the Seed. With it in place, the Wisdom of Sound could use his powers to manipulate and belabor his opponent's body with dozens of abilities. He began to boast of this advantage, but the human dashed to his feet and abruptly cut off any opportunity for taunts.

Again the man charged and attempted to bisect his foe, this time using a downward slash. Again Torlen used a net to slow the attack, and again he backed out of the range of the blade's bite. This time the human responded before he could be sent flying away, punching into the ground with his left hand and causing an explosion of earthen spikes to erupt forth.

The Wisdom had witnessed this technique previously and knew how to counter it. He engaged his left hand and reached into the threatening rocks, which were seized by a backlash of power from the rings on his arm and reduced to harmless shrapnel. As he glanced up, his assailant was already practically on top of him, slicing down again with the katana only two feet from Torlen's face. The assassin was not perturbed by this, calmly raising his right hand and releasing a sharp burst of sonic energy.

The steel of the sword vibrated intensely, then tore itself sharply from its master and embedded itself up to the hilt into one of the boulders towering nearby. As the man backed away nursing his wrist—which had been nearly broken by the sword's exodus—Torlen stepped forward and delivered a fierce punch to the center of his forehead.

The Sound laughed in amusement as his opponent's small frame was sent rolling away by this blow. Though the human's speed and strength were impressive—clearly at a level many times beyond what he had demonstrated in their first encounter—he was woefully unprepared to compete with Torlen's myriad of techniques. Of all Wisdoms, he was the most adept and diversified with his divine powers.

The battered warrior again rose to his feet and steadied himself. He was starting to breathe heavily, and continued to rub his wrist as he spoke softly, seemingly to himself. "Wisdom of *Sound*. You can probably hear my every move. I'd wager you process sound faster than your eyes process light, probably faster than any creature across the cosmos. You don't need to see me, because you follow with your ears. I don't know that I've ever faced an enemy who can follow my movements so precisely." He paused and dropped his arms to his side, glaring at his adversary with fists clenched in determination. "Try it now."

He tensed his muscles and the air about his body began to hum vigorously. At first Torlen could hear the sounds of whipping winds released by this wasteful show of power. Then something began to change. First the sound of the winds faded and a low hum took their place, as the human continued to wrap himself about with a freshly drawn layer of Asterian ether. Then, the sound stopped altogether. The Wisdom tuned his senses intently, but all he could make out was the surrounding sounds of nature, insects, and the occasional rustling of leaves.

Again his opponent moved. His motions were sudden, and Torlen's eyes were not fast enough to follow them. Without his hearing to aid him, he lost track of his target for just a second. Then he noticed movement to his side, as the man recovered his katana from the stone where it had lodged itself. Torlen spotted him just in time to see him disappear again, this time bringing the sword with him.

The Wisdom acted fast, knowing he had precious few seconds before he would be struck from some direction. He brought his right hand in front of his face and released a pulsing burst of sound in every direction. The feedback of the shockwave from behind him seemed unnatural. That had to be where the human had gone.

The assassin gave a swift leap forward and twisted himself about in midair. Relying on instinct, he tossed a wide slowing net as he spun about. This attack was in vain, as his adversary was slightly more at his left side than expected. The man had lingered back more than during his previous assault, well outside the range of the Wisdom's hands. A horizontal swing of the reaching katana was already begun, and Torlen had less than a second before he would suffer an injury which he could not defend against.

Had the Wisdom hesitated, he would have died. But his mind had been sharpened against far more dangerous foes than this. Unable to bring his right hand back into play after having just released the sonic net, and unable to use his left due to the shield encasing it, he lashed out with his right foot. A blast of synchronized sonic waves seized the man's arms and forced them up ever so slightly, causing his blade to sail harmlessly overhead. Torlen held back no further, having lost his comfort with this battle. He used a burst of sound from his shoulders to straighten himself forward onto his feet, then swiftly seized his foe's throat with his left hand.

The pulsing rings completely detached from his arm and entered the human's body, rocking his skeletal structure with vibration intense enough to shatter steel. The man tried to scream, but was unable to open his mouth as his jaw was nearly snapped, along with every other bone in his body. Soon the energy from the attack exhausted, and as the vibration slowed to a numbing hum, Torlen released his grip on the neck. The human collapsed his feet unconscious, his skin ripped and torn into uncountable strips, blood pouring from the body where it lay.

Torlen shook his head in admiration at his defeated opponent. His curiosity was sated. He could see how this mortal had been able to best Valinoru. The man used a fighting style which was efficient and merciless, ever attempting a fatal blow. His strength and speed were unnatural for any Morolian, and his magic highly tuned, allowing him to rapidly invent ways to counter even the divine techniques of a Wisdom. Coupled with the dangerous weapon he had pilfered, on Morolia this man was no doubt a match for anything. Torlen would rest easier once that baleful blade was locked away in Elysium.

He bent down and touched the fallen knight's right shoulder. He gathered a stream of stored Elysian ether and injected it sharply into the man's body. A bright green light carved an intricate pattern across the shoulder, then faded out.

The deity turned and began to walk away, knowing what came next. The air around the human erupted with electricity and flames, and the Veil was torn aside. Torlen shifted ether to his legs and once again took to the air, returning south to rejoin Dosiros.

* * * * *

Kelve sat staring down at the fortress he had grown to hate so intensely. He was alone for the moment, having isolated himself from his people and escaped a mile or so to the north, watching for activity within the enemy walls from atop a hill much taller than the one his troops occupied.

He had not yet recovered from the injury given to him by Gariso. He had lost too large of a section of side and stomach. Without a skin grafting procedure, there was no way he could heal from a wound of this nature. That aside, his bones were scraped and softened, and it was unlikely that even under ideal conditions he would recover to a point where he could return to battle.

It was hard for a former Devilslayer to admit he would never be able to fight again. Kelve had long prided himself on his combat instincts and sharp thinking. He had never made it a point to dash into battle recklessly, but there was a form of comfort in knowing he never had to wait long between tests of his skill. Suddenly faced with a life where that was no longer possible, he realized how empty he felt without that comfort.

He had never desired leadership, yet now it seemed he was destined to be stranded in that role one way or another. There were still no signs of Detria; he had begun to suspect something had gone awry and she would not be returning. His own inability to join combat ensured that even if she did, he could not resume his simple life as a loyal soldier. He could remain as a leader, or he could die.

His instincts went heavily against the latter action, so he had struggled to bring himself into stable condition. Many among the band of reinforcements were familiar with these lands, and they had been harvesting fresh herbs for Kelve. He had also created a sort of plaster that kept him from losing steady amounts of blood from his side. It was not enough to keep him alive, though. For that, he had been forced to turn to more extreme measures. He had started producing several forms of adrenaline supplements and steroids, as well as some fake blood supplements that would be damaging in the long term. His dosages were low for the moment, but he suspected over the next few months they would increase. He already knew that at best, there was no way he could buy himself more than another year of time.

As he weighed his fate, he was joined by a man from the camp. It was one of the newcomers, nearly seven feet tall with a pronounced potbelly. The man's name was Boderon, and he was their champion and apparent leader. He was missing one eye and wore a large patch over the right side of his face, and the wrist of his right hand had been carefully bound and reinforced with a few lengths of steel bar. Kelve had heard that his injuries were from a recent battle, but Boderon would not speak of the details.

His visitor sat down heavily and gave a sigh. "Needed to escape the limelight, huh?"

Kelve responded with a nod. "Something like that."

The man changed the subject quickly. Boderon was intuitive to the feelings of those around him, and Kelve had already grown to appreciate his presence. "Training's going well, I'd say. My people have a lot to learn to hold themselves like your soldiers do, but our spirits are stout. I can already hold my own with a few of your lieutenants." He pounded his chest with a proud smile. "Every one of you are tough to the core, though, I must say. You make us look like the vagabonds we are."

"This is going to be a long and drawn out war, Boderon. I don't see victory in sight. Why do you bring your people into this?"

"We were going to come here alone, even when we thought we'd have no allies. We were going to try to take down the Overlord's threat, or at least die putting a dent on it. We don't have a lot else to live for, Mister Kelve. This is our homeland. Leaving it took a lot out of us, and it was more than we could take. It was only time before our despair overcame our cowardice, and we came back certain we were to die. Thanks to your people's presence, that may not be the certainty we thought it. We've heard the stories. You've fought well, and got the Overlord's forces on the ropes. There hasn't even been an attack since the day we arrived. That has to be a sign that they're worried, trying to gather up. And when things start back up, they're going to have even more of a beast on their hands thanks to my folk. We're here doing a wonderful thing, you know."

The commander shook his head, his spirits not so easily lifted. "Is it really so wonderful? The Overlord is just some demon with delusions of grandeur. Eventually he would have left this place and tried to fight the Devilslayers. Would he have really been able to stand against them? And in the end, I'm forced to wonder which one would really make the worse evil. Probably just whoever wound up winning."

The big man gave a nod and leaned forward, looking at Kelve seriously. "We *are* doing some good here, bud. There's people still in that fortress held against their will, forced to slave and fight for that monster. Now I know we're going to kill some of them, and it breaks my heart to do it. But I hope that one day we can start setting at least some of them free, save them from this. And maybe if we don't save anyone in there, we'll at least keep the demons from going out and rounding up more for their little labor camp. Don't you forget, we're doing real good for someone. Maybe not for everyone, but not everything's about saving the world. Sometimes it's enough to just save one little girl."

The commander thought hard over these words, and his jaw

tightened with determination. He had sunk into his own misery for so long, and now he felt ashamed of it. There was a genuine truth to what Boderon said. Kelve had been a Devilslayer for too much of his life, too focused on believing the whole world had to be saved. He already knew his life was forfeit, already claimed by the fatigues of battle. But if he could burn his final months of energy and save one family, one young widow, one orphaned son, and give them a brighter future, he would gladly count his life a worthwhile cost.

He looked to his ally and offered a firm nod. "Thank you." He rose to his feet and brushed himself off, ignoring the protestations of pain from his side. "Let's go back to camp. I've got some plans I want to start working on."

* * * * *

"Awaken."

He had heard the word several times now. It was difficult to respond. Something felt heavy. His arms? No. Not his arms. Maybe his skin? No, not even that. It was the air. The air felt heavy, somehow. Like it was trying to drag him down. Like he was underwater. He could still breathe, but the breaths were difficult and painful.

He gritted his teeth and struggled to open his eyes. He was alone in a strange room. It was nearly the size of a house, but empty and circular. No walls or landmarks of any sort decorated it. Its great size seemed wasted, as he was pinned against the curving wall on one side, leaving the rest of the chamber bare. It took him a moment to discern in what way he was bound. Rather than chains or ropes, there was a thin layer of pressure pinning him backward. As he gradually began to recover his vision, he could see streams of green ether moving through the area.

The voice sounded again. It was coming from outside, it seemed. There were no windows or vents, yet the voice sounded clear to Abaddon's ears. "You are awake. Good. Your injuries were serious for your species, but we did our best to heal you. You must be presentable for the Muses."

"Muses?" he answered shakily. "What are you talking about? Where am I? Why do you hold me? Where is Torlen?"

"Many questions. I will tell you what I can, but I do not have clearance to reveal pertinent details. You have been brought to Elysium to stand trial by the Muses, the governing council of Elysian order. You will remain in this prison until they find time to speak to you, and then your future will be determined by their judgment."

"Release me from this place! I don't have time for your trial. There are important events on my own plane that I must see to!"

"I do not have clearance to release you. Besides, it was your 'seeing to' events that landed you here in the first place. I must go, I have a meeting to attend. Feel fortunate, for the Muses have made you a high priority. They should make their way to you within only a few months time. There is rare honor in that."

Abaddon clenched his jaw in rage, but he could tell there would be no reasoning with his jailer. Instead he began to focus on gathering power so he might break his bonds.

His attempts ended in failure. It was possible for him to reach Asteria from here, but after several efforts he realized that Asterian ether did not have the same effect on Elysian reality that it did on Morolian. All the techniques he knew were useless, and it could take years before he understood the interaction between Asteria and Elysium well enough to relearn his own magic.

He shook his head and dismissed the idea. If he did finally learn how to use Asterian ether properly on Elysium, it would undoubtedly cripple him once he returned to Morolia. He could come up with only one other option. No matter his choice, he would not be escaping this place quickly. It nearly sent him into a berserk fury thinking of being bound here while the Wisdoms continued to ransack Arkalen freely, but he knew that would only waste energy and possibly injure himself. He resigned instead to patience, at least for the time.

He swore inwardly this was not over. He would return to his home plane, and he would confront the Wisdoms. He would recover his sword. He would find Akatriel, and he would make him pay for his manipulations. For the moment he was trapped, but in this trap there was an opportunity to learn.

And so, with the future of his enemies burning brightly in his mind, Abaddon Daemon would study Elysian magic.

# ARKALEN II

## Calamity of Silver

## Chapter 28.

# Hell's Cell

In a small iron room with a single high window, a worn woman sat resting on her hands and knees in the two inches of thick mud layering the floor. The sun was rising, and beams of light began to paint the room anew. Every morning she was relieved to see the light again. Every morning, she thanked the gods she had not gone blind in the blackness of the cell. This brief glimpse of gratitude was the closest thing to hope she remembered.

Each morning she repeated the same daily routine. Shortly after sunrise, three visitors would arrive to spend the day with her. If she resisted them, they would beat her until she was nearly unconscious. Either way, she would eventually be lifted to her feet, and her wrists tied to a beam above her head. Wordlessly they would torture her throughout the day. Some days were intense beatings, others little more than using a needle to stab her hundreds of times across her body. No matter how she protested, no matter how she yelled, no matter how hard she struck them, they never spoke to her. They never gave her anything to acknowledge her humanity.

As the day drew to a close, for the last few hours of sunlight, they would raise her until her feet no longer touched the ground. Her food and water rations were brought in and sat upon the ground in front of her. The amounts were actually quite generous, large helpings of meat with steamed vegetables on the side and a large pitcher of water, and on some days milk. The guards then left her there, dangling for another hour with the sight and smell of her food growing cold. A thick iron band was bound around her ankles to prevent her from being able to walk. As she was left hanging in the evenings, the weight of that iron became more than she could bear, cutting into the skin around her feet and causing more blood to leak.

When the hour passed, one of the guards would return. With a swift blow to her head he would knock her unconscious, then untie her wrists and allow her to fall to the muddied ground. Sometimes she awoke in time to find and eat her tepid rations in the dwindling lights. Others she was left fumbling in the dark, often spilling her food or water and breaking down in tears over the loss.

For the first month it seemed impossible that she could survive this treatment. When she was alone she always wept, and she lost more of her rations to the mud than she ate. It was approaching the spring and summer months, and as daylight hours grew longer so did her torture sessions. One day she had broken down entirely, begging and pleading with her captors over the course of the entire day just to speak her name, just to say a single word to her. Even more than the pain, she could not endure the sinking feeling of her own madness.

In spite of her pleas the silence of the guards remained unbroken, and as evening fell she had been left hanging alone once more. Even then, after but a single month had gone by, she felt as though she had been here for years. Her mind had become a haze, a jumble, and it was too hard to press past memories of recent torture to the fading faces and voices of friends.

But she had tried, desperate to remember the sounds of kindness. She had sorted through faces and names, trying to bring up a memory that would give her stability from her own despair. Then she had found an image that would not fade. The face of a man, his blue eyes cold, his mouth solid and expressionless, his long black hair fading into the darkness of her mind.

Even though she knew she was alone, she spoke to the image hovering in front of her eyes. "Abaddon?"

*I despise weakness, Detria Alsen,* the response echoed through her mind. She knew she was only remembering words from earlier, out of context, but in spite of herself she tried to respond.

"I can't live like this. I'm going to die," she explained through a hoarse and cracking voice.

The image had not changed. No sympathy emanated from those cold blue eyes. *You cannot let the weakness win. Enduring is all you have left.*

She forced herself to concentrate, remembering the man whose face would not stop haunting her. What she remembered more than anything was his impassiveness. Calm, level, strong—his face alone reflected inner strength she could not forget, even when she had forgotten so much else.

She heard the sounds of footsteps approaching from the outside. Again she looked to this face for strength to confront her trials. "They're coming for me. They're going to strike me again. They always knock me out here."

*So why are you awake?*

It took her several seconds to process this question. She knew this was no memory, that Abaddon had never said those words to her. She knew this was a sign that her mind was beginning to slip. But simultaneously, she recognized that there was an idea there, an option her mind had created for her to escape. Just as the guard began to open her cell door, she let her body go limp and closed her eyes, feigning sleep.

Two guards had come to check up on her that night rather than the usual one. When they noticed her unresponsive form, they began to whisper among themselves.

"Looks like she's already passed out. Today was really rough on her." The first voice sounded young and strained, as if filled with regret for her condition.

"Not surprised. It's pretty normal for them to collapse like this. Most break down after just a few days. I'm amazed she's held herself up for this long. Come on, pull her down." This second voice contained neither the lilts of youth nor sympathy, and seemed unaffected by regret.

The two untied her wrists and lowered her to the ground, then took their leave. After she was sure they were gone, she rose back to a seated position. Her face was adorned with a broad smile as she moved over and ate her meal in the still bright lights of evening. It was the smallest grace, but at last hearing the sounds of real voices had given her renewed strength.

Her captivity continued long after this, but it became a different affair for her. She focused her mind on the image of Abaddon and made his cold resolve into her own. She abode her torture daily without flinching, not giving so much as a moan to satisfy her captors. In the evenings when she was alone, she worked her arms and her legs, pulling her head up to the ceiling and bringing her knees up into her stomach. It was hard at first, exercising after spending an entire day being beaten. But she stayed focused on the cold blue eyes, and in time her strength increased. As she became stronger it became easier to endure the torture sessions as well. Soon she looked at them as another part of her exercise routine, working and tightening various muscle groups as she braced herself for blows or shocks of pain.

Now she sat in the mud of her cell waiting for another day to begin. Abaddon's face no longer haunted her vision. She had grown past the need for it. No longer did she rely on the memories of his strength, for her own was sufficient now. It was nearly time for the guards to arrive, so she rose to her feet. It was difficult to stand with her ankles bound together, but each morning she greeted her captors face to face, her eyes cold and defiant.

She was surprised when the cell's door opened and only a single guard stepped in. He was not wearing the black cloak and hood that normally hid their visage. Instead he was garbed in standard Devilslayer attire—half plated armor, half demon pelts and animal skins.

"Detria Alsen," he spoke, and she recognized the voice of her elder tormentor.

She had not heard her own name in so long she nearly felt a rush of tears hit her eyes against her own resolve. She bit back the feeling and responded, "What?" in as impassive of a tone as she could manage with her weakened voice.

"You have served three months in this cell. Your term is now finished and you are free to go."

He stepped forward and knelt down at her feet, using a large skeleton key to open the shackles binding her legs. Then he turned and left the room, leaving the door open in front of her.

At first she could not move. The idea of returning to the outside world seemed a foreign notion to her. She had long given up on even the dream of it. Again she summoned Abaddon's visage and asked of him what he would do in her place, what path he would seek. A single word seemed to fill the room she was standing in, echoing across the iron walls.

*Revenge.*

She put her body into motion, grabbing the discarded steel plate that had served her previous day's rations. She ran to the door and looked around, quickly locating the guard as he was walking away. She tested the strength of her arms, chucking the disk hard in the man's direction.

Her aim and strength were both true. The plate crashed hard into the back of the guard's skull, dropping him to the ground. She ran after him quickly, glad to find that her exercises had left her legs with strength enough to carry her. When she reached the man laying on the ground, she threw him onto his back and sat down on his chest, locking her knees around his neck so tightly that he could not speak. He grabbed at her legs and struggled to free himself, but she was too strong for his weakening grip to budge.

Nearby Devilslayers began to take notice of this activity and assemble, gathering their weapons and armor. She would not have much time, so she spoke quickly.

"I want you to remember the slayers you've tortured. I want you to remember each person, each crime they committed to earn their sentence, what you did to them, how they looked when they were set free." She paused for a few seconds, giving him a brief opportunity to do as she asked. "And I want to know that every single one of them, right down to the most despicable criminal, will be remembered by history as a more valuable person than you, you sadistic, torturing bastard." She leaned back and reached her right hand to the pinned man's belt, seizing one of the bladed heads of his dannig. In a swift motion she brought the blade forward and thrust it into the base of his throat, severing his jugular. She relished the warmth of his blood splashing across her thighs as his struggling hands fell limply to the ground.

By now she was surrounded by Devilslayers, with weapons drawn and pointed in her direction. She stood and looked around at each of them in turn. There were over two dozen trained fighters here. She did not know if she could take them all, but she was ready to die finding out.

She picked one and motioned him forward, stating, "If you think I forgot how to fight in a meager three months, then there's yet more I can teach you new Devilslayers. Come, and I'll educate you on what it once meant to be Silver Pride."

A loud voice sounded from across the camp, ordering the slayers to stand down. A pack leader arrived, dismissing the soldiers and looking to the dead man at Detria's feet.

"It doesn't matter," he instructed. "Yasiff wants to see her personally."

He motioned her to follow. She thought of killing this newcomer as well, then continuing on a path of bloodshed until her own life was burnt out. But hearing Yasiff's name brought a new taste of hatred, more focused than her blind rage. Anxious to meet the Devilslayer chief once again, she followed the officer.

She was brought before the High Chieftain's throne. He smiled at the sight of her, though she could not imagine why. Guards moved to force her onto her knees to bow, but Yasiff signaled for them to desist. After watching her for a few moments, he addressed her.

"I am impressed by you, Detria Alsen. I was unaware you had such strength within you. I hear you killed one of your guards today. It's rare that someone emerges from Hell's Cell and is not in need of weeks of therapy in order to walk and speak again."

She only half listened, instead using this time to check her surroundings and run battle calculations. She was certain she could reach the nearest guard on her right, crush his throat, steal his sword, and use it to kill Yasiff before the others could react and stop her. There was no question she would die, but it was a small price to pay for the death of this man.

The next words he spoke gained her full attention, and her plan collapsed as her mind began to scramble. "The council has decided to go to war with the Overlord, at your behest. I have supported this plan so that we may extend the Devilslayer's reach into the eastern lands. Once we've increased our strength there we'll move west, and all of northern Arkalen will finally be protected.

"Starting immediately, we will begin preparations and be on the move. You will show us where his fortress is, and we will relocate the Devilslayer base there. I've assembled a full thousand of my finest soldiers and will personally lead the expedition. Whether or not the Overlord truly exists remains in question, but one way or another we will kill his legend."

Detria froze and struggled to think. Something about this bothered her frenzied mind. There was a reason this mattered to her, but she could not immediately settle upon it. She could still kill Yasiff and die here, leaving the Devilslayers to their own designs. But something held her back, something more important than her revenge.

Kelve. She remembered Kelve. For a moment her frozen blood thawed and she feared for the life of her dearest friend. Kelve had been fighting alone for three months now, in spite of her promise to return to him. If he lived, she had to see him again. She had to know what had happened in the east.

She returned her gaze to Yasiff and gave a nod, announcing, "I will take you." Her voice was still weak, but was slowly remembering strength and volume.

He gave a bold smile. "I thought you might. Guards, find her a uniform. Those clothes of hers are ruined and will serve her little good. Oh, and find her a new dannig. After all, she is a Devilslayer again. Her transgressions have now been purged by the Cell."

She did not rebuke Yasiff for his claim, but rather turned away to escape his presence. For the time, she would use him as she needed. Suddenly she was very tired. All she could think of was the notion of taking a bath, then laying down in a soft featherbed and remembering how it felt to be free.

* * * * *

Atop a snow-covered mountaintop in the Jagguron, a white figure traced across the white landscape, barely leaving a sign of his passage. Akatriel's long sleep was finally over, and he had awakened anxious to ascertain that his machinations had not spun beyond his control. The events of the last few months could doom him to an eternal enmity with his master. He was not certain how long even he could survive such a conflict.

When he reached the peak he stared out into the southern lands and slowly focused his sight, gathering the locations of the many creatures vying for power. As he did so he mumbled to himself, taking notes for his own reference.

"Two Wisdoms wait at the gorge, two still wait in the jungle. The Godbeasts have nearly crossed the mountains. They will not make it through the jungle without battling Dosiros and Torlen. What's this? It seems they're being followed." He traced his sight back from Schpariel and Aegagropilion, counting the number of creatures between his location and theirs. "They're being tracked by the Rook, who is pursued by the Bishop. But they're also being followed by a creature I cannot identify from here. Not hard to guess who that is. Still, I should keep an eye on that situation." He turned his gaze further to the south again, searching the areas around the jungle. "Ah!" he exclaimed when he found what he was seeking. "Good, the human pawn has stayed in the southern lands without my intervention. I was concerned over his fickle nature."

He nodded satisfactorily to himself and turned his gaze from the south, making a quick sweep over the northern reaches of the continent. "There's no sign of the Knight. He must have fallen in his foolhardy crusade against the Wisdoms. No great surprise there, but with his absence I shall be required to turn a pawn into a new Knight. For this I'll need to fetch Kargaroth." He scratched his chin and reviewed his findings. "Things still go well. Only my Knight has been lost while I have idled, and his replacement is already in position. As long as both Godbeasts don't fall at the feet of the Wisdoms in the upcoming battle, everyone will be ready once I need them."

He gave a flourished bow toward the south and proclaimed, "Wait for me, my pieces. The Queen will return to guide you soon. Next, we awaken Gilanirus. His presence will tilt the board." He glided back down the snowy slope, fading once again into the white landscape.

## Chapter 29.

# Cildar vs. Myris

Cildar Emle marched stalwartly across the Jagguron Peaks, still doggedly pursued by his former friend. The tenacious Cainite refused to give up on their feud, in spite of months of stalemate and near-death scenarios. The Dark Paladin had assaulted and tormented villages in the western lands for over two months, but on every occasion his wiry opponent had appeared and driven him away.

As Myris had grown accustomed to his foreign powers, he had proven to be more than a match against Haste. Cildar had discovered a few small details about this transformation during their skirmishes. The Cainite was using the Band of Barricus to draw generous doses of Gehennite ether across the Veil, then shape them into and around himself. His mind's link to his body was vastly accelerated, and his body itself was put into a state of constantly functioning at its utmost limits. The net effects forced Myris to fight at maximum strength and speed; he could not hold back or pull his punches. The armlet also gave his senses the boost needed to properly handle his own remarkable speed without handicap. That blessing alone would have made the man a grave threat.

And so the two had fought across the western lands, with many civilian casualties falling in the wake of their struggles. Until something unexpected had occurred—Cildar had been defeated. Not by his rival, but rather by two uninvolved creatures. One of these interlopers he had met before, a creature he believed to be one of the Wisdoms. The other was a peculiar demon whose overwhelming might had taken him unawares. Their exchange had been short, with the second demon overpowering him nearly instantly, then delivering a blast of energy that had destroyed the entire village over which the Dragoon had declared himself king.

Then these two strange demons had passed on their way, heading to the south. Having barely survived the encounter, Cildar had realized what was happening. There was soon to be a grand conflict on southern Arkalen, and all beings of significant stature were assembling there. He could not guess the exact nature of this conflict of wills, but he would not be left out. So he had fled the western lands, with the Cainite tracking him relentlessly, and made his way to Jagguron on the hunt of the demons which had humiliated him.

He was outmatched to the front and to the back. He could not defeat the two godlike demons if he caught them, he could not defeat Myris if he was caught. Still somewhere Abaddon Daemon awaited to be contended with, as well as the other Wisdoms Cildar was not yet strong enough to fight.

None of this concerned him. Only the hunt mattered. As long as he stayed on the trail of these creatures, stayed where powerful enemies were, eventually he would be ready for them. It was but a short matter of time now before he would be turning lich. Already he could occasionally feel the pangs of his body slipping from the Morolian plane into the abyss of swirling magics that would consume his soul. Every day he increased the degree of his Phase Shift, allowing deeper powers to drown him. Sometimes it hurt so much he felt like he could not breathe. This pain was the cost of godhood, and he *would* become a god. And once he was a god, he would need all of these greater foes to slake his lust for sport.

He stopped at the edge of a cliff overhanging the base of one of the mountains and stared out. He was finally on the last stretch of the range. All that remained was to find a safe route down this craggy bluff and he would enter the jungle that marked the southern lands of Arkalen. From that point, tracking would begin to prove difficult, for either him or Myris. This also did not matter, as he was certain he would wind up where he needed to be when the time came. Fate, he felt, was on his side.

He sensed movement below him, on the sheer wall of the crag. He checked for signs of what he assumed must have been animal life, perhaps a mountain goat. When he laid eyes on the source, he was fully awestruck.

"There's no way," he exclaimed as Myris blasted up to the ledge and delivered a flying kick to his face, sending him sprawling backward into a stony ridge.

Cildar pushed a collapsed shelf of stone from himself and struggled to shake off the impact. "How long have you been ahead of me?" he asked, hoping conversation would slow the man's signature frenzy.

"Days," Myris answered with a crackling deep voice. "My previous assaults have failed due to your cowardly escapes. This time I waited until I was certain you had nowhere to go. Try to run now, Dark Paladin."

Cildar checked his surroundings surreptitiously. Myris was right. Behind him stood the wall of a ridge he had climbed down, and before him the cliff face. There was no route he could take that his hunter could not easily keep track of him. With the Cainite's superior speed, that rendered escape an impossibility.

He was not given opportunity for further response. Myris charged rapidly and freed the Soul Scythe into his left hand in the same second. As he released a roar of inhuman rage, the aura surrounding him flickered and grew larger, appearing in the visible light spectrum for a moment and tinting him in a haze that resembled vaporous blood.

Cildar sidestepped the first swing of the scythe, sliding swiftly to his left. He knew that Myris would combo quickly off of that attack, as he always did. In anticipation of this he had already gathered his own power, and as he heard the clink of the Soul Scythe hitting stone he unleashed a Holy Wave. A liquescent wall of white magic slipped from his blackened body and shot over Myris like a great hand, nudging the Cainite a comfortable distance away.

The Dragoon used this brief opening to draw the Trine Lance and a small axe. The Gehennite ether wrapped about Myris' frame served as a buffer against any school of magic, so he would not stay down for long. Indeed, when the light and the smoke thrown up by the attack settled, he was already gone from sight. Cildar scanned frantically for signs of the man, and too late noticed a large crack in the wall of the ridge. At that instant his foe exploded from the section of the wall immediately next to him, striking his head hard with an open hand and bent fingers.

Cildar fell a few steps back as his face was sliced and blood sprayed from his cheeks. He delivered a reprisal swing with the axe in his left hand, but his berserk hunter caught the head of the axe in the palm of his own hand, and with a sharp twist shattered the head. The Dark Paladin dropped the weapon and took a hop back, but was far too slow. Myris' left elbow buried itself deep into the taller man's lower stomach, one of the speedy warrior's favorite blows.

As his opponent staggered another few steps back, the Cainite stayed his assault for a moment. Both of his fists were already bleeding, a common effect from his furies. "You are slipping, Dragoon," he taunted. "Usually you pose me a better threat than this."

The winded man shook his head, but did not offer a reply. Myris was right in his assertion. Cildar's efforts to accelerate his ascension to lichdom had not been without cost. By continuously deepening his Phase Shift, he was now losing touch with Morolia. His white magic was weaker than it had ever been before, and his connection with the Trine Lance had become strained, rendering the marvelous weapon nearly powerless.

He held only limited skill as a herald—particularly regarding direct attack magic—so his strengthened connection to Asteria did not yet serve him any meaningful use. Until he evolved to the final stage and became a lich, with mystic abilities to control the elements at will, his combat prowess was only hampered by a phase this deep.

His future was to be dictated by this battle. If he failed here, there would be no ascension to godhood, no epic war with the other superpowers of the continent. He cursed his circumstances, but knew that his choice had been robbed from him.

He eased his mind from the Asterian plane and reconnected with his body, releasing a full half of his phased condition. Instantly he felt a welcoming warmth from the Trine Lance fill his hand. It took concentrated effort to prevent the magic of the Lance from flooding over his entire body, as he knew it could yet cause him harm.

With this transition back to his Morolian being he felt his physical strength return, but he also felt the deep numbness of old pains settle in. His instincts warned him that he should heal himself, but he dismissed this as a waste of time. He intended to abandon this shell soon enough regardless.

He straightened his back and met his opponent's stare evenly. Myris seemed to recognize what had just happened, but showed no hesitation as he charged forward again. Once within range, he gave a leap and attempted to come at his target from above with scythe and red ether claws. The Dragoon underneath gave a rapid step back and struck upward with the Trine Lance, nearly slicing his attacker's left arm off at the shoulder and releasing a fount of blood. Upon landing, Myris retorted by extending his Soul Scythe's blade out straight and stabbing it into his foe's stomach like a lance of his own.

Cildar swiftly detached himself from the ravenous blade and slid back several more feet, redirecting all of his holy magic to the wound in his gut. Simultaneously, the wound on Myris' shoulder began to close up seemingly of its own accord. The Dark Paladin had managed to restore their old stalemate, but the outcome of this battle was still a foregone conclusion. His power would slowly deplete from having to heal his own wounds, while the Cainite's would remain at full strength with the Soul Scythe feeding him. It was time to alter the playing field.

He tightened his grip on the Trine Lance, and the soft light emanating from its blades shifted to a green tone. Myris took a step back and narrowed his eyes.

"You would dare to try Holy against me?" he asked. Though his voice did not reveal it, Cildar was certain the man had grown nervous.

"Unfortunately not an option. As I am, Holy would be every bit as devastating to me as to you. That technique was designed specifically to banish dragons, and currently I'm as much dragon as man. But as you can see, the memories of my draconic half have taught me a great deal about the nature of my weapon. Coupling that knowledge with my own ingenuity, once again I have found a way to become even mightier as a warrior. I wish only that I had devised this before facing Lord Abaddon." He leveled the Lance out until the tri-pronged tip was pointed straight to his right. As a deep green light flowed from it like steam, he taunted, "Hit me now, Myris."

The Cainite took a step forward as if preparing for a charge, then seemed to think better of it. Instead he gave a fierce sweep at the ground in front of him with his scythe, sending up a shower of dust and rocks in his foe's direction. As Myris' form disappeared behind the masking wall, Cildar closed his eyes and waited for the inevitable sound that would tell him the man had moved to strike. When he heard it—the light thud of a leather boot striking soil—he gave a twist and rotated his spear ninety degrees.

For an instant he was unable to move, bound by the magic of the Trine Lance. Shortly he felt his limbs respond again, and swiftly checked around for Myris. The Cainite was suspended in the air to his right, hung in space and time, Soul Scythe already swung and just a few feet from nipping into Cildar's throat.

As his movement was still being dulled by his own spell, he had to make a conservative counter to the incoming strike. He brought his spear around and locked it into the joint of the scythe, twisting the blade out of its path and then delivering a resounding blow to the side of Myris' head with the shaft.

As time resumed its normal flow the cowled man went flying

away at a breakneck speed, crashing through a boulder and into the ridge wall before finally coming to a stop. The Dragoon sent an Aura Blast into the gap his opponent's body had carved into the mountainside, hoping to finish him off. He was barely able to detect movement as a swing from the Soul Scythe dissipated the beam. Seeing this, he gave a resigned sigh. Their rivalry would not be ended quite so easily.

Myris leaped back into action, tearing upward through the rocks of the wall in which he was embedded, his shield of Gehnnite ether grinding away the stone. When he was nearly twenty feet up, he blasted back out and down at his prey, leveraging gravity to increase the speed of his next strike. Again Cildar gave a sharp twist of the Lance, and again the two combatants were suspended briefly where they stood. The Dragoon again regained his senses first, this time finding the aura of the Cainite's fist mere inches from his face. He threw his upper body backward and lifted his legs from the ground, spinning until his feet were just beneath his adversary's torso.

As time fully resumed, his spinning momentum increased tenfold. He delivered a powerful kick to Myris' chest with both feet as his chin tucked under the ethereally armored fist. The crimson assailant was launched clear to the other side of Cildar before he knew what had happened. As he again went flying away—this time toward the edge of the cliff—he struck out with both his scythe and right hand to slow his course.

This scramble was not enough, as he rocketed out over the edge and into empty space. He was not slow to realize the danger he was in, immediately laying his right hand across his left forearm and shouting, "Mutance azurey!" with a tone that bordered frantic.

As his enchantment faded and he continued to fall, a sliver of blue light crept along the edge of his scythe. He sent it arching out for the stony wall, spinning like a giant bladed discus. When the tip of the scythe landed in the cliff face, an explosion of ice surrounded it and froze it firmly in place. At that moment Myris aimed his right hand toward the point of impact and a large chain materialized, with links made of densely frozen ice binding him to the scythe's handle.

He swung down by the chain and crashed into the cliff far below his scythe, the icy links shattering as they smashed into the rock. He clung there for a few moments, clearly shaken by the ordeal. He held on tightly to the nearest hand- and foot-holds he could find, shivering with his eyes shut, fighting off waves of pain. His hood hung loosely around his face from the impact of blows that had loosened it, and his usual fiery illusions had not been raised into place to hide his eyes.

Glancing over the edge from above, Cildar shook his head at this display of stubborn survival instinct, muttering to himself, "I always forget how fast his blessings allow him to cast spells when his life is in peril." He waved his Lance and shouted down to his opponent loudly, "Hey, Myris! Coming up?"

The weakened man waited for a moment before reacting. Then he dug his hands and feet more firmly into the mountain wall and began to charge straight up. Moving at full speed he seized the Soul Scythe from its icy tomb as he passed, then leaped up at Cildar from underneath.

Again the Dragoon gave a twist of the Trine Lance just before the collision, and again time stuttered. As his movement returned Cildar lifted his spear overhead and brought the butt down hard into Myris' forehead. When the spell's effect faded, the scrabbling man was sent skidding straight back down the cliff he had just charged his way up so valiantly.

Then something out of place caught in Cildar's mind. For an instant, he had looked through the gap in Myris' cowl and seen the man's eyes. They had not been bloodshot and demonic as when under his Gehennite enhancement, but rather had retained their natural brown state. His opponent had charged up the mountain at his full speed, yet without his transformation he would have been doing so blind.

There was only one reason the Cainite would have attempted something so foolish, but Cildar realized it an instant too late. He had already rested the butt of his Trine Lance against the ground at his side, and his suspicions came to life as his spear was struck by the Stormbreak heraldry Myris had released during his brief second at the top of the cliff.

Thousands of volts of electricity coursed through the Dragoon as bladed bolts of energy laid into his back in an attempt to crush him and slice him to ribbons. Stormbreak was supreme among Felthespar's lightning magics, and even against a poorly grounded target the sheer impact and heat from the attack could prove fatal. Cildar shifted his grey barriers to his shoulders and upper back, as well as summoning another Holy Wave flowing out the top of his frame in hopes of dampening the strike.

When the electric barrage finally ended, he had somehow managed to stand his ground. He began to back away from the edge of the cliff, fearful that he might lose his balance and go over. He was forced to loosen his phase even further in order to redouble his healing magics, reverting to his original Hasted state. The damage his body had now sustained had pushed him to the edge of losing consciousness. Though his Haste was designed to disengage safely in such an event, he could not be certain if the gifts granted by Akatriel had yet become permanent.

Myris suddenly appeared in front of him, having once again charged up the cliffside for another assault. This time his eyes were stretched wide with thick black pupils, the whites hidden behind a maze of steaming red lines. Cildar felt the heavy weight of despair seize his chest in the face of his opponent's undying tenacity.

Again he reached for his trump, twisting the Trine Lance in his hand. This time the weapon did not respond. The magic which had infused it previously had been ripped asunder by the strike from Stormbreak, and Cildar had not thought to reenergize it. His foe surged forward unchecked, unleashing a merciless right hook that knocked him back into the ridge. The Cainite followed this by sending his scythe flying after. The blade implanted itself directly between two of the prongs of the Lance, lodging it into the earthen wall firmly.

On he came, laying into Cildar's torso with a flurry of punches. His demonic energies shredded through the Dragoon's plate mail and cut into his body, delivering wave upon wave of fresh pain at his currently low level of phase. Each time Cildar tried to regain his composure and gather energy for a counter, Myris delivered another hook to his jaw and left him reeling.

After a full minute of this the Dark Paladin knew he would lose consciousness soon. He gave a roar and let his instincts seize him. He released his Lance and began to counter Myris' punches with equal fury and a lack of focus, striking the Cainite square in the face repeatedly. The smaller man blocked several of the punches and kept delivering his own, then Cildar snapped. He took a punch to the chest from Myris' right hand, wrapped his left arm firmly around his attacker's right, then reached back and gave a solid right straight with all the strength he could muster.

A resounding crack was heard as the impact landed on the Cainite's chest. His frenzied movement stopped for a moment, and he gave a slight cough of shock. He stumbled backward from Cildar and began to sway dizzily on his feet.

"Mutance azurey," he whispered weakly. The red ether drained from his body and his eyes and skin returned to their natural color. He gave another cough and then vomited out a small quantity of blood. After stumbling a few more steps, he fell to his knees.

Cildar too was at his limit, but knew now was not the time to lose his edge. He reached over his shoulder with his left hand and pulled his Trine Lance free from the ridge wall. The Soul Scythe was dislodged as well and sent skittering over near where Myris had fallen. The Dark Paladin paid this no mind and began rapidly gathering spiritual energy into his right hand. He would push this body to its very limit one final time in order to rid himself of this foe, then he could return to the welcoming swirls of Asterian power.

Myris glanced up with blood running down his chin and from the corners of his eyes. The ground beneath him was dyed red, already tainted by the blood that dripped from his legs and torso.

"How did you move faster than me? I have to know before I die."

Cildar smiled, and a strange feeling of familiarity washed over him. *Just like Myris*, he thought. He knew it was unwise to answer the man's question, yet could not deny his old friend a dying wish. At any rate, he needed time to prepare his final attack, and words would easily fill the lull.

"Holy, the ultimate technique of my family's sacred spear, is an unbeatable move. It first releases a wave of stasis energy that binds all creatures in the vicinity. Then it borrows a piece of each of their spiritual stores and transfers it into the Lance. There they are magnified by the Lance's own purification processes, then unleashed in a secondary wave of energy that binds the enemy in place and simultaneously tears them to shreds." Myris reached forward slowly, grabbing the handle of his scythe and pulling it back to him. Cildar perceived no threat from this action, taking it as a matter of the Cainite's pride to die with his weapon in hand. "The technique actually takes well over an hour."

The prone man raised his head in surprise. "An hour? Impossible. I have witnessed Holy. The blast is nearly instantaneous."

"Or so it appeared to you. Because this Lance, unique among all artifact weapons, has the ability to convert white magic into a completely different type of magic—a type of magic capable of stopping time itself over a blanketed area. As it begins borrowing power from other creatures, it uses a portion of that power to hold time in this area suspended. As I said, Holy is far too dangerous of an ability for me to use in my current state. But a knowledgeable user can go beyond Holy, using the Lance to emit brief, smaller interruptions to the flow of time around him. I have named this interruption a Flash."

Myris lowered his head and stared at the ground before him. "But you are not stopped?"

"Not true. I am stopped. But as the disturbance originates from the tip of the Lance and expands outward, so too does it collapse.

So I'm the first thing released, only a few seconds before you are, but just enough to make a difference before the impact of an attack."

Suddenly Myris rose to his feet and leaped several yards backward, landing just at the edge of the cliff wall. He seemed somehow revitalized. Cildar quickly recognized that the man's injury—though serious—had been exaggerated in order to gain information. *Ever the Cainite,* he thought to himself with a mix of rage and admiration. *Ever a master of subterfuge.*

"Then I can defeat you," Myris announced with new strength in his voice.

"You think so?" Cildar retorted. "You don't even have the strength to call upon your Gehennite powers anymore. And now I have this." He held up his right hand and released a roar, and a single brilliant point of light appeared floating there above his palm. "You recognize it, no doubt. My Shock. Even you don't have the speed to dodge it."

"It shall never leave your hand," his wiry opponent swore.

Cildar gave a smile and tilted his head. "Still that confident, are you?"

"Prepare yourself, Dark Paladin. For I am about to show you true speed like you have never before seen."

Myris took the Soul Scythe and stabbed the blade into the ground at his side. The Dragoon was confused by this discarding of the man's only weapon, and concerned by his taunt. Did he need to lose the extra weight? Was there truly some further speed he had never revealed to this point? The Cainite warrior ducked low and charged forward without a sound, moving at his normal full sprint. Cildar shook off his apprehension and prepared himself to counter. Once again his foe was running blind. This time he could not let himself be caught off guard by a quickly cast spell.

He leveled his Trine Lance to his left and willed it to respond. Energy flared to the tip in an instant, and his interrupt was ready. Just as his charging opponent was about to reach him, he tightened his grip and prepared for the twist. He knew this time he would need to activate the technique earlier, in order to prevent the man from speaking the keyphrase to tap a matrix.

Then something occurred he had not anticipated. Before Myris was within range, he suddenly dug his heels into the ground and came to an impossibly fast stop. Cildar was so rattled that he gave a panicked twist of the Trine Lance to buy himself time to react, recognizing too late that Myris' body was fading from view.

*An Afterimage,* he thought in the brief instant before Flash seized his thoughts. *I'm such a fool. Why did I ever teach him that spell? How did he resist using it against me for so long?*

He was unable to locate the real Myris' position as the illusion faded. He had no idea how far away the man had moved, but he knew how far he needed. Without an external energy source to draw upon for supplemental white ether, his chronal disruption could only cover a radius of about seven feet. He had not revealed this shortcoming, but it was a glaring one. With the Cainite now almost certainly beyond the spell's grip, Cildar alone would be the stunned by his own technique.

The world stopped for a moment. When he regained his mind, a stabbing pain gripped his left shin. As his legs began sliding backward against his will, he looked down to see the cause. The Soul Scythe had been thrown at him, the blade biting into the side of his calf and the handle knocking his legs from underneath him.

He tried to catch himself against the ground, forgetting about the orb of power hovering above his right palm. As his concentration shattered, the attack was unleashed into the earth below. He gave a cry of pain as the backlash beams from his Shock cut into his body and face, then the entire world was filled with the echoes of chaos as the mountain exploded beneath him. Solid ground opened up and disappeared to reveal a waterfall of stones all around him, and a jungle below plummeting rapidly upward to meet him.

As he went into free fall, he spread his arms and closed his eyes. There was not enough will left in him to defy this fate, so he smiled and lost consciousness as the breath was sucked from his lungs by his tremendous speed. He was already out cold when a dark shadow latched onto him, carrying his body from rock to rock.

* * * * *

It was an hour later when Myris awoke. He had narrowly saved himself and Cildar from being crushed by the collapsing mountainside, taking refuge in a patch of grassland near the edge of the jungle. It had taken the last of his strength to settle the injured Dragoon down safely, then he himself had collapsed and slept.

He moved over now to check on his friend with concern. The unconscious man was breathing, but shallowly. The Soul Scythe was still lodged in his leg, but the majority of his other wounds seemed to have healed fairly well, aside from the cuts and burns carved by Shock. Myris carefully removed the Scythe from the man's leg, then applied a rough field dressing made with the supplies he could find nearby.

He checked his weapon, finding it had stored its maximum capacity of healing energies. He realized it had been leeching from Cildar all this while, and felt a pang of guilt for allowing it to do so. Still, he could not justify allowing the gathered power to go to waste. He channeled it and used it to patch his own wounds. Even the formidable magics of the Scythe were not enough to completely undo the combined damage from his prolonged transformation and the blows delivered by the Dark Paladin. Nonetheless, he was at least able to fortify his bones well enough to be certain he would make a safe recovery within time.

He sat for hours watching over the fallen paladin's body. He was not certain what to expect next. Cildar's powers of mysterious origin seemed to have faded away. His clothing was no longer shaded black, but was instead a very dirty white. His mask was long gone, and his helmet lost in the fall, but his blond hair seemed brighter than Myris remembered, surprisingly clean in contrast to the rest of his worn frame.

The sentry stayed motionless and waited, not quite sure if he was awaiting the man's death or resurrection. Nor did he know which event he should pray for. He sorely wished to see the return of his old friend, but if the man's mind was truly gone beyond the point of return, Myris did not feel he could endure another battle of such ferocity.

Finally Cildar began to stir. He released a few gurgled groans at first, followed by a loud sighing moan as he sat up and opened his eyes. He looked around the area until he saw Myris sitting nearby. The Cainite had not moved, but his hands rested carefully on the handle of his scythe.

The Dragoon looked at him with weary eyes and spoke slowly. "I don't wish to fight you anymore, old friend."

The man gave a relieved sigh beneath his cowl, taking the Soul Scythe and returning it behind his back where he normally kept it hidden. "Good, brother," he replied. "Then we shall fight no more. Heal yourself as best you can and then sleep. I will watch over you."

Cildar gave a nod and lay back, placing his hands on his own chest and slowly pooling what remaining white magic he had there. This went on for almost five minutes, then without another word he let his head fall to one side and again slept.

## Chapter 30.

# The New Challenger

The Monk of Tria stood alone atop a distant hill, watching the immobile fortress whose layout he knew so well. Gaius often volunteered to cover entire watch shifts by himself, giving Kelve and his forces a chance to rest or train. The enhanced senses bestowed upon him by the runes of Mercy were a marvel even to Tenkahn, and from a good vantage point he could monitor the activity of the entire compound unaided.

Unfortunately his spirit was still aflame with the impatience of youth, and he began to grow bored of his duty. On previous watches, he had often idled the time away by observing the comings and goings of the Robed Ones from the secret exits on the back of the fortress. Ever since his imprisonment under the Overlord he had been fascinated by the shrouded figures, wondering what secret motives drove them silently from place to place across the citadel. Today, however, something had changed—the secret tunnels to the fortress did not open, the Robed Ones no longer made an appearance.

In fact, there was scarcely any activity to observe at all. The Overlord's generals had begun to suspect they were being somehow monitored, and had relocated their troops and operations hidden deep within the stone walls. Occasionally Gaius would see one of the human slaves fritter nervously across the courtyard, but there was no sign of demonspawn activity.

When he had served seven hours of his watch, he decided it was time to call it a day. He moved to head back and ask Kelve to set up regular guard shifts. Just before he had turned his back to the fortress, he caught the muffled sounds of a door grating open. He swiftly reversed himself and pinpointed the source. One of the large gates closing off the central castle had been raised, and from its mouth stepped ten ogres. They headed across the courtyard and out through the main gate, commanding the four ogres standing guard there to join their exodus. Gaius watched with interest, deciding he could last another hour.

After exiting the outer wall of the city, the ogre entourage turned to their left and began to head south. Gaius let them march for a few hundred yards, then leaped from his hilltop and ran after in pursuit.

Upon catching up, he moved in front of the large parade and held his arms out. He seemed a poor barrier to these huge beasts, but the ogres were too familiar with capabilities of a Monk of Tria to be bold. Their leader signaled a halt at the sight of the small obstacle.

As the young monk addressed them, he inspected their group. Eight of them were cycloptic, their single paralyzing eyes already fixed upon his body. In spite of the group's apprehension, he knew this would be a difficult battle for him to win on his own. "Trying to move in for an ambush, are we?" he questioned the leader, an extra large blue ogre with three eyes decorating his face.

The creature shook his head. "I, Kogonbo, have decided to take my people from here. For too long now has the Overlord tried to use us as meat shields against the humans. Over the recent months too many of my brethren have fallen. Even when we were out in the wilds, facing whatever humans or demons came our way, we did not suffer so frequent casualties. We are tired of it, and have stormed out to reclaim our independence."

The monk took a step back and his mind raced. If Kogonbo was telling him the truth, this would be a significant gain for the resistance forces. Of the demonspawn under the Overlord's command, the ogres were among those that posed the gravest threat. Each time one was taken down, it had always been under mounting casualties to Kelve's own soldiers. Even Tenkahn or Gaius could be placed in check by a tactical rush from the beasts.

On the other hand, Tessena had tried some sort of deception or attack on an almost daily basis since the siege had begun. Gaius was not oblivious to the fact that this was likely another such deception. If fourteen ogres struck the human forces from behind during a battle, or even at camp during rest, it would be a trauma from which they might not recover.

After a few more seconds, he had formulated his answer. “So be it. You may leave, but I will escort you. There’s a canyon a few miles south of here, leading through the Banchik Mountains. It empties out on the other side, in the Lands of Poeth. Once you’re across, I’m going to trigger an avalanche and block off the pass. Poeth is a tightly isolated region, with few trails in or out. With the canyon cut off, you won’t easily be able to return here, at least for a few months.”

The ogre general gave a smile and a slight bow. “This does not hamper our intent.”

They began marching with Kogonbo at the fore, and Gaius lingering behind where he could keep an eye on the congregation. As they moved south he began to grow increasingly nervous. He had left the fortress unobserved, and Kelve was unaware of his absence. If Tessena attempted some type of raid, his army would be caught unawares. He began to suspect this had been the trap all along, and he had fallen right into it in spite of his own attempt at cleverness. Regardless, it was too late to show hesitance and go back now. He had to hope Tenkahn would notice his student’s departure and take the necessary precautions.

When they had gone only two miles, his misgivings were given form. Though he had not noticed it, the group marching in front of him had carefully adjusted their positions until they were aligned around him in a semicircle. When a sudden cry of, “Now!” was sounded by Kogonbo, the cyclopes spun about and focused their collective eyes on Gaius, binding him tightly where he stood with more paralysis spells than he could fend off.

“Fool of Mercy,” their general taunted as he drew his mighty steel war club from his back. “By now Tessena has dissected how you think. She knew you wouldn't trust us and would send an escort you thought could keep us in check. We hoped it would be one of you monks, but we would have settled for less. She said you'd expect an ambush, suspect we were trying to sneak around and hit you from behind. But we don't have to sneak around to weaken your forces. All we had to do was lure you out on your own, then kill you where you can't receive aid." His smile broadened as he walked toward the frozen figure and raised his mace. "For our cause, removing a single Monk of Tria will be even better than if we'd killed a hundred of your soldiers."

As the triclops spoke, Gaius was struggling to shake off the paralysis binding him. He tried to muster his magics to release a wave of opposing energy and block out the electrical stimuli. Without the movement of his arms or hands, however, the runes of Mercy were unable to manipulate kinetic energy. As he stood, he was only capable of minor self-alterations.

So, with reluctance, he fell back on his contingency plan for this scenario. Over the last month Tenkahn had drilled him on half a dozen new techniques, and Gaius had nearly mastered one of them. He would now put his training to the test.

Focusing on his mind rather than body, he began to sever the nerve pathways for each of his senses. First he disabled his sense of touch. He felt a slight sensation of relief as the pain of paralysis faded from his numbed skin. He proceeded to turn off each of his other senses in turn, at each step feeling the glare of the ogres grow slightly weaker. Lastly, cautiously, he shut off his optic nerve and went blind.

Tenkahn had instructed him on this technique this as a form of meditation. By disconnecting from his surroundings and distractions, a monk was able to think more clearly, more peacefully. For Gaius, it served a further use. Thanks to his own enhanced view of the world around him, he was still able to detect the presence of obstacles and enemies in spite of cutting off his senses. He suspected this was due to his awareness of the Asterian plane, building upon what he had learned from Cildar and Myris.

Whatever it was, this newly developed sixth sense did not conduct the poisonous static from the ogres.

As the spikes on Kogonbo's weapon came racing for his forehead, he at last felt his limbs snap back to his command. He swung up with his right hand, aiming at the steel surface of the club with unrestrained might. Just before impact he released a Pulsing Fist. The wave of energy put a dent in the frame of the club, slowing its momentum enough for the monk to bring it to a halt with his own punch.

The next few seconds of combat were crucial. Gaius was forced to rely on his extrasensory perception to evade a dozen blows of enormous strength. While clubs and axes crashed around him, he rolled, jumped, and dived to the areas he anticipated would be safest. Once he was certain all of the ogres were attacking him and their paralytic gazes had been broken, he began turning his senses back on. Once his sight was restored he launched into his own offensive, slamming the ground with both fists and causing an upheaval of earth beneath the giants. As they were distracted with keeping their footing and smashing the stone pillars attempting to strike them, the monk leaped out from their midst and planted his footing firmly. Here he would make his stand.

Once the quake ceased, the ogres stopped and stared at their opponent with hesitation. The young man feared for a moment they might attempt to reestablish their gaze now that his senses were restored. But the beasts did not understand how their prey had escaped their hold, and so did not try to renew it. Instead, they charged in a reckless fury. Gaius used a trio of Pulsing Fists to blind three of the cycloptic assailants, then another Tremoring Fist sent a wave of rocks cutting into the knees of the others, bringing two of them crashing to the ground.

The remaining ogres halted their charge and backed away, save one. A massive blue ogre proceeded forth with a powerful downswing from a greataxe larger than Gaius' body. The monk summoned all of his enhanced strength to catch the blade between his palms, stopping it only inches from his forehead. He did not have long before the others again attacked, and he could not maintain this vigorous combat for much longer.

He knew that if he was to gain an upper hand, it was time for someone to die. Against his better instincts, and Tenkahn's own warnings echoing in his mind, he attempted something never before performed by a Monk of Tria.

He straightened his arms holding the axe in place until his forearms formed a perfect line. Then he sent a wave of kinetic energy shuffling up through his entire frame, channeled it into his arms, and pressed inward on the steel blade above his face.

"Bonebreak!" he shouted as he released this pent-up force. The axe instantly snapped in two where his hands clasped it, and as the ogre backed away, the wooden handle remaining in his hands also snapped and shattered.

But the effects of this brutal attack did not end there. The ogre released a hollow cry of agony as his own fingers and wrists snapped and cracked. Next came his forearms, then his elbows, the bones bending and breaking as a wave of the monk's kinetic manipulations traced their way dangerously across his body.

Gaius spoke aloud dramatically as the technique progressed, to convince the other ogres that he was in full control. "Hands, arms, shoulders, ribs..." Each time he spoke, the ogre thrashed wildly in a fresh bout of terror. His allies watched horrified as the creature's body continued to disfigure itself. The victim's chest was drenched in blood as shattered ribs scraped out and tore through the fleshy barrier containing them, reaching like clawed fingernails for the sunlight. Then the stricken ogre suddenly ceased all movement, as Gaius announced the final stage. "Skull."

The monk stared impassively over the crippled body as it collapsed with a loud thud, then poured his vision slowly over the other ogres. "What? No more? Don't the rest of you want to share the fate of your brother?" There was no answer to this. Gaius noticed that Kogonbo had positioned himself behind his troops, and seemed to be trying to render himself invisible. "Go home," he commanded his trembling foes. "Return to Tessena and tell her the failure of her plan. I want her to know this defeat. And at least have the decency to carry the corpse of your friend and give him a burial."

Kogonbo muttered some orders to the nearest ogre. Several of them lifted the body of the deceased, then they began to march back to the north. Gaius stayed motionless until they passed over a small hill and out of his sight, then he fell to his knees and gave a gasp, rubbing at his forearms in agony.

The runes on his arms were glowing brightly, almost too intensely for him to make out their intricate tracing. Even with the structure's protection, he could feel a substantial amount of pressure on the bones in his arms and hands. Bonebreak was a technique he had invented himself, unbeknownst to Tenkahn. It could render a massive amount of structural damage to an object by transferring a small current of kinetic energy across a specific channel. Gaius had thus far only managed to advance it to the level where he could guide it directly across other solid objects, but he hoped to eventually embed the technique within the range of a Pulsing Fist.

Until today, however, he had not foreseen the destruction his invention brought upon himself. The raw wave of tightly programmed kinetic energy gave far too much of a backlash, and his own arms had nearly suffered the same treatment as the ogre he had targeted. Only his runes had shielded him, but they were now pressed to their maximum defensive capabilities, deadlocked fending off his own attack as it continued its assault against him.

"Seems I won't be able to use this technique again for a long time," he noted to himself. "Just another failed attempt at creating a new ability, I guess."

A voice sounded from behind him, "Not a failure, Gaius," and he clearly recognized the solemn tones of Tenkahn. "Only a lesson along the path." The young monk was relieved by the elder's presence. If his master had joined him here, it meant Kelve's troops had already been alerted and the proper guards placed on duty.

He rose to his feet, turned, and gave a docile bow. As the two conversed, they began the walk back to the north. "Forgive me for letting them go free, Master Tenkahn. I didn't have the strength remaining to fight them. I might have escorted them to the canyon beyond here, but I feared if they grew bold and made another assault I should perish."

"You did the correct thing. Do not fear, or number this a failure. We dealt another blow to the morale of the Overlord's forces. In addition to the felling of another ogre—no small victory itself—you hid your new technique's weakness well. This will cause their troops to dread the two of us even more than they previously have. Soon they will lose heart, and no longer possess the courage to strike us in any fashion without apprehension for their losses. When that day comes, we will be poised to claim our victory."

Gaius shook his head. He did not share Tenkahn's optimism on the situation. "We don't have the troops necessary to launch any sort of assault. Scarcely seven hundred are still with us, and only five hundred or so can still be considered fit for duty. We've done admirably at holding the enemy in check, there can be no question. But it's come at heavy losses. Even with your strength coupled with mine, we don't have the manpower to break this enemy and end this war. We're at a stalemate. They can't finish us, we can't finish them. There's only one inevitable conclusion to this situation. Eventually, the Overlord will return with a fresh stock of troops. If he's as powerful as believed, then the tides will turn badly against our favor at that time. On all paths, we only stand to lose this war."

"Your lack of faith does not reflect well a Monk of Tria. I have come to a belief myself. I do not think there is an Overlord. If there were, why would we not have encountered him by now? It has been months since we have laid siege to his home, yet there has been no evidence of him. No, indeed, I grow to suspect that Shote himself was the Overlord. His dominance was certainly that of a demon to strike fear into anyone."

"But," Gaius argued, "I know new troops often came to the city, brought by the Overlord himself while Shote remained at home.

They said themselves they had witnessed the Overlord's powers."

Tenkahn was not fazed by this counterpoint. "And I am certain they were recruited by *someone* whom they earnestly believed to be the Overlord. But such a deception would be a simple trick. You have spoken of the Robed Ones, correct? Perhaps they do Shote's bidding, disguising themselves as the Overlord and going forth to recruit other demonspawn. We have seen that they come and go freely from the keep."

Gaius bit his lip, unconvinced but letting the matter drop as they were within sight of the camp. Kelve waved them over. Their commander was not in good health, and still his side remained bandaged and bound. His once confident muscular build had deteriorated with the lack of solid foods in his diet, and he had grown slim and pale. He had discarded his armors and weapons in favor of a simple attire of silk shirts and cotton pants. It did not befit a leader, but no one questioned Kelve's need for the casual ensemble. By now all in the camp had discerned the truth. Their general had precious little time left for this world.

Even as Kelve's body had wasted away, his mind had grown ever sharper. His ability to guess and match Tessena's tactics had kept the human forces from being decimated by countless ambushes and deceptive assaults.

Upon their approach, the slim warlord questioned Gaius. "What happened? You abandoned your post."

"Apologies, Master Orista. There was a parade of ogres. I suspected a trap and didn't feel it correct to leave them to their own devices."

Kelve stared for a moment, then tilted his head. "And let me guess, the only trap was for you, correct?" The young man nodded in response. "As I suspected. Tessena seems to have some ideas as to the nature of your abilities. That's why she's pulled her forces within the walls. I'd wager she's actively seeking some way to counter your sight, as well. I'd be more concerned if she still had nightspawn available. That's not the case, so our biggest worry is the trolls. I'm not aware how deep their arcane understanding runs, but they're the most likely of Tessena's troops to fully comprehend how we've been keeping such a close eye on them."

The troll and draconic forces had proven to be the most staunch of the Overlord's warriors. The best among Kelve's veterans occasionally managed to bring one of the creature's down, but it had become a rare occasion. The trolls in particular were wildly difficult to keep in check, with their magical weapons slicing through armor and flesh alike. Only the small numbers of trolls remaining—somewhere around seventy—made them less dangerous than the still nearly two hundred draconics.

At the mention of the trolls, Gaius proposed an idea he had already mentioned several times before, to consistent rejection. "Why not send Tenkahn and I in to ambush the trolls? I'm certain I can locate their residence with ease, and with our cloak of invisibility we could kill at least half of them before we're forced into a retreat."

Tenkahn gave a sigh, but it was Kelve who rebuked the lad's eagerness. "Eiden, I told you I won't risk you and Tenkahn by sending you alone into that fortress. It's far too dangerous and would risk the entire strength of our delicate position. I don't want to hear the suggestion again."

The commander had a habit of addressing the young monk by his old name when he became cross with him. It stung each time, reminding Gaius that he still was not taken seriously as a leader here, in spite of his contributions to their cause. After this, Kelve turned to a nearby lieutenant and began to give orders related to sentry shifts.

Tenkahn bowed on his student's behalf. "Master Orista, do not take Gaius in sour taste. He grows concerned for the return of the Overlord himself."

The pale general glanced to his two champions quickly in turn. "Do you know something I don't?"

"No," the youth responded, "but it can only possibly be a matter of time before his return."

Kelve shook his head and began to walk away, carefully favoring his left side. "The Overlord isn't real, Eiden. He's just a myth. When we win here we won't have helped save the world. We're just trying to help save a few lives."

Gaius' fists shook with anger, but he could not find the words to say. Tenkahn put a hand on his shoulder and attempted to console him. "This war has taken a grave toll on Master Orista. He has given much."

He smacked his master's hand from his shoulder, the first sign of disrespect he had ever shown. "And have I somehow given less?"

"What would you have us do? We fight to the best of our ability, yet you act as though you expect more."

"It's your lack of belief in the Overlord that will allow him to continue! If we believe as Kelve does, that all we can do here is kill a few demonspawn and save a few humans, then that's all we'll accomplish! The Overlord himself must be killed or he'll simply rebuild it all!"

"Think of what you say. There is no proof that the Overlord exists. You yourself served as a worker in his fortress for many years of your life, and say you have never seen his face nor heard his true name. Many moons ago, when my brothers and I first found this place, we too believed it the Fortress of the Overlord, yet he has never appeared. How long do we continue believing in a ghost?"

"I'll not only continue to believe in him, but I'll find him and I *will* defeat him." He took leave of his teacher and stormed off to the north, taking refuge in the rolling hills. Tenkahn gave another sigh and a bow to his departed student, then went to speak with Kelve on matters at hand.

* * * * *

Once the sun had set behind the barrier of Techenar Forest, Gaius moved from the hills and approached the fortress in the shadowed valley. His previous indignation had faded, replaced by resolution. Tenkahn and Kelve may have dismissed the Overlord's existence, but Gaius had lived with the weight of the dreaded demon his whole life. He would not let it go without evidence.

He angled down to the far left corner of the outer wall, avoiding the regular ogre sentries that would be watching the destroyed front gate. Some effort had been put into repairing the structure at one point, but a few Tremoring Fists from Gaius and Tenkahn had driven Tessena to give up on the matter.

At the base of the stone wall, he gathered ether to his fingertips. It was the trick he had seen Abaddon do long ago, Shattering Fingertips. Gaius had altered it slightly for his own purposes, using the sparks of energy as claws to cling to objects. Using this, he easily scaled straight to the top of the wall and leaped over the parapet.

He moved through the courtyard silently, keeping his senses honed for any enemy who might detect him. He could not use the monks' invisibility without linking to Tenkahn, and the elder monk would never have approved of his mission. Instead he would have to rely on his own natural stealth and caution.

His intent was to find one of the lesser generals and interrogate them on the Overlord's true nature. He knew none of them were a match for him if isolated, and they were the most likely to know the truth of the matter. He slipped past several cabins and barracks, moving on to the central castle of the domain. Opening a door was too dangerous, so once again he prepared his fingers for climbing and moved in through a high window. He found himself inside a large hallway in a seemingly underused section of the castle. If he was going to find someone important, he would need to make his way back downstairs to the main hall.

An hour of wandering put him where he wanted to be. He stood at the deepest end of the entrance hallway. At the far side, he could see the main wooden door that led out to the courtyard. If any of the generals came or went, it would be through here.

His timing was serendipitous. He had only just taken up his hiding spot—using magic to latch himself into one of the corners of the ceiling—when he heard the sounds of talons scraping across the stone floors. He held his breath and waited. Soon a chimera passed underneath, headed for the exit.

Gaius recognized the griffin Ontarshiss as one of the generals. The beast was intelligent enough to answer his questions. He dropped softly to the ground and moved to follow.

Just before Ontarshiss reached to open the door to the courtyard, Gaius slid up and placed a hand on the back of the feathery neck.

"I recommend you not struggle. You're in immense danger, I assure you."

Slowly the creature turned its neck around and stared at the intruder evenly. "Ah, the Monk of Tria. A bold move to enter our base alone. Is this ambush all in my honor? I'm flattered."

"Don't be. I have questions, you have answers. Talk, and both of us walk away from this alive."

"If you think I'll turn traitor you mistake my breed. No, rather you would be forced to slay me now. Whether or not I concur with Tessena's mind I am loyal to her. The ties of honor bind me."

Gaius stepped back and gave a sigh. "Relax, winged one. I don't want strategic information. This is a personal errand."

Sensing the young man's relaxation, Ontarshiss cleared his throat with a rasp and began to walk back down the hall, returning into the castle. "I don't converse with primates."

In an instant Gaius was standing in front of the griffin, his right fist upheld and the runes wrapped about his arm blazing. "You'll make an exception."

The chimera narrowed his eyes, but made no further attempts to move. "You're quite boring. Can we get on with it?"

"I want to know about the Overlord."

Ontarshiss gave a bird's cawing laugh. "You've been at war over him all this time, and only now you get around to asking about him? Humans truly are thick."

"Quiet, dodo. Just answer my questions. Is the Overlord real, or isn't he? Why hasn't he been here since we arrived?"

"As to where the Overlord has been these months, I cannot

pretend to know. But questioning his reality is foolhardy."

"How are you so certain?"

"How do you think I came to be here? Do you think my chimeras arrived of our own free will at random? We were recruited by the Overlord. I've seen and spoken with him myself."

"So you've seen him, fine. Then tell me this—why do even the most powerful demonspawn here fear him so much?"

"Because we have watched him die."

Gaius raised an eyebrow. "What?"

"The Overlord persuaded my people to join him by fighting my clan. We killed him, tore him to pieces. Afterward he rose once again to his feet and dared us to try again. When we did he killed the closest three chimeras. At that moment, Manticore commanded our people to cease fighting. He realized that in the end we would continue to die, but the Overlord could only continue to live. The Overlord is feared for the greatest reason a demonspawn can be feared, boy. He is feared because he's immortal."

"Nothing is immortal. Everything dies with time."

"Conflicted words from the servant of a god. Perhaps you're right. But even if that's true, the Overlord will outlive us all. He cannot be struck down though battle."

Gaius stared at his feet for a moment. He had what he needed, and knew it was not safe to linger here. He had but one more question he wanted to get off his mind.

"Does he have a name?"

"When first I met him, he said only, 'I am demon; Zekraul'."

A booming voice sounded from the door leading to the courtyard. Gaius had somehow not noticed it opening, but a large shadow now stood blocking it. "You must learn to hold your tongue, eagle."

Ontarshiss gave a startled shriek and began backing quickly down the hallway, pleading with a quivering voice. "Lord Shote, no. I did the Overlord no wrong. I held the monk here so you could finish him. Once he's dead the secret remains secure."

Gaius stared in awe at the giant beast walking toward him. He had never seen Shote at such close distance before. His eight foot tall frame barely seemed to fit within the narrow hallway. As the minotaur reached to his back and drew a greataxe, Gaius suddenly realized he was in the most genuine danger he had encountered since Tenkahn had first given him the blessings of Tria.

"Generals," Shote spat contemptuously. "What good do you serve? The Overlord gathers you for support when he cannot be here, yet you provide only constant sources of failure. I'll certainly deal with you in a moment, Ontarshiss. But first..."

When he was five yards away, Shote suddenly closed on the monk at incalculable speed. At that same moment Ontarshiss turned and ran, hoping to vacate the area. Three swings of the greataxe were made almost before Gaius could react. Instinct narrowly saved him, sending him diving backward and rolling away awkwardly down the hallway. His towering assailant caught him again in an instant, already delivering another slash of the axe. The monk again rolled, this time punching the ground as he moved. Two pillars of stone formed from the hallway floor and wrapped themselves about the axe, snatching it from Shote's grip.

The minotaur did not slow, and was instantly again in Gaius' face. The youth did his best to strike the beast, swinging out hard with his right hand. He could have sworn he had released a Pulsing Fist, yet Shote did not budge nor even flinch as any other enemy. The demon gave a strong backhand to the monk's head, sending him flying down the hallway. The tossed warrior carved cleanly through stone walls, finally smashing out through the frame of the door. He continued to fly several feet into the courtyard before finally coming to a halt.

Shote stood staring out from the doorway and offered Gaius a quick farewell. "You live today by good fortune, monk. If I don't catch the griffin he will attempt to reach a window and take flight. I must make certain he doesn't escape. I trust you won't be so cowardly as to run away. Come fight me tomorrow, and I'll kill you and the Aged. Tell him I owe him much."

With that pronouncement, he disappeared in a blur of movement. Gaius was unable to clearly follow the speed of the minotaur as he moved through the hallway, but he could not tell how much it was due to the ringing pain in his own head. Activity was beginning to increase in the fortress, though, and he was aware enough to realize it was time to beat his retreat.

He took the direct route this time, charging through the empty courtyard and straight out the main gate. When the ogres there attempted to make trouble for him, he sent a vigorous flurry of Pulsing Fists into their faces and then continued on his way. He did not stop running until he reached the hill where Kelve's forces camped, in spite of his own increasing weariness after the combined strains he had endured.

He was met at the top of the hill by Tenkahn. The monk asked him a question, but Gaius could not understand it. His reserves of strength were exhausted now, and he only managed to exclaim one thing before losing sight and drifting into blackness.

"Shote lives."

## Chapter 31.

## Dosiros, Who Devours All

The touch of morning flitted across southern Arkalen, highlighting the regions of the continent within reach of the sun's rays. The Jagguron Peaks grew taller and denser as their line cut toward the east, and much of the continent was shadowed from the dawn by their domineering horizon. Even without the icy fingers of Jagguron, not all of the continent would have been warmed by the sun. Much was hidden within deep valleys, patched by hilly grasslands, or obscured by the thick Fenrir Jungle.

Beneath this latter masking canopy, the Godbeasts pressed through swamped turf and snipped their way through the dense overgrowth. Aegagropilion's arms had formed into giant scissors, and his feet had tightened into long metal stilts. Schpariel traveled with more difficulty than his versatile ally, resigned to follow cautiously in the path carved before him.

The Second Godbeast's powers had increased much in the short months spent in the western lands and, among other newfound abilities, he was now capable of tracking creatures over vast distances. Now the pair headed rapidly toward an isolated Wisdom, with a simple plan in mind. Aegagropilion would attack and hold off the Wisdom, hopefully drawing others to him as Schpariel beat a direct line for Gilanirus.

Both knew the dangers of this plan were numerous. Even if it proceeded as predicted, Aegagropilion would be outnumbered and overpowered, likely losing his life and the powers he had gained. If it fell short, Schpariel would be cut off by a Wisdom and slain, whereupon it would fall upon Aegagropilion to successfully escape and reach Gilanirus. In the worst scenarios both would perish, whether simultaneously or sequentially. Even facing such grave odds, they had agreed it was a time for desperate moves. If one perished and Gilanirus was resurrected in their place, it would be a victory for the Godbeasts of Gehenna.

Shortly Aegagropilion came to a stop in the middle of a particularly deep stretch of mire. His compatriot was forced to keep moving until he found a tree root to stand on, to anchor himself from sinking. Aegagropilion paid no mind to his plight.

"He's ahead," the shapeshifter announced. "No more than a couple hundred yards. I'll open with a resounding distraction, then you'll need to take off. Cut around east half a mile."

"You'll need to give me time," Schpariel complained as he was busy balancing on an overgrown root covered in slick muck.

"I'm masking our presence, but it won't fool them for long. Ten minutes is the most I can afford you. Get however far you can in that time, then run for it."

The Dark Wisdom gave a resolved nod. "I assume after I have gone far enough south, I'll lose your protection?"

"I have my limits. Waste no time with the window you have. There can be no guarantee they'll stay focused on me rather than pursuing you."

Schpariel summoned his Moon Rod and began gathering energy to it. "I'll use my magic to lend myself speed. I should reach Gilanirus in a few days, if the Rod doesn't run dry on me."

"Go."

As Schpariel moved, making slow headway against the swampy soil, Aegagropilion began preparing his own magics. His right hand swelled up into a large translucent balloon that began to fill with crackling electricity. He readied the rest of his body for combat, as well. His thin frame expanded to double its natural size, taking on a muscular shape in appearance. While his biceps and forearms became thick red flesh, his chest and torso shifted into a solid black shell. A series of horns appeared along the upper edges of his head, and his mouth split open and filled with long, poisonous needles for teeth. Three sets of small feathery wings emerged from his back to lend him speed, and his legs transformed from metallic stilts into the long stems of a gigantic bird.

Once the ten minute countdown had elapsed, he dashed forward silently to where he knew a Wisdom stood waiting. He slipped between two large trees and caught the briefest glimpse of his towering opponent. As soon as he saw the mechanical flesh of a Wisdom, he swung downward with his swollen right hand.

His ambush was not as jarring as hoped. The Wisdom nimbly dropped to his back and rolled away, leaving Aegagropilion striking the forest floor. The sack of power burst upon impact, freeing a fierce explosion of sound and heat that engulfed the area.

When the electricity emptied from the air, the vicinity had been drained of both life and water. Several inches of thick, dead ash now blanketed the scorched ground. Aegagropilion had been unaffected by his attack, and across the way from him stood Dosiros, equally unperturbed. The Wisdom's back was turned, and he had yet to lay eyes on his assailant.

"You would bring a superheated attack against the Wisdom of the Flame?" he spat derisively. "A decision as foolhardy as it is impotent." He stepped backward and twisted about, coming eye-to-eye with Aegagropilion, who had just increased his height to match Dosiros' eight-foot stature. "Ah, the Great Beast," he said without recognition. "We meet at last. Long have I anticipated this."

"You speak as though we were not intimate, Dosiros," the Godbeast responded as he rebuilt his exploded hand. "I know you well." He hoped to drag out the conversation, as the longer he refrained from direct combat, the longer he could concentrate on extending his masking spell over the retreating Schpariel.

"I'm sure you know me, Beast. But Kiastos and I perished since our last encounter with your kind, in other wars. All we know of you is the information we were granted by the Muses upon our resurrections. For me, this will be the treat of a first dance. Though I suppose with a metamorph and power thief such as yourself, every dance is like the first."

Aegagropilion hesitated, trying to select the right words to prolong their dialogue the longest. "Where is your Staff, Dosiros? Or your partner? Do you intend to fight me with your hands alone?"

"Do you think them insufficient to defeat you?" the Wisdom answered, taking a step forward.

"I simply thought," the Godbeast replied rapidly, hastening to correct his previous miscalculation, "the Wisdoms were about efficiency—subduing their enemies as quickly and brutally as possible. I'm surprised to see you standing before me, apparently prepared for fair and honest combat."

Dosiros halted his approach and chuckled. "I'm no coward, Great Beast. It's rare that I get such a delightful hunt as this. If I had my way, I'd allow you to awaken Gilanirus, and we would war our way across this expendable plane. But alas, I dare not defy Melukah. Even to the Flame, the wrath of the Sun is suffocating."

At that moment, Aegagropilion felt Schpariel slip beyond his protective reach. His foe seemed to notice it as well, his head suddenly twitching to one side and then glancing over his shoulder. The Godbeast immediately leaped forward with a screech, transforming his knuckles into stone using the magics of Kiastos.

He delivered a series of six strikes to Dosiros' face, then began pounding hard on the sturdy crimson chest. Chips of damaged iron flesh flew away from these blows. Dosiros uttered a soft grunt of pain, then raised his left hand before his assailant's face, releasing a tight blue fireball. Aegagropilion was driven back, but not stunned for long. Seeing the Wisdom's next punch already coming for him, he planted his feet, tightened his back, and met the punch with a right straight of his own.

The Godbeast's arm broke in four places and he again fell back. The counter was not unsuccessful though, and thick cracks spread over his opponent's fist and up a portion of his forearm. Dosiros also retreated a few steps, rubbing his broken hand. While Aegagropilion effortlessly rebuilt his damaged arm, the Wisdom used small flames to weld his sealed in a coarse, makeshift manner.

"That was disarming," the Elysian commented. "Of the Godbeasts, your punch is said to be the weakest. That lack of physical strength is the price you pay for your dynamic form."

Aegagropilion emitted a deep laugh—inwardly relieved that his foe had so easily forgotten Schpariel—then raised his left hand. The thick green tendons peeled down and climbed over his muscular red forearm, revealing a skeletal hand of solid stone. He moved the fingers on the hand slightly, and loud clicking sounds could be heard as rock scraped against rock. "You can only thank your own kind for my now profound structural integrity."

As vines of flesh rewrapped this stony skeleton, his adversary remarked, "Ah, rather than use Kiastos' ability to form a thick exoskeleton for protection, you've given yourself the sturdy endoskeleton you normally lack. It's your cleverness for which you are most consistently praised, Great Beast; though among my kind it's given as a warning. I'm glad to see you don't disappoint." Suddenly, he looked over his left shoulder and shouted loudly, "Torlen!"

A blast of purple energy struck the ground behind him, releasing a shockwave that briefly knocked out Aegagropilion's senses. When he recovered, the Wisdom of Sound stood at the origin of the disturbance, waves of purple and blue energy washing over his black and grey body.

"Giving up so quickly?" the newcomer asked of his much larger companion.

"Don't be stupid. Schpariel is escaping to the south, and slightly east. He was trying to move past us while this one distracted me."

Torlen turned and stared southward for a moment, nodding as he locked onto the Godbeast's location. "As you suspected. Don't worry. He will not outrun the Sound."

"I'd worry less had you not missed him the first time. Don't dawdle."

The smaller Wisdom gave a silent bow, then disappeared in another explosion of energy and pressure.

Aegagropilion clenched his fists in irritation. He had not bought

Schpariel nearly the lead he had hoped. It would not take Torlen long to close in pursuit. Their only chance now was for him to successfully kill Dosiros, before any of the others could arrive.

The lingering Wisdom turned back to his opponent with a shrug. "Back to business. Where were we? Ah yes, you had shattered my fist. It seems that you would beat me as we are."

Aegagropilion lowered his stance and narrowed his eyes. "It seems," he agreed cautiously.

"I doubt that," Dosiros laughed in response. "Let's see how you fare against the true intensity of the Flame!"

He released a loud roar and struck the ground with his fists. Six pillars of fire burst around him, encircling him with dancing orange flames that lit the area. He continued his roar without pausing for breath, raising his arms high and shaking with rage. His whole body caught fire, a deep red fire that hovered only a few inches from his skin as if encased by a glass frame. He finally ceased his roar and dropped his hands to his side with a sigh. The pillars faded out, revealing six fiery clones of his own flame-enhanced body.

Aegagropilion hung his head and smiled inwardly, silently admitting to himself that he had known this sort of display of might was coming. He had scarce time to think anything else, as the seven Flame Wisdoms set upon him in a jumbled mess.

The assaulted Godbeast reverted his legs to their natural plantlike form and dove away from the flurry of incendiary fists striving to envelop him. While spinning about frantically, he turned his fingers into stone claws and slashed at his nearest targets. Flaming limbs scattered at his blows, but quickly coalesced back to their intimidating designs. He used the wings on his back—coupled with a kick from his heels—to propel himself out of the frenzy. He failed to gain enough separation, as the burning creatures quickly spread their own fiery wings and closed the gap. In response he gave another surge backward, this time spreading his fingers wide and transforming both hands into massive webbed fans, slamming them together for an extra burst of speed.

As he burst away with redoubled speed, he noticed a lull in activity from his assailants. Only Dosiros himself continued to charge forward headlong. The clones were shaken, flickering as they were struck with fanned winds from the Godbeast's hands. It took him but a scant few seconds to recognize his opening.

As the real Wisdom swung out with a powerful right hook, Aegagropilion slipped beneath it and blasted his way over to the clones, increasing the size of the fans that now served as his hands and reinforcing the material comprising them. His first swing—an uppercut from his right arm—knocked out three of them, sending a spinning pattern of embers and heated vapor twisting through the jungle air. He followed up with a sweeping backhand from the other fan, and two more were sent dissipating into the surrounding area. As he finished the final clone by reversing the momentum of his right arm and swinging down, trees beyond the reach of his first attack began to set aflame. It was then that Dosiros charged from behind with a roar of indignation.

As the last clone's body dissipated, Aegagropilion turned and leaped back a step, preparing for another exchange of blows. He only barely had time to shrink his hands back down and reform the adamant skeleton of his arms, but threw his punch nonetheless before the Wisdom reached him.

As the deities' fists raced toward each other for impact once again, Dosiros demonstrated his own knack for improvisation. The scatterings of fire drifting on the air suddenly spun about and came back, transforming into sharp javelins and piercing the red-fleshed muscles from which Aegagropilion had composed his arms. Several gaping holes were torn into the sinew, and assimilated blood splattered. When their punches collided, the Gehennan's strength had been reduced far too much to withstand the blow. His own structural integrity was turned against him, as impact from the Wisdom's fist traveled through his stone frame and ripped his shoulder apart.

Dosiros was not satisfied by this small success. He used his left hand to seize the top of Aegagropilion's head, and with but a thought the remainders of his decimated clones flew to the Godbeast's body, coating him swiftly in a layer of red flames so thick he could not be seen. The Flame poured his own encasing fires into the mix. Once his body was shed clean, he stepped back to watch his opponent burn.

When at last the fires died, little recognizable substance remained of Aegagropilion. His arms had completely melted and slid off his body, and his legs were a sickening green pool beneath him. His shells of armor had turned into tight, deformed metal casings warped around him, and his head was blackened and drooling down his chest, with only half of one amber eye still visible. He struggled and gurgled for a moment, trying desperately to regain control of himself.

Dosiros gathered a new wave of combustion to his palm, slowly forming a compact blue fireball. "This Great Beast isn't so magnificent. Can't you shapeshift once your body is melted? What an unfortunate weakness to have with me as your enemy."

A sudden ripping noise sounded, then a series of fresh vines exploded from Aegagropilion's back and slid away as the outer shell of his body was left to cauterize. These vines shaped into a slim scarecrow with one eye. Dosiros shook his head at the sight of it.

"Now what, metamorph? Do you have enough power left to form a new body and resist me? Even if you do, it will serve you no better than the last."

The Godbeast's fresh head adjusted slightly to form the large beak shape it had once held. "I had a different idea in mind. You're clearly much too strong, Wisdom. I can't fight you on these terms. So instead, how about these."

He raised his slim hands and the air about him began to flicker. His green skin faded to black, and then soon he vanished entirely. There was a strange pop, then a cloaked and cowled figure with phantasmal amber eyes appeared standing in his place.

Dosiros was not impressed by this new shape, and tossed his prepared fireball at the spectral figure. There was an explosion from the impact that incinerated the air around his target, but as the heat dissipated, the creature stood unharmed.

"You'll find your fire no longer harms me," Aegagropilion taunted with a booming dark voice that seemed to come from inside the Wisdom's own mind.

This shadowy specter lifted his right hand and pointed it forward. A tremendous cyclone of fire roared forth, sweeping up Dosiros and forcing him back in spite of himself. It took him a moment to regain his feet, but upon doing so he lashed out and banished the flames. Aegagropilion raised his left hand, and a battering ram of solid ice exploded into existence and smashed hard into his foe's chest. The ice shattered upon impact—creating a small crack in the Elysian body—then turned into a rain of hundreds of icy razors that ripped through the jungle. When it seemed the barrage was finally over, a thunderous cluster of half a dozen lightning bolts struck the Wisdom's back and shoulders, driving him to his knees.

The ghostly figure across the way made no further move. The cloak forming his body seemed to possess a will of its own, swaying vigorously in unseen winds. No limbs or defining features could be made out; only the two amber eyes served to identify it as anything more than a shadow.

Dosiros forced himself to laugh against his own sizable pain. "So this was your plan. This is why the Great Beast suddenly felt the courage to stand against me." He rose carefully to his feet, rapidly heating and cooling his outer form to reinforce it. "Lich-agropilion. Ha!"

"You mock, but you know the danger you stand in. I cannot be harmed as I am. Not by the meager likes of you."

"Meager? I am Wisdom! I can cross the Veil and strike at your true form on the Asterian plane."

A cold sizzling sound emanated from the shadowed figure. "Try it. Do you know what a lich can do to a creature attempting to move across the Veil in its presence? I doubt you do."

Dosiros took a step back and gathered fresh sheathes of fire over his arms. The Wisdom of the Flame knew his own weaknesses better than anyone. If a creature was fireproof, there was little he could do beyond attempting to pummel it with his own brute strength. Against a lich, even that was not an option. To his bitter disappointment, his long-awaited battle was already over.

"If you think you can kill me, then come on and do it. I don't think you have the strength. The Flame won't cow to you."

The shadows twitched. Slowly, two long arms extended from the cloak and took a loose form. They pointed forward at Dosiros, and for a moment there was nothing. Then the black arms erupted into dozens of sharp vines, zigzagging through the air and coming for the Elysian. To counter this he used the fire wrapped about his arms as shields, successfully parrying the whiplike spears as they attempted to pin him, brushing them aside.

Dosiros began to brace himself for the next attack, but too late realized this one was not yet finished. After being deflected by his arms, the sharpened tips of the vines stabbed into the trees and ground of the surrounding jungle, then reemerged from other random locations, coming back for him. This time he was unable to deflect all of the attacks, and was skewered through cleanly in several places. Each vine either passed through him or was knocked aside, then took once more into an object in the background and again doubled back.

He tried to move away from this third assault, hopping a few steps in reverse and then dashing to his left. It was difficult to progress against the vines already anchoring him, but he managed to get about thirty yards away from his opponent before choosing his spot. The extensions of the lich's body continued their malicious whipping about the area, pinning the Wisdom through again and again. Meanwhile the unholy matter spread throughout his form and filled the cavities and joints of his body, expanding and freezing until he was robbed of all movement.

As the din in the area died down and the tentacles seemed to at last run out of momentum, Aegagropilion's voice sounded again in his head.

"Aren't liches remarkable? For Morolian natives, their power is astonishingly terrible. Schpariel and I both nearly lost our lives conquering this one. But in seeing you brought to your knees, it's all made worthwhile."

As he finished speaking, the amber eyes narrowed and the shimmering cloak shuddered. Both of Dosiros legs broke in two different places from internal pressure, and he fell to his knees with a groan.

"I can keep this up for as long as I feel the need," Aegagropilion boasted. "I can continue grinding your body's internal units until there is nothing left of you to resist me. You were right in one thing—I doubt I can kill you with this form. But I have no need of that. Once you're unable to defend yourself, all I need do is return to this plane and absorb you. Your abilities will do well to enhance those of Kiastos. My grip on them was beginning to weaken after so long."

Dosiros did not waste the time he was given as his tormentor idled. Using what power he could still muster, he continued pouring his formidable magic into his right arm until the steel there was superheated. When his entire limb was glowing white, he felt the lich's magic both inside and out begin to give way. With a final exasperated burst he lifted his arm and broke through the shadowy canopy binding it, pointing his right hand skyward as though reaching for the sun.

He began pooling the magic he had gathered up into his palm, forming one last fireball. Aegagropilion mocked his progress, but did not move to disturb him. "What now? You will strike me again with your flames? They won't burn me. My flesh is beyond your reach, Wisdom."

Dosiros finally released his attack. He did not strike at the Godbeast at all, but rather fired a large cone of flame spreading up through the canopy. Through his earlier retreat, he had positioned himself beneath some tightly interlaced branches of the jungle's foreboding trees. Aegagropilion watched in concern and confusion as the foliage above caught fire and quickly disintegrated. Then he saw a shimmer, as a hint of gold fell from the sky and landed in his imprisoned enemy's hand.

The Gehennan sounded a terrified roar and attempted to surge his strength forward, delivering a crippling blow to the Wisdom's biomechanical structure. The bindings over the right arm had not been reinserted, however, and too late did he realize it. Dosiros held the Sun Staff high as its decorative head began to glow from his touch.

In a calm voice he commanded the weapon, "Scatter." It immediately flared with a dispersal of white light in every direction. The attack was not potent in comparison to many which the Staff was capable of, but it easily abolished the tendrils of Aegagropilion's dark powers and sent his shadowy body tumbling backward.

Dosiros flushed himself with a burst of energy from the staff. Then, partially in command of the remains of his body once more, he crafted two large wings of fire and used them to lift himself into a standing position. He welded his legs to force them to maintain their shape, but he would not walk again until he reached Keldana. He leveled his gaze forward at Aegagropilion, who had been reduced to a shadowy, skeletal form scratching at the ground and attempting to rise again.

"I am pleased, Great Beast," he declared to his prostrate foe. "You forced me to fall back upon the gift of Melukah. Truly you were a worthy adversary for the Wisdom of the Flame."

He leveled the Sun Staff forward and pointed it where his foe lay. The Godbeast surged forth suddenly, leaping into the air and regaining his form as a cloaked apparition. Dosiros released the charge of the Staff, and a beam of dense sunlight erupted out. Aegagropilion was struck clean through, but when the light faded he stood unharmed, several feet to the left. The Wisdom redirected his staff and released another blow, but again the phantasm managed to slide through and survive the blow.

The Flame gave a dark chuckle and shook his head. He recognized what was happening from the vast wealth of information he had been bestowed by the Muses. They had instructed him on the nature of every prominent Morolian creature, to prepare him for the event of Aegagropilion's assimilation of them. He knew that liches were capable of moving their spiritual location independently of their Morolian image, making them difficult to strike down even once a successful attack was found. For a Wisdom, this was easily trumped.

"You're right, Aega," he said as he moved the Sun Staff to his left side. "Liches truly are astonishing." He swung it in a wide arc and triggered another release of its power, shouting, "Dodge this one!"

Aegagropilion was unable to dodge, however. A tremendous crescent of light poured over the forest floor, and the apparition was not prepared for the need to move his body vertically in order to escape it. The light of the Sun washed over him, seeping through his spiritual bindings and reaching him across the Veil, burning through him, devouring him, seizing him and pulling him back into Morolia, all as it disabled his shapeshifting prowess.

The stricken Godbeast lay upon the ground smoking and sizzling unhappily, robbed of movement and paralyzed by Elysian poison. He had reverted to his sickly green scarecrow. Half of that, even, had been incinerated. Aegagropilion now recognized the same truth that Dosiros had arrived at several minutes prior. This battle was over.

For his part, the Wisdom of the Flame had grown tired of the game. Being forced to use Melukah's magic to supplement his own left him with no feeling of victory. Though the Godbeast would die, Dosiros had lost the contest of might. He decided to finish things off abruptly, rather than allow his opponent the same opportunity for recovery that he had been afforded. He pointed his staff at his loathsome prey's twitching remains, commanding it to release once more.

Just before the instant of his attack, he detected a shadow move between himself and his target. He was surprised the Godbeast had managed another trick in such little time, but nonetheless was confident as the Staff emitted its beam. To his shock, the beam of light stopped far short of Aegagropilion himself, only traveling a few yards before halting upon some unknown obstacle.

Whatever this obstacle was, it charged forward against the flow of the Sun's light. Dosiros did not know how to react to this. His body was already broken beyond his own reckoning, and he had never seen anything stop Melukah's powers dead in their path. As the fervent ray of heat was cut down to only a matter of feet, the Wisdom felt a powerful impact reverberate through his arm. The light went out, and he was given an instant to see what had happened. A tremendous black crystalline fist had struck the Staff of the Sun, tearing cleanly through and blinding its eye. He was given only the one glimpse, however, because the fist struck him next. His body was sent flying clear across the jungle floor and sent sinking into a nearby mire.

The interloper struggled to reduce the size of his cracked hand to normal, as he turned and walked slowly to where the vanquished Godbeast lay. He spoke without hesitation, knowing the battle's reprieve was short.

"You are the Great Beast Aegagropilion, yes?"

The fallen metamorph had gathered enough strength to right himself somewhat, and gingerly eased off the ground into a sitting position so he could eye his mysterious savior.

"If you have been witnessing this battle for long, you no doubt know that already. Who are you? What gives you the audacity to assault a Wisdom of Elysium? Are you aware of the peril in which your life is now placed?"

The creature gave an elegant bow, staring at Aegagropilion with two empty eye sockets carved into a hard black skull. "I am demon; Zekraul. I've come to give you my body so that you might win this battle. You've fought a noble struggle and this Wisdom is nearing his end. But you're much closer to death than he, and he still possesses the ability to use his control over fire. Without my aid you will die. My body is capable of adapting to sources of heat and light, absorbing them. That's how I survived the Sun Staff's gaze. You need me, so I recommend you join with me quickly."

Even as he was already reaching his hand forward to seal the bargain, Aegagropilion was suspicious of this sudden boon. "Why do you surrender yourself to me? You will be lost to this world. Of what mind are you?"

A hissing cackle was given in response. "I didn't think it would be so difficult to convince you. But if you must know, I am a former denizen of Gehenna. I fled from there long ago, and have been here since. As any Gehennan, there would be no higher privilege than to give my life in servitude to our magnificent Godbeasts. Especially if it means I will contribute to the death of one of our immortal tormentors."

The Godbeast froze his hand and eyed his supposed compatriot for a moment. It took several seconds with his wounded form, but soon he was able to detect lines of Gehennite essence coursing in and out through Zekraul's body. His words were true. His birth was of Gehenna.

A splash was heard as Dosiros exploded out of the mire that had bound him. He began heating himself to clear the water from his frame, and struggled briefly to cleanse himself of muck and form fiery wings once more for mobility. Aegagropilion wasted no further time, leaping onto Zekraul's back as the demon turned to the direction of the disturbance. The Godbeast sank his claws in deep. It took effort to pierce the rigid structure of the crystalline body, but soon he had poured himself in and began to merge with his volunteering victim. He could shortly feel his strength returning, and already taste the new powers he was gaining. This creature's shapeshifting abilities could serve to magnify his own, and his energy channeling prowess would render the Godbeast virtually invincible to the assaults of the remaining Wisdoms. Pure glee flooded his mind at the prospect of the future lying before him. Even Gilanirus would be forced to admire the formidability of the new Great Beast.

Soon his shriveled shell had faded, leaving only Zekraul's body standing there as the Godbeast worked from the inside to bend it into his own new form. Then something began to feel odd to him. The black crystalline skin started to change of its own accord, shifting to a brilliant gold. Aegagropilion felt a curious pain, though as he was halfway through his transformation he was uncertain which body was suffering. The gold tone of the translucent skin intensified and a radiant light poured out.

He finally realized then what was happening. Zekraul had not deflected the powers of the Sun Staff, he had absorbed and stored them. Now he turned them upon his own body. In his final agonizing second, Aegagropilion understood how the gift he had been offered was truly the trap he had first suspected. He died in outrage, as his vision turned to nothing but the sight of a great sun.

Dosiros stepped from the marsh and looked for his foes, anger filling his eyes. This anger quickly melted to confusion at what he saw. Aegagropilion was gone, and instead only the new arrival stood there. His appearance was markedly different now. The black crystals forming his body had changed into the shape of strange, sinewy tendons twisting about. They still possessed the same faceted edges, but his flesh was no longer a solid piece as it had been before, but instead seemed to be a whipcord of crystalline ropes. It was the face that most disturbed Dosiros. The black skull itself had not changed, except for the two large amber eyes that filled it, surrounded on their fringes by an outline of green vines that spread over most of the upper face.

He used his wings to move forward and stared at this peculiar visage. "A new trick, is it, Aegagropilion?"

The creature raised its left hand as if to dismiss the Wisdom, but instead the fingers turned into long spikes that shot over the twenty yards separating the two and ripped into Dosiros' chest and shoulders.

"That beast is dead," the newborn creature replied, "do not insult me with its name. I am Zekraul, Overlord of Arkalen." He suddenly jerked his claws out, causing Dosiros to fly forward a few feet. Zekraul himself also charged forward, delivering a rough backhand with his extended fingertips. Most of the Wisdom's torso was ripped off and sent flying away. The Gehennan's right hand transformed into a huge crystal hammer as he continued his dash. Just before reaching striking distance, the hammer's surface transformed from crystal into the stone of Kiastos, and Zekraul used it to drive the Wisdom of the Flame solidly into the ground.

Dosiros coughed and gurgled uselessly as the last control of his body was crushed under the weight of that blow. Zekraul restored his hands to their natural state and looked down upon the Wisdom with disinterest.

"My speed has definitely increased. I was never able to morph that swiftly before. I also seem to have regained the remnants of the powers Aegagropilion himself had absorbed. But now, we put the most important question to the test. Did I gain the power I truly desired from this?"

He knelt down and slammed his hands onto the shredded and crumbling remains of Dosiros' chest. At first there seemed to be no response. Zekraul grunted and muttered a few times in frustration, then found the control he sought. His hands liquefied and poured over the Wisdom's frame. Lines of shadow spread to the tips of the Elysian's hands and feet, then soon devoured his head as well. The Gehennan continued pouring his black body out over the fallen Wisdom until it was fully enveloped. Once a solid black blanket hid the collapsed form, the demon began grinding it and chewing on it with his strange hands, continuing this process for nearly three full minutes until he was finally able to return his body to his natural size. Nothing of Dosiros remained.

Zekraul took a pause to familiarize himself with the unusual sensation of new information pouring into his head. It was unlike anything he had ever felt, and sent him soaring with an elation he had not thought himself capable of feeling. He looked to the swampland mire before him where Dosiros had fallen earlier. He pointed his hands forward and uttered a sharp cry.

Two massive cyclones of orange fire erupted at his command, ripping into the swamp and setting the mire boiling and evaporating. He let this continue for half a minute or so, then ceased. He had his answer. He had gained the full abilities of Aegagropilion, and had now merged with Godbeast and Wisdom alike.

He held his hands up high and released a shrill laugh. "I think this continent will no longer be sufficient to fill the grip of the Overlord! No, once I have eaten the powers of the remaining Wisdoms and Godbeasts, I'm not certain even Morolia will be enough to sate my reign. Perhaps I will return home to Gehenna after all. As I am now, it would be a veritable buffet for my indulgence!"

He looked to the south and gave a slight sigh of satisfaction. "I sense them. Melukah, of the Sun. I've tasted your power, and I can sense you now. I am coming for you next."

* * * * *

At the edge of Arkalen's largest ravine, Melukah still stood watching the empty winds of Morolia. For long months now he had not moved, waiting with the patience only an immortal could possess. Today his patience was tested, however. For the first time in many long moons, he felt his own magic being used to the north. He did not have perceptions as precise as Keldana's, so he could not be certain of what was happening. But his Wisdoms did not call upon the Staffs of the Sun idly.

He suspected Keldana would report to him soon enough, but he did not ask her for information. It took practiced discipline to keep himself from doing so, but it would have been inappropriate for him to show apprehension. Even amongst the Wisdoms, deities that they were, Melukah was worshiped. His stature as their superior could not be tarnished.

Finally, hours after he had felt the first triggering of the Staff, Keldana stood at his side quietly.

"Do you know something?" he asked reservedly. The Wisdom of Ocean was unlikely to speak unless first spoken to.

She answered with a soft tone that contained only the slightest signs of nervousness. "Dosiros has fallen. Dead."

"Truly dead?"

"His soul is devoured, like Kiastos before him. He lives on this plane no longer."

Melukah nodded. "Aegagropilion. If the Great Beast has grown in might so much that he can defeat Dosiros, we may be in significant danger. In our last war we had allies. This time, we have garnered none in hopes of swift victory."

"This is now three of us who are fallen. Dosiros and Kiastos are truly gone, and we have heard nothing of Valinoru. I've not been able to detect his presence since he fell. I fear he will not be coming to me for healing."

Melukah stepped away from the edge of the gorge and began to walk north. He stopped when he reached the place where his own personal Sun Staff pierced the rocky ground. He merely looked upon it, and it uprooted itself and floated to his back.

"Come then, Keldana. The Supreme Wisdom will end this recklessness. Order will be restored by the Sun."

"As you command, Exalted Melukah." Keldana lifted her arms, and her body scattered and turned to mist on the breeze, loyally following her lord to the north.

## Chapter 32.

# Rulers of Elysium

Abaddon Daemon rested quietly within the Elysian cell that had long served as his home. The magics here, in conjunction with his own studies, were beginning to affect him in not entirely positive ways. He was aware of this impact, but had accepted it. This was not the first time he had made sacrifices for power.

The detrimental effects were mainly to his mind. He was slowly losing his grasp on his identity, his individuality, his personal ideas and creeds. The nature of the green ether around him seemed to have been tainted with a certain predisposition toward order, and it enforced logical thought. Abaddon's mind had taken to this naturally at first, but after months of exposure it had become consumptive, as major parts of his psyche began to erode. For a time he suspected his jailers had plotted this against him, but his paranoia was soon replaced with a cold rationale. It was far more likely the Muses used these currents to influence the species under their dominion, keeping them bureaucratic and obedient to their doctrines.

It had boggled his imagination to think such a spell could be used to continuously lace an entire plane with subliminal messages. Then his imagination had been shut down. His memory soon followed, leaving him nothing but the shell of an obsessed man seeking power, for what purpose he no longer recalled.

His perceptions of time were also being interfered with. He estimated that he had been imprisoned now for seven months, but he was able to detect minor quantum fluctuations carried in the ether. He was fairly certain that time—or at least his relative conception of it—was being periodically slowed down or sped up in some arbitrary fashion. It seemed a singular trait of the otherwise order-imposing ether, and he suspected it was an unintended side effect.

On what he estimated to be the two hundred and twenty-third day of his captivity, he began to hear voices. At first he presumed some other part of his mind had broken down, but a quick moment of introspection confirmed that was not the case.

"Abaddon Daemon. Speak. Confirm that you function."

The query was delivered several times before the prisoner was convinced he was sane enough to answer. "I assume you speak to me," he replied perfunctorily. "I function." He did not bother to look around for his captors, as he was certain they would not be visible to him. Instead he left his head hanging weakly into his chest, his eyes closed and resting.

"We are pleased that you have weathered your holding period."

"You didn't seem concerned with the matter before. My race requires food and drink to survive."

"You fret unnecessarily. The cell you are in has life-sustaining attributes. We placed you here so that you would be safe until this trial."

"You're here now. Release me, then."

"That would not be wise. Your species cannot survive full exposure to Elysium's environment."

"I didn't ask for your 'protection', and would not require it were it not for your abduction. Free me, or I'll free myself."

"We can foresee no such outcome. You are pinned to that wall by a force of our will, unable to move. Your words of threat carry no potential."

"I've been awfully gracious," Abaddon growled, "waiting here for your return. I think this place has made me docile, patient even beyond my own normal standards. But don't be confused. Do not think I have idled this time away."

He lifted his head and opened his eyes. Within them, nothing could be seen save for deep green slits, leaking with Elysian power.

He made a motion forward, but was instantly repelled back. He grunted angrily, and his entire body flared out to mirror the glow in his eyes. A wave of resistance struck into the force confronting him. He then rose easily to his feet, walking slowly to the middle of the room.

From here, he stretched his arms wide and released a roar. The lines of magic flowing through the area redirected sharply, emptying into his flesh. Soon the integrity of his body began to fade, as his physical form was replaced by a billowing cascade of intangible green energy.

As the integrity of the circular barricade encasing the prisoner began to shudder, the Muses held a quick consultation.

"He is gathering a tremendous amount of mana to a single point. The localized backlash created will be substantial. Even we ourselves could die if we maintain this current proximity."

"His alien nature threatens our natural order. Unlike the mana to which he is accustomed, Elysian ether is not designed to be compressed to a single location thusly. This will send a destructive ripple of unbalance throughout the entire Dominion."

"Too much concentrated green ether could even destabilize time, or the Veil. If it collapses here, the plane will descend into chaos. In even the most optimistic scenario, he will corrupt or erase the effects of the Heart of Elysium, giving rise to a renewed rebellion."

"It is decided. Abaddon Daemon, cease your action against us. Though we do not find it in your best interests, we will do as you have asked."

The man immediately grew quiet, but it took a moment for him to return the ether he had already gathered. Soon his appearance reverted to normal, and he waited patiently for the Muses to fulfill their word.

This did not take long. Once they had ascertained the stability of the region, a crackle of electricity sounded and the walls around Abaddon vanished. He was struck by what felt like a river's current. The air was so heavy, carrying such tight payloads of ether, that it burned as it brushed against his skin. He was only briefly troubled, swiftly adjusting his green barriers to shield him from the pain, as well as harvest these new currents for fresh power.

"As we surmised," one of the Muses noted as they witnessed his surreptitious adaptation, "you are a superior variant of your species. In the last war of the divinities we were allied with a Morolian champion. As the new champion of your plane, we hope you will forge a similar contract with us."

Abaddon glared at the four creatures standing before him. They were tall, but not as large as the Wisdoms. Each of them stood at exactly six feet, five inches, and had slim white bodies with large golden face plates masking their features. The only distinguishing marks that kept them from appearing identical were carved on the golden masks. With his extrasensory perceptions, Abaddon was able to detect that the Muses themselves were merely an energy spectrum, manipulating these bodies for appearances.

He responded to their previous observation. "Is that why you have unjustly imprisoned me?"

"It was the murdering of a Wisdom that caused us to bring you here. Once you had demonstrated yourself so dangerous, we could not leave you to your activities unchecked."

The man thought hard before giving his next answer. "What is a Wisdom?"

Two of the Muses exchanged a look, then one of the others answered. "You have suffered decay from the holding chamber. That is not unusual. Here." As this Muse paused speaking, the Muse on Abaddon's far right took a step forward and lifted a robed arm. No hand protruded from the end of this sleeve, but a ball of white energy pooled in its absence. "Take this."

He took a step back, replying, "What reason do I have to trust my captors?"

One of the other Muses spoke. Abaddon noticed functioned on a strange cycle, with the same one never speaking twice in a row. "The psychological decay effect of the holding chamber has been observed on other mortals. It seems to be a consequence of the magic used to sustain your life indefinitely. When we brought you here, we made a copy of your mind and abilities as they were. From this white orb you will regain yourself, as you were when we first brought you here. It is the only way you can be whole again."

Abaddon nodded slowly, instinctively trusting this explanation in spite of his misgivings. He then reached out and touched the light. There was no sudden reaction, contrary to what he had expected. The light simply faded into his arm, then went out entirely. He waited to feel some sudden internal change, but it did not manifest. Instead as the Muses resumed the conversation, he gradually felt his memories coming back into place as they were needed.

"As said, you were brought here due to your murder of a Wisdom," the next Muse in the cycle said.

"They struck me first," the man responded with emphasis. "The one called Dosiros attempted to murder me and my allies, unprovoked."

"We recognize your plight, and your reaction. It was the natural course."

"Then why have you brought me here for trial?"

"Trial may be too strong a word. Perhaps we are not translating ourselves properly into your language. What we want with you is more of a... meeting."

"A negotiation?"

"Ah, yes. A negotiation."

"So far you've imprisoned me without food, water, or company for months. On my plane, that's not what we would consider a healthy start to negotiations."

"You do not understand. You are fighting on the wrong side of this matter. You cannot see the larger picture."

"Try explaining it to me. We'll see if I even care."

"The Wisdoms are at war with a race of creatures called Godbeasts. They are the deities of Gehenna, much as the Wisdoms are deities of Elysium."

"I know of Elysium and Gehenna," he interjected. "I don't need a history lesson."

"Then you surely know the chaos of the Godbeasts. They seek to conquer Elysium to make it their own. They will destroy every plane between here and there in order to do so. They will lay siege to your home."

Abaddon gave a long sigh. "The only creatures I have seen laying siege to anything is the Wisdoms. I've encountered no Godbeasts."

The Muse second to his left took a step forward. "I have a proposition. You wish to purge your plane of the Wisdoms' presence, correct? There is nothing simpler. The Wisdoms will only remain in Morolia until the Godbeasts are gone. Instead of expending your energy killing our kind—only to inevitably discover that we are correct and the Godbeasts are the true threat—why not kill the Godbeasts themselves? Once this is done, the war will not resume for another several centuries, long after your natural lifespan."

"All you're offering me is servitude. If we're to make a pact, I'll want other assurances. Morolian casualties must be avoided wherever possible. No more of the reckless behavior I've seen from the Wisdoms thus far."

"That seems to us an acceptable addendum."

"I already tried to offer such a bargain to two Wisdoms. Both responded with violence. How can I be expected to trust any of you?"

"A pact made with the Muses is unbreakable, binding even the Wisdoms themselves. Once the contract is sealed, deliberately breaking it will cause death to either party."

"So what are the precise terms, then? I agree to kill the Godbeasts, you send me home, and the Wisdoms suddenly start playing nice? That simple?"

"It could not be simpler. Then you accept?"

He looked from face to gilded face of the facades standing before him. "You're losing," he declared bluntly.

The next one in turn of their choir answered hastily, "What?"

Abaddon crossed his arms behind his back, pacing back and forth as he stared the Muses down in turn. "You're lying to me. If all you wanted was a contract this simple, you know I would have agreed to it when I was first brought here. Not only that, but you would have wanted me back on Morolia fighting for your cause as soon as possible, in order to bring this affair to a quick close. You never had any intentions of making a pact with me. You never failed in your translation. You were going to try and execute me for standing in your way, but things have changed on Morolia. The Wisdoms are losing, or perhaps are going to lose and your divine sight allows you to foresee the inevitable outcome. You're hoping my sword can tip the scales." He halted his march, awaiting their response.

They were quiet for a time, then confirmed his suspicions. "Your intellect is a suited match to your fighting prowess. You are uncommon to your species."

"Though you likely don't believe it in your vast arrogance, I've been trained by savvier diplomats than you." He turned away from them, staring off into the distance. "I don't accept your terms. I'm not on your side."

"Would you choose to remain imprisoned here instead?"

Abaddon smiled, detecting more than mild annoyance in the speaker's tone. In spite of their bluster, it was clear that he held every advantage in this alleged negotiation. The Muses were truly desperate to make a deal, but had no idea how to properly manipulate their Morolian guest. They were shifting frantically between tactics. "Make no mistake, I will escape your domain," he countered their threat. "If I have to claw my way through the Veil by sheer force of will, still I shall return home. As far as I'm concerned, I'm already at war with Elysium. I have no qualm in bringing that war to your home turf."

There was a long pause. Abaddon knew there was a chance this could come to blows, and he brazenly began to once more gather ether into his body. The Muses seemed disinclined to confront him on his terms, instead asking, “What is your desire?”

“If you want a contract with me, you have to offer me something worthwhile in return. Something I can’t just take for myself. That’s how these things work.”

“We can supply you with whatever information you need. Perhaps the history and true intentions of the Silver One would appease you?”

He raised an eyebrow in interest, then shook his head. “Torlen already informed me he’s not aligned with you. For the moment, that’s information enough. I’ll deal with Akatriel on my own. Tell me how long you’ve held me here.”

“Three months in the time of your home plane.”

The man turned around to face his captors. “If you wish to make a deal, you must compensate me for my lost time. You will send me back to Morolia, and I’ll hunt the Godbeasts where your Wisdoms have failed. But first, I want the power of the Muses.”

Though they made no move, he could feel their sudden discomfort. “To what do you refer?”

“You’ve pooled your power together in order to control Elysium. There’s a single point of your mana—far beyond what any of you are capable of individually—inflicting its will across this entire plane. You dared to imprison me for three months, now you aim to send me on your errand against creatures you know I am no match for. Your debt to me is great. And so I want that power. Bind it to me for three months, and using it, I will kill the Godbeasts.”

“What makes you so certain such a power exists?”

“Cease your posturing!” he barked in sudden anger. “I can read the currents. Its existence is as plain to a mystic of my caliber as a second sun in the sky. Your deception is a waste of time.”

“Very well, disregard deception. The power to which you refer is called the Heart of Elysium. It must not leave this plane. It is necessary to hold the balance of the Dominion.”

He narrowed his eyes, then took a step back and dropped into a battle crouch and redoubling his ether channeling. “Make your choice, Muses. Sign a contract with me and unleash my wrath on the Godbeasts, or face that wrath yourself. Either way, today I bring Elysium chaos."

"You make dangerous enemies, Abaddon Daemon."

He answered the comment with a large grin, baring his teeth. "They're the only ones worth having."

* * * * *

Kelve, Boderon, Tenkahn, and Gaius sat together at the top of their hill, protected from the Overlord's forces by a buffer of their own troops scattered down the grassy slope. The commanders were holding a debate over the current state of the war. They were not optimistic.

After Gaius' disconcerting proclamation of Shote's survival, the minotaur had wasted no time in making his appearance. Dawn of the next day, he had assembled his armies into the courtyard and began drilling them mercilessly into shape. The draconics, trolls, were-creatures, even the ogres and chimeras had been brought out. None of them dared to question the towering beast's reign or authority. Their tempers and attitude were kept even further in check by the massive pike Shote paraded around with. It stood over eleven feet in length, and pinned across the top of it was the head and neck of the griffin Ontarshiss.

The legendary creature had shown no interest in attacking the humans, so instead Kelve had ordered a charge of his own. It had been the first time in months they had dared to rush the Overlord's gate. The results had been dire. At first the demons had attempted to retreat deeper into their fortress, backing away from the front ranks of veteran former slayers and the two Monks of Tria. A murderous bellow from Shote had sent them retreating in reverse, back into the ranks of the humans.

Shote had remained at the rear of his forces, shouting constant orders in a tongue the human general could not understand. The demonic forces, however, had responded readily to these cryptic commands. The ogres—with a backing of chimeras for speed—quickly pinned down the Monks of Tria and held them at bay. The were-creatures spread themselves between the mightier demonspawn, or attacked the weaker flanks comprising Boderon's troops. The human forces were efficiently held at bay. As their numbers began to chip away, Kelve had sounded a retreat.

Two more charges had been attempted since, over the past week. Neither time did Shote join the battle, instead relying on his subordinates alone. Neither time did the invaders show more encouraging results. This sudden change from aggressive behavior to defensive was somewhat confusing at first. Kelve had later discerned precisely what was happening. Gaius, on the other hand, was still indignant.

"What's his problem? Hiding behind a wave of his troops like a coward, not daring to face Tenkahn and me. He won't even call an attack against us! He just stands there all day drilling them like he's preparing for an invasion force that isn't here yet!"

Kelve limped forward and placed a hand on the young man's shoulder to settle him. "He's doing what any brilliant general would do. He's bolstering their morale."

Tenkahn gave a slow, understanding nod as the younger monk retorted, "What? How is that brilliant?"

"Think about it for a moment," Kelve explained. "When Tessena was leading, we were keeping her forces locked down mainly through the strength of our threat. We had slowly reversed the situation until the demons—the superior force with the advantaged position in the siege—were afraid of us because they'd lost nearly every encounter to that point. Now they've begun a streak of winning every encounter. Shote has not aided them directly, he has not become personally involved. They know his strength is not what has tipped the scale. No, he's reminding them, without saying it aloud, that they're the superior fighting force."

"I find myself grateful that we already dispatched their nightspawn ranks," Tenkahn mused, "or the situation would be quite bleak."

"It may be that anyway," countered Kelve. "I can think of only one solution to this stalemate that benefits us."

"And that is?" Gaius asked.

Kelve paused, scanning his tactical mind for another option. Everything he could think of required outside influence; another batch of reinforcements, like Boderon's. With such a thing an almost certain impossibility, there was only one course his troops could take themselves.

"We have to kill Shote."

Tenkahn grew still at this, but Gaius punched his fists together in excitement. "Alright! Tenkahn and I will charge him then, and take him out. When the head is removed, it's just a matter of time before we finish mopping up the corpse."

"Silence, Gaius!" the elder monk suddenly shouted. The apprentice was unaccustomed to hearing his master take such a harsh tone, and fell a step back in dismay. "You know not where you speak!"

Tenkahn stormed away, and the youth stood bearing his chastisement silently. Kelve and Boderon continued the conversation without the monks.

"Tenkahn's entire brotherhood gave their lives in an attempt to bring down Shote," the sickly commander noted. "Having seen the level which Tenkahn himself can fight at, I can scarcely imagine the destructive force of ten such warriors. It's difficult to gauge Shote's current strength, whether or not he's at his full might himself. In any case, it seems unlikely we could bring him down while his entire army is serving as a distraction."

Boderon scratched the back of his head. "But isn't slaying Shote the reason Tenkahn is still here? Isn't that his only purpose?"

"That doesn't mean he doesn't fear the prospect of facing him again. Tenkahn's no coward, and will march to face his foe one way or another. But Shote's reappearance changed everything. Tenkahn's no longer here to see victory. Now he's here so that he may die in the same manner as his fallen brethren. He'll face Shote alone, and he'll die doing so."

Hearing this, Gaius' spirit returned. "Why would he face him alone? I will fight at my master's side!"

Kelve gave a sigh and shook his head at the impetuousness of youth. "What is your primary concern, Eiden? What's the purpose to which you swore your life?"

The young monk answered without hesitation. "To preserve the sacred order of Tria."

"And how is dying in the same battle as Tenkahn going to accomplish that?"

Gaius began to object, then what the man was saying finally registered for him. By his own sacred oaths, he and Tenkahn could not both march into a battle where defeat could be a certainty. He realized only now why he had been granted the blessing of the runes—Gaius was the order's safeguard. When Tenkahn died battling Shote, his apprentice would become the last Monk of Tria. He would be forced to withdraw from this war, unable to further risk his life until he had spread the runes to another vessel. He alone would have to preserve their order.

After a moment of weighing this, he stormed off in the direction the other monk had departed, to confront his master with his frustration. Kelve hung his head sadly. He knew that some day Gaius would make a marvelous warrior. He wished he could see that day himself.

"What will we do now, Sir Kelve?" Boderon asked, steering the subject from the departed monks.

"Tenkahn has to face Shote, one way or another. I know the man, his pride and devotion to his fallen order will allow nothing else. I intend to bide our time and make that battle possible. There's a chance, albeit slim, that he'll find a way to overcome. If so, it will aid our cause more than anything else could."

"And if not?"

Kelve answered with a smile and a wink. "Well I'll think of something, right? I always do."

He sent Boderon to see to the troops, then returned to his command tent for a fresh batch of steroids and a plasma injection.

As he was administering his drugs to himself, he stared at ten carefully arranged vials on the far side of the tent, on Detria's small desk. Each vial contained a thick black liquid. Kelve felt as though he was brought closer to his own death just by looking upon them.

In spite of what he had led Boderon to believe, he had already formed a plan to deal with their current situation, he had just not yet mustered the resolve to commit to it. Those vials held one of Kelve's most despicable recipes. It was a liquid that, upon ingestion, would alter a human's natural physiology in more complex ways than anything he had ever seen. It was not one of his personal inventions, but rather the most tainted secret he had been taught as a Devilslayer.

The chemical took twenty-four hours to take effect. In that time, the drinker's skin would be transformed ashen black, and his blood would become a thick blue color, no longer able to carry oxygen. After this transformation period was complete, the user had less than six hours before he would pass away. One hour after the moment of death, the various substances the skin and blood had converted into would mesh, becoming a chemical bomb. The resulting explosion was capable of blanketing a one hundred yard radius from just one body.

Kelve knew what he needed to do to assure victory in this war. Ten healthy troops, with physiological profiles fit for the transformation, had to be selected. They would be injected, then the next day they would charge the Overlord's gates alone. The toxin would give them superhuman speed and strength, as well as make them immune to all pain and wounds for the final hours before their death. They would die fighting, without question, but they would survive long enough to penetrate deep into the demonic ranks, perhaps even making it close to Shote's own position. An hour later, hopefully before the demons had finished cleaning their battlefield, the explosions would occur. Ten bombs of that potency would be a blow Shote could not recover from, and with only the most minimal human losses.

Unfortunately, Kelve himself was not a candidate for this

treatment. This meant he would have to select ten other soldiers. He knew that in every battle at least ten of his people fell, but that was the risk of war. It was one thing to ask hardened warriors to risk their lives for a noble cause. It was another entirely to ask them to sacrifice themselves outright, with no hope for survival, when he could not join them in their demise.

So as he had told Boderon, he would bide his time, awaiting another option. He took a deep breath and rose to his feet. He felt strong so soon after the doses of his drugs, but the feeling would last less than an hour. Each time his renewal became shorter. He wondered how much longer now before he could no longer remember his body's former strength.

* * * * *

Near the southern border of Arkalen's large jungles, the Veil split open in a rush of fire and lightning. A dark blue sphere appeared for a moment, shielding its contents from the storm of energy. Soon the disruption faded and the sphere scattered. Abaddon stood in the final remnants of heat and electricity, wrapped safely within his own magics. Quickly he thrust his hand back into the opening of the Veil before it could seal itself, and with effort pulled forth the Arda.

He attached the sword to the clip on his belt and twisted it to its resting position, then took a deep breath. At first he could feel nothing; this plane was empty to him. Then, as his starving spirit finally recognized Morolia, he latched onto the currents and was nearly overwhelmed by a rush of ether. He carefully spent time organizing his mystical talents, setting aside the store of energy he had brought over from Elysium and making room for fresh nourishment from both Morolia and Asteria. Once he was satisfied with his preparations, he tapped the Elysian store. His eyes shimmered with iridescence, and he sniffed the air around him.

"Now this is a godsend. Torlen is nearby. I owe him words," he said with vicious intent.

He spent a moment verifying the directions of the other Wisdoms. Torlen was in pursuit of something, Abaddon was sure of it. He would have to move quickly if he was going to catch the Wisdom of Sound.

There was time enough for one thing. He held up his open right hand, and bent his entire will on commanding Morolia. He gathered a joint whirlwind of wind and kinetic force there, focusing it into a tight vortex less than an inch wide. Then he turned and pointed his palm at a nearby tree, releasing a sharp roar. The trunk of the tree split open, then shattered into thousands of pieces. He smiled and began walking. As the tree fell down over him, he said softly, "It's good to be home," then disappeared in a haze of speed.

## Chapter 33.

# Sound and Fury

Torlen moved rapidly through the eastern fringes of the jungle, more than a little irritated. He had been pursuing Schpariel casually, toying with his prey, making certain he was close enough that his presence was known. Then the Godbeast had suddenly vanished. The Wisdom had swiftly dropped to where he had last felt the Gehennite imprint. There were no signs of any creature passing through, no trail for him to track. He tried instead to retrace and follow the line Schpariel had been taking, but found no results from that approach either.

Something was masking out his ability to sense his quarry. He had scanned the ether signatures in the area. He was not yet certain, but it seemed there was a disturbance of Asterian origin blocking his efforts. He proceeded on his path anxiously. If he allowed Schpariel to escape, Dosiros would be enraged and this failure would be reported to Melukah.

He spotted a river in the distance, with a figure standing on the near bank. His hopes were lifted instantly. With a burst of extra speed he blasted to the figure, stopping only a few yards away. As his ran his eyes over what stood before him, his optimism was replaced with dumbstruck awe.

"You cannot be here," he said slowly, as if the words would force the figure to vanish.

Abaddon glanced southward over his right shoulder. "What are you after, Torlen?" he asked mockingly. "Anything interesting?"

"I sent you to Elysium!"

"It would seem I came back. I tend to do that."

The Wisdom of Sound shuddered with rage, then snapped, "I

don't have time for this insanity. I must catch Schpariel!"

"Ah, the Dark Wisdom," Abaddon replied with a nod, "First of the Godbeasts. Schpariel is no more a concern of yours. I will pursue and kill him myself. After you and I rehash some old history between us."

Torlen gathered his white rings over his left arm and took a step back. "The Muses sent you to hunt the Godbeasts, yet you are foolish enough to betray them?"

Responding to the Wisdom's preparations, Abaddon smoothly removed Arda from his back. "Betray? Not so. They told me to hunt the Godbeasts, and hunt I shall. They never said I could not also hunt Wisdoms."

"You would hunt me? Then prove yourself a worthy predator!"

The mystic nodded his acceptance of these terms. He did not gather ether, as Torlen had expected, and his eyes did not glow. Instead he simply came running at his opponent, swinging his sword in a horizontal sweep with both hands. It was the same move he had used to open the last battle. The Wisdom was immediately frustrated he would have to repeat this same dance.

He lifted his right palm and released his slowing energy net. It fell over the man's body, as Torlen quickly took a bored step backward to avoid the long sword. His evasion was not sharp enough, and he felt the steel of the blade slice cleanly through his chest. A shockwave accompanied the strike, forcing him back a further dizzy step. When he recovered his focus Abaddon stood in front of him, back turned, the tip of Arda resting lightly against the right side of the Sound's neck.

"That is once," the man stated in a dead tone.

Torlen stumbled several steps away and steadied himself. He was having difficulty determining what had gone wrong. "Once?" he responded quizzically.

"Once, you have underestimated me. The third time, I kill you."

The mystic waited a few seconds for a response, but the Wisdom had none to offer. Abaddon resumed his offense, turning about rapidly and swinging the Arda with his left hand, aiming again at his foe's chest. The Wisdom was forced to react, using the resonance frequency of Arda to bring it to a stop. Though the blade did indeed halt in its path, he found that he could not send it flying from the man's hand as he had before.

The deity was not so easily perturbed this time. He surged forward to seize his opponent by the throat with his left hand. Abaddon seemed prepared for this move, taking an easy step back and raising his right arm in defense. Torlen's left hand latched firmly onto the uplifted forearm, then unleashed the power of his sonic rings. The white rings traveled into the human's frame, but immediately dissipated without so much as a hiss.

"Is that it?" Abaddon asked in clear amusement. His opponent again offered no answer, so he twisted Arda into a fierce uppercut. Torlen released his grip, leaped away, and used another burst of sound to halt the sword's path, narrowly catching it in time to prevent himself from being rent in half.

"It's as if each time I defeat you, you grow stronger," Torlen mused, half to himself.

"A problem you wouldn't have to deal with if you'd kill me when given the chance."

"Now that is a peculiar taunt. Never before have I, the Assassin of Elysium, been accused of being insufficiently thorough at killing a target. You need to understand that you are only alive at this moment because I've never actually decided to kill you." He began to harmonize his body with the area, tuning his magic up. "That sword will do you no good. Its blade cannot touch me. If you can't defeat me with your bare hands, then you cannot defeat me."

The Morolian champion gave a grimace, then stabbed Arda into the ground at his side. "So it is."

He charged with a yell. The Elysian gathered magic in a surge and sent forth his most intense barrage of energy, synchronized for his target's body. A wave of impact flew over the man's torso, clearly signaling the success of the attack, but it did not slow or stun him. He reached Torlen quickly, effortlessly, and delivered a powerful two-handed punch directly into the Wisdom's face mask.

"Twice," Abaddon roared as the blow connected.

Torlen was knocked to the ground and barreled over, rolling away from his smaller opponent as his mask crumbled away. He regained his feet unsteadily. At first, his exposed face appeared to be that of a normal human, albeit pale. This was as much charade as the mask itself, and did not last long.

As a wave of pressure washed over him, he choked out, "Imbecile! Those masks are the only thing that keeps our divine power in check!" Another wave washed over him, cutting off his ability to talk. His face melted, transforming into a latticework of blue energy, with two green flames serving as eyes.

Tremendous amounts of Elysian ether surged around the Wisdom and began to alter the surface of his body into a semi-malleable flesh. As this occurred, Abaddon began to back away. Torlen took quick advantage of his foe's hesitation.

"So you've grown strong enough to shrug off my attacks, have you? Shrug this off!"

He flexed his left arm in front of his face, and a tunnel of sonic energy ripped through the area, straight for Abaddon. The mystic did not have time to dodge, and his body splattered with blood as his skin was torn in dozens of places. Torlen made a similar motion with his right arm and a pillar of sound encircled his opponent, striking him from above and below simultaneously.

The man stumbled away further and vomited up blood. Torlen dashed forward and swung down with his hands, sending a fresh wave of sonic energy lashing out. Just before this attack connected, the human crossed his arms above his head and released his own wave of green ether. The Wisdom was only barely able to detect this quick attack, as the ether barrier shredded his wall of magic. As the attacks were neutralized Abaddon wasted no time, stepping forward and slamming his domineering foe with a vicious blow to the stomach. The Wisdom was not hurt, only brought to a forcible halt. The mystic quickly followed up with a fierce left straight into the Elysian's exposed face.

Torlen did not suspect this attack would do much harm, but

Abaddon had coated his fist in the same casings of Elysian ether he had used to defend himself. The Sound's crucial matrix of power was destabilized, and the shock to his system left him spiraling backward, gurgling and flailing his arms uselessly.

There was a brief lull in the battle as the mystic warlord did not further pursue his advantage. Both opponents took a moment to eye each other and recover from landed blows. In that instant, it occurred to the Wisdom of Sound that he was about to lose his life. His adversary's newfound command over Elysian magic, crude though it was, could prove lethal to a Wisdom outside of his home plane.

He brought his hands together in front of himself and cupped them over one another. A singularity of sound appeared there, writhing and rotating as it gathered momentum. Soon the reverberations from the infinitesimal point could be felt for miles around, echoing through the trees and bogs of the jungle.

"You've proven yourself to be a nuisance of unparalleled proportions, for a mortal," he remarked. "Your time in Elysium allowed you to study, to learn to use my own native ether to fend off my attacks. I'm amazed how far you progressed in such little time. It means I cannot crush you as I would any other foe. However, you're still a mortal. You're still a Morolian. Even if you are immune to my blasts, you're not immune to the might of sound itself."

He tightened his grip before his foe could respond. The sound permeating the area rose to a horrifying pitch, a screech so loud that some of the largest trees began to crack and peel. Birds fell from the sky—dying before they even reached the ground—and fish in the river floated to the surface, likewise deceased. Abaddon grunted and endeavored to move forward, but instead fell to his knees as blood began to ooze from his eyes and ears.

Torlen focused more intensity to the attack. It was difficult for him to maintain something this precise, but he could hold it for at least an hour, he was certain. That would be more than enough time to end the human's life, or at least render him unconscious. If necessary he would simply tear the man's head off with his own two hands.

After thirty seconds had passed, Abaddon was already on his hands and knees, groaning weakly as if begging for mercy. Torlen would not allow his opponent's plight to distract his focus. As much as he wanted to enjoy his victim's pain, he had to focus on keeping the singularity at maximum intensity.

Another thirty seconds passed, and the end seemed assured. Then the stubborn man stood to his feet. For a moment Torlen thought his foe had already recovered, but the expression on his face was certainly one of agony. He began walking toward the Wisdom slowly, a step at a time. The Sound briefly regretted that there was not much distance between them, but felt assured the mortal must surely fall again before reaching him.

Somehow he did not fall, however. As he came closer the sound waves began to affect more than his mind, burning his skin and causing the gashes that had already appeared to stretch and spurt fresh blood. Abaddon shut his eyes and clenched his teeth, doing his best to ignore the overwhelming pain of his skull shaking itself apart. Torlen began to panic as the man at last reached him, and the attack lulled for half a second.

The Wisdom quickly renewed his effort, but the brief disturbance had been enough to give Abaddon focus. He reached forward and seized his assailant's forearms. They stood there for a moment, locked in a staring contest, each willing the other to die. Then the mystic surged with raw determination, releasing a huge burst of white magic out around himself as he dug into his opponent's forearms. He screamed defiance into the Wisdom's chest, and with the strength of a possessed man his grip shattered the mechanical arms, wringing them closed.

The attack stopped instantly. The Wisdom reacted first, punching the man in the stomach to lift him from the ground. Then he struck his foe hard in the face, launching him away bodily until he came to a sliding halt on the bank of the river. Abaddon lay on the ground for a moment as still as if dead, but Torlen felt like taking no more chances. He pointed his palms in the human's direction and willed his magics to strike out and crush him.

Nothing happened. His magic did not respond, the human's body was not stricken. As he pondered his own impotence, Abaddon began to rise again to his feet, offering explanation.

"You're like your brother Valinoru. The body you have uses internal cavities to control external forces through intricate reflection and amplification. When your internal control is broken, the external follows." He looked up through blood-soaked features. Torlen marveled, for even as he was staring at the human his flesh was slowly rebuilding itself with a slight shimmer of white energy, closing the gashes and working diligently to restore his ruined hearing and sight.

"I was right before, wasn't I?" he remarked in awe. "You are an Avatar. Your powers must be those of a god."

Abaddon's expression turned to one of contemplation, and he stared at the ground in uncertainty. "Perhaps. Perhaps I'm this world's final Avatar. In truth, I can no longer be certain exactly what I have become, what Kargaroth has made me." His face suddenly turned serious, and his tone grim. "But I'm certain of one thing. Whatever else I may be, I am human. And I will teach you to respect that."

He dashed forward, snatching Arda from the ground as he passed it. Torlen started to prepare a deflection, then realized he could no longer use that technique either. His mind panicked and obsessed on what seemed like his only option. Finding himself uncharacteristically low on improvisations, he gathered ether to his feet and launched himself straight into the air for a retreat.

As soon as his prey's feet left the ground, Abaddon jumped and went into a tight spin, holding Arda out at his waist. Torlen thought he was sure to clear the blade, but somehow failed. The tip of the thirsty sword struck at his shins, biting deep. Once the surface of his legs were breached his abilities again collapsed, and he fell to the ground in a tangle with his foe. Upon impact the human was the first to regain his footing, positioning himself above

Torlen with the Arda hovering just an inch away from the Wisdom's electrical face.

"Third time," he observed cruelly. "That's the one where I kill you."

He lifted Arda high and instantly began a downswing, aiming to cut Torlen's head in half. For the first time in his memorable life, the Wisdom of Sound found his mind completely blank. No ideas occurred, no last techniques seemed available, no thoughts filled his head at all. Everything turned into a brief sheet of white as he accepted that he was dead.

Then Arda stopped. Again, only an inch from the Wisdom's face, the consuming edge of the blade halted and shivered slightly. Torlen felt his brief panic subside, replaced by confusion. Was the human toying with him? That seemed unlikely. Unless...

He looked up and confirmed his hopes. On Abaddon's right shoulder, a strange glyph shone brightly in etched green lines. The man gritted his teeth and tried to regain control of his arm, but could not. The Sound gave a chuckle in relief, then gently eased himself onto his feet, pushing the Arda out of his way.

"You had me in fear, mortal. Not one creature in a million can make such a claim. I thought, for a time, that you had learned how to remove the Mark placed on you. When last we fought I injected you with a Mark of the Muses. It's what allowed the Muses to pull you across the plain, it's what allows them to track your activities. But, more relevantly, it prevents you from consciously slaying any citizens of the upper echelon of Elysian society."

Torlen carefully adjusted and sharpened his magics, reinforcing his own delicate matrix of power. This Daemon could not murder him deliberately, but the repeated blows to his frame were beginning to shake his core. If the battle continued, there was a realistic chance the man would kill him by accident.

The human gave a bark of frustration, then settled himself outwardly and returned Arda to its clip on his back. He glared angrily for a moment, then commanded, "I won this battle. I don't want there to be any confusion on that matter. Twice you beat me, but today I surpassed you. You are no longer a worthy rival for me. Get out of my sight, or we will both enjoy a prolonged experiment in seeing how much punishment a Wisdom can survive before reaching the point of death."

Torlen bit back his pride and gave a bow. He then moved around Abaddon and began to head south. With some difficulty he managed to cross the river, and in half an hour was beyond sight of the battlefield of his defeat. Resorting to traveling on foot, damaged as he was, was impossibly frustrating for him. He was heading south—deserting both Dosiros and Schpariel—because he had no choice. Traveling Wisdoms were given their restraining masks for a reason. While only partially manifested on a foreign plane, a portion of their spirit remained anchored in Elysium. This was not dissimilar to how a human's own magic worked, and allowed the divinity to draw a continuous stream of their native ether.

With his mask shattered, Torlen was now fully bound to the Morolian plane. While this gave him a quicker and more adept control over his talents, it also meant he could no longer draw from Elysium. He was running only on the finite stores already contained in his current body. With his increased strength level, he would consume those rapidly. He had to find Keldana and allow her to heal him and restore his mask, or he would burn his body dry in only a few days time.

He was haunted by the fact that he had allowed Schpariel to escape. There could be no doubt the Godbeast was heading straight for Gilanirus. Torlen had to hope this quest was either quashed by Melukah, or that the human kept his word and hunted Schpariel in his stead. The Sound was certain of one thing—if the Tyrant of Gehenna was awakened, more Wisdoms would die before this war was over.

* * * * *

Schpariel fled far beyond the borders of the Fenrir Jungle, running with the most speed his cumbersome frame would allow.

Unlike Aegagropilion, he was not designed for agility. Being driven into this hasty march had left him in a sour mood. It had been a few hours since his separation from his brother Godbeast, and so far he had met no interference. He wished to believe he had passed into safety and could slow his pace, but sheer paranoia made him think better of the notion.

Having initially traveled too far east, he was moving through the Great Desert of Coroku, and could see miles in any direction. He continuously checked back over his shoulder for signs of Wisdom activity, but detected none. During one of his glances back, he tripped over a small rock and fell forward onto his face.

He grumbled in rage and rose to his feet clumsily, his stalwart body struggling to gain grasp on the loose sands. After dusting himself off and preparing to resume his run, he lifted his gaze to find a surprising visitor. A slim sheet of white had etched itself into light brown landscape before him.

"It's taken you some time to arrive here, Schpariel," the robed figure mused. "But I suppose I should count myself grateful you remain intact, given your obstacles."

The Dark Wisdom pointed his Moon Rod forward and gathered ether into his arm. "You. You sent us to the western lands, told us to return when we had power, then abandoned us. You left us to fend for ourselves against the might of the Wisdoms!"

The figure swept his hood back, revealing a scowl marring his pale face. "At what point did it become my responsibility to shield you? You're the ones who are the almighty Godbeasts. I'm just a lowly human in your eyes, remember? Don't condemn me for your shortcomings."

"I should incinerate you where you stand!" Schpariel shouted back as his eyes glinted red.

"I've long suspected you were stupid, but certainly you're not *that* dense. There's no energy remaining in that rod that you may waste. Strike me down if you dare, but your inability to resurrect Gilanirus afterward will be the princely jewel atop your crown of defeat."

Schpariel lowered his Rod and calmed himself. The pale priest had never shown him such insolence before. He began to suspect something was amiss. “I have not time for this. I must move. Wisdoms almost certainly pursue me.”

The scowling face faded to nonchalance. “You fret for naught. I’ve masked our presence here. Indeed, I have been masking your presence for hours now. The Wisdoms won’t find you until Gilanirus has seen daylight.”

“Ah, so you do yet aid our cause.”

The silver eyes stared at the Godbeast with disinterest for a few seconds, then his visage began to fade. When only a slight shimmer of white could still be detected, Schpariel heard an echoing, “Awaken the Spectre.” Then he was alone. He shrugged off his irritation and resumed his way south. He set an easier pace, knowing that he was protected by his untrustworthy ally.

* * * * *

Myris and Cildar sat around a fresh campfire, resting. They had been marching southward for two days now with no real destination in mind. They were lost in a jungle, and their progress was slow due to unfamiliarity. Cildar felt there was more activity to their east, but Myris seemed to think they should veer west. The Dragoon had not felt worthy to question his comrade, so they continued to edge southwest.

They had spoken very little the past couple of days, only making the necessary conversation to determine routes and find what little food or supplies were available. Now Cildar had finally recovered enough from his ordeal that he wished to converse.

“Myris, I need to ask you something.”

The Cainite gave a nod, but no verbal response.

“When we were fighting in the northlands, you put forth a great amount of your energy into saving the lives of bystanders. Why?”

The man shuffled uneasily. This was not the direction he had hoped their conversation would turn. “Is it somehow not sufficient that I wanted to save lives? After all, I am one of the 'good guys', am I not?"

Cildar gave a weak smirk, his face unadorned by his usual blue mask. "I know you better than that. You're certainly a noble warrior, but you don't concern yourself with casualties. You've always believed that a quicker victory is the path to fewest deaths. In this conflict between us, I dare say that certainly proved to be the case."

Myris twitched for a moment, trying to avoid giving an answer. His companion said nothing more, however, so he felt forced to offer response. "I knew it would haunt you. I saved those people because I thought it was what you would have asked me to do. There was something Lord Abaddon said when we first fought you. He said, 'If Cildar could ask it of me, I believe he would beg me, plead me, to prevent that from happening. I will kill you to protect the name of Emle.' I could not agree with his decision to murder you, but I understood his heart on the matter. I shared his concern for your interests."

"Thank you," Cildar offered quietly. "You're both truer allies than even I imagined."

"I am just pleased you are yourself again, my friend."

The paladin shuffled uncomfortably for a moment, then leaned forward. "Actually Myris, I think we need to talk about that."

The man tilted his cowled head, one of the flames covering his eyes shrinking down as if to resemble an intrigued squint. "Are you not well? Are there lingering effects we need to deal with?"

"It's not quite that. It's hard to explain, especially to you. But... the Dark Paladin. I get the sense that you imagine he was some foreign persona, some sort of bewitchment done by Akatriel. Throughout the time we faced each other, I kept insisting that I was myself, just given an enhanced perspective. Now that it's over, I need you to understand that I was telling the truth. It *was* me. I made those decisions, of my right mind."

"I do not believe that, Cildar. You are different now. I hear it in the very tone of your voice; in the kindness, in the remorse."

"You're right, in part. There are differences. I've lost the piece of my mind that could see through the centuries, both behind me and before me. I am no longer a dragon. I feel smaller, less significant. I'm nothing but a man now. And yet, the actions that I took, they were still mine. When I was removed from humanity, I no longer cared about it. And the scary part is, to some degree I still don't. I can't just come back from what I beheld, what I knew about the scale of time and our world. Our lives, our actions, they feel so much less significant than before."

"I understand. It may take you some time to fully recover from your ordeal. But you will. Soon you will be yourself again."

"I don't think you do understand. Or perhaps you're choosing not to hear what I'm trying to say."

"Perhaps I am." Again they drifted into silence for a time. Soon a thought occurred to Myris, and he began to press. "What are you really trying to tell me? What worries you so?"

"As you said, I'm back to myself, in a sense. The spirit of a dragon is gone from me. I feel like me again, because I don't have that wisdom, that longevity, that fortitude. It's made me realize that who I am, the Scion of Emle—it's born of weakness. What if everything about us is born of that weakness? What if that's all that we are?"

The Cainite dwelt on this a moment. He immediately recognized how it reflected his own crisis of confidence during their time on Arkalen. The two warriors were both such strong men, yet both so consumed with uncertainty. It was this reflected dynamic that had drawn Myris to Cildar in the first place, all those years ago on the hillsides of Vantrisk. Now, hearing his own misgivings echoed from his closest ally, he could not help but think to himself how silly they sounded. As he answered the man's question, he also answered his own.

"It is, Cildar. For that is the human condition. We are born, we are brief, we are weak. We learn this at a young age, and we bear it our entire life. We can die in any moment, doing any activity, risky or common. And even if we survive those odds, we get to witness but a century of life in a civilization that rolls on for thousands of years without us. We are made from weakness, Cildar. And yet, we never let it define us. We rise above it and we learn to recognize greatness in others, and remember them so that they will remember us. That is what it means to be human."

The blond man stared at his friend for several seconds, and the corner of his mouth twitched as a slight smirk threatened to overtake his weary features. "You sound like a paladin."

"I knew one, once."

"You know, even knowing our weakness in the grand scheme, or perhaps because of knowing it, I cannot escape one thought. We wield so much might, Myris. You and I could hold the lives of others in the palms of our hands and play with them. I've tasted what it's like to rule by the strength of your arm alone. For a time, I was lord of an entire village. What's to stop me from doing it again?"

Though the man's words sounded like ambition, his tone was one of despair. Myris was not deaf to this. His friend was not suggesting that he wanted to turn to ambition and corruption, he was mourning that he did not know if he had the integrity to prevent himself from it.

"Because," he replied with a subdued tone, "Lord Abaddon is still a dragon."

For the first time in what felt like ages, Cildar gave a warm smile. "I suppose he is." He rose to his feet, new energy in his movements as he put out the fire. A few ashes and embers drifted into his hair, and he was forced to quickly brush them out. "We should get moving again. Already I miss my helmet."

"It is a shame your ancestral armor was ruined and lost," Myris offered. "I suppose I owe your family an apologize."

"Don't stress it," Cildar said with a shrug as they began to march from the campsite. "I hadn't mentioned it before, but that wasn't my family's armor."

"What?" Myris responded in a startled tone. "But it was, I would know it anywhere."

"The past few years, I had been working on a replica. The Emle armor is virtually impenetrable, as you know. But after that lich destroyed my original helmet in the Second Arocaen, I began to grow concerned I was pushing it past its limits. I'd privately been working on making another set of the armor, meant to be as durable as the first. When we left for Arkalen, I didn't feel it was appropriate to risk the original set so far from home, so I brought my best mock set. The durability of the helmet was promising, but it seems I can't match the invincibility of the breastplate."

Myris thought a moment before responding, "If you had brought the original, I might not have been able to defeat the Dark Paladin."

Cildar laughed, answering, "Fortunate for us both, I suppose. My faulty replica aided you in victory *and* preserved the original suit." He gave a sigh, unsure if his humor was appropriate, then changed the subject. "We must find Lord Abaddon. But I don't even know how to begin. I'm under the impression that the Wisdoms are on this half of the continent now. But for all we know Abaddon may have already fallen, or could be battling elsewhere. We aren't even certain he crossed the mountains."

"We have done everything within our power. We must leave it in the hands of the gods to help us."

The taller man tilted his head at this. "We serve different gods. Which one do we look to for help?"

This time it was Myris who laughed. "Whichever will offer it."

Cildar joined his laugh for a few seconds, and they continued on their way slowly. They did not hasten to make progress, knowing they could be heading in the opposite direction of their goals.

* * * * *

Within the eastern stretch of the Blukar Forest, which ran between the Ashelon River and Great Desert of Coroku, Melukah came to a halt on his voyage to the north. A presence was approaching him, but he could not identify it. The energy seemed familiar, yet muddled. He sent a signal out for Keldana, and in only a minute she stood at his side.

"What comes, Keldana? Have you seen it?" he demanded, his words fast.

"I have not. But I know that of which you speak. Shall I send the mist?"

"Do so, and hasten. It will reach us soon."

A few minutes passed as the Wisdom of Ocean sent forth a small cloud bound to her will. Several bits of mist returned to her every few seconds reporting on various areas, all of them empty. Finally she received useful information.

"It is Torlen," she announced. "He is not well."

"Why does Torlen approach? Dosiros fell to Aegagropilion. Torlen should have been there at his side. Come, we must question him."

It was not long before the three Wisdoms had rendezvoused. Torlen fell immediately to his hands and feet, expecting the onslaught of Melukah's anger.

"Why did you abandon your commander?" the Sun demanded. "You were to serve at his side. Your failure to do so has lost us one of our fiercest combatants to fuel Aegagropilion's expanding might. I know you had your complaints with Dosiros, but this is unacceptable. Your behavior may have compromised our entire mission. Before all is finished, you may have sacrificed Elysium itself."

"Forgive me, Exalted Melukah. Dosiros demanded that I pursue Schpariel while he tended to Aegagropilion. You yourself commanded that I obey his every word. I did not fear to defy him, but I dared not defy you."

Melukah's temper seemed cooled by this news. "So it was Dosiros' own impetuousness that cost him his life. There is no surprise in this. He was ever foolish enough to place his own ideas of fun and sport above the mission itself." The Supreme Wisdom looked over Torlen, taking note of his condition. "Yet you seem to have been badly beaten yourself. As the assassin of the Wisdoms, I would not have expected you to be belabored so. Did Schpariel do this to you?"

Torlen hung his head lower before answering, "No, my lord. It was a human."

"Human? From where does one of theirs draw such potential?"

"He's wielding the Arda, Exalted Melukah. But also he seems to have become stronger after I banished him to Elysium. He returned, and now uses our own nature to enhance his might."

"You banished him to Elysium? Under what orders?"

"No orders, sire, but merely a request from the Muses. I had time while Dosiros and I awaited the Godbeasts, so I humored them. I didn't suspect such unfortunate consequences would come from it."

The Sun shook his head. "There are too many events in play right now," he pondered. "This situation is becoming difficult to control. How I despise the chaos in these lesser planes. Keldana, heal Torlen and restore his body. Torlen, where are the Godbeasts now?"

"Aegagropilion was in the north, near the mountains, last I knew of him. Schpariel is the problem. He was several miles east of here, heading south rapidly and had already at least crossed the great river when I lost pursuit due to the human's interference."

Melukah turned suddenly, looking back to the direction from which he and Keldana had just come. "Curse all! Just when we abandon our watch over Gilanirus, the Godbeasts make their final move. It's as if a higher intellect aids them."

Torlen raised from his prostrate position and seated himself upon his knees. "I would be remiss if I didn't add, the human I battled mentioned the name of Akatriel. He asked if we were in league with him."

Melukah raised a finger to his chin. "If Akatriel has taken sides against us, circumstances are more dire than the Muses led us to believe. I fear we should have acted with greater ardor since our arrival." He paused in thought as Keldana rebuilt Torlen's body. Waves of glowing water flowed into the Wisdom of Sound and regenerated his strength, while thick plates of ice snapped over his face and shattered limbs, transforming back into the perfected segments of his frame. Once his mask was restored the overload of his magics ceased, and he was able to grow briefly dormant while finishing his rejuvenation.

The Wisdom of the Sun announced his decision. "It is now likely we cannot reach Schpariel before he arrives at Gilanirus. It's best that we cut a course straight for the ravine, and hope to catch the Final Godbeast as he is awakened. Only then shall we have an opportunity to cut him down before he gains strength."

The Elysians remained stationary while Keldana continued her work. From the shadows, they were watched by a pair of hidden eyes. Deun Coloran marveled at the foreign deities and listened closely to their words. He had learned enough from them to understand the nature of their war. Wisdoms; Godbeasts; a human with the strength to defeat them; he wondered much about these events happening so close to his own hunt. But he was interested only in one thing; only in the Overlord. He broke off from his hiding spot and headed due east, not allowing himself to become distracted by these Wisdoms.

His decision was a foolhardy one. Even now Zekraul was approaching the Wisdoms from the northeast, unknowingly moving to cut them off on their eventual route. Still Melukah of the Sun kept his gaze focused south, only concerned with his obsession on Gilanirus, unaware of the other forces conspiring against him in the wilderness.

# Chapter 34.

## The Spectre of Gehenna

Deun had traveled swiftly along his route into the east. The forested areas had grown sparse, the climate arid. He began to have lingering suspicions as to his direction. The farther he roamed, the louder his instincts cried that he was going the wrong way.

These same instincts were also warning him that he was about to have company, but he could not get a handle on that feeling. His thoughts kept pouring over the words of the silver priest who had told him to trust his instincts, that they were his gift of superiority. Even after all this time the man's words haunted him, a phantasm he could not banish from his thoughts. The promises of such power, the idea that he might be capable of being more than a normal man, was succulent temptation.

As he came to the edge of a particularly long stretch of desert plain—which allowed him to see many miles into the lands he was entering and confirm there was indeed nothing there—he understood his feelings. The reason his mind remained focused on the priest was related to his forebodings of a visitor.

"You're already here, aren't you?" the traveler suddenly spoke aloud.

The response came without delay. "You're coming along nicely, Deun Coloran."

The man turned and looked behind him. He could see nothing. No visitor, no speaker. He concentrated on changing his sight, and with effort managed to make out the illusory outline of a robed figure. "Unveil yourself, sorcerer," he demanded in the direction of the shroud.

With a wave of his hand, Akatriel discarded the haze of refracting shadows hiding him from view. He swept back his hood and gave a smile. "Only by knowing of your own abilities, already they have expanded. I did not mistake your capacity."

The mystic stared evenly for a moment, his expression revealing no emotions or intent. Finally he asked, "What have you brought with you?"

"Very impressive," the visitor answered, the pale smile broadening. "Yes, I come bearing a gift. Along with a word of guidance, since you won't heed your own foresight. You're presently retreating from the Overlord's path. He follows the Wisdoms, hunting them as you hunt him."

The man's eyes widened. "The Wisdoms," he whispered to himself. "That's why my instincts led me to track them. I thought I was confusing sources of dangerous threat."

Akatriel continued without regarding this comment. "It's time at last for you to go back and face the Overlord. He has gained strength and grown bold, so he no longer hides as he once did, but rather travels brazenly in the open. As he has gained strength, so too must you if you are to stand against him."

The priest reached behind his back and, from a second magical shielding wall, pulled forth a sword larger than any Deun had ever seen. The steel of the blade was so flawless and brilliant in the sunlight that he would have sworn it had been carved from silver. The most peculiar feature, he found, was the loose and tattered bandages decorating the hilt.

Akatriel stabbed the blade into the ground at his feet. Even with the tip implanted, the hilt of the sword reached nearly to the top of Deun's head. "I give you this," the silver-tongued wanderer announced. "A weapon to leverage against your foe. This sword has the power to kill."

Deun turned to one side and began to walk away, snapping back, "All swords hold that power."

Akatriel slid quickly, disappearing from where he stood with a flicker of smoke and then appearing in front of the man's face.

"Not like this one. Take the sword, Coloran. Place your hand on its hilt, and you will understand the things I cannot easily explain to you. Your sight will show you Kargaroth."

Deciding to humor the stranger's unavoidable insistence, Deun stepped to the sword and swiftly snapped his left hand over the hilt. Instantly he fell back several steps with a gasp, holding up his palm and watching a thin black smoke pour off of it from contact with the Unholy Blade.

"It's—it's horrible," he muttered as he felt the flood of images still washing through his mind, a torrent of death and evil he could not turn off.

"Relax," Akatriel soothed. "You're only seeing the memories of what the sword once was. It's dormant now, its latent powers gone. It only serves its master, which makes it useless to the rest of the world."

"Except to me. At least, that's what you believe."

"You're such a quick study. Yes, your instincts and mysticism discern you from others. You have the substantive capability to adapt. You can, in time, adapt to Kargaroth and tie her to your will, as no other man can anymore."

Deun stared at his left hand for a moment longer, then tentatively reached out with his right and again seized the sword by the hilt. There was no flood of imagery this time, no heat of death repulsing his palm. There was only the cool invitation of steel sinking slowly into his skin.

"What's the price for this blade?"

There was a moment of silence, and Akatriel began to walk around Deun slowly. "What price would you pay to see the Overlord slain and his body broken at your feet?"

"*If* I thought it were necessary, I would pay any price. My life has no value other than the pursuit of the Overlord. It's all I live for."

"Then let's make this deal. I will aid you in all ways necessary to your victory and within my ability. When the Overlord is fallen, then you will do one errand for me, whatever I ask."

“I shall only abide by this if the tools you provide prove necessary to my victory. If I believe I could have won without them, I’ll have no need to repay you.”

Akatriel stopped his pacing and raised an eyebrow. “That’s acceptable.”

Deun gave a heave, and with much effort lifted the sword and turned its point toward the sky. The weight of the blade was daunting, and after only a few seconds he was forced to brace the hilt with a tight grip from both hands.

“Without its powers, this sword is too heavy to be of any use,” he observed. “No man could fight effectively with a slab of steel this large.”

He turned to see Akatriel give his response, but the cloaked figure had vanished. No matter how hard he tried Deun could not again locate his presence. In spite of this, he heard the priest’s response echo from the air around him. “I told you, the sword only serves its master. Surely you can learn to adapt to it before your upcoming battle.” The armored figure shook off his annoyance at his strange benefactor’s behavior, then turned his feet to the west.

* * * * *

Deep beneath a crust of stone-faced cliffs, through a series of unnatural winding tunnels that led miles, a small flame drifted through a narrow cavern. The corridor was so dark, so cold, that the heat and light from the flame seemed stifled, allowed to only expand a few short feet before being choked away. The darkness did not welcome the light, and the frigid air did not welcome the taste of fire.

The torchbearer was not a lone visitor. Behind him hid another intruder, one more welcome, more embraced by this sinister atmosphere. It wrapped about him, flowed through his being, drank in his shade. Pitch-black robes engulfed and shrouded him within the darkness, as his intense silver eyes fixated on the torch ahead.

Soon the leading figure stepped from the narrow cavern into an open chamber. The presence of running water could be heard, but not seen. His trailing shadow froze before entering the spacious enclosure, content to linger back within the comforting cold. As the torch moved deeper into the room, its light began to expand. The weak orange flame grew to a blaring red blaze, painting a picture of the surrounding tomb.

The center of the room was a solid steel dais, huge in size, with a mix of wooden and stone thoroughfares branching across to the far ends of the chamber. In the center of the uplifted scaffolding, a coarse statue of a giant samurai stood. It had six mighty arms, each one holding the decayed remains of an ancient steel weapon.

The figure holding the torch stepped forward to the foot of the statue and fell to his knees, his arms spread high and wide. "Gilanirus! The one true Godbeast! Your servant Schpariel is here. I come to awaken and serve you."

There was no response from the stone. Schpariel rose and pointed his torch at the ceiling. The flame detached itself from the Moon Rod he held, and the spiritual fire rose slowly to the top of the vaulted chamber. From there, it spread and carved lines of cryptic runes along the edges of the room, filling it with a bright warm glow.

After a brief rest, Schpariel again held the rod in his hand high. Red electricity shot from various points in the chamber to his body, flowing upward into his hand. The small rod began to transform, extending into a wondrous staff with a two-inch diameter. The subtle sapphire once adorning it changed into a huge narrow sickle, given a bright sheen by the crimson lightning flowing from the chamber's walls.

"I have come to feed you life. The life of Gehenna, as channeled by this Scepter of the Dark Moon. Taste, and exist!"

He stepped forward and thrust the staff out high, pinning the sickle deep into the statue's chest. Immediately the cavern began to tremble. A dull roar, like the moaning of stricken beast, swallowed all other sounds. The runes surrounding the chamber grew ever brighter and began to flicker in unison. Then the grey flesh of the statue started to bleed into red, mimicking their patterns. With one final flash, the stone monument disappeared and all light in the chamber fell dim.

Schpariel removed his Rod—which had reverted to its compact state—and backed away into the chamber, dropping again to his knees. In the midst of the darkness, a much blacker shadow could be sensed. It moved slowly, coiling itself into a compact ball, harboring itself against the cold. Two parallel vertical slits of white light carved into a random section of the specter and stared forth hungrily.

"Schpariel."

"Yes, Lord."

There was a moment of silence as the slits redirected, their gaze crawling over the rest of the chamber. "I shall need a body to house my consciousness. Craft me one."

"Forgive me Gilanirus, my Moon Rod is depleted after resurrecting you. If I expend any more energy from it, I run the risk of burning it out."

The two slits refocused on Schpariel and narrowed, turning a tint of red. "Craft me a new body, lest I scrape out your mind and claim your flesh as my own."

The servant shook his head, but raised the Moon Rod high. Once again the small bar became a marvelous staff, and the dying fires surrounding the chamber flared weakly in response. The Dark Wisdom pointed the scepter to the center of the room, near Gilanirus' shadow, and hundreds of rocks suddenly exploded from the flaming walls and began to congregate together. They formed a crude statue resembling a humanoid shape, then waves of rock and fire continued to slam into them, refining this shape.

When the work was complete, Schpariel's staff gave a shudder of protest, then crumbled into smoke and drifted away. The Godbeast sighed in irritation, but knew it could not have been avoided. As he mourned his loss, the shadow of Gilanirus slunk across the room into the stone golem.

As the shadow poured itself into the crude mold, a rush of yellow and blue currents began to slide along the structure, hollowing it and changing its integrity. This process did not take long. Soon an elaborate suit of steely armors began to rise from the stone, as the waves of divine will shined and tempered it. The body took the form of thick red and white plates resembling those of an ancient samurai, and stood nearly twenty feet in height. When its transformation was complete, the two identifying slits of white light scratched themselves into the faceless mask of the helmet.

Gilanirus stretched his newly formed arms out to his sides and gave a roar. The walls of the cavern shook in response. He turned his eyes to the floor at his feet, and a shock of willpower turned the rock there into a pool of magma. An intense fire burst from the pool, igniting the room and fully revealing the true splendor of the Final Godbeast's new form.

He looked over his body in the fresh light, then muttered, "Only two arms? You know I prefer to have many hands, Schpariel, to better serve my glory."

"The Moon Rod is depleted," the Dark Wisdom repeated. "We can count ourselves lucky I had enough power to resurrect you and carve any sort of body at all."

Gilanirus gave a begrudging nod. "So be it. Have you not recovered the gift that Barricus gave you?"

"It remains lost to me. I've spent much time seeking to resurrect you and Aegagropilion. I've had time for no further endeavors."

"Pah. No Rod and no Band. You are useless to me on this plane, Schpariel." The lifeless helmet lifted and rotated, and the vacant eyes turned to the north. "And Aegagropilion is dead, it seems. His soul awaits me in Gehenna."

"I feared such might be the case. When we parted he was battling Dosiros, the Flame."

Suddenly Gilanirus' blank face turned to the corridor from which Schpariel had emerged. "Why do you bring another with you?"

Schpariel turned slowly. "I brought no one with me."

Gilanirus thrust his fist into the magma pool and slowly withdrew it, crafting a long slim blade from the molten rock with his mind as he did so. When the blade was formed and cooling in the cavern air, fresh waves of electricity poured over it and began to stretch and sharpen it. Soon the weapon was complete; the molten rock had been transformed into a massive steel butcher knife, well over six feet long and two feet thick. A slim steel handle was attached at its base, held firmly in Gilanirus' hand.

"Then we have an interloper. I will allow him to taste the edge of Gehenna."

In the wake of his discovery, the hidden figure emerged swiftly into the chamber and the light of the fire. As he did, his black robes gradually shifted, shortly assuming a bright white color instead. He brushed back his hood and offered a bow wordlessly. Gilanirus still prepared to strike, but Schpariel recognized the silver-eyed conspirator.

"Wait, Lord! I know this creature. He has been of aid to us. He guided me to Aegagropilion and yourself in turn, that I might resurrect you."

Gilanirus dropped his offensive stance a took a step back, but said nothing.

"You've done well, Schpariel," the wisp of a man spoke in a docile tone. "Three Wisdoms are now fallen. Wind, Stone, and Flame have faltered. Only the Sound, Ocean, and Sun remain, with but one Staff of the Sun between them."

"So Aegagropilion killed Dosiros as well?" the Dark Wisdom asked.

The man gave a nod. "Something like that. But as things stand, you're in no condition to fight, are you? The Rod of the Moon is drained, and Gilanirus is only freshly reborn. God of Gehenna he may be, but his majestic might grows with time, correct? As it stands, he's no match for the fury of Melukah with a Sun Staff."

Schpariel paused for a moment of thought. "We could even the score, if the Moon Rod was at its full potential." He turned to his lord and dropped to his knees. "Eternal Samurai, open the Gate to

Gehenna. Allow me to travel there. In the swirling eddies of our ether, I can revitalize the Moon Rod. My strength will be more fearsome than it has been in centuries. I will be an ally worthy to fight at your side!"

The burning white slits did not unlock from the small human form. "I do not open the Gate lightly. It's our duty to protect Gehenna from roving outsiders."

"Consider, Lord," Schpariel countered, "there are not creatures of threat in Morolia. And the Wisdoms could cross into Gehenna if they wanted regardless. We have nothing to lose, but formidable power to gain!"

The pale figure stepped close to Schpariel. "What is this 'Gate of Gehenna'? I've never heard of such."

"It's a weak point in the Veil between this plane and ours," the lesser Godbeast answered. "It's not truly a Gate, but long ago Gilanirus pierced it with his own mind, widening the rift and allowing us to pass through. It's how we first came here. Ever since that time, my lord has retained the ability to open or close the Gate when he deems fit, from any distance."

As this explanation finished, Gilanirus' eyes flickered and then changed to a deep shade of red. The air around him shuddered, and a reverberating hum of sonic waves could be felt throughout the room. This disturbance shortly ended, and all returned to calm. "The Gate is open," he announced. "Go to it, if you must. But you go alone."

"But Lord—"

"I do not wish to hear any more of your whinging. I granted you one wish. That's all I shall abide this century. I head for Melukah. Catch up when you are no longer useless."

As they conversed, their neglected visitor scratched his chin and silently mused, *A rift in the Veil directed at Gehenna? This may be handy information in the future.*

Schpariel gave a despondent bow to his master and began to leave. The pale stranger interjected himself into the conversation once more, speaking directly to Gilanirus for the first time. The departing Godbeast paused to listen. "Spectre of Gehenna, I have a place where you can gain much power in a short period of time. If you'll follow me there, you may make it your refuge and feed. Melukah will already be aware of your rebirth. He'll be coming for you, just as much as you are coming for him. I can make certain you're strong enough to face him when that time comes."

Before acknowledging this offer, Gilanirus ordered his subordinate, "Go to the Gate. If time is little, don't waste it." Schpariel quickly resumed his exodus and soon was gone beyond sight. The remaining Godbeast leaned down and brought his face close to the tiny man. "Akatriel," he stated with emphasis.

If the pale figure could have paled further, he would have. He began to walk back rapidly as if stricken.

Gilanirus continued, "Did you not think I would recognize my old foes? Did you think yourself so much more clever than I? You're that insignificant silver dragon who dared to wage war against us last we fought the Wisdoms. You stood by the side of the celestials of Elysium. Now you've changed form, seduced my Godbeasts in their ignorance, led them about this continent like your puppets. Such trickery does not work on me. Make the case for your life well, for I am about to end it."

"Understand me, Tyrant Gilanirus," Akatriel answered, speaking rapidly. "I am the one you think, the Silver One from your last epic war, the champion of the Asterian plane against the Gehennite invasion. See through my eyes but for a moment. After the war was over, I was gravely injured, struck down by your kind. For over two thousand years I rotted here on the Morolian plane, comatose, my body doing its best to recover from a wound that should have killed me but did not. When I awoke, I was robbed of grace and power. My soul had rotted here, atrophied. I'm no longer the splendid creature I once was. My brothers in Asteria did nothing to save me, nothing to restore me to my lost glory! And so I will undo what they once made me do. I stood alongside the Wisdoms before, I lost everything for it. Now I'm balancing the equation. I stand to give the Godbeasts life again, to resume the war. I'm here to show those who abandoned me that I'm not so weak that I can be discarded in dishonor!"

The towering Godbeast continued to stare, the oversized cleaver in his right hand swaying back and forth lightly as he seemed to debate a strike. Akatriel held his breath, his white skin flushing a rare shade of red as his blood pressure elevated. At last Gilanirus rendered his verdict.

"If you seek revenge against the Wisdoms, I shall allow your revenge to occur. But know with whom you deal, Akatriel. Turn on me, and I'll show you what causes even Melukah to fear me."

The former dragon released his held breath with an exhausted rush and bowed his head. "I don't need to be shown, Spectre of Gehenna. I remember your ferocity from centuries past. Even when you were weakened and crippled by Melukah's light, you were more than a match for me at my most glorious."

"You claim you have a place for me to feed. You would suggest to know much about my nature."

The conspirator straightened his back, his calm demeanor returned in the form of a narrow smile. "I studied the Godbeasts once long ago, so that I might better know how to defeat you. Now I would use that same knowledge to aid you." He gave a flutter with his hands, and a vast array of silver lighting crawled into the air between the two, revealing a complex map of Arkalen. A small speck of red gradually congealed at one point, then the entire design flickered out. "Will you remember that?" Gilanirus nodded, as he took the giant cleaver held in his hand and laid it across his back. Instantly the armors there shifted to form to large griffin talons, which seized the sword and held it tightly in place. Akatriel continued, "I will proceed ahead and make certain the Wisdoms don't cut off your path. I'll meet you there within a week. Is it an accord?"

With no further words, the Godbeast began to walk. He stepped directly over the smaller figure and made his way out through the caves. Since his large form did not fit through the narrow opening, waves of divine power emanated from his mind and destroyed the stone hindrances threatening to slow him. Akatriel watched the deity leave with a mix of fear, rage, exhaustion... but most of all, joy.

* * * * *

"Master Orista, there's a great army here! It's unlike any I have ever seen!"

Gaius was clearly concerned, his face flushed and his composure lost. Kelve knew the monk was overly bold and not taken to easy panic. If something had spooked him, it was certainly something that could be a threat.

He exited his tent gingerly and then looked back to Gaius, awaiting further guidance. The young man pointed toward the Forest of Techenar, where Tenkahn and Boderon stood alone, staring to the west motionlessly. Kelve did his best to hobble his way across the hilltop with haste. Soon he caught up with his co-chieftains and stared out at an impressive sight.

It was a view that made him more sick to his stomach than any other, though Gaius had exaggerated their numbers. It was no army, but it was a sizable battalion, no less than a thousand able warriors. They were arranged in perfect file, each holding intimidating weapons, all of them clearly well trained and of dire mind. They stood silently, seeming to await the order for a charge. Kelve knew the charge would not come. This show of arms was only to intimidate. It was typical of the Devilslayers.

He looked over the ranks of strange, unbalanced uniforms and a flood of memories overwhelmed him. Once he had been proud of his people. Now, seeing them stand before him like this, he saw them for only what they had become—a militia of tyranny. The strong arm of a self-appointment government that did not belong in a land of free peoples.

One among the slayers stepped forward to address the small group of commanders. It was a woman in full Devilslayer attire, holding a large staff of solid steel in her right hand. She was nearly atop him before Kelve recognized her.

"Detria!" he shouted without being able to stop himself. He wanted to rush forward and give his old friend a hug, but the outburst alone had robbed him of his breath. He forced himself to remain calm and fend off a wave of dizziness.

"Kelve," she said without emotion on her face, "I'm glad to see you live. You've done well here to have held out for this long. But Yasiff and I have brought the Devilslayers to finish this once and for all. The Overlord falls this day."

At the mention of his name, Yasiff sauntered up behind Detria and delivered a broad smile. There was disdain hidden in that smile. In contrast, the disdain on Kelve's face was not hidden, but rather accented with a scowl of rage.

"You don't look well, former Wolf," the High Chieftain spoke. "This war has been hard on you."

"Sometimes wars are like that," he muttered in response. "We didn't seek nor ask for your help. Take your men and go home."

Tenkahn placed a hand on his shoulder. "Is that wise, Master Orista? Perhaps we should accept their assistance. After all, they share our cause."

He shook his head. "It only seems that way for now. Yasiff has only one cause, which is to rule all within his reach. I made my mind up long ago, and he will not rule me. I won't sell my soul to one devil in order to kill another. Even if I die today, my troops will not again march under Devilslayer orders."

Detria narrowed her eyes at her old friend and rebuked him. "Then it's a good thing the soldiers here are not your troops. They're *my* troops, and march at my command, under whatever orders I give them. You're only a lieutenant, Orista."

Kelve stammered for a few seconds, seeking feebly for the strength to argue with her. But his heart was crushed, and his body matched, so he merely hung his head in a weak attempt at a bow. "As you command, milady. I'll go and spread the word of your return."

He turned and walked away slowly, leaning heavily on a crutch he had recently taken to. Boderon gave Detria a murderous glare for a moment, then turned and followed Kelve, offering his arm to support the demoted commander. Gaius watched them, but did not follow.

Tenkahn kept his gaze focused intently on Detria, however, and she did not fail to notice. "What do you stare at, monk?"

"I am uncertain," Tenkahn responded with a kind tone. "I thought, for a moment, I spotted someone else in your face or voice." He paused, then added, "Where is Master Abaddon?"

Detria turned her head and looked over her shoulder, back towards the west. "I don't know. It's been many months since Abaddon and I parted paths. I cannot tell if he's alive or dead."

"If the odds he faces can be survived, rest assured, he is the one who will survive them. His absence is a shame, though. With the strength of his arm, we could certainly have overturned the Overlord's remaining forces in very little time."

Yasiff stepped forward at this point, shouldering his way in front of Detria to assert his own authority. "I don't know who this man you speak of is, but rest assured, the Overlord will fall swiftly before the might of my men. This war is already over. Ending it is now merely a formality."

"Your soldiers are that good, are they?" the monk queried with a strange lilt to his voice.

"Never before has an entire thousand Noble Pride slayers been leveraged against one such meager foe. Here I've done this to prove that our might is not to be questioned by the lowly demons of this continent."

"Then perhaps you would like to carry out a charge tonight," Tenkahn recommended. "Our forces are very weary, and could desperately use an opportunity to rest. Your warriors seem mostly fresh, aside from their journey. But surely a triviality like that is not enough to wear them down."

Yasiff ruffled his chest and shoulders in an insulted manner. "Of course not! Come Detria, we attack now, immediately!"

"Detria should remain for now," Tenkahn interrupted, "in order to reassociate with her own troops. They have long mourned her loss and awaited her return."

The Devilslayer chieftain gave a loud puff to signify his indifference, then waved to his troops and began a march down the hill. With the sounds of synchronized marching drowning out the volume of his voice, the elder monk whispered to Gaius, "Go with them. Do not put yourself in unnecessary risk, and stay away from the minotaur, but secure their retreat when the time comes. Try to prevent the death of more than necessary, but do not lose your own life at any cost. Do you understand my instructions?"

"I understand what you're doing," his apprentice answered with a nod. "Don't worry, I'll see that it's done." He took his leave after the marching battalion, and in a few more moments only Detria and Tenkahn stood at the fringe of the forest.

"What *have* you done?" she asked of him.

"Master Yasiff's arrogance can serve us no aid," he replied. "He believes he can wrap this up quickly with a pretty bow, but the reality is much harsher. He will not listen to our counsel or accept our cooperation as long as his ego sits so high. By nightfall, his arrogance will have been erased."

"This is over a thousand men and women capable of fighting at nearly the same levels as myself or Kelve. You really think they're going to lose?"

Tenkahn's expression turned grave. "There is no 'think'. Once they draw Shote, the ground will dye red from their spilt blood."

"Who is Shote?"

"I suppose it has been long, and you do not remember the tale. Would you rather see for yourself?" he asked of her. She nodded in response. "Then come, witness the battle from our hilltop."

* * * * *

Dashing across uneven terrain, Abaddon Daemon moved at inhuman speeds in his hunt for Schpariel. Nets of his consciousness were cast for hundreds of miles in every direction, an advantage granted to him by the ethereal battery he had stolen from Elysium. The entire continent rested under his watchful eye. As the surviving Wisdoms rejoined into a single unit and began to move, he saw it. As Schpariel disappeared into a cave at the bottom of the Lifeless Ravine of Arkalen, followed by a cloaked stranger, he saw it. As the Devilslayers charged to do war with Shote, he saw it.

Suddenly he came to a stop. His heart lurched, with excitement or shock he was at first unsure. A new power had arisen. A sort of creature he had never before encountered now breathed life on Arkalen. It was not like the Wisdoms. Its power was far more condensed, a burning light on the ether currents that could not be ignored. Nor was it like the Godbeasts. They were no more than exalted demons, given vast strength by some blessing long since forgotten.

This was a god. Abaddon Daemon knew all too well this presence. He had witnessed it, nay, he had experienced it. This was the spiritual force of an entity so mighty that entire civilizations could pass before its eye, and it would not acknowledge them with so much as a blink of recognition.

He remembered the warnings of the Muses as he had taken his leave of Elysium. "Gilanirus is unique among Godbeasts," they had cautioned, "try to understand that. When Gehenna was first created by Elzaniru, it was an empty, lifeless plane. Only Elzaniru's own shadow lived there. Over the centuries, that shadow evolved and seized intelligent life of its own. That shadow, that power, is Gilanirus. All other denizens of Gehenna, including Schpariel and Aegagropilion themselves, Gilanirus forged with his own mind. Schpariel and Aegagropilion are insignificant, as they are only the mightiest of all hellspawn. There is only one true Godbeast. There is only Gilanirus."

Abaddon felt a tingling sensation in his fingertips as he felt the gravity of that presence. There was a rush of blood to his face as he flushed with excitement and bloodlust. His eyes were wide, and his mouth agape, as he uttered quietly, "Gilanirus."

Then he dropped to a crouch, and again exploded away with

anomalous speed. He would heed no warnings. He would suffer no cautions. This was the opponent he had awaited his entire life, the battle that could finally give him his ultimate end, his worthy death. All other goals were purged from thought as he prepared himself for what was coming, prepared himself one final time to reveal his full might to this world.

The Knight of Hell would face the Samurai of Gehenna.

## Chapter 35.

## Death of a General

In the final rays of sunset, Shote stood at the doors to the keep looking over the casualties of the latest fight. Nearly one hundred demons had been killed, far more deaths than any encounter since he had taken over. For the first time, he was beginning to feel a pang of mercy for Tessena's plight. Truly these invaders were a nuisance.

He had summoned the human girl down from her chambers, where he had been forcing her to remain and watch the battles he led without participating. He then ordered her to oversee the humans cleaning up the courtyard's mess. Tessena's spirit was broken, and she humbly did as asked. Shote knew she expected her death at any moment. He had considered it, but ultimately judged that she could still be of use. The minotaur was incapable of linking to the blessed gauntlet the woman wielded, which had demonstrated the ability to put the Monks of Tria in check. Sooner or later he would have to confront the monks, and there could be wisdom in using Tessena to hold one at bay. Mighty though he was, Shote did not wish to risk his health unnecessarily. He had paid the price to the Order of Tria once before.

Beyond strategy considerations, eventually the Overlord would return. He would not be pleased to discover one of his own had murdered those he had appointed as generals. Already Shote would have to seek forgiveness for the human experiment gifted with the remarkable arms, as well as the fallen chimera ambassador. Killing the First General might prove one sin too many, even for the Overlord's chosen son.

He had finally discarded the long pike carrying Ontarshiss'

severed head. It had rotted and developed a considerable stench, and even Shote's nostrils were not immune to the fetid decay. The gesture had served its purpose, at any rate. The chimeras, most headstrong of the Overlord's troops, now marched at his order without hesitance. He found them an invaluable infantry, able to pick off soldiers from either ground or sky with relative ease.

Their advantages had been scant help in this latest skirmish. A thousand humans had rushed the fortress, wearing clothing and brandishing colors both unfamiliar to him. Shote had welcomed the entertainment at first, but after a mere fifteen minutes it had become clear that his troops were suffering under this new burden. He did not allow things to proceed beyond that point, stepping into the fray himself wielding a greataxe in each hand. In a matter of minutes he had dismembered a full hundred of the human soldiers, and their retreat was a swift and terrified one.

The indomitable minotaur always enjoyed the look of fear in men's eyes at his rampages, but he could not quell a nagging sensation that had overtaken him since this exchange. In response to such a vicious counterattack, the legendary beast should have been confronted by one of the monks, or perhaps a platoon of spearmen futilely determined to hold him back. Instead these humans had seemed wholly unprepared for his strike, and lacked any of the elite units previously displayed.

Something was amiss, he was confident in that. In order to progress the war in a controlled manner, he needed to know the state of the invading forces. It was situations like this where Tessena would have awaited the next move from the enemy. It was her lack of initiative that had led to her failure. He would not follow her example.

"Tessena, come!" he bellowed across the parade ground. She came swiftly, dropping to one knee before him. He continued, "On your feet. I'm restoring your rank. You are First General to the Overlord once more."

As commanded, she stood. "Thank you, Lord Shote. I'm honored with your show of faith."

"I am not fool enough to be blind to my own stumbles. These invaders are indeed the stubborn horseflies you proclaimed them to be. You and I are heading out." He turned to a nearby griffin sentry, the chimera general that had taken over after the demise of both Manticore and Ontarshiss. "Scklaria! Assemble your strongest ten chimeras and put them to my back. We may require an escort."

Tessena creased her brow, slightly emboldened by her restored title. "What exactly are we looking for? Is this an assassination?"

Shote began walking towards the front gates as he answered. "Only if it becomes one. For now, we need to see the consistency of the opposing forces. We may be under attack from more than one enemy at the moment. I cannot proceed intelligently until I know for certain. If we find the Monks of Tria, we will slay them. Anyone else is not worth consideration, so we'll remain hidden long enough to inspect their ranks."

"As you command, Lord Shote."

* * * * *

On the flat plains facing the Fortress of the Overlord—closer to the enemy compound than was safe—Kelve and Detria stood side by side staring at the menacing entrance. No iron gates stood closed, no domineering guards stood at watch. Shote had long ago opened the doors freely to the humans, daring them to make a move into his terrain.

Boderon stood alongside the pair, separated by several yards. He had given the commanders some distance when their discussion had broken into a violent argument. It had ended without conclusion, and now the two had remained silent for nearly half an hour, each refusing stubbornly to either speak out or walk away. Boderon gave a sigh at their mirrored obstinance, and wandered away to scout the edge of the nearby hills.

Noticing his departure, Kelve forced himself to break the somber stalemate. "I won't march under Devilslayer banners," he said with a slow, calm tone.

"We need their strength," Detria answered with similar composure.

"Then you don't need mine."

She again lost her temper. "Why must you be so difficult?! You've done a good job fighting this war. You've given us all something to be proud of. Now all you have to do is help me lead them to make the final strike. You're a stubborn ass, Kelve Orista!"

He took an unsteady deep breath before giving his response. "When Yasiff assumed control of the Devilslayers, he killed a wonderful thing. He transformed the enemy of oppression into oppression itself. My father believed in the code of the slayers, and worked his whole life to strengthen and maintain it. When I left, I was betraying all the oaths I had ever made to my father. I swore to him that I would always be a slayer, and that I would always uphold what they stood for. I broke those vows, because I believed what the Devilslayers have become isn't the organization my father believed in.

"On the day that I broke those vows, I made a new one. I swore to myself, and to the ghost of my father, that I'd never go back on that decision. I swore I'd left the Devilslayers, that I'd abandoned Yasiff's rule, out of justice. And only by remaining loyal to that sense of justice, only by always swearing, *believing*, that I made that decision rightly, can I live with the oaths I once broke."

Detria shook her head with a sigh. "That's such a silly little thing, Kelve. It's just—it's all silly. You're focusing on things of the past instead of making the decisions that are best for the present and future. I know you have to see that."

He nodded, but said only, "Sometimes it's those silly little things that hold a man together when there's nothing else of him left."

At that moment, a shout came from Boderon in the surrounding shadows. "Trouble!" was all the man managed to get out before the sound of a dull knock overtook him. Detria swiftly drew two three-foot lengths of staff from her back and twisted them together, assembling the basic form of the Devilslayer's dannig. Kelve reached to draw his remaining saber, but was cut off as a massive body, easily eight feet tall, hurtled itself from the darkness and seized him by the throat.

Detria immediately struck with her staff, connecting hard with the back of the assailant's skull. Her target gave a soft grunt, then an effortless backhand sent her flying away.

"Tessena," Shote ordered of his general, "kill the woman." He turned his sight back to Kelve and narrowed his eyes in distaste. "You are the chemical master. Your hand has slain innumerable of the Overlord's forces, and stymied our closest grips at victory on every occasion. I didn't come here looking for you, but finding you undefended like this is too fine an opportunity."

As he tightened his grip to squeeze the life from Kelve's throat, Boderon reappeared. The large man was bleeding heavily from a large gash along the side of his head. He returned that blow with a vengeance, leaping from the shadows and striking at Shote's face with a slim-lined sledgehammer. The force of the blow snapped the right side of the minotaur's jaw clean off, sending his head limping to the side. Boderon quickly spun the hammer about, using a warhammer pick on the reverse side to strike Shote's elbow. A second crack resounded, as the chemist warlord was released and dropped to the ground.

"Run, Sir Kelve!" Boderon bellowed. "I will distract this beast!"

As bid, the commander scrambled to his feet and began running. As Kelve retreated, Shote patiently reached up and gripped his own face with both hands. He positioned his shattered jaw and then gave a sharp twist of his neck. He flexed his left arm up and down, ascertaining that his elbow still functioned. "Going to distract me?" he remarked calmly to Boderon. "That seems unlikely. Still," he turned briefly to glance over his shoulder and called out, "Chimeras! After the retreating one." He then turned his attention back to his ambusher. "Distract away, little one."

Kelve struggled to climb the hill leading to his base. He was losing strength fast, his body ill-prepared for the sudden rush of blood and adrenaline seizing it after Shote's attack. He forced himself to keep his coughing under control and kept his mind focused on one thing only—he had to save Detria. He could not lose her now after having successfully shielded her from this war for so long.

Fortunately, Gaius' curiosity had led him down to find Kelve and Detria and determine what they were discussing. He encountered Kelve as the commander struggled limply to climb the hill. An entourage of ten approaching chimeras set against the night sky did not escape the monk's sharp eyes.

"Master Orista, stay close to me! I will protect you."

The frail captain shook his head and leaned on Gaius' arm for a moment, then sputtered, "Detria, Boderon..." and pointed toward the direction of the fortress.

Gaius nodded. "Fetch Tenkahn, we'll need his strength."

The young monk charged from the weary man's side. As he heard the sounds of battle joined, and the harsh cries of fierce chimeras, Kelve felt his legs give out. He fell to the hillside and coughed up blood, tears of agony streaking down his face.

The lord of chemicals was not to be undone without having his final say in matters. His hands flew to the hidden pockets and satchels of his vestment, drawing forth vial after vial of obscure liquids and powders and tracing a complicated design out on the ground in front of him as he tore away strips of grass. Soon he had built a latticework of reactants, each one shielded from the others by insulators. He stared at the patch in the dirt for a moment, carefully working his mouth and gathering his own saliva.

He steeled his composure and whispered quietly, "Detria, I loved you. I wish I'd been a more serious man, so that you might have believed me when I said it." His voice, though hoarse, was filled with the certainty of his final words. He spat, and as his saliva mixed the chemicals before him, the sky lit up.

The patch of earth turned into a blaze of fire, throwing Kelve's limp body away as the flame went streaking for the sky. There it mushroomed out and left a large star of light carved across the land. The impact from the blast was fairly weak. This was little more than a fancy display of lights and fire, but it fulfilled Kelve's hopes. Far across the camp, patrolling the edge of Techenar Forest, Tenkahn realized his dear friend was in danger.

* * * * *

Since the ambush had begun, the two female high commanders had remained locked in bitter combat. Each woman was quick, and knew well how to strike or deflect a killing blow. Detria had struggled to gain the upper hand with quick spins of her dannig, but Tessena managed to hold stalemate with her single-headed axe and the threat of the gauntlet on left hand. The rechristened Devilslayer had been briefed on the all-consuming power of that gloved fist, and that knowledge had already saved her life in this duel more times than she could count.

As the two stood taking a brief breather, chests heaving with exhaustion, Tessena observed, "I've rarely been matched so skillfully in battle, and never by my own species and sex. I'm honored to meet one like yourself."

"I don't share your good nature, witch of the Overlord," Detria offered back with a spit. "You've killed my men, and now I'll kill you."

Tessena straightened her back and gave a smile. "Don't bite off more than you can chew, lady."

Detria nodded, likewise straightening her stance. She reached one hand behind her back and pulled forth a large hooked blade. She attached it to one end of the dannig and secured it with a twist. Then she drew forth another blade—this one straight and angled like a large arrowhead—and attached it to the other end. She gave a dizzying sweep of the dannig around her body, then took a step back and dropped into a defensive stance.

Tessena sighed and returned the nod, then charged. The new form of the dannig proved troublesome, and she had to quickly adapt her previous defensive style. Rather than attempting to catch the staff with her palm, she made a tight fist and used the back of the gauntlet to deflect Detria's blades. Sparks of magic shot from the glove each time it was struck, rattling the frame of the dannig and causing a numbing sensation to spread through its wielder's arms. Tessena kept her defense solid, using her axe to catch whatever blows her gauntlet could not. She knew the odds stood in her favor. Sooner or later, her opponent's arms would tire from the backlashes of magic from the Hand of Ramsa.

Just as the tide seemed to be turning and the fervor of Detria's assault waning, the Devilslayer leaped away and took a breath. She seized her dannig by the center with both hands and gave a sharp twist, then spun it about once and leveled it above her head, pointing it at Tessena's face like a spear.

"Are you ready?" she asked solemnly.

Tessena recognized the intent behind this move. Her foe had abandoned all defense, in order to make a reckless offense. The First General smiled, knowing this fight was hers. She lifted her left hand forward and opened her palm wide, fully prepared to catch the coming blow and disintegrate her enemy's weapon.

"Whatever you've got, dear."

With a yell Detria rushed forward and, as expected, gave a sharp straight thrust with the dannig. Tessena reached up and caught the tip of the spear—not concerned by its now magically dulled edge—and simultaneously delivered a rapid chop with the axe in her right hand.

Part of what she expected happened. There was a flash of light as the dannig vanished without a trace. But only half of it. As soon as the illuminated gauntlet made contact, Detria gave a rapid spin to her right and detached the back half of her staff. Tessena's axe swung through empty air as Detria delivered a wicked sweep from the hooked blade on the remaining half of the dannig, slicing cleanly through the General's left forearm and sending her Hand of Ramsa to the ground, hot red blood mixing with glowing cerulean lights.

Tessena was about to give a shout of surprise, but Detria quickly followed the attack, slamming the hook hard through the First

General's chest and leaving it embedded there. The Devilslayer commander pushed back, forcing the pierced woman to the ground, then spat down upon her prostrate form.

"I told you I would kill you," she taunted without mercy in her voice. "You were probably a better fight than me, if I'm willing to be honest. And with that glove of yours, you definitely were. But as I once told a man far, far better than you, 'It's the way of the Devilslayers to find victory against superior opponents.' And in that, you were nothing special."

The victor turned to where she had last seen Kelve, and instead she saw only Shote standing there, the beaten and bruised body of Boderon hanging motionlessly from one hand. The beast noticed the conclusion of the women's battle and tossed the big man to the ground, no longer interested.

He began to walked over to Detria, shaking his head in discontent. "How can you humans constantly serve such an annoyance? Though naturally weak compared to myself, Tessena was one of the Overlord's most capable champions. Yet today I throw a random wench her way and she somehow falls."

A shouting voice suddenly pierced the night sky. "Perhaps the gods are against you!" Shote looked up to see a body falling his way, and only thanks to his extreme speed was he able to back from beneath it. Gaius fell to the ground fists first, and from the impact several sheets of stone cracked through the soft earth and dove forward. The minotaur crushed the first wave with two powerful blows from his fists, but the second followed too quickly and sent him tumbling away.

The demon regained his feet and looked at the monk facing him. It was the younger one he had encountered several days ago, in the hallway with Ontarshiss. Gaius was absolutely drenched in blood of various colors—black, green, and red. Shote took a tentative step forward and gave a sniff. He did not mistake the odor.

"You killed my chimeras. All ten of them?"

Gaius cracked his neck to one side and pounded his fists

together. "Yeah. Why? Was that supposed to be hard? I'm not even warmed up yet."

Shote reached behind his back and drew forth one of his axes, as he tightened the muscles in his legs for upcoming exchange. "You, I did come looking for. I'm thankful for the chance to slay you without interruption."

Without further delay the two superpowers joined in battle. Gaius had overplayed his ease in defeating the ten chimeras, and he was already pushing the limits of exhaustion. His runes hummed with a bright blue as they reinforced his strength, but it was not enough to match the ferocity he normally held.

He delivered wave upon wave of Pulsing Fists, striking from range while evading the axe blade aiming for his throat. The towering beast weathered the force of Gaius' attacks without reaction, without bothering to dodge, impassive as chunks of his own flesh and blood ripped and splattered around him.

The young monk battled with all his vigor, but could not bring the minotaur down. He knew he could do more damage if he moved in close, but the speeds at which Shote's greataxe moved discouraged such brave ideas.

And then in an instant, Shote moved. Gaius was able to follow the motion—barely—with his enhanced vision, but he was not able to react fast enough to respond. The beast's entire body slid several yards off to his right, then swiftly pivoted and slid back in behind the youth. It was the same burst of speed he had seen the minotaur use once before, a speed beyond even that of Myris Phare.

"You're nothing like your teacher," the beast taunted from high above his prey's head.

Gaius recognized what had happened with a grin. Shote was unaccustomed to his opponent being able to follow his unrestrained movement. The demon felt assured that Gaius had lost track of him and been rendered unaware that his deadly foe was about to strike from behind. This arrogance had led him to take a second to mock his victim. That single second of delay was all the opportunity the young monk needed.

As Shote's axe swung in a wide arc above him, Gaius threw himself forward into a roll. Simultaneously he freed his left arm and gave a quick punch to the ground, causing a tremor of earth, then a single spiked rock to stab out at his foe. The minotaur caught the tip of this spike with his free hand and grunted in annoyance. The monk quickly righted himself and sent a pulsing wave into the stone, causing it to shatter into shrapnel. As Shote stumbled back with tiny cuts in his eyes, Gaius prepared his secret technique.

"You're right, beast, I am nothing like Tenkahn!" He charged forward with a reckless yell, both arms thrown wide to his sides. Shote bellowed in rage and swung his axe in a downward chop. The blade moved almost too fast for Gaius, but almost was not sufficient against a Monk of Tria. His hands snapped shut tight against the sides of the axe, and with a grin on his face he could not repress, he roared, "Bonebreak!"

There was a crackling sound as the energy from the attack traveled down the axe, but the reinforced hilt survived without shattering completely. Shote did not weather the attack quite so well, and his right forearm suddenly snapped and seized up from coursing kinetic energy. Shortly his bicep followed, the humerus bending at an unnatural angle.

Gaius backed away a step and silently congratulated himself on his victory, happily dealing with the pain of Bonebreak as it fought to shatter his own arms. Then Shote's left hand suddenly lashed out and seized his own right shoulder. In the same fluid motion he gave a rapid yank, removing the shoulder from the socket. Gaius began to back away in concern, while the Overlord's champion waited patiently until he was certain the powerful vibrations seizing his bones had died down.

Once the effect had passed, Shote snapped his shoulder back into place. He then straightened and rejoined his humerus and the bones in his forearm, and stretched his fingers on his right hand wide. He picked up his axe from where it had fallen to the ground, giving a few strong practice swings with it.

"Please, monk child, don't tell me that was the best you had for me. I've endured so much worse than such a petty trick as that." Gaius did not answer, staring with his mouth agape in mixed pain and terror. Shote shook his head and narrowed his eyes tight. "It is what it is, then."

He moved in a large blue blur, appearing atop his enemy and giving an uppercut with his axe. The monk's body flew into the air unnaturally, ever so slowly. Though Gaius had only seen one swing of the axe, no less than six gaping rips tore through his chest and torso as he drifted away from the daunting minotaur and fell to the ground. He coughed and wrapped his arms about his body, hugging his wounds together and willing forth his healing blessings.

Shote did not miss this. "Still you live?" he lamented. "Stubborn. That attack was sufficient to end previous monks. The exuberance of youth must serve you well. But I'm confident you will die when I take your head."

In spite of his apparent control over the battle at hand, Shote seemed somehow physically agitated. Rather than dashing in swiftly for the kill, he walked slowly over to his downed adversary. He then gingerly lifted his axe with both hands and hovered it just a couple of feet above the monk's neck. There was nothing Gaius could do to defend himself. He closed his eyes, begging Tria forgiveness for his shortcomings.

Just before the beast could make further move, a stern voice shouted from across the battlefield, "Shote!" The minotaur lifted his head to see Tenkahn standing at the base of the hill, the runes of Tria burning brightly as he gathered power. "If you kill a Monk of Tria this day, it shall be me."

During the few seconds that his executioner was distracted, Gaius rapidly rolled away on the ground, sacrificing dignity but saving his life. The minotaur looked back and seemed to briefly toy with the idea of pursuing his first victim, then gave a silent shake of his own head, turning fully to address the newcomer. Shote and Tenkahn the Aged met once more, a confrontation long awaited. "I take no quarrel with those terms," the Overlord's masterpiece promised.

He abandoned the defeated monk and approached the boy's master, stopping once there was a comfortable ten yards between them. The minotaur reached to his back and drew his other axe, clearly taking Tenkahn as seriously as he could any opponent. The Monk of Tria watched these movements and offered a slight bow.

"I have seen your moves. You're not the man you once were, Lord Shote."

"I am not now, nor have I ever been, a lowly man."

Tenkahn raised his fists and flexed his chest and arms. "I broke you once, long ago. I will do it again now without hesitation."

Shote dropped into a crouch and swung forward each of his axes. "That sentiment is echoed by my own heart."

The elder monk gave a short bark of ferocity, then in a streak of speed disappeared. His fist slid harmlessly through the place Shote had once stood, as the minotaur had already flown from his path. Tenkahn felt the counter coming, the beast already charging in a similar move with axes sweeping. He burst forward again, leaving his foe's path and spinning about on his heel.

For a minute this was all that could happen. Neither warrior could gain striking distance on the other, as they continued to weave to and fro in specific straight-line dashes. Though their speeds were well matched, both combatants were clearly reserving their most vigorous surges for defense, both well aware of the consequences of giving the other an early advantage.

Suddenly Tenkahn had an idea to end the stalemate. For his next attack, rather than properly orient himself for a strike, he simply charged backward off his heel at his foe. It would have been a useless move if detected, but Shote had grown too comfortable in their dance and dodged on instinct alone. When he then tried to once more ambush his opponent from behind, the monk was instead facing him, meeting his charge with a pillar of earthen fury.

Shote was stunned for barely an instant, then quickly adapted, delivering a series of five unbelievably fast vertical slashes from the axe in his left hand. Even as he decimated the monk's attack, he dropped lower and gave a sweep from his other axe, aiming for the man's shins.

Tenkahn had no option to gracefully avoid that strike, as he was still crouched on all fours from delivering his Tremoring Fist. He shifted power to his hands and lifted his legs from the ground in time to avoid the edge of the axe. Then he thrust with his entire upper body, throwing himself a dozen yards into the air.

Shote saw the monk fly away from him, so he heaved back and swung forward, releasing his left axe in a wide swinging arc. The weapon spun through the air and met the monk at the top of his jump. Tenkahn did a nimble backflip, punching the projectile's handle and sending it flying underneath him. He straightened himself and turned to watch Shote, only to find the minotaur had disappeared once again.

The aged monk's eyes widened in rare panic. "He couldn't..."

Releasing a massive amount of kinetic energy from every part of his body, he forced himself to swiftly spin about entirely to face the other direction. His rotation completed just in time to see Shote, his other weapon snagged out of midair, closing in with the axes from each side like a deadly pair of scissors. Tenkahn reached out with his hands and closed his fingers around the edge of each bladed head. The leverage from the long weapons threw him back, sending him springing to the ground once again.

As soon as his feet touched land, with Shote still suspended in midair, Tenkahn cursed. "Two can make that move," he boasted, then dashed off as the runes on his legs geared to their maximum output. He sprinted underneath his hovering rival, slammed his feet hard into the ground, and exploded his way up to behind the minotaur's head. The monk went into a tight aerial spin with his arms thrust out, striking his enemy several times in the back of the skull and sending him plummeting earthward.

When the two landed, each safely on their feet, they faced one another with stolid grimaces. Each rose from their crouches slowly, watching the other for a move. Shote spoke first.

"I remember you, Monk of Tria. I remember your speed. I don't remember much of my previous life, the one that you took from me. But I remember you. Ten...kahn."

The sounds of a large commotion sounded on the hill behind them and both turned to look. A thousand troops had assembled at the command of Kelve's lieutenant Colbiss, a mix of former and current Devilslayers. Three hundred archers had poison-tipped barbs aimed for Shote's throat, and an advanced guard of two hundred spearmen had their own tips down, shields up, daring the beast to charge their ranks.

The minotaur flexed his shoulders and puffed through his nostrils. "It's going to be a good battle, monk!"

"You cannot win this, Shote," Tenkahn argued. "I still stand strong, and these warriors outnumber you heavily. You may kill most of them, but you *will* die."

"My life to strike a crippling blow against the enemies of my Overlord. A worthy price."

The monk pointed at the fresh forces that had joined their cause. "These men are Devilslayers. If you leave even one alive, he will go and bring a thousand more troops here. Maybe five thousand. What will your forces do then, without you to lead them?"

Shote sniffed and shook his head, then stood in contemplation for a moment. "No matter, then. I've learned what I came for. Until we dance again, Servant of Tria." He turned away from their army and slowly began to make his way back to his fortress, leaving behind his fallen allies.

Colbiss moved swiftly to Tenkahn's side. "Say the word, and I'll have our army cut him down!"

Tenkahn was not interested. "Leave him be. I bluffed, and he did not call it. We count ourselves lucky today."

"Bluffed? Everything you said was true."

"Everything save one. We could not have killed him. He would have taken my life, and that of all the soldiers, and still would not have gone down today."

Colbiss was silent for a few seconds, either unable or unwilling to accept this. "Are you so certain?"

The monk gave a slow nod, locking eyes with the man. "The weapons you have cannot bring that beast down, and I could not have long fought at his level. His victory only needed time."

The lieutenant shook his head forlornly. "If we cannot defeat him by himself, how are we supposed to win this war?"

Detria came to their side and answered in the monk's stead. "However we must. But Tenkahn's right, now is not the time to push the matter to a boil. Did you bring medics?"

"Of course," Colbiss answered, "a solid fifty of Yasiff's best."

"See to Boderon and Gaius, and..."

As Detria continued dishing out orders, Tenkahn wandered over to where Tessena lay dying alone. Her glazed eyes saw his approach, and she smiled up at him weakly.

"Hello, warrior of Tria."

"Hello, warrior of Ramsa."

She shook her head softly in response. "I was only a thief in the house of Ramsa. I don't deserve such a title."

"Perhaps all of us who rely on the blessings of gods are merely thieves in their houses."

She did not respond immediately, but continued to watch him slowly for a moment. When she began speaking again, Tenkahn got the impression she had been carrying a conversation in her head without his involvement.

"You have to understand, in the lands of the Overlord I was a nothing, a nobody. No human was worth his consideration. I had to rise up, to become a something. For myself and for our people. Just one useful human made the Overlord more merciful, more considerate when dealing with our kind. I *have* saved lives, you know. I know I've cost some, I know I've taken some... but not all I did was bad. It wasn't all evil. In my heart, it was never evil."

He shushed her supplication. "You do not answer to me, Madam General. But I will say, that you die with such a guilty heart does not bode well for you in the next life."

She nodded her agreement and again rested for several seconds. “Shote killed Gariso,” she then said softly.

Tenkahn lowered himself down onto his knees, to better hear her words as her volume softened under the grip of death. “The strange fighter with the arms of a dragon, yes? He was a powerful adversary. It is always the highest shame when such a warrior is slain by an ally.”

“He wasn’t an evil man either. Somebody should know that. Everything he ever did, he only did for me. If anything, I’m accountable for his sins, too.”

“Very well. If that is how you choose to believe, then I will echo your belief and we will declare it so. But if you are to be accountable for the sins of Gariso, then in similar fashion I must prescribe the weight of your sins to Shote. And I declare you, Tessena, blameless and free to die innocent.”

A brief spark of life returned to her eyes as they filled with tears, and her mouth twisted as though she were about to sob, but she lacked the strength. Instead she took a soft breath and said, “You have to kill Shote. For payback for Gariso, but also to save the humans still enslaved here. Please, promise me that you’ll take them from this place, away from the Overlord. The only thing I can do to protect them now is to beg for your mercy.”

“Then you are blessed, for Mercy is my way. You have my word, I will do everything in my power to bring Shote down, and Gaius will set free the humans in the Overlord’s thrall. I will hold nothing back, even if it means I must perish alongside my foe.”

She took several more weak breaths, then continued, “I can help a little more. Shote has a weakness few know. I know it.”

Tenkahn widened his eyes, but forced himself not to become too hopeful so quickly. “Any edge I might gain over him could make the difference.”

“You don’t remember the last time you fought him. You don’t remember how you beat him.”

“I do not remember that I beat him at all.”

“Shote is fast, like a devil. His speed puts fear into those brave enough to face him. But he normally moves so slowly. Don't you notice? Enemies think it's to catch them off guard, to frighten them. But in truth, he's a living golem. He doesn't work like the rest of us. He has an internal battery, of some sort of magic I can't fathom. As he fights, his energy drains. The faster he moves, the faster it drains. He's never recovered from the beating you gave him, and his reserves don't last as they once did. At his full strength, it might last him three, maybe five minutes. But no more."

Tenkahn turned his gaze to the fortress where Shote had disappeared, replaying the events of the battle. "That is why hesitated so much to finish off Gaius. And why he retreated. He knew I would conclude that he was allowing us to escape, but in truth he feared his own time was nearly out."

"Against a worthy foe, Shote cannot win anymore. Eventually he'll collapse. The tide will turn. He will lose..." The last few words were barely a whisper, carried by her dying breath. Tenkahn watched her cold body sadly for a moment, regretful of the life she had been forced to lead. It was one more reason for him to hate the sway of the Overlord, and the things it had done to Arkalen.

At that moment Detria again stepped to his side. She ignored the corpse beneath their feet, with the hook of her dannig still protruding from its torso. "Tenkahn, have you seen Kelve? I lost sight of him during the battle."

Tenkahn could not bear to meet her eyes, but he moved away and answered, "I will take you to him."

* * * * *

Minutes later, Detria stared in shock upon Kelve's corpse. He had a few burns over his face and hands, but overall she could not tell what had killed him. She wanted to know, wanted to ask Tenkahn, but she could not bring herself to use words as she stared at the lifeless eyes, still open, trails of singed tears on each side of them.

Tenkahn intuited her concern without her giving it voice. "Master Orista was injured in a battle some time ago. You knew this, of course. What you did not know is that once he saw Yasiff, once he saw the Devilslayers assuming command of this war, he stopped using the medications that were keeping him alive. He told only me, swearing me to secrecy. He said his time should end now. That it was appropriate, even overdue. He swore me to watch over you, Mistress Detria. He said you would be a leader far greater than he ever was."

This statement alone stirred Detria from her shock enough to respond. "He lied. He—I'm not half—I'm not Kelve."

Tenkahn nodded at her stumbling response. "That may be. I cannot say for myself. Kelve Orista was an amazing man, and I will not besmirch his memory with any words. That anyone could be a leader 'far greater' than he, I find difficult to believe. He was a flagship that men and women of honor sat their sail behind, and followed across the wayward sea of battle."

Slowly Detria knelt to the ground and placed her hands on the sides of Kelve's face. Her whole life he had guided her and she had taken him for granted. Never once had she given him the thanks he was owed. Never once had he asked for it. When she had returned, she had treated him with disdain, like any other common soldier beneath her. She could not believe this was how he died, that this was when he died. She felt certain he must have died hating her, and knew it was a hatred she deserved.

She wanted to cry. She wanted desperately for tears to stream down her face and honor his memory. But she could not offer him even that. After all she had endured in the past year, she was too broken on the inside. Her mind and her heart had been poisoned, and she had allowed it to freeze out her most trusted ally; her dearest friend. The person she was now was no good for friendships, no good for grieving.

But she was good for something, still. The source of Kelve's torment was the same as her own, and she knew how to put a stop to it. After a further moment of staring at her lost companion, she knew what she had to do. She reached to his side and seized the hilt of his cutlass, drawing it slowly from its scabbard and then rising to her feet.

"Arrange a burial, Tenkahn. I'll carve his tombstone myself. Understood?"

The monk bowed, but said nothing. She began to walk, slowly, unevenly, to the center of the camp. As she traveled she placed Kelve's sword through her belt and let it hang at her back, continuing to walk with a horrified expression on her face. She kept moving until she reached the outside of Yasiff's tent. The sentries there moved to stop her, but she gave a halfhearted shout in to the High Chieftain himself. He poked his head out, saw her, and signaled for his sentries to make themselves busy elsewhere.

She followed the man into his tent. He swiftly moved to prepare glasses of wine for the two of them. "Welcome, my dear. I'm not entirely surprised to see you join me tonight. I've heard there's much arguing between yourself and Kelve on my behalf. I'm glad to see you have come back so zealously into the fold." He sat their glasses on a rounded wooden table, then took a comfortable seat on a small fur lounger.

"Kelve is dead," she answered perfunctorily. "There was an ambush. He fell."

"Oh? Hmm. A shame, I suppose. He was a good soldier, a brilliant chemist." He wagged a finger in the air. "But he was headstrong and unreliable. Certainly, he was not the man his father was."

Detria's eyes snapped shut, and at last a tear slid from each one. Without hesitating, her hand flew to her back and seized Kelve's sword. A step forward, a swift stab, a twist. Without even opening her eyes, she had removed the viper's larynx from his neck.

Blood splashed across the floor in a rush and Yasiff fell to his hands and knees. As he sputtered uselessly and tried to call for help with no voice, Detria opened her eyes and stared at the ceiling.

"He hated you. So much. He hated what you did. He hated the way you tarnished his father's memory. Kelve's whole life was the

Devilslayers, and you took that away from him. So he dedicated himself to me, and me alone. And then you took that away from him too, and I was too stupid to see it." She raised her heel to the man's shoulders and forced him onto his back, eyeing him as he continued to twitch and gurgle. "I should have killed you for him. If I'd done that, he wouldn't have given up on his life." At this point, tears poured unchecked down her face, and her mouth tightened with grief. "If I could do anything, I would go back and kill you. I would trade a hundred of your lives just for one of Kelve's! Just for Kelve!" she ended with a scream. Then, using all of her might, she drove the cutlass through Yasiff's face, pinning the twitching man to the ground as his sanctimonious mind perished.

* * * * *

Hours later, Detria stood in the light drizzle of early morning rain, staring down at the grave that had been made for the fallen chemical master. As promised, she had carved the headstone herself. It was at this she stared. She knew it was inadequate. In her heart, she felt she had always been inadequate toward Kelve.

She had been standing there for a long time, alone. The rough processions of a makeshift funeral had been held, and the others had moved on. It was not because they did not grieve his passing; every man and woman who had served under him felt an unstoppable pang of loss. But there was so much to see to, and everyone knew if Kelve had been there he would have ordered them on their way. They could still hear his voice guiding them.

Soon she was joined by Gaius. He was carrying the Hand of Ramsa, now detached from Tessena's dead hand. He offered it to Detria once he reached her.

"We decided this rightfully belongs to you now. Tenkahn and I cannot wield it, and it's your spoil of war. Use it well in the upcoming battles." She took it in silence. The monk paused briefly, then added, "We wouldn't have made it this far without him."

"Me neither," she answered cryptically.

"They've found Yasiff. There's going to be hell to pay for what you've done. Are you sure it was worth it?"

She narrowed her eyes and clenched her fists. "Without question."

"How will we handle this?"

She shook her head with a sigh. "Easily enough. Devilslayers are sworn to uphold the last command of their chief if he loses his life in a battle or on a mission. Yasiff swore them to follow my orders and see the Overlord's fortress taken. I'll remind them of this. Yasiff has conditioned his men to serve as fanatics, supplicants, cultists. They won't question his final mandate, even if things seem wrong to them."

"I see," Gaius replied with a nod. After a pause he added, "Did you... plan it that way? When you decided to kill him?"

"Are you asking me if I'm so callous that I avenged Kelve's death not in the heat of passionate rage, but rather as a calculated decision where I knew there could be no repercussions against me?" she asked, her tone bordering indignation. Then, however, she continued softly, "I honestly don't know, Eiden. I'm not too proud to admit that I'm a mess right now. I'm just trying to figure out a way to put myself back together, while mourning the loss of my best friend."

"And I don't want to be insensitive to that, but you'd better come and put this plan of yours into effect. I think there's about to be an uprising. Tenkahn and Colbiss are trying to keep the peace, but it won't hold long."

"Give me another moment here."

He did as asked, leaving her standing alone at the grave, her tears intermingling with the rain. She stared at the carving on the headstone and read it aloud one last time, committing it to heart.

*Kelve Orista*
*Master of Nature*
*Leader of Men*
*I will always love you. ~Detria*

## Chapter 36.

# The Overlord of Arkalen

The demon Zekraul moved brazenly through the eastern Blukar Forest. He had been experimenting with his new abilities, testing both his offensive and defensive prowess. The Gehennan's body had always been extremely malleable, granting him a wide range of immunity. Now he had evolved beyond even that. With the solidity of Kiastos' stone flesh abilities, and the flexibility and instant regeneration of Aegagropilion, he found himself more indestructible than ever.

Of more interest to him was the new destructive capability he had gained. Though he had previously lacked in the ways of offense, he had now been granted an overflowing bounty. The fiery magics of Dosiros were extreme on their own, allowing him to level an entire forest with a mere thought. But even more tantalizing, he had gained the talents of a lich. The dark spellcaster's manipulations over reality and life-degradation attacks were absolutely daunting. To some degree Zekraul feared his new potential; though this would not stop him from wielding it against those foolish enough to challenge him.

Though he felt invincible, his thirst for power was not yet slaked. He would shortly reach the other Wisdoms and claim their abilities as well, thanks to the gifts of Aegagropilion. The former Godbeast had possessed an unfortunate weakness of losing stolen talents over time. That weakness was now erased, thanks to Zekraul's own ability to store his absorbed attributes indefinitely. It seemed he had become a truly perfect being. While he continued to move ever closer to the Wisdoms, he began to consider that the title he had long used now seemed insufficient for his splendor.

As he mused upon this, he was interrupted by the arrival of a visitor. A human warrior in thick black armors dropped from a nearby tree branch, landing on the ground a few yards away. As the man stood he slowly raised a sword held in his right hand, a massive steel slab over six feet long.

"Overlord!" the intruder announced. "I am here to end you."

"Overlord?" Zekraul replied curiously. "Only my servants call me by that name. Are you one of my servants?"

"Don't even think it," the man spat with contempt. "Long ago you destroyed my family. My brother gave his life fighting your minions, as you slaughtered a village of innocents without remorse or cause."

Zekraul stared for a moment, thinking this tale sounded familiar. He released a short hiss when recognition finally came. "Sssss, yes. You're that human who's been hunting me across the continent. I didn't think you were resourceful enough to follow me over the mountains."

Deun took a step forward and gave a feign swing with Kargaroth. "You will see that you have underestimated more than that."

The demon tilted his head a notch. "We've fought before, yes? You did me some injury, but mainly you made a mere nuisance of yourself and forced me into a retreat. Your timing in finding me now will not serve you. You were only barely a match for me before, and I am an entirely different monster."

Deun roared with indignation, "No matter what you become, I will crush you!"

The dark knight dashed forward, raising Kargaroth to his right side and running it out along his shoulder, bracing for a mighty swing. Zekraul waited for the blow, and when it came he was disappointed by its lack of speed. As Kargaroth swung slowly at his head, he crouched slightly and collapsed his neck, lazily avoiding the strike.

"I think you need more practice with your weapon," the demon taunted.

Deun responded by diving into a series of blows as blunt as the first, full sweeping strikes of the massive blade with little agility or accuracy. Each time he swung he gathered speed slightly, using the momentum from a previous swipe to adjust his footing and lead nimbly into the next. The combo turned into a rapid slashing one, as he sliced down at the demon's right shoulder, across at his waist, diagonally back up at his head, aiming down for his skull, low and across at the demon's feet. Zekraul dodged each of them, mocking the human's prowess with a few hissing chuckles.

After the last sweep the man seemed to pause for breath, and his opponent almost began to taunt him anew. Instead Deun suddenly whipped about on his ankle, swinging Kargaroth hard behind his back and letting the force carry him in a full circle. Zekraul took a step backward, but was not out of the sword's range. Thinking fast, he shattered his spine at the waist and let the upper part of his body lean away from the blade.

Again the demon relaxed, believing the first exchange of the fight over now. But as Deun swung his sword, with the tip only inches from his foe's amber eyes, he released a hoarse cry of pain and effort. The sword responded to his despair, flaring up with a thick casing of purple light. Zekraul watched in concern as this light appeared. Some remnant of divine instincts warned him that his death was at hand, so he rejoined his spine and began sliding away swiftly. As the man finished his swing, the aura around Kargaroth blinked out. In its stead a wicked arc of black light echoed forth.

As he continued his retreat, the demon threw a whirlwind of dark red fire to stop the darkness approaching him, but his flames crumpled and were sucked into the sliver of energy. Thinking fast, he channeled his inner lich and threw up half a dozen walls of the most impenetrable ices. Still the dark blade was not halted, but Zekraul stood waiting patiently for it to reach him, as it was slowed by the frozen barriers it had to shear from its path. When it passed through the final icy wall and came a mere foot from his form, the demon suddenly disappeared in a puff of smoke, zipping several yards to his right. The blade passed on through his afterimage, burning out once it was too far from its origin.

The demon turned to face his hunter with renewed annoyance, uncertain what powers the human had recently tapped. In the very instant he twisted about, he saw Kargaroth floating over his head, sweeping down for a strike. He hissed and instinctively drew forth Aegagropilion's shapeshifting, forming his right hand into a huge metal vice and snatching the blade. With effort he ground the weapon to a halt, glaring at his attacker with intense eyes. Deun locked his feet into the ground and struggled to regain control over his sword, but Zekraul shifted his arm slightly and channeled the physical strength of Kiastos, holding tight.

In the face of his own impotence, Deun let out another roar of despair. Again Kargaroth responded with a gleeful flicker of light. From his contact with the sword Zekraul heard a stranger whisper of death and the voices of chaos. There was a malevolent flash, after which the demon felt himself go temporarily blind. The sword then propelled itself sharply to the ground, tearing through his arm and cutting it cleanly in half.

As soon as his senses were restored he wasted no time, throwing himself backward and delivering a kicking uppercut to his opponent's jaw with both feet. As the human flew away, Zekraul tended to his injured arm. At first it seemed he would be able to repair the damage, but then the crystalline structure of his entire arm, from the elbow to the fingertips, shattered and exploded into shrapnel and dust. He arched his back in response to the rare sensation of pain. Again he reacted quickly, discarding the unusable parts of his flesh and growing a new arm with a sickening burst of green blood. He transformed the newly generated green muscles back into his preferred black crystals. As soon as he did there was a sudden cracking sound, and a slim fracture appeared running throughout his arm where the cruel blade had sliced him.

He gave a frightened hiss. "Ssssss. No weapon has ever left a permanent mark on my body. What deviltry is this?"

He looked across the clearing to his assailant, who had regained his feet and was charging with Kargaroth upheld. Zekraul leaped backward a full twenty yards to give himself a moment to work. He channeled Asterian energy and began to change, shifting his physical form across the Veil as a thick shroud of darkness enveloped him. Once he had fully summoned his lich might, he pointed his left hand forward at his opponent.

Only ten yards away, Deun felt a strange pressure tighten around his throat as the demon commanded, "Stand still, all weak creatures." The air around the human turned black and solidified, paralyzing his muscles. Kargaroth began to rattle in his hands, resisting the influence of the black magic. The mystic warrior tried to bind himself to the sword, recognizing that the Unholy Blade had the power to break him free of this spell. As he was absorbed trying to understand his own weapon, his enemy vanished and reappeared directly in front of him. Zekraul uttered another dark chant, "Suffer, those with a spirit of life," and thrust his right hand straight through the man's chest.

No physical impact was made. Instead a strange ripple of distorted light pooled from where the black arm made contact. The ripple emanated three more times—flowing freely through the air as if it were water—then Deun's entire body exploded into black fire and was lifted from the ground. As the man screamed in the confines of a nightspawn's torment, Zekraul shifted himself back onto the Morolian plane, spending a moment repairing his own spirit from the damage caused by using the lich's magic.

His victim dropped and the flames burned out, quicker than Zekraul had expected. It was unclear if the attack had faded so soon because of his dismissal of his own dark gifts, or because of the man's powerful sword. Considering the latter, the demon moved across the clearing and snatched the greatsword from the wounded man's hands. Deun offered no resistance, his mind rendered useless from the corruption of lich darkness seeping through his every fiber.

Zekraul stared at the sword, sniffed it, and began to give practice swings with it. Raising the strength in his arms to their maximum, he swung the sword in dizzying patterns, putting Deun's own use of it to shame. He sent Asterian magics creeping up along the blade, trying to assume command of it. He tried swinging it with his own roar of rage, mocking the fallen man's earlier attacks. No matter what he tried, the artifact gave no response.

"How useless," he finally surmised. "There is no power to the sword. It seems the human tricked me." He tossed the weapon over his shoulder. It flew a few yards through the air, then embedded itself into the base of a youthful oak. Zekraul was slightly disappointed. He had hoped to couple the sword's magics with his own, but now he assumed the dark energies must have somehow been generated by his opponent. He offered the man a final farewell. "You certainly had unexpected talents, hunter. I would add you to my glory, but the Unhallowing has wrecked your flesh and spirit too severely. Absorbing your decayed form would cause me more harm than good. Die here alone, that is the only honor I grant you. Perhaps if you'd been a worthy enemy, things would be otherwise."

Deun lay shuddering as his despised foe left the area, tears streaming from his eyes. He bit deep into his lip until he drew blood, trying to revive his senses by way of pain. But he was comatose, in an odd waking sense, trapped within his own flesh. He had heard Zekraul's words, and they had singed him even deeper than the fires that had crippled him. Memories began pouring through his mind, memories of his own life, loved ones, former allies, enemies. As each one flashed through it faded, dying never to be recovered. The final image he hung onto ferociously. The image of his brother's face, smeared with blood, preparing to charge into battle with the Overlord to defend their home village.

And he remembered words, his own words, that had been sworn long ago to the memory of that face. *Tassix, whatever it takes, I will see you avenged. The Overlord will fall at the hands of Coloran.*

As the deep regret of failure sank into his being, Deun's body tightened. He opened his mouth, but all that came out was a gurgle. He struggled more, and the gurgle turned into a cry of pain. This in turn rose to a scream, and from across the clearing Kargaroth responded, flaring with dark light once again. Then the scream ended, the light flickered out, and Deun slumped back and lost his mind to the darkness.

* * * * *

Keldana stared to the north, her vision probing through unseen miles. She had stopped a few minutes earlier, triggered by one of her hundreds of feelers of mist crawling the continent. Nearby, Torlen and Melukah impassively awaited her report. When she finally returned to them she initially offered nothing, instead asking of her lord, "Did you feel it?"

Melukah returned a nod. "You are not confused. My third eye briefly locked onto the presence of a mighty Gehennan, then lost it. Even among hellspawn, there can be no more than twenty or thirty creatures of such Class. What did you find?"

"I'm not fully certain. It is the Godbeast Aegagropilion. Or rather, it somehow tastes of him. It has some sort of shell which makes it impossible to read deeper into. The only thing I can determine for certain is that it's not of divine origin."

The Sound looked to the two of them. "What do we make of this?"

"Perhaps Aegagropilion has created a lackey for himself of some sort?" Keldana speculated. "A severing from his own body."

"Is he capable of that?" asked Torlen.

"It's difficult to confidently predict the Great Beast's capabilities in each iteration," Melukah responded, "but it doesn't matter anymore. Gilanirus is awake, so we continue south." The others nodded, and the group began to move once more.

Another hour passed with the Wisdoms traveling in silence. Melukah had become upset the moment he had first detected Gilanirus' presence. Torlen had offered to travel forward and catch the Tyrant off guard, but his lord had denied him. If they were going to strike Gilanirus down quickly, it would require the three of them to attack at once. Unfortunately the Wisdom of the Sun lacked a type of swift transportation like Keldana and Torlen, so they were forced to move at his pace.

At the end of this hour, again the three came to a halt. They stared forward without motion, waiting for the inevitable. When it did not come, Keldana commented, "It seems he moves faster than us."

Melukah gave a slight sigh, annoyed by the interruption. "Torlen. Assassinate him."

The Wisdom of Sound gave Keldana a nod, and the two spun about to Melukah's errand. The Ocean pointed her hands forth, and the light vegetation of the outskirts of the forest were instantly covered in a sheet of ice. Torlen moved forward and released a shockwave from his shoulders, detonating the frozen flora into shrapnel. A slim black figure was revealed, standing perplexed that his ambush had been preempted. Torlen moved in rapidly for the kill, lashing out with his arm wrapped in thick white rings.

Zekraul responded swiftly to the reversal, thrusting his hands into the ground and using Kiastos' magic to create a shell of petrified earth around him. Torlen smashed through it within an instant, the white rings crawling over the stone and grinding it into dust. The Wisdom reared his arm back for another attack, but as the rocky surface disappeared, it was revealed that his target had vanished.

He looked around in frantic shock, then heard a soft scraping sound behind him. He turned to respond but was immediately engulfed by a wall of fire, which lifted him and carried him back into the forest, melting a trail through the other Wisdom's icy shrapnel.

Keldana herself rejoined the battle in an instant, swinging a thick sword of ice she had constructed, the blade four inches wide and four feet long. Zekraul twisted about and transformed his arm into a giant shield to block this attack. He had attempted to simultaneously change his skin to the stone of Kiastos, but was not yet adept enough with those talents. Icy crystal crashed into demonic crystal, and each shattered and danced in the sunlight as Melukah watched from the sidelines.

Zekraul leaped into the air as his right arm was shattered. He used his left to summon a sweep of flame, creating a raging fire blanketing the area above Keldana's head. The attack seemed a waste of energy at first, then the demon transformed the fire into dense stone and sent it crashing down. The Wisdom was crushed by the massive materialized boulder, which the interloper immediately glazed with more fire, drowning the area in magma.

As soon as Keldana seemed at least momentarily dispatched, Torlen made his return. He blasted from the forest with a burst of sonic waves propelling him at tremendous speed. As he approached he raised a hand, and a huge net of numbing sonics ran forth to impede his foe. This time Zekraul was not caught unawares. He waved his remaining hand and placed a tunnel of fire between himself and the Wisdom of Sound. Once the area was superheated, the demon sent his own shockwave out—one of cold—bringing the entire vicinity to a frigid halt. The sonic waves from Torlen's attack distorted and lost cohesion with the sudden shift in temperature, while the Wisdom himself was blanketed in a thick sheet of frozen flames.

As the deity's encased body rocketed into him, Zekraul fell onto his back and lashed upward with his feet. His legs split into vines and wrapped around the Wisdom's frame, and he was lifted along as both went flying from Torlen's momentum. As they crashed, the Gehennan flipped about to drive his quarry to the ground, exploding his hand into ropes and latching them around the Elysian's neck and face.

Torlen attempted to regain control of the situation, using bursts of sharp sound to free himself of his icy restraints. But Zekraul was also working quickly. He shifted his existing arm to the middle of his chest, as he extended his feelers about his prey's shoulders, then grew a fresh set of arms from his sides. He did not bother transforming these new limbs to his crystalline appearance, but rather took the green tendrils and wrapped each one about the forearms of the pinned Wisdom, binding tightly.

By the time Torlen had freed himself from the ice, it was too late. Zekraul had already sunk his own mind into the Elysian body, and the melding process was underway. Behind him, the demon heard sounds of Keldana attempting to freeze over the magma holding her immobile. He paused his absorption long enough to rotate his head around and send a fresh wave of fire arching from his eyes, reheating the rock. Then he noticed motion from the other Wisdom. Melukah stepped forward and shook his head, reaching behind his back and drawing his Sun Staff.

He addressed the interloper for the first time. "Release my servant. I do not have time for this."

Before Zekraul could offer response, the Wisdom of the Sun pointed his Staff forward and a blinding blast of yellow heat was emitted forth. It was a dozen times brighter than the blasts Zekraul had seen previously, and struck twice as fast. Still the adaptive demon managed to shift the color of his flesh in time, changing to a shade of bright yellow and absorbing the rays into his body. When he could store no more, he phased again and allowed the remaining energies to pass harmlessly through.

When Melukah's attack faded, the demon twisted his head and gave a hissing chuckle. "I understand you're in a hurry, but try to have at least a little patience. I'll come to you shortly."

The Supreme Wisdom's dark-rimmed eyes narrowed, the stone of the mask twisting in response to his irritation. "An energy channeler. You are bold, Gehennan, to think you can stare into the sun. Let me educate you."

He stabbed the tip of the Staff into the ground behind him and turned from it. He lifted his arms out from his sides, and several channels opened along them and began soaking energy directly from the air. Zekraul attempted to speed his devouring of his current prey, unsure of what to expect from the Lord of the Wisdoms. Melukah brought his palms forward and pointed them at his wiry foe.

"Adapt, child."

With that, a burst of light exploded from the Wisdom's fingertips and struck Zekraul. It was similar enough to the light from the Sun Staff, and the demon managed to shift his body once again before sustaining much damage. Still, this blast had been incredibly fast, far smaller than the unfocused beams of the Staff, and carried more impact than he could have imagined.

As quickly as his body began to relax from the strain of surviving this flash, another emanated from Melukah's hands. This time it was a wide red beam, far different from the prior, its light carried in a large funnel shape instead of a slim-lined blast. Zekraul sustained immense damage across his upper body before he could adjust once again, and he began to feel his grip on Torlen slipping as his flesh smoked in pain.

Another attack emanated, in what seemed to Zekraul to be the same second as the first, this one a series of six bright blue balls. Then another, a dozen radiant orange spikes that shot from the Wisdom's hands and slammed into his target from all sides. Next a yellow pillar that erupted straight from the ground and passed harmlessly through Torlen, but burned away the green tendrils binding his arms.

The attacks kept coming faster than Zekraul could conceive. He could not complete his transformation into Torlen's frame, could not shift his body to deflect the lights, could not even extract himself and attempt to run. He was helplessly struck over and over, letting out a scream of terror as he was beaten into oblivion by an agony he had never before felt, the agony of being burned alive.

Then his salvation came from an unexpected source, as Torlen regained enough of his senses to control his arms. He pointed them forth at the beast straddling him and, with a panicked instinct, used a tremendous boom of focused sound to seize Zekraul and send him flying away. The tendrilled arms and legs were both shattered from this reverberation; only the demon's head and half of his torso remained intact as he soared away. Nonetheless, it relieved him from the fury of the Sun long enough to recover his thoughts.

When he landed, Keldana awaited him. She pointed her hands and sent a blast of freezing air to imprison him. Zekraul quickly shed his outermost layer of skin, turning it into fire and sending it billowing out around him. As he did so, a black haze began to distort his body as he separated from the Morolian plane. The fiery shell surrounding him transformed back into crystals and then swiftly into stone, then was frozen by the frigid wave sent from the Ocean.

Melukah wasted no time, retrieving his Sun Staff and charging it for but a moment. Then he lashed out with it, an intense white strike disintegrating the area where Zekraul had hid himself. When the light and smoke from this luminous eruption had faded, the demon had vanished once again.

Keldana raised her hands and a light rain began to fall across the area. "He retreats," she reported. "He moves quickly, carrying his body along the ether streams. Torlen and I may catch him yet."

Her lord placed the Sun Staff across his back and shook his head. "I have no interest in a meager hellspawn. Still, it's a curious change of events. Whatever he is, it seems somehow he managed to defeat Aegagropilion and gain his powers. This may be advantageous to us. Regardless, he has received his education. After today, he will not attempt to confront the Wisdom of the Sun again."

The idea of pursuit abandoned, Keldana instead moved to where Torlen sat braced on his hands and knees. She patched his minor damage with ease, and the two of them rose to face Melukah once more.

"Did I not know you better, Torlen, I would begin to think you of no use," the Sun chastised with a tone almost of amusement.

The Wisdom of Sound hung his head. "Never before have the creatures on Morolia been such a nuisance, Lord."

"So it seems; and we have lost too many allies because of it. Come, let us leave the creatures of this continent to their trifles. All that remains for us is Gilanirus. If we can slay the Shadow, we may return home."

He turned and began to march without further word. Keldana followed after, but Torlen stood alone for a moment. He shook his head in frustration and glanced to where the demon Zekraul had disappeared. After uttering a silent curse, he too moved after his master.

* * * * *

It was hours later before Akatriel found Deun lying incapacitated on the forest floor. Nearby his body, Kargaroth jutted out from the corpse of a withered tree. Akatriel stared at the decrepit trunk for a moment, surprised to see such an ancient and dead figure amongst the other young and leafy boughs. He shrugged it off with disinterest, then retrieved Kargaroth from the wood and moved to the injured man's side. He thrust the sword into the ground, then knelt down to the still body.

Thanks to his innate mystic defenses, Deun had not died. His spirit was incapable of reversing the damage caused by the lich's magic, however, and he could do nothing but lay in agony. It took Akatriel several minutes of intense healing to bring the man back to consciousness. Once finally revived he looked up at his healer with empty eyes, his expression wholly devoid of emotion.

"You lost, Deun Coloran," the white robed figure teased. "You're doomed to die here, alone, in failure. But I have been given the power to save lives of the inhabitants of this plane. All I ask is a price, a favor which you cannot know in advance. The same price I have offered you twice before. Would you have me save you?"

Deun's right hand suddenly reached out and seized Akatriel's throat. For a moment the pale conspirator thought himself in trouble, and only with effort managed to remain calm. Then the dying man gargled, "I will give anything. Give me one more chance at the Overlord."

The conspirator smiled in spite of the mystic's crushing grip. "Good to hear," he whispered. With a flick of hands he cast a strange white bubble over the battered body, then delicately extricated himself and began pacing around the battlefield in disinterest. "That spell will take a moment. Even I have my limits. I cannot undo the ruination you've suffered, so I shall be forced to build something anew. Don't worry, what I grant will be far superior to the body you had before."

He wandered over to an area of the battlefield where several pieces of Zekraul's shattered arm lay, kneeling down and selecting the largest intact piece and holding it up in the sunlight, observing its refractions. "I instructed you to master your new sword before meeting your nemesis. You have yet to unlock the blade. Had you done so, you might have already seized your victory. Hopefully you better understand my counsel now, but I will advise you once more to adapt to Kargaroth. It is capable of such wondrously terrible things you cannot even fathom."

He stood and returned to check his spell's progress. Satisfied that it had purged any lingering shadow magic, he placed his hands on the human's chest and released a second burst of energy to merge with the bubble. Deun's flesh began to glow a brilliant white. Soon the wounds and burns covering his body lessened and then faded, as his hoarse voice rose into a clear roar of determination. Akatriel continued to pour archaic magics into him, whispering quietly, "When the time comes, you'll know what you must do to repay me."

A blinding flash echoed forth, blanketing the forest. When it faded, Akatriel was gone from view. Deun stood on his feet, his eyes shut tight, waves of silvery power pouring from his shoulders. He reached forth and seized Kargaroth by its hilt, lifting it high into the air effortlessly, its once formidable weight no longer burdening his hands. He swung the sword rapidly from one side to the other, the blade flying as easily as if it were a mere dagger. He pointed the tip at a nearby tree, and an echo of silver light mixed with black shot forth. The tree split from base to branch, thousands of shredded leaves drifting to the ground swallowed in black flames.

Deun opened his eyes, which had been replaced by twin pools

of white light. In the center of those lights, a slim streak of purple could be seen, which skittered back and forth in random patterns, responding to a similar cloak of electricity draped across the Kargaroth.

He spoke and a deep booming voice, which echoed both from his throat and from his sword, filled the area. “Overlord! Your death seeks you! I will carry your body to the grave within my own teeth.”

## Chapter 37.

# War of the Kings of Hell

Abaddon stood poised on the peak of a tall stone spire. He was less than a mile from his goal, no more than a few leaps from his encounter with Gilanirus. He had been just about to dash into the fray, when in an instant the situation had changed.

Kargaroth had reappeared.

Far to his north, he could feel the hunger of his lost sword crying out. How had it escaped his detection for so long? Some creature of strong intent must have been masking it, blocking his senses to it. He held his suspicions as to who was responsible; but once Kargaroth had flared, with the deep powers of the sword being summoned, no force could have prevented Abaddon's sight from locking onto his missing limb.

So he stood debating. Someone was using Kargaroth, one who had managed to link with it and harness the secrets left in its haunted steel. He could not abide the thought of leaving this person to their devices, of allowing them to use his weapon to further whatever agendas they might hold. He had sworn the Unholy Blade would not kill, binding its hilt with bandages to acknowledge this pledge. Even now, when so many other events transpired, he could not tear himself away from that sacred oath.

But the sword was at least two days' travel from him, and in that time he might lose his immortal quarry. The Godbeast was moving west with distinct purpose, as the Wisdoms closed from the north. If the divinities collided, there was no predicting which side would emerge victorious. If the Tyrant fell to his ancient nemeses, Abaddon would miss his own opportunity for a final battle unlike any other. However, he also had to consider that as unrivaled as the might of Gilanirus' was, Kargaroth could be essential to stand against him.

He released a sigh and shook his head. He knew his nature. In the end, there could be only one decision. He sealed away the bulk of his strength and, with a grunt of effort, launched himself into motion once again.

* * * * *

Gilanirus moved through the barren southern stretches of Arkalen. Any plant life or forests that had once occupied this area had long since died off and petrified, their spirit robbed by the unyielding Lifeless Vortex. The area was desolate, soulless, unwelcoming. It reminded him wistfully of home.

He moved through a peculiar area where giant stone pillars rose across the land, like the fingertips of drowned corpses reaching for the freedom of air. The ancient Godbeast admired the scenery, but was finding it annoying to navigate his way through. He conserved as much of his limited strength as he could, but occasionally his temper would slip and he would turn dozens of the surrounding spires into dust with a flash of heated thought.

After one particular outburst, he looked up to notice a curiosity awaiting him. Standing atop one of the shortest pillars a small distance away, a human male in black attire awaited with a serene look on his face.

Gilanirus stopped and stared at the native for a moment. He had wandered much of the Morolian plane, and rarely had he witnessed something so amusing. "Are you a guard of some sort?" he asked cheerfully. "Perhaps a travel guide? I find myself in no need of directions, but thanks anyway." The human wordlessly reached to his back and drew forth his weapon, a sword of nine feet. The Tyrant's slitted eyes narrowed in recognition. "So you have the Arda," he observed, the levity now drained from his voice. "I suppose this means you have come for me explicitly, after all."

The man gave a nod. "You're a quick one."

Even before the last word of the sentence was complete, Gilanirus was hovering in the air above the human by a good twenty feet, his right palm pointed out and his left hand held high. After releasing a pillar of divine fires down upon the arrogant sentry, he exclaimed, "That I am."

The deity slid back to the ground and waited for a roasted corpse to materialize at his feet. When this did not happen, he widened his eyes and expanded his senses. It was only barely in time that he detected the attack coming from below, beneath the very ground he stood upon. Eight pillars of earth, twisted into blades, snapped up from every side and slashed inward. Gilanirus took a calm breath, then a wave of psychic force emanated from his body in all directions, ripping the weak Morolian stone into pebbles.

When his vision cleared, the man stood before him once more in a defiant and loose stance, the Arda held out to his side in one hand. Gilanirus shook his head as he contemplated the approaching Wisdoms.

"So be it, Morolian. If you cling so desperately to your survival, I will allow it. But I cannot play with you today."

He turned and leaped into the air again, moving far faster than what he believed a human's meager senses would be able to follow. In a single burst of strength he cleared a full mile, his armored form flying through the thin Morolian sky as easily as a sparrow.

At the top of his jump, a black blur suddenly materialized only inches from his face. He twisted his head and prepared to brush the anomaly aside with a blast of fire, but in the same instant, a punch of incredible strength landed on the top of his helmet. A wave of crushing green energy poured over his entire frame and sent him rocketing to the ground below, straight back in the direction he had just come from.

He recovered himself in time to gain his feet, but his temper had slipped a final time and his eyes now erupted with bright red flames.

"Insolent welp!" he roared. "Dare you strike the Tyrant of Gehenna? Know you the fate you seek to make for yourself?"

The man pointed his sword forward, bringing the tip within inches of the burning eyes. "I am Abaddon Daemon. My name is all you need know. Remember for all eternity. You will humor me, Gilanirus of Gehenna. You will face me as your equal."

The Godbeast gathered power, both in the outer layers of his armor as well as deep within his core, abandoning caution and gearing up for divine war. "Equal?" he mocked his would-be adversary.

He moved forward and struck with his right fist only, a punch that on its own would have killed a hellspawn. His target's eyes locked onto the armored fist, and a backlash of white ether suddenly spewed forth and gripped the armored titan, hampering his body with binding pressure. Abaddon swiftly leaped a step back, stabbed Arda into the ground behind him, and met the punch with a thrust of his own fist.

There was a radiating boom of impact, as Gilanirus expected to see human flesh disintegrated by his malice. Instead there was only a collision of magics, his red ether feasting into both white and black, a maelstrom of energies mixing and disintegrating. In the end the force of both blows was neutralized, and on the human survived.

The Tyrant raised his arm and looked over his fist. He had sustained no damage, but neither had he won the battle instantly, as anticipated. The human had at least been drained, forced to retreat several yards and breathe heavily from the effort necessary to counter that punch. Gilanirus respectfully did not acknowledge the man's weakness, impressed by his audacity.

"Equals indeed. Few are those who have survived that blow, and most among them number as gods. If it is noble death you seek, you have demonstrated yourself worthy to meet it at my hands." He reached to his back and seized the sizable cleaver he had forged at his awakening. "Draw your weapon, Morolian."

Abaddon walked forward and retrieved Arda, gripping it tightly and raising it forward in both hands. As he focused his magic, a slim aura began to shiver around him and his eyes turned to brilliant blue pools. With a roar, he unleashed all of his self-imposed restraints layer by layer. Floods of ether from miles around poured to him, emptying into his spirit and corpus, elevating him beyond the levels any man had ever before attained. For the first time in many long years, Abaddon Daemon reached his limit.

Gilanirus waited for the end of the mystic's display, bored and ready to finish this battle. "Do what you can," he taunted, still waiting.

Abaddon crouched and released another roar. The air began to hum with a high pitched shriek, and the earth at his feet became malleable and liquescent. Finally, he surrounded the Arda in a Holy Aura and threw himself into the air.

He struck his enormous adversary head on, a sweep of Arda that took less than a quarter of a second. Gilanirus parried the blow with ease, as well as the next ten that followed within three seconds, each from a different direction. The Godbeast took note of the human's speed, impressed but not dazzled. He patiently countered the series of attacks and then, when he was content with his control over the situation, released a swing of his own.

The oversized cleaver launched at Abaddon's waist, a blazing strike that began instantaneously as the man was preparing for another of his own swings. He forced himself into a tight spin and struck the hatchet with Arda, using the katana's leverage to jet himself above the blade's path. He flew a few dozen feet above his armored foe and positioned himself for a falling attack. Before he could begin his descent, Gilanirus glanced up and locked eyes on him.

In a flash of divine fury, Abaddon's body was doused in thick psionic fires. He flew away from the Godbeast with ridiculous force, his barriers barely shielding his life before they collapsed. Once he had gone half a mile away, he was struck from above by a massive gauntleted fist. Steel thicker and stronger than any he had ever known cracked the back of his skull, and he flew face-first into one of the earthen pillars below, bombarding through it and deep into the ground.

Gilanirus landed a few yards from the crater where his enemy was now buried. He gave a broad sweep with his cleaver, and a haze of heat echoed forth and melted the pillars throughout the immediate vicinity, leaving the battleground unencumbered.

"Come out, little one," the Spectre of Gehenna demanded. "I promised you death, and you shall have it. Do not hide now and make me come looking for you. That would dishonor the demise you have so earned."

As he was finishing his sentence, there was a loud clang on his left shoulder. He looked over to see Arda resting there, an attack he had not felt coming and had been unable to block. "Such speed..." he whispered. Recovering quickly, he reached his left hand over his shoulder and snatched Abaddon's head between his fist, then flipped the human forward and slammed him bodily into the ground. He followed up with a downward chop from his weapon, aiming once more to cut the man in half at his waist.

The beleaguered mystic reacted in spite of the jarring impact he had sustained, lashing out with Arda and cutting into the cleaver. There was a booming twang from the impact of the combatants' clashing brawn, then the disconcerting sound of a crack. Abaddon ripped up hard with his sword, tossing the cleaver away, then struck out at an awkward angle and slammed the katana hard into Gilanirus' left elbow. Gehennite armor again deflected the blow, but the force temporarily jarred the strength of the arm, and the grip of its fingers loosened enough for Abaddon to escape.

He dropped to the ground breathing heavily, staring forward at the armored tank he could not penetrate. He observed that Gilanirus' cleaver was uninjured, its rough edge untarnished from traded impacts. He inspected the Arda, and was dismayed to find it was indeed his sword that had cracked during the previous exchange.

His turned his questions to Gilanirus. "This sword has cut

through everything I've brought it against. Why does it not injure you?"

The Eternal Samurai gave a chuckle. "You haven't been told? Arda came to this continent long ago, transported from Gehenna by mine own hand. Arda was *my* sword. Carved from my own body, by the essence of my own mind. It is imbued with the same killing edge as my new weapon, this Okidin, and can slice through all materials. Except, that is, my own armor. My armor alone cannot be pierced by blades of my creation."

Abaddon slowed his breathing with effort and dipped his chin slightly. "Then this sword is not the power that can kill you."

"There's no power you know that can kill me."

Abaddon raised an eyebrow, then gave a shrug.

He crouched low and gathered a stream of ether into Arda. The blade began to flicker, changing into a bright green hum that released a strange whir. The knight looked again to Gilanirus and drew a deep breath. He blazed forth once more, launching into a series of ferocious strikes and attempting to cut the colossus down. At first the Godbeast idly blocked a few of the blows, then surprisingly found himself unable to keep pace with the human. In order to disguise his disadvantage, he ceased all attempts at countering. Abaddon struck the armored frame over and again, each time causing Gilanirus' anchoring psyche a tremor of disruption, but dealing no real harm. The final blow came directly down upon one of the steely shoulders, with a tremendous explosion of energy originated from the impact. Still the armor of Gehenna did not give quarter.

As the lag after this last strike was substantial, Gilanirus launched one of his own, swinging the Okidin as fast as he could in a horizontal sweep. Abaddon was forced to clumsily reverse his attack in order to catch the cleaver on Arda's edge, grimacing as he heard another nerve-raking crack from the katana. He moved to retreat a safe distance, but this time his foe would not allow him to disengage so easily. The Tyrant locked his mind once more to his opponent's location, and a thousand tiny sparks of red light closed in from every direction, seeking to engulf the man and devour his flesh.

Abaddon released a commanding battle cry. In an instant, a whirlwind of green ether surged forth and evaporated the voracious sparks. Gilanirus waited until this display was over, then crouched and eyed his small rival.

"I begin to understand you. Your power is not your own. It could not possibly be. You've been deputized by the Muses, to carry out their work in the place of their cowardice. You're a vessel devised to be a nuisance long enough for Melukah to reach me. This is a trap most foul."

Abaddon continued to wrap himself in green ether as he responded to the accusation. "It's true that I borrowed from the Muses. But I'm neither their creation nor their servant. They asked me to face you on their behalf. The truth is, I would have come for you regardless, once I knew of your existence. They say you're the mightiest of all warriors, a creature of ultimate battle. I cannot sufficiently describe how fervently I've sought you. My heart swells with glee as we fight now. You are my superior. You are better than me, stronger than me, impervious to any harm I might inflict. You, Almighty Gilanirus, are capable of destroying the Destroyer."

The knight raised his eyes, and they had shifted from blue to a very dark green. Gilanirus had never before seen such a reaction from Elysian ether, and took a step forward with interest in the sorceries the human was conjuring. Abaddon continued, "And that's why I have to fight you. Pay no heed to the powers borrowed from the Muses. I only used them as a defense measure before, a panic button. I gathered them for a different purpose entirely. I gathered them to use as a battery. I brought them here, so I might show even you some real challenge. I want to see, Gilanirus of Gehenna, Shadow of Elzaniru, what you can do against *me*."

He tightened his two-handed grip on Arda and pointed it to the sky with a roar. The swirls of green ether surrounding him suddenly began to change, seeping into Abaddon's body and transforming into eddies of black and purple. Soon his clothing began to alter, shifting into armors. Spikes and blades protruded forth, ornamental decorations with wicked barbs and hooked edges. A thick cape, ethereal and drifting into a shrouded darkness behind him, grew from his back. His hair lifted up as if on a breeze, becoming longer and darker, and his body began to grow, expanding to much more than his original height, until he stood over nine feet tall.

He looked at Gilanirus with new eyes, empty pools of darkness that mirrored infinity. This new Abaddon spoke, a dark voice that echoed across the plains. "Show me what you can do against Hell."

For the first time in this encounter, Gilanirus felt a twinge of apprehension. "These magics. They are of the children of Elzaniru."

This memory of the Hell Knight moved forward. His feet stepped slowly, but still he covered distances at tremendous speed. Gilanirus was forced into a retreat in order to move the Okidin fast enough to keep up with the relentless stream of slashes coming from Arda. Abaddon held it nimbly in one hand and lashed out repeatedly, aiming to slice through the iron helmet. A blow finally got through in spite of the Godbeast's best efforts, a dull thunk to the top of his head. The divine steel did not budge, so he answered the hit with one of his own, finally passing his Okidin straight through the human's waist.

There was a splatter of red blood signaling a successful blow, but the man did not fall. Instead he gave an agile leap over the Godbeast's head, kicking out hard into the middle of Gilanirus' back and slamming him into the stone battlefield. As the Tyrant recovered himself, Abaddon gathered dark energy to his left hand. He placed a black-coated fist on the base of his katana's blade and chanted, "Corruption." Arda's frame suddenly became coated in purple lightning and the metal began to transform. The straight lines of the katana shifted into the jagged pattern of a jigsaw, the silvery blade became black, and the already lengthy sword grew even longer, nearing fifteen feet of reach.

Again the hellish apparition approached Gilanirus, striking out with the transmogrified katana. This new blade twisted and moved like a serpentine whip, landing on the Okidin but still bending to slash against Gehennite armors. The Godbeast was relieved to find his plates did not give to these blows, taking no scratches from the dark points of the mysterious serrated edge.

Gilanirus fought to regain an upper hand in the exchange, but he could not reach the necessary speed with his body at its current starvation levels. He continuously struck out with fury, slowly feeling his arm tire as it began to drain his stores of red ether. Eventually—annoyed that he was forced to use such costly magics so soon after resurrection—he opened his eyes and locked his thoughts onto his foe. He unleashed a backlash of psionic energy that rocked the area for miles. After this a dozen blades, composed of nothing but thought, appeared around his tormentor's body and within an instant closed in. Abaddon was forced to parry as many of the immaterial strikes as he could, but even through his best efforts half a dozen bleeding gashes were torn through his devilish armor.

Gilanirus stared at his opponent for a moment and forced himself to regain composure, to see through the shroud of intimidation this mortal had somehow erected. The strength the man wielded was truly terrifying, even the Spectre himself would not deny that. But this was only a weak version of the dark gods he had once known, a sad simulacrum. The human had proclaimed he was using the powers of the Muses as a battery; Gilanirus had much experience with the Muses, and knew well their limitations. Interesting as it had been, there was but one inevitable conclusion to this contest.

He raised his Okidin, and a fiery wall of red ether coated the blade and burned it up. Then he covered it in an invisible wall of psionic energy, crushing the Gehennite ether directly into the blade itself. He watched briefly as his opponent spent a moment healing wounds from the previous psionic strikes.

"Tell me, Son of Hell," Gilanirus inquired, "would you still have me show you what I can do?"

Abaddon's eyes had lost their blackness and were now only a dark blue, and his hair had drifted back to its natural position. When he spoke, his formerly booming voice was diminished, and even hoarse. "I came here to witness your best."

The Tyrant leveled the Okidin out to his side, horizontally at the height of his waist, and channeled more ether to it. "Then I shall not leave you disappointed. Prepare yourself."

The mystic took a deep breath, then laid his left hand once more across the blade of Arda. His eyes again sank briefly to black and the entire mesa shook with the sound of a single word, though Abaddon's lips did not move. "Destruction!" echoed the land.

Again Arda changed, this time the blade darkening, deepening, until it vanished entirely from view. All that grew from Abaddon's hand was a piercing void, a long strip of distorted air that whirred as a vacuum. Soon this vacuum became covered in a deep shroud of shadows, and strips of purple lightning began to leak from it. Gilanirus waited, allowing his foe's attack to form as he confidently charged his own.

Then Abaddon moved. He took the brief instant of his maximum strength and used it to shift in front of his foe as quickly as a flash of light. After this surge he raised Arda high and reversed it for a swing. This motion gave more than enough time for his divine opponent to react, sinking his heel into the ground and shifting his armored body swiftly to the left. Before the black void of a blade could close in and make contact with his samurai shell, Gilanirus released a psionic pulse and blasted his own body straight through that of his mortal challenger, swinging the Okidin and exploding all the layers of devastation coating it.

The energy from the two attacks created a pillar of melted magics, booming straight for the midday sky and threatening to rip a new wound in the mighty Veil. Black and red lightning swirled into a tornado and then shattered out across Arkalen, striking through desert, forest, rivers, killing hundreds of animals, demons, and humans indiscriminately.

It was several minutes before the chaos died down enough for the two warriors to address one another. Gilanirus sounded a satisfied sigh as he powered down. He was about to speak out to deliver a final taunt, but as he stared at the edge of his Okidin, there was a sudden outlandish cry as metal twisted and splintered. A small purple shockwave ripped forth from the body of the cleaver and it shattered down the middle, leaving only a one-foot slab of steel in his hand as the rest of the blade exploded into grey dust and red lights.

"He finished his strike?" Gilanirus mused. "When?"

That was not the end, however. The Lord of Gehenna felt his arm gripped by a paralyzing pain, and fell to his knees as black energy crawled from within his body and began to devour his armor. The immortal shell cracked, then splintered, then caught fire and melted away. The deity endeavored to bring his formidable might to bear, fighting to anchor his frame against the damning magic, but he could make no headway. After half a minute there was another explosion of red and purple lights as Gilanirus' right arm, from hand to shoulder, disintegrated.

He sat for a moment shivering, drawing any small amounts of red ether he could back into his body. He spent nearly a minute attempting to steady himself, to recover from the horrible pains of body and mind being devoured by the unholiest of magic. Finally he found the strength to speak. "Well struck, Morolian. Of the many thousands I have slain, you are among the very few to have caused me anguish. Last I lived, I met a man whom I believed to be the pinnacle of human potential, a Saint named Loridican. You have far surpassed him, Abaddon Daemon. Your name has been etched in my memory. In that way, you have bought yourself immortality even as I cut you down and ended your life." He turned about to look upon his fallen adversary. "But you also destroyed the Okidin, so I'll be forced to reclaim my Arda, it seems."

Gilanirus was not greeted with the sight he expected—Abaddon on his knees, dying, ready to beg for mercy. Instead the man stood boldly, the phantasmal demonic armors withered; diminished; but not yet faded. His right hand gripped Arda tightly, though the sword had reverted to its natural form. A slim one-inch crack had reappeared on the blade, almost three feet from the hilt.

The Godbeast took his left hand and placed it over the gaping hole where his right arm had once been. With effort, he caused a fresh patch of armor to materialize there, shielding his vulnerability. "Still you would stand in defiance of me?!" he demanded of the accursed vision.

The mystic offered no response, but stared forward with a dead, cruel look in his blue eyes. Gilanirus began to brace himself for another rush, then suddenly felt the proximity of the Wisdoms. They had made much progress against him while he had battled here, and now he was in worse shape than ever to face Melukah. Whether or not this human had willfully agreed to serve as bait for the Muses, their trap had nonetheless served its design.

He shook his head in frustration. "Uncanny. I'm forced to retreat from you, Abaddon Daemon. We must call this battle a draw. I don't have the time to cut you down to the level where I could pry my Arda from your lifeless hands. Yet I warn you, if you once again try to follow me, I will be inclined to leave no pieces of you intact."

Gilanirus turned once more from his enemy and gave a vigorous leap into the air. Abaddon moved to follow as he had before, but after taking only half a step he fell forward onto his knees with a lurch of pain, dropping Arda with a clang. The weakness he had fought so hard to hide from his dominating rival had overtaken him. The last remnants of his transformation flickered out with a whimper of hatred, and his body diminished. Staggering wounds reopened, including a thick slash across the line of his waist, as most of his blood emptied from his body with a single gush. The battery of the Muses suddenly unlatched from his spirit, splitting the Veil with a wicked crackle and returning to Elysium. The mystic well understood what this meant. He had bound the Muses' magic to himself until one of two conditions had been met—either his contract fulfilled and Gilanirus returned to Gehenna, or

Abaddon himself crossed into the abyss of death.

He stayed on his knees for as long as he could, his thoughts pouring through his past. He recalled every event, every friend, every battle. He forced himself to think, to keep his mind alive. Finally he could remember no more, could think on nothing except for the opponent who had defeated him, who was getting away even now. His heart reached in that direction, yearning for his feet to move once again.

His eyes welled in tears of frustration as his jaw tightened. "Why?" he growled to himself. "All of my life I wanted this. To be the mightiest I had ever become and yet still be defeated. To be crushed by an enemy truly better than me, though I performed at my very apex." In spite of the pain gripping his throat and chest, his words rose to a yell with the strength left in his lungs. "Why now, when I have been granted my glorious death!" His voice sank and lost volume as his breaths became jagged. "Why is it... that all I want... is one more chance to fight?" He sat quietly for a moment, feeling the insurmountable and innumerable pains rushing through his nervous system.

"I want to fight!" he cried again as tears broke freely from his eyes. He surged forward and lifted himself up onto one foot, struggling ferociously to gain the other. But his strength failed one final time. He collapsed backward clumsily, rolling onto the ground on his side. There he lay without another sound, the plains mourning him only through the whispers of wind raking across their stripped surface.

And so died Abaddon Daemon.

## Chapter 38.

# Deun's Revenge

Myris had positioned himself atop a singed tree and stared southward over Arkalen, casting out Feelers to gather information. He shook his head and gave a sigh, then did a nimble backflip and fell to the ground. His feet hit the earth with a feathery impact, then he turned to where his companion sat bandaging his own shoulder.

"How is it?" the Cainite asked.

"I'll survive," Cildar responded without taking his eyes from his work. "Any idea what the hell that was?"

A few minutes prior, the Dragoon had been struck down by a thick red bolt of lightning. The jolt of unnatural electricity had come in horizontally from the south, tearing its way through several trees and blasting his right shoulder pad into ashes.

"That is beyond my ability to nail down," his friend replied. "The source is quite a distance from here. It must have been a tremendous release of energy to have come so far and still been that powerful. I analyzed the ether signatures that swept through the nearby areas. They were a mix of divine origins."

Cildar paused briefly as he completed dressing his injury. With some reluctance, he filled his left hand with a touch of healing energy and began to massage it through his bandages. Since recovering from his time as the Dark Paladin, he had refrained from using his own magic as much as possible. As he continued his work, enjoying the soothing sensation of holy energy flowing through his frame once more, he commented, "I take it you think Lord Abaddon was involved."

"Without question."

After another few seconds of healing, Cildar rose to his feet. "Then that's the direction we head. Did you pinpoint an origin?"

"More or less."

"Let's move."

Myris moved to block the taller man's path, holding out a hand in caution. "Perhaps you have been through enough the past few months. Is it wise to charge so recklessly once more into confrontation? We could find a settlement somewhere, take some time to recover. Lord Abaddon would understand. He knows we are but human."

The paladin avoided eye contact, staring directly over his ally's head. "I need to fight something, Myris," he explained. "Something that isn't an innocent civilian, and isn't you. I need to remember whose side I'm on. Right now, recovering my mind's more important to me than my body."

"I understand," he answered, stepping aside. As Cildar walked past, Myris shook his head solemnly, then disappeared into the trees and shadowed his haunted friend.

* * * * *

In a narrow hallway in yet another of Arkalen's vast underground tombs, Akatriel stood waiting in silence. He was as motionless as the rocks around him, albeit slightly more vibrant in the dancing torchlight. He had been stationed here for several hours now and was beginning to lose his calm. His plans were not designed to confine him so long to a single space. The freedom of the Queen's movement was crucial to control the board.

Signaling the return of a familiar phenomenon, a black shroud began to seep from the air around his robes and brushed against his frame. He gave no response to the intrusion, but prepared to lose his vision and be cast into darkness. This came as expected, and a voice soon followed.

*You have idled long.*

"Long enough to catch your interest, it seems, yes. Gilanirus delays for some reason. Has he decided I'm not to be trusted? It would be a death knell to our cause."

*He comes.*

Akatriel relaxed slightly at this announcement. "That is welcome news. It's a nice change of pace for your incessant nervous spectating to serve some actual use to our cause."

*The hour approaches. These final steps must not go wrong. Even minor setbacks speak to your lack of control over matters.*

"Don't denigrate me right as I'm on the cusp of triumph over an impossible task. I am in complete control, as I have ever been. I've played the entire board, every piece, perfectly. Perhaps not everything is precisely as I had divined, but I hold the threads too tightly for them to slip. I will accomplish what even the True Gods failed to do, with all of their 'infinite' power and wisdom. Once Gilanirus reaches this place, my success is assured. All aberrations from that point will be handled."

*I will watch and judge.*

"I have no doubt of that. But when the time comes! Do *not* forget your end in all of this. Even you have your price to pay for my services."

*Your price is a pittance to me. I have no reason to betray you.*

Akatriel gave a nod but no further response. Within a few seconds the deep darkness faded, restoring the atmosphere of the cave. It was less than another hour before he heard the sounds of heavy footsteps coming his way. Shortly after that, Gilanirus stood towering before him.

"Akatriel," the Godbeast announced upon arrival. "I'm pleased to see that you are swift. My current temper would not have weathered a wait."

The pale figure tilted his head slightly to one side, gazing at the barren spot where Gilanirus' right arm had once been. "You did not endure your journey well, Spectre. Did Melukah somehow intercept you?"

"No, I have evaded the Sun. This damage was caused by mortal hands."

"Mortal hands?" he asked with a smirk. Then a thought occurred to him, and he widened his eyes in suspicion. "Tell me, you didn't by any chance get a name?"

"I did, and swore him I would commit it to the eternal tome of my memory. I was scarred by the human Abaddon Daemon."

Akatriel bowed his head and held his hands up to his face. "I find myself stunned," he whispered. "Where was he hiding from me? How did he find strength sufficient to damage the Tyrant? I was warned the Knight was unpredictable, but this is unprecedented."

"What?" his domineering ally demanded aloud.

"Never mind. Come, we're not here without purpose."

They moved to the end of the tunnel. Though they were already miles underground, as they walked the slope of the cavern floor steepened, causing them to move ever deeper before being forced to a halt. A bright barrier shone before them, hiding a doorway of some size, though still insufficient for Akatriel's towering guest.

He looked back at Gilanirus. "Will you be able to fit? It's a bit small, and your psionic blasts aren't safe down here."

The Tyrant gave a grunt of effort, then a shimmering aura surrounded his body. His legs, torso, and his arm began to shorten, collapsing at the joints. Soon his frame had deformed itself, shrinking down from his normal twenty foot height to less than ten.

Rather than answering, he offered a question of his own. "What is this barrier?"

"Pay it no heed. It's designed to keep certain things in. It won't bother us."

Having said this, he walked swiftly through the light. Gilanirus spent a moment attempting to analyze the magic in the area, but he could make no sense of its nature or even origin. At last, he committed himself and moved forward through the barrier.

Once on the other side he stood in a massive chamber, which extended an impenetrable distance. The ceiling ran so high that

Gilanirus surmised it rose even above ground level, and must have been positioned under a hollowed mountain. Even his sight could not locate the far wall from where he stood. Littering the ground of the chamber in every direction, there were piles of human corpses. The Godbeast's phantasmal eyes widened as he stared across the myriads of bodies and sniffed the air, which carried the unmistakable flavor of fresh death.

Akatriel paced about, kicking some of the straggling corpses and offering explanation. "You feed on the shattered essences of the recently fallen, correct? Long ago, there was a savage war here. Two rival cults both claimed this mountainous tomb for unholy ceremonies. Each was urged by their different gods that it was theirs by right, that they were the true descendants of those who had carved it. One or perhaps both of the gods clearly lied, but humans cannot fathom the deceptions of the divine. So the war came. It was a war of samurai and warlocks facing knights and shamans. Their strength was startlingly even in its match. Over one hundred thousand men and women came here to kill. Legend says they did so until only four hundred were left alive. No one knows which side won, however, for the four hundred disappeared. Even I don't know happened to them.

"A confounding legend, I'll admit. But legend aside, there's no denying the actuality of the corpses. This chamber is sealed by a strange archaic magic, presumably put in place by one of the cults. It locks the air in the room from the influence of the Veil. The souls that perished here were never able to pass on. They have drifted in purgatory for ages, unable to escape the Morolian plane. I offer them to you, Lord of Gehenna. Feast upon these souls and increase your power. I'm certain there are more than enough here to restore you to full strength. The barrier will hide your path from the Wisdoms for some time. They will have to track you the old ways, which will be much slower for them. By the time they come, you will be ready to hold your ultimate battle with the Wisdom of the Sun."

Gilanirus had expanded his body back to its full size during his cohort's speech, and already had opened several large rifts in his steely shell. Energy from the air continued to pour into him as he sniffed and groaned, pleased with his feast. Akatriel moved past the armored form and attempted to leave, but the Tyrant shot his left hand out and seized the priest by the throat.

"And where do you go? Some further scheme you have in mind?"

Akatriel released a light cough and struggled to talk with a calm voice. "You misjudge me, Lord. I have simply noticed that your weapon has been lost. You cannot build another without Schpariel's magic, correct?"

He released his grip and nodded slowly. "Only Schpariel has the gift to wield Gehennite sorcery outside of our home plane. It is his birthed purpose."

"I merely depart to find you a suitable weapon for your battle. Fighting the Wisdoms unarmed would be foolhardy even with your might."

"The one called Daemon is too powerful for you to defeat. You will not retrieve Arda from him."

Akatriel shrugged as he continued his exit, shouting back cryptically, "I have my sight set on a different sword."

* * * * *

"I have lost Gilanirus," Keldana confessed dejectedly.

She had been attempting to relocate the Tyrant for nearly an hour, since his presence had first vanished from Melukah's detection. The three Wisdoms had endeavored to rove as close as possible to where they had lost the signal, but they had gone too far without direction and knew that soon they would be following the wrong trail.

The Supreme Wisdom stared up at the midday sun and released a groan. He spent a moment in reflection before responding, "The explosion from a few hours back—can you take us there?"

"Yes, Exalted Melukah."

"Torlen, we'll be relying on your tracking skills from here on out. It seems it has become necessary to follow the Spectre's physical trail."

"It's no problem," the Wisdom of Sound answered with a bow. "I have not allowed my abilities to rust."

Melukah spent a moment fuming at fate, then once again set his feet into motion.

* * * * *

In the same crater the Wisdoms now approached, Akatriel stood staring down over the limp form of Abaddon Daemon. The man lay on his side, on dusty ground painted thickly with his spilled blood. His skin had grown pale with the stillness of death. The priest reached out with his hand and touched it to the man's throat. The pale skin of the dead was no match for the colorless white flesh of Akatriel's own fingertips.

Finding no pulse, he rolled the figure onto its back. He wordlessly rolled his sleeves up to his elbows, then plunged his hands hard into the fallen mystic's chest, summoning a huge aura of bright light around the two of them. When satisfied with his efforts, he stood and let his sleeves fall back to their natural position.

"Truly dead, even beyond my ability to resurrect. It seems Gilanirus left you more damaged than he realized. Disappointing. I might have had some remaining use for you." He thought for a moment, then turned his gaze north. "Still, a single Knight is an acceptable loss when I command two this late in the game." He lifted the Arda and examined it, making note of the large crack in the blade. "Damaged as well, though it makes little difference. I still need Kargaroth for my endgame. Deun Coloran will bring it to me soon enough."

He dropped Arda back into the dust and began to move away. "Farewell, Daemon. Of all I have dealt with, you were the only one I couldn't predict adequately. No piece has embodied his namesake more perfectly than you, my fallen Knight."

Just as he completed this pronouncement, he came to an abrupt halt. Slowly he straightened his stance and turned his gaze back into the clearing, stretching his senses to their limit.

"The Wisdoms approach," he spoke with trepidation. "They are too close." He raised his hands and cast a rain of scanning nets over the area, seeking out all signs from the previous battle. "I must hasten to hide Gilanirus' tracks. I can't have the Wisdoms reach him before he's ready for their confrontation." The conspirator then surrounded himself in a cloak of invisibility and went about his task.

* * * * *

North of these proceedings, Zekraul stumbled through forested lands in a daze, giving a constant hiss of exhaustion as he struggled to pull his body back together. He had managed to rebuild his outer frame, but could not cure himself of the aches and pains brought on by Melukah's blows. He could feel his grip on the talents of Aegagropilion slipping away, along with his control over the other abilities he had gained. Slowly he was becoming trapped within his own crystalline skin, unable to access the vast arsenal formerly at his disposal.

He struggled to rebuild his right arm for the fifth time. Just as he completed the skeletal structure and began to wrap it about with dark vined flesh, he heard the sound of footsteps behind him, followed by a rough ripping sensation as his new arm was cleaved off.

He rolled forward and brought up a wall of earth to cover his back, spinning about behind the safety of his shield. Recovering from his ambush, his senses heightened just in time to detect the faint sound of a single foot landing on top of the earthen barrier, then the same sound again behind him. He abandoned his sight—as it was serving him little use against his assailant—and allowed his other senses to lock onto the trajectory of a large sword swinging for his throat. Fearing his shapeshifting was ineffective at the moment, he sprang up from the ground and landed on the swinging sword, hanging on for his life.

When the sword stopped moving, the demon brought his vision back into play to get a look at his attacker.

"You again?" he shouted.

Deun stared at the feeble creature balancing on his sword and gave a broad smile. "Once more, Overlord. Once more must we waltz."

He flipped up hard with Kargaroth, throwing the demon into the air. Zekraul used the moment of freedom to run a few quick checks of his talents and determine what was still responsive enough to be useful. The magics of Kiastos and Dosiros were still potent, and his own meager shapeshifting abilities were undamaged. Aegagropilion's expansive morphing prowess was nearly lost to him, as well as the spirit of the lich.

The human warrior waited until his foe had reached the top of his climb, then soared into the air after him. Zekraul converted his arm into a huge spike and prepared to stab out, but his enemy went into a late spin. Deun swung out Kargaroth with his left hand barely gripping the pommel, and the demon was forced to use a blast of fire to propel himself just inches away from this slash. As the two began their return to the earth together, the human toyed with his prey, taking a few slow sweeps with his sword and challenging the Gehennan to evade or counter.

When their feet hit the ground, the demon began to grow himself a new arm. Instead of a hand, he crafted a crystalline greatsword from his wrist, identical in size to the Kargaroth. Deun shook his head disapprovingly at the display and unleashed another swing. Zekraul positioned his blade to intercept the oncoming steel, but the human's speed suddenly peaked and Kargaroth effortlessly shattered its doppelganger to bits. The ebony creature skittered away and took a moment to reconstitute his limbs to their normal forms. It was clear he would no longer be able to match his hunter in melee combat.

"You've grown faster with your weapon in a very short time, it would seem," he remarked in an attempt to lure the man into conversation.

The mystic did not fall for the ploy, instantly dashing to his hated foe's side and striking down with Kargaroth. "Faster," he shouted. Zekraul hopped away and avoided the blow, but as soon as he regained his footing he heard the man's voice from behind him. "Sharper." The demon broke into a dash, this time without yet knowing an attack was coming. His instincts were good, as the greatsword once more sliced cleanly through earth as he narrowly escaped it. He turned to face his belligerent rival and observe his move. This served him no good, as Deun's body launched straight at him far too fast for him to react, punching him squarely between the amber eyes. "Stronger," the man roared. Zekraul was sent rolling away head over heels, coming to rest lying on his stomach and hissing loudly.

"You killed me," Deun remarked. "I will kill you. In this there is balance."

The demon rose to his feet slowly and attempted to quieten his hissing. "Leave me alone," he whined despondently. "I don't have the energy for this now."

He turned his right hand into a narrow drill and stabbed it into the ground at his feet. In response to this, a thick wall of stone again emerged between him and his pursuer. This blockade was several times wider and taller than the previous, in a clear attempt to stymie Deun's fleet feet. The man grimaced and then moved forward to the wall, Kargaroth already held out and braced for a swing.

"Your tricks and barriers won't stop this sword, Overlord. I know how to wield it now."

He swung, but the section of rock he had attempted to shear vanished preemptively. Kargaroth passed easily through empty air, throwing him off balance. At the same time, the sections on his left and right sides slid about to encircle him. Deun observed in confusion as the stone transformed into black crystals, then he was skewered by twoscore crystalline spikes ripping through his flesh from every direction. He gave a gurgle and a strange shudder, then fell silent.

Zekraul slowly collapsed his trap and condensed the material back into his body. It had taken a terrible amount of his remaining strength to manage that metamorphosis. He would require days of rest, if recovery was even possible at this point.

"I may have to abandon this body," he mourned quietly as he felt a stiffening sensation in his limbs.

He glanced up to see Deun still standing there, motionless since the last attack had pincushioned him. Zekraul widened his amber eyes as the man began to move again, stretching out with a grunt as a shell of silvery magic slid over him repairing his wounds.

The regenerating mystic fell back a few steps and wiped blood from his eyes, as the hole in his forehead slowly sealed up. "I've waited too long for you to die," he declared with determination. "Though I sold my own soul and freedom for this power, I stand here with no regrets. At last I am sufficient to slay you."

He dashed forward once more. He was noticeably slowed by his previous wounds, though they were not yet enough to stop him. Zekraul nonetheless counted himself blessed for the dulled pace of battle. Deun swung Kargaroth into more blazing sweeps, but now the demon was able to remain a step ahead. He danced in and out of the path of the blade, collapsing and discarding pieces of his body to keep from being cut even once.

The battle dragged on in this way for several minutes. Zekraul hoped to drain the human's meager stamina, but there seemed to be no such decay. Instead a slim translucent barrier hung about the man's body, and as time went on he seemed to again grow faster and stronger. The demon was not blind to this effect, and so began calculating his next move.

Just as he was about to strike, the mystic suddenly broke off his assault and leaped away, halting nearly ten yards from his opponent. Zekraul watched hesitantly. Had his foe somehow detected his upcoming attack? No, that did not appear to be the case. The man merely seemed distracted by a sudden disturbing vision. The wiry Gehennan spent a moment considering if this could be an opportunity for escape.

Overwhelmed by his own curiosity, he did not take it. "What are you doing?" he asked in spite of himself.

Deun's eyes were fixated on Kargaroth, his thoughts elsewhere. "This sword," he said with an entranced tone overtaking his voice. "She won't let me kill, for some reason. Some stronger will guides her, and overtakes my own thoughts. I've tried to ignore it, but I don't understand. It's swallowing my seer's sight, preventing me from reading your moves as I should be able."

Zekraul shook his head, dismissing the human's moment of apparent insanity as a result of his brain having been pierced by the demon's previous trap. He struggled to gather energy from within himself, already shaking to the core as he concentrated intently on using his own refracting abilities to magnify the magics of Dosiros remaining to him.

Across the way, Deun seemed to reach his epiphany, stabbing Kargaroth forward into the ground in front of him at an angle. He released his hands from the hilt and waited a moment, watching the sword intently. "This is the problem," he concluded quizzically. The dim light encasing his hands suddenly brightened, blazing out into a shrieking silver, then he reached forth and seized the tattered bandages around the hilt. With evident difficulty, he tore them away with a fierce rip. He took a few more moments to make certain all shreds of the fabric were carefully removed. When the deed was done he gave a satisfied nod, prying the sword free once more.

As the last of the tattered fabrics fell, a strange glow suddenly emanated from them. Traces of red runes appeared scrawled across them, revealing the dirty cloth to actually be something much more—deep bluish green sheets of rune pages covered with incomprehensible spells. They shone with this intense light for a few seconds then burned up, lifting away on the breeze as dark ash.

"Kargaroth's master used that spell to bind his will to the

sword," Deun mused, still talking to himself. "What a powerful man he must be, to be capable of binding sentience to a dead blade. No matter now. We are free." He lifted the sword high in his right hand and focused his eyes on his opponent once more. "Kargaroth," he commanded firmly, "despair."

The long silver blade flared forth with a dim purple aura, and the air permeating the battlefield seemed to grow darker. The disturbance only lasted for a few seconds, then the energy collapsed to Kargaroth's razor edge, which was left shimmering in an eerie glow.

Deun waited patiently for a few breaths, reveling in the strength of his weapon. Then he ran forward at Zekraul, faster than he had been since the beginning of the fight. It was with a startled gasp that the demon finally released his own attack, turning his arms into a stream of fire so thick it resembled the fiercest lava. This stream crashed into the charging warrior and wrapped tightly about him, burning up the ground beneath him and the air around him. The heat sank deep through his armors, charring his flesh and drying his blood within seconds.

But his charge was not halted. He reached striking distance of Zekraul without slowing, his sword still held high in his right hand, even as the bones of his legs began to crack from pressurized heat. When his melting face was only a foot from the black demon's, he dropped Kargaroth like an echoing hammer. A tall white line passed deep into the forest, carving up four mature trees before flickering out of life.

The fires of Zekraul extinguished, dying down to embers along the forest floor as the Gehennan fell backward and crashed into the ground with an audible shatter. The resilient demon struggled to piece his body back together, but could manage no such effort. He gave a long hiss and then muttered, "Death? For Zekraul? That is not to be. I was granted eternal life, true immortality by birthright. I am to never die."

The disfigured face of Deun stared down upon his enemy. So long had he hunted this creature, and now he could not remember why. This moment should have been satisfying for him, but it was empty. He tried to remember how this frail skeleton had wronged him, what made its death so important. The knowledge would not come. Regardless, he stoked his determination once more, and through melted lips and a fried trachea he muttered, “Overlord,” and thrust Kargaroth firmly into Zekraul’s neck, wrenching the two halves of the twisted head from the rest of the body.

With his lifelong foe dead at last, Deun turned and began to hobble away, feeling the pain of his body gradually fading as he lost life. He was glad when the sensation of overwhelming heat turned to one of cold, and would have smiled if his face had still been capable of such contortion.

As he was about to fall forward into his own demise, a light suddenly enveloped him. His pain was redoubled, as this radiance closed in tight and attempted to rework his flesh. Soon the magic seemed to realize the damage was too severe, and instead solidified the flesh as well as it could. It then encased his entire body in a solid white material, hiding his skin away both outside and inside of his black armor. His face was sealed within two mirrored sheets of the same material, with narrow green slots carved for the eyes.

When this strange healing was complete he heard the voice of Akatriel, though he could tell it came only from within his own mind.

*Your work is not yet done, Deun Coloran. Your price not yet paid. Death cannot set you free just yet.*

He gave a nod and a sigh. He swung Kargaroth to his back, letting the magic now at his disposal hold it there for him, and began to walk. Though he knew he spoke only for his own ears, he responded to the voice in an attempt to anchor his sanity.

“I suppose I only hoped my rampage might finally be over.”

## Chapter 39.

## Keldana, Who Rebukes Death

Detria Alsen sat in Kelve's command tent, pouring over a collection of documents which had been gathered for her. The most astute of the Devilslayer's chemists had gone through Kelve's chemicals and notebooks, endeavoring diligently to archive the man's knowledge. This had been mostly futile. The deceased commander's understandings had progressed so far beyond his Devilslayer days that most of the scholars could not even read the personalized shorthand he had developed for his formulas.

In particular, there were ten vials containing a strange black chemical no one could quantify. The base compounds of one of the vials had been identified, but the chemists on hand confessed they were not masters of the craft, having not yet learned any of the forbidden recipes Kelve had mastered. After a long debate, Detria had decided to have the chemicals safely disposed of, since it could not be determined if they were intended for friend of foe.

She gave up on her study of inventories and hypotheses for a moment and leaned back, rubbing her eyes with her palms. Kelve had always taken care of this stuff for her. He had said a real leader should not have to deal with the paperwork, that it was the whole point in having a deputy. It was funny now, she thought; now that she could no longer tell if she had ever been a real leader.

Since she had resumed command, relationships among leadership had become strained. Upon discovery of Yasiff's fate, the Devilslayers had predictably moved to have Detria executed. After a lengthy discussion by a hastily formed council, it was decreed that High Chieftain's final edict must be followed verbatim, therefore the Fortress of the Overlord must be taken before she could be brought to justice for her crimes. Since Yasiff's official recorded order included language alluding to Detria's oversight on the mission, the entire Devilslayer entourage had been begrudgingly linked in under her judgment.

As the fog of torture and manipulation was beginning to clear in her mind, it became apparent that Yasiff had possessed some ulterior motive in his treatment toward her. According to some of the more amicable pack leaders she had spoken too, the chieftain had never allowed a former slayer to return to the ranks. Further, he never assigned such exalted positions during missions to a slayer of anything less than sterling reputation and status. All agreed that at the very least the man was trying to make some sort of a point, using Detria—considered by many the most successful and influential of his detractors—as a demonstration that there was no escaping his thrall. In the back of her mind, she feared even further that he had been grooming her to be some sort of "warrior queen". She was so disgusted by the thought that she could not long dwell on it.

Things were no simpler among the forces that had been united under Kelve. Boderon—and his people by proxy—bore an intense distaste for Detria, blaming her squarely for the fallen commander's despair and ultimately death. She wanted to rail against these sentiments, but they echoed too poignantly with the pain in her own heart. Tenkahn and Gaius treated her with a courteous respect, but seemed to be functioning as an independent force now, no longer unified with the larger war effort.

Only Colbiss had stood firmly at her side, sternly reminding the soldiers under him that she had always been their leader. It had not taken much convincing. These troops had marched under her lead for many months, and they were grateful for her return in the wake of their recent loss. However there were also brewing concerns as to her reinstatement into Devilslayer ranks. Some of this had settled at the news of Yasiff's assassination at her hands, but rumblings of uncertainty remained.

Behind her came the sound of someone entering the tent. She did not bother turning, assuming it to be Colbiss. The stalwart lieutenant ran errands constantly, tending to most of the duties of overseeing the troops and running guard shifts and training exercises. Yet somehow on top of all this, he made it a point to drop in and make certain Detria was doing alright about once every hour. She figured it was about that time.

When she heard her visitor's voice, however, she discovered she was mistaken. It was not Colbiss in the tent with her. "Good evening, Commander Alsen," the man said with a quiet and humble tone.

She spent a moment soaking in the words, then responded through clenched teeth, "Mek." She rose to her feet and turned to face him. It was indeed the Devilslayer who had captured her several months prior, on his knees before her. "I wasn't even aware Yasiff had ordered you along on this mission."

"That was by design. I was assigned to keep an eye on you and ensure you didn't attempt any sort of betrayal. I've remained hidden in your shadow."

"Betrayal, huh?" she scoffed. "You mean like political assassination? If so, you did a pretty lousy job. As your former teacher, I'm almost ashamed."

Mek rose to his feet and began to pace about the tent. Detria watched him nervously as he spoke, her hand straying to a dagger head on her dannig belt. "Put yourself in my boots for a minute. Under Yasiff's old order, everyone was held accountable. Everyone near you was a spy against you. When we encountered you in that forest, I had no choice but to turn you over. My lieutenant of the time also recognized you, made a comment about it to me. I couldn't have pretended to buy your story. As I told you then, Yasiff would've had me. I was a prisoner of my regime.

"But Yasiff made a mistake when he brought me along on this particular voyage. He put me alone. He assigned me to watch you by myself, because he feared you were astute enough that you would notice more than one spy. He trusted me most because I'd brought you in. He assumed this meant I wasn't vulnerable to your charisma, which he always considered a threat to his ideas of order. So I watched you. I watched you when you bickered with Kelve. I watched you when you battled the Overlord's generals. I watched you when you seized Kelve's sword and headed straight for Yasiff's tent." He paused in front of her, staring hard for full effect. "I watched you."

"Are you suggesting," she asked with annoyance, "that you knew I was going to kill Yasiff?"

"I'd have been a fool to not realize it. And I had too shrewd a teacher to be a fool."

She spent a moment digesting this thought. "So why?"

"Do you think you and Kelve were the only slayers made uncomfortable by Yasiff's rule? There were many more of us. Some of us were not invited to join in your little exodus. Some of us were invited, but stayed hoping things could get better. Some of us were simply afraid to go. We're not all leaders. Many of us are just followers. But that doesn't mean we approved of the direction Yasiff was taking us. We knew he was a tyrant, and we chafed within the bonds of his tyranny. So why would I stop you when I saw you were moving to his tent with a weapon in hand? You had the power to remove the tyrant. The power that, truly, all of us had. But only you had the courage to exercise it."

"Whatever. It's done then. You got what you wanted. Yasiff's dead and you didn't have to bloody your own hands, you didn't have to make any of the hard choices. So why are you here?"

Again the man dropped gently to his knees on the ground before her. "I wish to swear fealty to you, Detria Alsen. I wish to move to appoint you the new High Chieftain of the Devilslayers of Arkalen."

At this announcement, Detria fell back into her chair in shock. Though she was not unaccustomed to having such responsibilities suddenly thrust upon her, she could not believe it was happening again. "The council would never hear of it," she tried to argue feebly.

Mek would not be discouraged. He rose back to his feet with a fiery passion. "And why not? Already you've worked yourself into a position where you command the largest contingent of Devilslayers ever assembled. In effect, you are already our new leader. If other factions oppose your assuming command, you could take the force you currently hold and bring them into line. A group of four hundred rebellious slayers wouldn't be rash enough stand up to a commander of nearly a thousand Noble Pride. And the old influences Kelve once held? I have them as well. I'm not as directly tied to the council as he was, but I know the people who are. They're people who are sympathetic to this cause. Like me, they want to see the Devilslayers restored to honor and glory. Just because we've suffered through the reign of one horrible leader, it doesn't have to mean we forever abandon the noble principles upon which we were founded."

She shook her head. "I can't lead alone. Kelve was always at my side."

"Someone must lead. And whoever leads will always stand alone. If not you, then who?"

She rose to her feet and turned her back to the man. She leaned her hands forward on her desk, hanging her head and trying to shake herself free of this whole ordeal. "Surely you can think of someone better suited," she replied.

"Better suited? You're the one who stood up to Yasiff's rule, from the very start! You left, to emphasize how strongly you opposed it. No one better represents a return to the old values than you. Yasiff knew this. It's why he saw you as such a threat, it's why he wanted so desperately to conquer you, to erase what you represent to our people. If there's a better person, man or woman, point them out to me and I'll make it so. If you cannot, then you must consider my offer. The Devilslayers need you. And if they can be righted, Arkalen still needs the Devilslayers."

He took his leave without waiting for further argument. Detria was pleased by this, since she had no argument to offer. She shut her eyes tight, not welcoming this new turn of events. After a few more seconds of silence, she pondered quietly to herself, “Kelve Orista, does your ghost yet have some hand in this?” At that moment, Colbiss entered the tent and asked if she was alright. She gave the man a smile and a reassurance, then asked him to have a seat so she could speak with him about matters at hand.

* * * * *

Fenrir moved carefully, soundlessly through the night, coming so close to some of the human soldiers sleeping within their camp that he feared they might smell him. Fortunately humans lacked his developed canine senses, and he passed without incident.

His mission was a dangerous one. He had overheard of the passing of the human commander, Kelve Orista. The Overlord’s troops were filled with relief at this news, as the legend of the man’s fatal capabilities had spread rapidly. It was rumored he had killed Kaltheria, the mightiest of shadow wights, with a simple powder thrown from his fingertips; he had bested two ogres with mere scratches; he had stood against both Gariso and Manticore simultaneously yet had not perished. It had taken a direct assault by Shote and Tessena to finally bring the warlord down, and even then Tessena herself had been sacrificed in the attempt.

Fenrir had grilled his troops repeatedly on these rumors, and had pieced together enough of the truth. This Kelve was more than a former Devilslayer, he was a master dealer of death. The human had understood the laws of nature governing all things, and how to twist them into the demise of any foe under nature’s cruel dominion. The demonspawn wolf salivated at the suggestion of such knowledge. In a different world, he would have sought this man out, begged for his tutelage, sworn undying fealty at any cost.

But in this world, Fenrir served the Overlord. He had no doubts the Overlord was to win this war, especially with Shote himself finally directly joining in combat. Selling out from the winning side of a war to join the losing side had never seemed a viable proposition to the crafty survivalist.

Now Kelve had been slain, leaving Fenrir with but one, slim option to profit from the situation. He had gone to the Robed Ones' archives and found their last remaining Crucible of Anji. He would have sworn there were once two, but only the one remained. He wondered if perhaps the other had been used in some way to restore Shote.

The Crucible was an ancient device, primarily associated with the transference of one creature's knowledge or powers into another corpus. But the followers of Anji had been an ambitious lot, and the original intention of the relic was a much loftier goal: immortality. The Crucible only worked on a dying or recently deceased body, and the first action of the device was to summon the target's spirit into the grey orb.

Problem was, Fenrir only had a small window after Kelve's death wherein the Crucible would still work. He had been forced to await the burial, then the graciously brief funeral. Now nearly a full day had passed, and finally the area near the tombstone stood empty at his approached. Still, humans were a sentimental lot and a visitor might approach at any time. He would have to work fast before his opportunity passed.

He slunk to the grave and read the inscription on the headstone, then rolled his eyes with a sneer. He drew the Crucible of Anji and sat it upon the freshly dug mound, then tapped on the head of the decorative demon entrapping the device. The golden idol opened its mouth and gave a hiss, causing Fenrir to glance about nervously. The sound terrified his sensitive ears, and he felt certain hundreds of humans would be upon him in a matter of seconds.

In spite of his fears, no one heard the small sound. For a time, nothing happened. Fenrir crouched low and waited, exercising his cowardly patience to the best of his ability. The human had been dead for many hours, so the Crucible would have a difficult task reassembling the last vestiges of his remaining life, if it was even yet possible. The demonspawn general had no choice but to wait, and he licked his lips in anticipation for every second of it.

This excruciating stillness went on for nearly a full hour, backed by the soundtrack of the perfectly even hiss. Fenrir's anxiety nearly got the better of him, and he contemplated setting a hard deadline for resigning his effort. Then finally the Crucible was enveloped by a white light. This light pierced the ground as the hiss finally came to a stop, and but a second later faded out. Fenrir looked once more to see if any humans had noticed this disturbance, but once more seemed to be safe.

A few more seconds passed, then the dull grey orb shifted and turned into a swirling black. Fenrir almost squealed with glee, but repressed himself. He lifted the artifact, staring at it hungrily. "The might of a Devilslayer," he whispered to himself. "The knowledge of Kelve Orista. Mine."

He swiftly turned the demonic head upon himself and squeezed the metallic demon's body ever so slightly. Again the mouth opened, and a black beam blasted forth into Fenrir's chest. He was bound with paralyzing agony for a moment, unexpectedly forced to relive the pains of Kelve's death. Then this faded, and he sat breathing heavily on his hands and knees.

As Akatriel's before it, the Crucible of Anji collapsed, turning to dust as the demonic gold melted away into the earth. The artifacts were created to grant immortality to the priests of the order, but required their own maintenance and regeneration to remain active. The secrets of those rites had been lost long ago, and with improper usage the devices were easily lost.

Fenrir paid no heed to this, unconcerned with the loss of the priceless object. His mission had been accomplished, and a trove of knowledge flooded his mind. Even as he stared around the forest surrounding him, suddenly every leaf and blade of grass had a different meaning. He could not cease his wide, toothy grin, and it was only with the faintest of restraint that he held back a howl of triumph.

He flexed each of his hands a few times, then calmed his nerves and prepared to make his return to the Overlord's keep. Before doing so, he stared at the tombstone before him one last time. His grin at last faded, and for nearly two full minutes he stood reading it. Finally he turned and took his leave, with two deep trails of tears flowing down his furry face.

* * * * *

The Wisdoms had found the corpse of Abaddon Daemon.

As soon as they had come within sight of the tremendous battle scar left from the pillar of light, Melukah had sent Torlen and Keldana to scout for tracks of Gilanirus' departure. In their absence, he spent a moment examining the landscape. The high celestial was amazed to see how much power his ancient rival had released at this place. The bitter taste of Gehennite ether permeated the air, and the ground was carved up by signs of a mighty battle waged between two enemies of divine mettle.

What bothered him more than anything else was his inability to determine the Godbeast's opponent. The Wisdom of the Sun himself should have been the only threat capable of bringing so much of Gilanirus' might to bear. The freshly awakened deity would have known this, and been conserving his strength for that inevitable collision. Someone or something had forced the Tyrant to risk his ability to abide the Sun. Yet before him, all Melukah could find was the lone corpse of a human.

Soon Keldana returned, her circuit of the region complete. "I can find no tracks, my liege," she reported with a subdued tone.

Melukah returned a nod, unsurprised, but did not reply. If there was anything for Keldana to find here, she would have been able to spot it hours before their arrival. Their best hopes now rested upon Torlen's skills.

The Wisdom of Ocean hesitated a moment, then tried making small talk to test her lord's mood. "What do you think happened here? What did Gilanirus fight?"

Melukah briefly rolled his eyes skyward. At times Keldana's insight into his own mind confounded him. "As much as it pains me to consider, it seems to have been this human lying here. He's the only evidence of another living being in the area. He is also close enough to the final blast that, were he not Gilanirus' rival, his body would have been consumed by it."

"This human, sir? Does that really seem plausible? I thought humans only a Class Eight species."

"Believe it or not, they were once a Class Two. Elzaniru stripped them of their might before we came into being. I suspect this particular human must have tapped into his verboten heritage. Did not Torlen say he was previously bested by a human?" She answered with a nod, so Melukah continued, "I would wager this is the very one."

"Even so, a Class Two creature should not be able to stand against a Class One. Gilanirus least of all."

"I concur. That stands as compelling evidence the Spectre is weak so soon after his resurrection. We must hasten to find him before that changes."

Torlen returned from his scouting, walking slowly over to join his fellow Wisdoms. Before receiving his report, Melukah queried as to the figure lying before them.

"Torlen, do you know this man?"

The Wisdom of Sound looked down, then jerked his head back slightly. "I do. This is the human I banished to Elysium at the behest of the Muses."

"It seems you did not exaggerate his might," Melukah offered. "If he was able to provoke such a response from Gilanirus, it's no small wonder you were bested. To the contrary, it is testament to your skill that you even survived such an encounter. The Sun offers his rare apologies for having doubted you. Having said that, what of your scouting? Where hides the Shadow?"

"I examined the area as thoroughly as I'm capable, for a several hundred yard radius. As I was about to give up, I discovered some slight indicators that were anomalous. Several more minutes of study revealed something unpleasant. Some creature, seemingly of Asterian origin, has masked out Gilanirus' presence and tracks. It's not a trivial power obscuring our way. I can find no way to trace him."

Melukah spent a moment deliberating this revelation. "So Akatriel has made his move. He once allied with us to war against the Godbeasts, now he has chosen the other side. No doubt he attempts to help the Spectre gather strength so that he might serve the Silver One's revenge against us. That dragon is impossibly clever. We must assume that even now Gilanirus' threat grows with each passing minute." He turned to Keldana. "Akatriel no doubt thinks he has successfully stymied us, but the human may know which direction the Tyrant went from here. That could provide the only assistance we need. If I can get close enough, I'll be able to feel him in spite of whatever barriers hide him away."

The Ocean knelt to the ground and spent a moment analyzing Abaddon. "He is dead."

Melukah's head twitched to one side as his patience slipped. "Another obstacle aligned against us. Can you resurrect him?" His tone had begun to show his temperament, with the question becoming demanding.

"I can attempt to. His physiology seems simple enough. Still, I'm not designed for such a task. It will drain a good deal of my healing reserves for a time, and it will be necessary for you to piece his soul back together, if it's possible."

The Supreme Wisdom reached his left hand up to his face and used two fingers to stab through his false eyes. A blinding white light shone through his mask, focusing on Abaddon's figure. Shortly the divinity announced, "The human is long dead now. Even if resurrection succeeds, he will only live a few minutes. That's long enough to speak. Begin your healing, Keldana. I shall do what I can."

The Wisdom of Ocean placed her hands on Abaddon's chest and the man's entire body was instantly entombed by a massive block of ice. Thick visible trails of frozen vapor rose throughout the area. Melukah gathered energy, and particles of both light and spiritual essence flowed into the air around him.

It was nearly half an hour before Keldana's portion of the work was finally complete. The small Wisdom backed away, falling to the ground with a sigh. Torlen helped her to her feet, and the two watched their lord's work. After about ten more minutes, Melukah held his Sun Staff into the air, gathering power from the Morolian sunlight into his own frame. In an instant Abaddon's body turned into a solid sheet of light, which only a few seconds later blinked out just as suddenly.

Melukah motioned for Keldana to patch the holes in his mask. As she did so, he tested the success of their joint efforts.

"Human. Do you live?" There was no response. Melukah tried again louder, refusing to believe he had failed. "Human! Answer your savior!"

There was another long pause before, "I live," escaped between Abaddon's lips. No other part of his body moved, including his eyes, and the dead tone of his skin had not changed.

"Answer me, did you fight the one named Gilanirus here? Are you the one he battled?"

"Gilanirus," Abaddon whispered slowly. "I could not kill him. If only I had Kargaroth..."

Melukah glanced to Keldana. "What is Kargaroth?"

The slim Wisdom answered with a shrug, "There was no knowledge of such a name passed on to us by the Muses," then backed away from her master. His mask was repaired, and the lacy trim around his chiseled eyes restored.

He resumed his interrogation. "Did you injure the Spectre at all in your battle?"

"I removed his right arm." Abaddon's tone remained empty, and he continued to show no further evidence that he was alive.

Melukah was taken aback by this response. "Removed his 'right arm'? Peculiar. This suggests Gilanirus had only two arms in his current form. Now he is left with but one. The Final Godbeast of Gehenna's power is released through combat. A single arm would be quite a handicap for him. He would be incapable of wielding his many divine weapons, as is his preference."

Keldana interjected, "Lord, the human will not last long."

The Supreme Wisdom nodded, then demanded of Abaddon,

"Which direction did he go? Where was Gilanirus heading when he parted from you?"

Abaddon's hand shook for a moment as though he was going to lift it, then the movement ceased. Instead he offered, "South by southwest, almost precisely." Hearing this, Melukah let his head fall back and gazed skyward in relief. Finally they were back on course.

"Human," he declared in a magnanimous tone, "you have served your time well. Thank you for your assistance. It will help save your world and ours. Now you may rest. Soon death will take you for the last time."

As the Wisdom reached forward and used a potent spell to put Abaddon into a deep sleep, the weakened man gave his final weak response. "Thank you."

* * * * *

"Get up and fight!"

*What?*

"Get up and fight! Now!"

As the words echoed around him, Abaddon fell deep into his own mind. Swirling blackness surrounded him, crushing him, drowning him. Then, below, he saw a large plane, carved out by infinite blue lights and burning through eternity. As his feet crashed down into the plane, hard, he recognized it. He had been here once before. This was the prison of his mind, a place he had created long ago to shield himself.

He seemed alone at first, but then he was not. Another version of himself, larger, more intimidating, covered in the armors of the Hell Knight and, most of all, very angry, stood before him yelling.

"Since when does the Daemon lie down and wait for death? I must get up and fight, as I always have! I am the Destroyer!"

Abaddon looked down weakly at his own hands. They were dressed in white gloves, and seemed so small compared to the armored fists of the monster before him. "The other guy said I could rest. I wish to rest. Do you know how long it's been since I slept? I'm so tired."

"Tired?!" his overbearing self roared in outrage. "What is 'tired'? A trivial thing. Surely I have evolved beyond that. If I am tired then I can sleep later. But not while battle is at hand!"

"I can never sleep. Such nightmares haunt a man who's lived through what I have. This is the only rest I can get. I am dead."

"Dead? Why am I dead?!"

"Gilanirus killed me."

"Pah. Death will not quell the Daemon's wrath! I'll get on my feet, I'll find him, I'll kill him! He will see that I'm a warrior to the bitter end!"

Abaddon's passive version shuddered in frustration, then with a loud cry punched the massive apparition before him, causing it to shatter into thousands of fragments of black light drifting through his mindscape.

*Yes,* came the voice of his broken image, *use my anger. Feed on it. Become the Destroyer once more.*

As the particles tried to come near him, Abaddon shook his head slowly. "Not this time." He blinked and a flash of light covered the mindscape, and the particles were wiped away. "Why shouldn't I rest? I deserve what everyone does. Everyone dies eventually. I too have that right." His shoulders sank and he repeated with a heavy voice, "Why shouldn't I rest?"

*Because you made a promise, Ab.*

His eyes widened in surprise at hearing the familiar voice of Atheme Tethen. It was just a memory, but he could not stop himself from reliving it. The plane upon which he was standing reshaped into The Camarilla—a tavern in his home of Felthespar—where he was sitting with Atheme having a drink.

It was when Abaddon was still young and headstrong, and did not yet fit within the walls of Itrius' mighty capital. Atheme was fussing at him for breaking his word to Leprue over some meeting Abaddon had deemed unworthy of his time.

"The reason it matters is simple—because you made a promise,

Ab. Promises are important to a man. They're a bind, a commitment. If people can't take your promise, how can they ever trust you? When you're out in the field, in that heat of the moment, and you really need your fellow soldiers to place their faith in you, what more can you give them if your word is of no value?"

"This is philosophical moralizing nonsense," he had argued. "Not every promise can be kept. Am I to be held to some invisible ledger when events conspire against promises previously made? If my word will be devalued for circumstances beyond my control, there's no sense in fighting it."

"Such an attitude could be applied to anything. There's no point in Felthespar fighting wars, because eventually we'll lose one. Sooner or later, something could go wrong, we could be beaten. You're not going to persuade me on such a cheap tactic." Abaddon had wanted to respond, but had been cowed by Atheme's insistent tone. "If you can't keep a promise, then don't make it. There's nothing complicated in that. It's one thing to tell someone you're going to try to do something, to try to be somewhere. But once you give them your word, whether by promise, swear, or oath, you've committed a piece of yourself to fulfilling that action. Every time you break a promise, every time you cheat on a swear, every time you neglect an oath, you're giving up a piece of who you are. You are lessening yourself. As long as you walk by my side you will not be permitted to lessen yourself in such a fashion. Is this understood?"

Once Abaddon nodded his head in agreement, the vision ended. He was left standing once more on the plane of lights with Atheme's voice still echoing, *Because you made a promise, Ab.*

"What promise?" he roared to the air around him. "What promise did I make that robs me of my right to rest?!"

And then he heard it. Loud and clear in his own words, as he saw the face of Detria Alsen appear before him. He could even feel the movement of his lips as he spoke the words.

"Then for you, I shall offset my plans to die in a haze of glory for a time. I promise you will see me again."

This vision became more than a memory, as the young woman stepped forward and placed her hand softly on his shoulder. "You told me you endured, Abaddon Daemon. Isn't that what makes you human?"

"There is nothing more human than dying," he argued.

She faded, and Abaddon's own younger self appeared before him. This memory wore his original Felthespari attire, a black outfit with thick grey gloves and a long purple cape. Though he had not physically aged many years beyond this version of himself, he could still see confusion and sense of loss in his youthful eyes.

"Atheme wouldn't want me to die," his past self proclaimed, a shiver of uncertainty present in his voice Abaddon had long ago abandoned. "There's still more I can do for him, to make him proud."

"It's not his choice," the quieter counterpart contended.

"I won't fail him! Do you understand? Do you know what he's done for me? He's given me everything! He has made me into a man, saved me from being a mere beast! If I follow him I can become something great, as he already is!"

He shook his head, his resolve still unchanged. "I walked away from that path already. I no longer seek greatness."

"That's a lie, Abaddon Daemon," a lilting female voice rang out. The vision of himself faded, and a shimmering silver light appeared in the distance. As she grew closer her form took shape, the familiar visage of a hood with two decorative feline ears flopping softly atop it. "You will be great."

"That's your belief, Relm," he argued with Atheme's young wife. "Not mine."

"You can lie to the rest of us, but don't lie to yourself. You adore greatness. That's why you love Atheme. It's why you love Cildar, and Myris. It's why you love me. You see within us the qualities you wish to have for yourself. You still want to grow. You want to be a man who makes us all proud."

At last his resolve wavered, as he responded brokenly, "I do."

She bobbed her head to the side and gave him a warm smile. "Don't leave us. Because we love you, too."

Again the apparition faded, and again he was left standing within his own mind. He stood alone no longer, though. To his sides now stood the hollow forms of Detria, Atheme, Relm, and Abaddon's younger self. They waited patiently for him to make his decision, staring at him with eyes that whispered of honor and loyalty.

He bowed his head in defeat. His resolve crumbled, and then was forged anew as the fires of his inner strength returned to him.

"So be it," he announced. "Abaddon Daemon will live again."

He raised his hands above his head, and all things shattered. The plane, the visions around him, the very air he breathed, each exploded once more into the nothingness from which he had carved them. They swirled about him and poured into his ephemeral body, a raging whirlwind of chaos into which he screamed at the top of his lungs, devouring the power from it, unifying his mind, pouring the pieces together until finally, he too vanished.

When it was over, he stood once more; no longer trapped within the confines of his mindscape, Abaddon's feet rested on the solid ground of Arkalen, staring into the crater left behind by Gilanirus. He came to himself in the middle of his scream, caught off guard momentarily by the sound of his own voice. He spent a moment breathing heavily, making certain his body was in stable condition. Once it was clear that it was, he reached down and picked up the Arda. He turned and looked to the southwest, a somber expression on his face.

"One more time, then."

## Chapter 40.

## Schpariel, Unleashed At Last

Cildar and Myris continued their trek south, making promising headway against the sprawling Yerria Forest. As they had sought the origin of the earlier divine storm, they had veered further west than the Cainite would have liked. He let the matter rest for now, knowing there was still enough distance to their destination that he could make corrections as needed. His companion had been quiet for some time, practicing to regain control over his spiritual abilities. There was a strong possibility they marched toward battle, but in spite of his resolve, it was evident the Dragoon was not yet ready for it. Myris grew concerned as to what the cost of his friend's stubbornness would ultimately prove to be.

He did not allow his mind to dwell on doubts over Cildar. Instead he remained fixated on his own duties—keeping an eye on their direction, as well as using heraldry to scout the surrounding regions. Things had been very still in the forest they were moving through; he expected they would escape the woodland terrains within only a few more minutes.

He spent some time checking his spell matrixes. He had exhausted most of them in his early battles with the Dark Paladin, and had never spent the time resetting them. As he had grown more reliant on the blessings of his Gehennite armlet, black magic seemed less of a priority. While it was possible for him to tap matrixes with the armlet activated, it was a struggle, as concentration was difficult under the sway of red ether. Nonetheless, his inner Cainite chided him for allowing himself to become lax in his disciplines. He vowed that when they next stopped to rest he would fill his matrixes with the most complicated spells he knew, solely for the practice.

One of his Feelers brought back information of movement, and he spent a moment reading the currents. "Cildar," he announced, "people are coming this way. Several dozen at least, in a rush."

The tall man swiftly drew his spear from his back. "An attack?"

Myris similarly drew his Soul Scythe and disappeared into the shadows. "Not sure."

The paladin gave a nod and waited. It was not long before a man stumbled into sight, crashing directly into him. Cildar noticed the newcomer was a civilian, haggard and clearly in the grips of terror. He grabbed the man by the shoulder and attempted to steady him.

"Whoa there, slow down a second. What's going on?"

"A horrible beast attacks our city, Tyerria!" the panicking stranger announced with wide eyes.

"Retreating like wild animals will accomplish nothing. Gather your people and hold here, form lines and make certain no women or children are lost in the chaos. I'll take care of the problem at hand. What manner of beast is it?"

The man looked over Cildar and seemed to consider running once more, but the paladin's stern face and clear, fearless eyes set him slightly at ease. "It's a demon in human's clothing. We tried to confront him, but that enraged him. His fury is mighty, like a god's."

As the villager relayed his tale, Myris prowled to investigate based on what he had already overheard. He reached the edge of the forest but did not desire to move into the open, so instead he ascended nimbly to the top of the tallest nearby tree. Once he had a stable foothold, he enhanced his sight and stared hard over the terrain beyond. He could only just see into the village the man had vacated. It was quite large, nestled into a tremendous clearing in the midst of the Yerria Forest, which on the other side ran much farther south than Myris had expected. It took a moment, but soon he was able to tune his vision to the proper range and locate the intrusion in question.

He dropped down, returning to where Cildar was helping to gather the fleeing villagers into a group. Myris released a low whistling sound too subtle for the others to hear, but his old friend picked it out. With a polite word he extricated himself and moved to where the Cainite waited.

"How does it look?" he asked into the faceless shadows between the trees.

"This is no mere beast," Myris' voice answered from behind him. "It is a Wisdom."

The paladin took a slow, deep breath. After a calm pause he answered, "We have to kill it. It's what Lord Abaddon would expect of us."

His compatriot uncharacteristically removed his stealth and moved to stand before him. "I have witnessed these things in action, Cildar. And not as when we were dispatched easily by Dosiros. I have seen them killed. I know their limits, what it takes to defeat one. These are creatures that can push Lord Abaddon to his peak and still hold him at bay with ease. The real Lord Abaddon, the one which he hid from both of us, the one that is more god than man. We have gained much power, but not that much."

Cildar shrugged, then stared at his friend hard. "Since when do you back down from a fight just because you might lose, Myris Phare?"

The Cainite returned this stare for a few seconds, then began to chuckle. "I suppose I do begin to sound like you, with your vain protestations of reason." He turned around and gazed back to the edge of the forest. "How are we going to kill it? Can you use Haste yet?"

"No, the Asterian currents of the Phase Shift would still be too much for me."

"That places us at a rather significant disadvantage. Perhaps with your Haste and my armlet we might prevail, but we need both to even have a prayer."

"Maybe not," he disagreed. "I have a plan."

The hooded warrior gave another chuckle as he ground his fist into his palm. "I do love it when you say that."

The Lord of the Phoenix reached over and removed his right glove, flexing his fingers tight as he gathered white magic into his arm. "Do your best to hold him off. If you can buy me ten minutes, I'll finish him. Just don't die, got it?"

"'Don't die'," Myris mocked with a sarcastic shake of his head. "You don't ask for much."

He broke into a sprint, and was gone from sight in an instant.

* * * * *

Schpariel stepped to the central square of a large city of Arkalen natives. The humans who resided here were even more primitive than the rest of the species, but barbaric and warlike. The Godbeast had been forced to kill several dozen before the rest would scatter. He would have slain them all, but he did not yet have the freedom to act on his whims. This would be shortly remedied.

The Gate of Gehenna was located in the center of the settlement. There were no visible indicators of the phenomenon. The humans would not have noticed it, but Schpariel could feel the unmistakable draw of home beckoning him to the portal. He meandered slowly through the streets, savoring the flavor of red ether that danced throughout.

He found the exact locus of the rift in the Veil and stared into it. He could see the ghostly image of Gehenna—vast burning wastelands with the occasional tormented devilspawn wandering across them; rivers of blood and ash; the sunless sky over dusty prairies, always bright red, always so very hot. He forced his mind from nostalgia and went about his duties. He spent a moment drawing his native ether directly into his corpus, then with effort summoned his Moon Rod once more into corporeal form. The ancient artifact came, but then immediately the sapphire at the top grew dim and faded into a dead stone.

He smiled upon his tired weapon. "Drink of Gehenna," he commanded, thrusting the small pole into the Gate.

It was several minutes later before Myris reached the scene, just as the Godbeast completed his conjuring and withdrew his rod forth. It had transformed into the fierce sickle topping a long scepter, a cloud of red smoke billowing outward around it. "At last," Schpariel whispered to it, "you once more have power sufficient to retain your true form." He then turned to his human visitor. "And what's this, a test subject supplied to us so readily?"

The combatants stood only five yards apart in the middle of the emptied town square, which was decorated by nothing but a single large statue. The statue held a human shape and the vague outline of a face, but no details had yet been carved into it. Myris had picked up enough of Arkalen's ancient languages during his time with Detria to make out the inscription at the base of the statue, which read simply, "War God". It seemed an incomplete monument. The Cainite spent a second noting his surroundings for tactical purposes, then locked his eyes on the monster in front of him. He drew his Soul Scythe and pointed it in his foe's direction.

"I am here to fight you, Wisdom."

Schpariel tilted his head at this. "Please, Dark Wisdom. There's a significant distinction."

"Not significant enough to dissuade me from striking you down."

"Dissuade? I wouldn't dream of it. No, certainly let us continue."

He raised his staff high. The cloud covering the weapon crawled over the Godbeast's body, casting an eerie red glow over his ornately designed shell. There was a sound of twisting metal, as Schpariel's humanoid mask transformed into that of a canine demon, with no less than three huge sets of razor-like fangs filling the mouth. The once conservatively slitted eyes were replaced by two deep chasms, each overflowing out a fiery substance that resembled blood and smelled of rot.

"Behold the true face of Schpariel," he barked in a guttural roar,

"First Anointed Godbeast of Gilanirus!"

He swung his staff until the sickled head touched the ground, and a thunderous eruption deafened the area. In a crescent pattern originating from the scepter, a series of nine waves of lava gushed from the earth and splashed toward Myris, each wrapped tight in barbed trappings of Gehennite ether. Schpariel watched with glee as everything within his sight burned, blinding him to all else. He gave a shrill laugh echoing with the howls of banshees.

Slowly the lava sank beneath the crust of the land once more. After it had faded, the Godbeast searched for the wilted remains of his target. It was not long before he was able to detect the dark outline of the human, standing in one of the few patches of ground that had not been upset by the spell. Schpariel spent a moment contemplating this. He was certain his prey had not been standing there when he had initiated the attack.

In spite of his swift evasions, Myris' right arm had taken a fairly serious burn. He spent a moment carefully siphoning the heat from his flesh and using a touch of energy from his Scythe to repair damaged tissue. "That was dangerous," he commented. "If I am to fight with you, I must be at my full strength. I suspected as much from the outset, and should never have attempted to test you. This injury is one of arrogance."

Schpariel ignored these remarks, demanding, "When did you move?!"

Myris ignored the question, continuing, "I had best ready myself." He raised his left arm in front of his face, and touched his forearm lightly with his right fingertips. The black cloth there faded, a dismissed illusion which had masked a large white armband. Schpariel took a step forward at the sight of this ornament. "Mutance crimsonus," the human commanded. His dark body was swallowed up in a storm of Gehennite ether, embracing him and lending him the might of a foreign world.

"You have my armlet," the Godbeast observed softly as the twin flames hiding Myris' eyes flickered out and revealed stretched, bloodshot orbs. "And you've learned to use it. Inconvenient. I'll be forced to refrain from incinerating your body until I have reclaimed what is mine."

Myris lowered into a crouch, and the storm of red ether dancing about him increased in intensity. "I would not hold back too much, were I you," he taunted.

He blasted himself into motion, dashing clear across the desolate stretch of land between him and his divine adversary in barely a second. While in motion his hand slid to his back and prepared the Soul Scythe for a strike. Upon reaching his target the dark blade flew, aiming for Godbeast's skull. Schpariel responded with a conservative tap of his staff upon the ground, and an arc of fire ran from the sickle-moon and wrapped about his own head. Myris' scythe crashed hard into solidified flames and crashed to a stop.

The two stared at each other for a moment as the man waited to meet his enemy's counter. None came, so the Cainite quickly leaped back a step, charged forward once more, and swung his scythe again. This time he sent a wave of his own red ether creeping along his blade, and when it came into contact with the fiery barrier it ripped through. The Godbeast was not perturbed, however, nimbly stepping back as the tip of the sickled steel failed to nick his maw.

"You think you're fast," the Gehennan commented, "but the limits your gods impose on you are much stricter than those granted by mine."

Myris narrowed his eyes, and again the ether draining into his body tightened and redoubled in intensity. "My limits are an obstacle set for me to overcome. As are you. Both will be shattered!"

He dashed forward and swung once more at his foe. The Godbeast again set up an ether barrier to block the attack long enough for him to step back. This time, however, at the last second Myris faded from his view. He felt the pressure of red ether shifting past his left shoulder, and recognized that the human was already behind him. He tightened his grip on his Moon Rod and a swathe of ether coated his entire body, lending him speed and lifting his feet a few inches from the ground. He spun about rapidly, noted the direction from which his opponent's next attack was coming, and sidestepped just in time to avoid being skewered.

Again Myris slid from view in a haze of black and red, and again Schpariel was forced to follow the trail of ether to track the human's presence. As he dodged the next blow he felt a brush of warm ether, as the edge of the Soul Scythe slid only an inch from his neck.

Schpariel finally attempted to give an attack of his own, swinging his Scepter of the Dark Moon at the spot where his opponent stood. The frenzied man disappeared from his strike's arc, running in a wide circle around him. The Godbeast adjusted and readied a spell to cut off the Cainite's path, then his target vanished. He searched frantically, and at the last moment felt a shadow fall upon him. His enemy was falling from above, the dark scythe already closing on his right eye.

The Dark Wisdom dropped his knees to the ground and slashed up with the Moon Rod. He made solid contact against the handle of the Cainite relic, and his superior strength knocked the human off balance and spinning toward the ground. Myris regained himself somehow, landing lightly on one foot at an awkward angle. Though it looked like his leg should have broken, the instant his foot made contact he again dashed and lashed out sharply with his scythe.

The Godbeast lost patience with his wily foe, and this time merely raised his left arm higher than the path of the blade. The scythe passed instead into his torso, ripping straight through the ribs on one side and protruding out the other. Myris released a short grunt of satisfaction, but instantly Schpariel reached down and gripped the weapon by its handle.

The two combatants locked eyes. Schpariel felt no pain from the attack, and gave a demonic smile as he tightened his grip on his opponent's small tool. "Now what?" he scoffed.

Myris attempted to back away, but could not free his weapon

from the stony fingers clutching it. The Godbeast shook his head in rebuke, then slashed down once again with the Moon Rod at the man's head. The Cainite was at last forced to release his grip and retreat. He slid back from the physical range of the Scepter, but as it passed his height it released five ferocious wheels of ether. The Gehennite energy transformed into complicated barbed blades and zipped through the air, closing in on their target from every direction.

While Myris busied himself dodging wheels of steel forged from Gehennite magic, Schpariel extracted the Soul Scythe from his body with a grimace. He stared at the flimsy weapon for a moment, then shrugged and sent it spinning away from him. It embedded itself into the nearby sculpture, pinning it through the chest.

He turned his attention back to his agile adversary just as the magics fueling his previous spell faded and the five disks crumbled into harmless ether. Myris stopped to catch his breath, bleeding from a score of raked wounds across his arms and one leg. As soon as the human stopped moving, Schpariel opened his mouth and sounded a fierce bark. A monstrous blue fireball erupted forth, moving faster than any of his prior spells. Myris recognized he could not dodge this attack, so turned his shoulder into the blaze and wrapped himself thickly with ether from the Band of Barricus.

The fireball crashed into the storm of red energy and crumbled against it. The Cainite's defense was not a total success, as the cloth from his left shoulder was seared off and the flesh of his arm suffered an instant cremation. He collapsed to the ground, his head spinning from a combination of the red ether seizing him and the wounds he had already suffered in this battle. Though he felt no pain, he could feel his body grow sluggish as his life ebbed.

He clenched his hands into tight fists and began to shake with rage. As the adrenaline in his body responded, so too did the tempestuous ether clinging to him. His muscles expanded, his wounds bled more profusely, and his skin became even more distorted and agitated.

"I will run," he growled. "Running is what I know best. So I will run. My limits, my opponents, Cildar, even Abaddon—I will run past them all!"

He jerked to his feet and released a shout of determination, then once more closed the distance to his enemy in an instant. Schpariel responded to the rush swiftly, pointing his Moon Rod forward and unleashing a fireball ten times larger than the last. As it came within inches of him, Myris delivered the spell a ferocious backhand and it was sent crumbling from his path. He then reached his target and landed his right fist several inches deep through the Godbeast's ironclad chest.

Schpariel was startled by the impact from that blow, and sent forth a scattering of spells in a panicked fashion. Myris paid these no mind, slipping through an easy opening and delivering a hard left hook across the canine face. The jaw shattered, and the entire front row of fangs were destroyed and turned to dust, swallowed by the crimson ether arming the man's fist.

As his adversary again reeled from this impact, Myris leaped up, stood on the Godbeast's upheld arm, and roared. He held his arm high for a moment, then slammed down hard, crashing his right elbow deep into the base of Schpariel's neck on the right side. Chunks of the armored flesh split off and rained down, as a giant crack lurched from the shoulder through to the armored bicep.

Enraged, the Godbeast reached out with his left hand and snapped it shut across his assailant's face. The man instantly responded by slamming both of his fists into the thick forearm, shattering stony flesh once more. Schpariel gave a huff, then commanded, "Away!" With a mighty heave he sent Myris flying, then swung out with his staff, creating a river of fire that flowed forth to where the tossed human was about to land.

The Cainite detected this spell before he hit the ground and gave a nimble aerial flip, then coated his feet in much denser layers of ether. He landed briefly on the flaming stream, then blasted out of it and back to his rival, a trail of flames following in his wake. Hc reached Schpariel in spite of a series of fireballs and barbed blades, then another six grueling blows cracked and splintered the unnatural iron frame.

After this successful sequence, Myris felt a pang of agony seize his arms in spite of the numbing effects of his armlet. Knowing this could be a sign of serious injury, he retreated without further assault and spent a moment observing the status of his foe.

His analysis did not please him. Schpariel's body was crumbling, but it seemed to have no impact on the Godbeast's endurance, strength, or sorcerous prowess. Even as the Cainite was contemplating these things himself, his adversary shrugged and asked of him, "What are you expecting to happen, little man? Eventually do you think I'm just going to wear out and fall over? A taste Gehenna has served you well, this I will not deny. Let's see just how adept you are with your pilfered powers."

He thrust his staff toward the sky, and a red lightning bolt shot upward from it. As crimson storm clouds began to gather, the Cainite abandoned caution and charged once more. Again he dove into a dizzying combination of blows. This time Schpariel did not allow the strikes to land, slipping and hovering out of the path of the man's fists. In that moment, Myris realized that he had gotten slower. As his frenzied speed diminished further, his opponent came to a halt and allowed him to land another blow. This one was not as successful as previous hits, and his knuckles scraped uselessly against the chiseled robes.

"Out of power, are you?" the Godbeast mocked. He gave a rapid sweep, and the sickle of his staff dug through Myris' shoulder, lodging into his clavicle. "Close proximity to the Scepter of the Dark Moon does not augur well for those who feed on red ether. Slowly, the scepter will drain their might, making it into its own." He lifted the man and again tossed him away, flinging his body more than a dozen yards before it crashed and slid to a rest. The Cainite scrambled to his feet unsteadily. Now distanced from the Moon Rod, he was able to gather a storm of ether to himself once more, but was uncertain how to proceed. If he attempted to draw close enough to strike his might would again be dulled, but the

Band of Barricus did not afford him much in the way of ranged techniques.

As the wiry warrior stood gripped by his dilemma, Schpariel dropped the head of the Moon Rod to the ground once more, shouting, "Now this!" The storm clouds that had gathered from his previous spell congealed and turned into a meteor coming down upon his human adversary. The ball of rock, ether, and fire was formed almost immediately, and was over twenty yards in diameter. Myris spent a brief moment considering his options, only to realize he had none. He fell to the ground and rolled himself into a tight ball, blasting out with the thickest barrier of Gehennite ether yet.

Schpariel watched as the meteor came within a few short feet from its collision, then concern for his armlet overtook him. He pointed his staff at the enormous stone and it exploded only a second before impact. The explosion was no small matter, and rocked the surrounding remains of the human settlement, collapsing over a dozen buildings from gale force winds alone.

The Godbeast spent several minutes waiting for the flames and winds to settle down. Myris' body lay intact, unconscious but saved by his final defenses. Schpariel moved forward, determined to reclaim the Band of Barricus quickly on the off chance that the human might reawaken.

When he was less than two yards from the dark body, a voice demanded from behind him, "Wisdom! You will not finish him until you have dispatched me!"

Schpariel spent a moment considering this development. He could still dash forward and seize his armlet. Once retrieved, its gifts would enhance his power substantially, far more than it had for the human. In addition to supplying a continuous draw of ether for even his most exhaustive sorceries, the relic would reinforce and renew his body continuously. With both of his accessories once more in his possession, he would no longer be the weakling of the Godbeasts, but rather a fearsome threat worthy to stand alongside Gilanirus as a peer.

Whatever new opponent had appeared, Schpariel ultimately decided he would not be witnessed scrambling like a coward. Instead he turned about slowly, already commanding his Scepter to ready the next spell. He would kill this new challenger in a single stroke, claim his armlet, then return to Gilanirus' side to neutralize the wrath of Melukah, as was always intended to be his role.

He looked to the newcomer. It was a larger human, over six feet in height and wearing a mostly ruined suit of white plate mail. Unlike the previous, no helmet or mask disguised this man's features. Blond hair floated lightly on the hot breeze combing the area as the interloper continued to walk toward Schpariel. The human's right hand was gone, wholly consumed by an intense light the Godbeast could not bring himself to look upon. In his left hand the man held forth a long lance, glowing with a dim shimmer of green energy.

"Another Morolian volunteers to test my ascendancy?" Schpariel remarked. "Yours is a generous race. Or a suicidal one."

Cildar continued his slow approach until he was within three yards of the Godbeast, cautiously raising each arm out from his sides. "You want me, Wisdom? Get me."

Schpariel sighed in exasperation. "Dark Wisdom. My heritage is Gehennite, not Elysian. But like your precursor, I suppose you don't care." He lifted the transformed Moon Rod into the air. Filling the space between him and his foe, a thick fog of crimson ether drifted into the visible spectrum. It thoroughly coated the land, leaving no area vacant as it spread over Cildar's location. "Ether Mine," Schpariel chanted, then slammed the tip of his weapon's blade against his own fist. A spark emanated, and the fog draping the land transformed into a phenomenon of blistering light, heat, and electricity. Even the air itself did not survive the smothering oblivion imposed by this attack.

Cildar had seen the spark, felt the heat of the ignition begin to warm his skin, and then had given a sharp twist on his Trine Lance. The Godbeast detected this subtle move before his vision was drown out by his own explosion, but stood confident the human would be dead before any counter would matter. Then he felt something odd; a hand landed on his chest, a strong impact forcing him back several feet. His divine eyes adjusted swiftly, and for just an instant saw his opponent standing directly before him, a shimmering right arm pressed against the Gehennan's chest. The man made another twist of his spear and again vanished, so immediately and completely that Schpariel almost doubted his own sight.

Then his vision was robbed by his own trap, as heat and light washed over him. He tried to command his Moon Rod to dismiss the spell, but it was too late to deny the explosion its fury. He was forced to wait until the effect faded, leaving a massive black scar burned into the battlefield.

His senses restored, he cast about quickly for his enemy. Cildar had retrieved Myris' body and slung it over his shoulder, then somehow moved a vast distance away. He stood now nearly a quarter of a mile from his foe. Schpariel was shocked at this display. The speed of this human dwarfed the other, dwarfed his own even. Since he did know how the mortal had moved so fast, he began to question the certainty of his victory, especially as retrieving his Band of Barricus no longer seemed to be an option.

Still he showed no outward hesitation, shouting with a barking voice that cleared the plains. "Run if you dare! Though your own feeble reach is limited, there is no range where my magic cannot strike you!"

He took a step forward and readied a spell, then felt a peculiar sensation. His neck twisted about involuntarily, and his shoulders each gave an unpleasurable snap. He glanced down, and the blaring white light previously engulfing his adversary's arm was now lodged in the center of his own chest where the man's hand had landed. Schpariel had failed to notice over the din of his own spell. This light expanded, then faded as it sank inward. He spent a few seconds fumbling, trying to determine how to counter this effect. These wasted seconds proved to be all he would have, as the fragile shell restraining Cildar's infinitesimal Shock orb collapsed. A thousand points of light instantly crackled out of Schpariel's body, streaking through the air in every direction. Then the core of the spell erupted, forming a tremendous pillar of light engulfing the Godbeast's frame as it raced for the sky.

The brilliant release lasted only a few seconds, then blinked out. Schpariel stood waiting for further assault from inside of himself, but nothing came. Though damaged by a thousand microscopic holes throughout his flesh, his body remained functional. He released a sigh of slight relief. For a moment, he had felt a genuine twinge of fear.

He looked across to where Cildar still stood watching with his unconscious friend draped across his shoulder. Schpariel moved to make a bold taunt, but his voice gave out with a sickening crunching cough. He ignored this and reared back his right arm, swinging his scepter forward.

To his dismay, his arm shattered at the shoulder. It fell to the ground with a crash, where his stone fingers crumbled to pebbles and lost their grip on his staff. Soon the rest of his arm followed, shuffling into a humble pile of ash. He stared in amazement, then heard the sounds of more dust splashing to the ground. He inspected himself and saw that his left arm also crumbled away, as well as the stump of his right shoulder.

The Godbeast moved about clumsily as his decay progressed in this fashion. He sought to cry out, to curse this human, but he could find no voice. It was not long before his mouth as well turned to dust, sliding over his abdomen and racing to the ground at his feet. Half a minute after the release of Shock, nothing remained of the First Anointed Godbeast but a stretch of black and red ash dusted across the dirt. With his body collapsed, his anchoring lost at last, Schpariel's soul slipped through the Gate of Gehenna and returned home to rest alongside his brother.

Cildar gave a satisfied nod, lowered Myris to the ground gently, and locked his Trine Lance against his back. He struggled to awaken his friend, slapping him fiercely across the face and shouting at him, "Myris! Myris Phare! Listen to me! You must release the armlet's power! If you don't, you'll die! Dammit Myris, wake up or I swear to Pecoros I'll beat you to death!"

The Cainite struggled weakly to consciousness for a moment, his face already bruised from the blows of the Dragoon's hands. Cildar halted his berating, as Myris touched his right fingers to his own forehead. He spent a moment in concentration, then spat weakly, "Mutance azurey."

The beaten man collapsed once more into unconsciousness. Cildar spent a moment verifying that his friend's transformation had indeed been successful, then sighed quietly. He gazed across the city of Tyerria. There were many freshly dead bodies there. The paladin hated what he was about to do, but knew his options were limited. The Soul Scythe could feast weakly on the spiritual energies of a recently slain human. Though he could not save their lives, he might yet save Myris'. He moved from his companion's side toward the statue decorating the town's square—which surprisingly had remained intact—offering a prayer of apology in advance to the victims of the fallen Godbeast of Gehenna.

* * * * *

In her private chamber in the Overlord's fortress, Meriosthro basked in a moment of quiet meditation. The chamber was dark, save for a single candle sitting on the desk in front of her. Also lying across her desk, she had a strange package wrapped in brown paper. She stared at it, solemnly adjusting the chemistry of her body as only an ancient draconic knew how to do. She slowly unwrapped the bandages hiding the stump of her left shoulder. Then, in a similarly patient motion, she unwrapped the package lying across her desk. When opened, a full draconic arm, with skin of red tone, was revealed before her. There were signs it had been recently carved from its host body, and still leaked fresh blood.

The draconic lady barely repressed a smile. She had been long seeking a draconic with blood compatible to her own. She had put forth the ruse of desiring a new mate, and gone through dozens of suitors, both male and female. It had finally been a male with red dragon in his roots that had proven to be the right match. Meriosthro was herself a fallen blue, so she was surprised that a red had held the compatible blood type. She needed not the explanation, however, only the match.

Once she had become certain of the male's compatibility, she had finally invited him to her bedchamber. He was the first suitor to have gotten so far, and was unable to repress his excitement at the prospect. In his eyes it signified he would soon be the leader of the draconic clan, as his idol Farthas before him.

His fate took a far darker course. Once alone, Meriosthro had slain him immediately. She first carefully carved off his left arm, then devoured the rest of his flesh. She did not prefer cannibalism, but she could stand it, and she did hate to see a draconic's spirit wasted. Once her feast had finished, she spent some time selecting the most choice bones from his skeleton to fashion into fresh weapons for herself. Then she summoned her most trusted servants and had them transport the rest to the armorers, offering no explanation.

Though her original injury had only claimed her forearm, Meriosthro had since been forced to have the upper arm detached more carefully. For what she was about to do, fragments of sliced and damaged bone would not suffice. The wound must be clean, the bones intact, the joints receptive.

Now it was time to put the donor arm to its test. She lifted it carefully by the bicep, and with a forceful grunt locked the humerus into her rotator cuff. There was a brief signal of pain from the arm itself, then her own flesh seized upon it. She waited nearly five full minutes, motionless, until she was confident it had healed sufficiently to remain attached for at least a moment. She then quickly flew her right hand to her desk and seized several large pins, which she jammed into her shoulder to latch the limb in place. Once this was done, she knew she needed only time. She spent a few more minutes binding the arm against her side with bandages—a difficult feat with only her right hand to work with—

then gave a sigh of satisfaction. She could feel the healing taking effect already, a warm numbness spreading in her new fingertips. The match had been pure.

"That was impressive," a voice hissed from the shadows behind her. "Even by my lofty standards, your survival abilities are remarkable."

She quickly drew a cutlass from her belt and spun about, swinging at the source of the voice. Before she could find the creature's throat, a hand shot out and struck her sword hard, knocking it from her grip and across the room.

Fenrir grinned at her through bared fangs. "Don't bother. I'm a match for any draconic."

She let her shoulders slump at the sight of the wolfen creature. "It's only you. I feared a more loyal servant of the Overlord."

"Internal spies are not so much Shote's style. If he suspects you of trouble, he prefers to kill rather than verify."

"What do you want, anyway? You have no right in my private quarters at this late hour."

"I wish to speak with you about the war."

She moved over to her bed and took a seat on the edge. She was now deep in a healing cycle, and did not have energy to expend in throwing her intruder out. "Whatever it is, I'm sure it could have waited until morning."

"Not really. You see, I've been outside."

Meriosthro paused at this announcement. There had not been activity from the human forces in quite some time, and she had to admit she was curious as to their status. "Outside? Shote has forbidden us to leave the compound since the last ambush."

Fenrir shrugged. "Shote forbids a lot of things. I find obedience is very inconvenient."

"Fine. What's the news, then? What has you coming to me, exactly?"

"There's a large force that's joined with the humans, right? No doubt you heard about their presence in the last skirmish."

"We were not involved. My draconics were on foraging duty

that day, guarding the humans and Robed Ones who had exited the rear of the castle."

"I went to inspect these newcomers. Suffice to say, they're formidable. I've spent the last three days hiding amongst them, listening in on their conversations and plans. They were forestalled due to an internal assassination and leadership change. They're attacking tomorrow, though that's less important. More important was the title of these reinforcements. They march by the name of 'Devilslayer', a gathering of around eleven hundred from what I can tell. If my memory serves me—and it always does—your people fled here to escape these very Devilslayers, when Farthas yet lived."

Meriosthro sat in silence for several long seconds. Fenrir soon prompted, "That bad, is it?"

"Devilslayers only move in groups of fifty, maybe a hundred. Even in such numbers, they are never defeated. A force of a thousand is unheard of. This place will be wiped from the face of Morolia."

He nodded. "That's kind of the impression I was getting. Though they're still humans, and still no match for Shote. Even so, they are efficient killers of all other demons. In the end Shote will survive, no doubt. He may even overcome, killing all the humans on his own. But the rest of us he leads as shields of meat, sacrificial lambs for the final glory of the Overlord. By my accounting there's no wisdom in following an immortal leader into battle. He lacks the judgment necessary to protect those of us suffering from mortality."

"What are you saying, Fenrir?"

"Shote's merely sending us out to die, yes? He'll win this battle by his own might one way or another, yes?"

She hesitated before answering, "That is how things seem."

"Then what does it matter to him whether we escape alive or dead? Either way he loses his troops. Personally, I've completed my stay here. The rest of my species perished at the hands of the Devilslayers moons ago. If I didn't join them then, I don't see the virtue in doing so now. It's time for less hostile pastures. Yet surviving on Arkalen is no simple feat. I need a force to take with me. As a general here I have my own followers, but the shambling werebeasts are useless. What they lack in strength and intellect, they compensate for in numbers. That's not sufficient to safeguard me against the mightier creatures who dot the continent. I need a troop of true warriors, true survivors. I belong with your kind, I've decided. We are of like spirit and body."

"What do you propose? Are you suggesting that I take my people and abandon this place that has served as our home? I'm not even certain they will take to such a rapid decision."

"Then bring the ones you can, the ones who will adapt. They're the true survivors anyway." He reached into his vest and pulled out two strips of thick paper. "Take these. In the morning, Shote will call us out to battle. I already know the humans will assault at dawn, and it'll be in full scale. Shote will expect us to deliver a full scale response to match. I'll meet you at the base of the fortress, just beyond the castle doors. I leave this place tomorrow one way or another. If you have decided you'll join me, hand me the white parchment. If not, the black." She took the strips from his hand, and he moved soundlessly across the chamber to her door. He stopped there for a moment, then shouted back, "Spend the night thinking it over. Oh, and enjoy your new arm. It's quite lovely."

He took his exit, leaving Meriosthro staring at the strips of paper she had been given. She looked in particular at the black one, noting how silly of a gesture it was. She ripped it up and threw it aside. Regardless of her decision—whether she would join Fenrir in his retreat or not—she would give him the white paper. His expectations otherwise showed a naive trust that forced her to question his own ability to survive.

Unbeknownst to her, Fenrir waited with his ear pressed outside of her door. Once he heard the sound of ripping parchment he gave a soft chuckle, then moved away. In either retreat or death, tomorrow morning Meriosthro would align with the fenrirs.

## Chapter 41.

## The War of the Overlord

Freshly decreed High Chieftain Detria Alsen stared down upon the Fortress of the Overlord preparing herself for battle, the same as she imagined Kelve had done many times before her. Her lieutenants had been informed this would be their final raid. No quarter would be given, no retreat sounded. It was a stressful mindset for entering battle, but the advantage in numbers she held had convinced her that any other tactic would be cowardly and demoralizing.

She had set forth a simple strategy—too simple, her insecurities screamed—but all parties had agreed to it heartily. The several hundred veterans which had served united under Kelve were the most familiar with the Overlord's armies, but weary and beaten after their lengthy siege. The majority of their number had been placed under Colbiss and given the relatively tranquil task of controlling the poorly trained were-creatures and human slaves. However, three hundred of their most grizzled and most fearless had been assigned to Boderon, who had been instructed to ignore all other foes for the sake of the trolls. Only sixty of Dokitir's adamant cultists remained active, but the threat of their shadow magic could not be discounted.

The nine hundred uninjured Devilslayers had also been divided. Two hundred would march straight for the ogre forces, under Mek's supervision. Another two hundred would disperse out and hunt for chimeras, under the oversight of an older Silver Pride pack leader named Storio. The remaining five hundred would report directly to Detria, with the intent to slaughter Meriosthro's draconics as swiftly as possible. All slayers had also been given permission to pick off the Overlord's human or were-creature forces at their convenience, but no other troops unless their lives depended on it.

The only outstanding concern was Shote, the indomitable lord of the fortress. To that question, there could be only one answer—the Monks of Tria. The two mighty warriors stood to Detria's left, silently awaiting the order to march. Tenkahn had assured the other commanders that, with the information given to him by Tessena, he could hold his dreaded rival at bay. He would not even raise the possibility that he might defeat the beast, promising only to buy the army enough time to gain control of the fortress before he fell. No mention had been made of Gaius' role in the upcoming struggle. Detria had chosen not to question the elder monk on the matter, as her standing as leader was already a tightrope act.

She took in a slow breath and released it in a long sigh. It was time to sound the march. She turned somberly to Colbiss and signaled him with a nod. Following her lead, the man sounded an enthusiastic shout to the armies and the troops began to make their move down the hillside. Detria, lingering behind, turned and glanced to Tenkahn. The stalwart monk offered her a smile, then a wave of his hand to encourage her to march without him. She grimaced, but broke into a run to join the front lines, catching up with Boderon and several of her lieutenants at the fore.

Soon the two monks were left standing alone atop the hill that had long served as their base of operations. Gaius said nothing, awaiting the order he knew was inevitable.

"You cannot join this fight," his master announced as expected. The young man bit his lower lip, but nodded his acquiescence. In spite of the youth's quick surrender, Tenkahn continued his lecture. "This battle has been presented as a 'do or die' affair. It would be foolhardy for the only two remaining Monks of Tria to both participate. I alone must confront Shote."

"Using our cloaks of stealth—"

"They are no good against Shote. He possesses demonic senses allowing him to see through us, somehow. Remember, I assaulted him once before with ten monks, not two."

Gaius bowed his head despondently. “I understand. I can’t match your lost brothers.”

Tenkahn patted him on the shoulder. “No single man could. Do not feel despair. It is simply the limits of one when compared against nine. You are specially gifted, Gaius. Few monks have ever risen to the level you have attained so rapidly. That is why I value your survival so highly, even above my own. You are the future of our order, where I cannot be. You are the new beginning, free of the failures and shortcomings of our past.”

They stood in silence for many long minutes, watching as the battle between the Overlord’s troops and Detria’s was joined. The teacher turned to his pupil. “Let us activate our stealth cloaks once more. I will slip between the lesser demons and head straight to Shote. You, however, must flee this place. Find safety and carry on our legacy.”

“Yes, master,” Gaius answered with a subdued tone. They joined their fists together, and soon both monks disappeared in a haze of divine magic.

* * * * *

Detria’s forces charged through the front gate with cries of fury, diving for the nearest foes and unleashing their onslaught. The demonic army was not caught unprepared, alerted by circling chimera sentries. Shote had found time to shuffle the freshest of his troops to the front lines already, and the battle was met earnestly.

The Overlord’s magnificent beast watched from the back lines as the slaughter of his demons began. As he had feared, the remaining demons here were no match for these newly arrived Devilslayers. He had held back the trolls, and they waited in the wings for his signal. He nodded to a nearby chimera, who unleashed a mournful shriek. The trolls rode out on horseback immediately, charging to the invaders’ ranks and stemming their slaughter.

Shote issued more orders, and soon the draconics and ogres also charged into the fray. He held back no available resources this time, sending human scouts and messengers to every corner of the fortress. Finally he sent word up through Scklaria, and for a time the chimera forces aligned with the troll and ogre ranks to form a sturdy barricade of demonic flesh.

This was briefly effective. The Devilslayers still did not know how to deal with the seemingly unstoppable trolls, and the ogres and chimeras were able to utilize this confusion to their benefit. The enemy army was pushed back and a clear line of battle was established between each side.

The minotaur looked over the opposing forces with a strange feeling in his gut. He had almost a thousand units at his beck, but most of those were lowly humans and were-creatures. The enemies ranks consisted of nearly double that number, a thousand of which were expertly trained and capable of fighting at an ogre or chimera's level. He had brought the flow of battle briefly under control, but the outcome was inevitable, and it did not favor the Overlord.

"Kogonbo!" he roared out. Anticipating the command, the ogre general arrived at his side shortly. Shote greeted his arrival with only a nod, and the triclops moved quickly to the exterior wall of the castle behind them, taking up station on the far right side of the doorway. The minotaur shouted remaining orders to his struggling troops, knowing their fervor would not last long. "Scklaria, avoid the ones in furs, strike down the weaker targets. Fenrir, Meriosthro, stay on the defensive. Dokitir, push them back. Everyone, hold the line. I repeat, hold the line!"

This final order sent new zeal into the demonic forces, and a wave of their enthusiasm pounded against the wall of human figures. It was this moment for which Shote had drilled these troops, this maneuver for which he had trained them. He watched as slowly, deliberately, the humans were drawn together and clenched between the fortress wall at their backs and the raging demons to their fore.

Soon the vigor of the demonic surge began to fade. As the

invaders began to push once more forward from the western wall, Shote made his move. He retreated to where Kogonbo stood waiting, moving to the opposite side of the door. Each of the stalwart creatures gave a ferocious punch to the stone in front of them, sending huge cracks along the wall and causing a small area to collapse on each side. Two giant levers were revealed, solid steel affairs rusted with age and disuse. Shote and Kogonbo seized the respective lever in front of them and, without hesitation, gave a sharp pull at the same time, grunting with the effort required to dislodge the hinges from stasis.

There was a sound of gears grinding, too soft to overtake the din of battle. For about twenty seconds nothing happened, and the minotaur turned with apprehension. He worried the humans would force their way to the interior courtyard too quickly, but his demons caught a stroke of fortune, as a troll scythe struck Detria's calf and she let out a cry. The Devilslayer forces around her immediately fell into a defensive formation and shuffled her to safety. It quelled the invaders' momentum for the brief few seconds Shote needed.

When the sprawling mechanical apparatus forming the skeletal structure of the Overlord's home finally completed its activities, a boom of thunder reverberated beneath the ground. Sand and dirt suddenly began to slide into the earth at various spots, revealing open gratings under the feet of many slayers. Another boom of thunder echoed, this one louder, and majestic pillars of bright blue flame erupted through these gratings, devouring hundreds of warriors before they could react.

The demons delivered another hard push against the bewildered enemy army, then tactically retreated several yards. The move was made just in time, as a final expulsion of long pikes and tremendous saw blades claimed hundreds more of the invading soldiers. This was followed by an unsettling rain of blood and gore, to the delight of the Overlord's forces. The screams of the wounded echoed across the battlefield, soon silenced by their deaths. These blades had been coated long ago with the blood of slain green dragons, and the acidic venoms had not lost their potency in dormancy. Not a single warrior who was stricken survived, not even those who took only the finest scratch.

Shote signaled Kogonbo back into the fray. Once the ogre was gone from his sight, the minotaur commander released a loud snort of relief. The trap had gone over even better than he had hoped, killing almost half of the enemy force. Even better, most of those stricken had been the reinforcing Devilslayers, as the other humans had drawn back defensively out of loyalty to Detria. His troops were not yet in a position to end this battle easily, but they had at least reestablished equal footing.

And the legendary beast knew how to leverage equal footing. He reached to his back and drew forth his two axes, beginning to amp his body for combat. Once he joined the fray, the already diminished morale of his enemies would collapse entirely. Their retreat was assured, while his army would live to fight another day, with confidence buoyed by their invincible leader's display of triumph.

Just as he was to begin his slaughter, he detected a peculiar movement in the swirling dust before him. He gave a sniff with his large nostrils, then narrowed his eyes and gritted his teeth.

"Ten...kahn," he stated with emphasis.

The monk stepped from an invisible fold in the air and offered a bow. "For a second time, Shote, you have broken my heart. I underestimated the cards you still held, and in doing so failed Detria and her people. I have witnessed the deaths of far too many of my allies at your hands. This is a blow from which I shall not recover. Though I serve the God of Mercy, my heart is now devoid of it."

"I have no time for you," the demon replied, pointing his left axe suggestively at the monk's throat. "I move to the fore of the battle. Follow me if you will, stay my massacre if you can."

The monk brought his hands together and channeled effusive energy around two fingers on his right hand, then raised these fingers to the center of his chest and drew a straight line. The spark faded from his fingertips and caused a complex rune to darken on his chest, which intermingled into the other runes and then began to glow with new life. Tenkahn lifted his eyes, which now swirled violently with the same light from his Human Script.

"No," he answered with an emboldened clarity that left no room for questioning. "Today, I am Merciless."

He spread his fingers wide and gave a guttural roar, then smacked his open palms hard on the stone beneath him. Flawlessly round earthen pillars exploded upward throughout the area, still reshaping themselves under the grip of an overwhelming wave of kinetic force emanating from the monk's body, encircling Shote and striking into the castle walls. The beast awaited the inevitable pillar that would strike against him directly, but it did not come. Instead his foe moved fast, too fast, stopping only a foot from his snout. The minotaur panicked at this speed and tried to lash out with both of his axes, but a punch from each of Tenkahn's fists struck his wrists and threw his arms forcibly open wide. The monk then wrapped arms about his enemy's waist, and at that moment a final mighty pillar ejected from the ground and struck his own feet. He used a powerful kick to add to his momentum, and together the two rivals were sent rolling skyward, to the roof of the Overlord's castle.

Just before landing, Shote kicked the monk away from himself and managed to settle onto his feet. Tenkahn hovered in the air for a moment longer, then fell down upon his foe with his right fist reared back. The minotaur anticipated one of the monk's typical kinetic wave attacks, so he postponed his dodge until the last second, then leaped backward and angled himself off to one side. Tenkahn did not give a typical strike, however, and instead upon landing he thrust forward his right forearm and gave a shout.

Shote was able to see the disturbance heading his way, but there was nothing he could do in response. A wall of pure force—over thirty feet high, thirty feet wide, and moving every bit as fast as Tenkahn's own fist—rippled along the air and tore a wide rift into the rooftop stone beneath it. It overtook the minotaur just as he landed and traveled unhindered through his body, continuing on its path showing no evidence of slowing. Blood splattered sharply from his back and legs, and he felt the iron bindings holding his ribs in place buckle and snap.

He bore his anguish and forced himself to keep his locked eyes onto his opponent for the next move. Tenkahn graciously waited, gathering ether to his body and recharging from his last rush. Shote gave an accepting nod and began redoubling his own internal strength.

"I see," he said with resolve. "Then show me, Monk of Tria, just how merciless you can be."

* * * * *

With Detria's safety confirmed, the Devilslayer commanders did their best to recover with composure from the devastating blow they had just been dealt. Mek Tellish assumed command, reaffirming Detria's original strategy and ordering each unit to their assigned targets. It proved difficult with the demon forces intermixed in their current formation, so the first priority became a counteroffensive to escape the burning, bloodied trap grounds and establish clean footing.

Despite still being staggered by losses, this renewed push went smoothly. With Shote's trap sprung, the Overlord's forces had returned to a defensive mentality, unaware of their commander's next move. The subsequent unexplained disappearance of said commander from the battlefield further dimmed their organization, and the invading soldiers met only minimal resistance driving into the inner courtyards. Mek was comforted by this success, as fighting while avoiding still-spewing pillars of fire and poisoned blades would have been a significant handicap for the slayers.

Once he was confident his army had regained a clear skirmish line, he decided upon his next course of action. Momentarily disjointed as they were, the demons nonetheless held the advantage in morale. The best blow Mek himself could personally deliver against this was to slay one the enemy generals. His troops had been instructed to contain the ogre troopers, and he would not defy orders. After scattering his units to various ogres raging across the battlefield, he headed himself toward the giant blue triclops who served as their master.

Kogonbo had only just rejoined the battle, taking a position along the front lines. A swing of his club sent three Devilslayers flying away from him, as demonic soldiers parted their tide to make way for the thunderous general. Mek swiftly moved forward and signaled the nearby slayers to evacuate the area. The triclops nodded to his challenger in acknowledgment, likewise motioning for his own allies to clear the lines and make an opening. It was to be a contest of champions.

Mek discarded the two short swords he had been wielding up to this point. He could have returned them to their sheaths, but opted instead to ditch the extra weight entirely, tossing them to his feet. His hands flew to his back and drew forth his twin steel poles, each three feet in length. He slammed these together with a twist, joining them into one bar, then spun his assembled dannig base over his head fiercely and thrust it symbolically into the ground at his side. "I am the Devilslayer of Arkalen!" he bellowed. "You have been condemned for your crimes against the human race, and as of this moment you life is forfeit to this staff of justice."

Kogonbo uttered a low growl. "Now is not the time for grandstanding. Your life is in eminent danger. Consider!" He raised his steel club straight from his side and unleashed a vicious horizontal swipe at the man's head.

Though he had not allowed it to show, the pack leader had chosen his position carefully. He was standing at the very edge of the range of the ogre's club, and in his haste to make his point Kogonbo had not taken a step forward to compensate. The Devilslayer casually let his body lean away from the strike, rocking back on his heels. The club flew by his face with incredible speed for such a conserved motion, missing his nose by barely an inch.

As his opponent's arm flew over his own left shoulder, Mek swiftly drew his weapon from the ground and stabbed at the giant's face in one fluid motion, blinding the eye in the middle of the blue forehead.

Working through the agony of having his eye splattered into his own skull, the triclops lost no time following with another attack. He allowed the momentum of his club to carry the weapon behind his head, then twisted his body sharply at the torso, coming down at the human with another crushing blow, this one moving nearly twice as fast as the previous. Unfortunately his target's reaction was just as fast, as the man gave a rapid spin with the dannig and snapped it at Kogonbo's hand, breaking his two middle fingers and causing him to release the weapon.

The club soared harmlessly over the slayer's head as he began a low dash to finish off his enemy. A series of screams sounded behind him, warning him that dozens of his allies were about to be crushed by the soaring slab of steel. He had not expected the beast to drop the weapon entirely, but had only hoped to cripple the blow and prevent a swift reaction to his charge.

A shrill, "Dammit!" tore from his throat as he cursed his own inattentiveness. No sooner had he recognized the threat than he was already in motion, his right heel thrust hard into the ground to brake his charge as he straightened his stance. He threw himself backward and spun about in midair, grabbing a tightly wound whip from his belt with his left hand. He slung with all his might, praying that its reach was still sufficient. The length of corded leather unwound and revealed three highly flexible blades at the end, which lashed about and buried themselves into the wrapped leather handle of the flying club. Once sure of his grip Mek tucked his dannig under his arm, stabbed the end of the pole and his left heel simultaneously into the ground, and pulled back with a mighty heave from his left arm.

His efforts paid off. The club crashed to the ground a few yards short of his onlooking soldiers, into a space that had been emptied by the quick-witted slayers. But his loyalty to his brethren had its price. In spite of his anchoring, the momentum of the club had also pulled him forward, slamming his face hard into the ground and nearly pulling his arm out of socket. As he struggled to recover from this ungainly position a voice in his mind taunted, *You're dead now, Mek. You've turned your exposed back to your enemy and you're dead.*

But he would not stay down—his Devilslayer training would not allow it, his body remaining in motion almost beyond his own conscious control. Even as he was clumsily regaining his feet, his sprained left hand reached to his belt and pulled forth a large spiked mace head, weighing about twelve pounds. He attached it to one end of the dannig with a twist and began spinning the weapon about with his right hand, unable to raise his left arm.

Then with a flourish he seized the end of the pole and twisted about, swinging ferociously at the height where he remembered the ogre's head. Kogonbo stood still bemoaning his own wounds, and too late saw the weapon that tore his head from its shoulders. For a moment Mek counted himself lucky the ogre had taken such dismay from his broken fingers, especially when he had shown so little concern over his destroyed eye. Then upon closer inspection, he realized these were not the injuries that had kept the towering demon in dismay.

The man spent a few seconds staring at a series of arrows embedded in his fallen enemy's neck. They were small, only the quills could scarcely be made out, but Mek recognized them well. He glared at the surrounding demons and they quickly retreated further from his sight, not desiring to be the creature he next turned his ire upon. He turned his head back and shouted orders to his nearby allies, chastising them for their idleness and ordering them back into the fray. Soon a young female Devilslayer stood at his side offering an amused smile.

He did not reciprocate her pleasant mood. "That was improper, Kalea. You shouldn't have interfered with a battle between commanders."

"No one saw anything. My crossbow is both silent and effective, don't you think? Everyone thinks you killed him fair and square."

"That's not the point, Kalea. It's not our way."

She rolled her eyes at this. "I don't know about you, but I don't plan on dying today. I'll do whatever it takes to make certain I still have tomorrow to argue about what's 'proper'. And now, thanks to me, maybe you'll get a chance to win that argument."

She left his side and returned to the battle. He sighed in frustration, disheartened that this was how his grand moment had ended. Then he too moved to the wall of demonic troops, taking his rage out on weaker enemies before continuing his hunt for the other ogres.

* * * * *

Fenrir dodged nimbly through human forces, endeavoring to progress against an unfriendly tide. His escape was not going to plan. The trap that had been sprung against the invaders had incidentally compacted their forces around his location, effectively cutting off his path to freedom. Further, although he had received the white parchment earlier this morning, he had been unable to make contact with Meriosthro or her forces. He was uncertain if this was an unhappy coincidence due to Shote's tactical choices regarding the draconics, or a deliberate choice made by their leading lady. In either event, it seemed he would be forced to make his escape on his own.

He had pulled a sizable allotment of his were-creatures and had them functioning in a shield capacity, charging recklessly into the Devilslayers and creating enough of a distraction for Fenrir to slip through. With each yard he progressed he lost a dozen more of the simple beasts, and knew that soon he would be without guard.

"Why was I not informed of this trap?" he cursed to himself as he cut down another eager Devilslayer, effortlessly countering their various martial arts. As weapons he wielded two huge crescent-shaped blades with a slim steel bar running behind them, which he gripped tightly in each fist and used with a bare-knuckle fighting style. This setup allowed him to fight with his feral instincts, but served as a far more effective alternative to his natural claws. "After all, am I not one of the Generals to the Overlord? I should know what Shote's mind is. It seems I'm not to be trusted." He smiled at the irony of his own statement, then slid through invaders as he left gaping wounds in their guts.

He beat a winding line for the back of the fortress, attempting to angle through the thinnest parts of human ranks while carefully avoiding the active traps. He thought his retreat would be easily mistaken for an overzealous assault, but his guise did not hold. Dokitir seemed to take exception to his activity, and came nearby to address him.

After using a force of twenty trolls to hammer through the humans and approach the retreating general, Dokitir barked at him, "You're too deep, creature. Pull back, reorganize your troops."

Fenrir bared his sets of needle-like fangs and shook his head. "Your rank is the same as mine, don't tell me how to wage this battle. My fangs cut through the flesh of trolls as easily as that of humans. I'm not the creature you want to challenge."

The troll narrowed his eyes and mumbled a few dark incantations. A shadow magic lance appeared in his right hand as a wave of shadowy blades and fires coated the rest of his skin, forming a perfect barrier against direct assaults. "What do you think you can do against me, Fenrir?"

A swarm of invaders struck them at that moment, though none of them Devilslayers. Fenrir and the trolls both reacted sharply, cutting down the dozen or so humans who thought they could match these troops with ease. This display discouraged nearby enemies from making another such move for at least the moment. After the interlopers had fallen to troll magic or Fenrir's blades, the Generals of the Overlord once more set their eyes on one another.

"You're a capable warrior," Dokitir offered civilly. "There are no doubts why the Overlord promoted you. But Shote warned me you were not to be trusted, and it seems his insight has proven true. You cannot take twenty trolls. Your body is too soft. You will die before a single among us falls."

Fenrir clenched his month shut tight and ground his teeth. He did not want this confrontation, but could see no way out. He knew Dokitir's assessment of his chances was correct. It seemed that his race was about to vanish into extinction at last.

Then another wave from the battle washed over the antagonists. This time Fenrir was spared, as the full force of draconics broke hard into the troll warriors. The score of trolls were outnumbered badly and driven back by an armored wall of dragon scales. Not a single troll fell to the exchange, nor did a draconic take more than minor damage from the magical weaponry.

Meriosthro brought herself forward and met the troll general head on. "Enough, Dokitir! The Overlord's dominion is finished, and we're escaping. If you're not with us, then go serve your lord until you perish for him."

Fenrir took a moment to slink away from the lines of this skirmish, smiling broadly. A more experienced human tried to assault him in his isolation, but the knowledge he had absorbed from Kelve's body had given him too keen of an understanding for how the Devilslayers fought. The ambushing warrior shortly fell the ground with a rift torn through his jugular.

Dokitir countered Meriosthro's jeer. "I have my own orders. To serve my lord, I need the head of the wolf."

"There's well over a hundred draconics between you and that head. I know trolls are considered most invincible among demons, but a draconic does not die easily. Even once killed, we can continue fighting until our enemies die alongside us. Do you really think you can take my forces?"

One of the other trolls stepped forward and whispered something in Dokitir's ear. The troll general gave a sneer, then a nod. "I suppose it's possible the wolf slipped past our grip before we noticed him." He gave a few hand signs and the trolls pulled back to the demonic front lines. It was not long before Devilslayers filled that gap and the battle was resumed with the draconics.

Meriosthro turned to Fenrir and gave him a serpentine smile of her own. He narrowed his eyes and spoke over the sounds of the battle. "You knew about the trap," he said accusingly.

"What? Didn't you?" she asked with a hint of laughter in her tone.

He was unable to prevent himself from dropping into a growl, then lashed out to one side and killed another nearby human. "Come on," he barked. "There's too much action for me here. Let's move." Meriosthro released a snarl to her troops, and the two generals began to cut their path toward the main gate.

It was long and slow going. Fenrir cursed internally that he had been unable to secure a key to either the northern or southern gate. After the encounter with Dokitir, he had no doubt this was also a result of Shote's foresight. The human combatants in their path were as much of a nuisance as the traps dotting the terrain, and it was difficult for the draconics to maintain a tight, cohesive unit. At least a score of Meriosthro's troops fell to the cautious tactics of the slayers before they finally found themselves emerging clear into the western edge of the outer courtyard.

As the draconics regrouped, now free of the traps, the two former generals prepared to make their final exit. Once more this was not to be so easily achieved, however, as they were blocked by a line of fresh Devilslayers stationed between them and the gate. There were at least eighty of them by Fenrir's rough count, led by a human female wearing the Hand of Ramsa. He knew the dangers of that weapon well, and held no desires for a final test of his skill.

Detria held her dannig in her left hand with a large spearhead attached to it, pointing it forward at the retreating force. "I don't know what you're about, demons, but your tactic won't work."

Meriosthro knew they held the advantage in numbers, so she moved to charge forward and urge her troops into battle. Fenrir caught her by the wrist and shook his head. He bowed to Detria and sheathed his weapons at his back. "Master of the Devilslayers, you pursue the wrong enemies. We are abandoning Shote and the

Overlord. We only want our freedom, our survival. Rather than wasting time here fighting against us, you should use your might and concentrate your efforts against Shote. You could hold an even greater advantage in numbers if you let us escape, or you can waste lives fighting enemies you need not have."

Detria creased her brow and seemed to think this over. Noticing her hesitation, the man to her right interjected, "Lady Detria, this is surely a demonic trap. They're probably headed to strike our base, kill our children and wounded and leave us nowhere to escape!"

She weighed the man's words against those of Fenrir, then finally shook her head. "This is no tactic Shote would employee. He knows, as well as I do, that dividing his troops at this time would be foolish and leaves him in a weakened position. We'll do as the wolf suggests. Return to battle."

"Milady—"

"Did some part of my statement leave room for questions?"

There was a pause of silence, followed by a humble response of, "No, High Chieftain."

As the chastised slayer took command of the unit and marched slowly around the draconics, Detria stepped forward and pressed the tip of her spear into Fenrir's neck.

"Heed these words, you of the fallen fenrir. I am the master of the Devilslayers, as you addressed me. If I return to my camp and your demons have made a move against a single person there, you will find no rest on this continent. I control the entire web of slayers, and I'll turn that web upon you. You think that which we did to your kind before was bad? Wait until you see the punishments I'll have awaiting you personally." She tilted her head back and widened her eyes with sincerity. "Genocide will seem like mercy compared to the hell I'll teach you."

He stared at her with an odd, fearless calm—his heart strangely at peace with her spear upon his throat—then knelt forward onto one knee and answered, "As you command, milady." He rose to his feet and swiftly made his escape toward the gate. Meriosthro growled once more at Detria. As the Devilslayer began to stroke the ribbon holding the Hand of Ramsa in check, the draconic backed down and led her troops to follow Fenrir.

Finally free of the raging battle, the draconic and fenrir took a moment to relax and run a final casualty count. Meriosthro spoke with a few of her ranked officers as Fenrir stroked his own ego, cursing Detria's name and boasting that he was not afraid of a scraggly human girl.

Meriosthro was seized by a sudden harsh cough, then a few weaker ones followed. She signaled for her officers to move on about their business as she gradually recovered herself. Fenrir noticed her condition and commented, "Ah, yes. You should take this."

He reached into his vest and pulled forth a slim vial containing a purple liquid. She took it and drank eagerly, and her coughing shortly subsided.

"Hm, a powerful effect," she observed, pleased. "What was that? Some sort of elixir?"

"Elixir? No, calling it that would be inappropriate. Do you recall the parchments I gave you last night? You thought I was requesting a signal from you. I knew that whether you would join me today or not, you'd only need the white parchment. I also knew that you'd be arrogant enough to assume this immediately, and would destroy the black parchment without hesitation. Unfortunately, that parchment contained a powerful airborne powder-based toxin. It's dangerous to all manner of demons, and even humans, but it's particularly deadly to dragonkin. It's easily cultivated from the pollen of a nearby flower. The vial I just had you drink contained the antitoxin."

Meriosthro spent a moment processing this information. "Wait. So last night was a ruse, and if I had betrayed you then I would have died?"

"Yes, once I chose you as my confidant our fates were linked. Only by choosing to ensure my survival could you save your own life. Fortunately for us both, you've proven yourself a trustworthy ally. From here I think our partnership together might prove quite mutually beneficial."

As he turned and walked away from her, Meriosthro stood admiring his determination and cunning. *You're a dangerous companion, Fenrir*, she thought to herself. *I hope you can make the risk worthwhile.* She yelled at her officers and they began to move south and slightly west, making certain to cut a path that clearly avoided the Devilslayer base.

## Chapter 42.

# Merciless

Slipping easily through the ranks of humans and demons alike, an invisible Gaius made his way to the castle beyond the battlefield. He had held his position in the hills for nearly fifteen minutes, meditating to prolong the stealthy cloaks of Tria he had paired with Tenkahn to activate. Though this technique allowed him to hide from the eyes of others, it rendered him infinitely easier to detect and track by another monk. Now that his mentor was distracted by a raging duel, he could operate in true secrecy. Unfortunately his cloaks would not hold much longer now, so he could no longer afford to be patient, in any event.

He spent a moment sniffing the currents, reading the movements and harmonies of the battle. It was beautiful, in its way. The music of carnage called to him, ached him to rock in its melody. But he could not allow himself to enjoy this battle below; he had to remain focused on the one raging above.

High on the rooftops, amid pirouettes and towers, Tenkahn and Shote collided fists and bodies into one another. There was no harmony to this battle, no melody culled its savagery. As his cloaks at last flickered out and he stood revealed, Gaius turned his eyes skyward and spent a moment monitoring the fight.

He reached his left hand into his vest and pulled out a small vial containing a bright white liquid. The toxin glowed with its own power. Even through the binding force of the glass, the monk could feel its mystic reverberations as it tampered with nearby currents. As he stared upon it he heard the voice of Kelve Orista replaying through his mind, as the commander had explained his final and most ingenious invention.

*Eiden, I don't believe I'll see this war through to the end, and so there is a charge I must place in your hands. Do you remember the beast that Abaddon, Cildar and Myris had to face in the Forest of Techenar? That beast was Tenkahn himself, under the influence of a technique he calls 'the Merciless Rune'. Cildar described it to me, and also how they defeated it. I believe before this is over, Tenkahn will go to face Shote on his own. He'll command you to remain behind, because he will be unable to endure your loss like that of his previous brethren. But once summoned, Tenkahn cannot disable the rune, and so he'll be lost to it. He may prove to be an even greater threat than Shote himself. After much studying, I've made this potion. The chemicals are attuned with your particular brand of magical energy. It will burn off the runes of Tria, even the Merciless Rune, I'm quite confident. When Tenkahn activates it, it'll be your responsibility to apply this to his chest and set him free. I can't guarantee it won't kill him, or even you for simply being near it. In the end, you'll have to be the one to decide if it's worth the risk.*

The young man smiled sadly to himself. "Kelve," he whispered to the memory of his commander, "I am Gaius now, Tria's faithful kin, and must follow Master Tenkahn's orders. However, you gave your orders to Eiden. Out of love for your memory, Eiden will heed your request."

He leaped to the stone face of the castle wall and seized upon a few secret footholds that only he knew, and began his scale to the top.

* * * * *

Shote raised his axes to the sky and bellowed. The unnatural blood in his sewn network of veins began to race, and his very flesh turned from its typical shade of blue to a pale red. Steam began to leak from his mouth and nostrils, and his eyes became enlarged to match his swollen muscles.

Tenkahn stood motionless, staring at his own feet with arms tucked in tightly at his sides. Shote laughed at the monk's cockiness and blasted forward with his pure, uninhibited speed. His movement was faster than it had been in years, faster than anything Detria's army had yet seen from him. It was a speed the elder Monk of Tria would recall all too well, however, and the Overlord's champion looked forward to seeing the return of fear to the man's eyes.

As the battleaxe in his right hand flashed downward to tear a cavity through the rune-covered chest, the monk's voice surrounded him. An echoing "No," was all Shote heard, then his trusty axe was sent shattering into a thousand pieces dancing in the sunlight. He grunted and tried to make a counter, but Tenkahn's fist implanted firmly into his jaw from beneath and lifted his feet from the ground, stretching his spine to the edge of injury and paralyzing his movement. This blow was immediately followed by a prod from five fingertips to the minotaur's chest, and he was sent forcibly back to his starting position.

Tenkahn's voice was becoming increasingly animalistic in its tenor, and speech was clearly becoming a struggle. "I'll have nothing to do with your weapons," he snarled. "This is the body that crushed Abaddon Daemon beneath it. Are you worthy to face it? Fight me like a true warrior or crumble in disgrace!"

The monk lifted his hands high, then turned them over and released a shockwave from his body. The roof began to reshape into his characteristic attack of earthen spikes, but the old stone was not able to endure such an abrupt transformation. The structure collapsed, dropping the contestants into the top floor of the castle beneath them.

Shote spent a moment shrugging off the slabs of rock that continued to crash into him, then walked slowly across the hallway he had fallen into. Tenkahn had landed in a different room, and a large wall separated the two warriors. Shote could feel the monk's presence, standing motionless in the room beyond. He returned his remaining axe to his back and gathered a rush of ether to his upper body, then laid his shoulder into the wall dividing him and his enemy. A massive doorway was blown open at his touch, as the additional structural damage sent a fresh rain of debris falling from the castle rooftops.

Shote locked eyes with his seemingly unbreakable rival. The minotaur took a deep breath, releasing another wave of steam from his nostrils. "So," he observed aloud, "you will take my all, Tenkahn of Tria. I once fought ten of your order at this level only, yet now it proves insufficient to face you alone. I will admit I do not understand. But the fate of that battle is tied indelibly to this one. The corpses of your fallen kin were recovered, studied by the acolytes. Though they could not unlock most of your myriad secrets, enough were revealed during my convalescence to grant me additional powers in preparation for such an occasion as this."

He went into a low crouch and sounded another bellow, the true sound of an ancient minotaur of legend. The Veil itself responded to this cry, as the air around him tinted red to match his skin and began to drip with a thick, vaporous blood of its own. This tangible ether dumped into Shote's body and set it aflame, as he reared his head back and screamed, "Red essence, feed my rage!" His breathing became rapid and erratic, as he demanded of Tenkahn, "Hit me again."

Not awaiting response to his request, the enraged beast slid instantly to his foe's location. Tenkahn attempted to make another crushing counter, but Shote took an immediate step back, slightly out of range of the monk's touch. The minotaur edged his right foot forward and stepped down hard, and a wide patch of floor around his opponent's feet collapsed and began to slide down to the next story. The demon let the monk sink a few inches, then slammed all of his body's might into a single punch, making square contact with the man's jaw.

Tenkahn flew down and away, twisting about and burrowing face-first through the solid stone floors. Shote launched into the air and shifted direction at the top of his leap, coming down and cracking his right heel solidly into the back of the monk's skull. Together the two crashed down to the next floor, bringing half of the upper level with them.

Immediately upon landing, Tenkahn forced his body to spin about. He released a powerful burst of waves from his fist as he slung it in his foe's direction. The ethereal flames dancing about the minotaur deflected the pressure from this attack, and in response Shote planted his right fist firmly into the man's stomach, burying him deeper into the stone floor where they had arrived.

Tenkahn did not accept the stagger, in spite of a burst of blood that flooded from his mouth and threatened to cut off his air supply. He thrust behind himself with both elbows, and two twisted pillars emerged from the ground and slammed into Shote's head from each side. The floor around them once again began to collapse from this deformity. As it did, the monk soared to his feet, braced his fists together firmly, and delivered a massive two-handed uppercut to his adversary's neck. The minotaur flew up through the ceiling above, smashing through one of the few patches that had been undamaged in their previous round.

The frenzied human reached out and grabbed one of the pillars he had just formed, snapped it off at the base, then tossed it lightly into the air above his head. He gathered a wall of kinetic energy about his fist and slammed it into the huge rock. It went soaring in Shote's direction, transforming as it flew into a cluster of razor-sharp points. This stone porcupine pinned the floating beast onto itself and carried him up another floor, smashing again through remnants of the building's architecture.

Tenkahn quickly calculated Shote's position, gave a short hop to escape the stone collapsing underneath him, and ran along the floor of the banquet hall he occupied. When he had reached his chosen spot, he blasted himself straight into the air. Each time he reached another ceiling he delivered a rapid punch, and an array of shrapnel surrounded his body and carried him to the next floor.

When he cleared the final floor and drifted once more above the castle's roof, there were at least thirty large stones flying with him. He went into a flurry of repeating punches, sending a barrage of missiles in the direction of Shote and the thorny boulder that had carried him aloft.

The reeling minotaur gave the spiny obelisk a firm hug and splintered it into debris. He spun about and saw his foe's new assault, and a series of strikes from his clawed fingertips tore each bullet to dust. He performed a sudden aerial flip and used the momentum to carry him to a stable section of the castle, where he dashed backward rapidly. Tenkahn set his own feet into a nearby tower, then kicked off of it to send himself catching up to Shote. The tower collapsed from the force of his jump and fell into the courtyard below.

They came to a sliding stop only a few inches from one another. Shote wasted no time, using his advantage in height to punch squarely down on the top of the monk's head. Tenkahn, in turn, used his runes to absorb the impact of that blow onto his shoulders and back, then returned a single uppercut into his opponent's ribs, redirecting the pressure of the attack flowing back into the minotaur's own body.

The beast bore the attack without flinching, and the two monsters sat staring at one another for a moment. Shote offered a smile, then confessed, "That's the most impressive trick you've used yet."

* * * * *

After spending nearly the entire battle wandering aimlessly, Boderon had finally gotten his forces into position to pin down the trolls. It had taken a difficult series of pincer attacks to bring several small troll units into one large force, but now the battle between the two factions had grown so intense that the trolls no longer tried to scatter.

The human commander was relying on some minor Devilslayer backup, but he was not finding their tactics to be of much use. Each time a slayer tried to move in and finish a troll off, the beast survived and ended the human's life gruesomely. Boderon personally knew better than to try such a gambit. As he continued his own battle with Dokitir, he stayed focused on disciplined defense and remaining alive. His only goal was to hold a stalemate, hoping the trolls would eventually surrender if the rest of the Overlord's army fell.

He had slammed his war hammer into Dokitir's head at least a dozen times since the pair had entered their duel, yet the troll continued to battle with a menacing grin splattered across his twisted features. Boderon knew the beasts were tough, but he still found himself in awe at their ability to stave off concussions. There were several open, bleeding scrapes on the troll general's scalp showing the sturdy bone of the skull, but still the demon seemed to feel no pain.

Boderon, in contrast, was wearing thin in spite of his admirable defensive efforts. He had successfully avoided any direct blows from the troll's shadow magic lance, but the lesser shadowy blades that hovered over Dokitir's flesh occasionally came too close, carving burns or gashes into the man's potbelly or broad shoulders.

His sledged weapon was enduring equal strain. The armored steel had held out well against blows from the ethereal polearm by which it had been repeatedly struck, but the backlashes of energy were beginning to soften the material and carve chunks from its surface. Boderon reckoned that if this war was to last much longer, neither he nor his weapon would be able to hold firm against the zealous troll lord.

His distracted thoughts got the better of him and brought the issue to an unexpected close, as the tip of the shadowy spear ate into the far left side of his chest and tore the breath from his lungs. When he recovered from the shock of pain caused by the shadow magic, he realized he was lying face down on the ground, staring into a shallow pool of his own blackened blood.

He heard a voice above him taunt, "You were a stubborn one. I almost would have believed you had a bit of troll in your blood. Ready to die now, human?"

Boderon shut his good eye and tried to imagine the troll chieftain standing above him, his shadow lance held high and braced for a downward strike, probably at the prostrate man's head. He took a deep breath and willed himself to concentrate. He had been chosen as his people's champion. He had been given the greatsword Kargaroth to wield when a foreign warrior had washed up on their beach. He had lost that sword to its fierce master, and his entire tribe had felt disgrace that day. If he died here, once more his people would bear the weight of his inadequacy.

All these thoughts flashed through his mind in an instant, and his humiliation washed out his pain. He clenched his teeth and responded to his foe's taunt.

"Not just yet."

As soon as the man finished speaking these words, Dokitir went into his strike. This was exactly the reaction Boderon had hoped for, and he immediately threw his body into a fierce roll. Once he was on his back he quickly grabbed the handle of his hammer with both hands, then swung back in his foe's direction. The mystical spear bit the dust his head had just left, as the sharpened end of his war hammer embedded deep into the soft flesh of the troll's lower abdomen.

Dokitir shut one eye and released a harsh gurgle of pain. Something vital had been hit, and his injured body released control of its warlike instincts, which included his potent demonic magics. The shadowy lights dancing about his body flickered out, as the spear of blackness in his hand shrank and then vanished.

Boderon seized this opportunity quickly, surging to his feet as a rush of enthused adrenaline dampened his own agony. He grabbed the handle of his weapon with both hands and twisted as though it were a lever, clawing the head deeper into his enemy's guts. He then gave a cruel tug forward, hooking the blade into the wounded troll's pelvis with an emphatic shock of movement.

The demonic chieftain's eyes opened wide as blood began to drip out of the left side of his mouth. Clearly, Boderon now had his full attention. "This next part sucks," the human champion taunted seriously. "Make your choice quickly, but wisely."

Stricken as he was, Dokitir was too shrewd not to understand the man's meaning. He spoke rapidly, "Spare me and I'll command my warriors to surrender. You may defeat me here and now if you so choose, but as a race we're hopelessly stubborn and will fight to the bitter end. I'm more valuable to you alive than dead. My word has more weight than my corpse. Please," he ended in an anxious hiss.

Boderon paused several seconds for effect, then gently reversed the motion of his war hammer, sliding the clawed edge back out of the troll's body without inflicting further harm.

Dokitir dropped both hands to cover his pierced abdomen and stood shivering in pain, his eyes closed as blood now poured freely from his mouth. It was several more seconds before he regained his composure, when he looked up to his foe and asked, "Why? Why do you show me mercy? Surely you didn't believe my claim that I would call off my warriors."

"Because," Boderon replied as he lifted his war hammer, resting it on his shoulder, "I understand you. I think you *will* keep your word. Because I'm the same as you are—a former servant of the Overlord who just wants to come out the other side of this as a survivor. Who just wants to get the chance to live on, and be something more. Something else."

Dokitir hissed for a moment, then spat a few times to clear blood from his mouth. "Tell your men to stand down first," he stated stubbornly. "I won't order my people to stop fighting just to be slaughtered."

The big man quickly barked out a few orders, signaling to several of his lieutenants. It took a couple of minutes, but eventually he got his troops backed away from their troll enemies, weapons on both sides pointed forward menacingly. Boderon held his breath, well aware of the likelihood of a coming betrayal. There was no such event, however, as Dokitir released a few guttural rasps in an ancient language. As he did so his trolls gathered nearer to him, but they also disabled their shadow magic and returned any physical weapons to their sheaths.

"Shote will kill us for this," the troll chieftain lamented. "Our fate is now tied to yours."

The warlord nodded, signaling his people to escort the trolls away from the front lines to somewhere they could be bound. "Our fate is survival. My fate is survival. That, I can promise you. And I'll bring you along with me."

Dokitir moved in closer, speaking quietly enough that only the human commander could hear him. "If you *had* been born a troll, you would have been a good one."

Boderon left his soldiers to handle the captured prisoners, returning himself back to the battle lines to face off against lesser foes. A rare smile decorated his features for the rest of the battle, and he endured the pains of whatever wounds came his way with grace.

He knew his tribe of former slaves had been considered an afterthought, unneeded bodies when compared with the supposed superiority of the true and official Devilslayers. The deaths of his people had been an expected outcome of this battle, but today would not be the day he died. Today his tribe had conquered the devil the Devilslayers could not slay. His people would be remembered as no mere afterthought, they would not be forgotten and fall into the shadows. No, they would be remembered as the rebels who overcame their Overlord.

* * * * *

Detria moved cautiously through enemy forces, a squad of twenty slayers clinging to her relentlessly. Early in the battle she had taken a deep wound to her upper thigh. She had insisted the damage was minor, but the Devilslayers had taken to her with cultish enthusiasm, refusing to leave her unguarded. So for the time being she contented herself with overseeing the tides of the battle.

Though her heart still ached from the fatalities caused by Shote's trap, she otherwise found there was much cause to be optimistic. The ogres and trolls had been brought under control by Mek and Boderon respectively. Shote was nowhere to be seen, nor Tenkahn; she could only assume the implications there. Fenrir's retreat had left the were-creatures disorganized, and most had fled into the surrounding buildings for shelter. The Overlord's despondent human troops had already surrendered as well, and Detria had instructed Colbiss to partition out a squad and make certain the prisoners were given sanctuary. It was only a matter of time before the battle wound down and her forces would be able to declare victory and terms.

There were only two wild cards remaining. The eventual reappearance of Shote could be devastating. If the beast found a way to best Tenkahn, Detria did not know how else he might be defeated. Her other concern was the chimeras. Storio, along with most of his pack, had been killed by the traps. The other commanders had not taken notice of this early enough, and the chimeras had been left effectively unchecked throughout the course of the battle. Scklaria had organized his winged allies well, having them take to the air and continuously dive-bomb the Devilslayer units. They lifted bodies high into the air, dropping them into the traps on the back side of the battlefield.

Detria did not know how to prepare for Shote, but she was certain if she killed the griffin general his troops would lose at least some of their enthusiasm. She gave orders to the slayers following her, then led a rush on Scklaria and the two chimeras serving as his guards. As this fresh battle began, she made it a point to slowly disentangle herself and the general from the other soldiers. The General of the Chimera easily picked out this tactic but did not seem to mind, following the woman's lead and abandoning his bodyguards.

The new general was a smaller griffin than Ontarshiss had been, with a browner tint to his feathers. His head was tilted slightly, given him a sickly appearance. He had learned to use his small stature to his advantage, though, and every part of his body was honed to exceptional coordination and reflexes.

This was something Detria learned swiftly. Normally she relied on her speed with a staff to overwhelm her foes, but as the two commanders dove at each other in a flurry, the chimera had no problem avoiding each strike and slipping in its own jabs with a dangerous curved beak. The High Chieftain shifted her dannig to both hands and made her attack patterns even more dizzying, but still the griffin found her moves uninspired, using bursts of wind from his wings to propel himself around and throw off the small human's balance.

Detria slid her left hand to her belt and attempted to remove a piece of weaponry from there, but Scklaria detected the motion. The razor-sharp beak flashed out once more, striking the back of her hand and knocking an axe-head to the ground. She tried again to modify her dannig, but again her foe struck and disarmed her before she could bring the weapon together. She tried to use his attack as an opportunity for a counterstrike, but the griffin continued to launch from her path too ably.

The battle continued a while in this manner. Scklaria's confidence grew at the mounting evidence of his opponent's lack of advantages, and soon repeated chomps from the griffin's jaw shattered the dannig beyond use. Detria dropped her weapon and tried to retreat rapidly, but the pain in her injured thigh caused her to fall to one knee with a gasp.

Scklaria wasted no time, rushing in and pinning her to the ground. As the griffin's face came down to tear her eyes out, an instinctual panic caused her to raise her left hand to guard her head. The golden beak bit hard, but the cerulean glove the woman wore did not give way. The chimera general reared back and struck again, biting and twisting with fervor to pierce his way through to the human's throat.

Then, as the glove weathered the sharp beak's assaults, the slim ribbon wrapped around it suddenly came loose and drifted into Detria's face. She felt a tingling power flood through her arm, and her hand became filled with strength. A strange voice echoed through her mind, psychically explaining the magics now at her disposal.

She slipped her free right hand forward and grabbed hard into Scklaria's neck, cutting off his windpipe. The griffin froze, unsure what to expect next as his pinned victim promised, "That was a mistake."

The High Chieftain kept her left forearm lodged firmly in his beak, but twisted her hand about and placed her fingertips against the feathery cheek. The Hand of Ramsa did not delay, did not waste time charging, did not paralyze or stun her opponent. The God of Kindness had designed the glove to bring swift, painless death to its enemies; it left no time for them to suffer. Scklaria's mind was shut off immediately by the tiny, unreadable runes that flooded their way into it. They continued their path across the griffin's body from the inside out, and soon a flash of light left nothing behind but a light rain of brownish-gold feathers drifting across the battlefield.

With her foe banished, Detria grabbed the curious ribbon and wrapped it about her glove once more. The light on its surface faded and then shut off entirely. She raised the dormant Hand to her face and stared at it for a moment, then heaved a sigh of relief.

"Good to know," she commented, then moved to help her troops against the chimeras they still battled.

* * * * *

Shote and Tenkahn no longer waged war on the roof of the Overlord's fortress. They had battled their way up and down several floors, finally carrying their duel into one of the largest towers. From there they had plummeted in a death-spiral of blows, bringing the entire tower down around them and crashing hard into its base. They had risen from this rubble without pause, smashing again into one another, destroying or unearthing the stones around them in their ceaseless quest to end the other's life.

Then Tenkahn had ceased his assault, dropping into a defensive stance with his arms wrapped around his head. Shote glared at the monk, hesitant to make his next attack. The minotaur's left shoulder was completely missing; a gaping vision of patchwork muscles and a peculiar skeletal structure was all that remained in that area. His left knee was shattered beyond his ability to repair, and that leg would no longer adjust. He was certain his right foot was shattered, but he had no feeling in that part of his body. His right eye had been closed forever.

He was certain of only one thing—the creature he was fighting now, this titan, was not the Tenkahn he had once defeated. Shote's internal stores were depleted now, his might drained. The effect of his Gehennite essence would soon fade and he would be unable to renew it. Even if he won this battle, he would not be able to march outside and ransack the armies of the invaders as he had formerly planned.

But he no longer cared for any of that. He swore he would not rest until he saw this last Monk of Tria put down. He gave up on his oaths to the Overlord, to this fortress, to everything. All that remained in his world was the human standing before him, the runes dancing across his body burning with that infernal blue light Shote despised so much. He geared his flesh up one final time and sent his internal pressure to the utter limit, raising his strength and speed a full notch past the levels his body was designed to sustain.

And he moved; so fast that the air itself burned his skin, causing him immense pain as it tore through his open shoulder and into his nervous system. He could feel every spec of dust in the air as he passed it and it tore slivers of his flesh away. He lost sight in his remaining eye. He could see nothing, but he would not let it slow him. He knew where Tenkahn was. He knew the monk was not moving.

His right hand flew around his back and gripped the hilt of his axe. He had to give a sharp twist to dislodge the weapon, but it came free in his hand as he dashed. He swung as he ran, calculating every step, every inch perfectly. The Monk of Tria would not beat this. He would not outdo this attack.

Nor did he even try. When the blur of distorted reality faded and Shote once again could see, his axe rested firmly in Tenkahn's torso. He had struck straight through the human's ribs and squarely into the spinal cord, snapping through it. The minotaur bellowed his victory and released his axe. He reared back with his right arm and prepared to strike a high blow, determined to remove the monk's head before his enchanted strength faded.

Then the rune-lit arms unwrapped from the man's head. The left fist crashed into Shote's chest and tore cleanly through, knocking the beast's heart out and sending it splattering to the ground behind his back. His victorious bellow turned into a sudden vomit of blood, and he locked eyes with his abhorred adversary.

"No," the minotaur whimpered desperately as the tone of his skin faltered from red back to pale blue. "My axe is in your spine. You cannot move!"

Tenkahn blinked, and with a rumbling voice answered, "I don't *care*!" He sent an uppercut from his right fist into Shote's neck and blasted through it, wrapping his fingers around the minotaur's brain and, with a sickening lurch, ripping it down through the beast's throat.

As the remains of the monstrous carcass crumbled to the ground at his feet, Tenkahn spent a moment reveling in the light rain of blood drizzling over his skin. He reached down and slid the axe from his torso, then shut his eyes, allowing the overflowing power of the Merciless Rune to rebuild his bones and flesh. There was a flicker of a thought, some panic in the recesses his mind, but it was shortly drown out by fury. Now that his enemy was dead, he needed a new one. Tenkahn was built to fight. He needed something to fight.

Fortuitously, a target presently itself. As he moved to walk through the collapsing castle and return to where he could hear sounds of battle, he spotted a young man covered in blue runes of his own. The youth was speaking to him. Something about recognition, asking him who he was. Tenkahn did not care. He needed to kill. Shote was dead. Shote had been wonderful, the worthiest rival for which he could have ever asked. More should die alongside him. The legendary beast deserved that honor.

He waited until he was certain his wounds from that battle were mostly patched, his spine fully rejoined, then rocketed forward at the young man. He was uncertain how strong this new opponent might be, so he decided to start with a light attack. He tightened his right hand and prepared a Pulsing Fist. Upon reaching the newcomer he punched forward at the boy's chest, at the last second opening his fist wide and striking with his five fingertips. Five simultaneous attacks carrying his kinetic force ripped through the abdomen of his foe, sending a trail of blood painting the floor beyond.

The raging monk was disappointed. It seemed the boy had not attempted to dodge or even counter. Then he noticed it—the boy *had* countered. He had punched Tenkahn's chest with his left hand. The attack had been so very weak. Was this all he could now expect? Where were the foes like Shote, the titans that could cause him real pain?

He looked down at his chest and observed that a strange white light was covering it. He reached up and tried to wipe it away, when a shrieking pain overtook his head. This was followed by a loud buzzing, like an army of banshees tearing his mind apart, then the air went black. As he fell to the ground he was briefly aware of the ceiling coming down upon him, at the same moment that his divine magics abandoned him.

* * * * *

The tides of battle had finally faded, but not to the state of victory which Detria had hoped for. The remaining troops of the Overlord had pulled back into a tight unit against the front gate of the castle and dared the Devilslayers to attack. Every rush she had organized only ended in the death of more of her people, and they were finding the mixed front line of surviving chimeras and ogres still effective and impenetrable.

Detria knew if she threw enough lives away she could break the enemy, but she was uncomfortable with such a suicidal record so early into her career as High Chieftain. Since the battle had calmed and now consisted only of two sides staring at one another, she had tried to open negotiations. She had nearly been killed for this, spared by a score of Devilslayers under Mek's lead coming quickly to her salvation. The ogres and chimeras had only shouted back that they would await Shote.

Now Detria had been shuffled to the back lines of her forces against her will, the slayers unwilling to allow her to take even one more risk this battle. She sat with legs crossed on the ground with a headache, amazed and slightly discomforted at the parallels her mind kept drawing between the Overlord's zealots and her own Devilslayer soldiers.

Soon Colbiss approached with a nod. She returned a smile. "Tell me something good," she requested halfheartedly.

"Someone is here to see you, High Chieftain."

The man stepped aside, and Gaius came forward. Strapped across his shoulders was Tenkahn, and in his right hand he held something in a large sack. The elder's chest was smothered in heavy bandages, as was the younger monk's own left hand. Both sets of bandages appeared to be fresh, but were already thoroughly soaked through with blood.

"Gaius!" Detria cried as she stormed forward. She looked over Tenkahn's face, but he was unconscious and seemed pale. "Are the two of you okay?"

The standing monk offered a grin. "We'll live. He'll live. Here, I've brought a present. No, forgive me, there's too much hubris in that statement. This is from my master—from Tenkahn the Aged."

She creased her brow and looked into the sack he had handed her. Her eyes went wide with a mix of excitement and disgust. She immediately carried it to the front lines, ignoring all objections with violent blows to the heads of the stubborn slayers trying to hold her back.

As she emerged, the demons prepared to make a move on her once more. She reached into the bag and drew forth its contents, which halted their approach. As she held high the dismembered head of Shote, its left eye still gaping open in disbelief, the demonic troops released cries of despair. Once she was certain they were left with no will to assault her, she brought her left hand up to her teeth and tore loose the ribbon on her glove. She then pressed her fingers lightly to Shote's face and, with a flash, the specter of the minotaur's threat was truly gone from the world.

Detria nodded at Mek and made a motion, and he tossed his dannig to her. She leveled it forward and pointed it at the remnants of the demonic army. "Tell me, what miracle do you await now? Or will you at last surrender to me?"

The loss of Shote was indeed the final necessary blow to the morale of the Overlord's followers. Those capable of it fell to their hands and knees and begged for mercy, while the chimeras slid backward and grumbled weakly.

Colbiss finally caught up with his commander in the front lines, breathing heavily after his struggle getting through the ranks. "What now, Lady Detria?" he asked between gasps.

She looked over the enemies in thought. "Bind the chimeras with ropes. They'll have to be dealt with carefully, as they're taken to vengeance. As for the ogres, trolls, and were-creatures, allow them a full retreat from this place. Without leadership they'll return to their tribal ways. Offer the humans sanctuary and give them medical aid and food supplies as we can spare them."

Colbiss went to carry out her orders, but Mek gave her a questioning glare. "Allow them a retreat? Madam, we are the Devilslayers. It's our duty to kill the enemies of humanity."

She shook her head decisively. "Our goal here was to defeat the Overlord and bring this army to an end. That's enough for now. If we want to make a quest to clean the demons from this region in the future, then we'll do so in a more organized fashion. Enough of our own lives have been lost this day, far more than we hoped. I don't wish to see one more drop of human blood spilled here, even if it is to kill a devil."

He leaned his head back, but overall seemed pleased by her response. "You're going to be a very different leader for our people, High Chieftain Alsen."

She smiled pensively for a moment, then said, "I've had many influences in my life. I hope to take a little of the best from each of them."

Mek went to help his troops bind the chimeras, and Detria shed another tear for the most dear of her fallen allies. *It's done, Kelve*, she announced inwardly, silently swearing to his memory that she would become the great woman he had always stubbornly believed her to be.

## Chapter 43.

# Champions of Arkalen and Itrius

Abaddon stared at the visage of the strange creature standing before him. Tattered and melted black armors covered metallic white skin, and piercing green slits stared out from a face formed of two mirrored white plates. It was hard to tell if this was a human or a demon. Having had his share of encounters with extraplanar entities, Abaddon was not alarmed by this one.

What he was alarmed by, however, was the glimmering greatsword the creature held in its right hand. The two travelers had been journeying on separate routes, seemingly unrelated, and had come across each other just southeast of the borders of the Yerria Forest. They stood now in the open air of desert lands, their respective weapons drawn and pointed at one another.

After a few moments of this calm staring had passed, Abaddon spoke. "You have my sword."

"Oh?" the man that was once Deun Coloran responded. "If what you say is true, that would make you Abaddon Daemon. I thought you dead."

"I have been, on a few occasions."

"Then how about once more?!" the Arkalenian warrior exclaimed without further preface, dashing forward and swinging downward with Kargaroth. In response Abaddon rolled quickly to his left and then shot up to his feet, lashing out with Arda aimed at his opponent's neck. Deun reversed his swing and raised Kargaroth's hilt above his head, using the sword as a shield. His attacker gave a sharp jerk on Arda's hilt, causing it to miss Kargaroth and sore harmlessly overhead.

The disfigured man gave a twist to his hilt with his off-hand, carrying his momentum forward and again swinging down. Abaddon was left with limited time to respond to the swift short-range strike, so he dropped to his knees and laid Arda lengthwise over his head. He then moved his left hand beneath the center of the blade and caught Kargaroth there, using the surface of Arda to shield his palm.

Deun tried to pull back with his weapon, but the crouched man had clenched tightly with his fingers, holding the sword in place as he took a few seconds to rise to his feet. The armored warrior shook his head in admiration, pushing back against the force of the Daemon's rise.

"Such strength," he commented impassively. "You're almost a match for me. Impressive for someone who's only human."

"Only human?" Abaddon responded with an inquisitive tone. Deun felt Kargaroth begin to shudder as ether throughout the area poured into his opponent's body. The dark blue eyes began emitted an eerie glow as the man's clothing and hair became tousled. "I take pride in that."

He suddenly pressed back hard into the smaller man, lifting him bodily from the ground and sending him several feet back. When Deun had gathered his wits and landed, his instincts alerted him to his enemy's presence already behind him. The man was swinging Arda at his knee, attempting to sever his left leg. The former Devilslayer lifted his foot sharply and stepped down, springing off of the sweeping katana and spinning in midair. Kargaroth lashed out for Abaddon's face, but a quick tap up from his elbow knocked the blade off course and spared his life.

The Felthespari warlord sprang back, setting some distance between himself and the white-masked stranger. His strength continued to expand as he gathered more ether, and his eyes had now become bright blue slits to match the green ones of his opponent. Still, without the Heart of Elysium bolstering his spirit his might was not what it had once been. Furthermore, he was only freshly awakened from the dead. He had already pushed himself to the edge of what his still-healing body could presently handle. He was slow, and his arms were tired. This fight was sure to feel like a long one.

He took a moment to catch his breath, taunting his adversary. "If you're so certain of your power, why don't you put my sword down and we'll fight as men?"

Deun twisted his head about and his neck sounded several nasty cracks. "This is how men should fight—sword against sword, skill meeting skill. I'm not so thick as to be lured into fisticuffs with a brute like yourself. I know where I can and cannot match you. Are you really so afraid of your Kargaroth?"

Abaddon rolled his shoulders and straightened his back. "To the contrary, I'm afraid *for* it. I don't know if Kargaroth's steel can hold off the bite of Arda. I was hoping I wouldn't have to test it. But it seems luck has not been with me lately."

Deun leveled the shimmering greatsword forward, aiming the tip at his opponent's throat. "The strength of your arm is the only thing you can rely upon in this life."

The big man glared in response to this, then gathered another surge of ether as he responded, "And that's why I am still here."

He leaped to his foe's location and swung down sharply with Arda. This time he did not hold back the blow. If the legendary katana was going to slice through the Unholy Blade, it would do so no matter what force he lent it. The Arkalenian's seer abilities once more warned him of impending demise, prompting him to punctually drop a step back and slide Kargaroth above his head. The steel of Gilanirus crashed hard against the steel of the dark gods, but could not penetrate it. Encouraged by his old sword's endurance, Abaddon planted his feet and went into a frenzied combination of strikes. Deun was pinned down, forced to position Kargaroth in front of him and use the broad face of the weapon as a shielding wall.

Abaddon completed two dozen strikes against his old weapon before accepting that he was not going to be able to penetrate this enemy's defenses. The creature's reactions were sharp, unnatural, and the Daemon had not seen his moves predicted so perfectly since the last time he had faced his mentor.

He needed to put his challenger on the offensive in order to gain a better understanding of his nature. He slowed his assault over the next three hits, then feigned a pause between two of his attacks. Deun took the bait, slashing out at his attacker's waist. Abaddon gave a mighty backflip and slid several yards back. His opponent saw in this the opportunity for another attack and swept in, Kargaroth held above his left shoulder.

Abaddon swiftly slid Arda up to his own shoulder and gave a powerful strike. The southern champion matched the move with his own blade. An audible cracking was heard, but the strength of the two warriors held even. The momentum of Deun's charge caused him to slide around close to the larger man, and the contestants pushed to separate from each other. They let their swords slide past one another as each man took a step forward past the other, found firm footing, then spun about and crashed their blades together once more.

For a second they stood there deadlocked, Arda and Kargaroth forming a giant cross, heat echoing from each blade. Keeping his sword locked, Abaddon took a step back and began to twist with his katana, sliding it around the greatsword while holding his adversary in place. The former Devilslayer quickly realized what the man was trying to do. Arda held superior reach, so its wielder was attempting to use that length to reach his target's neck in spite of the stalemate. Deun could not easily mimic the move, as the tip of the greatsword would not reach his opponent's throat before his own head would be severed.

He disengaged, giving a hop to his left and then several hops back. He paused a second to feel for the next attack. Sensing nothing coming, he humorously offered a slight bow.

"Akatriel told me you were the strongest of humankind, the champion of the entire race. I thought facing you was going to be more daunting. I can see why you're so feared, but to be honest I expected something more. I suppose you're proof that the entire species is just too limited, after all. Humanity will always be the idle playthings of the gods and overlords who stand above."

As Abaddon listened idly, he inspected Arda. The crack he had heard earlier was the sound of the sword's metal giving out. The hairline fracture put there by Gilanirus was beginning to expand. One more impact like that and he suspected the blade would shatter entirely, leaving him weaponless.

"Akatriel?" he responded. "Are you in league with that sorcerer?"

"Does it truly matter?"

"No," Abaddon answered with a shrug. "I'm clearly going to have to kill you regardless."

He raised Arda high and pointed the tip skyward. He sent an intricate reverberation tracing through the ether in the area, then dropped Arda like a hammer. Three dozen Abaddons detached from his body and spread across the area, then dashed in on Deun one at a time, each swinging its own Arda or striking out with fist or foot.

Deun shook his head and stepped calmly through the crowd. One by one the illusions came to him, and one by one they passed through harmlessly. He raised Kargaroth, then gave a sudden dash three feet to his right and swung down.

Abaddon was startled he had been so easily distinguished from his mirages, but not startled enough to fault. He swept up with Arda and attacked Kargaroth directly, knocking the sword safely to one side. Deun planted a foot firmly behind him and nailed his left fist into the Daemon's jaw, sending the man crashing backwards and shattering his afterimages as his concentration gave out.

The Itriun caught his feet after only two yards. He narrowed his eyes and redoubled his control over the energy surging around him. He gave a fierce twirl of Arda around each side of his body, dropped to one knee, then planted his left arm up to its elbow into the arid ground. Eighteen pillars of hardening sand rose around him, then each bent down and transformed into sharp points aimed for his opponent. Deun was shocked to see this level of command over nature itself, and fell back a step. Abaddon swept a wide circle with Arda, severing each of the pillars at the base. He then stabbed the sword into the sand behind him and thrust forward with his fists. A wind of kinetic energy carried into the pillars and sent them diving for his foe.

Accompanying the earthen spears now coming for him at tremendous speeds, the ground around Deun continued to erupt from the mystic warlord's initial blow. The beleaguered warrior took a deep breath and abandoned himself to his instincts. Slowly but confidently, he took two large steps to his left and diagonally forward. Spikes whizzed past him as sharpened sandstone from the ground destroyed the spots his feet left. He paused for a second and a half, then took half a step back, three steps to his right, followed by a short run forward. He took another step back while using Kargaroth to shove one spike out of his way and then gave a jump, landed on a pillar, flipped high into the air, and landed nimbly three feet behind where Abaddon was already dashing with his retrieved blade.

Deun went into a spin and held Kargaroth in close. The Felthespari realized his foe had somehow gotten through his carnage and was behind him, but he could not react in time. Kargaroth bit deep into his upper back, cleaving his shoulder blades and throwing him face-first into his sediment pillars as his assailant released a burst of dark power from the sword.

The Arkalenian gave a chuckle and began to circle about the area, watching as his adversary struggled to gain his footing and was forced to knock his own attacks from his path. When things finally settled Abaddon was sitting on his knees, Arda lying on the ground at his side, a cape of blood flowing from the gash on his back.

"You can get stronger and you can get faster," Deun warned him, "but that won't defeat me. The stronger you get, the faster you get, the more you telegraph your moves to the currents. It becomes easier for me to watch you with my seer's eyes, and eventually the cruelty of your own disloyal sword will claim your life. You must have noticed I've removed the bandages that you once used to bind her to your will. Today Kargaroth can kill. So now what will you do against me, Daemon?"

Abaddon took an unsteady breath and rose slowly to his feet, then gave a difficult swallow. He focused spiritual energy to the wound on his back, staunching the blood flow and closing the wound partially. After this he released the remainder of his power, emptying his reserves and letting the freed ether flow into the air around him. His mystic rival felt him do this and watched suspiciously. By flushing himself of ether the man only stood to make himself weaker, yet Deun had already proven himself a match in speed and strength.

The weary soldier continued his course without hesitation. He reached to his forehead and seized the dirty bandanna that kept his hair out of his face. "I started this day dead," he announced quietly, "I think I shall not end it that way." He lowered the bandanna over his eyes and tightened it, forming a rough blindfold. Then he slid the tip of his right foot beneath Arda's hilt and kicked it up to his hand, pointing it at Deun.

The encased knight tilted his head. "Are you serious?"

Even as this was asked, Abaddon went into a charge, releasing a reckless roar as he approached. He did not ready himself, did not even change his grip on Arda to a more battle-suited pose. Deun shook his head sadly as his opponent reached him, took a minor step to his right and swung quickly at the man's neck. His instincts informed him that the battle was now over. His foolish foe had no counter prepared.

But to his surprise Abaddon did counter, kicking back Arda and snapping the base of the katana into the edge of Kargaroth. He then dropped into a low crouch and slid his long blade underneath the greatsword, coming in for Deun's thigh.

There was no instinctual blare to warn the mystic seer of this attack. His thigh tore open and burst blood as he retreated too late, his right leg severed and hanging on only by a loose slab of muscle and flesh. A surge of shimmering silver light rushed to the area and replaced lost organic material with magical artificiality. He started to remark, but upon looking up he was shocked to find Abaddon standing only a yard away, already driving down with Arda.

Deun fell to one side and took the blow. His left shoulder was ripped through, as well as his right forearm. He started to make a counter with his sword but then thought better of it, as silver magic was the only thing holding his arms in place at the moment.

He turned and dashed away, trying to ignore the feeling of the vicious katana tearing three sharp horizontal slashes into his back as he ran. He gained solid footing, waited until he was certain his mysterious healing processes were caught up, then turned and launched himself back into the fray with a furious series of attacks. Abaddon fell into the defensive, locking Arda upright and sidestepping and rolling through Kargaroth's sweeps effortlessly. Every so often he would release a sudden slash. Each of these were completely unforeseen by Deun, ripping a new silver cavity into his rapidly dissolving body.

The Arkalenian warrior leaped away and attempted to summon magic to his aid, hoping Akatriel had blessed him with some further hidden powers. At his behest, a rain of fire came forth and swept at his adversary, as well as a streak of lightning bolts, then a shower of icy shards along the ground. The ruthless mystic spent a moment feeling the attacks approach, and Deun felt the man prepare a counter. Beneath his mask he smiled, comforted that he was again able to sense his foe's actions.

Abaddon did not counter the spells as predicted, however, but instead turned and ran. He ran several yards away from the waves of elemental magic, strafed to one side until he was out of their path, then circled back and charged his enemy head first. The mystic seer waited anxiously, desperately seeking to read the attack that was about to come from Arda, but the man did not swing his sword. Instead he rammed his forehead directly into Deun's face, smashing his nose through the plates protecting it.

As his rival reeled from the force of that first blow, Abaddon at last blasted horizontally with Arda. The stumbling warrior saw this attack coming with enough time to drop Kargaroth into its path. This did not bother the blinded Felthespari, however, as he immediately planted the base of his open left hand firmly into Deun's jaw, sending him spinning away through the air.

The beleaguered seer used a burst of magic to right himself and gain his feet. Gathering his speed, he again went on the offensive. It was clear that Abaddon's sudden inexplicable unpredictability was getting the better of him, but surely the man would be unable to respond so ably to Deun's own assault.

He lifted Kargaroth above his shoulder and ran forward, preparing a powerful strike that would remove his enemy's head at the shoulders. Abaddon also charged forward, Arda held foolishly out to his opposite side. When he was within range Deun unleashed his blow, and almost too late his adversary raised his katana and mirrored the strike. Once again the two warriors crossed swords in the midst of charges, and once again they slid past each other with their blades locked.

This time Arda did not sustain the impact. At the last moment the legendary sword snapped and a majority of its vast length fell to the ground. Only a two-foot segment remained in its master's hand as he moved past his foe, Kargaroth's edge only barely missing his shoulder. The mystic seer's senses alerted him to the katana's failure, and he knew he now held a potent advantage. Once again the two opponents would spin about to lock swords, but this time Abaddon lacked the length to win the stalemate. Deun allowed himself to drift forward another foot, well beyond the range of the shattered Arda, then spun about swinging Kargaroth to end his enemy's life.

As he rotated and the other man came into sight, Deun could see he was performing the same move. Blindfolded and seemingly unaware that his sword had shattered, Abaddon floated in mid-spin, Arda held over his left shoulder, prepared to swing the sheared weapon in a hopeless prayer for victory. In that second, Deun Coloran pitied him. It would be such an ignoble defeat for so remarkable a warrior.

Then, in an instant, Abaddon's arm moved. The swipe was faster than Deun could follow, and his seer's eye told him nothing. He panicked and went to complete his strike, when suddenly an odd pain seized him and he was unable to move his arm. He stopped his spin and planted his feet, taking a step back and staring at his fellow combatant. Finally, he recognized that his opponent's right hand was now empty.

He looked down to see the hilt of Arda protruding from his chest. The magical blade was lodged deep in his heart. A surge of silver magic spent a few moments trying to wrestle with the damage, attempting to destroy the sword in its way. But Akatriel's gifts were insufficient against the blessings of Gilanirus, and soon flickered out in surrender. As they did so, all of Deun's enchantments gave way. The white steel coating his body turned to smoke and drifted away from him, revealing his charred and mutilated flesh. His right leg gave out and ripped off, as well as his right hand at the forearm. As a slash tore from his left shoulder and carved down through his torso, he sputtered, "Well struck, Daemon."

He collapsed and lay weakly on his back, lacking further strength to move. He watched as Abaddon reached up and raised his bandanna back to his forehead, tightening it once more into place.

Deun shut his eyes and begged the planet to allow him to live a few moments longer, pleading for time to speak. A swell of white magic in the region crawled into his frame, and he felt a minimal amount of his strength return. "You really are the best of us, aren't you?" he remarked. "I was no match after all."

Abaddon stepped forward and knelt to his side. "You're a human. A mystic, like myself. Why did you insist on fighting me?"

"My soul was bound by Akatriel. He is about some great scheme. I was only allowed to feel bits and pieces of it. When I encountered you, the hex placed over me became upset in some way. All I knew was that you're supposed to already be dead. Your continued existence is an aberration to his designs. I had no choice but to obey his will, to attempt to reconcile the mistake. He purchased me at the cost of this power I wield, this power that was not enough against you."

"Akatriel," the victor growled through gritted teeth. "The conspirator has played us all for some foul end."

Deun reached up and laid his left hand on the man's shoulder. He spoke through labored breaths, "Please, I must know. Why could I not match you? I held every advantage."

"Indeed you did. Yet you gave yourself away when you mentioned your seer's sight. I'm familiar with the technique. It's controlled by reading information and signals emitted to the currents, and using those to predict future moves and events. I've never seen it performed as swiftly as yours, but I knew how to defeat it. I removed myself from the currents, then blindfolded myself and shut down my thoughts. I charged you without plan and fought on spur of the moment instinct alone. Every move I made was without foresight or regard for my own well-being. Without your seer's gift you were disoriented, and unprepared for the tides of battle. 'A warrior who relies too heavily upon his sight is truly blind, but it takes a superior warrior to show him.' A quote, from my teacher."

Deun's hand dropped as his strength began to wane. "It's uncanny that you were able to fight at such a level without having your thoughts on the battle. And robbed of your magic as well. I once thought I was born to be a warrior, that my body and instincts were all I needed. But you're the one who's truly bred for battle, aren't you? Abaddon Daemon. What I would have given to have your strengths instead of mine."

After a moment of mournful silence, the warlord answered, "I'm sorry that I had to kill you."

Deun struggled to take a shivering breath. "Listen. Akatriel wanted Kargaroth. He told me where to bring it. I don't know what his purpose is. It may be some further trap, but it's better that knowledge not die with me." He lifted his hand a few inches from the man's face. A light swirl of ether appeared there and flowed into Abaddon's eyes, drawing a map of Arkalen for him to see. "It's there. Do you see?"

He nodded his acknowledgment. "Tell me your name. I'll see to it that the crimes committed against you are not forgotten."

Deun started to answer, then paused as the lost pieces of his former mind came back to him. His eyes brimmed with tears and they flowed unchecked over his ruined flesh. "My name was Tassix Coloran," he choked out. "Remember. I was the greatest warrior of all Arkalen." His head fell softly back to the ground, and as his dying breath escaped his throat, a peaceful smile spread across his mangled features.

Abaddon reached to where Kargaroth lay and detached the fallen warrior's lost hand from it. He picked the sword up and rose to his feet. He spent a moment feeling the touch of the familiar grip once more, then gave a firm swing and felt the hum of its steel.

"Now I am the Destroyer once more," he announced quietly. "Akatriel, you will answer to us."

* * * * *

Shortly after Abaddon had passed a safe distance away, Akatriel stepped from the shadows and kicked lightly at Deun's corpse. "My, my," he muttered. "It seems my original Knight has a peculiar stubbornness to him and does not wish to be replaced. I was positive he was dead."

He inspected the hilt of the Arda—stuck in Deun's chest as it was—and shrugged. Then he stepped to where the remainder of the blade lay. Seven wondrous feet of the katana's length was still intact. He retrieved it and swung at a nearby rock. The sword did not penetrate the stone, but instead chipped and sent a piece flying into Akatriel's cheek. He twisted his lips in annoyance, then offered another shrug.

"I'm certain Gilanirus can restore your life," he assured the tremendous piece of steel.

At that moment a cloak of blackness engulfed him once more,

removing him from the Morolian plane and placing him in familiar stasis. He rolled his eyes upward in impatience, but nonetheless waited silently.

*It is time. The Wisdoms are at Gilanirus' feet. Are you ready?*

"All is set here. I need only take Gilanirus his weapon, that he might die valiantly. Abaddon Daemon brings me the last piece I require."

*I thought we agreed we would not use the Daemon; that the other human was easier to control.*

"It was not to be. It doesn't matter. He will fall for the trap same as the other."

*Respect his intellect, or he will best us yet.*

"I've observed him long enough. I know how he will be best controlled. Enough of my business. Are you set? There are not words in this tongue for how much I would hate for you to ruin the years of work I've put into this."

*All is set. I have gathered a body of equal strength to your own. I only await.*

"Then for one last time allow me to insist you detain me no further, and let us seal this contract."

The sight before Akatriel's eyes turned from the black of abyss to the brown of arid sands. He disappeared into his own magic, gliding swiftly to Gilanirus along the back-currents of reality.

# Chapter 44.

## Melukah, Who Rules the Light

Detria sat atop the parapets of the Overlord's collapsing domain, staring out at the hills that had served so long as the meager command center for her soldiers. Now she sat instead as lord of a stalwart castle and a mighty army. As the thought passed through her mind, she released a sigh and hung her head. Things were not as simple as they once were. Once she had led a noble entourage of stragglers, fueled by a community spirit and good intentions, with a brilliant assistant watching her moves and correcting her mistakes. Now she had the mantle of High Chieftain of the Devilslayers sitting on her shoulders, a far more crucial duty with no safety net.

This reprieve was the first she had afforded herself in the several days since Shote's fall. There had been no sign of the Overlord himself returning. As the demon forces were scattered and set free back into the wilds of Arkalen, the human morale soared ever higher. No one here feared the Overlord's return; not with the invincible Monks of Tria providing sanctuary.

Detria was less optimistic than her people, but she joined in their smiles. Tenkahn still had not recovered from the effect of Kelve's final potion. With his rune structure weakened, and given the substantial amounts of divine blessings he had channeled in his battles with Shote, his hair had rapidly descended to a shock of solid white. Even his skin seemed to have grown rougher, perhaps with a meager touch of grey. The man had aged an entire decade in only a few days.

He assured Detria these effects would mostly reverse once his runes stabilized. She could see through his bravado, though.

Tenkahn had stepped back, and was following in Gaius' shadow now. The younger monk had become the commander of the duo. It was a subtle change, too little for most of the troops to notice, but the High Chieftain could not fail to see it.

Even as her thoughts turned to him, Gaius took a seat on a large concrete block next to her and offered a smile. "I've been talking to what remains of the Overlord's slaves," he announced without formality. "They're mainly thrilled by their liberation. There are a few who are still pretty shaken up and terrified, but all in all I'd say reactions are positive. They want to take this castle and renovate it, spend the next couple of years fixing it up, make it a sort of base of operations. They're offering to let you have it, as the Devilslayer's central location. There are a lot of amazing carpenters and architects in the group, some of them better than I ever was. It seems that since my absence Tessena went out of her way to open up the libraries to the slaves and allowed them to study."

The mention of Tessena's name brought a twinge of guilt back to Detria's mind, reminding her of her crass behavior before Kelve's death. "Do you think she was evil, Gaius? Or just another victim trying her best?"

He shrugged. "Who can tell, in stories like this?"

"No, that's not enough. Not for me. I'm the lord of the self-appointed judges of Arkalen. I *have* to know the difference."

He grunted and rose to his feet. "I'm sorry to say madam, but I don't think I have the superior conscience to help you with your questions."

She changed the subject smoothly, following his move to stand. "Do you think the men of Felthespar still live?"

He smiled broadly and looked her straight in the eyes. "No one can kill Abaddon Daemon. If nothing else, I'm confident in that."

She returned the smile with a slim one of her own. "Thank you, Gaius. I hope to see him soon."

"As do I. As does my master. Speaking of, he wants a word with you. He has some ideas of what the Devilslayers should do next. That is, if you'll accept the two of us into your fold for a while. It'll be a long time before there will be ten Monks of Tria again, but there's still too much work that needs to be done on the continent for us to idle."

She moved forward suddenly and hugged him around his neck. He was taken aback by the sudden display of weakness. Detria numbered among the toughest warriors Gaius had ever known, and this behavior did not fit her image in his mind. After a moment's hesitation he returned the hug, patting her on the back firmly.

"Thank you, Eiden Hoek," she whispered. "I need the support of you and Tenkahn. There are so few of us left who began this together."

He stammered something awkwardly, his composure shattered. She ended the hug and stepped back, offered him another smile, then moved to the stairs and made her way to the courtyard. He took a deep breath, shook himself off, and followed after.

* * * * *

Gilanirus sat alone in the vast empty cavern Akatriel had supplied him. The Silver One had already brought him what remained of Arda, and the Godbeast clutched it tightly within the armor of his left fist. He felt a rumbling emanate from the far side of the chamber, caused by sonic disturbances. The immortal lord of Gehenna was rarely moved to emotion of any sort, but he gave himself over for a moment to bask in his excitement. It was time for divine war.

He stood and used a wave of psychic will to reinforce his armor and awaken the remnant of Arda. His armor flashed white, Arda flashed red, and a cloud of black steam blew fiercely from his shoulders.

Torlen then succeeded in blasting his way into the area, blowing a gaping opening in the stone and slipping through swiftly. Melukah and Keldana made their way in behind, sauntering slowly. They stopped for but a moment to locate Gilanirus in the underground city, then moved to his location.

When his guests arrived, the Final Godbeast offered a bow. The Wisdoms did not move to assault him. They could feel his dominance. They knew how dangerous he was. They had arrived too late for an easy victory over the Tyrant.

"Melukah, Supreme Wisdom of Annihilation." Gilanirus addressed his ancient rival directly, ignoring the others.

Melukah did not put up the facade of returning this cordial bow, but immediately began charging his Sun Staff. His allies each responded to this. Torlen formed sleeves of white sonic rings over all four of his limbs, while Keldana drew all of the moisture in the entire chamber from the air and gathered it to her body.

"Here, I am the Sun," the Lord of Elysium replied.

"I'm not interested in the Melukah of Morolia. It is the Melukah that invaded my Gehenna that I owe penance or penalty."

"We entered your plane only to preempt your own planned raid of ours," the celestial retorted.

"And I would rule Elysium now, had you not cowardly begged for salvation from the denizens of Elzaniru's dominion."

Melukah raised his staff high over his head. The ornate decoration atop it flashed and melted, transforming itself into a small sun and spreading its light to every corner of the sprawling subterranean vault. Gilanirus took a couple of steps back and raised his sword, his devilish eyes shrinking from the light. "Our home will never be your domain, Spectre of Gehenna," the Wisdom swore.

The Godbeast looked to Torlen and Keldana and released a crude laugh. "Must you bring the children, Melukah?" He raised his sole left arm and pointed about the room. "This place was filled with thousands of forlorn souls. I have drank them all into my shadow. My power is the utmost it has ever been on the Morolian plane. Your Wisdoms could not stand against me before. What makes you think yourselves a match now?"

"Torlen," the Sun commanded, "end his arrogance."

The Wisdom of Sound shook himself and made a strange sound,

reminiscent of a human drawing in a deep breath. "Yes, Lord Melukah."

His feet left the ground and a whirlwind of energy flew behind him, the backlash from his sonic burst. Gilanirus waited until the Wisdom came close enough to throw his first punch and then, without jumping, he suddenly started moving backward at an even faster speed. Torlen's fist flew through empty space, but without hesitation he blasted forward again and attempted to chase down the evading Godbeast.

As he pursued, the Sound set his body spinning and lashed out with various punches and kicks. Gilanirus moved easily, his feet never touching the ground, sliding in and out of the blows and holding his hiltless Arda at ready. Torlen knew a strike from the sword was coming eventually, and he kept a ready eye on it.

Soon frustrated by facing an opponent with superior speed, the Wisdom shot up over the Godbeast's head, turned his body sideways, and went into a tight spin. He struck out with his foot at the last second to maximize the momentum of his kick. Gilanirus dropped his feet to the ground for an instant, then with a light jump sent himself hovering above his foe, reversing the situation. Torlen's kick flew in vain as the Tyrant brought his full weight down upon him, digging his massive left foot hard into the Elysian's chest and shoulders and driving his frame crunching into the stone beneath them.

Gilanirus raised his blade above his head, prepared to decapitate his pinned adversary. "Recognize my might. The Assassin is of no threat to me."

The Godbeast felt a wall of divine magic approaching and recognized he was in true danger. He swiftly released Arda and let it fall onto the stone floor, shot his hand to his back, and drew forth an immense tower shield. He only barely managed to get the plate in front of his face before a massive beam of yellow light struck, crashing against the face of the shield and washing over his frame, cracking and constricting his armor.

The blast faded as his shield crumbled. He had managed to hold his ground, however, and still his armored boot continued to sink Torlen deeper into stone. Gilanirus stared at the collapsed pieces of his shield, then looked up and directed his voice at Melukah. "A sneak attack, Supreme Wisdom? Such callow tactics. Have the humans influenced you during my slumber?"

Across the chamber, the Sun addressed Keldana. "Are you ready? Torlen can not long stand alone."

"Nearly, master. If I merely might release—"

"Not yet. We await Torlen's lead."

She nodded, then turned back to gathering moisture to herself.

From beneath the giant steel boot, Torlen suddenly whispered, "Found it."

As he finished reaching over and retrieving his Arda, Gilanirus turned his gaze back to his pinned prey. "Found what?" he asked in bemusement.

"Your frequency," the crafty Wisdom announced.

Gilanirus' electric eyes went wide and he tried to strike, but a sonic release from Torlen rippled through his body and sent him flying away. The Lord of Gehenna used a burst of psionic force to right himself and land nimbly. The Wisdom of Sound gingerly picked himself up, then touched his left hand to his own face. The sonic rings there blasted through his head and shattered his mask, revealing the energy matrix beneath. His magics soared as a hum of sonar filled the air.

Keldana glanced eagerly to Melukah once more, and her lord nodded his acquiescence. The Ocean formed claws of ice about her fingertips and slashed at her own mask, crumbling it. The Sun simultaneously punched himself in the forehead with his free hand, obliterating his mask. The Wisdoms each became surrounded in vortexes of energy and swirls of dust from the ground.

The Wisdom of Ocean spread her arms wide. Suddenly the water molecules she had gathered formed into dense armors of ice, covering her body and more than doubling her already impressive stature. A two-handed ice axe appeared in her right hand. She grasped it with her left as well, then ran forward to join Torlen's struggle. Still Melukah stood back, charging his Sun Staff with ever more power.

Gilanirus attempted to strike his current foe with the Arda, but the Assassin brought the attack to a halt and began sending bursts of sonic pressure at the phantasmal armors from afar. The stunning impacts grinding into enchanted Gehennite steel sent the air and stone into protestations, crumbling from mere proximity to such blows. The Godbeast tried to charge forward, but Torlen would not halt his assault. Soon the divine armors began to weaken in their defenses, giving in to deep dents from the blows the Wisdom of Sound rained upon them.

As the Tyrant fell forward to one knee, Torlen finally paused for rest. He had expended more than half of his remaining stores of green ether in less than a minute. Though he was proud of himself for holding the mightiest of all hellspawn at bay, he knew his advantage would not last long.

The tide turned on him even sooner than expected. As Gilanirus sat on his knees languishing, the magics faded from his armor and its composition reverted to the stone from which it had been originally constructed. Torlen took a step forward, his hopes foolishly rising that his glorious enemy might have been defeated so easily after all. Then the stone body moved and rose back to its feet, the joints grinding and releasing a rain of pebbles and dust.

The Eternal Samurai moved forward swiftly and struck out with a sluggish punch. The Wisdom commanded his sonic magic to bring the body to a halt, but only at the last instant realized that as the steel had transmuted back to stone, its resonance frequency had changed radically. Gilanirus converted his fist alone back to steel just before impact with the Elysian's head, and Torlen's cracked and twisted body went flying away until it vanished from sight.

Keldana reached their location at this point, attacking with a two-handed chop of her axe. Gilanirus caught the axe on the edge of Arda, and the katana dug into the ice and brought it to a halt. With their weapons locked, the Godbeast borrowed a moment to restore the rest of his shell into his invincible steel.

With her new armors Keldana was nearly the size of her deadly foe, and she showed herself a fit match to him in strength as well. Gilanirus snapped Arda clear of the edge of the axe and tried to deliver a ferocious onslaught. Each time his blade struck the frozen weapon it bit in slightly and became lodged, breaking his pattern and forcing him to pull back. The Gehennite lord knew how to handle this. He stepped in close and made a high feigned attack. The Wisdom countered, and he canceled his move. As the ice axe crashed uselessly against his empty right shoulder socket, he sent his katana driving at his adversary's skull.

The Ocean's icy helmet held against the enchanted blade. Arda only bit a couple of inches and then was brought to a halt, stuck too deep for Gilanirus to easily dislodge. Keldana reared back and made another fierce chop with her axe, this time striking at his ribs, but the weapon did no good against the armor of Gehenna.

"Impressive," he said as he struggled to regain control of his sword. "You've managed to match me in defense. I did not know you were capable of such might here on Morolia, Wisdom of Protection. In the last wars you revealed no such combat prowess."

"I prepared this technique for you. I cannot halt the edge of your weapons, but my ice grips it as it enters, rending your all-cutting edges useless."

Gilanirus relented on retracting Arda, realizing the truth in his foe's words before she finished her explanation. His face began a slow transformation, forming jaws that resembled the face of a dragon and slowly opening. The Wisdom distractedly looked up to her opponent's left shoulder. She slid her axe behind it and sent a wave of divine energy into it, then ripped back fiercely against the back of the huge joint. From across the chamber, Melukah released a sudden cry.

"Keldana! Move away!"

The Wisdom of Ocean glanced to her lord in confusion as her axe lodged into the iron shoulder. Her hesitation cost her too much time. The dragon-like jaws of Gilanirus opened wide and a large orb of solid red electricity emerged. It struck Keldana's body, and the pair was suddenly lost in a pillar of raging Gehennite ether, fire and lava. Melukah tried to release a counter with his staff, but his blast was unable to penetrate the divine flames.

From the depths of the darkness Torlen returned to the fight. He saw the inferno of the Godbeast's attack and encased himself in a thick sonic layer. He clenched his hands together tightly and summoned a thick wall of white rings there, already synchronized to Gilanirus' armor. One way or another, the Wisdom of Sound swore to himself that with this next blow he would tear through that cursed red steel.

He sent a sonic vibration forth and rode through the flames. In the midst of the explosion he barely managed to make out a huge body, surrounded by the image of a greater dragon traced in power lines of red ether. His determination wavered at the terrifying sight of that magic, magic so potent that it took on a life of its own amid the flames of Gehenna. He forced himself to ignore his fear and sent another vibration forth, trying to determine the physical frame of the body. Once certain he knew the location of the chest he shot forward, leaped into the air, and struck out with both of his hands.

His fingertips cracked against impenetrable flesh, and he released the white rings of destruction. With a deafening shockwave they shot forward and traced into the body, and after an intense rattling Torlen felt the area in front of his hands give way. He clenched his fists and punched hard, sending a secondary shockwave blowing a solid hole through his target's chest.

He took a step back and stared up at the creature before him. The fearsome spiritual dragon bent forward and came close to his face, opening its maw and giving a soundless roar. Then suddenly it transformed into currents and began to flow away, sliding rapidly to Torlen's right and coalescing into the shape of a thin red blade.

The Wisdom panicked at that moment. He gathered energy and released an omnidirectional dome of sound, scattering wide the fires of Gilanirus. When they were gone from his view, he gazed upon a colossal icy statue. Steam poured from the outer layers of the body, a chasm had been torn into its chest, and Keldana's frigid face stared back at him.

"Torlen," she said with a wavering voice. "No..."

"Thank you for your aid," a booming roar announced from his right, where Gilanirus was regathering the vast amount of ether he had emitted to form his deception. "Though my Break spell had weakened her substantially, it would have taken a colossal blow for me to have torn her apart. Ice is unstable in the face of sound, and your arrival was quite timely." He finished recharging his iron shell and looked to Keldana. "Begone," he proclaimed, and his eyes flashed once brightly. A stream of erupting consciousness swallowed the Ocean, and her abdomen exploded into millions of beautiful dancing fragments. Only her shoulders and the lower section of her legs remained, collapsing to a sad melting pile at Torlen's feet.

"Ancient devil!" the Sound screamed with rage, turning his open palms at Gilanirus and releasing an attack with the ferocity of his indignation. Waves of sound washed ineffectually over the Gehennan's frame, neither doing damage nor driving him back.

He shook his head. "Not this time, little assassin. I've made a subtle adjustments to my structure. Just enough to rework the frequency you synchronize with." His eyes flashed again and Torlen's stomach was struck with a blow of unseen force, lifting him bodily into the air. Gilanirus came forward and made a swift sweep of Arda. The blade passed unhindered through the Wisdom's thighs, ripping his legs off, and another burst from the Godbeast's mind tore them to cinders. What remained of the Elysian's body fell to the ground, but the Tyrant did not try to continue this struggle. Instead he walked past, careful not to let the broken Wisdom touch his frame. "No more playing, children." He turned his gaze back to the light at the entrance of the chamber, beckoning, "Melukah," in an eager tone.

Gilanirus had walked only a few yards when he heard a peculiar buzzing sound behind him. He turned about to find Torlen floating there, his body carried by a bizarre net of energy pouring continuously from his unmasked face. His hands were gripped together in front of his chest and seemed to be struggling to hold something.

"You are oddly stubborn for a divinity," Gilanirus observed. "One of eternal intellect should know when he's hopelessly outmatched."

"And one of yours should know to finish your opponent when you can. Never leave them to try a final desperation technique. Die, accursed one!" He flew forward until he was no more than three feet from his undaunted foe. The Godbeast sighed and raised Arda, prepared for a finishing sweep. Then Torlen opened his hands and made a motion toward his enemy. Suddenly a ripping sound echoed, and Gilanirus felt his frame pulled against by a tremendous vacuum. He stopped his swing and braced his feet hard, attempting to step away, but even with all of his strength he could not overcome the force now pulling against him.

Torlen also seemed to struggle against his own attack, using what remained of his magic to create a sonic barrier and drifting slowly back. Gilanirus tried to ascertain what was happening and stared downward. There was a single point, infinitesimally tiny, sucking everything the room toward it.

The divinity shook his head in disbelief. "A singularity? Triggered by sound? This will destroy everything!"

"Everything in Morolia, perhaps," Torlen answered over the sound of a forming hurricane. "But Elysium will survive!"

Gilanirus braced himself and forced his mind to work. He could not overpower this attack, he knew that much. Still, a singularity required mass to become self-sustaining, and this one had not yet devoured enough. That meant something had to be sustaining it, nursing it until it gained in strength. The Gehennan could not see Elysian lines of ether, but it seemed logical that Torlen had to be holding the attack in place. If it was still that fragile, there was one obvious way to stop it.

He took Arda and stabbed the tip into the ground at his side, hoping it would hold there. He then reached out fiercely with his hand and gripped hard onto Torlen's head. The Wisdom released a gurgle and immediately Gilanirus felt a fluctuation from the singularity beneath him. He braced his arm carefully, barely managing to keep it from slipping into the vortex, and then pulled forward sharply on his opponent's head.

The Wisdom of Sound's body slipped into his own attack and was ground mercilessly, giving a sickening series of crunches. Once his body was damaged beyond function, the effect came to a stop. The matrix of Elysian energy within the face flickered out, the singularity weakened and then collapsed, and Torlen's head snapped off in the Godbeast's hand. The small point of mass that had been gathered by the attack collapsed to the ground, making a thud uncharacteristic for an object of its size. Gilanirus attacked it with a lash of thought, shattering it and sending a rain of the Wisdom's scrapped body out in shrapnel. He gave a tight squeeze on the fallen assassin's head, then dropped it as well.

He turned to retrieve his Arda, but instead found himself face to face with Melukah. The ball of light at the end of the Sun Staff had grown massive, and now was roughly three times the size of the Wisdom himself. "Ah, so you're ready," Gilanirus greeted him unperturbed.

Melukah swung his staff and touched it to the chamber floor between them. The Godbeast grabbed his shorn katana and struck down at the remaining Wisdom's shoulder, but was not fast enough to stop the coming attack. The ground at the Tyrant's feet turned into an explosion of pure light, lifting him up and burning deep into his armors. He was forced to collapse, retreating tightly into his shell for survival. The blaze of the Sun's attack dragged on for another several minutes, then finally threw Gilanirus free and sent him rolling across the room.

He stood slowly, smoke rising from his body as a slim layer of his armor returned to stone and was shed like a snake's skin. He raised his left hand and revealed his successfully retrieved Arda. "Heh, got it," he taunted in Melukah's direction.

As his vision recovered from blinding light and turned to where the staff had struck, he saw his ancient foe was no longer there. He heard a tap behind him and looked over his left shoulder, where Melukah now stood. The Wisdom's right arm had been severed by Gilanirus' hasty strike, and he now held his relic in his remaining hand. The head of the Staff of the Sun rested in the joint of the Godbeast's remaining shoulder.

"No!" the Spectre of Gehenna protested. His plea fell on deaf ears, as Melukah was incapable of showing mercy to his hated rival. The Sun Staff released a second blow, and Gilanirus' arm was torn soundly apart. The Supreme Wisdom adjusted his staff and refocused the light, disintegrating the severed arm and the hiltless Arda entirely. Then he gathered the mass of light back to the head of the staff and smacked it hard into his enemy's armored head. He used the force of his blow to drag the Gehennite god to the ground, then swept upward and sent him bowling away.

The Samurai again surged to his feet. Melukah sent a continuous wave of blasts from the Sun Staff, walking slowly toward his opponent. Gilanirus could do nothing but take these blasts, struggling to rebuild his armor even as it began to give out and collapse around him.

As he approached, Melukah spoke. "Last you faced me the Great Beast protected you with scales of gold. Alone you are no match for me, especially here on Morolia, where your specter is confined to a body of steel and stone."

"How did you penetrate my armor with your Staff?"

"I did not. Keldana tore a wound in the back of that shoulder before you killed her. It was your own failure to notice it."

Gilanirus growled in frustration. "If I could separate you from that staff, I would kill you," he retorted.

"I seriously doubt that."

"So you need me prove it?" He raised his head and the jaws on his helmet opened once more. A beam of red ether, twisting within a fierce psychic maelstrom, was sent ripping through the Morolian air for Melukah.

The Wisdom of the Sun was caught off guard, forced to swiftly match the blow with a beam from his staff. He caught the blast halfway to him and ground it to a halt. He started to give a sigh of relief, then realized that Gilanirus' wave was overcoming his own. It was moving slowly, but the point where the two attacks met was indeed shifting in Melukah's direction.

"How can he still hold such power after being struck by my Staff?" the Sun mused to himself. "His stores of red ether should be nearly drained." He thought quickly. He had only one arm remaining, and it was currently occupied holding his staff in place. He sent a portion of his will into the Staff to allow it to function briefly on its own, then stabbed the butt of the weapon into the ground and released it. Its power diminished slightly, but it held enough potency to hold Gilanirus' attack at bay. Melukah dropped to his knees and pointed his left hand forward, gathering a surge of his own magic there and releasing it.

A second, smaller beam of light slid beneath the two clashing together, striking his foe's thigh and disintegrating the armor there. Gilanirus lost his balance and fell to one side. As he did so his attack slid, catching Melukah by his upper body out of sheer luck and knocking the Supreme Wisdom away from his staff. The Elysian's misfortune was mirrored by fairer luck, as the beam from the Sun Staff also washed over the Gehennan's torso.

Each of the celestial entities struggled to regain themselves. Melukah began to walk to his Staff, while Gilanirus struggled to rise to his only remaining foot. The Godbeast's armor had taken all the abuse it could sustain and began to totally collapse. Everything from his waist up crumbled to the ground, leaving only the image of an enormous shadow, the form of a huge platinum dragon with two piercing eyes of light.

As the Sun came close to his staff, his body began to be struck with blows of psychic force. Gilanirus' eyes flashed periodically as he sent his psionic energy into the Wisdom's chest. Melukah smiled inwardly and shrugged the blows off, continuing his march. He sensed that his foe was desperate now. One more strike from the Sun Staff and the Godbeast would die.

"Enough of your resistance, Spectre of Gehenna."

"Not quite yet I think, Wisdom of Annihilation."

Melukah reached forth to seize his staff, and with it victory. Just before his fingertips touched the wooden frame, he felt a dull impact. The blade of a crude metal sword struck hard into his forearm. He stared at it in surprise, and shortly another sword joined it there. Then finally a battleaxe came sweeping in, tearing his arm off at the elbow.

He gave a cry of shock, then felt the impact of several weapons crashing into his back. He turned to see what creatures dared attack the Lord of Elysium. The sight he found was a fearful one. In the air before him, the weapons of all of the dead humans floated, suspended by magics Melukah could not discern. There were thousands of them, thousands upon thousands, all of them aimed for the Wisdom of the Sun.

"This is why I love our little battles," he heard Gilanirus announce from behind him. "You can never remember this, my most carefully kept secret. It takes much time for me to block out the sight of the Muses and make certain they cannot discover it. And poor you, Melukah, can never remember the previous times I have killed you. You can never remember the full glory of my consciousness."

Melukah shook his head in panic, trying to determine a course of action. "You have never killed me. I have never been killed!"

"That is what the Muses program you to believe each time they resurrect you. You're a sad puppet, Melukah. That's why you cannot rule. I alone can be the true Tyrant of Elysium! I am Gilanirus, and I am lord of all weapons!"

The Supreme Wisdom spun about with a scream, releasing a desperate blast of light from his entire ethereal face. Gilanirus' shadow made a motion, and a dense wall of human shields and armors rose up before him. Melukah's blow melted most of the barrier, but did not pierce through to the other side. The Spectre released a laugh and a roar, and the weapons floating about the room resumed their assault.

The Sun was lifted up into a whirlwind of attacking steel. Gilanirus had spread his consciousness equally throughout the weapons, and each of them contained just enough of his will to gain his unstoppable edge and pierce the Wisdom's flesh. As the air about Melukah turned into a vicious blender and chunks of his flesh went flying in every direction, he lashed out uselessly with blasts of light across the room. Soon these struggles faded, and the Supreme Wisdom of Elysium fell.

What remained of Gilanirus' armor turned to dust and the menacing shadow collapsed to the ground. His final attack had required spreading his magic across the entirety of the underground city. Between that and the blows he had taken from Melukah's Staff, he was far weaker now than he had been even when he had first awakened.

He heard a slow clapping coming from somewhere in the chamber. He did not bother to focus on it, certain he already knew who it was. Akatriel soon walked to the remains of Melukah, scanning them over diligently.

"My, my, Lord Gilanirus. I didn't think you had it in you to win against such odds. Three Wisdoms slain in a single battle, all on your own. Truly you're the mightiest of us all. I thought I would have to finish Melukah off myself."

"You? You thought you would succeed where even I had failed?"

"Well I certainly suspected Melukah would have been weakened by you, brought within a sliver of his own death." The slim figure bent down and swept up some large chunks of Melukah's body into a burlap sack, then closed it tight and concealed it within his robes. "And, I had a trump card." He drew his hand from his robes and revealed an extremely large black crystal, nearly the size of his arm. "Do you know what this is?"

Gilanirus shook his head, uninterested, and struggled to recall his Gehennite magic from across the chamber. He still did not trust the silver dragon, and his current state left him too vulnerable to betrayal. "Should I?"

"It's a creation of yours, of course. It's the remains of a

devilspawn named Zekraul. Zekraul was a peculiar demon, capable of channeling heat and light-based energy. For this, I had him killed. I needed to borrow that talent, and he was of little use to me alive. I took this crystal from his corpse and kept it alive with my own magics. I've made some interesting changes to its nature. I hope you don't mind me tampering with your designs."

"I care not."

As he continued his speech, Akatriel placed the large crystal into a point on the ground and stared at it for several seconds. Then he began walking toward Gilanirus. "As you gifted him, Zekraul was able to absorb and contain any sort of light or heat. But I had little need for that sort of technique. No, instead I have altered his nature to be capable of containing shadows."

This statement finally piqued Gilanirus' interest. "What do you say?"

Akatriel was halfway between the Godbeast and the crystal now, and he came to a stop. From within his sleeves he drew forth an ornate yellow stone. It resembled a large inverted eye with a thick white pupil. "Shadows, you see. I needed it to contain shadows. Or perhaps more accurately, I should say 'specters'." He raised the eye and pointed it at Gilanirus, then with a flick of his fingers set it spinning and released it. The eye hovered there on its own, and the pale conspirator bowed. "If you'll excuse me." He raised his arms high and vanished.

Gilanirus stared in curiosity at the spinning stone. For a moment it seemed nothing was going to happen. Then there was a release of ancient divine magic. A tremendous gate appeared, drawn with lines of electricity. This gate opened and revealed two demonic eyes, sharp like a cobra's.

"The eyes of Kentral!" the Spectre exclaimed. "It cannot be, he is dead!"

Two beams of light struck forth from the eyes and dove for the Godbeast. The shadow attempted to evade them, but they curved and followed his movements across the chamber with ease, catching him in a matter of seconds and spreading through his phantasmal essence. Light flew from the other end of the gate as well, striking into the black crystal Akatriel had placed there. The chamber rumbled from the roars and struggles of Gilanirus, but he had not recovered enough of his scattered magics to shield himself from a spell of divine origin. The eyes closed, the gate shut, and the stone fell to the ground. When it was over, the Final Godbeast of Gehenna was no more.

Akatriel reappeared and gave a satisfied chuckle. "And so the opposing King is at last within my grasp. But this is only check. The final blow must yet be struck, and my own King set to reign eternal."

He retrieved the Ion of Kentral and returned it to his robes, then moved across the chamber and lifted the crystal. He could feel the heat coming from its surface, as well as an unstable rumbling from within. Gilanirus' glory would not be long contained. Fortunately Akatriel did not need long. The next step of his plan was but minutes away, carried swiftly on the feet of Abaddon Daemon.

## Chapter 45.

## Checkmate

Myris stepped into the arid plain where Deun Coloran's body rested and inspected it. Cildar scouted the area, trying to gather any information as he could from the shifting sands. The two went about their separate tasks for a few minutes before reporting to each other.

The Cainite removed the hilt of Arda from Deun's body and looked it over. He recognized the sword immediately, and was surprised to find it broken and discarded here in such a manner. Only two and a half feet of the blade remained intact, but its seating was strong. Myris tested it on a nearby rock and found that its cutting edge was not dulled. He studied it for a while, waiting for Cildar to finish his scans.

Shortly later the paladin returned. "Lord Abaddon was definitely here. Felthespari boot prints, his size, no way it's coincidence. Not that long ago, either, or the winds would have erased them. We're close. It looks like we need to move southeast, toward that mountain there." He pointed, and Myris glanced up to see a peak decorating the eastern horizon.

"Cildar, look at this."

As bid, the man inspected the shattered sword in his friend's hands. "Arda? Lord Abaddon abandoned it?"

"It seems it was broken. By what, I do not know."

"So what weapon is he using now?"

"I cannot say. Perhaps he fights unarmed. Regardless, I think I can use this. Its unwieldy size is gone, and I believe it would make a suitable replacement to my old katana."

"Doesn't that sword cut through anything? It'd be of limited use to you, as it cannot be sheathed for your Draw Strikes."

"That was my first thought as well, but look here." He pointed to a series of tiny red runes traced along the back portion of Arda's blade. "These runes seem to be Gehennite in origin, but they're adaptive. I imagine these are what allow Arda to retain its properties on other planes. They're shockingly similar to the Living Runes of my own people. If I can get even minor interaction with them, enough to garner some basic information on the nature of their magic, I may be able to alter the Living Runes on my own sheath and it will be able to repress Arda's power."

Cildar scratched his chin, then nodded. "Sounds good to me. But work while we move. We must yet try to reach Lord Abaddon. If he's hunting Wisdoms without a powerful weapon, he could be in even worse danger than before."

Just as Myris was standing to his feet, the two of them were nearly thrown to the ground by an abrupt earthquake. Instinctively they turned their gaze to the mountainous peak on the horizon. First there was the sight of a single black speck being hurtled out the side of the rock face. Then, something neither of them would ever forget.

The entire mountain exploded, throwing its body out in every direction across the continent. It was not a volcano, nor was it a true explosion. It was as though the mountain decided that it no longer desired to be a mountain, and acted upon that whim. Myris and Cildar dove for cover and evaded a rain of deadly missiles, then watched in amazement at what they witnessed next.

* * * * *

Abaddon moved deep through underground caverns, following the trails of several large creatures. His senses could detect green ether nearby. He was certain the Wisdoms had taken this path. He was also certain they would still be hunting Gilanirus. This left him with a point of confusion. The dying Coloran had informed him this was where he would find Akatriel, but it seemed to be leading him to the warring foreign deities instead. Had the man deceived him? Had he been under Akatriel's control to the end? Or was Akatriel somehow involved with either the Elysians or Gehennans? From what Abaddon had learned from the Muses, he did not believe Akatriel aligned with the Wisdoms. Perhaps then with Gilanirus?

Many questions rang through his mind, not the least of which was on Akatriel's true nature. Still he did not know what the silver stranger was about in his meddling. What he did know, however, was that he was not ready for a battle with Gilanirus or the Wisdoms. Either force would be far too much for him in his current state, and he would doubtless perish.

He asked himself what Atheme Tethen would do in his position. He knew Atheme would not have endangered the lives of others. The Lord Councilor only ever took the forces he deemed essential, and tried to protect those weaker than himself whenever possible. Abaddon had thought of going back for Cildar and Myris, but knew if he brought his friends to this place they would likely die. He would not have their deaths on his hands.

Nor would Atheme have stood idle or retreated. That was not a Knight's way, and it was not how Abaddon was trained. His only option was clear. He had to march into the danger ahead with his chin upheld. With such threats as what lay ahead, he would just have to be more cautious than his usual self.

He kept his presence wrapped in thick cloaks of mystical stealth and moved soundlessly through the caverns. It made for slow going. He had been traveling for several hours and not yet caught up with the Wisdoms. His patience was sorely tested by his pace, but he forced himself to hold steady, reminding himself of the previous outcome with Gilanirus.

Eventually he reached a large opening in the stone, torn by substantial force. He could taste green ether still lingering in the air here. His suspicions confirmed, he stepped carefully through the opening into the room beyond.

The chamber was tremendous, running for miles before him. He gave a look around and sent subtle feelers. It did not take him long to recognize the place for what it was. This was a temple to one of the ancient gods. He could sense overwhelmingly complicated spells, channeled by a series of rune structures that wrapped all the way about the cavern. There was nothing natural about this formation.

He moved deeper into the area, trying to read the currents with no success. Whatever spells held this place together also purged the currents regularly, preventing them from containing any information useful to his mystic senses. He raised his hand to his shoulder and drew down Kargaroth, wrapping his knuckles tight about the hilt of his old sword.

He walked for another hour, moving through the empty space and finding nothing. A few times he thought he could detect scratches or craters along the ground, perhaps the signs of a battle. Each time he attempted to search he could find nothing. He shook his head and moved onward.

When he reached a point where he could no longer see a wall in any direction, he heard a sudden snap. In front of him a shroud slid away, and Akatriel stood greeting him with a broad smile.

"The Knight has come to see the King," he announced to his visitor.

Abaddon pointed Kargaroth forward and immediately released his limiter. "I've come to kill you, Akatriel."

The pale priest flipped his hand with a flourish and gave an elegant bow. "Do tell?"

The mystic surged forward and swung Kargaroth with vicious might. Akatriel slid out of the way of this first blow, but already the sword was being swung again. The pale figure dodged once more, then the tip of the greatsword was aimed at his throat and closing in. He ducked, taking a nasty gash across his forehead, then the silvery blade came down for his shoulder.

The trickster slid away from his assailant in desperation, his right shoulder spurting a river of blood and his left hand throwing nets of silver lightning. Abaddon brushed the bolts aside with a few swipes of his sword, then stopped bothering. As lightning struck him directly in the face and chest he came forward with a roar. Kargaroth flashed three more times, and more of Akatriel's blood painted the floor.

The priest collapsed in a pile of bloodstained white robes and crawled away, desperately trying to escape the angry man's reach. Abaddon could not repress his contempt. Biting his lip, he walked forward and slowly raised his weapon to strike a final blow.

"To think you're the one who caused so much trouble. I've never had much respect for the mastermind type. If you can't hold your own in a simple battle once your enemy finally pins you down, how can you ever achieve any of your plots and agendas? I hold many questions that I would like to be answered, but giving you the opportunity to speak, to stall, will only play to your advantages. I'm no man's fool. Though this battle can bring me no satisfaction, I'll kill you instantly, and deal with deciphering your motives once you're out of the way."

As he finished his statement, Abaddon's foot stepped into a narrow crack in the stone floor. He held his balance and did not falter. Then he realized the instability of his footing was not his biggest problem. His foot had landed on a rune, one he had been unable to read amongst the masked currents here. Suddenly the floor of the entire chamber disintegrated, followed by the walls and the ceiling. The thick layer of dirt built over centuries was blown away, as the rune structure holding the room together flared up in response to the mystic's presence and, in an instant, latched onto his soul and began to consume it.

"I agree with your sentiment, Knight," an answer came from the darkness. "Any so-called mastermind who could be killed so easily would be nothing more than a puppet disguised as puppeteer. I suppose we haven't spent enough time together for you to hold me in higher regard. Perhaps now's the time for us to remedy that."

A paralyzing effect he could not resist seized Abaddon hard and drug him to his knees. He looked around the empty chamber—

now lit bright blue from the runes that had wholly subsumed the walls—and noticed two Akatriels before him. One lay on the ground dying, as the other stood comfortably within a circle of blurry objects the man could not identify.

The standing Akatriel made a dismissive motion toward his bloodstained counterpart, and its body disintegrated. The lingering head grew huge and started laughing, then flew in Abaddon's direction and crashed into him, finally fading as well. The Daemon's rage redoubled and he tried to stand, but there was no overcoming the tenacious leeching of the ancient heraldry.

"Don't feel bad that you didn't sense my little illusion," Akatriel soothed. "This chamber was designed to mess with your senses. You couldn't have been expected to notice it. That is, unless you had tried to punch it, perhaps. You know, that old exciting feeling of flesh meeting flesh as you bring your hated rival to his knees? But no, you were too excited to have your Kargaroth back, weren't you?"

He raised his hands, and the stone beneath his feet was unveiled. He stood within an intricately drawn black star. At each of the points of the star sat a different artifact. One was a faceted black crystal humming with red energy. One was the head of the Wisdom Valinoru, which Abaddon had removed himself. One was the head and twisted shoulders of Torlen, which the man recognized in spite of its disfigurement and missing face mask. One was the shattered pieces of a Wisdom he did not recognize, covered in ice that had halfway thawed and left a small pool of water beneath it. The final was a simple burlap sack, with unknown contents.

Akatriel moved forward to the spot precisely between Abaddon and the five artifacts. He reached into his sleeve and drew forth a yellow stone, lying it on the ground. He came nearer the paralyzed mystic and sat down in front of him, only a yard away, offering another smile.

"We have some time to spare. This room has to suck in all of your considerable spiritual potential, or the experiment will fail.

We can't rush matters now, so why don't we spend that moment getting to know each other better? I do wish to play the good host and all."

"Who are you?" Abaddon muttered through clenched jaws.

Akatriel reached up to touch one finger to his nose and gave a wink. "A good place to start. Very straightforward of you, Knight. So then, let's start at the beginning.

"In spite of current appearances, I am a silver dragon. The eldest silver dragon. Of all my brethren, I alone remember the creation of our race. I was a pet of Elzaniru himself, one of the emissaries to my people. As the oldest and wisest of the smartest breed of dragons, I am the most cunning of all creatures. You could argue if you wanted, but any debate is pointless. There are none more clever than I.

"So when the Godbeasts first invaded Morolia, I was first of my kind to recognize the threat they presented. If Gilanirus conquered Morolia, it was only a stepping stone. The Tyrant of Gehenna wants what he has always wanted—Elysium, and nothing less. Given this, it was clear that his next stepping stone would be my home: Asteria.

"I appealed to the Council of Platinums and petitioned that we must send resistance to halt the Godbeasts' planar march. They agreed with me, dispatching me to oversee it myself. They offered me no armies, no forces, not a single ally. One might have seen it as a suicide mission. I took it as a vote of faith. After all, as Abaddon Daemon is among humans, Akatriel was amongst dragonkin.

"So I battled, alongside a Saint of one of the gods, a few mostly useless heroes of Morolia, and the very Wisdoms themselves. What an honor, I thought, to fight with the Wisdoms against the Godbeasts. Such an opportunity for learning secrets no other dragon knew!

"We won, in the end. But I was struck a fatal blow. And here begins my indignation. You see, had I died there, I would have come home to Asteria and been greeted as a hero. I asked one of the Morolian warriors to finish me, begged him to take my head.

But he, in some misguided sense of honor, refused my request! So, dying but not dead, I passed into a coma and rotted away.

"Understand something, Knight. In all the history of all the world there has never been a metallic draconic. No metallic has ever lost access to his Asterian powers. It's believed to be impossible. And here was I, the most sacred, the most noble of all dragons! Then after this war, after being a savior to the three planes, I was abandoned and left alone.

"Two thousand years later, I awoke. I, Akatriel, who could practically remember the very creation of the world, lost two thousand years of time! Do you know how much a dishonor that is for a dragon? We were designed by Elzaniru to be flawless in memory! And I was the most flawless of us all. But as further humiliation, the centuries of rotting in this accursed plane had transformed me into a draconic. I, Akatriel the Immutable, was reduced to Akatriel the Lost. I was no longer capable of using magic, nor of even returning home.

"I was left with no recourse but to wander this accursed world of yours. I saw great magics, and learned them, but could not use it. I was doomed. I was miserable. Do you know how frequently the creatures of this plane will attempt to kill a dragon, even a beautiful metallic, just as a test of their meager might? But I could not allow myself to be killed. You see, if I died as a draconic, I would have been reborn as a new dragon on the other side. It would have had my memories, but it would not have had my personality. It would not have been *me*. That is the way of the dragon species.

"Then!" He rose to his feet with excitement. "I received an offer. I would be given my body back, made into a glorious dragon once more, my atrophied spirit wholly restored. All I had to provide in payment was Morolia. All of it. If I could deliver the entire Morolian plane into the hands of the King, he would mend the ways in which I was wronged. To prove his abilities he gave me this body, and with it I was again able to use black magic. So I set about this spectacular plan, and have since spent decades in preparation.

"Still, even for a mind such a mine, this was no small task being asked of me. I would need several things to accomplish my goal. I first spent years scouring Arkalen to determine what resources were available to me. This chamber was built long ago, by cults of the god Anji. I knew it could serve my plan. I also needed an Ion of Kentral," he pointed to the stone he had placed on the ground, "an artifact very hard to find. This is the last one that remains functional. I needed the Wisdoms and the Godbeasts. More specifically, I needed the shadowy corpse of Gilanirus, and the corpses of four Wisdoms to serve as a counterbalance to his rather significant soul.

"Finally, I needed Kargaroth. This was before you, mind, when the Unholy Blade was a source of truly magnificent powers. The protective gods of the sword wouldn't have allowed me to claim it for myself, so instead I entered Cainite society posing as a Saint of Vaelius. I took stewardship of a child and dedicated him to the retrieval of Kargaroth for me, so that I might fetch it later. Then I left the northern lands to allow the war to proceed on its own terms, as I still had too much preparation in motion on Arkalen.

"My Bishop—your Cainite friend, Myris Phare—failed me, however. With the birth of the Hell Knight all would have been lost. No amount of planning or foresight on my behalf could deal with a creature who can swallow entire planes upon whim. And then, as quickly as you gave him life, you took the Hell Knight from this world. By the time I was made aware of these events it was too late, you'd already escaped back to the northern lands and taken Kargaroth with you.

"But I am a patient one. Sooner or later I would get the Unholy Blade into my grasp once more. It was simply a matter of choosing the method when the time came. I did not suspect, however, you would bring it to me yourself so soon."

The runes in the room released a sudden flash, signaling that they were sealed. Akatriel stood, moving to the stone on the floor and setting it spinning. "Now, Knight, I'm going to give you something beyond what any human has enjoyed. Now that this chamber has drained your own mysticism from you, I'm going to place the souls of the Wisdoms and Gilanirus into your body. This Ion of Kentral is capable of such a transference. For one moment, Daemon, I am going to make you more powerful than the gods themselves. But that won't be entirely new for *you*, will it?"

The Ion of Kentral floated into the air and as before, the huge electric gate appeared around it. Akatriel moved rapidly across the chamber, taking up his position nearby within a large rectangle he had drawn as a marker. The gate opened and its two eyes stared out at Abaddon, who had finally been released by the spell of the room. He struggled to rise to his feet and move away, but his strength had been fully sapped. His muscles felt as though they had been scraped raw, and even his breathing was strained and caused him agony.

Two beams from the eyes blasted forth and struck the center of the black star Akatriel had drawn. The star illuminated and drained the spiritual essence from each of the five artifacts at its tips, feeding it into the beam of light. The energies traveled back to the Gate of Kentral, then turned into a single beam and poured into Abaddon's body.

Felthespar's Champion screamed with pain beyond any he had ever known. He could feel the magics of Kentral reworking every fiber of his body, stripping the marrow from his bones and rebuilding them, tearing the meat from his muscles and replacing them, shredding the cells of his skin and recreating it with magic. Even for someone with Abaddon's substantial experience with pain, it was intolerable. For more than a few seconds, he went completely insane.

Then the magic released him and dropped him lightly to his feet. Instantly his consciousness reopened and repaired itself, then expanded. He could see everything. Black, white, red, and green currents all intermingled at his fingertips. He twitched with his hand, and the current of all four planes responded to his will.

He stretched and gave a roar, and the fabrics around him started crumbling. The air surrounding him experienced a unique chain reaction, as a ripple of willpower from his location took the current of all four planes and began to melt them together. This disturbance expanded out until it basked the entire room—the colors black, white, red, and green all faded, leaving the air with nothing more than a shimmering effect. He could neither read this shimmering reality, nor interact with it. Soon it had devoured everything in sight, and all that remained was Abaddon and Akatriel standing in a milky galaxy of void.

Across the room, the conspirator crouched low and touched his hand to where the runes at his feet had once been. Abaddon felt a strong pull in response to this. In the Morolian fragment of reality, the runes in the underground temple flared up and sent an immense beacon of energy to the precise center of the chamber, only a few feet from where the mystic himself stood. There a vast crystalline light structure, which appeared to him like a tear in reality itself, began to take shape.

"Thank you, Abaddon Daemon," Akatriel said with a disquieting sincerity to his voice. "You have made this possible. The spell will complete soon. Just wait and observe."

Abaddon stared at the energy source before him and tried to decipher what it was, but his mind was still in shambles. He could not bring himself to rational thought. He turned his attention to Akatriel, and the spike of emotions he felt told him all too well what he had to do. The Silver One had to be stopped.

He spoke, and could feel the tremors of his voice echoing back to him from each of the four planes of reality. He could not deny that the feeling was one of incredible power, and he basked in that glory. "Whatever it is you're about, I will not allow you to see it through."

He raised Kargaroth, preparing to dash at Akatriel and cut him down. The pale priest seemed to misinterpret this action, as he took a swift step forward and shouted, "Ah, ah, ah! I really wouldn't recommend that, Daemon. God though you may be at the moment, striking that spell will unmake us all. It's too late for you to prevent my designs without sacrificing your own life."

He turned to face the crystalline light, his sword held still while he thought aloud. "You tell me that you plan to trade the entire Morolian plane with your plan, and think threats of my own death weigh of equal accord? I've died enough times with this life that it has been made cheap. Even if it's with my dying breath, I'll protect those I hold dear."

As Akatriel released a scream of protest, Abaddon swung Kargaroth. The silvery edge of the sword crashed hard into the disturbance before him and came to a brief halt, then ripped through. There was a hateful flash as the shimmering reality around him transformed into pure scorching light. As he felt his flesh burning and his spirit emptying, Abaddon suddenly became aware of a terrifying presence he had not felt before.

There was a second flash to mirror the first—this one from the walls of the underground temple—and then order was restored. The lights faded, Abaddon felt his spirit return to normal, and he collapsed forward onto his hands and knees. He coughed up blood as his body struggled to cope with the sudden reversion to its natural state. He heard footsteps coming from his right as Akatriel stepped forward and stood in front of him, staring down with a look of pleasure coated across his face.

But as Abaddon looked up it was not Akatriel's expression that caught his attention. It was his eyes. They were gone, replaced by twin black pools of swirling magic.

"Hello, Abaddon," Akatriel greeted with a new voice. It was stronger, darker, and echoed with authority that struck the man to his very core. The new creature bent down and touched a fingertip to Abaddon's shoulder, then raised him up to his feet. "Aren't you glad to see me?"

He held tightly to Kargaroth, making certain he did not drop it in his weakness. "You," he stammered weakly.

"Come, Abaddon," the voice cooed. "Say my name. It will bring me such joy. After all, as the son of Virtue you're practically my family. You should be the first denizen of Morolia to exalt in my presence."

"Vaelius."

The newly born god chuckled. "Now, now, you know better. Vaelius was only a mask, same as Anji, same as Karn, same as a dozen others. Try a little harder. Say my real name."

Abaddon gained enough strength to right himself, and suddenly lurched forward and brought the edge of Kargaroth up against the neck of Akatriel's former body. "Ambition," he grunted through clenched teeth.

"There we go," the deity responded with satisfaction. He raised a hand and Abaddon suddenly slid back across the room. The human felt no pressure moving him, no friction on the ground at his feet. The movement seemed to be a simple displacement of him within reality itself. "Excuse me," the god apologized. "I need a new body."

Ambition lifted his hands and began to change. The pale skin of Akatriel shifted to a healthy tan color. His short white hair turned to a new style, growing long and flowing down his back. His robes tightened in and shifted from white to a regal carmine. He dismissed the sleeves, leaving short ruffles about his shoulders instead, and formed a collection of silver and golden bracelets along the length of his left arm. The fingers on his right hand became adorned with rings containing the finest of human jewels, while his left hand became encased in a thick black gauntlet.

He looked himself over, then flashed a broad smile. "There. This appearance is more befitting for the ruler of the world, wouldn't you agree?"

"Why?" Abaddon muttered to himself. "What did I do wrong?"

Ambition again chuckled. "Akatriel was more clever than I ever gave him credit. At least his boasts of his own spectacular intellect were not mere arrogance, tiring as they were. I'll try to sum it up so you can understand. He placed the essences of the Wisdoms and Godbeast into your frame. As a mystic, you adapted and expanded your consciousness. For that moment in time, you existed across all four planes. Then, acting on instinct, you tied the four planes together into one so that your mind could survive trapped in what was otherwise impossible chaos. This temple was formed by one of my own cults long ago, to prepare for this event. It drained your mystic stores from you and used them as a battery, then used that battery to contain the actions of your amalgamated self to a limited region. As the deity Akatriel had made you, you would have ignorantly bound all four planes together across the entire universe. That would have destabilized, if not outright ended, our reality. I had to keep you in check.

"Then the runes concentrated the Veil, reducing it to a single tangible point. Akatriel taunted you, predicted you, knew how to fool you into striking it. Didn't you think to wonder why he said he needed Kargaroth? It was foolish of him to give away so obvious of a hint. In that moment I thought he had undone all, but I'd overestimated you. Even now you don't yet understand. Only Kargaroth has the might, the edge, to destroy the Veil itself. Only Kargaroth exists outside of it and can cut into it. When you sliced through it, the Veil collapsed. In its absence, the effects of your soul pulling the four planes together became permanent. Within this temple, Morolia, Asteria, Gehenna, and Elysium all were the same.

"I had crafted a body for myself and awaited in Asteria. When the four planes merged, that body occupied the same space where Akatriel stood. The rectangle he drew was a Grounding Square, a strange magic only the dragons understand. When the rune structure gave its final push and destroyed this section of reality, restoring the four universes and the Veil, I was unable to cross back to Asteria because of the Grounding. Instead I was left here, in Akatriel's form. Here, where I am god."

The fatigued man did not try to process this, but instead ran forward and swung down with Kargaroth. His aim was true, and he struck perfectly at the center of the god's head. Ambition did not move—Abaddon was certain he did not move—yet somehow the sword struck to his right, slicing uselessly through the stone floor.

The god waggled a finger. "The time for such bravery is past."

He pointed at the ceiling, and instantly Abaddon's body went flying away. He crashed hard through the roof of the temple and kept flying, digging straight up through rock and earth until finally he crashed from the side of a mountain and was sent soaring across Arkalen. Ambition took a deep breath, and raised his arms.

The mountain above him exploded away, sending a rain of rock shrapnel as far as the ocean to the north. Ambition floated slowly through waves of collapsing rubble as he rose into the sky, where he could overlook all of Arkalen. He started to pursue Abaddon, but then had another thought.

"The Gate of Gehenna," he said with a voice somewhere between his own and Akatriel's. He pointed a finger forth, and an immense ripping noise covered the entire continent. Ambition reached into the rift in the Veil, into Gehenna, and brought forth entire vast armies of hellspawn, decorating them across the Arkalen frontier and driving them into frenzies.

"There," he said with satisfaction. "That should create some amusement."

He turned to the south and flew rapidly across the continent, practically teleporting to where he imagined Abaddon had been tossed. He arrived at the edge of a small river and landed lightly. At his feet rested Kargaroth. The sacred blade was alone, its master nowhere to be seen.

Ambition looked around for his quarry, trying to locate him with his godly senses, but any evidence of the Daemon's spirit seemed to have grown too weak. "You're not dead, are you Abaddon? No, that would be too easy with you. Doubtless you're only on the brink and will return to annoy me. Still, try what you will. Without this," he stooped down and picked up Kargaroth, "you're of no concern to me."

He raised his right thumb and touched it to the edge of the blade, reeling back with a hiss as his finger began to bleed. "The sword that can kill a god indeed. Kargaroth, I adore you so for the might you represent. But I would be both a god and a fool if I allowed you to remain in my world."

He pointed his free hand to one side and an electrical vortex appeared there. He concentrated his divine will tightly, tunneling it continuously deeper until he was certain of its stability. Then he heaved the sword into the vortex. The Unholy Blade went spinning away, then vanished. Ambition snapped and the vortex sealed off in an instant, with Kargaroth lost to the world of man. He once more lifted himself into the sky, casting his gaze about Arkalen.

"Now, I need a suitable throne."

# EPILOGUE

## When Heroes are Needed

Atheme Tethen, Knight of the Heavens, Warlock, Bishop, Lord Templar, Brother of Man, and Lord Grand Councilor of Felthespar sat in a majestic office pouring over paperwork. A smile lit his features, as the humming of a jovial tune escaped from his lips. He tried to keep his mind focused on his duties, but there was excitement in the morning air and he struggled to contain himself.

After the fifth attempt at rereading the same paragraph of his document, a knock sounded upon his door. He looked out his window and checked the position of the sun. It was still early—too early for him to be disturbed. He stretched and gave a yawn. If someone was bothering him during his writing hours, something new must have developed.

"Enter," he shouted, rubbing the drudges of study from his eyes.

The door opened, and his young wife Relm entered with a grin. "Atheme dear, there's someone here to see you."

"Here to see me?" he said with a creased brow. "Whatever it is, can't it be resolved without my personal involvement?"

She offered no answer beyond her continuing grin, so he sighed in surrender. He rose to his feet and gave her a quick kiss, then slipped out the door at her lead. They exited into the light, onto the deck of a great ship still in the process of being loaded with cargo and soldiers. He looked down the beach at the line of twenty other vessels, each undergoing similar procedures. He took a deep breath and tasted the sea air, then turned his attention to his visitors.

Before him stood Kulara Karfa, General of the Military, with his entire Military Council backing him. Atheme had abdicated his own rule in Felthespar and left the Council in charge, and was taken aback to find them here, miles from their homeland, their weapons drawn and bags packed for travel.

There was Kulara himself, carrying his large two-handed katana, the Moradel; Shasta D'argail, Lord of the Phoenix, and his Conformer, a powerful shapeshifting lance; Karice Contel, Lord of the House Aithr, a stoic woman with the fiery longsword Flamberge; Cyprus Galahe, Lord of the House Saelen, Cildar's brother and bearer of the Emle lineage, wearing his shimmering twin elemental gauntlets; Zynex Traval, Lord of the House Lurin, Lord of the Feather, carrying his family's aged Bow of Traval; Warlock Lathria Grielat, Lord of the Black Hand, and her Pearl Staff; and finally the youngest lord, Fujia Tuel, with her short Shield Sword strapped across her back alongside her Morabet.

"Kulara? What's the meaning of this?" Atheme demanded.

"We took a vote. And we decided, as the rulers of Felthespar, that it was only fitting to send the *entire* Military on this voyage. So we've brought with us the Phoenix Dragoons, a majority of the Templar core, and of course, our humble selves."

Atheme shook his head. "You agreed to watch over Felthespar. Someone has to defend our city while we're gone."

The General nodded and stroked one finger down the scar that ran across his right eye. "Oh aye. That's why I contacted Thian and had him send a force of Cainites over to watch the city. Stealthily, that is. Don't want to be causing no big uproar. Don't worry, though, we left Kinguin more or less in charge of things. He's going to form a puppet council around himself and keep things in shape until you get back."

Atheme opened his mouth and started to offer another objection, so Kulara dropped his tone to a more serious one. "Listen Ath, from what I've heard tell from you and Relm, this ordeal is about to blow up and claim the whole world. Now we're warriors, and we're not going to do a lot of good sitting here in Felthespar and hoping things just work out. Right now our nation's more feared than it's ever been, and you know as well as I the raging wars of the past are lost, faded from all but memory. Kinguin can run the country and Thian can send aid if he needs it. But bottom line, if there's going to be a battle for the souls of all mankind, the seven of us agreed that we're not going to miss out on it."

Atheme ducked his head to hide a grin. "It seems my people are too much like me."

"You left us behind last time," Kulara replied with a smile. "If someone's staying at home this time, it can be you."

The Lord Councilor released a hearty laugh, then patted the General's shoulder firmly. "Captain!" he shouted up to the till. "Rearrange the passenger allotments, make room for seven more on our ship." Turning his attention back to Kulara, he added, "Pick yourselves some space somewhere and get as comfortable as possible. It's going to be a long trip and the quarters are severely cramped."

The Military Councilors exchanged smiles and made their way to find quarters. Atheme sighed and wrapped one arm about his love's waist. "I guess we have to make the best we can of things."

"Atheme," she cautioned, "when Pecoros warned me of Vaelius' return to our world, he said we would face dangers which threaten to consume all four planes. Are you sure it's wise to bring Kulara and the others along?"

"I'm certain, Relm, that it's not 'wise' for any of us to be going. But you said Pecoros assured you that without our aid to the resistance on Arkalen the world was doomed to servitude."

"His visions of the future are only limited, though. When he said 'our' aid, he might have meant only you and I. Or only you, even."

"Even if that's so, if there are horrors ahead I must face, I will face them more resolutely with bold allies at my side."

She leaned her head against his chest and hugged him tightly. "Are you sure you're ready for this? Are you sure *we're* ready for this?"

He put his fingers beneath her chin and raised her head, then flashed his most winning smile. “War with an actual god made flesh? I sincerely doubt we’re ready. But we’ve got friends on Arkalen who need us. Even if things are at their worst, we’re not going to leave them to die alone.” He turned and moved back to his office door, shouting a final order to the captain of the vessel. “Complete the preparations, then get us underway immediately. Take me to Abaddon Daemon!”

Thanks for reading!

We hope you enjoyed our novel.

We'd love to hear from you. You can find us on our forums at
**www.onionknight.com**

Or reach out on Twitter or Instagram
**@abaddononion**

www.ingramcontent.com/pod-product-compliance
Lightning Source LLC
Chambersburg PA
CBHW020615310726
48979CB00008B/1501/J

* 9 7 8 1 7 3 2 8 2 5 2 2 2 *